Lies of Stone

Leona R Wisoker

The Necessary Legal Stuff

First Edition published 2024

Printed in the United States

THE SCRIBBLING LION LLC
Sandston, VA 23150

https://www.thescribblinglion.com

Trade Paper: ISBN: 979-8-9889349-0-5

Acknowledgments

This book has taken a longer and stranger journey than I could ever have expected. The first draft was reviewed by my writing group sometime in the early 2000s. One of the group members declared that Tank was a terrible person, a moral degenerate, completely unsympathetic, and so on. As I quite liked Tank, I took dire offense and began to write a whole other book to defend him by way of explaining his backstory.

Unfortunately, a smart mouthed street thief walked onto the first page of that attempt and ran away with what eventually became *Secrets of the Sands*, in which Tank wasn't even featured directly (although Idisio does meet Tank's father). I started fishing for a publisher at that point, and by the time I landed one, I'd written the sequel, *Guardians of the Desert*, and the series was underway. Tank had to wait for the third and fourth book to have his day in the sun.

Along the way, I kept returning to the original story (which I'd given the working name of *Kingdom of Salt*, a reference to how the Northern Kingdom started), and applying my increased skill set to making that story better.

Looking back now, I totally agree with that early review. Tank was much less palatable in the first two dozen drafts, and Lia was completely hopeless. In fact, I only really nailed what I was originally going for in the last few months of 2023, and only because of external pressure from readers and editors.

So I have to thank Ed Morris, Tanya Wisoker, and Barbara Friend Ish for not letting me settle for good enough. Barbara especially was so encouraging and supportive that I got a huge burst of energy and confidence on fixing various issues. She deserves a massive accolade for doing me the favor of coming in at the last minute and spending quite a lot of her time on this project. It was absolutely delightful to work with her again. Any remaining mistakes are mine alone.

I have to thank that early writing group for making me mad enough to launch into what became a truly epic project. The group scattered years ago, and the only person I kept contact with was the indomitable, unique Angela P Wade.

Angela and I read each other's drafts, edited one another's work, and I typeset several of her books over the years; we went out for hot chocolate and commiserated over our woes, laughed and cheered about our successes. Angela passed away after a prolonged fight with cancer a couple years ago now, and the world is much, much smaller without her boisterous personality in it. I so badly wish I could have put this book in her hands.

I owe thanks for so much to so many: my beloved oak tree of a husband, Earl Harris, who patiently listens to me wail, rant, brood, and ramble about my writing; reads my early drafts, brings me coffee and takeout sushi; and cheers me on when I'm stuck or despairing. My best friend and beloved rock, Russell Schroeder, who grounds me, makes me laugh, stabilizes me, and keeps me going.

My sister Sue Wisoker, whose support and encouragement means the world to me. My fabulous friends Chris Addotta-Smith, Amy Addotta-Smith, and Ame Morris, whose incredible love, understanding, and support have kept me believing in myself and laughing along the way. They have also been the best possible live audience for read-aloud tests on so many manuscripts that I've lost count at this point.

My second mom, Georgia Schroeder, another amazing cheerleader who's gotten me through bad patches since I was a teenager; my second set of brothers, Travis and Darren Schroeder, whose sturdy support and unwavering welcome are an unlooked for blessing in my life.

My daughter Kristie McWilliams, who I hope won't mind that I took the "step" out of that statement; she and her daughter are utter delights in my life and lift my mood on a regular basis. My grandkids Kye and Kyler, who continue to teach me new ways of seeing the world.

I offer a sincere bow of appreciation and respect to Monica Marier, who created the new, lovely double map; also to Christina Yoder, who created the lively, vibrant cover. Both were abolutely wonderful to work with.

Goodness, so many more.

All the folks at the conventions and events up and down the East Coast: MarsCon, ConGregate, RavenCon, AtomaCon, ConVivial, and several others. From con runners to attendees to fellow panelists: I have learned so much from all of you. Knowing you're there and interested in what I have to say and in reading what I have to write is just so, so much excellence in my life.

There are more, there will always be more. As I think I've said in previous Acknowledgments, I could fill page on page with the people who made this book possible. But listing everyone back to my second grade teacher would be tedious, and I want you to get on with reading the story.

I'm incredibly excited to be unleashing this book on the world. I've been telling stories about this story at conventions and events for over ten years now, and working on the book itself, in fits and starts, for twenty. I truly hope you like reading it as much as I loved writing it!

Dedication

For Angela,
who was there
at the beginning.

I miss you so much.

Contents

ROYAL LIBRARY MAP
no. 151: The Northern Kindgom
N
NW
NE
W
E
SW
SE
S
Ice Tundra
Scarpane Mountains
Harsh Hills
Assiasan
Belpost
Stecatr
Cold Hills
Orhon
Kismo
Wastelands
The Bone Plains
Kio
Arason
Ghost Lake
Isata
The Hackerwood

Sea of Gold
The Hackerwood
The Ugly Swamp
Salt City
Obein
Sandsplit
Sandlaen Port
Heybrook
Bright Bay
The Horn
Sea of Kings
ROYAL LIBRARY MAP
no. 150: The Northern Kindgom
N
NW
NE
W
E
SW
SE
S

Lies of Stone

Chapter One

The night wind ran chill, this close to the sea in the king's city of Bright Bay, whispering and stirring the sandy dirt underfoot. Clouds scudded across the sky, covering stars and waning moon alike in a shifting haze. Torches snapped and guttered by the doors of western dockside taverns and warehouses, all of which were firmly shuttered at this late hour. Better quality areas had hurricane lanterns hung outside, but here, a windy night meant walking in the dark more often than not.

It was a good, if cold, night to lurk in an alley between warehouses. Tank told himself to enjoy the cutting wind; the morning would once more bring brutal heat. He couldn't quite convince himself. He didn't like this side of town, never had, and he loathed being cold.

There were no drunken sailors roistering along the docks. Guards stood outside nearly every warehouse door, stolid and severe. Their night uniforms were leather and wool for warmth against the chill, and they held clubs or staves. The cheaper warehouses hired their door guards for appearance rather than skill, but at least one truly skilled guard waited inside each building.

Sailors went to the eastern dockside for their fun these days. The western docks, as evidenced by the ostentatious overpopulation of warehouse guards, weren't safe for careless drinking and brawling, and the taverns were filled with F'Heing supporters. Of all the Families that could have essentially bought themselves a chunk of Bright Bay, F'Heing was arguably the most dangerous. Certainly they were the most viciously inclined.

In the harbor, tall masts swayed with the push and pull of an incoming tide. Smaller boats bumped and clicked. Lanterns glimmered like earthbound, swaying stars on the decks of the larger ships as watchmen made their rounds. The wind ran through Tank's hair, working strands loose from the already untidy braid. He began to raise a hand to tuck them back, and caught the sound he'd been waiting for: a shuffling step, a shoe in need of mending that dragged at the heel.

Tank dropped his hand and lowered his eyelids, listening more than watching as a stooped figure hurried past, just over arm's length from the alley mouth. A waft of sour tobacco and old sweat drifted in its wake. Tank curled his lip in distaste.

The guards took a cursory glance as the man went through the few thin puddles of light, then collectively ignored him as a non-threat. The wind stilled briefly. Tank caught the tiniest intake of breath from someone nearby: two warehouses butted up against one another not far from his alley, and the tiny corner formed by mismatched walls offered enough shelter for a slender person to hide in. He'd considered taking that spot himself, but he was too big to fit safely. More intrigued than concerned, he marked the location as one to stay aware of.

The man paused near a lantern at the edge of the walkway, glancing around anxiously.

A moment later, two men materialized out of the shadows to stand on either side of the stooped man, who squeaked in noisy alarm. Guards along the dockside snapped to attention, then retreated into their various buildings, taking their shielded lanterns with them. The lantern above the newcomers went out. Darkness suffused the area.

A glowing light coalesced. One of the men held up a hand filled with pale amber illumination that held steady, unbothered by the wind. He was taller than Tank, with a sharp, lean frame, and moved with cold precision. The man beside him, shorter, had a rounder build and held himself with the complacency of the truly powerful. In the discolored witchlight, their clothes looked to be a nondescript gray and tan, but gold glinted along their ears.

Pressing himself gently back into the wall behind him, Tank shut his outer mind to complete blankness, drawing a breathing calm around himself. He became nothing more important than the stone around him, beneath him, above him. A speck in the night, a moment among moments, nothing in the least remarkable. With care, he folded his inner self sideways into the most private, most shielded part of his mind.

Once secure, he allowed himself to think: *Fucking desert lords. Fuck. Fuck, fuck, fuck.*

The stooped man had straightened, clearly alarmed. Wisps of graying hair fluttered at the edges of a frayed red head scarf, and his clothing was dull from wear rather than design. Standing straight, he was a height match for the smaller desert lord.

He'd presented himself as hailing from Stecatr, earlier in the day when he'd asked to join Tank's group on their journey north. *Toad*, he'd called himself without a flinch. Tank was dearly interested in the story behind that nickname; perhaps he'd have time to get it out of the man on the journey north. If they were even accepting the old man, after whatever this meeting showed.

Toad had stopped far too close to Tank's hiding spot. Tank couldn't afford to move a muscle. Couldn't withdraw, which would have been by far the smartest option. At least that allowed Tank to hear the conversation, even through the gusting wind.

"You're late," the taller of the desert lords said. He lowered the hand filled with light, nearly shoving it into Toad's face.

Toad tensed but held his ground. His voice shook as he said,"I got lost. Er. My lord.

I'm sorry."

The tall lord lifted his hand away, his thin lips twisting as though he'd tasted something revolting. "I'm not *your* lord, you soggy little ragpicker. I wouldn't have you in my service for all the gold in your king's vault. You're clumsy, and you stink."

Tank couldn't help smirking in agreement. Toad shifted uneasily, finally backing up a pace. Both desert lords sneered this time, one muttering something in a western dialect Tank didn't know well enough to translate. He picked out the unmistakably aristocratic accent well enough, though: clipped edges here, drawn out syllables there. Not an unbound lord, then, not with that attitude and that accent. Meaning he was Family. Meaning, given this particular location, F'Heing.

F'Heing desert lords had a reputation for unusually sadistic violence. Tank kept his eyes almost shut and most of his attention on being completely uninteresting.

"No need to be rude," the shorter desert lord said. "And there's no need for names or titles, northern. We aren't so easily offended."

Tank knew Toad wouldn't understand the soft-voiced insult: *You are not important enough for your manners or lack thereof to mean anything at all to us.*

"I ... I thank you," Toad stammered, clearly relieved at the apparent forgiveness. "I ... um." He peered at the ships again. "Should we ... go?"

Apparently he'd been expecting to go aboard their ship. Whatever game Toad was involved with, he was absolutely terrible at it. The soft-voiced desert lord chuckled condescendingly.

"I think not." That biting derision came from the lord holding the light, which he shifted to the other hand as he spoke, an impressive display of power. Toad flinched backward. "We can handle our business right here. Do you have an answer for us?"

Tank slitted his eyes open enough to see Toad twisting round as though searching for eavesdroppers.

"There's nobody listening," the tall desert lord snapped. Tank put that aside to feel smug about later, and stayed very, *very* quiet. "Talk, ragpicker!"

Toad's voice wavered in a desperate attempt at bravado. "You tell me! Do you have the medic — the package?"

"Do fish swim?" The light was shoved forward into Toad's face once more. "The *answer*, ragpicker! Give me the words of your betters!"

"I'm told to say we have an agreement," Toad said sullenly, backing up a step and squinting as though the dim amber light hurt his eyes. "All the proposed terms are satisfactory."

"Good. Here."

"*Tas-shadata*," the soft voiced southerner muttered: *Cowardly fool.*

Tank wasn't entirely sure he agreed. For all Toad's quavering, he'd tried to stand up to them. Foolish, definitely. Cowardly, no. Standing in the presence of desert lords for the first time was a deeply unsettling experience. He wondered if Toad had the slightest idea of what even an unbound desert lord could do. Probably not, or he'd never have dared even that small defiance.

The tall desert lord handed a small package to Toad, who took it with clear unease.

In that soft voice, as though talking to a difficult child, the second desert lord said, "Tell him we'll be in place by next spring. He'll get the rest of what he asked for then."

Toad stiffened. "Wait. Wait, no, that isn't what he told me — he said I was to bring back —"

"There were difficulties." Soothing and chiding at the same time. "He'll have to make do until spring."

"But that's not the agreement!" Toad protested, and actually took a step forward.

"*When* was never specified, ragpicker," the taller lord snapped. "Shuffle along, now, we're done here." He closed his hand: the light disappeared.

The northern let out a small gasp as darkness coalesced, audibly staggering a step as though he'd lost his balance.

Tank hadn't looked at the light long enough to lose his night vision entirely. The desert lords vanished as smoothly as they'd appeared. Tank cut a glance along the docks, trying not to move more than his eyes, not daring to stretch his senses, and found nothing.

The men hadn't literally teleported. That was a ha'ra'hain trick, not one desert lords had ever mastered, as far as Tank knew; but then, he hadn't known they could transfer witchlight so casually from hand to hand, either. Still, it seemed more likely that they'd used a more potent version of the *being insignificant* trick that Tank himself was deploying. The men could very well be standing nearby, watching to see what happened next.

Tank stayed very still. The guards began to emerge, relighting the lanterns and taking up their silent posts. Toad turned and hurried away with as little stealth as on his arrival. After a few moments the watcher to his left slipped from hiding, a lithe form in dark shades, and set off after Toad. Nobody leapt after them. The desert lords were well and truly gone. Tank eased from concealment and followed.

The stranger was *good*. The desert lords hadn't picked up on their presence, which strongly implied some damn solid aqeyva training, which meant a southerner. Perhaps a F'Heing spy, sent to make sure Toad wasn't playing games, but that seemed redundant after a meeting with desert lords. Those *ta-karnes* could practically smell a lie.

Maybe the spy was someone in training to be a master assassin, a *shay-nin*. That would make sense, regardless of Family affiliation. Quite possibly Toad was about to get mugged, if not killed outright, and the package stolen.

Tank wasn't sure whether he wanted to intervene if that happened. He definitely wasn't pleased with the phrasing at the end of that conversation. "The Agreement" had a very specific implication, a nuance Toad couldn't possibly have understood. If there was any sort of new *Agreement*, with a capital A, being built, it would have to be stopped, and fast.

For hundreds of years, if not thousands, the original Agreement had dictated a tenuous balance between humanity and an ancient race called ha'reye. Most modern humans didn't even know about the deep-dwelling ha'reye. Most humans thought desert lords drew their power from politics, not from the abilities ha'reye bestowed on their servants for a hellish price.

Tank dearly, sometimes desperately, wanted to be most humans.

The Agreement had been broken, not long ago, and was now dissolved, hopefully forever. It sure as scalded shit oughtn't to be restarted in any form, most certainly not under F'Heing auspices.

The only good thing about the recent disasters cascading from that breach, in Tank's opinion, was that desert lords were clearly weakening. If those two *fesh'ii* could access their full strength, he'd never have been able to hide so close at hand.

The spy flitted from shadow to shadow, twice ducking neatly into cover as a city guard patrol went by: four men with two lanterns, dressed in sternly cut white uniforms. Both patrols looked narrowly at Toad. He raised a limp hand and asked directions each time, as though entirely lost. The guards pointed him onward and dismissed him without a second look. Tank followed, dodging the patrols with ease, increasingly intrigued.

Streets widened, taking on a distinctive slant as they moved into the middle city. Drains that should have channeled water cleanly into the swamp had broken down in recent years, frequently leaving a large swath of town near the swamp's edge flooded and muddy.

Tank tested each step to be sure it was dry, swatted at night gnats, and hoped they'd be out of this area quickly.

Toad turned down a narrow side road, then up onto the stoop of a shabby hostel. The battered lantern by the door gave Tank a clear view of Toad's sly, weathered face. He'd taken off his headscarf at some point, and his thin hair was wild and kinked from the humidity. In this light, his worn linen shirt was a washed-out green, his leggings a faded bluish gray.

Toad whirled on the doorstep, peering around with belated suspicion, then went inside. Already in hiding, Tank waited, curiosity about that second watcher holding him. He counted to a hundred, then again.

Halfway through the third repetition, a shadow broke from cover, stepping into the lantern light: a young woman in dark gray and darker green clothing that covered every bit of skin besides neck and hands. She stepped up, reaching for the latch, then paused, not quite touching it.

Tank took a careful study of her face as she hesitated. Pale hair, sharp features. Definitely northern, definitely not a southern assassin in training, and an established assassin wouldn't have hesitated. How in the hells had she gone undetected by two desert lords?

The young woman dropped her hand and turned away. Tank watched her slide, with remarkable grace, back into shadow. He took a half-step to follow, then it was his turn to hesitate. It was no short stroll to his lodgings at the Copper Kettle, and Dasin was waiting. He really didn't have the time or energy to go chasing after a mysterious girl. He needed to report back, then try for what sleep might be left to the night.

Reluctantly, he decided to let her go. Her presence was more than likely unrelated to his own business with Toad, and he'd probably never see her again.

Maybe Dasin would be properly asleep, or too lazy on aesa to ask after what Tank had seen, and Tank could get the sleep before the arguing for once. *No harm in hoping*, he thought sourly, and started the long walk back to the Copper Kettle.

Intersection: Reincorporation

The wind was cool here, at the edge of the ocean. Teilo had stood at this liminal point at two critical points in her life. First, after her part in bringing about the death of a mad hakrakha — which modern humans, unwilling to make the effort, had corrupted to the far too soft *ha'ra'ha* — those monstrous creatures who'd shaped the world for millennia. That had triggered her unexpected ascension to hakreye-kin and the theft of her child. Then had come her binding, her captivity, and, eventually, her escape. The second time had gone no better, for all that her new powers should have made her invulnerable.

Liminal indeed. Salt water before her, brackish marsh beside her, a very dark and dangerous forest behind her. The air around, above, and beneath her surged randomly from clear to tainted in a way humans could never sense. The final key to catastrophic chaos lay in the deep, immortal fire within her own body, should she choose to unleash it.

The humans had no idea what sort of intersection they'd built their proud city upon. No wonder a wretched, outcast hakrethe had settled here, gone completely mad, then spawned an even worse child. No surprise at all that the city had descended from there into unstable rulership, diseases, fires and catastrophes.

Not at all shocking that the humans hadn't figured it out, even to this day. They didn't hear the world properly. They never slowed down enough to listen.

Teilo didn't like this place. It reeked of human-kin pain, other-kin pain. Her own pain. She shouldn't have come here at all. But she was hakreye-kin, at this point, and certain patterns compelled. Even after so many years of watching that weakness erode the hakreye, even knowing better, she'd been drawn back to this small stretch of beach, to this moment between the fading of the dawn stars and the rising of the sun.

Not so far from this spot, she'd almost died. Shortly after that, she'd almost been killed. Then, like a fool, she'd once again been careless with her trust and been thrust into horrific agony.

She'd survived it all. She always would. She carried the fire of her transformation. Perhaps more importantly, and thankfully untainted by the hakreye, she still held her connection with water. She'd been afraid, during the long centuries of seclusion in the Jungles, that her service to the hakreye had severed that. Finding it only smothered, not lost, had been a joint-weakening relief.

She was the First. The first to speak to the hakreye, the first truly successful hakraiknin. The first full conversion to hakreye-kin, always theoretically possible but never before realized. Her power came wholly from the world and the creatures that roamed it. She should have long since been granted the deference due a god. It grated that she'd been met with the exact opposite.

The Jungles had tried to have her killed. She'd walked out on them, disobeyed a direct order, and gone on to upend rather a lot of comfortable arrangements. One might even lay some of the blame for the eventual burning of those same Jungles and the overall destruction of the hakreye at her feet.

Only some. Hardly all. Human arrogance had provided most of the push.

Teilo frowned out at the ocean, then realized she was pouting. That was an unattractive and foolish expression. She smoothed her face, still only a basic framework, to blankness once more and went on brooding.

The Jungles had been a good home. A safe home. A smothering home, one she'd never expected to return to and now couldn't, because it was ash.

Hakreye lived far below ground everywhere else in the world. The Jungles had been hot enough, and their servants devout enough, for them to move much closer to the surface.

The teyanain had burned hundreds of miles of rainforest, launching vicious explosives that ate through wood and stone alike. The human-kin died immediately. The hakreye, never quick to react, had only just started to move when the corrosive liquid reached their lairs.

By then, it was too late.

Teilo didn't hold any anger against the teyanain for the burning. More specifically, against Lord Evkit, their leader at the time. There was simply no point. She couldn't possibly get *more* angry at him than she'd been when he stole her child.

In any case, the Horn had been destroyed as well, Lord Evkit's little kingdom shattered by human stupidity, the remnants stolen from him by his own daughter. Evkit's peculiar mystics, the athain, held little to no power now, leaving Evkit vulnerable to his many enemies. Teilo didn't have to lift a finger towards revenge.

She did want revenge on her most recent captors, the attiara. The other-kin had fled during the collapse of their den beneath the Qisani, leaving her behind to die. Since her emergence, she'd been unable to locate them. Thinking of them still made her genuinely angry. They'd dared! They'd dared bind *her*, once First among those called to serve!

Her lips distorted in resentful anger. That wouldn't do. She drew in a few breaths, calming herself, and built dry humor from the ashes of the rage, a recognition of the immobility of the past: *Ah, well, once.*

Once lay long and long ago, and there were other matters to hand in the moment. If she found the attiara, she'd take her revenge. She contemplated a visit to Peys:mun Family, far to the south of where she stood, for some extremely sharp words with a certain First Born hakrakha, regarding how he'd abandoned her to the thoughtless tortures of the attiara.

Words, and more than words.

Let it be, let it go. She didn't have the strength for that long a trip purely for vengeance. They were both functionally immortal; her anger with Deiq could wait. Now was the time to focus on rebuilding, pulling together scraps and bits, proteins and salts, bone chips and muscle fragments. She could combine them into a cohesive form that humans wouldn't flee from with shrieks about demons and *shia-banse*.

Shia-banse wasn't actually all that far off, depending on how one viewed matters.

Focus. Focus.

She let herself sink down through the water, releasing what little coherence she'd held while thinking. From sand and shell and fish, seaweed, bone, and stone, she began to create a new body. It would look nothing like her previous form, but that was a relief. Being a blind-eyed crone had been getting — she snickered to herself — old.

Time for something *new*.

Chapter Two

Bright Bay didn't have a proper church. Lia had trouble wrapping her mind around that idea. This was the heart of the kingdom, the home of the king, the place where the Northern Church creed had been *born*; and yet, unbelievably, the southern religion had recently taken full hold here instead. Dozens of small shrines and symbols to the southern Three, rather than the northern Four, were scattered openly about the city.

She'd known to expect it, of course. Her local priests, in Stecatr, had been very clear in their condemnation of the king city's impious behavior of late. Seeing the proliferation of southern heresy here of all places still came as a shock. As did the realization that even two months ago, she would have said *The Northern Church had been very clear*, rather than *my local priests*. She was still coming to terms with the reality that worship of the Four was handled differently from town to town — and that *none* of those others matched the version she'd grown up with.

Equally startling had been Sanben's warning not to talk about anything Northern Church related in Bright Bay. "It's not in favor, down this side of the Forest," the mercenary told her firmly. "Don't you go calling on your gods or making your warding signs. You won't like what you get back in your face."

Lia hadn't entirely believed that. It was simply too vast of a concept to accept. No Church? No priests? No followers at *all*? Impossible. The Stecatr priests must be wrong, and Sanben was pulling her leg.

Lia had hired on alongside Sanben in Orhon, a small village not far from Stecatr and, coincidentally, her mother's birthplace. They'd served merchant Kennet as guards, occasional packhorses, and, in Lia's case, backup for the sales table on market days. Kennet was generally surly and cynical; Sanben started out coarse, rude, and sarcastic. Sanben's attitude, at least, had softened over the days and miles, as she earned his good regard.

Even then, he retained a streak of jagged humor and liked to poke fun at her ignorance. She had been absolutely sure the matter of the Northern Church's presence in Bright Bay was one such case.

But among the colorful clothing and sprawling architecture, only the smallest signs remained of the Four. A mosaic on the side of a fountain, weathered from neglect. An inscription on a wall, heavily scratched as though someone had tried to remove it and gave up halfway through. A small pot of clover, set unobtrusively to one side of a doorway.

Lia almost knocked on that last door, suddenly desperate to make a connection with something familiar. Common sense and an uncommon sense of dread stopped her. She walked on, increasingly bewildered.

The Bright Bay Hall of Arms, her first and most obligatory stop in the absence of a church, was as oddly built as the rest of the city. It consisted of a series of long, low-roofed stone structures, connected by walkways overhung by massive tropical trees. A floral smell hung in the air, not unpleasant but nearly overpowering in spots. Enormous windows, draped with insect netting, were framed by heavy shutters that spoke volumes about the seasonal hurricanes Sanben had mentioned in a conversation along the road.

"Like a blizzard," Sanben said, "but *wet*."

Then he'd explained tornadoes. That concept had given her nightmares in which her entire family was swept up into the sky and lost to her forever. She still eyed any accumulation of southern clouds with deep distrust.

The master of the Bright Bay Hall of Arms didn't meet with Lia directly, of course. She wasn't nearly that important. Instead, she spoke to a clerk, updated her information, signed up for a free room and a meal a day, and found herself wandering the city before noon.

Kennet had offered her a job working his market stall until she found a northbound contract, but he wasn't setting up for two more days. She had time to explore, and Sanben was meeting her at the center of the market.

"You'll know it," he'd told her. "Bunch of food stalls. Tents. Everyone gossiping. Wear light clothes, it'll be blazing by then. Don't wear that damn ata." He flapped a hand at her, cutting off her protest, then walked away.

She wore the face covering anyway. Her oath to the Stecatr Hall required wearing it whenever she was armed. Daggers were considered unremarkable, but they didn't feel obvious enough. Lia knew her slight build invited underestimation, so leaving her sword behind always made her far too twitchy in strange areas. She did make sure her wooden mug was tightly attached to her belt; no point paying for one, once she got to the center.

Lia regretted the choice to wear the mask as the dense humidity glued the cloth to her hair, face, and mouth. She frequently had to shift the folds to uncover her mouth or nose for a time. People stared at the mask, some edging away with suspicious care. She did her best not to glare back. They didn't know. They couldn't know.

The slightest credible suspicion that Lia had broken the oaths required of her by the Stecatr priests would rebound on her family, on her younger sister most of all. Gossip ran faster than water down a steep cliff, and she wouldn't be there to protect them if things went sour. It wasn't worth the risk.

The market stalls ran for what seemed like miles. Brightly colored tents and pavilions offered customers shade. Distinctly expensive stalls boasted servants waving fans to provide a breeze, and clouds of birds wheeled overhead at erratic intervals, chirruping and squawking.

The noise and the smell varied from thick to overwhelming. In one section, chickens, sheep, horses, cows, pigs, and a double dozen exotics Lia had never even heard of before cast their distinctive voices and aromas into the air. The ata, slick with sweat by that point, did nothing to help the smell.

She paused to look at a tightly woven cage holding several small brown snakes. The merchant, a thickly built man in a sweat-stained robe, grinned unpleasantly at her without rising from his stool. He said something in a desert dialect; registering her incomprehension, he switched to Kaenic, the standard kingdom language.

"Desert adders," he told her. "*Micru*. One bite is deadly."

There was only one customer for that kind of item, and she certainly wasn't it. Incredulous that an assassin's tool could be sold so blatantly in open market, Lia backed up a cautious step. The man's grin widened to mockery. She ignored him and moved on to a less brazen display.

A line of canines caught her attention next. Thin and long-legged, with finely boned muzzles, they looked like an aristocratic version of wofics. This merchant, a dumpy little man with lank brown hair, looked her over and chose Kaenic.

"Asp-jacaus," he informed her briskly. "Excellent sense of smell. Nobles use them to pick out snakes."

Lia couldn't help glancing back towards the *micru* stall. The asp-jacau merchant grinned with the same sour amusement as the previous man. Once more, she backed up and moved on. Her next stop was involuntary and delighted:

"Firebirds!" she blurted.

The handler looked up, his lines face creasing into an indulgent smile, and waved her over.

"You're northern, then," he said as she approached. "We call 'em chachad birds, here. They're lovely to look at, aren't they?"

Some of the firebirds — chachad birds — stood nearly as tall as Lia, although most only reached to her waist. They were, as the name implied, a ferocious shade of red, their glossy black legs tipped with wickedly taloned feet. The males had a crest of feathers that could lie flat or poof out around their heads like a lion's mane, while the females had a more delicate, golden fringe down each side of their necks.

She'd heard stories about firebirds her whole life: fierce protectors of humans and livestock alike, favored by both of Patyi's incarnations, the kindly and angry alike. They lived for hundreds of years, in the stories.

These birds looked very mortal, to her. Still incredibly impressive, but not gods-touched. Hoping it wasn't an embarrassingly ignorant question, she asked, "How long do they live?"

The handler's grin widened, but not mockingly. "Not as long as the hero tales would have it. A dozen years, maybe twenty at the outside. Depends on how well they're taken care of. Royal creatures, these, and the tales do get one thing right: they're excellent guardians. Are you in the market for one, perhaps?"

Lia shook her head, stepping back. "Thank you for letting me look at them, *s'e*."

"You're more than welcome, *s'a*. You have a good day." He waved cheerfully as she moved on.

Lia wished she could sketch some of the animals for Kia, especially those chachad birds. But not only was drawing living things forbidden to women by the Ch — the *Stecatr* Church — Lia's best effort would be stick figures. Instead, she looked closely, asked questions, collected stories to tell her little sister later, and decided to write down as much as possible that night. Kia would be annoyed if she forgot or muddied the details of something so exciting.

One stall offered drawings of several animals. She hovered uncertainly, then passed it by as, again, too risky. She did buy a sheaf of drawings featuring southern plants and buildings; that was safe enough, and the artist offered a stiff leather carrying tube for a reasonable fee.

From there, Lia passed into a section that seemed designed to offset the pungent mixture of animal smells with perfumes, incense, oils, herbs, spices, and soaps of every possible variety. The wind swirled more strongly here, keeping the pleasant aromas from becoming overwhelming.

Lia spent some more of her carefully hoarded coin on spices. Her mother loved cooking with unusual ingredients. Cinnamon, nutmeg, and a red-tinged variety of clove would delight her. They were hard to come by and expensive in Stecatr.

After some consideration, she bought a small bar of exotically-spiced shaving soap for her father. He'd likely never use it, but it seemed worth the gesture all the same.

Her nose was running freely by the time she escaped that row. She was relieved to find herself at the center of the market at last. As promised, it was a large, erratically covered courtyard with bench tables at which to rest. A few stalls stood around the edges of the dining area, offering pastries and pies, skewered meats and, most importantly of all, drinks.

Lia negotiated a dipperful of fruit-scented water from a small-ale vendor, then retreated to a table with a sigh of relief. Sanben was nowhere to be seen. Well, he'd just have to find her. She wasn't moving for a while.

The three women already seated there turned their heads, looked her over, then rose as one and stalked away. In the northlands, it would have been an intolerable insult. Lia had no idea if it carried the same weight here. It seemed likely, but she'd seen enough odd differences to be wary of assumption.

She picked at the ata, resignedly shoving stray hair back under cover, and wished for the breeze that had made the perfume and spice stalls bearable. Even at the height of summer, Stecatr sat high enough in the mountains that there was generally a breeze to shake the heat apart. Here, Lia felt flattened by the stifling moisture. She envied the locals their loose, flowing clothes, even as she tried not to stare at how much skin was showing.

Words like *redstone, charcoal,* and *leather* came to her mind when looking at the people here. The broader, paler features she'd lived amongst all her life were merely sun-reddened accents. Many of the darker-skinned folk had completely shaven heads. Others, men and women both, wore their hair long, plaited into thin braids woven through with brightly colored threads or beads.

And the women! Lia *tried* not to stare, but gods, she'd honestly never seen so much exposed skin. Nobody appeared to view it as the least bit indecent. The women didn't strut or show themselves off. They moved normally, and were treated normally, and —

Lia froze as two women, dressed in brightly colored, fluttering gauze that covered damned near nothing, walked by arm in arm. They openly exchanged flirtatious gestures and the occasional kiss. In Stecatr, with a properly gendered couple, the ostentatious affection would have been scandalous. These brazen women would immediately have been taken by the Church, and hanged within a day, with or without official approval from the Lord of Stecatr.

Lia's eyes stung. She looked elsewhere, wiping away what had to be sweat, and focused on a child of indeterminate gender running past. It tripped, fell, rolled to its feet without pause or complaint, and dashed off again.

Is it different, in the city? a young woman in a small town had asked months ago, blue eyes swimming with misery. *Do they hang you here?* Lia replied, deliberately brutal.

But in *this* city ... oh, yes. Matters were, very obviously, very different indeed.

Two men went by, casually holding hands as any couple might do. Lia's mug creaked in her grip. She made herself relax her hands.

Dear gods ... Isla....

For a searingly bitter moment, Lia considered staying. She could get used to the heat. She could get used to anything if it meant —

No. *No.* Isla was gone, and Lia had to get back to her family. She couldn't allow herself to think of any path which allowed such indecent behavior. She had to leave those thoughts, those days, behind her. She'd made a choice. She'd sworn a sacred oath. Payti was tempting her. That was all.

Wae, cool my intemperate nature, wash me with Your holy waters and calm my soul. Aspna Pay'nianth, aspna, aspna.

She shifted the folds of the ata aside and took several long swallows of water, trying to forget the sight. Isla was gone, that was all. She'd never laugh at Lia's fear again, never spin round in a blue dress, never cheerfully mock the world's expectations, never greedily inhale the smell of Lia's freshly washed hair. All those memories belonged firmly in the small, spiky mental box that contained Lia's most painful moments. She didn't need to ever think about Isla again.

She couldn't bear it.

She slammed the imaginary box shut as a large form loomed in her peripheral vision.

"There you are," Sanben announced grandly, and plopped down on the bench across from her. He wore a light, sleeveless shirt and red linen pants. His dark hair was neatly washed and braided back, no blond streaks showing now. The way his skin was already bronzed from miles of walking, he could have been a local. He made a sour face at her and demanded, in his broad northern accent, "Why in th'*hells* you wearing that damn thing? Like to suffocate in this mess."

"Hello, San'," Lia answered. "I'm wearing my sword. I have to wear the ata."

"Stupid, wearing the sword. What, you think you'll get into a fight inna open marketplace? Stupid." He snatched her mug away and peered into it. "Thought so. Water! Pfeh." He stood and crossed to the small-beer stall, taking her mug with him.

Lia leaned her elbows on the table and worked at the edges of her ata, loosening it to get some relief. She wondered, with cynical resignation, what stink-brew he'd inflict on her this time. He'd been trying to make her like ale the whole road south.

Sanben returned with two mugs, hers and his own, both filled with a pale amber liquid. "There you go. Try that."

"It's blazing hot and you want me to eat porridge?" she retorted, sniffing at the mug gingerly. It didn't smell like swampwater, but with her nose running she couldn't tell what it *did* smell like.

"Nah, not this," he said, laughing at her. "I got you sommat good this time. Try it." His hands were heavily bruised, the knuckles split in spots. He rubbed at them, wincing a bit.

She eyed him warily, but parted the ata and took a sip all the same. Ginger and citrus blazed across her tongue, and the liquid actually felt *cold* going down. She took a second, larger gulp, then lowered the mug. Sanben roared with laughter.

"Your expression! Gods," he said, still chuckling. "You look like you expected to lick a pig's ass and wound up with a mouthful of good cream instead."

"More or less," Lia admitted. "All right, this isn't bad. How is this cold, though? You can't tell me there's ice here!"

"Things are different here," he told her cheerfully. "There's witches here as *make* ice when they want." He motioned towards the stall he'd bought the beers from. "Got a partial over there, he can do some marvelous tricks."

Lia's hand fell away from the mug as though shocked by lightning. *Witches*? Had she just drunk a witch-brew? "A partial? What's that mean?"

"Eh, it's …." Sanben hesitated, sobering. "Eh. I shouldn't'a started talking on that. Just … just forget I said anything."

Lia stared at the man, abruptly suspicious. "Is this like that … thing in Arason?" she demanded.

That thing. Gods, that was a using bit of sand to indicate a mountain. *That thing.* That non-human — inhuman? — personage, Idisio — *ha'inn Idisio* — who'd witched Lia twice. The first time she'd woken up in her inn room. The second time, she'd woken up days out on the road. The memory still put chill horror up her back. *That thing*, indeed.

"Sommat like, yeah." Sanben studied his mug with a frown. "It's a lot different here. Your Church wouldn't like a lot of it." He laid enough emphasis on *your* to be clear that he was talking about Stecatr.

"I believe I've figured that out already," Lia said dryly.

Sanben glanced up, searched her face for a moment, then sighed. "Yeah, well. I figure you don't want to have to answer questions, when you get home. So what you don't know, you can't say on, and you can't get in trouble. And your family's safe then. Yeah?"

That put her at a loss for words. She'd only mentioned her worry for her family once. She couldn't believe he remembered.

Sanben studied her eyes, not smiling. His own gaze was flat and subdued. He said, "You ought to stay, Lia. You'd like it here, I think."

The words slipped out: "I think I would too." She caught herself there and added, acerbically, "Maybe in the winter, though."

Sanben laughed. "Nah, this's cool for this time of year. Humidity, yeah, that's bad, but in another few tendays we'll be at full blaze. Everyone stops moving, pretty much. Then there's the rain, when you only got a couple hours a day to get anything done outside."

"Why would Kennet want to stay here, then?" Lia demanded. "It can't be profitable!"

"There's more than profit, even for Kennet," Sanben said. "He's got two lovers here as want a fair chunk of his time now and again. He can't stand 'em more than every other year, though, so he switches out where he ends his route each spring. That widow in Orhon don't like Kennet any more often than that, so it works out well enough."

Lia couldn't think of a thing to say to that casual recitation of utterly heretical behavior. Sanben laughed at her expression.

"You're just poking at me, aren't you?" she accused.

"Nope," he told her. "Damn, you're wet still. Thought I'd knocked that priddity out of you on the way down."

"*Priddity?*" It didn't sound like a southern word, somehow.

He waved a hand impatiently, then winced and lowered it to inspect the trickling blood from a broken scab. He muttered a curse under his breath, then said, "Priggish. Prudish. Twitchy. Whatever. You ought to stay, is the point."

"No thanks," she said. "I'm ready to turn around and go home as it is."

"What, you been here a day, two days, and you're cutting out?" he demanded, incredulous. "You can't be serious. You can't even have put your toes in the ocean yet. I know you said you were leaving, but come on!" He looked at his hand thoughtfully, then shrugged and licked the blood away.

Lia leaned back, her lip curling. Sanben smirked at her.

She retorted, "I'm completely serious. I have to be back by Winter Festival. I told you that."

"And *I* said you oughtn't make any such promises, living this life," he shot back. Then his lips thinned and he shut his eyes briefly, making a careful, dismissive gesture with one hand. "Eh, whatever. Look. I did some asking around. Any merchants headed back up to the North Road far as the mountains done already left. Only ones still here aren't going past Isata, or Arason maybe. Nobody wants to get trapped in an early blizzard." He drained his mug, then looked at it thoughtfully, as though considering whether to get more.

"Are you saying there's *nobody* here traveling north at this point?" she demanded.

Sanben set his mug down with a grin and swiped hers. "You gotta drink it afore it gets warm." He drained the contents in three long swallows. "There, that was just in time to save it," he added, setting it back down in front of her with a wink just shy of a leer. "An' saved me the cost of a new one."

She hooked her mug back on her belt with an exasperated glare at him. "There must be *someone*," she insisted.

"Eh, well." Sanben, sobering once more, sighed. He turned on the bench to scan the area. "Yeah, all right, you hardheaded bitch. You're lucky in your timing, for sure. Half the tent is all merchants gaggling about at each other. See — there's Kennet."

Lia wouldn't have recognized the man if Sanben hadn't pointed him out. Like Sanben himself, the merchant now wore clothing that matched the local crowd's bright, thin garb. His hair was done up in bead-studded braids, and he was more cheerful than she'd seen him in weeks. She hadn't noticed before, but he'd definitely lost weight on their journey south. Not that he'd ever been chunky, as such, but his frame showed through more clearly than when they first met. She wondered if she also looked leaner.

Sanben, mangling his sentences as he did when distracted, said, "So from as I can see, what's sitting here are folks as go from here to Sandsplit, which don't get you nowhere useful, since you don't want to chance not finding a reliable group in Sandsplit for the Forest Road. It's a nice enough town, but it's small, yeah? And a few crazies live there. You don't want to hang around looking needy."

He sucked on his front teeth, considering, and glanced at her. "A couple groups I know as might be headed out to Isata, at best, but those ain't people I'd tell you to walk with. They're … they're dubious sorts. Me, yeah, I'd watch my back and take the chance, but you gotta think about rumors more'n I do, and these folks lean towards hiring unsworn. That ain't no good for your name."

Lia reflected, not for the first time, that Sanben had proven to be considerably more perceptive than she'd expected. His eyes gleamed as he grinned at her. She suspected he knew what she was thinking.

"One set left," he continued. "Best of a bad lot. Well, maybe that ain't fair. But whatever. See the big redhead sitting with his back to us, at his own table but near the gaggle, over past my left shoulder? Looks like one of your northern lot, don't he? He's southern, believe it or not. Name of Tank. He's sworn through Bright Bay Hall and runs alongside a merchant called Dasin. Both of 'em crazy as a bat drunk on dashaic, but the redhead's solid enough."

His mouth drew aside, and he cut Lia a glance as though waiting for her to ask what *dashaic* was. Given that she'd already learned enough to shock her into silence three times over today, she kept her mouth shut this time.

Sanben grinned briefly, apparently guessing her thoughts, then went on. "They do a route to Assiasan, deal with herbs and such. They normally leave earlier'n this, but they've had some schedule trouble this year. Way I hear it, they've decided to risk a winter layover up north. Might be they'd take you on. I think they might be down a guard."

He rubbed his knuckles again, absently nodding to himself. "Yeah, that'll do. Tell him I sent you. He'll know my name." He pulled a half-gold round from his belt pouch and passed it to Lia, who regarded it with surprise. "Buy him one of them ales I got you. It's called ginger-gold. Tell him that's from me, too. Might sweeten his mood a bit."

She glanced at the small-ale stall in disbelief. "Gods, is it that expensive?" *Do I have to pay you back?* hovered on the back of her tongue. She held it silent with an effort. Sanben had been the one to insist on the drink; she didn't owe him anything.

He smirked, as though once more guessing her thoughts. "To fill your mug and one for him, yeah," he said. "Why you think I snatched yours up? Heh. You want his attention, that'll do the trick. Well, that and your damn headwrap." He laughed and lumbered to his feet, hooking his mug back onto his belt. "Go on, then, talk to the batshit redling. I'll go find me another drinking companion."

The small-beer stall vendor was a thin man with mismatched eyes and a pleasant smile. Lia, the word *partial* ringing far too close to the surface of her mind, tried to return it in kind. By the way his expression cooled, she hadn't succeeded.

She held up her mug. "Two mugs of ginger-gold, please."

"Half a gold for two and a mug," the vendor said, voice and eyes flat. She handed over Sanben's coin, wondering if her momentary slip had inflated the price. It didn't seem safe to haggle the way she would have in Stecatr.

As far as she could tell, he didn't spit in the ale as he drew it. When he handed the mugs to her, though, his stare remained no friendlier than that of a micru.

"I'm sorry," she blurted. "This is my first time here. I don't mean to be rude."

His mouth quirked into a more amused expression. "You're not the first northern to be upset by my eyes," he told her. "Go on. No harm."

Taking that as an easy excuse, although his eyes weren't actually the most upsetting part, she retreated with relief. As she approached the table Sanben had indicated, the angle took her behind the sole occupant. The line of the man's broad shoulders tightened, his head lifting.

Recognizing that reaction, she swung wide around the table. As she'd expected, the moment she entered his peripheral vision his gaze locked on her: not hostile, but sharply assessing.

Lia sat down, placed one mug in front of him, and took a reluctant sip of her own. She set her mug on the table before her, then flattened her hands on the warm wood.

"Afternoon, *s'e*," she said calmly into his bright blue stare. "Tank, isn't it?"

His gaze tracked over her, examining the ata, her hands, her shoulders, then back to her face. She took the opportunity to study him as well. He seemed to be in his twenties at most, with a head of Stecatr-bright red hair and a dense array of freckles that almost blended into suntanned skin. His clothing was simple and light, both in color and material, leaving his muscular arms bare to the shoulder. He wore no jewelry, no marks of status or rank, but he had the air of a seasoned commander.

"Take that mask off," he ordered. "I don't talk to people I can't see."

Lia unwrapped the ata, then dropped the cloth into her lap and finger-combed her hair into a rough semblance of order, painfully conscious of how rumpled, creased, and red her face must look.

Tank studied her with an entirely blank expression for a moment, then blinked and leaned back a bit. An odd smile stretched his mouth.

"Well, then," he said. "And what can I do for you today, *s'a?*" His voice was a pleasant baritone, with a distinctly southern cadence and frequently blurred vowels.

She made herself quit smoothing her hair back. "I'm looking for a contract to take me up along the North Road. I'm from Stecatr, and I need to be back by Winter Festival." She was talking too fast. Something about his intent regard was throwing her nerves to all the hells. She tried to pace her next words more steadily. "Sanben said I should talk to you. The beer is a gift from him."

His smile faded, eyes narrowing thoughtfully. "Is it, now." He lifted the mug and sniffed the contents. "Ginger-gold. Huh." He set it down without tasting it, never taking his eyes from her face. "Sanben, was it." None of those phrases were properly inflected as questions.

"He ... he said you might be down a guard." She barely managed not to turn it into a question. The conversation seemed to be hurtling toward an invisible cliff, and she had no idea how to turn it aside.

"He should know," the redhead said, no smile on his face at all now.

The cliff loomed close. Lia shut her eyes, already wincing; remembering the fresh bruises on Sanben's knuckles, she knew what Tank was about to say.

"Sanben's the *ta-karne* as put our third guard out of shape last night. Gint was just back on his feet after a bout of flu. He went out to have a beer, wound up in a brawl." His face settled into grim lines. The beer hadn't been enough for him to forgive Sanben. No wonder San' hadn't walked her over for introductions himself.

Lia silently cursed Sanben through every one of the hells, then sent a hasty apology to the gods for such unkind thoughts. *Aspna, aspna.* She was losing her way again.

After what seemed a dreadfully long time, Tank said, "You didn't know."

"No. Sanben didn't mention that detail." Lia hesitated, considering a polite retreat followed by a mug of something scalding thrown in Sanben's face at the first opportunity. But if this was her only option ....

"Your name and Hall, then," the redhead said, expressionless.

"Lia of Stecatr Hall," she said. His eyebrows climbed sharply, and he gave her another swift, sweeping assessment. She spread her hands on the table and set her jaw, annoyed as always by that reaction.

"Tank of Bright Bay Hall," he offered after a moment, his expression smoothing back to blankness. "Stecatr. You did say, earlier. I didn't hear it properly. Stecatr. Huh. So you're the one that's been on the gossip tree."

Next he'd ask about the restrictions the Church had imposed. People always did, usually with leers or mocking grins. Lia thinned her lips and offered up something her mother had often said, when confronted with gossip: "There are always people with more mouth than sense."

Tank grinned, although a cool appraisal lingered in his eyes.

"That is the truth," he agreed. "So, then, show me your Hall coin."

She handed over the large wooden disk. The Stecatr Hall of Arms crossed-dagger sigil was burnt into one side, her own circle and stars mark on the other. Tank studied it briefly, feeling along the edge as though that told him something, then handed it back.

He let out a small, thoughtful humming noise, looking her over yet again. She couldn't tell if he was inspecting muscles or curves this time, and her jaw tightened in rising anger.

Tank met her eyes and blinked, leaning back a bit. "Eh," he said as though by way of apology.

A burst of laughter to the side drew Lia's attention. Kennet was grinning at the table around him, most of whom were roaring their amusement and even slapping the table. Probably he'd told them the story about the women and the pigs in Starst. Kennet turned his head, meeting Lia's eye, and hoisted his mug in cheerful greeting. Then his gaze settled on Tank.

Kennet's smile faded to a thoughtful, wary expression. He raised an eyebrow in question, or perhaps warning, at Lia, then pointedly turned back to his companions.

Tank didn't seem to have noticed the brief exchange. He pointed at the mass of black fabric puddled on the table in front of her. "Tell me about that thing."

Lia made herself focus on him again, noting the slight crease around his eyes. For all his relaxed poise, he hadn't actually missed a thing. "It's called an *ata*. I have to wear it any time I'm carrying anything larger than a belt knife."

The child ran by again, in the other direction, apparently unaffected by the dire humidity. Lia envied that resilience. She already felt herself wilting into a lake of sweat. There had to be a bathhouse somewhere along the way back to the inn. She would spend any amount of coin for cool water and soap right now.

A breeze swirled by, nearly sticky with salt. She considered excusing herself and leaping into the ocean, fully clothed. It couldn't be all that different from a lake, could it?

Tank observed, "That's not standard rules."

"I'm the first woman to graduate the Stecatr Hall of Arms," she said.

His blue eyes narrowed. "Meaning the Church demanded it."

She returned his flat stare with one of her own. Sweat trickled down her neck and down her chest, and her face increasingly felt sunburn-hot.

Tank nudged her mug with a knuckle, frowning. "Drink, northern, before you faint." He waited until she'd drained half the mug, then said, "Church rules are endlessly fucking stupid, that one more than most. I won't have it. Lose the wrap or find someone else to ride with. Wait." His words had sharpened, losing the soft edges and taking on authority.

He rose, picking up her half-empty mug and his untouched one, and went over to the small-ale stall. The vendor offered him an amiable grin and swapped out the ginger-gold for the same fruit-scented water she'd started out with. Tank came back and plunked Lia's mug down in front of her. "Half of this. Now."

She drank, resentful but unable to argue the sense of the command. Then she said, "I have to wear the ata. I'll lose my standing. You said it yourself, people are gossiping. Word would reach Stecatr before I did."

"Not my problem." He drained half his mug of water, then leaned well back and poured the rest of it over his head. "Fucking heat," he muttered, swiping his free hand over his hair to spread the moisture out, then sat up with a sigh. His light shirt clung to his torso, water beading down his arms and across his face. As though he hadn't paused, he went on, "Wear it in Stecatr. You can go ask the Bright Bay Hall for a letter of exemption for undue hardship. They'll grant it. And you'll feel better for dumping that over your head, too, you know."

"And give everyone a show," she retorted. "No thank you."

He grinned. "No more than anyone else is offering, by your standards," he pointed out, glancing sideways as a group of women settled at a nearby table. Like the two women Lia had seen flirting earlier, they wore barely enough to cover essential areas and seemed entirely unselfconscious of it. One woman laid a piece of thick fabric on the bench before sitting, which won her a round of mockery from her companions.

Lia tore her gaze and her thoughts away from that display, and found Tank looking at her with a thoughtful squint.

Abrupt anger crowded her throat. She said, voice gaining strength with every word, "I'm wearing the ata. I swore an oath. This is *my choice, s'e*. This is what you're hiring. And you're going to hire me, because you're down a guard and late on the road. I'm honest, and Hall-sworn, and the best you'll find on short notice. Sanben might be an ass, but I can tell you respect his judgment. So unless you're feeling rich enough to layover here until next Secondmonth, let's be done with you telling me what oaths I'm allowed to honor and start talking money."

She made herself stop there, sucking in a deep breath of the salt-thick air. The women at the nearby table had stopped chattering and were staring her way. Apparently she'd been louder than intended. A glare at the women turned their attention quickly away. A glare at Tank just made his thoughtful squint deepen.

A long moment of silence hung between them. She kept eye contact, her spine defiantly rigid.

At last, his face relaxed, a bemused smile appearing. "Does the damned thing have to be *black?*"

Lia let out a long, slow breath, adjusting her temper. "It's what I was given," she said with care. "I actually never thought about getting a different one."

His grin widened, then vanished into a brisk, businesslike attitude.

"*Allipa* over." Tank pointed to the stalls behind her. "Two rows over. Wolf's Cloth Shop. You'll see the wolf head sign. Tell him I sent you, and get him to sew up something lighter, color and fabric both, rush order, by the end of the day. He'll put it on our bill. An' by the way, you ought to go without that mask for a while, you're getting a stripe." He drew a hand across his eyes by way of illustration. "Few hours in the sun here an' there and it's sorted, but don't wait much longer."

"...All right. Thank you," she said, slightly dazed by the abrupt turnaround.

He went on, words rapid enough now that she had to pay close attention, all softness gone. He could have been a northern rattling off orders. "Terms. We take the North Road through Assiasan. Pay is two and eight in silver a day if you have your own horse, two and a half if you don't. Merchant's name is Dasin. We run spices and herbs. One wagon, three guards." He held up three fingers, then pointed one at himself. "I'm trail captain. Cilif's my second." He pointed at her. "You make the third. As newest, you get scut work, cleaning up dishes and such at the end of the day. Whoever gets up last in the morning does the breakfast dishes. Cilif and I do the cooking. You bring your own tent if you want one, or you can share a tent with one of us. Problem with any of that?"

She took a moment to sort through what he'd said, making sure the speed and her surprise at his vanished accent hadn't blurred anything in her head.

Finally, she said, more calmly than she felt, "No. I'll get a tent of my own." *And new boots. And clothes that aren't a sack of sweat by noon. And I'll definitely have enough of a tithe to make the Church happy.* Relief made her briefly dizzy. How could spices possibly be *that* profitable? To cover her reaction, she drank off the rest of her water in three large gulps.

Tank picked up his own empty mug as though to drink, then grimaced in annoyance and set it down again. "Talk to Wolf about a tent, too," he advised. "He takes 'em in trade now and again, might have something cheap. Horse?"

The child trotted by again, much more slowly. Its face was beginning to flush. Tank turned his head to watch, muttering something under his breath.

Lia said, "No." Tank looked at her, frowning, and she clarified, "No horse."

His face relaxed. "Ah. Can you ride? Groom and tack up and all that?"

"Yes."

Tank half-rose, looking in the direction the child had gone. He waved to someone, pointed after the child, then sat back down with a thump. "Good. Go to Cross's Stable, north and east two blocks of here. Tell 'em you're there for Rooster. Was Gint's horse. Now it's yours, while you're with us anyway." He paused, looking past her again. "That's handled, at least," he muttered.

Lia held herself firmly straight, as much from dignity as from a sense that Tank was testing to see if she was nervous about things happening out of her direct sight.

Tank grinned at her, his sly amusement confirming her suspicions, then went on, "Rooster's a splotchy, leggy gelding. We supply the feed, the tack, all the basics. You care for your beast and help with the others as asked. Again, you're junior, you'll be given the heavy end of the load. Understood?"

"Yes." She so, so badly wanted to turn and look for the child, even knowing that Tank was baiting her. Probably he'd signalled the child's parent to collar it and douse it with water, but he could just as well have waved guards after it.

None of it was her business, in any case. Feral children ran everywhere in any large city. She'd been one herself.

"You speak anything but Kaenic?" Tank asked abruptly, and seemed pleased when she shook her head. She tried not to scowl, guessing that he'd be chattering away with his companions in a southern dialect whenever they didn't want her to know something. Rude, and insulting. Maybe she could angle for language lessons along the way. That might help her nerves, if nothing else.

Tank heaved himself to his feet, picking up his empty mug. "All right. Let's go introduce you to Dasin, then I'll cut you loose to go handle what you've just taken on. We leave before sunrise."

She stood as well. As he detoured to drop off his mug, she drained her own, hooked it onto her belt, then turned to scan the crowd. The child was nowhere in sight. Unsurprised but vaguely disappointed, she trailed after Tank, hoping that Dasin would prove to be less bewildering than the big redhead.

Chapter Three

Dasin, predictably, was in the wine-seller's section of the dining tents, sipping pale wine from a fine glass goblet and talking with three fellow merchants. His fine blond hair, gathered into a series of beaded braids and looped up into a style that kept it off the back of his neck, looked shorter than it actually was.

Tank's fingers twitched a bit as he remembered the previous night. *Gods*, Dasin looked good with his hair down. He'd been awake when Tank got back from his dockside vigil, and in an unusually amorous mood.

Focus.

It was cooler here. Servants flapped broad palm-leaf fans, and a partial sat quietly in a corner, eyes closed. Tank ignored him, knowing Lia wouldn't see anything other than a small, dark-skinned man in pale blue and silver clothing. As long as he didn't draw attention to the man, Lia wouldn't start twisting her hands about her precious Stecatr morality.

Stecatr. Godsbedamned Stecatr. Tank would have refused anyone else from that ridiculous place, but Lia intrigued him. Gint had been starting to piss him off anyway, so this was as good an excuse to switch him out as he'd likely get.

Dasin's clothing and jewelry were expensively simple: a white peasant shirt and beige trousers of finest linen, two silver hoops in each ear. Intricately etched silver bracelets clinked on his left wrist and circled above his right elbow.

His fellow merchants were all similarly attired. Two had the dark hair and features of southerners, but the third was a pale-haired northern Tank had met before. Gen something. Genic? Genvic? Garvic? It didn't matter. The man dealt in fine silver jewelry, if Tank remembered correctly. The other two were likely in related trades. Dasin chose his conversations strategically.

Dasin's aloof expression remained intact as he watched Tank and Lia approaching.

"Excuse me, *s'ieas*," Dasin said lazily as Tank paused a respectful five paces from the table. "My trail captain *apparently* needs a word with me." The last words held the impatience of a noble being bothered by an underling; Dasin's way of rebuking Tank for interrupting.

Tank bit the inside of his cheek and stayed stolidly expressionless.

As the three merchants rose, Gen grinned amiably at Tank, then shifted his gaze to Lia, who hadn't restored her face wrap yet. His grin slid into something considerably more personal. Tank moved a step sideways, breaking the merchant's line of sight, and delivered a flat stare. Gen, blanching, retreated hastily.

The two southerners chuckled. In a dialect that Lia wouldn't understand, and which they probably didn't think Tank would, the broader of the two remarked, "That one has a type, and one day it'll put a knife in his ribs." He bowed to Tank and tugged his companion away, linking arms as they went.

Tank turned to find Lia giving him the same flat stare he'd aimed at the silver merchant. She obviously wasn't impressed by his intervention. He shrugged unapologetically and waved her to a seat on the bench. She didn't move.

Dasin's pale, blue-gray stare swept thoughtfully across Lia, then fixed on Tank. Tank half-lifted one shoulder, grinning into that silent query. He said, with expansive courtesy, "Merchant Dasin, meet Lia of Stecatr. I'm hiring her to replace Gint. Now we can leave in the morning as we'd planned. *S'e*," he added with servile humility, just to make Dasin twitch.

Dasin's eyes narrowed into distinct hostility that boded ill for a repeat of the previous night.

Lia shifted her weight uneasily. "Greetings, merchant Dasin. I —"

"Sit down," Dasin snapped. He kept his stare pinned on Tank.

Lia sank onto the bench.

Dasin's mouth thinned. "I thought we'd agreed that Gint could catch up with us." He didn't even glance at Lia.

"He doesn't need to, now," Tank said easily, and tucked his thumbs into his belt because he knew the casual disrespect of it would annoy Dasin. "Town to town is the deal, like always. We've swapped out guards on the last day before."

A vein beat in Dasin's forehead. In Aerthraim dialect, which even a passing southerner likely wouldn't understand, he snapped, "You're pushing your authority. Yuer approved Gint. This one isn't going to be accepted."

"*This one*," Tank said, in the same dialect, "is the first woman to graduate the Stecatr Hall of Arms. And she had the guts to face me down when I pushed her. Gint's a stale noodle with his nose up Yuer's ass, and you know it."

Dasin shifted his gaze to study Lia for a long moment. Since Tank was standing behind Lia, he couldn't see her expression, but the set of her shoulders was not friendly.

Dasin looked back up at Tank. Still in dialect, he said, "And are you going to tell me she's not the one you saw trailing our northern *friend* last night?"

"Nope, she's the same one all right," Tank said, grinning just to piss Dasin off. "That's the part got me curious enough to talk to her in the first place. I want to see what she does when she comes face to face with him. And we'd best stop talking in dialect before she loses her temper."

Dasin looked at Lia and switched back to Kaenic. "Keep your fucking around outside the crew," he told her, voice flat.

Lia's chin lifted, offended pride nearly visible in the air around her. Tank cut in: "Crew means Dasin too. I know he's pretty, but he's off-limits." In dialect, he added, "Damnit, Dasin, she's *Stecatr*. The hells you trying to do, have her gut you here and now?"

Dasin directed a sharp glare his way. "If her temper's that quick, she's no use to us," he retorted, not bothering to switch out of Kaenic.

Lia interrupted before Tank could answer; just as well, since his reply would have set off far too public of a row. She said, voice clipped and harsh, "I understand, *s'e*. And no, my temper isn't that quick, and *yes* —" she turned her head to glare at Tank. "I *am* sworn to celibacy."

Apparently she'd guessed at his comment. Not difficult, given Dasin's response and that *Stecatr* sounded the same in both languages.

"Go on, then," Tank said, wanting her out of there before either he or Dasin said something else provocative. "Go find Wolf and Cross, sort out what you need. Collect Rooster in the morning, and meet us at the far side of the eastern merchant yard. There's a redcone pine tree taller'n damn well everything else, we're near that. Before sunrise, mind."

She rose, winding the ata back around her face. "I understand," she said again, as crisply as before. "Thank you. Good day, *s'es*."

She stalked away without another word. Dasin looked up at Tank and said, scathingly, "*Pretty*? And why the face wrap?"

Tank shrugged and sat down where Lia had been, folding his arms on the table. He ran his gaze deliberately along Dasin's lean frame. "Did you want me to lie? I do like how you're built. You might have noticed that, on occasion?"

Dasin growled in the back of his throat. He hated any sort of public flirting. "What the *hells* are you trying to do this time?" he demanded. "Yuer is going to be *pissed*."

"Yuer can take it up with Gint. This time it's not our fault. Gint could have walked away from that fight. He knew we had to get on the road."

"Gint will be on his feet in a day or two!"

"He's got at least one cracked rib and a concussion. He won't be any damn good for over a tenday and you know it. He'd be useless in the Forest. We can't afford that on a moondark run."

Dasin growled again. Tank regarded him with patient stoicism; Dasin tried and, as always, failed to stare him down. Finally dropping his gaze, Dasin grumbled, "Well, at least we've only got the northern to worry about, not any *sti'shaa-teyhieas*. Toad said his nephews have decided to stay here after all."

Tank frowned, uneasily remembering a cold southern voice on a windy dockside saying: *There were difficulties ....*

No. There was no connection. That was too far a stretch. F'Heing didn't deal in children. *Anymore,* a darkly pained voice added in his mind, and, *Allegedly.* He ignored it. He was being jumpy over nothing. The katha villages had been entirely destroyed. Anyone trying to restart them would find a similar fate. Those days were over.

Gathering his calm, Tank observed, "That's odd. I thought that was the whole reason for his trip."

"Apparently Toad's content just having seen them," Dasin said, oblivious to Tank's moment of distraction. "They're happy here, he says. I'm not arguing it. I must have been out of my mind to even think about hauling a couple of weeping brats along. Oh — I finally found those damn candles you've been asking after." His eyes narrowed. "They're *fucking* expensive."

"I figured they would be."

"*And* black market."

"Not surprising."

Dasin snorted, mouth thin and hard. "Go find Gint. Give him his parting bonus and apologies. Try to avoid starting a fight with him." *I'm not the one who starts the fights,* Tank thought dourly. *I'm the one who ends them and cleans up the mess.* He laughed, just to make Dasin scowl again, then left the merchant to finish his expensive wine in sour-mouthed peace.

Chapter Four

Pre-dawn in Bright Bay was chill, foggy, and damp. This was turning out to be a city of bewildering extremes, from the people to the weather. Lia wanted to overwinter here. She wanted to learn more about this place, understand the tangled social rules, walk along the ocean edge until it stopped being terrifyingly huge.

She couldn't afford to take the time. The Hall of Arms wouldn't mind a bit, and technically their authority was what counted. But while the Stecatr Church might be gracious about a short extension that brought in a higher tithe, *they* wouldn't accept another six to ten months. Especially if those months were spent in such decadence.

Lia knew perfectly well she wouldn't hold to her oath in this setting. Not with so many beautiful women walking by, shameless and provocative. Not with the obvious, blatant freedom on display.

She focused on the muffled *clonks* and *clups* of Rooster's hooves as they paced through the quiet streets. He was a big gelding. Not the largest Lia had ever ridden, but leggy enough to be mildly intimidating. Rooster probably had some Western Highlander in him, and the peculiar dappling down his flanks reminded her of a Flatbrush. He seemed intelligent, if a bit reserved about whether to trust her. She'd walked him round the stable yard for a time the previous night, getting to know him without trying to ride him.

This morning, she'd decided to lead him again. Riding a strange horse through unfamiliar streets in poor light was rarely a good idea. Walking also let her test out any tight spots in her newly resoled boots. So far, her only complaint was that they were thicker than her old soles, muffling the feel of the road underfoot.

Her new ata felt strange. It was too light by half, and added pale edges to her vision where once there had been black lines. But her face was still properly hidden and her clothes, now of a much lighter cloth, still properly modest. Hands and eyes were the only skin visible. Nobody could carry tales of her flaunting indecent attire back to Stecatr.

If there was time in Isata, she'd see about trading out her worn, unadorned leather armor for something newer. Maybe even something with a discreet pattern. She could stroll back into Stecatr without having broken a single Church rule and still put a thumb in their eye with evidence of her success.

Improper thoughts. Selfish thoughts.

She didn't care. It was far too early in the morning and she'd expected at least another two days of rest before heading north again. But she had a *horse*. She was going to be able to ride, not walk, the long miles home. She was going to be able to *ride!* That alone made her giddy with excitement at odd moments, and that unsteady happiness was yet another reason she'd hesitated to mount Rooster this morning. It was too much like a dream she'd wake up from if she tried to reach for it in reality.

She'd been this excited about her first contract, road guard for a portly merchant named Elrin. He'd offered her a surprising amount for a one way run from Stecatr to Arason, better wages than she'd expected straight from graduation.

Of course, as she should have anticipated, the second day on the trail he'd pressed her hard for *extra* services. She'd grabbed a dagger and laid his cheekbone open, then used the hilt to knock him senseless. She gathered her gear, took what he owed her for the day's travel, then bolted for the nearest town, a small village called Orhon where her mother had grown up.

Rooster snorted. The entrance to the eastern caravan yard lay ahead, and he sniffed the air, eyes alert. His pace changed to what could only be called a strut: hooves lifting a little higher, setting down a bit harder. He was clearly intent on making an impression on the other horses. A stallion or an irritable mare might well take exception to the rangy gelding's challenge.

Lia slapped the side of Rooster's neck warningly. "Don't you start," she told him. He ignored her with magnificent disdain. She shook her head, caught between annoyance and amusement, and kept an eye on the horses they passed.

A northern draft in an unusual dapple-roan pattern caught her attention. Its ebony-dark tack was immaculate and trimmed with silver, while a browband of silver and gold beads drew attention to the horse's large, gentle eyes. Lia stumbled, missing a step in pure astonishment: what under the love of the Four would prompt someone to fussy up a *draft?* That gorgeous work would be covered in muck and sweat in under a mile, and probably permanently ruined within five. But then, there was no sign of any kind of wagon or cart being readied, so whatever the task of the day, it didn't involve hauling anything.

The south was *so* odd sometimes. She'd never understand these people. Maybe the draft was being readied as a gift, and its presence at the back edge of the caravan yards was deceptive.

Gift made her think of the small stash of presents she had carefully packed away, and the ones she hadn't thought to get. *I should have bought something for cousin Anaya in Orhon.* Dasin carried herbs and teas; he'd probably have something suitable. *Should I look for a gift for the Stecatr priests? Or the Hall masters?* No, that would be too much like fawning. They'd have to take her presence home as good enough.

Lia should already have been safely home, or nearly so. But in Isata, she'd heard news about a man from Stecatr, nicknamed Toad, who'd passed through not long before, headed to Bright Bay. If she'd ever known the man's real name, she'd long since forgotten, and didn't care to remember. He was too contemptible a creature to be dignified with a proper name.

Years ago, Toad had murdered his wife with a poison from his own apothecary stock. He should have hung, but a shifty nobleman had intervened. Toad had only been stripped of everything he owned, including his apothecary license. He survived, these days, by telling stories for coin and drink. The Church — the *Stecatr* Church — watched him closely, eager to find anything they could hang him for, but secular law appeared to have lost interest.

Lia raised her head at a sudden thought, looking around with a frown: she hadn't seen any guards so far, which seemed both unlikely and unwise. A tall man dressed in neutral colors, leaning against a tree, caught her eye and grinned amiably; she assessed his too-casual pose and the discreet club at his belt. Knowing what to look for now, she saw similarly unobtrusive watchers at regular intervals. Why this area had such understated guards, when the western docks had been so overly patrolled, she couldn't understand. She put it down to more southern oddness and kept going.

The caravan yard was pragmatically divided into incoming and outgoing sections. The incoming camps, to her left, were largely quiet save for guard patrols. To her right, most of the camps showed considerable activity. The striking roan draft had been to the left side, so it was inbound, and almost certainly intended as a present. Not so odd after all.

Tents were being broken down, horses groomed for the road. An array of dialects wrangled over, at a guess, final inventory tallies, discussions, and directions. She passed merchants with but a single wagon and more affluent trains of two or three wagons. One family, their youngest child petting their weary, graying mule, was busy shifting the load around on an open cart that looked to hold all their worldly goods. Four groups were sorting themselves into a roughly organized caravan; their cheap torches guttered and spat a foul smoke. Lia resisted the urge to hold her nose as she went by.

It took some time for the coarse smoke to fade from her nostrils, replaced with Rooster's comforting, horsey mustiness, underpinned by the leather and metal of his tack. Now and again a waft of damp earth and wet sand drifted by. Bands of other smells regularly disrupted the chill, damp air: horse dung, human sweat, oil and metal, among other aromas.

The thick cloth of her original ata had filtered out the worst of the odors along the road. The new, lighter one proved far less useful in that regard. Lia wrinkled her nose and tried to breathe through her mouth, which promptly coated her tongue in noxious off-notes.

Noxious made her think of Toad again, because that was a good description of him.

Nothing that man did was innocent. Going so far out of his usual routine as to travel to Bright Bay had seemed flatly sinister. He certainly wasn't moving to Bright Bay. Her contact in Isata had implied that Toad was carrying messages south, no doubt from that same corrupt nobleman who'd saved his neck.

Lia had stayed with Kennet in order to follow Toad to Bright Bay. Now she had to get back to Stecatr before the noxious old man, pass along what she'd seen to the appropriate people, and ruin whatever evil pact he'd entered into with the southern witch-lords.

Abrupt worry that Toad would be leaving today as well prompted Lia to search the outgoing groups as closely as she could without causing offense. She saw no sign of the disgraced apothecary. Her anxiety lessened with every enclosure she passed.

The tall red oak Tank had mentioned lay to the far end of the row. Dasin's crew would be the first allowed through the eastern gates when they opened. Toad wasn't leaving yet. She'd easily get to Stecatr ahead of him, while he'd have to hop from group to group. He'd be slow on the road. She had plenty of time. Everything was going to work out fine.

Someone began to sing a cheerful ditty about greeting the sun and the road ahead. A barrage of shouts that it was *entirely too fucking early for that sort of shit* erupted. The song faltered to silence. Lia laughed, quickening her pace, and let herself go back to the free-flowing happiness about having a horse to ride.

The last enclosure held a strange wagon of a subtly odd, if obviously new, construction. It resembled a regular merchant's wagon, square-sided and round-roofed, but Lia saw extra doors along one side and what looked to be an unusually sturdy undercarriage. It was harnessed to a gray draft pony that probably outweighed Rooster. The draft looked like a northern Grenka, but the head was a bit too narrow and the feathering on its legs too thin for it to be a pure line. It stood patiently still, long ears flicking lazily.

Lia ran a critical eye over the black horses, her eyebrows rising. She didn't know the breed — an unusual blank, for her — but they would have been entirely suitable for a lord's stables. They were *far* too fine to be trail horses for mercenaries, no matter how much money spices brought in. There was a story there. She made a note to ask after it when opportunity presented.

Tank held the bridle of one of the black horses, which shifted its weight frequently as though impatient to be moving. Dasin stood beside him, talking animatedly, waving his hands for emphasis. The horse didn't appear bothered by the random motion so close to its head, which spoke to excellent training somewhere along the line.

A stocky, scowling man wearing a dagger at each hip sat atop the second black horse. He stared down at her with frank dislike in his murky green eyes. A thick, brassy looking ring sat high in his left ear, and a matching band graced each dirty thumb. He wore no armor beyond a thick jerkin, and the pale, thin sleeves of his shirt reached his wrists.

Tank, in a similar long-sleeved shirt and jerkin, looked up as Lia led Rooster into the enclosure. Dasin turned, a sour expression on his face.

"About damn time," he carped. "Walking? What, are you afraid of the horse?"

"I'm guessing yeah," the mounted man said, sneering down at her. "Tiny little thing, ain'tcha?"

Lia drew in a breath, holding back her first and second responses to both comments.

Rooster let out a whuffling nicker, lifting his nose into the air briefly. The draft pony turned a disinterested eye his way, but the two black horses gave return greetings.

Tank said, mildly, "Easy, Dasin. There's time yet." She glared at him. He shrugged it off, as he had before; looked her over, then added, "You don't need full armor until we get to the Forest. Take it off. I'll stow it in the wagon. Keep the bracers. The rest is gonna be too damn hot by midday." He grinned at something he saw in her eyes. "Sanben let you wear the whole kit all the way south, didn't he?"

Lia bit her lip, grateful the motion was hidden beneath the ata, and began to unbuckle her brigandine. Dasin snorted, hauling himself onto the driver's seat. The draft pony stomped an oversized hoof once, then lifted its tail. Dasin swore irritably in a southern dialect, one hand over his nose, as a hot, grassy smell filled the air.

The stocky man hooted laughter. "You'd think you never smelled horse shit before," he said, then something in dialect.

"Fuck off," Dasin snapped. "*Ta-karne, ta-neka, sanahair, adruu!*"

"And there's your lesson in southern swear words for the day, Lia," Tank said lightly. He took her armor and walked to the back of the wagon.

Dasin smoldered. The mounted man smirked. Lia rubbed Rooster's neck and tried not to meet anyone's eyes.

Returning, Tank said, "We're only waiting on one person now." He raised his voice to a carrying pitch: "You done shaving yet, there?"

"Yes, yes," a thin voice answered briskly from the other side of the wagon. "Just packing everything away. There. All set." A gaunt man with flyaway gray hair scrambled up onto the far side of the bench to perch beside Dasin. He leaned over to tuck a knapsack and battered lute case behind his feet, then straightened, grinning.

He turned his head and met Lia's eyes. They both froze.

Tank moved to stand in clear view of everyone. "Introductions are in order, I believe," he said cheerfully. He pointed to each in turn as he said, "I should think everyone knows Dasin and me. Cilif's the one who's forgotten how to smile; *s'e* Toad is the one just climbed onto the wagon seat; our new hire, Lia of Stecatr, is the one holding Rooster. Hey, *s'e* Toad, didn't you say Stecatr is where *you're* from?"

Lia sucked in a deep breath, as quietly as she could. The air cut at her throat like a million tiny ice shards, and her stomach felt pierced by every one of them.

As always, Toad's clothes boasted a riotous mixture of primary colors that didn't look as absurd here as they had in Stecatr, and the once-foreign, wide-cut style of shirt and pants was now a familiar sight. In fact, after seeing the lush decorations of the south, his outfit actually seemed a bit drab. His gray hair, normally tucked tightly under a cap, swung in a wild, frail corona around his head.

Lia glanced to the side to find Tank watching her intently. The big redhead's expression immediately turned bland.

"*Lia?*" Toad's voice cracked. He shot a hasty glance at Tank and Dasin, then cleared his throat. His tone took on a smooth, rapid confidence, the sound of a storyteller hooking his audience's attention. "My goodness! Is that *you* under that, that ata? I heard you went into the mercenary Hall, but I didn't know you'd graduated! Much less made it this far on a contract. My goodness, how astonishing."

Lia wished she could drill holes in the man with the fury of her stare. *Traitor, murderer, liar*: she barely kept her teeth shut on the words. She should have mugged him when she had the chance.

Toad beamed at her as though oblivious to her expression, but his eyes held no warmth at all.

Tank cut in, "So, now we've all met. Cilif, with me. Lia, to the back of the wagon. Watch out for beggars as we go through the gates, they'll grab your boot on the one side and another will have your coin pouch while you're busy fending off the first."

Cilif grunted and swung his horse around to line up with Tank's.

Lia checked the tack and girth one last time, then swung up into the saddle. Rooster shivered, ears swiveling, but stayed still. Lia patted his neck, murmuring praise and gratitude until the horse relaxed. Then she looked *down* at Toad, way down. Abruptly, she realized that he was considerably smaller, in every way, than her fear had painted him.

She had a good horse under her and good coin coming to her pocket. *He* had nothing, and in Stecatr, less than nothing once she passed along word of what he'd been up to. She had nothing to worry about. She straightened her back and cast Toad one last, disdainful glance; then, letting that wild joy swell within her once more, nudged Rooster to take up rear guard position as the wagon began to roll forward.

Chapter Five

Kybeach had changed since King Oruen's ascension, but travelers who only passed through on their way to a nicer place wouldn't have noticed. It looked much the same from the outside: dilapidated, swampy, and stinky. One ramshackle set of buildings served as the only inn, tavern, and stables.

On any closer inspection, though, travelers would notice that the inn boasted a reasonably fresh coat of paint, and well-tended flowers nodded in pots along the edges. The stables stayed clean. The feed wasn't bug-riddled. There were no rats — well, *fewer* rats — in the tavern and its kitchen.

The inhabitants were still surly, especially at dawn, which was when Dasin's wagon drew to a stop in front of the inn. But the people came out with coin in hand, thin in quantity and clipped in quality though it might have been.

Tank had mostly convinced Dasin to take a calculated loss here. Mostly.

A small woman, hair shorn nearly bald, hurried up before the wagon had even properly stopped. She held up a sack commandingly and said, in a surprisingly deep voice for her size, "The salt, if you please! The Horn salt! A big scoop! An' I'm not paying more'n I did last time, neither."

Dasin climbed down from the wagon, his expression deceptively beatific. Tank signalled Cilif and Lia to stay on their horses; Kybeach never took long.

"Now, *s'a* Beita," Dasin said as he unlatched the side door and began pulling items out, including the box of Horn salt. "You wouldn't expect me to take a loss, would you? You know I never charge you more than a flat ten percent above what I pay myself."

As Dasin spoke, Cilif took Blackie round the wagon in a loose circle to keep the horse from fretting, then drew up a few yards away to watch. Dasin, ignoring the movement, splayed a hand to his chest, looking at Beita gravely.

Ten percent, my ass, Tank thought, but kept his expression blank. Beita always brought out the worst in Dasin. He was about to quote her something outrageous.

Dasin said, without any shame, "It's six full silver for a big scoop."

"Outrageous!" she declared. "You asked for four last time!"

Dasin only ever paid one full round per scoop. Tank stayed silent — he didn't much like Beita either — and waited to see what number they landed on. He made a private bet on five.

Catching movement, Tank looked sideways as Rooster backed up a few steady, precise steps, then stilled. Lia was staring at the horse's ears, her own expression startled and pleased. Tank guessed that she knew dressage, and hadn't expected Rooster to recognize the commands. Interesting. Most mercenaries wouldn't have the faintest idea how to do what she'd done.

Tank contemplated whether to put her up onto Sin at some point. That would be amusing, at the very least, starting with if she could stay on. He put that aside for later and went back to watching Dasin.

Dasin was saying, grudgingly, "I suppose I could go as low as five-six. Since you're such a steady customer for the Horn salt. Not everyone likes the taste."

"Four-five!" she shot back.

A pudgy man with deep pox scars and a cast eye came up to stand beside the woman. "Ah, Beita, settle on five flat already and get out the way," he whined. "I've tea waiting on me, and the wife as well."

"Your tea's warmer than your wife," Beita snapped at him. "Let the tea cool as you like, that won't change."

Cilif let out a choked sound that earned him a ferocious glare from the pockmarked man.

It was time to step in. Tank dismounted, looping Sin's reins loosely over the saddle hook. "*S'ieas*," he said, pitching his voice to cut through the rising squabble. "We can't stop for long. Could you carve one another up after we're gone?"

The arguing couple glowered at him.

"Five," Beita muttered. She handed Dasin five uncut silver rounds. Dasin filled her bag and handed it back. The small woman cast a venomous look at Tank and stomped off.

Three more women and a young man were approaching as the pockmarked man gave Dasin his order. Tank recognized them all: no troublemakers in the lot. Beita was the only truly sour apple left in Kybeach. He could step aside for a few moments to make a delivery of his own.

Sin swung his head irritably. Tank touched the horse's soft nose and said, in Aerthraim dialect, "Behave yourself, asshole. I'll let you run a bit after this."

The horse flicked his ears and stomped once with a back hoof. Tank patted the side of Sin's face, smiling with real affection, then looked up at Lia. The ata hid most of her face, but he saw the lines of amusement clearly enough.

"So I like him," Tank said a bit defensively. "Most horses are assholes. This one's not bad."

She widened her eyes and delicately put a hand to her chest, miming high-class denial of having said anything at all.

Tank laughed, then said, "Sin will hold still as long as you don't let Rooster crowd him. This is a short stop. Don't bother dismounting. I have to talk to someone. Be right back." He dug a heavy pouch of supplies from his saddlebags, patted Sin once more, and went into the inn.

The inn was dim, the large windows still shuttered. A single lantern burned, flame steady, in the corner of the commons room, and a faint smell of vinegar hung in the air. Nobody was sleeping on the floor, for a wonder, but a slight figure watched the room from a rocking chair near the lamp. As Tank came in, she turned the wick up and stood, smiling at him.

When he'd first met Rania, she'd been coated in dirt, begging him for help escaping a madwoman. She'd been bony and angry, spitting curses as often as stealing his coin. Nobody would connect that surly street rat to this elegant young woman. She wore a dress of fine, pale fabric, cut tight and low in strategic spots; the shoulders were left bare and the skirt flowed as she moved. It suited her dangerously well.

Tank stopped, unable to help staring. She'd put her auburn hair up in an aristocratic bun, tendrils trailing around her face. The commons room seemed less worn and more sophisticated from her presence.

Rania swayed her hips suggestively as she advanced, her smile taking on a wicked slyness. "Good morning, *s'e*," she said in a low, cultured voice that put a warm burr up his back — and elsewhere. "Can I ... *help* you with something?" She looked him up and down, slowly, and her smile widened. "I think maybe *so* ...."

The neckline of that dress ran *far* too low, and the shift in his perception of her was sharp enough to muddle him briefly. He blinked hard and brought his gaze up, then held out the pouch like a talisman against temptation. "I brought you some —" he began.

Rania stopped moving, her sultry smile melting to a frown. "Damnit, ghost-rid'!" she snapped, cutting him off. Her gaze raked the air around his head. All seduction left her stance, her relatively refined accent dropping back to street dialect. She planted her hands on her hips, glaring at him. "D'you know, I told myself that the day you walked in and looked at me like that, I'd have your pants down before you knew what hit you. But —" She made picking motions at the air between them, her mouth contorting in distaste. "You went and got yourself another damn set of trouble. It's all round you. I can't touch you without touching *it*, and I *ain't* doing that."

Tank drew in a steadying breath. "Thanks for letting me know I'm carrying ... trouble again. And for the, uh, offer. But you're ... look, you're still a —"

Rania's gaze snapped up to his face. "Don't you dare say I'm a child," she cut in, furious color washing across her cheeks. "I ain't all that much younger'n you, and I been on my damn knees since before I got my cycles. *You* know how it is."

He shut his eyes briefly, irritated with himself. He did know. And Dasin certainly wouldn't have hesitated to take what was being offered.

All the more reason to say no.

"Doesn't mean I have to help keep it happening," Tank said, and tossed the pouch at her. Rania caught it without taking her glare from his face. "Black pepper. Horn salt. Nutmeg. A few coins. Put a gift on Seshya's grave for me, and say a prayer." Pointedly, he turned his back and started for the door.

"Tank, wait," she said, all flirtation gone. He paused, half-turning to look over his shoulder at her. "Do *you* know what you're walking into?"

His mouth thinned. He almost said, *I'm always walking into trouble, I travel with Dasin.* But she clearly meant something more serious. He probably didn't want to know what she was seeing. He probably needed to.

Tank sighed and turned all the way around. "You tell me."

"It's not clear." Rania wavered a hand in the air, her thin face intent. "I'm wondering if I'll see you again. There's a, a prickling sort of haze ... I know you always walk with trouble on one shoulder, but this is different." She made that picking-at-air gesture again. "Sommat's off in your future, ghost-rid'. Sommat's shifting ahead. Sommat dangerous. You're ... you're going to change things, whether you want to or not. And they're going to change you. Be careful." She hesitated, then addded, reluctantly, "You've done kindly by me, and by this place. I'd like to see you at peace without a grave being involved."

"That would be nice," Tank said, half-laughing. Her eyes narrowed. He patted the air in a settle-down gesture. "*Ha'vash, ha'ne.* Peace. I take your warnings seriously. Thank you, Rania."

She turned away, carrying the supplies toward the kitchen without another word.

At least his arousal had faded completely. She wouldn't try again, now that he'd refused once.

Maybe. Probably. In any case, he'd be forewarned. And he'd make *damned* sure Dasin didn't stop inside next time through. Seshya had clearly trained Rania well in their short time together.

"Changes, hmmm?" he said under his breath. Absently, he cracked his knuckles. The sound caught him away from brooding. He shook his hands out and went back into the steadily brightening dawn.

The storyteller was as good as he'd declared himself to be. Tank kept getting caught up in the swaying cadence of the man's words.

The old man also seemed impervious to distraction or heat exhaustion: a black gerho fly landing on his wrist was evicted with a gesture that blended perfectly into the tale he was spinning. Sweat plastered his thin shirt against his wiry body and his gray hair into limp straggles, and none of it mattered against the images he presented.

It was a good thing the draft pony knew how to walk a straight line without help, because Dasin wasn't watching the road most of the time. It was a good thing this stretch of road was never any trouble, because Cilif rode alongside the storyteller, a faintly glazed look on his normally sneering face.

Lia alone seemed unimpressed. She rode at the back of the wagon, her gaze flicking from side to side, picking at her own sweat-damp clothes from time to time. Tank dropped back to ride beside her, making sure to keep Sin well clear. Sin and Rooster occasionally decided to snap at each other. He wasn't in the mood to wrangle a horse fight.

She glanced at him as he fell in beside her. Tank was beginning to be able to read her expression through the ata. The lighter fabric helped, but he was also good at reading body language: she was still furious about traveling alongside the storyteller.

Her earlier glare at Toad spoke to a startling level of hatred. Dasin had already started taking odds on the storyteller disappearing some night along the trail, with Lia looking sunnily innocent come morning. Cilif had taken the contrary side from Dasin, as he almost always did regardless of the bet. Tank had demurred.

He needed to dig into Lia's anger and find out what was going on before they went much further along the road. To test her temper, he observed, "Watch your balance with Rooster. Nothing against your riding, but he gets cranky if his rider shifts around too much."

She cut a suspicious glance at him and said, stiffly, "Yes, I picked up on that. I'll keep it in mind. Thank you." She paused, then added, even colder now, "Just ask already, *s'e* Tank."

He resisted the urge to pinch the bridge of his nose. He was trying to break himself of that habit. "All right. What's your history with the old man?"

"It's a long story, and a boring one, *s'e* Tank. Not worth the telling."

Rooster's ears flicked, flicked again. Sin gave his odd little shimmy that meant annoyance. Tank checked his position: too close. Edging Sin a bit further away, he waited until the horses settled, then said, "You don't care for him, that's clear. It's a long way north, and I like to know what I'm dealing with. I suggest you risk boring me."

Lia's chin lifted. She stared ahead, stiff and resentful. "We disagree on a few things. It won't cause any trouble on the road, *s'e*."

"He ever laid a hand on you or yours?"

Lia glanced sideways at him. "No," she snapped, then looked away too quickly. So it was more complicated than a yes or no answer.

Time to poke at a suspicion he had about the old man. "Is he a thief?"

She startled. Her shoulders hunched forward defensively. "Um. No," she said, the words scarcely audible and more like a question than a statement. She avoided his gaze.

Tank decided he wouldn't get anything else useful out of her right now. "All right," he said. "Good enough."

"I didn't say —" she started. He waved a hand to silence her.

"You didn't say anything," he agreed. Ignoring her smothered curse, he nudged Sin forward. As he moved past Dasin, he said, in Aerthain dialect, "I'm in. He'll live."

"Optimist," Dasin said in the same dialect. "Ten silver bits."

"Done."

Toad cracked his knuckles cheerfully. "So, then, another!" he declared. "You've maybe heard the one about the *shia-banse* in Assiasan who won a wager with a priest?"

Tank exchanged a startled glance with Dasin. Toad rattled on without the least flicker of a pause; either it was a bizarre coincidence that he'd picked that topic hard on the heels of a comment he damn well shouldn't have understood, or he was that good an actor.

"No?" Toad asked the air in general without waiting for an actual answer. "Well, good, for it's a fair load of nonsense. *Shia-bansain* don't place wagers! Foolishness. They're mad creatures that go wailing round the rooftops on a cold night, looking for men who don't hold faithful to their wives. Now, there's a *true* story about a *shia-banse* that I know, happened to my second cousin ...."

Coincidence. Had to be. Tank made himself smile tolerantly at Toad, then nudged Sin to ride point before he could get caught up in the story.

Obein, as usual, came as a relief to Tank's senses. After the chaotic vegetation of the swamp around Kybeach, which took several miles to peter out, the clean lines of the town felt restful. The people of Obein put considerable care into their plantings. Round, glossy-leaved bushes stayed neatly trimmed to shape, flowers in complementary colors filled strategically placed pots of various heights.

Tank vaguely recalled hearing that desert Families used movable displays of vegetation to convey subtly coded messages to visitors. He'd never been particularly interested in learning complicated details like whether lavender meant health or worry or indigestion depending on what it was next to plus how many branches it had on the north facing side while a snake bit a pig somewhere indelicate.

He laughed a little at himself and stored aside the small rant to share with Dasin another time. He could use it to draw Dasin into talking about southern symbolism. It would at least make for a neutral conversational topic, which often fell few and far between.

Obein was arranged in a sensible, easily navigable layout. Most buildings were of stone, but a fair few showed sturdy timber framing. The pathways were neatly raked sand, gravel, or, occasionally, carefully placed strips of cobblestone. Obein was obsessive enough to have laborers patrolling the city all day, sweeping up horse droppings, raking out paths, and repairing any incremental damage before it could spread to a larger issue.

Dasin had said it set him on edge. He found the dedicated tidiness deeply suspicious. His sour moods, and his fondness for provoking unnecessary chaos, were always more prominent here. Today, though, relaxed from hours of listening to increasingly improbable stories, he seemed nearly cheerful as he gave directions involving lodging, stabling, behavior, and tomorrow's plans.

Unfortunately, his mood darkened as soon as he finished those responsibilities, and he disappeared into the nearby tavern before Tank could catch him.

"He's a thirsty one today," Cilif observed with ostentatious innocence.

Tank turned to scowl at him.

"Must have been a long and sandy ride — hey!"

Tank had picked up a small stone and lobbed it at Cilif's head. The big mercenary dropped Blackie's reins to dodge, laughing; Blackie stomped a hoof and whuffled impatiently.

"Yeah, yeah, I know, I know, feed time. Come on then," Cilif told Blackie, retrieving the reins and leading the horse towards the waiting stableboy.

Tank caught Lia looking at him with a raised eyebrow, clearly puzzled. He pointed her firmly after Cilif, unwilling to explain the very southern, and very dirty, joke.

The stableboy, remembering Tank's standing request, took Blackie to the far end of the row, well away from Rooster and Sin, because Blackie and Rooster didn't get along in close quarters. Rooster and Sin went to adjoining stalls near the entrance, the stableboy took the draft pony to a box stall, and everyone set to work settling the horses for the night. The stableboy would have groomed all of the horses, not just the draft pony, for a reasonable price, but Tank felt the riding horses, at least, deserved better than to be turned over to a stranger after a long day's ride. Cilif agreed, and even took over grooming the draft when he wasn't too tired.

Sin certainly earned his name that day. Normally he was quiet and amicable; some days, though, he was nearly impossible to manage. Today was the latter. By the time Sin was properly groomed, fed, and watered, Tank had been crowded into the walls, knocked to the ground, drooled on, and snapped at. He'd reflexively jumped sideways on that last — stomping right into a fresh pile of manure.

It took a tremendous effort for Tank not to slam the stall door behind him. As he latched it, adding an extra twist of strong wire — Sin had proven himself *absolutely* capable of undoing a standard stall closure when in a mood like this — he glared at the horse, muttering promises of dire revenge in the morning. Sin sneezed, majestically turning to hang his head out the pasture-side window.

Turning to face Lia, who was waiting outside Rooster's stall with her ata wound around one arm, Tank held up a warning finger and said, "*Don't*. Not a *word*."

The merriment in her eyes remained, but she managed to compose her expression to a more serious neutrality. She put her attention to lifting her sword belt from the hook by the stall door and fastening it, then cleared her throat. "I think I really ought to ask, though, if you'd like to change before you go to dinner?" She looked him over, smirking.

Tank glared at her. She took on a demure expression, as Cilif had done earlier, and once more put her hand to her chest in that mock protest of innocence.

"If there are local baths, perhaps," she added helpfully.

"Shut it," he growled. "Just —" Glancing down at the disaster of his clothing, he let out a rueful bark of laughter, unable to stay annoyed any longer. "Yeah. A bath and a change."

Cilif latched Blackie's stall, adding the extra wire, as Tank had done, then sauntered towards them. His clothes, while dusty from the road and stained from lunch, didn't show any signs of being knocked around by an annoyed horse. For all Cilif's grumbling about Blackie not being *his*, he had a surprising bond with the beast. Blackie almost never caused him the trouble that Sin gave Tank.

"Sin was fussy today," Cilif observed as he looked Tank over. "Best clean up before

Dasin sees you if'n you want any *dessert* tonight."

"Get out of here," Tank ordered.

Cilif winked and left the stables. Tank turned to find Lia watching him with a bland expression. She'd obviously understood *that* remark fine.

"Yeah, so?" Tank snapped at her, braced for a moralizing condemnation of *ii'ne* behavior.

She hesitated, then said, "So nothing. I'll see you at dinner." She moved around him towards the stable doors, not quite *not* limping.

Tank cleared his throat, regretting his flash of temper. She'd started to thaw from her prickly defensiveness, even if it had involved laughing at him. He didn't want to lose that. "Sorry," he offered.

Lia paused, turning back to face him. There was something odd in her expression, a moment of tautness; then she shrugged, lowering her gaze.

Tank, wondering about that pause, said, "You're limping. How long since you've been on a horse?"

She glanced away, then made a sour face and wrapped her ata into place, obscuring her features. In a stifled tone, she said, "It's been a while."

"Then you'll want a good hot soak. Go tell the innkeep to take a tub up to your room." She began to protest; he cut her off. "Dasin pays for rooms *and* baths. I take private baths every chance I get. Only reason I'll go to the men's baths tonight is that the inn would toss me out if I tried walking in like this." He paused long enough for her to nod reluctant assent. "Come get a meal over at Grayfeathers, the tavern Dasin just went into. Don't come armed. Don't wear that damn mask. And don't get into a brawl."

"I avoid brawls," she said, her tone aiming for light and only achieving shaky.

He didn't have the energy to dig after whatever had rattled her. "Yeah, well," he said, brushing past her, "Dasin and Cilif *love* 'em once they start drinking, and they're both in there already."

Chapter Six

Short hair dried quickly in southern heat. By the time Lia stepped up onto the porch of Grayfeathers, the only dampness on the back of her neck was from sweat. The air hadn't cooled much, if at all, with the setting sun. An erratic cloud of tiny black gnats hovered near the door. She batted at the insects and ducked inside.

Lanterns lined the walls, set high enough to be almost out of reach. More of the same sat on each bench table, long or short alike. The western wall had three large, wide window openings, shutters thrown wide to let in air and light to diffuse the pipe smoke and alcohol fumes. The floor was surprisingly clean, and the serving girls wore unexciting, long-sleeved dresses fashioned for utility, not display.

Lia hadn't been in this tavern before. Kennet had taken lodgings on the other side of town, at a much finer establishment. Mainly, Lia remembered the girls at that tavern. They'd all worn shamelessly provocative dresses. She'd had to keep her nose almost in her drink to avoid staring.

She took several steps into the room, assessing the layout and ambient mood.

A shout came from her left: "Oy, here's the pretty dancer I asked for after all! Here, then, sweet —"

Lia was already skipping to one side as a large hand reached for her arm; immediately regretted the motion as her thigh and calf muscles complained.

"Hey, what?" the big man who'd grabbed for her complained, frowning.

He stood considerably taller and broader than Lia, with an untidy mop of curly brown hair. Multiple tattoos ran up his bare arms. Lia took in the symbols with a quick glance and felt her heart sink. Some were well done, others rough road pokes, but the story they told was all of a piece.

Red snake wrapped around a black frog; a splayed blue hand, outlined in red; a red star; a bull's head in shades of red and black. *Experienced fighter, multiple kills, unsworn and proud of it.*

She'd been warned never to trust an unsworn. They weren't beholden to any Hall or authority beyond whatever contract they held at the moment; most of them were perfectly happy to break even that if more profit came along; and *amoral* didn't begin to cover their general behavior.

Lia stepped further back, well out of his long-armed reach. Doing her best to sound as frosty as a Stecatr winter, she said, "I'm not entertainment, *s'e*. I'm sworn through Stecatr Hall of Arms."

The man let out a drunken bellow of laughter. "Now that's entertaining," he drawled. "You already have someone who's paid for your night, say so, but don't hand me horseshit. You, from Stecatr Hall?" He leered at her. "I ain't that drunk. They don't take *women*."

In peripheral vision, Lia noted that the tavern had gone largely silent, the dozen or so patrons turned to watch with varying degrees of interest and intoxication. She counted four women in that quick glance, only one of whom seemed remotely concerned by the developing incident. The other three, respectively, looked bored, amused, and annoyed at being interrupted. She didn't see Dasin or Cilif anywhere nearby, and couldn't take the time to look more carefully.

The big man shoved forward an aggressive step. "You think you're a fighter, then?" he demanded. "How about you prove it!" He shifted to a brawling stance, fists raised, and grinned as he surveyed her thin frame. "I c'n break you with one hand, y'damn sheath!"

The woman who'd been watching rose to her feet, her frown deepening. She was shorter than Lia, with flat features and copper skin, but the wary glances of the nearby drinkers told Lia she'd gained at least local respect.

"Hold on," Cilif said, coming up from Lia's right.

He'd changed into a dark, sleeveless tunic with a wide belt and trousers, displaying an array of thin scars along one arm from wrist to elbow and a black snake tattoo wrapped around each bicep. He'd taken off all of his jewelry, but his belt had a silver buckle worked into a swirling snake design.

"She's telling the truth, Feenie. Stecatr changed the rules last year. This one's part of my team, working for merchant Dasin. And Tank," he added meaningfully. He glanced over to the still-standing woman and made a patting gesture at the air; she sat down, but continued to watch.

Feenie eyed Cilif with distinct suspicion. "Last time I believed you I wound up giving you my godsdamned horse," he growled. "I'm not likely to make that mistake again. And *fuck* your redheaded whore, he don't impress me."

"You never went up against him," Cilif retorted. "Aw, leave it already. Shit, Feenie, lookit how she's dressed! You think one of your women would wear that? An' I know damn well you were told your girls aren't allowed in here."

"Ain't nothing wrong with my dancers," Feenie said, folding his arms over his broad chest. "Maybe this one's new enough to not know how to dress. Or maybe she wants to look respectable in a classy place like this so's we don't get thrown out by you judgmental bastards. Anyways, I still ain't believing she's *Stecatr*."

Cilif hooked his thumbs into his belt. "Look, Feenie, you don't believe me, go ask merchant Dasin. He's right over there. He'll tell you straight."

Feenie didn't even turn his head. His thick lips curled contemptuously. "The fuck he will. He's more devious than you are. An' you lot never travel with women. I know damn well your employer wouldn't let you do that." Somehow, he managed to make *employer* sound filthy. "Nah. I ain't that stupid. Whatever. Your road toy's too skinny for me anyhows, I'd break her." He sneered at Lia again, then turned away, bellowing to a server to bring him more ale.

Cilif cast a frowning, sideways glance at Lia. "You gonna let that go?" he asked. "Him calling you that?"

She discreetly took in the room once more before answering. The patrons were returning to their card games, dice, and drinking; even the woman who'd been watching earlier had turned back to her conversation. Three young men with strikingly similar features and hair ranging from ash to dirty blond were the only ones staring at her, and something about them ....

One of them leered. Another dropped a salacious wink at her. The third wiggled his fingers in a mocking wave. She'd seen that specific gesture before, from someone else who looked a lot like these three. With a gathering sense of dread, she checked their shoulders: yes, their shirts were all marked with a fine criss-cross pattern of red and silver threads.

Oh gods. A stone settled on her chest, and her breath ran short. *Nahonna spawn.*

Three other women had entered freewarrior training with her. Lia was the only one who'd made it all the way through. Isrin Nahonna had led the harassment and eventual attacks that drove the other three out — one so physically broken that she'd never leave her house again.

Nobody could ever prove a thing, of course. Certainly not against the kind of money Nahonna threw around like blossoms at a wedding. Lia had a feeling that these three not only knew who she was, they knew Isrin; knew about the women who hadn't made it through training. She also suspected, from their eagerly intent expressions, that they were already planning to lure her into a dark alley, or break into her room in the middle of the night, or find some other way to provoke a no-win situation to bring her down. Quite possibly they'd spin false tales to Dasin and get her dismissed without recommendation.

Searing resentment burned at the back of her eyes. It wasn't *fair*. She'd worked so hard and come so far, and here, weeks of travel from the place where such concerns properly belonged, she was once more painfully vulnerable to malice.

"Oy," Cilif said, nudging her shoulder with one thick hand. "You off in dreamland, Stecatr? You gonna let that *fesh'ii* call you that and walk away? In public? He's *expecting* you to go after him!"

Lia turned away from the smirking men with an effort. She allowed resentment to make her icy-sharp with Cilif. "I'm not here to brawl, Cilif. I'm here to get a fucking meal. He doesn't matter."

She finally caught sight of Dasin at a short, narrow bench table across the room.

Trying not to noticeably grind her teeth or limp, Lia headed his way. The hot bath had helped immensely, but she still felt like a solid mass of bruises from head to foot, and a headache was starting up.

"Aw, what?" Cilif said, following behind her. "I dunno, *I* think you were scared of him."

Deliberately or not, his voice carried across the noise of the room. She shot a glare at him over her shoulder, noting that the Nahonnas were looking like Cilif had handed them a basket of gold rounds.

Ignoring her anger, Cilif pushed past her to plunk down next to Dasin on the bench seat, He announced, again far too loud, "I don't think she's gonna work out, merchant Dasin. Feenie scared her about to pissing herself."

The bench seat only ran long enough for himself and Dasin, leaving two chairs that would put her back to the room. The tables to either side were taken, their occupants intent on card games that didn't allow for outsider interruption. As she glanced over the games, she saw one of the players deftly swap out a card in his hand for one in his sleeve.

She considered raising a fuss over it, by way of distracting Cilif and the Nahonnas. But honestly, she was too damned tired and hungry. She wanted to sit and eat in peace. Surely Dasin, as her employer, would shut Cilif's belligerent nonsense down.

As soon as she thought that, she hated herself for the weakness. *Don't ask men for help,* her mother had often warned her, all the more stridently after Lia's acceptance to the Hall of Arms. *They always want something back, and you'll never get free once you start that.*

That had surely turned out true enough so far in her life. She had to shut Cilif down herself, that was all. She'd faced off with worse.

Lia sat down across from Dasin, her back and neck straight and proud even as her shoulderblades itched from putting her back to the Nahonnas. Dasin took a long pull from his tankard, his eyes gleaming with a viciousness she'd never seen in him before. He'd obviously hit the ale hard from the moment he walked in, and at this point had cast common sense and responsibility for his hires to the wind. He didn't say anything; he didn't have to. That smirking grin said it all: she was most definitely on her own.

Mad as a bat drunk on dashaic, Sanben had said of Dasin and Tank both. Apparently that involved a cruel streak once Dasin, at least, had gotten to drinking.

"Let it *be,* Cilif," Lia snapped. "I want a meal, not an argument." She turned, looking around for a server, carefully *not* looking at the Nahonna table.

Cilif scratched his ear, looked at his fingers, then demanded, "What the hells are you going to do when someone comes charging at you with a sword out, if you can't even handle one drunk *fesh'ii?*"

"I'm not afraid. There just isn't a good reason to fight." Lia took in Cilif's uncompromising expression and reluctantly admitted to herself that she couldn't shut him down. This situation only had one ending. Cilif would keep baiting and pushing, as Sanben had done along the road from Orhon. He wouldn't be satisfied until he'd drawn her into some sort of brawl. And Dasin wouldn't intervene.

Tank did try to warn me, I suppose.

At least Sanben had taken her aside for a private sparring match to test her competency.

Cilif seemed determined to test her ability to withstand public humiliation. Dasin was in too malicious a mood to stop matters from escalating. Tank hadn't arrived yet.

I don't need any of them, anyway, damnit. Lia flexed her fingers under the table, testing to see how much strength she had left after the day's ride. Not much. On an empty stomach besides, this would have to be settled quickly.

"You were *scared* of him," Cilif insisted. He scratched his ear again, grimacing. "I saw your face. If all it takes is someone bigger'n you to back you off, we ought to send you off and hire someone with actual guts."

Lia glared at him. "I'm on this crew *because* someone got into an ill-advised bar brawl." Dasin's eyes narrowed at that. "I don't see the point in brawling with an unsworn. That's a short road to an early grave."

Dasin motioned Cilif silent and studied Lia with increasingly sober-eyed interest. "You're assuming a brawl with Feenie would end in your death?" he asked, rational and crisp. Apparently he wasn't overset drunk after all, which made his malice all the worse.

Lia snapped, "Mine or his. I wasn't trained to play games."

"Holy flaming gerho farts," Cilif said. He let loose a bellow of laughter, slapping both broad hands on the table. Dasin snatched up his ale and steadied the lantern before it went over from the impact. Cilif's mug jolted sideways but stayed upright. "Are you saying you don't know how to have a good *brawl*? Fucking *hells*, you've some training missed along the way!" He picked up his ale and drained the mug, then shoved to his feet, rocking the thin table.

"That's *not* what I —" Lia began.

Cilif lunged round the still shaking table, yanked her to her feet with one hand, then reared back and lobbed the empty mug across the room. Someone shouted. Feenie roared angrily.

"Cilif," Dasin said, belatedly reluctant. "Wait — don't. Tank said —"

"Oh, fuck his fucking moralizing. *Feenie!*" Cilif bellowed. "You fucking puddle of gerho shit! *Get over here!*"

Dasin let out a high, savage crowing sound, all hesitation disappearing. "Make it worth the price, girl," he shouted at Lia, then raised his voice even further. "Oy! Taking *bets*! Two silver on the girl! Over here, Delin, Abra, I know you want in on this!"

Lia shot him a furious glare, then turned to face the unsworn lumbering rapidly towards her. Rapidly cataloging his weak points, she found her mouth stretching in a wild grin.

If I have to do this, I might as well have fun with it, she thought, and moved into a clear space to meet the man's charge.

Chapter Seven

A brawl was, of course, in full uproar by the time Tank stepped up onto the tavern porch. He ducked inside, edging along the wall, and took a moment to study the situation.

Four of the six bench tables had been shoved aside at erratic angles. One, splintered, was being trodden into further pieces as fights shifted around the room. Food was splattered and smeared underfoot, and some combatants bore signs of having been the target of a flung trencher.

The chairs had mostly been tossed aside rather than taken up as weapons, which was a pleasant change. Tank had caught more than one chair to the face while pulling Cilif and Gint out of previous brawls. Two of the servers had already gathered up the table lanterns and taken shelter behind the bar. Denil, the thin, grim-mouthed man serving as barkeep today, stood with his arms folded and a thick club waiting before him on the bartop.

Feenie, the unsworn that Cilif often drank with, sat in a corner protected from the brawl by several chairs that had been thrown in the way. He was nursing his drink as he watched the fight with a sour expression. Tank would have expected him to be in the middle of the brawl. He put Feenie on peripheral watch as a potentially problematic variable and looked at the rest of the room.

Most of the female patrons had already, sensibly, left. A handful of mixed gender combatants, none any older than Tank, staggered through attempts to pin one another down, tag one another with thrown objects, or just land a square punch. They were all too drunk to be a threat to anything but the floor. Even as he watched, three of them — including one woman — went down and stayed there, laughing breathlessly. Tank shook his head in disgust and looked for Cilif, who would inevitably be at the core of this mess.

Cilif wasn't throwing punches. He stood beside Lia, facing off with three young men. Tank studied the strangers, gathering an idea of what he was about to step into.

They had similar shades of blond hair and narrow builds, although one was distinctly heavier-set. Their finely tailored clothing was cut from expensive cloth, and they wore more jewelry than any decent southerner would dream of stacking on. They looked to be closely related if not triplets, with identical malicious grins.

Cilif wasn't laughing, the way he usually did during a brawl, and Lia —

Oh, that's not a good look in her eyes. That's murder, cold and blue, right there.

Tank's heartbeat juddered once. His perception slid sideways into a cold, glassy acceleration. Before he consciously decided to move, he was already across the room and stepping right into the middle of the brewing fight, facing the triplets.

"*Stop*," he said, barely managing to haul back on projecting the sort of force a desert lord could summon.

He felt more than heard Cilif shifting back a step, pulling Lia along; heard the burly man muttering, "Get clear, get clear, you don't fuck with him when that look's in his eye. Stay behind him, damnit."

The triplets backed up as well, still grinning. "Good of you to ride to her rescue," one of them said, the words loaded with salacious implication.

Tank growled, momentarily unable to form words without using that *other* voice. The men's cocky smiles vanished. The two skinnier ones moved another step back and aside, their eyes narrowing warily.

Tank's voice emerged rough and thick with restrained violence as he said, "Not protecting her. Stopping you from getting yourselves hurt."

Cilif moved to stand at Tank's right shoulder but made no move to restart the brawl.

The heavyset young man brayed laughter.

"From *that*?" he demanded, pointing past Tank to Lia.

"By her, and by *me*," Cilif snapped. "You crossed a line, *ta-karne*, with that remark."

The young man sneered. The other two visibly assessed the opposition, glanced at one another and backed up a bit more. One tugged at his earlobe, digging his short nails in anxiously.

Cilif let out a low growl of his own and jerked forward a step. Tank smacked him hard on the shoulder; Cilif grumbled but came back to stand even with Tank.

Tank focused on the apparent leader and remarked, "I take it you know her."

"Everyone *knows* her," the young man said, tone dripping with innuendo. "You think she came by that Hall coin on her feet?"

He laughed again. His companions joined in a bit nervously, their gazes flicking from Lia to Tank to Cilif to Tank and freezing there. The one tugging his earlobe jerked as though he'd pinched too hard. He dropped his hand, lips moving in a silent curse.

Tank, still swimming in that crystalline clarity, felt Lia starting to lunge around him. He swept an arm up and out; she checked just shy of clotheslining herself.

"*Stop*," he told her, making it an absolute command, and felt her stagger under the force of it. "*Stay there.* Lia. What's the history here?"

She sucked in a breath. Then, in a clipped voice, she said, "They're from a rich family in Stecatr. Nahonna. I knew their cousin." The last word held murderous savagery. "I've never met these three."

"And it's our cousin as would know how she earned that coin," the leader pointed out smugly.

Lia pushed up against the arm Tank still held out. Momentarily impressed — she shouldn't have been *able* to move — he dropped the angle of his arm and shoved, driving her back. Lia let out a feral sound. Cilif stepped around behind Tank to pull Lia clear without a word needing to be said.

The leader of the Nahonna trio smirked, entirely complacent about his own safety. "You're giving her far too much credit," he said. "She couldn't put a fist into a brick wall, way I've heard it. *Fesh'ii*, you call it, right? More strut than substance?"

He mangled the pronunciation: *fishy* rather than *fess-hee*. Cilif snorted contemptuously. Ordinarily, Tank would have laughed, himself. At the moment, he wasn't capable of anything but barely leashed rage.

"You lot are fucking *fools*," Cilif retorted, pronouncing each word with ostentatious clarity.

"Enough," Tank ordered. "You three don't look like mercenaries."

They all drew themselves up, looking haughtily offended. "We are *Nahonna*," the leader snapped. "We are *craftsmen*, not common brawlers."

"I see," Tank said, forcing his tone to a deceptive mildness. "Craftsmen really shouldn't risk their hands. Broken fingers take an awful long time to heal, you know. Especially after someone's stomped on them a few times." He stomped one foot with a grinding, twisting motion to make the threat unmistakable.

The two standing back exchanged another, more worried glance than before. "Eh, Gisi," one muttered, "Maybe this isn't such a good idea ...."

The leader's chin came up, arrogance in every line of his body now. "Look, friend," the leader — Gisi — said in a superior tone, "you needn't get so upset. We've no complaint with you, nor even with her. I made a joke, that's all, and she overreacted. As women do."

"You lying, rat-dicked sacks of rotted pig entrails!" Lia yelled. Tank heard her fighting to get free of Cilif's hold.

Gisi laughed. "See?" he said. "Totally irrational. Overreacts to everything." He folded his arms over his chest, still looking down his nose at Tank. "You really ought to discard her, you know. I'm sure she'll find another customer soon enough. Unless you *want* to wind up with whorepox. I wouldn't know, maybe she's worth it." He sniggered.

Glassy detachment broke into shards as Tank's temper snapped. Moving, again, without conscious intent, his fist connected with Gisi's stomach, knee to face as the man folded; then a hard shove put Gisi on the floor out of the way. The other two had started moving back, separating sideways, but they weren't moving nearly fast enough to evade him right now. Tank repeated the maneuver with each Nahonna. Basic as the sequence might be, still their bodies made a satisfying *thunk* when they landed on the floor. Absently, Tank picked up a stool and snapped a leg off, then moved to stand over Gisi as the man began struggling to his feet.

Tank poked the man in his lower back with the makeshift club, aiming for the kidneys.

Gisi yelped and collapsed. Tank leaned down and said, rapid and low, "One word, *fesh'ii tas-shadata* — and you fucking well learn how to say the words properly before you take my language in your mouth again — no, *stay down*, I'll put this right through your fucking kidneys next —"

Tank set his foot on one of Gisi's hands hard enough to trap it as he spoke, then thunked the end of the stool leg twice on the floor by the man's shoulder. Gisi whimpered, turning his head to stare sideways up at Tank with wide, terrified eyes.

Tank went on, "If I hear *one word* against this woman's reputation that traces back to you, every single bone in both your hands will be in more pieces than a glass dropped on stone. You and your friends here. I'll find you. I'll break you. Name's Tank. Ask around if you have any doubt about how serious I am. Are we entirely clear?" He put more weight on his foot, twisting a bit.

Gisi squealed, "Yes! Enough! Gods, you're insane!"

"Yes," Tank agreed, stepping back. "Good of you to notice."

The Nahonnas staggered to their feet and fled the tavern, the lesser two supporting their stumbling, shaken leader. A damp patch stained the floor where Gisi had lain.

Tank drew in a harsh breath as the cut-glass clarity faded. His eyesight felt weaker, his hearing muffled, and a foul taste coated the inside of his mouth. He took a deeper breath, listening to his heartbeat as it slowed, regretting and not regretting what he'd just done.

The room was silent. The various brawls had stopped completely. The combatants were edged back as far from him as they could get. All eyes were fixed on him — most wide and startled, some narrowed and calculating.

Anger still simmering far too close to eruption, he glared around.

Denil's steady voice carried in the quiet: "*S'e* Tank. If you'd come over this way."

Tank turned away from the staring patrons. The servers came out from behind the bar; they began picking up scattered debris and shooing patrons to the remaining tables. On his way to the bar, Tank paused to pick up a particularly large piece of table that a server had been eyeing with dismay. He leaned it securely against the nearest wall and kept going.

Denil drew Tank a drink, tapping the bar in a signal for Tank to keep his back to the room. That was smart, if unsettling; it would avoid accidental re-escalation from a sour glare. Tank trusted the man enough to obey, but as he wrapped his hands around the mug, he realized that Lia hadn't been one of the people staring at him. He risked a casual look over his shoulder. She was gone. As were Dasin and Cilif.

"*S'e* Tank," Denil said in low-voiced warning. "If you set things off again, I'll personally skin you alive."

Tank ignored that. He tracked the various glances still being aimed his way, two of which were considerably more intent than the others. From different places in the room, a small, narrow-faced man in News Rider leathers, and a much larger, muscular man in unremarkable colors, studied Tank with too much interest. Somehow, he didn't think they were planning to start a new brawl, which meant they were connecting old rumors to what they had just seen.

Not good. Not good at all.

"I'm sorry, *s'e*," Tank said aloud, setting down the untasted mug. He reached for his belt pouch. "I'm not as thirsty as I thought I'd be, but a meal for myself and my crew would be a kindness. What do I owe you?"

"No charge," Denil said, his attention on the too-quiet room behind Tank.

Tank lowered his voice. "Put the damages to merchant Dasin," he said. "I'm well aware it's his fault, somehow."

"Not this time," Denil said, smiling a little. "Feenie actually started this one rolling, way I see it. And those three *fesh'ii* said something that lit your hire right up. I won't let them in again. Arrogant little asses." His gaze flicked to survey the room again. "I'll send food to the back door," he added. "Best go."

Tank headed for the door, deliberately avoiding meeting anyone's gaze. He made it out into the humid night, took one step clear of the porch, two —

"*S'e?*" The cautious tone said more than the word itself.

Tank turned, forcing a strained smile. He said, "No. I'm not who you think I am. I've been told who I look like, and —"

The man shut the tavern door behind him and came down from the porch, keeping a goodly amount of space between himself and Tank. He stood a head taller, and showed considerably more muscle, but regarded Tank with the wariness of a fighter knowing himself outmatched.

"I *know* who you are," the man said. "I've a message for you."

Tank backed up a step, then set his stance for a fight he didn't particularly want.

The man laughed a little, holding up both hands. He wore no rings, on hands or ears, and his clothing was the sort of unremarkable that came from deliberate design. For all his size, he moved with the grace of a dancer; for all that he'd plainly enjoyed brawling, Tank had a feeling he was more comfortable with less open conflicts. Quite possibly an assassin. At the very least, a spy or dark-market courier.

"Not that kind of message," the man said. "I was told to start by saying: *plucked feathers grow back.*"

Tank's temper stirred again, his vision wavering in and out of that dangerous crystal clarity. The man watched, unafraid but ready to dodge. Tank drew in a difficult breath, forcing the anger down. This wasn't a fight that could be won with violence.

"Not on me, they don't," he said roughly. "And if that's supposed to be subtle, it's flat failing. *No.* Take that answer back to —"

The man held up a broad hand, expression apologetic. "That wasn't the message, *s'e*. That was just to get your attention. And to make sure of who *you* are, of course."

"And who do you think I am, then?"

"I think you're a red-haired northerner who talks like a southerner and moves like a desert lord," the big man said levelly. Producing a small, sealed envelope, he held it out without moving forward. "I don't know what's in it, I don't want to know any more about who you are, and I don't have any interest in pursuing you. But I'm bound to deliver this." His mouth went thin for a moment. "If you know who sent me, you know what that means.

Please, take it."

Tank twitched it out of the man's grasp and said, "So, your part is done. Go away."

"Happily," the man said. He offered a slight bow, then went back into the tavern.

Tank stuffed the envelope roughly into his belt pouch and went round the side of the tavern.

As he'd expected, Dasin, Cilif, and Lia were waiting there. Enough light spilled over from the lanterns in front of the tavern to show that Dasin and Cilif bore the bright merriment of drunks. Lia had her arms crossed and was looking distinctly displeased.

"Fucking ta-karnes," Tank said, shoving Dasin's shoulder hard enough to stagger him sideways. "Why'd you run out on me?"

"Thought it best to let you handle it on your own," Cilif said, grinning broadly.

"You're lucky," Tank observed. "They're not blaming us this time. Stuck it on Feenie and the northerns."

Cilif sobered. "Yeah, well, they're nasty business, those three." He cut a sideways glance at Lia; she shook her head. Cilif shrugged, then broke out into a forced laugh. "Ay, though, you shoulda seen the scrap with Feenie! That was *fun*."

Lia scowled at Cilif, not at all amused. Tank snapped his fingers to draw everyone's attention, then said, "Food's been brought round the back. I'm getting a meal and going to sleep. I suggest you two do the same, you're damn near talking to the wind. Lia, I'm assuming you didn't get anything to eat either. Come on."

They followed him around to the back of the tavern. A small lantern hung from a hook by the door, showing four large bowls of stew, topped with equally generous chunks of bread, on the step. Tank handed a bowl to Lia and took one for himself. Dasin and Cilif took theirs and left, presumably to eat at the inn. They'd bring the bowls back later.

Tank motioned Lia to a row of overturned crates nearby. They sat and ate without speaking for a time. Eventually, Lia said, "Cilif cornered me into brawling with that big unsworn — Feenie? I tried to avoid it."

"I did warn you," Tank said. "I'm glad Gint isn't along. He and Cilif would get to drinking and would scrap with each other if they couldn't find anyone else to fight. At least you had to be forced into it." He munched on the last of the bread thoughtfully. "So he set you against Feenie? How'd that go?"

"Quickly," Lia said, the ghost of a smile in her voice. "He was slow."

"Wait." Tank stared at her. "You *won*?"

She looked down at her bowl, shadow making her expression unreadable. "I clipped him along the knee and the elbow just right," she said. "He lost interest after that."

Feenie never *lost interest* in a brawl when he'd been drinking. That light comment evaded what had to be the reality: that she'd hit at least one nerve point hard enough and precisely enough to temporarily paralyze the targeted area. That would have backed the big unsworn off immediately, especially coming from someone of Lia's relatively slight build; and it explained why Feenie had retreated to a corner.

She'd hit his *knee* like that without destroying it? *Damn.*

Deciding to keep his response light rather than shocked, Tank let out a low bark of laughter. "Damn. Yeah, those aren't proper brawling moves, you know that, right? You're supposed to throw punches, maybe grapple, toss people into the furniture."

Lia's thin shoulders moved in a shrug. She rubbed at a small smear of dirt on one arm as she said, "I didn't want to brawl in the first place."

"*Alli-na-kii*. Two hits and done," Tank said, and laughed again. "I like you."

She stood and set her empty bowl on the crate where she'd been sitting. "Thank you for the food, *s'e*," she said, voice abruptly colorless, He had a feeling that she'd seen through his surface amusement to the astonishment beneath.

"You can stop being so formal," he told her. "Far too long a road ahead for that. And I don't know when Dasin and Cilif got you out of there, but those assholes won't bother you again, or spread tales."

"Dasin hustled me out the door while they were still talking. He said you were about to snap and it was best I not be nearby. Cilif came out almost on our heels." She hesitated, then said, "They both looked ... odd. I might have imagined it. But ...."

Tank let go of any attempt at levity. "They looked scared," he supplied quietly.

"Yes."

Tank sighed, tilting his head to squint at the star-dappled sky, and reminded himself that it was a mark of trust that she'd even gone that far towards asking.

"I lost my temper," he said. "That always gets a bit unpredictable." He glanced at her. "You lost yours, back there, too. What set you off?"

She didn't answer immediately. At last, she said, voice stifled, "I had a friend who died, a while back. They implied that they were involved in her death. It's complicated. I wasn't expecting it." She paused, her voice turning cold. "I shouldn't have let them bait me. And I thank you, but I don't need to be protected, *s'e*. I had it handled."

"There's different kinds of protection," he said amiably, storing the spots where her voice had faltered, and the *it's complicated*, to think about later. "You're on my crew to fight bandits on the road, not fools in a tavern. I'm not inclined to replace yet another guard twice at short notice, and if you'd laid hands on those three, you'd have been taken in for brawling."

"Everyone was brawling," she objected.

"Locals and regulars," he corrected. "Every single person there is paying triple for their drinks for the next tenday, believe it, including Cilif, Dasin, and me. You don't have that kind of tab here. Those three you were up against are lucky they didn't get tossed to the guards, just banned for life."

"Lucky," she muttered, the word savage. She scratched her right forearm, then smoothed the area with sharp sweeps of her palm.

Tank, deciding not to prod, yawned. "You'll likely be on your own with Dasin at the morning market tomorrow. He'll be hungover and cranky, so don't take anything he says seriously and don't let him chase you off. I've errands to run before I come out to the stall. I'll take over sometime after noon. Goodnight."

"Goodnight," she said, and walked away.

He watched her move through shadow and lantern-light, admiring the soft-footed grace of her stride. She had better training than he'd expected if she could bring Feenie down so fast. It was tempting to assume aqeyva training, but as far as he knew that discipline hadn't made it to Stecatr yet. Who the hells had trained her?

Well, that was a mystery for another day. Right now, he had to go yank on Dasin's ear about letting Cilif goad Lia into a brawl. It was most definitely going to be a dry night, after that.

He sighed and slouched towards the inn, already sorting through which phrases to avoid in the pending argument and which would land with the precision of an aqeyva strike. If he had to have this fight, he wanted it to be like Lia's brawl with Feenie: short, savage, and definitively over before it really started.

Intersection: Contemplation

Light cycled in slow, steady rhythm as the First worked on her new form and new name. The water warmed and cooled and warmed again under the vagaries of local weather patterns. On occasion, a human wandered too far into the shallows. She accepted those gifts, drawing their feeble strength into herself to fuel the process.

At last, satisfied, she walked calmly out of the water, rising from the ocean like one of the gods she'd once worshipped. It was night: stars scattered across the clear sky, shining down like a benediction. She looked up for a long time, enjoying the feel of water slowly evaporating from her body, enjoying the feel of breath moving through her lungs once more.

She'd considered leaving herself without pesky human organs. She could breathe perfectly well through her skin, if she so desired, and she had almost no need at all for the other tedious functions. In the end, simple habit had won out, and she'd gone with the usual array of linked processes.

So, then. She'd accomplished two momentously difficult tasks: escaping the *attiara* and rebuilding a complicated human body to an entirely new appearance. She found herself at a loss, now. Those two matters had required such intense concentration as to leave no room for future plans.

Who am I now, and what do I want?

She thought about that for a time. She'd been Teilo, once, but that name didn't suit any longer. Neither did *the First, the sacred mother, windspeaker,* or any of the other names and titles she'd held over the centuries. Nothing came to mind, so she set that question aside for later. It wasn't all that important just now.

As for *what do I want* ... Revenge? Of course, but that was a small matter, not one worth pursuing as a primary goal. It would fold in along the way. Opportunity would arise.

What to do now? If not revenge, then what?

Exploration, perhaps. See how the world had changed during her captivity, see how long it had taken her to scrape together enough substance to rebuild to this point.

Yes. Exploration. And perhaps ... she looked down at herself. Clothes. Yes, humans expected clothes. She laughed a bit at an amusing memory linked to that phrase, then stretched her fingers out, enjoying the play of human muscle. She'd take some clothes along the way. Perhaps, if the target had any interesting heritage, she'd feed to satisfy pleasure instead of hunger for once.

Then she would find out where the dangerous ones had settled. The First Born, the Calcen, the *attiara*. There were other creatures, as well, that might be able to slow her down, interfere with her forming plans, perhaps even harm her. That determination had to be next.

After that, she'd have leisure to decide her path. Food, water, shelter were all matters of concern for lesser creatures. She'd long since moved past that. If necessity did arise, she could easily take what she needed along the way. No, next would be ... *amusement*, perhaps, although that didn't quite seem the right word. Experience? Entertainment? Interests?

She shrugged aside precise wording. Perhaps she could track down her former pupils. That was an intriguing thought: she could see what they'd become. Find out if they'd turned out *useful* in any way. Seeing them might help her decide what she wanted.

It took a moment to bring their names to mind: *Tanavin. Dasin.* She tucked those names away with care, surprised and annoyed at herself for having even briefly misplaced them, then set off towards the night-darkened buildings of Bright Bay.

Chapter Eight

Southern sun and an overnight downpour had left the air even thicker than the previous day. Lia stood in the dubious shade of a wide-limbed pine tree and tried to breathe without gasping. Even this early in the morning, sweat trickled down her face and soaked her clothes.

At least she didn't have to wear the ata. Obein forbade weapons larger than a belt knife in their open market, and armor wasn't necessary either. Lia had opted for a blue linen tunic over her long-sleeved white shirt this time, which allowed for reasonable modesty and didn't add much weight.

Merchant Dasin, once more wearing deceptively simple white clothing, seemed completely comfortable. Not in the least grumpy, he laughed and called out to passerby, his silver bracelets and earrings gleaming and clinking as he gestured people over. He greeted more than one visitor by name, drawing them in for a chat about personal matters. Most left the stall with at least a small purchase in hand; usually, from what Lia could see, a packet of dried basil.

Best thing in the world for an upset stomach, Dasin promised, and spoke of mixing it with garlic as though it were a dish fit for a king's table. Nearly as often, he sold something called *ravann*, at a much higher price. He insisted it was the perfect answer for women who had trouble sleeping. *Unless the s'a is pregnant, in which case I'd suggest ....*

Lia admired his easy confidence. He drew people out about their troubles, found something in his stock that was absolutely perfect for that problem, and without ever seeming to press had money in hand within moments. She'd never seen anything quite like it. Kennet, while skillful, had been considerably less graceful.

Not for the first time, Lia considered telling Dasin that Kennet had trained her to run a sales table; once more decided against it. Dasin sold *himself* as much as the product. She couldn't match that. She didn't want to try. Besides, she didn't know nearly enough about the herbs and simples on sale to speak with confidence as to their uses.

Motion to her left brought Lia around, sharply alert. A muscle-broad woman in a yellow and green dress spread her hands in a peaceful gesture, smiling, then came forward another few steps. She waved at Dasin. The merchant's eyes narrowed, not quite hostile. He jerked his head in a return greeting, flipped a hand to Lia to indicate the woman was known, then went back to talking with the current customer.

"He always sees to business first," the woman said with an ostentatious sigh, then offered Lia a bow. Her skin was dark and lightly ghost-marked along her right cheek and neck. She said, "I'm Priana. I can see you're new. I decided it's only kind to stop by and introduce myself."

Lia hesitated, then put her attention back on watching the table as she spoke. "Lia, of Stecatr. I'm afraid I don't have time to talk right now, *s'a*, I'm working."

"Of course," Priana said. "You're so dedicated. It's quite inspirational. Tell me, have you replaced Cilif?"

"No," Lia said. "He'll be along later." Eyes narrowing, she watched a young, dark-haired woman approaching Dasin's table.

"How are you getting along with Cilif?" Priana inquired. "He can be quite the ... *handful*." She chuckled salaciously.

The dark-haired girl stumbled, catching herself on the edge of the table. Lia moved without hesitation, stepping up to trap the girl against the table. "Put it back," she said into the girl's ear. "That wasn't even a good attempt."

The girl froze. Then, with a resigned shrug, she tossed two small spice packets back into the table baskets.

Lia didn't move. "Now put back the other three."

"Damn," the girl said, turning to look at Lia with open admiration. "You're sharp, you are." She dropped three more stolen items into their proper places. Lia stepped back, releasing her. The girl offered a mocking bow and disappeared into the crowd.

Lia met Dasin's gaze straight on, measuring the amusement in his face. "I don't appreciate being tested, merchant Dasin," she told him.

He made a face, thin lips twisting. "Wasn't me," he said. "That was all *her*." He nodded over her shoulder.

Lia turned to find Priana grinning at her broadly. The big woman came over to the table and slapped Lia on the back.

"She'll do, merchant Dasin," Priana said. "She'll do."

"Thank you for your approval," Dasin said, voice dry. He wiped at his hairline, grimacing at his damp fingers. "Lia, may I introduce you to Priana of Obein, head of the local market and the most *remarkable* pain in the arse I have yet to encounter." He pulled a soft cloth from beneath the table, wiped his hands, then dropped it back out of sight.

"Ah, sweetling, you only say that because I won't pleasure you," Priana shot back without an ounce of shame.

Dasin rolled his eyes, expression somewhere between amused and disgusted. "Go on, then, have your talk, I'll manage for a bit," he said, and waved them away. Priana laughed, drawing Lia back to stand in the shade once more.

"You're a sharp one," she said. "You know what to look for. Much better than the usual run of tit-gazers he hires. I could use you around here. Feel like staying? I pay well, room and board included."

"I can't, *s'a*," Lia said stolidly. "I'm due home to Stecatr." She caught herself scratching her forearm, an old, bad nervous habit, and made herself fold her fingers and cross her arms.

"Well, so," Priana said. "You ever change your mind, I'll have a spot here for you away from all that cold weather, and I don't say that to many northerns, trust me." She paused. "Watch out for yourself," she added, more soberly. "Dasin's got a temper, and a mean, dark streak. Don't cross him, or the redhead."

Yeah, I noticed that last night, Lia thought but managed not to say aloud. Priana's eyes glittered as though she'd heard the unspoken words.

A skinny young man stopped in front of Dasin's booth to inspect the herbs. He didn't show any tells of being a thief, but Lia found watching him was much easier than enduring Priana's knowing gaze.

Cilif's voice cut in. "You trying to steal another hire, 'ana? You got no shame in that overboned body of yours."

Lia let out an incautiously loud breath of relief. Priana laughed, said something to Cilif in dialect, patted Lia on the shoulder once more, then left to harass someone else. Cilif, grumbling under his breath, moved to stand beside Lia.

"Good morning," Lia said. "I didn't think you'd be up this early."

Cilif grunted and waved a hand in what could have been greeting or dismissal. "Fucking 'ana and her fucking games," he said. "She pull the thief at the table shit on you already? Yeah. She likes to test anyone new. Dasin's given up telling her to lay off. Last time he yelled at her, she doubled his table fees and put him to the worst corner of the market. You didn't run into her on your way through to Bright Bay?"

"The market was closed. Kennet wasn't willing to wait two more days."

"Yeah, no money in that." Cilif rubbed his nose, surveying the area thoughtfully. He added, "I went up against 'ana once. Lost my temper at her needling, took a swing. She laid me out flat with one hit. Bitch has a fist like a brick house. Go away. I got this. Dasin don't need both of us, no matter what Tank told you. Go walk the market. Come back if you get bored."

Lia hesitated, measuring his unexpectedly civil tone against his previous behavior.

Cilif cut her a sideways glance. "There's a place next row over as sells practical stuff women like, or maybe need," he said. "Couple mercenaries I know say it's a useful stop on a long trip. Teas and...." He made a vague gesture in the air. "You know. Stuff."

She blinked, taken aback, and couldn't think of a thing to say.

"I been on the road a while," Cilif said, not looking at her. "Worked with a fair few women. Go on already. Come back when the day's wrapping up and I'll take you to a better tavern. One with wine and decent ale, where you can have a drink there for the taste, not to get stupid drunk."

It sounded like the closest Cilif could come to apologizing for the previous night. She considered for a moment, then decided it would do well enough.

"I'll wander a bit and come back," she agreed, then added, warningly, "I'm not brawling."

Cilif grinned, rubbing his nose again. "Nah," he said. "Not at this place. Tank already raked me over about the fight. And you ain't no fun, anyhows." He mimed two quick jabs and a body falling to the floor, then waved her away again. "Go, go, I got this."

She shrugged, unable to come up with a better answer, and went to advise Dasin she was stepping away. His sunny demeanor disappeared as he listened, and he looked over her shoulder at Cilif. "Very well," he said. "One moment, before you go." He set a small red spice bag on the table. "Call it a bonus." He wouldn't meet her eyes.

Lia hesitated between irritation and relief: irritation that Tank had, clearly rattled both men into apologizing to her, relief that her employer hadn't turned against her. She picked up the small bag, wondering what spices Dasin was giving her.

It clinked.

She froze, weighing it in her hand reflexively. "What is this?" she demanded.

"Your winnings." Dasin's expression curdled briefly. Then his benign grin resurfaced as he waved at an approaching customer. "*S'a* Benialla! I've had a special blend of ravann, pepper, and ginger made up just for you. Lia, go if you're going, get out the way in any case," he added in an undertone, waving her aside.

She went, tucking the small bag into her belt pouch, and resolved to have a word of her own with Tank at the earliest opportunity.

Chapter Nine

"You sure she's not interested in Cilif?" Dasin said as he snapped the lock shut on the last chest. His manufactured cheer had, as usual, disappeared along with the last of the customers. "She looked awful happy walking off beside him." He cut a sideways glance at Tank and added, "Maybe she thinks he's *pretty*."

I should have known he wouldn't let that go easily. "He's making up for being an ass last night," Tank said. "Something for you to think about, maybe."

Dasin shot him a poisonous glare. "I already gave her the winnings! The hells else you want out of me?"

"How about straightforward apologizing to her? How about apologizing to *me*?"

"Oh, fuck you." Dasin dropped the waterproof cover over the table, twitching the edges to even them out. "If I apologized every time you took offense, I'd be on my knees to you twenty out of twenty-four."

Tank bit his tongue against the obvious answer to that. In the moment of silence, a dark flush crept up Dasin's neck.

"That didn't quite ...." Dasin muttered. "Never mind. Leave me alone. Go find someone else to annoy for the night. I'm sure you can find *someone* who doesn't offend you."

Tank balled one hand into a fist and rested his knuckles gently atop Dasin's shoulder. "Once, Dasin, *once*, make it easy on me," he said in a low voice.

Dasin swung his head to one side, pulling his shoulder out from under Tank's hand: not entirely rejection, as he didn't move any further away.

Tank said, neutral, "Kaya's place is open again. They're calling it The Glass House these days. Might be a bard there tonight. And I need to talk to you about something."

Dasin cast a last, distrustful glance around the emptying market, watching the evening guards take up their posts. Since the recent disruption, Obein's market was rapidly growing to be *the* coastal market, instead of Sandsplit, in large part because of Priana's controlling hand. Yuer's heavy-handed mismanagement of the Sandsplit open market had shifted the balance even further. Not that Tank was ever going to point that out to his employer. He liked living.

Back when Tank and Dasin had signed on under his hand, Yuer — while not officially in charge of anything — had been the dominant power along the entire Coast Road. Politics and catastrophes, such as the recent destruction of the Horn, had eroded his hold. He'd retaliated for his loss of range by tightening his grip on Sandsplit itself. Outside merchants had to pay increasingly high stall fees for poor locations, and were particularly forbidden from undercutting anything sold by the locals.

Priana, in sharp contrast, kept the Obein market thoroughly staffed and guarded with her own people, day and night. There was a nominal fee for merchants who wanted to leave their merchandise at their stalls overnight. A nominal fee for risers. A nominal fee for weatherproof covers. Bit by bit multipled by hundreds of merchants times invaluable goodwill, it added up. Priana was a rich woman these days, and fast becoming a frighteningly influential one. It didn't do to piss her off, and hanging around glaring at her guards was a quick path to doing just that.

Tank wrapped a hand lightly around Dasin's upper arm and steered him from the market square, releasing his hold the moment he felt muscles tighten towards pulling free. Dasin's rejection of anything even approaching public affection set a rough ache into Tank's chest, as it always did; as always, he pushed it aside. Things were as they were. Dasin needed someone to keep him steady, and Tank was the only one willing to step up to the task.

Dasin did his fair share of balancing Tank out. They had similiar scars — on the inside, at least — and the mutual understanding served as solid comfort on bad days. *Tore up as we both are*, Tank reflected, flattening his palm briefly against Dasin's mid-back, *not likely anyone else would want either of us anyway*.

Dasin shivered like an annoyed horse, stepping sideways to get away from the touch. Tank dropped his hand, settling his face into an indifferent, hard-eyed expression, and led the way without any further attempts at conversation or connection.

The newly reopened Glass House turned out to be more crowded than Tank had expected. It had rarely been busy under the previous owner. It looked the same on the outside: weathered, more than one board a bit out of true, and in need of a fresh coat of paint; but four more bench tables had been added inside, and most of them were full. The room hung as thick with smoke as with ale fumes, and the ambient conversation made for a steady rumble of noise. Tank hesitated, not sure if this was a good idea after all.

Before he could suggest retreating to somewhere quieter, Dasin shoved past him, grumbling under his breath, and chose a seat on a nearby bench.

Tank held back an annoyed snarl and plopped down across from Dasin with a deliberate lack of couth. He let his irritation show as he stared into the assessing glances of the other people around the table. One by one, they looked away. The closest two even moved to an entirely different table, leaving Tank and Dasin with plenty of space to themselves. The ones who stayed looked resolutely forward at the musician near the fire, a sallow-faced older man with deep pox scars who was currently checking something on a lap harp.

A server with a dark birthmark prominent on his relatively pale face appeared at Tank's elbow. He set a mug of the house ale in front of each of them and said, "Bread or noodles?" in a tone of utter disinterest.

That wasn't typical tavern fare, but Tank wasn't inclined to ask questions just then. He held up a silver round and said, "Bread for me, noodles for him." The server took the coin and went away.

"What if I wanted bread?" Dasin demanded. "Can't I order for myself?"

Tank took a sip of the ale. It wasn't bad at all. Keeping his gaze to the side of Dasin's narrow face, carefully non-challenging, he said, "All right. Call him back and change it. Or I could just eat the noodles, give you the bread."

A thread of sound reached him as the bard ran a few tentative chords on the lap harp. The man looked around as though gauging the room's attention and noise level, tilting his head a bit as he ran though a few quick sequences. Apparently dissatisfied, he set the lap harp aside and pulled a large wooden box in front of him.

"Do you want to call him back?" Tank prompted when Dasin didn't say anything.

"No. Never mind." Dasin glanced at his mug, his expression turning sulky, then went back to watching the musician.

Tank drank his ale, partially to shut himself up. It had an oddly smoky flavor that reminded him of a good whiskey, not something he'd ever expected from an ale. Maybe he'd actually ask about how it was made. He probably wouldn't understand above half the answer, but asking would at least convey his appreciation.

The bard's wooden box featured variously shaped holes, cut in what seemed like random patterns. As Tank watched, he sorted out a stack of strikers that looked to be made of different woods. One set gleamed like metal, but Tank wasn't close enough to be sure.

The bard put the strikers into a neat, easily accessible line, then picked out two. He launched into a simple rhythm. The hammering grew rapidly louder, silencing the chatter and drawing the room's collective attention to the musician. The bard grinned. His hands moved more quickly, the rhythm changing to a pattern that invited dancing. A few people stood up and stomped in place briefly, bumped into tables and companions, then sat down, laughing. The remaining people at Tank's table moved to find seats closer to the bard.

The bard began switching out mallets, somehow without losing a beat, and ran through some astonishingly complicated sequences. Assured of the patrons' attention now, he dropped abruptly into a barking beat and began to sing. His voice, strong and deep, filled the room as he belted out the words:

Oy, hey, time to play
Oy, hey, take the day,
Oy, hey, make some time,

Oy, hey, drink your wine ....

He pointed at someone nearby. The customer yelled out, "Oy, hey, keep it neat!" The singer pointed at someone else, who chimed in with, "Oh, hey, thresh the wheat!", and the crowd was off, several people eagerly waving their hands to be the next one called on.

Tank had heard similar work chants before. He suspected a tavern crowd wouldn't be able to hold it for long. Sure enough, five people later, the target fumbled the line, and the room burst into laughter.

The server came by with a basket of rolls, a bowl of wide noodles drenched in butter, and a chunky wooden fork. She tossed a few squares of dry cloth down as well and said, "Use these to wipe your hands and faces."

Tank looked up, startled, but she'd already turned to work her way back to the bar. "That's new," he said, watching her go.

More delusions of nobility," Dasin said, nudging the cloths with one finger. His mouth twisted in contempt. "Gods, they're fucking *embroidered*."

"Well, there's no tablecloth," Tank pointed out. Dasin grumbled something indistinct.

The bard rattled an impressive staccato on the box, then settled into a different beat and began to sing again.

The lord of crown, you walked a-tilt, with silver mule and pack
The mule went down, you took his gilt, and used him for a sack
The sun came back, the moon came dry, with silver in your hand
The tithe was lack, you gave mulesack, bent silver to a brand ....

Tank smiled a little, settling back in his seat. Not so many years ago, those first, apparently nonsensical lines would have promptly cleared the room as terrified patrons scrambled to remove themselves from the vicinity of a treasonous song.

Lord of crown was a disparaging reference to the king, implying that the only real authority he held was over the crown on his head; *a-tilt* was the madness the recent rulers had labored under. *Silver mule and pack* Tank wasn't sure of, but thought it probably referred to the noble houses who had propped up the failing rulers, since the next line definitely pointed at the collapse of financial stability as the kings stripped every treasury they could get their hands on, noble and mercantile alike, using the most specious and threadbare charges of treason. *Sun* and *moon* probably pointed to the desert Families, *moon* for the east and *sun* for the west — or was that the other way round? Tank wasn't particularly good at untangling allusions.

He was glad Lia had gone off somewhere else with Cilif tonight. She might not have taken this song particularly well. That thought led him to wonder if Toad knew it, himself; if he might have the brass ass to sing it on the road at some point, just to antagonize Lia.

The singer wrapped up that tune in short order and promptly launched into another, even more dangerous song. It featured an overzealous priest being targeted for pranks and tricks by the villagers, and held a heavy implication that all priests of the Northern Church should be similarly mocked.

It's a very good thing Lia isn't here. She'd probably attack the poor musician at this point. Not that I'd blame her.

Tank found himself frowning at some of the wording. He didn't hold any fondness for the Northern Church himself, but these lyrics went well past blaming the priests and edged towards advocating violence against their followers. He'd have to warn Lia to be especially careful about speaking of her home city along the Coast Road, if this was the prevailing sentiment.

He finished his ale and began working his way through the warm, surprisingly light rolls. Dasin stared at the steam coming from his bowl, his expression morose, and made no attempt to eat. With nobody else at their table and the bard holding the room's attention, the moment felt safe enough for delicate conversation, as long as Tank was careful. Gods only knew if he'd get a chance to talk in proper private. Dasin was far too erratic for Tank to count on something so theoretically simple.

"Dasin," Tank said. He paused, breaking a roll into several pieces. He picked out and shredded the soft inside, then began squishing the loose crumbs into tiny flat bits. Wasteful, but he absolutely needed something to do with his hands for this conversation. Dasin watched, frowning, but didn't comment. Tank took a deep breath and went on, as steadily as he could: "After that brawl. Last night. Someone came up to me with a message. From our Family." Even with the ambient noise, *Aerthraim* was too risky a word to voice aloud. As was *the mahadrae* or *Mahadrae Kallaisin*.

Dasin's eyebrows rose. "For *you?*"

"Yes." Tank wiped squashed crumbs and oil from his fingers. He reached into his belt pouch. "Here." He passed the folded piece of paper to Dasin, darting a side-eye glance at the nearest people. They remained reassuringly oblivious. "Careful opening it."

The song ended with a viciously unhappy ending for the religious zealot it had been mocking. Several patrons burst into loud applause. Others, notably older and mostly female, showed less enthusiasm and wore uneasily disapproving expressions. Apparently they'd also noted the overreach in the lyrics.

The singer, sweat beginning to trickle down his stubbled cheeks, grinned amiably. He picked up his lap harp again and began a folk song about a farmer endlessly chasing a neighbor's goat out of his garden. The room relaxed into concerted laughter by the second verse, and people began belting out the chorus by the third.

Dasin ran a finger gently along the outside of the paper, his gaze not leaving Tank's face. Finding the broken seal, he opened it with care, revealing a lock of glossy red hair as long as his hand, streaked with gray, tied with a silver ribbon. He stared at that for a few moments, then read the short, unsigned message on the paper itself. His breath hissed between his teeth.

"'You look a great deal like your father,'" he read aloud, his voice tight. He turned the paper over and looked at the broken seal. The paper sagged in his suddenly loose grip. "Oh, Sun Lord's *cock*."

Tank reached out, taking the paper and hair before Dasin could drop them. He folded the message up, keeping his hand over the seal in case anyone glanced over, and tucked it away. "Yeah," he said. "Yeah, I know."

Dasin didn't say anything for a few breaths, his eyes still shut. At last, he looked at

Tank, eyes bright with misery. "That's K —"

Tank held up a hand in a warning gesture, deliberately flicking his gaze from side to side. "Yes. It's her seal. I know."

Dasin's lips folded in briefly. Then he said, barely loud enough to carry to Tank, "What are you going to do? Or should I ask, what are you asking *me* to do?"

Tank shrugged, blinking hard. "Nothing."

"*Nothing?*" Dasin stared, clearly not believing it.

"She wants me under her control," Tank said flatly. "If I go charging off south, I'll never fucking come back. Doing that for a man I've never even met? Leaving you, for *that?* No."

Dasin opened his mouth, closed it, then looked away, his nostrils pinched.

"There's nothing you can do," Tank said. "I know that. And I don't think you had anything to do with this. If I did, I'd have put a knife through your gut already."

Dasin shut his eyes and dipped his chin to his chest, lips tight. "I *didn't* have anything to do with this. I wouldn't. Gods, Tank, that's — that's *cold.*"

Tank bit his tongue to stop himself saying something openly dangerous, like *Why are you surprised?* It wouldn't be fair. Dasin had never wanted to see that side of Aerthraim Family, and Tank had never pushed it. Instead, he said, as placidly as he could, "I know. So let it be. May she have joy of waiting on an answer."

"She'll kill him."

Tank didn't say anything.

Dasin straightened, studying Tank's face. Then he said, "It's a good thing she didn't aim that at me. If she'd found my father ...." His lips sucked in again, as though to stop himself from saying more.

"She doesn't need to," Tank said as gently as he could. "You never broke ties. You'd go back anytime she called. She doesn't need this sort of leverage on you."

This was the first time Tank had ever put matters so bluntly. Dasin clearly didn't like it. His distress faded into a scowl, and he looked away as though watching the bard.

Tank let him be, in part because he found his eyes unexpectedly blurring. *I have a son myself,* he wanted to say. *I saw him once, after I made a stupid, stupid promise that means I'll never see him again. And every time we go through the Hackerwood, I can't help looking to see if he's staring over the wall at me. I'm no better than my own father.* He swallowed hard, surreptitiously wiping the back of his hand across his eyes, and gathered his composure.

Still watching the performance, Dasin said, "Something's not right."

Nearly grateful for something immediate to focus on, Tank took a casual survey of the room, searching for out-of-true patterns. Two people with ghost-marked skin; one, besides the server, with a visible dark birthmark — this one on his forearm. Two people with noses that had been broken and badly set. One person who was nearly as short as a child. Women, men, indeterminates ... visible heritage markers, accents, clothing ... everything seemed to be reasonable. He focused on sounds, riffling through tones and tenors, searching for strain in the wrong places, but nothing felt wrong there either. He began to inhale through his nose to check nearby aromas.

"Not *here*," Dasin said, impatient. "The last few tendays. Something's off."

Tank refocused on Dasin, irritated by the wasted effort. "How so?"

Dasin rattled his fingers on the table, his signal for uncertainty. "What's being bought. What's being sold. What's being said and not said. What you saw at the docks. Those songs." He tilted his chin at the singer, who had switched to an older, well-known song about the dangers of sailing. "And then ... that message. It's all got the hair up the back of my neck. The patterns are all wrong. Something ... something's *changing*."

Rania's voice came to mind: *Sommat's shifting ahead. Sommat dangerous.* Did it involve Aerthraim Family after all?

Tank checked his muscle tension, made himself relax, and forced his expression to a sleepy amiability that wouldn't alarm anyone who glanced their way. "Keep us out of politics," he said. "We can wait it out as long as you don't drop us in the middle of a mess."

Dasin shot Tank a brief, ambigious glance, then picked up the fork and poked at the noodles in his bowl, head bent.

Oh gods. "Dasin, tell me you didn't."

"I'm not stupid," Dasin retorted, which was no answer at all.

"*Dasin.*"

Dasin didn't lift his head. "I'm doing my best to give you what you want — your *precious* simple life." The words carried searing resentment. Tank let out a frustrated breath; picked up his mug, remembered it was empty, and set it down harder than he needed to.

"If you don't want me to hold you back," Tank said, and left the statement hanging.

Dasin looked up, scowling. Tank waited, keeping his expression flat. He might not be good at distraction, or selling at a profit, or being charming, but he could wait in ominous silence worthy of a desert lord when he wanted to. Eventually, Dasin dropped his gaze and said, in a scant whisper: "I need you."

"All right," Tank said, a familiar sense of exhausted cynicism settling over him like a heavy blanket. "So trust me, and stay out of their games."

Dasin stared at his ale with a dispirited frown. "I want to be alone," he said. He tossed back the rest of his drink and rose to his feet.

Tank began to shift his weight to stand, but Dasin's expression — tired, not restless — stopped him. Dasin wasn't going to look for trouble this time. And this was Obein; the only *trouble* here was so mild-mannered, compared to what Dasin normally hunted after, as to be laughable.

"I'll see you in the morning," Dasin said. He set a gold round on the table. "Give it to the bard. Enjoy his company, if you like. Good night."

Tank opened his mouth, irritation flushing up his neck. Dasin turned away without giving him the chance to answer and made his way to the tavern door.

"Godsdamnit, Dasin," Tank muttered under his breath, then scooped the far too bright coin into his pocket and began eating the noodles.

Intersection: Redemption

Being drunk would have been a relief. It was so very long since Ebe had allowed himself a drink. *Surely I've earned one. Surely I've paid enough.*

Ah, I think that every day of my life. The answer never changed: no. He hadn't earned it. He hadn't earned anything, not even the breath in his lungs. Drinking would put him deeper in debt to whichever of the gods had seen fit to preserve him this long.

Ebe sat on a bench near one of the few taverns in Obein, enjoying the warm southern sun as much as testing his sobriety yet again. Besides, this was an excellent spot to watch beautiful young people go by — and they were all beautiful, and all young, no matter their actual age or appearance. The gods didn't care about such things, and so he wouldn't either.

That even the kindly faces of the gods also didn't care enough to save their most faithful was a problem Ebe considered every day. Of course the unkind sides of the Four wouldn't care, but Ebe couldn't understand why so much, so terribly much, was allowed to happen even to those who were steadfast followers, as his Linera had been. He knew it was a heretical thought, but if the gods weren't going to do anything to earn or reward human faith, what was the point of bowing to them?

The priests, who knew Linera had been devout, who knew Ebe hadn't ever done anything ... well, *significantly* sinful ... they showed no care for years of dutiful tithes and contributions. They offered no softness, no forgiveness at all. A corrupt nobleman had saved Ebe's worthless life, not the godly representatives he'd expected to intervene on his behalf.

Enough. He didn't need to revisit the increasingly sour memories he'd been chewing on for most of his life. *Most of my life.* He turned that over in his mind, surprised to find it true. It had been well over half his life ago that everything fell apart. He'd lost his reputation, his wife, and his profession. The cruel, amphibian nickname of *Toad* assigned in the wake of that disaster had been insignificant, except that he'd been angry enough to take it on publicly, as an act of defiance, rather than allow people to see him hurt by one more thing.

He'd stopped counting the months, then stopped counting the years, then stopped counting the decades, and here he was: a lonely old fool, far from home and yet no less a stranger here than in Stecatr.

Ebe wished he could stay in the south. He quite liked the sun, and the people laughed more, appreciated a good story more, *gave* more in every way.

Mostly.

The negotiation for the medicine had been extremely unpleasant. Worse was Ebe's sure knowledge, after meeting the sneering southerners, that Jener wouldn't use the medicine as promised. He'd exploit it for his own profit, never mind his protestations of higher purpose and justice. The southerners hadn't been men of honor. For Jener to choose *them* as a source confirmed Ebe's worst fears about what he'd agreed to be a part of.

Stecatr was an insular, isolated city, and the Northern Church did their best to block unfettered access to outside news and certainly to outside ideas. Once on the road, however, traveling further from home than he'd been in many years, Ebe had picked up on a growing discontent about the king in Bright Bay.

Why, people asked irritably in every village and town and city along the way, did they pay taxes to a king who'd never seen their lands and never would? What were they paying for, when the taxes given to local lords went south with scanty returns on a practical, local level? The merchanting guilds, people grumbled, put more money and effort into keeping the roads and city streets useable than the king. When was the last time any of those supposedly excellent southern engineers had been sent to restore some of the crumbling buildings that had once been so fine? The king was more concerned with the southerners than his own people, and the Northern Church wasn't, to date, picking up the slack.

Ebe knew that in Stecatr, the Northern Church most certainly had their hands on all such things and more besides, but he also knew better than to remark on that aloud. Better to remain a quiet, amiable old man and store up what he heard, piece by piece. Jener might have to adjust his ambitious plans to a considerably narrower scope. And if the lands north of the Hackerwood split away from the lands south of the Hackerwood, a regular supply of the medicine Ebe had in his pack would likely come dearer than Jener had expected. Which meant Jener would definitely put it to a use more profitable than healing the poorest of the city.

Ebe shut his eyes, chewing his lip gently, until the sudden, painfully intense desire for a drink passed.

He couldn't *not* turn the medicine over to Jener. He couldn't claim that he'd never received it. Jener was far too sharp for that, and he had ways to detect lies. Methods that would bring the fury of the Church down on the man, was he ever discovered.

Probably. Unless the rumors of what the *Church* used for inquisitions was true. If so, there was a high chance that Jener knew the truth of it, and had proof, and held that as a shield to protect his own activities.

Never mind. Think of the best path, then set about building it.

If the medicine really worked as promised, if a supply could be established ... if Ebe could, perhaps, find a leverage on Jener that would force matters along the *right* path ... the lives saved would make this entire, miserable trip worthwhile. Building that path, that success, would balance out the weight on his soul enough to allow him the joy of a drink one last time. Then he'd step over a cliff, secure in his redemption.

The medicine, if it worked as promised, might have saved Linera. How bitter that thought was, here in the warm sun.

Anger choked in his throat, a living, writhing thing. He forced a deep breath, another, fighting to loosen Payti's grip one painful, rasping inhale at a time. Even in the drowsy, lovely sunshine, it was more difficult than it should have been.

Someone laughed, a high, amused sound: a cross between a chachad bird's challenge and a shrieker-bird's startling cry. Ebe turned his head sharply, searching for the source. It hadn't been a natural laugh. He had the instant, irrational conviction that it was directed at him, that his thoughts had been overheard.

Irrational, perhaps, but he knew better than to assume *impossible*. Things were different this far away from Stecatr, and there *were* creatures here who could read minds. He'd been thinking of killing, and had drawn unwelcome attention. Best to proceed as though a god-servant was watching.

He drew himself up and said under his breath, "Gods be blessed, I offer no harm and ask to pass under your interest, wise one." That seemed a safely generic address for any unknown he could think of.

Silence. He waited a moment more. The raggedy laugh came again, more thinly this time.

He pulled out phrases from the stories he told, ones that had always resonated in his bones as *true*. "I offer you respect," he said to that cruel amusement. "I offer you honesty and kindness, and a wish for your well-being. Pass by, wise one, pass by, I beg of you."

Silence. A rough, slightly kinder chuckle.

You know the forms well enough, little human, someone said. *I shall pass by, as you ask, after one question: Who do you travel with? I smell something on you I have not smelled in a long time. Tell me who walks near you.*

"Eh ... Merchant Dasin," he said, not at all sure he ought to be answering. But one didn't offend a god-servant, and his traveling companions were hardly a secret.

Ahhhhh. It might have been a breeze passing by. *And does this merchant have a companion?*

"T—three guards, gracious one. Lia, Cilif, and Tank. "

The rough chuckle returned. *Ahhhhh. Yes. Interesting. Amusing. You may go, little human. Forget me, forget, forget ....*

Silence: lighter this time, with a sense of danger dissipating.

Ebe drew in a shaky breath, wiping sweat from his forehead; and without being quite sure why, went to find a more densely populated area in which to sit.

Chapter Ten

The second day after the brawl dawned clear, with an improbably strong breeze chasing away the usual stifling heat. Rooster was unusually restless, nearly dancing under Lia as she waited for the others to be ready.

Tank paused in checking Sin's tack to glance her way. "Once we get moving, let him run a bit," he advised. There was a fresh bruise forming on the left side of his face, and a small cut near his right eyebrow; he looked like he hadn't slept at all the night before. He met Lia's startled gaze and shook his head slightly, his eyebrows dipping into a forbidding frown. She bit the inside of her cheek and put her attention on managing her horse.

To her right, Cilif mounted Blackie, settling into the saddle with a grunt. Dasin finished checking the draft over and climbed onto the wagon bench. Toad scrambled up, looking tired and out of sorts; then they were off, rattling through Obein's tidy streets out onto the wide coastal road towards Sandsplit.

The day went by, sullen and uneventful. Tank said even less than usual; Toad begged off telling stories for most of the journey, claiming a headache. It was, Lia decided, a tossup as to which man looked worse. Dasin, by contrast, seemed nearly cheerful. He even sang a few bits of song in a dialect Lia didn't know, but the tunes were similar to those of her childhood games.

Trees with variegated bark began to appear between the cross-hatched palms and feather-fern bushes. Long, sturdy limbs arched over the road in spots, creating a dappled shade that came as a relief from the intense sunlight. Twice, a large crow-like bird flapped across the road, startling Rooster the first time and Sin the second.

Tank had more trouble than usual bringing Sin under control afterwards. Dasin had to stop the wagon so that Tank could let his horse kick and fuss, and seemed amused as he watched the struggle. Rooster, by contrast, skipped sideways when the crow went by, then turned in a tight circle, tail swishing. He settled almost immediately after that.

Cilif didn't laugh at either incident, just kept Blackie well clear and watched Tank with an unsettlingly intent, sober expression.

As Dasin's wagon trundled into Sandsplit at last, an elderly chachad bird screeched thin challenge, strutting along the fence line in a noble attempt to reclaim its glory days of terrorizing travellers. Its long black legs were crusted with yellow, its proud, fiery plumage falling out in patches. Lia had a sudden urge to dismount and go pet the poor creature. Then she looked at the still savage beak, the glaring eyes, the wicked talons; laughed at herself a little, and stopped pitying the beast.

The common stables, not far past the guard bird enclosure, were an odd configuration: a series of rectangular buildings, offset together along the long ends and internally connected by several passageways large enough for a draft horse to pass through with ease. During her stop with Kennet, even though she hadn't been riding then, the odd layout had drawn her in and she'd been unable to resist poking around.

"You look as you know what you're seeing," a stable boy had commented, leaning on his broom and grinning at her. "We've spots, if you're looking for hire. No? Come on, anyway, I'll give you the tour. I need a break from this."

It was one of the larger public stables Lia had seen, and well run, with almost too generous a roster of staff, including a skilled veterinarian, tack repair and cleaning services, *and* an exercise yard suitable for dressage work. She had been severely tempted to hand in her Hall coin in favor of this life. And now she would be stabling a horse there. The thought brought a wide grin to her face.

Not far past the stables stood an equally impressive barn for storing carts, wagons, and carriages. Kennet had remarked that it was the best place beyond Assiasan he'd ever dealt with. He hadn't said why, and Lia hadn't been interested enough to tour that building.

Tank dropped back to ride beside her as they came up on a fork in the road, one path leading to the public stables, the other on a meandering northwestern course around the town. Rooster cast a sidelong glance at Sin, then ignored the big black horse entirely. Sin whuffled and stayed placid.

"That way," Tank told Lia, motioning her to follow Dasin as the wagon turned onto the northwestern road. She caught sight of Toad hopping down from the bench and hurrying off into town.

"We're not going to the stables?" she asked, disappointed.

"Not the public ones, no. Our employer lives here. We use his." He tilted his head from side to side, stretching his neck, and winced, muttering something unintelligible under his breath.

Lia reined Rooster to a stop. "Wait," she said, an unpleasant shock running through her. "You work for — what's his name? Youner? You never said anything about that!" Kennet had adamantly refused to set up at the market in Sandsplit. They'd stayed one night at the Gray Rooster Inn and left before dawn.

Tank gave a light tug on the reins. Sin halted immediately. From what she'd seen, other than that one incident with the bird, Sin had been remarkably well behaved so far today.

Tank rubbed the back of his neck, grimacing, then dropped his hand and said, "You, specifically, work for me. I hired you, I have first responsibility. The rest of us work for Yuer. If he approves of you enough to take your hire, you get to negotiate your contract with him, and then we're all on equal footing there." He hesitated, then added, "I'd rather you keep things as they are." His face closed off, as if he'd said too much, and sharply waved her to follow Dasin's wagon, nearly out of sight around a curve.

Lia looked longingly at the public stable, even as she obediently turned Rooster to follow. "I didn't know I was working for him, even at a remove," she said. "I'm not happy about this."

"I didn't lie," Tank said mildly. "So you've —" He paused, looking ahead with a frown.

A noisy procession wound towards them, young women dressed entirely in black, waving multicolored streamers on long black poles. One of them, a sturdily built girl with glossy black hair that swung loose to her waist, wore a large drum harness. She was enthusiastically beating out a rhythm that moved from simple to complex and back again. Two of the girls, both blond and similarly long-haired, were singing a soaring duet, their voices weaving under and over one another. The group was still too far away to make out the words, but Lia recognized the underlying tune well enough.

"The hells?" Tank said, scowling.

Lia couldn't help laughing at his dismay. "It's a coming of age celebration," she told him. Girls with their hair down will be considered an adult after today."

"Why are they wearing *black*?" Tank demanded.

Lia shrugged. "Different communities use different colors."

He looked sideways at her, one eyebrow going high. "Don't tell me you have this in *Stecatr*."

She reined Rooster in, delivering a hard glare. He pulled Sin to a stop, regarding her with a bafflement that slowly shifted to remorse.

"Yeah, okay," he said. "Sorry. That was a little stupid of me."

"Just a bit," she said. "Stecatr isn't some terrible, joyless prison, you know."

The procession swirled to either side of Dasin's wagon. Lia and Tank moved to opposite sides of the road to let the dancers through. Lia ran a quick count: fifteen girls, six of whom had their hair down. The other nine wore their hair in simple, unadorned braids and wore no jewelry, while the newly declared adults had large silver hoops in their ears and an array of silver bracelets clicking at each wrist. All of the girls had large red flowers secured in their hair and wore light slippers with leather soles.

Rooster shifted uneasily as the dancers went by. Lia patted him reassuringly and backed him up to stand a bit further away. The words of the song were in an unfamiliar dialect, but it would be about the joys of childhood changing to the joys of adulthood, the antics the new adults had gotten up to, and the things they were looking forward to in the days ahead. The Stecatr songs were all formulaic, even abstract; she had a feeling, looking at the changing expressions and bursts of laughter, that these were far more individually crafted.

One of the younger girls looked up at her, waving merrily. Lia laughed back at her, bowing as best she could while mounted. The girl whirled and bounced up against one of the older girls; turned back with a silver bracelet in one hand, and tossed it up. To her own surprise, Lia caught it easily. She held it up in triumphant gesture, then held it against her heart in a gesture of gratitude and blessings. Several girls were looking her way at that point. They laughed, twirling in an extra complicated pattern briefly, then went by without another glance. Over their heads, Lia saw Tank catching a flung bracelet himself, his expression entirely bemused. He duplicated her gestures awkwardly, clearly mimicking her without really understanding what he was doing.

She laughed again, giddy delight filling her, and slipped the bracelet onto her right forearm as the last of the girls danced past and went on into the town. Coming of age celebrations always made her feel nearly drunk with reflected joy. Her own had been, quite possibly, the first time she'd felt genuinely free.

Shame that didn't last, she thought, then pushed the sourness aside.

As the procession faded out of view around a corner, she rejoined Tank in the road, following the once more moving wagon. Tank took up the previous conversation: "So you've heard of Yuer, then?"

Lia's good mood faded rapidly. She looked at the silver bracelet on her arm, trying to hang on to joy.

"Here," Tank said, offering her the bracelet he'd been thrown.

She shook her head, holding up a hand in refusal. "It's yours. It'll bring you luck today." And if she'd taken it, that would have signaled the beginning of a relationship neither one of them wanted, but she wasn't about to explain that part to him.

He blinked at her, his expression souring. She tried not to look at the bruise, which was taking on a particularly vile color.

"Luck," he muttered. "Wouldn't that be nice." He glared ahead at the wagon, then shrugged and slid the jewelry onto his left forearm. "Go on with it," he said. "Yuer."

She took a moment to center herself in the moment, deliberately releasing annoyance and anxiety, then said, "Kennet absolutely refused to set up here, even though it was market day. Said he wouldn't have anything to do with Yuer. Sanben told me he was bad news and best stayed well clear of."

Tank pinched his nose, his expression once more bleak. "Damnit, Sanben," he muttered. Then, with audible care: "Yuer is ... challenging to talk to, if you don't know southern custom and history. You don't. Cilif has some but not enough. If you're accidentally rude, it comes back on me and Dasin. I'm not real keen on that happening. Yuer knows that. He won't ask to meet you directly, as long as you don't make a spectacle of yourself. So once you get Rooster stabled up, I want you to discreetly disappear until we ride out in the morning. Your room's already booked at the Gray Rooster. You know where that is?"

"Yes. That's where Kennet had us staying. We're not selling here?" The breeze had died down, leaving a sticky heat behind. She worked at her ata, loosening it around mouth and forehead, shoving stray hair back under cover, then patted the cloth back into place.

"No." He hesitated, as though considering a longer explanation, then shook his head. His tone went back to crisp command: "Get to your room tonight and *stay there*. I'll bring you dinner and come collect you in the morning."

She stared at him, a deep unease growing in her chest. "Am I in danger?"

"Not as long as you do what I said." Something about his tone indicated that the conversation was over. His face was once more hard and uncompromising.

A distant cheer signaled that the procession had reached the end of its route. Six new adults would be leading the revels at a huge feast lasting most of the night.

The silver bracelet bought outsiders entry to the celebration. There would be games, and prizes, and an abundance of home cooked food. A sharp ache settled into her chest. *Sneak out, maybe, he wouldn't really know, would he?*

Dear gods, I sound like a child myself.

Maybe Tank would understand, if she told him about the open invitation they both wore; but he was already riding ahead to catch up with the wagon. His back and shoulders were too tight, and Sin was already edging sideways, tail switching fractiously. Lia had the feeling Tank wasn't in the mood to have any kind of fun.

Which made her think of those bruises, and the difference between his demeanor and Dasin's over the course of the day, and how Tank's unhappy tension had gone tightrope-taut during the conversation. Abruptly, she didn't feel much like joining a coming of age celebration either.

She rode on in pensive silence.

Chapter Eleven

As always, the oversized fireplace in Yuer's receiving room had a healthy blaze going. Sweat broke out across Tank's neck and back before he'd even settled into a stiff-backed wingchair.

Yuer's horrifically wrinkled face was usually hard to read, but his current displeasure was entirely plain. No teapot graced the low table between them, just the battered accounting books. The old man sat rigidly, precisely straight, his hands resting on the heavy lap blanket that hid his legs. He stared at Tank, then at Dasin, allowing the silence to stretch out.

Tank stayed quiet. Yuer considered it proper manners for the host to speak first, especially when the host was also the employer. Dasin, in the chair to Tank's right, sat as stiffly as Yuer, his gaze aimed at the table, although his jaw worked from time to time.

"I am *dismayed*," Yuer said at last, his voice as crackling and dry as the fire. "I thought we had come to an understanding about you dismissing my hires without first consulting me."

Dasin raised his gaze to meet Yuer's. His voice entirely steady, he said, "Gint removed himself from our service, *s'e*. We waited past our window for him to recover from the flu; he knew we had to leave. He still jumped into a bar brawl that left him unfit for the road. We had to leave, and we need a second guard at least through the Forest."

Thank whatever gods existed, Dasin had phrased it as *his* decision, not Tank's, and definitely not one they'd argued over. Tank was never quite sure Dasin would have his back, when dealing with Yuer, especially after the previous night's clash. Now to see if Yuer bought the version Dasin presented.

The old man considered Dasin for a thoughtful moment, then said, tone still abrasive, "You did not, however, need an extra hand along the Coast Road. You could have managed with Cilif from Bright Bay to Sandsplit. I would have provided another hire for you."

Dasin was ready for that. He said, tone still civil but taking on a distinct edge now, "We've discussed my requirements, *s'e*. I only work with Hall sworn. I'm not certain you could have found one, on such short notice, more qualified than the one who —" He paused, visibly rearranging words in his head, and went on, "— who approached us in Bright Bay."

Tank blinked sleepily to hide the fierce bubble of pride in his chest. He'd worked with Dasin for *years* to get him to the point where he could stand up to Yuer without crossing into impropriety. Dasin had the skills for this sort of conversation, much more solidly than Tank; what he'd lacked was the self confidence and strength.

In a corner of his mind, Tank began to sort through some very detailed ideas on how to show Dasin, once they were alone, how pleased he was about this moment.

"You were about to say *who dropped in our laps,* I believe," Yuer said acerbically. "Which I tend to see as more accurate. Why else would you hire a *woman?*"

Tank didn't know much about Yuer's origins. He was definitely from south of the Horn, and connected to Darden Family: whether as ally or relative, Tank had no idea and didn't really want to. Yuer's attitudes were very southwestern desert, though: women in general were weak, shallow creatures, and certainly any born and raised north of the Horn weren't worth any consideration at all.

Yuer's information network was less extensive than it had been, with the recent shift to Obein as the dominant force along the Coast Road, but he'd still likely known about Lia before Dasin and Tank had even gotten past Kybeach. Tank kept his muscles relaxed and sent a fervent prayer to any gods that might be listening that Yuer's informants had missed Toad's dockside meeting with F'Heing representatives.

F'Heing and Darden did *not* get on. At *all.*

"Lia is a Stecatr graduate," Dasin said. "That's fairly remarkable, *s'e* Yuer. Stecatr has an exceptionally tough Hall of Arms, and they've never allowed women through before. For her to pass means she's very good indeed." He paused. "We also checked with the Bright Bay Hall," he added. "They have a letter of high praise on record from her Hall. So it's not just a guess."

Tank held back a smile at the blank look in Yuer's eyes. They'd managed to surprise him.

"*And,*" Dasin went on, "because Lia is northern, if we are forced into a winter layover as I expect, she may well provide us with valuable contacts to make it through the lean months. In any case, having her on the crew will help in places where Stecatr's Hall reputation opens doors."

Yuer, his intent stare unwavering, said, "I see. May I safely assume you plan to retain Cilif, at least?"

"Absolutely," Dasin said. "He's been exceptionally reliable."

Unsaid, the understanding hung in the air: *you'll always have at least one person of my choosing on your crew, like it or not.* Tank was under no illusions that Cilif would ever choose Dasin's — or Tank's — interests over Yuer's, and his own, if pressed.

"Good." Yuer bent his head and was silent for a time.

A log snapped and settled in the fire, setting off a wash of renewed heat. Tank felt sweat trickling down the back of his neck. Dasin fidgeted, working his shoulders, then stilled again, grimacing.

Yuer looked up as a servant came into the room: a small, pale boy with long arms and fingers, who paused on entering the room. He looked only at Yuer, whose wrinkled face moved into a strange expression it took Tank a few moments to identify as *fondness*.

"Yes, please," Yuer said, as though the boy had asked a question.

Without so much as a glance at Tank or Dasin, the boy went to the fire, adjusted the logs to a new balance, set the tools tidily back in their places, then bowed to Yuer and left the room.

Yuer's expression faded back to chill once they were alone in the room once more. His gaze settled on Tank for a long, thoughtful moment, examining his face. Tank, abruptly recalling the marks from last night, did his best not to flinch. Yuer's gaze moved, with that same detached interest, to Dasin; after a much shorter survey, he looked back to Tank.

The old man said, "I am aware you prefer to avoid political entanglements. That is no longer possible. If that means you wish to leave my service, so be it. I'll provide you with a reasonable ending payment and find someone more ... flexible to work with." On the last sentence, he focused on Dasin once more.

Tank couldn't stop himself from drawing in a sharp breath and shooting a sideways look at Dasin, who sat unmoving, showing no surprise at all. He'd known this was coming, damn him.

What are you doing, Dasin? What have you done? What am I about to find out?

There were times Tank wished he was capable of a desert lord's mind-speech trickery. It would have made moments like this much safer to navigate.

What it would have done last night, though, didn't bear thinking of. Better this way. Much better.

Yuer lifted his hands, one at a time; clenched each into a fist, stretched the fingers out wide, then put them gently back down onto his legs. "You've been in my service long enough to have grasped my loyalties," he said. "I doubt you've missed the struggle between the west coast Families to gain influence in the northlands, especially in the wake of the recent disruptions."

Disruptions. Such a polite way to describe an enormous chunk of the southeastern coast destroyed, most of the Horn caved in, a tsunami wrecking a good quarter or more of Bright Bay, and sea traffic to the northwest hobbled by a mysterious series of misfortunes.

Yuer's gaze flicked to Tank, as though he'd heard that thought. Tank hastily rebuilt his shields from the hissing crackle of the fire, the sweat trickling down his neck, the feel of the wingback chair around him, the movement of air past his nose. Yuer's stare turned less dangerous, edging into what might have been amusement. He said, "F'Heing has captured the western sea trade quite thoroughly. The Horn is impassable. Darden is boxed in and hemorrhaging resources."

That half-hidden smile felt like a deliberate provocation. Tank reacted before good sense could stop him. He said, tone entirely too sharp: "And Peysimun Family is the new star of the south. What's your relationship with *them, s'e?*"

Yuer's face creased in a distinctly unfriendly fashion. Dasin sucked in a tiny breath through his teeth. The old man stared at Tank; Tank met the gaze without flinching or aggression for several heartbeats, then, deliberately slow, lowered his eyes.

Yuer stayed silent for another few beats. Then: "Peysimun Family has not been overly helpful. The other Families...." He spread his hands again, set them back on his lap. "The north has a great deal of undeveloped land. Darden is making arrangements to relocate to one such area."

Tank's breath froze in his throat. Not so much at the information, which he'd already guessed from various bits of gossip over the past year, but that Yuer was so blatantly saying it. Desert Families didn't relocate. They couldn't. They were locked in to their home ground, reliant on the support of their ha'rethe, no matter how arid and difficult their lands were.

But: *Things are changing*. That bond might not exist any longer.

Dasin dipped his head in a slow nod, still far too calm for Tank's liking.

Since his earlier rudeness hadn't gotten them ejected, Tank gave up on caution in favor of gaining support for his guess. He said, bluntly, "I wasn't at all sure that a desert Family *could* relocate, s'e Yuer. That's fairly remarkable, isn't it?"

"It is," Yuer agreed, with a brief, unamused smile. "The constraints that kept the desert Families bound to their geographical areas are ... well, not there any longer." A wider, darker smile this time, as though Yuer could see the sinking twist that confirmation put into Tank's stomach. "I'm not willing to go into more specifics than that. Call it superstition. Some names will never be spoken within my walls." He looked pointedly at Tank.

Dasin shot Tank a tight, hard glance. Tank groaned inwardly. They'd once more hit an intersection of *Dasin, I don't want to talk about my past* and *Tank, what the hell is going on?*

There was no negotiating that in front of Yuer's too-sharp gaze. No saying the words required to take this part of the conversation any further: *ha'reye* and *ha'ra'hain*; *Deiq* and *Lord Alyea Peysimun*; quite possibly *Aerthraim Family* and *teyanain*.

Five out of those six were not safe to talk about in front of Dasin. Tank had refused to answer questions for too many years. Discussing them now — especially if Tank's *encounters* with Alyea came out — would set off an instant firestorm of a fight with Dasin, which one *did not do* in front of Yuer. Tank had already pushed their employer well past the point of wisdom. An open fight in his sitting room would be a leap too far.

"Understood," Tank said as blandly as he could. "Forgive me for asking, but how will any of that force us to be involved in politics, s'e? I'm not hearing anything that would impact our role as merchants."

The young servant appeared in the doorway once more. This time, Yuer shook his head, flicking his fingers. The boy retreated.

"Your route would change, in time, to support the new Darden enclave as it develops," Yuer said. "More immediately, in addition to your usual business, you will be escorting certain people as they relocate. Your role, from this point on, leans more towards assisting the resettlement efforts and less towards selling ...." Again, he flicked the fingers of one hand in a dismissive gesture. "...herbs and simples."

"We've done well for you with those *herbs and simples*," Tank said, stung. At Dasin's small, pained noise, he belatedly added, "*S'e.*"

Yuer's mouth briefly moved as though he were chewing something, and his hands shifted restlessly, rubbing his legs: signs that his patience was beginning to wear thin. Dasin needed to wrap this up soon and get them out the door.

Yuer said, "The amount of money you've brought in is insignificant against what a small group of these people will pay for a one way escort trip. Perspective, if you please. Your work to date has been aimed at building contacts, precisely for this eventuality. Do please reassure me that you haven't been so very foolish as to miss that, *s'e* Tank?" He came down hard on the word *foolish*, a stark warning that he was done accepting Tank's aggression.

"*Knock it off*," Dasin said in Aerthraim dialect, clearly seeing the same thing. Yuer smirked, just as obviously understanding what Dasin had said. Tank hung between anger and anxiety for a moment, then bent his head, internally retreating to a focused consideration of what was being said.

Dasin's exuberant charm with customers hadn't been simple salesmanship. It had been about building connections. Being *known*. Tank had missed it. He'd actually thought Dasin was happy as a merchant.

Tank recalled Dasin's bitter words from two nights ago: *I'm doing my best to give you what you want — your* precious *simple life.*

Turning his head, he met Dasin's gaze. In that moment, he was glad he couldn't read Dasin's mind. The pained hope in his eyes was devastating enough.

Tonight wouldn't be nearly as friendly as Tank had been planning. Dasin wouldn't forgive Tank for seeing this moment of naked need.

"You decide," Tank said, then tried to lighten his voice to a less sullen cast. "I'll follow your lead."

Dasin blinked, blinked again, his expression flattening. Without looking away from Tank, he said, "*S'e* Yuer. When would you require an answer?"

"Now," Yuer said. "I have someone who requires an escort. If I can't send him with you, I may as well collect your earnings and send you on your way. You may keep your wagon, of course, as you've had that built from your own funds." His tone made that a generous concession.

Dasin's eyes slid shut, his lips thinning. Tank watched, unable to look away from Dasin's pale features, resigning himself to the inevitable. The silence hung heavier by the breath. Dasin's lips turned in, his jaw so tight Tank expected to hear teeth creak.

Recognizing the signs of complete decision paralysis, Tank breathed out hard through his nose. He said, not bothering to warm his tone above freezing in spite of Yuer's warning moments before, "Where are we escorting this person to, *s'e* Yuer?"

"Only to Isata," Yuer said, his now-glittering gaze fixed on Dasin's taut, motionless form. "After that you will continue on your route to Assiasan as planned. When you come south again, you'll turn around here, not in Bright Bay, with a small group to escort, so it's best you sell out of inventory before you return."

Dasin bent his head, his shoulders hunching miserably. Then he straightened, looking to Yuer. As crisply as though he hadn't frozen at all, he asked, "Will this person be ready in the morning, *s'e*?"

"Yes."

"Good. Does he have his own horse?"

Yuer's head tilted slightly to one side. He regarded Dasin with what might actually have been a genuinely amused expression. "He chooses not to ride. He will have no difficulty in keeping up with you, however."

"May I have his name?"

"Ganne." Yuer was definitely smiling now, beneath the wrinkles.

"Thank you, *s'e*." Dasin stood and offered a short bow. Yuer waved one hand in a lazy gesture by way of reply, the closest he ever got to acknowledging gratitude.

Tank followed suit, fighting to keep his expression safely neutral in spite of a rising sense of disconnection. Dasin never risked veering that close to rudeness with Yuer, and certainly not after Tank had gone so far out of line, but the old man seemed unconcerned.

If Dasin was taking on *this* sort of mood, there were two ways the night could go, one considerably more pleasant than the other.

Dasin went on, tone brittle, "When you're done with the books, *s'e*, please have your servants leave them in the wagon, so that we don't disturb you in the morning. We'll excuse ourselves, by your leave. It's already late, and there's a long road ahead tomorrow."

"Of course," Yuer said gravely. "Good night, *s'es*."

Tank offered another quick bow, just in case, before turning to follow Dasin out into the muggy evening air. He thought Yuer let out a faint chuckle, but under the snap of the fire and the wobbly roaring in his ears, he couldn't be sure.

"Bloody hells," he said as he caught up to Dasin a few steps later. "Dasin. *Dasin*."

Dasin kept marching, his expression ferociously bitter. "Damn you," he said. "*Godsdamn you*."

"What? *Why*?" Tank swatted Dasin's shoulder lightly, then dodged back as Dasin turned on him, fists at the ready. "Dasin! Stop. *Stop*."

Dasin stepped back, dropping his hands to his sides. He glared at Tank. "Go get some sleep," he said tautly. "I'll be in later." He began walking again.

Ah. That sort of night, then. Tank's chest went thick and hot. *No. Not tonight. I can't — no.* He lunged forward, grabbing Dasin's arm and yanking him back around in a staggering arc. His hold slipped: Dasin pulled free easily.

Dasin snapped, "I'm going for a drink." Tank couldn't help moving to grab after his arm again. Dasin moved out of the way, putting a hand up in warning. "I want to be left alone, damn you!"

"Not tonight. *Not tonight*, damnit. Are you going to Spinner's?"

Dasin turned his back and stalked away. Tank followed, a scant step behind.

"We've talked about this," he said to Dasin's back, and received an openly rude gesture in response. "*Damnit*, Dasin!"

Dasin kept walking. Tank ground his teeth and followed him to a small, neatly constructed building at the edge of town. It had no sign, no formal name; it was more of a farm than a true tavern, with working fields spread out in a thick arc on three sides.

A patterned knock on the back door and a half gold round bought them entry.

The rooms beyond were well-lit and comfortably furnished. Easily a dozen people relaxed on large, well-stuffed chairs. A few more sat carelessly on the floor, slouched in chairs around square tables, or perched atop the tables with brash disregard for propriety. Most had a drink in hand and, by appearances, several already down. Pipe and aesa smoke swirled through the air. Two card games were in progress, and a game of dice.

Conversation paused briefly as Tank and Dasin entered, heads turning to assess the newcomers. A few hands raised in a wave of welcome, then the patrons politely went back to their various amusements and discussions.

"A drink, *s'es?*" a voice said at Tank's elbow.

"Aesa," Dasin said absently, his attention on the patrons. A moment later, he simply walked away, headed toward an ethereally thin, blonde woman wearing an outrageously colored mishmash of loosely sewn fabrics.

Tank sighed and looked down. "Water, please," he said. "Thank you, Spinner."

Spinner's mouth curved in what passed for a grin on his misshapen face. "He can't get into trouble tonight," he said. "Back rooms are shut. Had an incident a few days ago. Need to let things settle out."

Tension drained from Tank's entire body, leaving him briefly lightheaded. "Sorry to hear that, but thank you."

"Something more than water, then?" Spinner's large eyes gleamed with humor, their odd shape accented by the lumps in his shaven head.

"I'll stick with water," Tank said, offering a real smile.

The water Spinner served actually tasted good. Tank had asked about it once, and Spinner had shown him a complicated-looking distilling setup. *Why go to such bother?* Tank had asked. Spinner shrugged and said, *It tastes good, doesn't it? There you go, then.*

"Water it is," Spinner said now. He turned and waddled away on stumpy, twisted legs. It always surprised Tank how quickly the man could move, and with no apparent pain, at that.

By common wisdom, Spinner should have been living a miserable life as a beggar, reviled and mistrusted. He certainly hadn't started out with gold in hand, from what little Tank had managed to coax out of him over the past three years. He didn't have any particular alliances, or enemies. His tavern was neutral territory for those who, like himself, had never quite fit in — and who had, by and large, vastly exceeded expectations.

How he'd come by ownership of the farm was a mystery that Tank and Dasin, in a rare moment of complete agreement, had decided not to investigate. No point poking a beehive when the honey was already on the table.

Tank liked talking to Spinner, his staff, and the house guard. He liked sitting in a corner with a drink, peacefully secure that nobody would intrude. Normally, Dasin liked the same. In moods like this, though, he went straight for the back rooms, from which he tended to emerge in need of bandages and, occasionally, stitches.

Gods, what a pair we make, Tank thought ruefully as he folded into an empty chair that gave him a clear view of Dasin's activities. He let out a long sigh, rubbing his eyes with the back of one hand.

Dasin was already in deep conversation with his target, their heads bent close together as they passed the aesa pipe back and forth. Dasin's body language showed no sign of anger or tension, only loose, confident grace.

"Nursemaiding the boy again?" a gravelly voice said to Tank's right.

Tank put out his right hand without answering; exchanged a hard grip of greeting, then said, "Just doing what needs doing, Horse."

The short, burly man — Spinner's best house guard — laughed and hauled a chair to rest close beside Tank's. Horse had trimmed his red-blond hair back since their last meeting. It now ran prickly-short on the sides and fell in a long, thin braid to his mid-back. The hue of his skin and shape of his face spoke to primarily southern heritage, but his hair, mannerisms, and accent could all have been from Stecatr. Tank had carefully never asked after Horse's background. He didn't answer questions about his own, after all.

"One of these days," the guard said as he settled into his chair, "you're going to have taken enough of his shit. My offer's still open. Work here. I'll pay you more than you make on the road." He laid a thick wooden baton across his lap as he spoke, keeping one hand on it and his gaze moving around the room. His leather tunic had no sleeves and laced halfway down his torso, displaying muscular, scarred arms surprisingly bare of tattoos.

"He's getting better," Tank said. A stout young woman in Spinner's house colors of blue and white brought him the requested mug of water. Tank handed her a half-silver piece and flicked his fingers to indicate she should keep the extra. She motioned silent gratitude, then left them alone.

"— damned northerns," someone said at a carrying volume. Tank held still, his eyes sliding half-closed, and waited. The speaker went on, slightly less strident: "All they ever do is complain. Whyn't they go back to their homes, if it was so grand there? And more than a few of them astounded when they're not given a warm welcome. Act like they came here to bring civilization to a backwater. Feh."

Tank cut a sideways glance at Horse. The bouncer returned the look, expressionless, and said, "People get to grouse."

"True enough." Tank forced his shoulders to relax and casually looked around. The complainer was at a table with another man, who was frowning and motioning for his companion to lower his voice. Both men had light brown hair, thin beards, and lean, sharp builds, with skin bronzed from time in the sun, not heritage. At least they weren't likely to discriminate based solely on appearance, but accent and attitude.

Across the room, Dasin seemed to be telling the woman a story. His hands waved in wide gestures, and she was laughing. *Probably the one about the ant and the asp-jacau,* Tank thought. Dasin was good at telling that one.

Horse snorted. "Not but so much mending a cracked pot can take, and being glue is a damned tiring job," he observed. "Never mind, never mind, all right. Opal."

"What?" Tank took his gaze from Dasin, startled, and looked at the guard.

"The woman he's talking to. Calls herself Opal, while she's here. She's an odd one. Showed up a handful of tendays ago. She's an artist. Comes from Bright Bay, apparently. Doesn't talk about herself, likes to be left alone. I don't think I've seen anyone approach her before without getting rebuffed right off."

"Wonderful." Tank rubbed at his eyes again. House rules discouraged staff from addressing anyone by name, while also encouraging patrons to use an alias. Tank had never bothered with the latter. Neither had Dasin, but Horse was always precise about following his employer's wishes. For him to name Opal was worrying, a warning in and of itself. He said, unable to stop himself, "An *artist?*"

"She's got money. She's renting one of Spinner's cottages. Every so often I see her paintings set out in the sun." Horse cut a glance at Tank, grinning. His teeth were small and discolored; one lower canine was missing.

"All right, I'll bite. What does she paint?"

"Nightmares," Horse said. "Twisted lines and colors that don't add up to a damn thing except a headache if you look too long." He paused, watching Dasin for a few moments, then added lightly, "Now and again she paints pretty flowers. Those sell well, at least."

"*Wonderful,*" Tank muttered again. "I think I'd have preferred nudes."

"I had my hopes," Horse admitted. He scratched at a lumpy scar on his upper left arm. "Even offered to pose for her."

Startled, Tank met Horse's dark eyes. They stared at one another for a moment, then Tank burst into helpless laughter. Horse grinned amiably and went back to scanning the room. After Tank recovered, the guard said, "You're having that bad of a time, then?"

The last of the laughter drained from Tank's chest. He cradled the mug in both hands and tilted his head to stretch his neck, then looked up at the ceiling. "Is it that obvious?"

Horse took the time for a slow, assessing look around the room, then said, quietly, "You don't laugh like that unless you're a step shy of the breaking point. And you both walked in looking somewhere between gutted and gutting." He paused to look pointedly at the bruise on Tank's face, then went on. "You know my rule. Don't drag it through these doors and I don't have to pay it no mind. Tonight I'm wondering what you're dragging along."

Tank watched the way the lantern light refracted from Opal's eyes, frowning. The white seemed *too* white, and the blue had an oily sheen. She laughed at something Dasin said, gesturing with bony hands as she responded. Her nails were chewed back to the quick and stained with unsettling dark lines.

"No," Tank said, returning his attention to Horse with a nearly physical effort. "Nothing dragging after us that I know of. Just...." He tilted his chin towards Dasin, grimacing.

"Leave him be," Horse said. "Let him clean up after himself for once."

Tank didn't say anything. The server came back, this time handing a mug of water to Horse. The guard took a healthy draught, looked around for a table within reach, then shrugged and set the mug on the floor between his feet.

"There's change moving around in the air," Horse said. "I'm seeing more News Riders go through of late, and some of them aren't just messengers."

First Rania, then Dasin, now Horse. *Change. Things shifting.* Tank kept his face neutral as he asked, "King's Riders?" Those carried political messages, between people of influence, rank, and power. A flurry of King's Riders moving about was a damn bad sign.

"More than like. They're wearing casual clothes, but there's no hiding that attitude."

Horse's hands ran restlessly along the rod in his lap as he spoke. With anyone else, Tank would have cracked a joke about fondling one's stick, but he knew better than to try that with Horse. The guard would toss him into a wall and then out the door without hesitation. The comment about posing for the artist had been shockingly coarse by Horse's standards; he'd no doubt only made it to startle Tank into laughing.

Dasin's smile shifted to something more predatory than amiable. Opal's expression matched his, her eyes gleaming. They stood; Tank stood.

Horse tapped Tank's hip lightly with the rod and said, "Sit down, boy. Let him be."

Tank, ignoring the guard, took the few steps forward that allowed him to wrap his hand around Dasin's upper arm. He dug his fingers in hard enough to compress muscle. Dasin yelped, tugging to get free. Tank locked his grip, met Opal's gaze straight on, and said, "Excuse me, *s'a*, we have to get on the road early in the morning. He asked me to remind him if he looked about to forget."

Opal's smile sent a chill down Tank's back. There seemed to be too many sharp teeth in her mouth. He blinked. Her grin became a perfectly ordinary, if yellowing and gapped, display. She swept her gaze over him from head to toe, managing to convey amusement and dismissal all at once.

Dasin yanked, trying to break loose. Tank kept his feet planted and his attention on Opal.

Horse loomed beside him. "House rules," he rumbled gently, "are that people get to be whatever they want to be, here, *s'ieas*. I suggest letting go and walking away, *s'e*."

"I'm making sure that my friend knows that *the back rooms are closed* today, *s'e*," Tank answered. He felt Dasin's arm droop from the shoulder and loosened his grip. Dasin immediately jerked free and aimed a sharp jab into Tank's stomach.

Tank had enough warning to tighten his muscles, and the blow was far too weak to really hurt. Dasin snarled and backed up two long steps, hands up defensively. Tank stayed still, all too aware of Horse at his elbow.

"I think it's time you took your problems outside," Horse suggested. "Good night, *s'es*."

Opal grinned at Tank, then yawned widely. Tank had an abrupt image of a cat showing its teeth to a mouse. "You're very boring," she told him, then looked past him to Dasin. "So are you," she added. "So sad."

"Don't incite anything, *s'a*," Horse said stolidly. "They're leaving now. You're welcome to go with them, if you like."

"No," she said with a regal shrug, and took her seat, pointedly putting her back to Dasin.

Dasin took a step forward, staring at the back of Opal's head with a faintly wild-eyed expression for a moment. Tank moved sideways, cutting off Dasin's view. The blond growled; Horse grunted warning; then Dasin turned and stormed from the building.

"Goodnight," Tank said to Horse, and went after Dasin.

Several steps outside, as expected, Dasin spun and launched himself at Tank, with more focus and ferocity than before. Tank turned aside punches until an opening came, then dropped his shoulder and bulled in, sending Dasin sprawling.

He stepped clear and waited as Dasin scrambled to his feet. The blond stood still, breathing hard, making no effort to resume his attack.

"You fucking *ta-karne*," Dasin said at last, his voice cracking. His eyes had taken on a manic gleam. Tank sighed. Now the night was moving into a rare pattern, one he really preferred to avoid: but for the second night in a row, Dasin needed to either be hurt or hurt something, and Tank wasn't willing, was *never* willing, to do the former.

"Yeah," Tank said resignedly. "I know. Come on. Let's get out of the open and finish this in private, huh? I'll try not to be boring."

Chapter Twelve

Lia had promised to stay indoors, but the room was small and oppressively stuffy even with the window open. The aroma of dinner — fish stew — hung rank in the air, as did the lamp oil — probably also fish, at a guess.

It's unreasonable to stay indoors. Go outside for a bit of fresh air, what harm can it do?

It was full dark outside. Everyone was asleep. Nobody would see her if she stepped outside for a stroll around the inn to get some fresh air. For the love of the gods, she'd already *been* through Sandsplit once, headed in the other direction. Kenret hadn't offered such dire warnings. It seemed highly unlikely that there was real danger in this sleepy town. More than likely Tank had been testing to see if she'd obey even irrational orders.

She latched the window shut, then settled her shortblades into place along her forearms, checking to see that her sleeves covered them properly; added a dagger at her waist and another in her boot, and called it good enough. She didn't want to wear the ata.

Walk, that's right, walk around a bit....

A stroll around the inn took the fish smell out of her nostrils but did little to manage her restlessness. The thought of returning to that stinky little room turned her stomach. One more time round. Maybe two more. Then she'd go to bed.

She found herself starting to drift away from the inn proper.

Just a bit further, around that corner there, nobody will know ... asking you to stay indoors is so unreasonable, a bit further ... there's that interesting tree not far away, you could climb it ....

Lia stopped and turned around, annoyed at herself. A walk around the inn was one thing. That was defensible, if Tank decided to step out for a breath of air himself and caught her doing the same. Going further couldn't be explained as anything but disobedience, and she had no doubt that he'd fire her on the spot for that.

A disappointed sigh seemed to ghost through the air as she sat down on the bench near the inn door. Or perhaps she sighed. She wasn't quite sure, and frowned at the darkness, abruptly uneasy.

"Lia," a familiar voice said nearby.

She drew her dagger as Toad moved into the small circle of lantern light.

"I'm not going to attack you," the old man said, sounding exasperated. "Gods, I'm not violent. You know that."

"But I *am*," Lia said. She noticed his breath held a stronger wheeze than usual; the humid air was affecting him. She could reach him in two steps. He was slow. He was old. He was lousy at fighting. He'd never know she was moving. "Aren't *you* a bit worried that I'll lay a knife up into your ribcage?" It was empty bravado and she knew it, but *he* might not.

"For what cause?" Toad retorted. "I'm unarmed. I've not done a thing to threaten you. Put the knife away. You're being childish."

She'd never heard him speak so crisply when not telling a story. "Spare me your insults, old man," she said, but sheathed the dagger. "Go away."

"I'm not your enemy, Lia," he said. "I've never been your enemy. There's a lot you don't know, and more you've misunderstood."

"*Hsscchht*," she said, turning her head to direct the hissing insult directly at him. "You've done enough harm to others that I don't need to give you the chance to hurt *me*."

With unexpected passion, he snapped, "You throw *hsscchht* at *me*? I turn it back to you! Would your father appreciate knowing what *you've* done?" His voice turned gray and weary. "No, that's not a threat. I'm not in a position to make threats. I'm well aware of that. However, *neither are you*." His tone gained strength on the last words.

She sat silently, tucking her chin to her chest, and listened to him shift in place. He clicked his tongue thoughtfully several times.

At last, he said, "I won't harm you, nor steal from you, nor speak against you, while we travel together. In return I ask the same of you. Is that a fair enough arrangement?"

Restlessness abruptly became recklessness. She said, "I want to know what made you come all the way to Bright Bay."

"I have relatives there," he said. "One of them died, and I —"

"Horseshit."

"Oh-no-no, it's quite true," Toad snapped. "I did not hatch from an egg in the deep desert, my girl. I have family still, no matter what stories in Stecatr may say of me." His voice turned chill. "I've made my offer, and I'm not about to explain myself to someone who pokes at my every word. Take it or leave it, but *do* remember, if you please, how the stories claim I murdered my wife."

Her lips drew into a thin line. "That *is* a threat."

"It's a recommendation to think clearly," Toad retorted. "Do we have a deal, or not?"

Her teeth sank into her tongue. After a long pause, she said, "Yes. While we travel together. The moment we part ways, the truce is over."

"Agreed," he said. "Good night."

She listened to him walking away, more quietly than she'd expected. He must have gotten better shoes. And the way he'd talked! She'd never heard him like that. The trip south seemed to have given him strength.

Lia admitted to herself that she'd gotten used to seeing him as nothing more than a clumsy old man scuttling through the streets of Bright Bay, cringing under the glares of people who knew what he'd done. She'd forgotten Scarpy's warning not to underestimate him.

"Kill him outright," Scarpy had said once, "or leave him alone. Don't *ever* play games with someone who's used poison to kill."

The urge to walk, to move, to stretch, maybe even to climb a tree returned, stronger than before. It had been years since she'd been able to climb, carefree, into the security and freedom of the upper branches of a stolid oak. She'd been *good* at shimmying up trees, and it had been an excellent escape on the far too frequent bad days. She missed it, now, with a ferocity that mildly alarmed her.

Restlessness abruptly drained away, replaced with a dreary exhaustion. Her tiny room, with its heavy latches across door and window alike, seemed preferable to open air after all.

As she stood, a movement flickered in peripheral vision. She turned her back to the inn wall, knife once more in hand.

A gaunt, blonde woman, dressed in colorful clothes a scant step up from rags, stepped out into the lantern light. The smirk on her face immediately put her into the *dangerous/ mad* category. Lia shifted her stance to face the newcomer, preparing for a fight.

The woman's bare feet made no sound at all on the stone as she advanced without hesitation. "Quiet now, quiet, good girl," the woman crooned, her voice scarcely audible. "You're strong, aren't you? Just like that foolish man who got in my way earlier. And then another foolish little man got in the way when I called for you. Men always get in the way, don't they? Ah, but now it's just us. And you're strong, so lovely, lovely strong, but not strong enough. There, there, I've got you. Hold still, nice and still ...."

Lia's arms drooped to her side even as terror shot up her spine. She couldn't move, couldn't yell: she stood helpless and frozen as the woman eased closer, that too-wide grin showing ever more yellowed, gapped teeth.

"You're going to like this. I'm *telling* you to like this," the woman whispered, her voice crackling like frozen silk. Lia felt a wave of heat run through her entire body, found herself beginning to breathe heavily. The woman purred. "Oh, yes, you've been tying yourself down for so very long now, oh yes, my, yes, *I'm* going to enjoy —"

Another figure loomed up behind the woman. She began to turn, her grin shifting to a fierce scowl. There came a brief flurry of movement: then the woman dropped to the ground, unconscious.

Lia pressed back against the wall of the inn, gasping. The knife slipped from her trembling hand.

The newcomer, a burly man with red-gold hair shaved on the sides and left in a snake-thin braid down his back, bent and scooped the woman up. He draped her carelessly over one shoulder, then paused to look at Lia, his gaze grave and thoughtful.

"You all right, *s'a?*" he asked.

"I ... I...." She couldn't make anything more coherent emerge.

"You oughtn't go out at night around here, not alone," he said, perfectly calm. "This isn't the only one locally as gets overset at odd moments. Go to bed, *s'a*. The inn's warded properly, you won't have any troubles if you stay indoors."

Overset? Warded? She couldn't make herself say the words aloud. It was all simply too bizarre.

He turned and walked away. Lia, finally catching breath and sense, grabbed up her knife and bolted for the safety of her room.

Chapter Thirteen

An ancient, spreading creek tree marked the turnoff for the southern Hackerwood edge camp. A few late blossoms dappled the branches, and the star-shaped leaves were full and glossy despite the afternoon's growing heat. On a homeward trip in the fall — it always amused Tank to realize that he thought of Bright Bay as *home* — he'd seen the tree flushed a gorgeous, defiant shade of red, with clusters of small black fruits dotting the ground around it, drawing in squirrels and birds. Once, memorably, Tank had seen a wild boar snuffling through the fallen berries. It had looked up at him, slow and wary, then trundled off towards the line of the Hackerwood, proof that not only monsters lived beyond the aenstone barriers.

The aenstone-walled camp was enormous, with fifteen small, separate campsites and a large communal area capable of hosting five more. On the busiest day, Tank had counted twenty horses, ten full wagons, five small carts, and forty people; that had been close to uncomfortably crowded. Once, a train of heavy ore wagons had taken up most of the communal area, shunting all other traffic to the smaller camps. The most interesting, in Tank's opinion, was the time they'd shared space with a troupe of dancers on their way to a birthday celebration for the Lord of Isata. They'd made for enjoyable, vibrant company along the road, entirely undimmed by the looming menace of the Forest.

Their current *company* would be far less fun. A short, stocky southerner named Ganne walked beside the wagon, listening to Toad's tales with a small smirk. He had winding black tattoos along both arms that ended in elaborate wristlets, and wore plain, homespun style trousers and sleeveless shirts; but the shirt was bright red and the trousers bright blue. A thick scar ran across the knuckles of his left hand, and he wore no earrings or jewelry at all. From the holes Tank could see, he'd once had the full set of earrings, which made their absence more than slightly disturbing.

Ganne didn't seem much older than Tank himself, mid twenties at most, but he held the arrogant confidence of a seasoned warrior. Tank hadn't suffered a moment's doubt, on their initial introduction in the dimly lit barn that morning, that Ganne was a desert lord. The sense of leashed power was unmistakable.

Tank had very nearly quit on the spot. Dealing with a Darden noble would have been bad enough, but escorting a desert lord wasn't just walking into politics, it was jumping into a volcano of them. The strained look on Dasin's face had been, barely, enough to stop him. Then Ganne had introduced himself, and Lia had arrived, and the moment to retreat had, somehow, been lost.

Ganne glanced back at Tank, his smirk widening as though he'd felt the sour regard; not at all unlikely. Tank grimaced, tightened his shields, and pointedly looked ahead, over the desert lord's head.

On the east side, the wall looped around a small cottage and garden housing Kwri, a follower of the southern god Comos. Tank had first met the *comosain* on their first trip through the Hackerwood, years before: an attack by a decidedly non benign Hackerwood resident had left Tank drenched in the creature's blood and half out of his head from the non-physical part of the attack.

Tank took a moment, as he always did on entering the southern camp, to offer a heartfelt plea to any gods that might exist: *please make this time through peaceful. No disruptions. Please.* Given that they were on the ending sliver of the waning moon tonight, and facing a moondark trip through the Forest itself, that plea seemed unlikely to produce results. Especially now, with Ganne in the mix and Dasin increasingly leaning into being his worst self.

Tank took one hand off the reins and flexed it gently, wincing as sore muscles pulled around a bruise on that forearm. While painful, it was necessary to avoid stiffness making the arm useless; and for some reason he didn't want to examine, he liked the feeling of stretching a bruised muscle. At least the long-sleeved shirt hid that and other bruises from the previous night. He should probably go see Kwri tonight, though. Like most comosain, Kwri was an accomplished healer and herbalist.

As Dasin steered the wagon towards the communal section, Tank glanced over at the cottage, half-hoping to see the man out in his garden. A private visit would be considerably less embarrassing.

The comosain's house was built of pale yellow aenstone, and a low wall of the same material circled his tidy little garden. The campsite wall ran in hip-high sections, since there needed to be substantial gaps for wagons, carts, and horses, but it was a far more useful barrier than the lines of salt superstitious fools still insisted on casting.

There was, wisely, no opening on the northern side of camp.

As he always did, Tank looked at the massive amount of aenstone with a sense of bewildered incomprehension at how much the setup had to have cost, and wondered who, exactly had financed it. King Oruen, of course, but this much aenstone was beyond even a king's reach. Especially a king fighting through the aftermath of too many viciously poor rulers and a relatively recent catastrophe.

Aenstone came exclusively from Aerthraim Family, and they charged outsiders exorbitant fees. Tank wasn't sure how it was made; he was certain it wasn't mined. It was a human-created composite that warded against the uncanny abilities of desert lords, ha'reye, ha'ra'hain, and all of the latter's lesser relatives.

As Dasin drew the wagon to a halt, Toad climbed down and headed for Kwri's cottage, a heavy belt pouch in one hand. Cilif drew up beside Tank, looking bemused.

"Don't know as I'd have the stones to knock on a comosain's door without invitation," he remarked. Ganne seemed not to have noticed Toad's departure, or, more likely and thankfully, didn't know enough to care.

"I'm guessing it's ignorance, not courage," Tank said.

Dasin, climbing down from the wagon, waved sharply at them. Tank started to nudge Sin forward.

"Wait," Cilif said, putting out a hand. His expression shifted from bemusement into something more complicated. He shoved a strand of dark hair back behind one ear. "Look, Tank, I don't put my hand where it ain't wanted, but ...." He glanced at Dasin, who was facing away from them and saying something to Lia; then, pointedly, looked at the bruise on Tank's cheek. "This is maybe getting a little much, yeah?"

Tank felt his face twist into a snarl before he could control it. Cilif leaned back in the saddle, eyebrows high, and raised a hand defensively.

"Okay!" the stocky mercenary said. "My hand ain't wanted. Okay." He turned Blackie away, angling around the far side of the wagon.

Tank let out a harsh breath through his teeth, his hands tightening on the reins. Sin snorted, sidling sideways as he caught Tank's abrupt shift in mood. Dasin, visibly irritated, waved again. Ganne jerked round to look between them, his eyebrows going high.

Something small and sharp shattered inside Tank. Before he quite knew what he was doing, he was yanking Sin round and riding out of the campground. Reaching a clear patch of road, he thumped his heels in; Sin shimmied once, joyously, and exploded forward.

Tank lost himself in the thundering, the wind, the vibrations. Little by little, that broken feeling faded into the deep background of his mind, leaving behind a swirling calm. The world came back into slow, easy focus. He brought Sin back to a trot, then a walk. The big horse wasn't even breathing hard, and seemed reluctant to stop, but at Tank's urging obediently turned to amble back towards the camp.

The deep calm lasted until the turn that would take him back into sight of the campground wall. He checked Sin to a stop, breathing hard as the quiet turned fragile and shaky. Sin turned, unprompted, and began walking steadily away from the campground; Tank gathered his wits and checked him once more. Sin stomped a hoof, once, ears flicking, but held still.

Tank shut his eyes, cradling the globe of calm, breathing into it, building supportive and protective braces around it; centered it, solidified it, *became* it. Took a deep breath, another. Opened his eyes to look at the clouds scudding across the late-afternoon sky.

"Fuck it," he said aloud, and turned Sin back to the campground.

As afternoon settled into evening and everyone withdrew to their tents or, in most cases given the still-warm air, their bedmats, Tank found himself watching the fire with only Ganne for company. Dasin, for once, wasn't snoring fit to shake the trees. Toad, Lia, and Cilif weren't thrashing or snoring either, and the three other travelers sharing the campground — bound south, and carrying no news of any concern about the state of the Hackerwood road — were equally quiet.

Too quiet. The hair prickled on the back of Tank's neck as he registered how quiet everyone was being. Out of eight people, someone should have been making a noise in their sleep. Tank could hear crickets, night birds, and small foraging animals. Once or twice over the past hours, he'd heard an owl's long, mournful song. That was reassuring. In his experience, owls never showed up near the odder sorts of trouble.

Still. It was too damn quiet.

He looked over at Ganne, who was watching him with sleepy contemplation. They stared at one another, the only sound the pop of the fire as the largest log began to catch at last.

Nobody had said anything at all about Tank's abrupt departure. The camp had been entirely set up on his return, a communal dinner cooking, Dasin and Toad in lively conversation with the strangers. Lia had been cleaning her riding boots, Cilif mending a shirt. Ganne had sat quietly watching everyone without much expression. No doubt Dasin would have something to say later tonight, with or without words, when Tank came to bed.

Tank was entirely certain that tonight, at least, he wouldn't put up with any shit from Dasin. He was fairly sure that Dasin knew it as well.

For the moment, Tank had a desert lord to deal with. He'd avoided it all day; there was no putting it off any further. He said, mildly, "You don't like to hear snoring, I take it."

Ganne's mouth widened in a brief smile, revealing small, uneven teeth. "I do not," he agreed. "It gets in the way of hearing important things." He motioned north, towards the darker shadows of the Hackerwood. "My hearing isn't as good as it used to be. I prefer to avoid unnecessary sounds."

Tank dipped his chin to his chest, thinking over the implicit and explicit admissions in those few sentences. Desert lords had been very nearly gods at one point. Rumor suggested that with the destruction of so many ha'reye and ha'ra'hain in the recent catastrophes, their legendary powers were waning sharply. Apparently rumor, in this case at least, had been right.

At last, he said, "Are you taking a watch tonight?"

"Is the storyteller taking a watch?" Ganne inquired, another brief smile twisting his mouth. "Are you paying me as a guard?"

Tank grunted. "No," he said. "Sorry. Forget I asked."

Ganne shrugged. "I doubt I'll do more than doze until we reach Isata," he said more seriously. "Consider me as backup if something happens."

"I'll do that." Tank felt his hostility easing. Ganne wasn't nearly as arrogant as he'd expected from a Darden noble, let alone a desert lord.

"The world is changing, *s'e* Tank," Ganne said. He ran his left hand over his other forearm, looking down at his tattoos as he spoke. "Some traditional behaviors simply don't work any longer. That's why *I* am the one traveling north at this time. I don't find it offensive if those of lower social standing and even less *under*standing treat me as inconsequential." He looked up at Tank and smiled, hard and feral this time. "Those who do know better, on the other hand, I expect proper respect from."

Tank let his face fall into flat, hard lines. "I don't recognize your superiority, *s'e*," he said bluntly. "If we were on Darden lands, sure, but we're not. You're on *my* walk right now. My job is to get you to Isata alive. Best not to tinker with *social standing* if you want that to work out. And *don't* pry at my thoughts."

He'd thought it would be impossible for Ganne to read him while surrounded by aenstone, but Tank wasn't entirely certain about desert lord abilities, not to mention what having so many large openings for traffic did to the protective barrier.

"I'm not," Ganne said, sobering. "It was obvious what you were thinking. No prodding necessary. I was warned not to try that on you, although I'm not quite sure why."

So Yuer hadn't told him about Tank's actual background. Quite possibly he'd decided it would be more amusing to see Ganne sandbagged by the truth too far along the trail to turn back.

"That was a good warning." Tank made no attempt to take up the implied question.

Ganne's face creased in genuine amusement. "As you say. My apologies. I believe I'll turn in." He rose, offered a deep bow, then retreated to his bedmat, which was laid out some distance from everyone else's.

Tank let out a long breath and rolled his neck in a series of deep stretches, releasing the tension he hadn't noticed until that point. Looking up at the thin sliver of moon, he judged it about time to wake Lia for her watch. He started a pot of coffee. The familiar, simple movements drained away more of his worry, bit by bit.

Then he glanced up at the moon again, and anxiety came roaring back. It was nearly gone. He'd argued with Dasin over taking a moondark trip. This was the worst possible time to go through the Hackerwood, and they'd never risked it before. Dasin had been firm in sticking to the schedule, and Yuer had been as unyielding about getting Ganne to Isata with best speed.

On consideration, Tank found himself, reluctantly, glad that Ganne was along. The desert lord might draw more attention onto them, but he'd also be more capable of handling trouble than a simple noble would have been. Crippled abilities notwithstanding, Ganne had experience. He'd know what he was looking at if something happened, and he wouldn't stare in superstitious bewilderment if Tank had to haul out the special candles.

Salt and herbs were utterly useless. *Diomersha* candles, normally only available to desert Family nobles, were essentially condensed aenstone in candle form. They cost more than ten times their weight in gold, and were worth every bit.

Lia sat up, rubbing at her face with one hand and sniffing the air dubiously.

"Coffee," he said, motioning her over.

She rolled to her feet and into a series of slow stretches before approaching the fire. He used the time to pour her a cup of coffee, well aware that watching her would be a bad idea.

She wasn't conventionally attractive by southern standards — too thin in the wrong places, including her face and hair — but Tank most certainly appreciated the muscle laid along those long bones, and the grace in her movements. He needed to find a time and place to test her, to spar with her. He'd intended to do that along the coastal road, but between that stupid bar brawl, the letter in Obein, and the tension of Sandsplit, he hadn't been able to focus. He'd find time after they left Isata.

He was quite looking forward to having a valid excuse to study her closely. *Hands off crew* didn't mean he had to be unappreciative.

But she likely wouldn't take it as a compliment. And if Dasin ever caught a hint of Tank watching her, Lia's life would become very difficult. She didn't deserve that. So Tank kept his attention on the fire, and the coffee, and listened for sounds that didn't belong.

Lia settled down on the stump beside his not long after that, finger-combing her hair back from her face. Laying her sword harness across her knees, she took the cup he offered, sniffing at it dubiously. "What did you say this is?"

"Coffee. You never had it before?"

She shook her head.

"Well, I brew it strong and bitter, so I'm guessing it's going to taste awful at first. But it wakes you up, and you get used to it in time." He grinned, unable to resist adding, "You'll likely take a run to the latrine, too."

She started to hand the cup back to him, her thin face wrinkled in clear distaste.

Tank waved it away. "Nah, drink it. I'll cover you if you get the shits. Happens to everyone eventually. Didn't you have that arranged with Sanben?"

"I woke him up once or twice, and he did the same," she agreed, and took a sip of the coffee. "Huh. Not bad, actually."

"I put extra honey in," he said.

"Thank you." Her gaze traveled around the campsite as she took a few more sips. "Are we the only ones holding watch tonight?"

"Bell's going on after you," Tank said. "That's the big blond over there —" He motioned to the other group of travellers. "Don't get too close when you wake him, he warned me he's twitchy."

"All right. So nobody's walking perimeter right now?"

"You don't, here," Tank said. He pointed at the aenstone walls. "Stay inside. If there's trouble, it'll come through the gaps. You use your ears, pay attention to the horses, and you'll know trouble's coming a half mile away. Same as we'll be doing in the Forest proper. Sit still. Listen. Watch the gap in the wall. No sense pacing around unless you need to stay awake."

Her pale brows drew down sharply. "That's not how it went on the way south with Sanben," she objected. "I mean, we stayed inside the campgrounds, but he had me walking around more than sitting down."

"Everyone runs their crew different," Tank said. The look on her face told him that wasn't going to be good enough. He was going to have to upset her superstitions. "Look, we're going through on a moondark cycle. The quieter everyone is, the less chance of trouble."

Her frown intensified, and she crossed her arms. "Quiet," she said, not quite a question.

"Emotions," he clarified. "Don't get into a fight. Don't brood over things that upset you. Don't pace around and be anxious. Nothing that will turn you towards night terrors. Those are bad."

She didn't seem as surprised as he'd expected. She said, "Sanben asked me whether I had nightmares. Any sort of odd dreams. He asked me that almost every night on our way south."

Ah. That was why. *Thank you, Sanben.* "Did you have any? And what moon cycle was it?"

"Beginning moon. And I didn't dream at all. I normally don't."

"Good on both counts," Tank said. "This run'll be different. You got to be *calm*. There are creatures in the Forest that can hear you when you're emotional. You have any dreams, you see anything odd, you tell me — *me*, not nobody else, right off, even if it means waking me up, yeah?"

She uncrossed her arms, still visibly unhappy. He had a feeling she was biting her tongue to keep from asking about demons and witchcraft.

"Listen," he said, making a decision. "How's this? I never sleep well on this leg of the run until we reach Isata. You and me, we're going to sit up and talk most nights until someone I trust takes over. I'll doze a bit then. But I'm not making you stand watch alone, not on a moondark run."

Her back went stiff and her chin went up, offended pride washing through the air like the heat from the fire. "I don't need —"

He held up a hand and gave her a forbidding scowl, *pushing* without meaning to. She stopped almost mid-word, her eyes wide and her face losing color. He hastily reeled back the push, irritated at himself now. *Careless. And lazy.* He'd need to spend some time tonight on self control exercises. Every night, until it went back to being as reflexive as breathing.

"Stop," he told her. "That's exactly what I mean. Don't get mad. Don't get prickly. I know you're capable. I wouldn't have hired you if I didn't think you could do the job. But the Hackerwood is *different*, and at the dark of the moon, it's going to be fucking *dangerous*. We're about near the only people going through, more than like. Anyone who knows anything won't risk it. I'm a fool for letting the schedule fall on this point —"

Taking the blame for a mistake not his stung, but it was better than saying *Dasin's a fucking fool* to a new hire. Her expression already held enough mulish discontent.

"I've been through already!" she said. "I know it's dangerous."

"You're *not* understanding," he said. "You went through on a beginning moon. That's reasonably safe. Best time is a full moon." He paused, thinking of how to explain, then went on, "Everything goes to sleep, like, on a full moon. Everything comes all the way awake on a dark moon. And we're walking into at least two days of full dark — of *hat'naa-iti*, of *shiaq'ree* — do you know those terms at all? — before we come out the other side."

"They're not familiar, no. But I think I understand." Lia dropped her gaze and sipped coffee for a time, her frown reappearing on occasion as she worked through what he'd said. "Are there demons in the Hackerwood?"

He started to laugh, more because he'd been right than because it was actually funny; caught himself before she could get offended, and made a show of considering the question. "I wouldn't call them that," he said with ostentatious care. "I think your Stecatr priests might, though."

"What would *you* call them?"

He looked north, sorting through answers. "Old," he said finally. "Old, and dangerous, and hungry." *And they have my son. Or, at least, Balby has my son ... our son ... and lives among them. What are they teaching him? What are they* doing *to him?* He blinked hard and shoved that aside, focusing on the topic to hand. "I'm not saying more than that. Lia, you've got to go back and look your priests in the face. Don't ask what you don't want to confess to knowing about."

Her scowl reappeared, although her anger held a considerably quieter burn this time. "I'm getting tired of people telling me that."

"Are we wrong?" Tank asked, meeting her eyes. "Should we answer you completely and openly? Do you want *me* to do that, right here and now?"

She held his gaze for a moment, then looked at the ground. "No," she said, scarcely audible. "But I don't like being pushed into choosing ignorance."

Tank let that be. It was her business to sort out that particular issue.

Lia drained her cup and sputtered. Tank laughed, careful to keep the sound quiet, and said, "You don't drink it all the way down. The dregs are pure grit. Here —" He snagged the cup from her and refilled it, adding a lesser dollop of honey this time.

"Thank you. Urgh. You could have warned me."

"Well, now you won't do it twice," he said, still chuckling.

She set the cup down and stood, buckling her swordbelt around her waist, then sat, more carefully than before. Tank handed her the cup.

"You ought to get a shoulder harness like this one," he said, tapping the strap of his harness. "Your sword's shorter than the standard, looks like, would make an easy balance."

"I've thought about it," she admitted, "but wouldn't the draw be —" She stopped, blinking, and looked around. "What's that?"

Tank shut his eyes, listening intently. "I don't hear —" he began, opening his eyes, then swore. She was halfway to the wall, moving slowly, staggering a bit. He made it to her side before she stepped through the eastern gap; grabbed her arm and hauled her back around.

She stopped walking, but half-turned, staring to the north. "It sounds like someone's singing. It sounds like ... it sounds like my *sister* is singing. What's Kia doing here?" Her voice warbled, bewildered and childish.

Tank swore again and pulled Lia, unresisting, back to the campfire. Ganne was already on his feet, his dark face alert. "Trouble?" he asked.

"Something's calling her," Tank said shortly. "Hold her. I'll deal with it." Of all the people in this group, a supersititious, ignorant northern shouldn't have been a target — but then, maybe that made her the perfect target.

Ganne locked his hand around Lia's arm and drew her down to sit on a stump, murmuring in her ear. She sat, obedient as a child, but her eyes were fully dilated and she shivered from time to time.

Tank drew his sword and moved to stand near the eastern gap, where she'd been heading. The night was silent. Far, far too silent. The crickets and frogs had stopped entirely, and a familiar, hazy non-sound ran round his inner ear.

"Go away," he said to the silence. "Go *away*. There's nothing for you here."

Ganne swore, abruptly and loudly, in southern dialect. The camp roused, people scrambling to their feet, alarmed inquiring noises breaking the foggy silence into bright, painful shards. Tank jerked around to grab Lia, who was moving considerably faster this time.

"Watch her knees!" Ganne yelled. "*Taneka.*"

Tank adjusted his hold and got tender regions out of the way just in time; adjusted his hold again and slammed her down to the ground.

"*Cilif,*" he said, voice aimed to carry but less than a shout.

The big mercenary loomed up a moment later and sat on Lia without needing to ask for direction. She writhed, swearing, but there was no budging Cilif when he didn't want to be budged. Tank had learned a long time ago never to grapple with the man.

"*Taneka,*" Ganne said again, a dangerous edge to his voice. He was crouched, hand cupping his groin and hissing occasionally.

"Save it," Tank said, already turning back to the gap. "Ganne, hold the camp. Kick up the fire. *Shut everyone up.*"

The desert lord huffed incredulous contempt, straightening with a pained wince and a glare down at Lia. Tank ignored him, his entire attention focused on the space beyond the walls of the campground. Sound slowly died away, replaced once more with that thick, charged not-quite-silence. Light built as someone stirred the fire back to life, pushing the darkness steadily back.

A *push* washed through the air at Tank's back: Ganne, binding everyone to silence inside and out. They'd pay for that later, but it would save lives in the moment.

A piece of darkness pushed forward as though fighting to hold its territory against the firelight. Shadow gathered into a tall, vaguely bird-shaped space. A *churkling* sound drifted through the air as the bloodbird's head dipped down and forward, like a stork chasing a frog.

Lia screamed and thrashed. Cilif grunted and swore. Lia went silent. The only sound was the bloodbird's bubbling chuckle. It moved sideways, craning its neck as though looking past Tank.

"She's out," Cilif said, voice low. "Ganne's got everyone still. We got this side."

Tank moved forward a step to stand square in the gap, sword ready, and let the always-ready, acidic anger rise. "Go away," he said, pushing fury into each word with increasing force. "There's nothing for you here. *Piss off.*"

The creature moved sideways, clicking erratically, and flared its massive wings, blocking out swathes of star-dappled sky.

"*I will take you apart joint by joint and piss on your remains,*" Tank growled, channeling his many, involuntary lessons from desert lords and ha'ra'hain, and *pushed.*

The bloodbird stopped moving. It let out a faint, distressed chittering sound, then retreated, the darker shadow of its presence seeming to simply dissolve.

Tank stayed still, listening to the silence, listening to his heart pounding in his ears, counting his breaths. Twenty. Thirty. Forty. His heartbeat slowed. The gloss over his hearing faded. Another ten breaths. Twenty. Nothing happened.

He stepped carefully back from the gap, turning to survey the camp.

Cilif stood, his own sword drawn, well out of reach, watching Tank with a grim concentration that said more than words. He'd obviously been ready to attack Tank if he'd gotten overset. That was reassuring, although unnecessary and even a bit amusing. It took more than an oversized stork to rattle Tank's defenses these days, and Cilif would have been no match for Tank in a crisis. But that was a conversation Tank refused to have with anyone, much less within earshot of Dasin.

Dasin was on his feet, his own dagger drawn, watching Tank with a much more panicked expression. Ganne stood a bit apart, his arms folded, studying Tank with an entirely new interest. Tank could almost see the pieces clicking together in the desert lord's mind.

Damnit. Well, consequences and questions alike could wait.

Tank lifted a shoulder in a hard shrug to all three, sheathed his sword, then knelt to check on Lia. She was already stirring. Cilif had probably used a chokehold rather than knocking her out. He felt along her throat, checking for damage, but Cilif had astounding precision when he felt like using it. She might have a small bruise or two come morning, nothing more.

"I'll sort out the camp," Ganne said, scarcely audible.

Lia coughed, the sound raspy, and let him help her sit up. "Slowly," he said. "Breathe easy. Don't talk." He hoisted her gently to her feet and steered her to her sleeping mat. "Settle there. Dasin, water."

"Here," Dasin said from behind him, and handed him a waterskin. He passed it on to Lia.

"Thank you. Slowly, drink slowly, there you go. Sip on that and breathe, and go to sleep."

"What — was —"

"Don't talk. Wait for tomorrow." He laced compulsion into the words this time. She coughed again, yawned, and drooped over into sleep. He caught the waterskin away from her before it could fall into the dirt, and handed it back up to Dasin.

Standing, he turned and scanned the camp. The southbound travelers were on their feet, their worried gazes switching between Tank and Dasin. They seemed to not even register Ganne's presence.

"What was that?" Bell demanded. His dark eyes were inclined to cross, giving a mildly ridiculous aspect to his expression as it wavered between bewilderment and annoyance.

"Someone had a nightmare," Ganne said, the words echoing through an entirely non-verbal range. "She shouted and roused everyone into a panic. Nothing more. You can all go back to sleep. Very annoying. Very rude. But nothing to worry over."

Tank bit his lip, watching the tension drain from the suspicious travelers. None of them looked at Ganne; they seemed to think Tank was the one speaking.

"You ought to hire people less prone to night terrors," one of the men sniffed, already turning away. "She's too young to be out on the road," another one said, darting a supercilious glance at Lia. Bell stared, eyes narrow and thoughtful, his gaze going from Tank to Dasin to Lia, passing over the spot where Ganne stood, then hitching back to almost focus on the quietly standing desert lord. After a moment more of consideration, he said, "My turn on watch, then."

"Yes," Tank agreed neutrally. It was early, in truth, but Lia was in no shape to go back on watch, and a time-muddled Bell was better than one in full clarity just now. Tank was fairly sure there wouldn't be any more trouble tonight. He glanced around, counting heads, and frowned. "Where's Toad?"

Ganne snorted and pointed at the wagon. "Underneath," he said, voice rich with contempt. "Wiggled fast as a snake going to ground."

"He's got good sense, then," Tank said. He went to the wagon. "Come on out, s'e Toad, the fun's all over."

The old man didn't answer. Tank crouched, frowning, to peer beneath the wagon. Enough light from the renewed fire crept into that space to show him the old man curled up, snoring gently.

Tank laughed a bit as he retreated, and managed to keep that good humor through sorting out Bell for the watch and everyone else back to their own beds. He shifted a still-dazed Lia to his left, set Cilif to her left, and put Dasin to his own right. Ganne retreated to the edge of their informally claimed area, as before. Tank had a feeling Ganne would be awake most of the night, quietly watching.

Good enough. Despite his own intention of not sleeping, himself, Tank could feel his hands shaking from the ferocity of that push. He hadn't done anything like that for a long time. Hadn't wanted to. Had tried to forget he *could*.

All I want is to be like everyone else, he thought despairingly. *Why is that so fucking hard?*

He shrugged at himself and sank onto his sleeping mat.

Dasin leaned over him a moment later. Voice low and hard, he said, "We're not waiting on her to recover from being witched."

Tank hadn't even thought of that part yet. Lia would be entirely useless in the morning. She might not even be able to stay on her horse. Come to that, Tank wasn't at all sure how functional *he'd* be.

Tank shut his eyes, ignoring the feel of Dasin's glare on his skin. "I'll sort it in the morning, Dasin," he said. "Let me sleep."

He didn't quite push, but it was a near thing.

Dasin rolled onto his back with a displeased grunt.

Tank let himself feel a brief moment of relief, then dropped into blessedly empty stillness.

Chapter Fourteen

Lia woke with a splitting headache, vomit-sour mouth, and the threads of nightmares just barely beyond recall clouding her focus. She staggered to the necessary without really seeing anything, then made it to a fireside seat before her knees failed. Someone pressed a mug into her hand; she drank, too dazed to make a face at the bitter taste of unhoneyed coffee. It tasted better than the inside of her mouth, at any rate.

A biscuit was pushed into her other hand. Tracing a thumb across the texture, she felt an embossed pattern that identified it as one of the cinnamon sweets Dasin favored for breakfast. She blinked, momentarily befuddled with both hands full. Which one would bring coffee, which one a biscuit? Giving up, she lifted both at once.

The mug began to slip from her right hand. A slim, warm hand wrapped around hers, steadying her grip, then gently tugged the mug clear.

"Eat," someone said. Not Tank. Not Dasin. No, maybe Dasin. But not — who else was there to not be? She blinked, then tried to wipe the persistent gumminess from her eyes. A moment before she smeared cinnamon crumbs all over her face, a larger hand caught hers, a burst of laughter ringing out from somewhere nearby.

"Damn, she's tanked," another voice said. Another peal of laughter followed, and a sour grunt. That last sound *was* Tank. She knew that irritated sound. The laughter was … was Dasin, probably. And he'd been the one to take the coffee from her, and probably to put it in her hand to begin with. Which made the second person … Cilif? No. Tank.

Her sense of proportions and locations began to return. She lifted her free hand, carefully, and rubbed the back of her wrist across her eyes. This time, blinking produced a narrow band of sight: only people registered, little of the surrounding area.

Tank knelt beside her, watching gravely as she sorted herself out. Dasin stood behind Tank, arms folded and a distinctly impatient expression on his thin features. Cilif was busy checking the horses over; Toad sat on a nearby bench, his gaze shifting sideways to Lia every so often, then jerking away. Ganne glanced up from prodding the remnants of last night's fire together, regarded Lia, then went back to coaxing a small flame from the coals.

"Can you ride?" Dasin asked irritably.

"Dasin," Tank said, voice flat and reproving.

"I *said* we're not waiting on her," Dasin snapped.

"And I heard you fine. Piss off already. I got this."

Dasin stared at the back of Tank's head, eyes wide; then his expression fell into severe lines. He turned and stalked away, headed for Cilif.

Lia caught Ganne watching Dasin with an oddly calculating expression. She shut her eyes and bent her head, nausea muddling her focus.

Tank nudged her shoulder with a knuckle. "Hey," he said. "Drink the coffee, eat the biscuit. We're due on the road. It's a long one today, we're aiming for two campsites along this time. There you go, good."

The mug was back in her hand. She sipped coffee and chewed cinnamon biscuit, half-listening to Tank's steady voice as he told her what order the horses were being tacked up in, that Cilif would take care of Rooster for her but she wasn't to expect it after today; that Toad had already promised three of his best stories today, none involving any sort of haunting or high dramatics. They were bypassing the next campsite because Dasin wanted to push almost to nightfall before stopping. There wasn't going to be any significant traffic, so there shouldn't be anyone ahead to get in their way and slow things down.

The mug was empty, the biscuit gone. Lia set the mug down carefully, then brushed crumbs from her fingers. "Thank you," she said. Her voice emerged as a hoarse croak.

"Already got your gear sorted," Tank said. "Let's get you up onto Rooster."

She looked around, too fast. Dizziness leaned her sideways. Tank caught her before she could sprawl to the ground.

"Easy there, easy, steady. Slowly now, there you go, up, up, good," he said, and she was on her feet, frowning at Ganne for some reason. Oh, Ganne was grinning at her, that was why. And Dasin had a poisonous look going. She tried to pull away from Tank's support, but the big redhead leaned in, nearly picking her up, and steered her towards the horses. He had his armor on: the smell of oiled leather and metal filled her nose.

"Might not be the best of ideas," Cilif said dubiously, eyeing Lia. He, too, had kitted out in a light leather hauberk, bracers, and leather chausses.

"Nothing for it," Tank said. "Help me get her up. There. Good. Lia, here, these are the reins, right? You hang on to these. Don't drop them."

She stared at Rooster's mane, not at all sure how she'd gotten up onto the gelding's back. Oh — right. Tank and Dasin — no, Tank and Cilif had lifted her into the saddle. She felt leather strips in her hands and reflexively caught them into a familiar grip: not too tight, not too loose. Saddle. Seat. She checked the placement of her feet in the stirrups and adjusted her posture.

"Right," she said aloud. "Right. Good. So." She looked down at a loud snort of laughter from Cilif. "Oh, piss off," she told him.

He stepped back, laughing openly now. "Gods damn," he said. "You an' I *got* to go get soused together one a' these days. You'll be the gods' own fun, won't you?"

She couldn't think of an appropriate answer, so she said, once more, "Piss off."

"Enough," Tank ordered.

Her vision started to blur. She sat grimly still, eyes shut. The searing pain in her temples surged back, distorting thought. Speech was impossible. She went through a set of silent, stuttering prayers, unhopeful that the gods would bother to intervene.

"Godsdamn, she's white as bone," Cilif said. The words weren't loud, but they echoed as though coming at her from every direction at once. Someone said something else. Ganne, maybe? Something about *sensitive*, and that was bad, that was exactly what she didn't want them to think her. She tried to open her eyes and protest. She couldn't move. She felt locked in place, stuck in a timeless moment of dizziness and stabbing pain.

Words came through in blurts: "We'll have to … turns. Ganne, can you … I'll take a … campsite …." She wasn't at all sure the same person was speaking throughout.

She *was* sure that she didn't want Ganne anywhere near her. Not after she'd nailed him in the tenders the night before and *gods* only knew why she'd done that. He had to still be angry about that, and so was definitely not the right person to ask for help. Maybe they were asking him something else. To drive the wagon. Or something.

She'd welcome Tank's help. She trusted Tank. He wouldn't let her fall. Fall? Why would she fall? Leather moved against her fingers, recalling that much of the moment: she was on Rooster, high above everyone, and he was being unusually calm, as though aware of how unsteady she felt.

"Lia," Ganne said in her ear. That should have been impossible because — because — she couldn't remember why. There was a strange off-echo to his voice that ran counter to the ripples going through her ears, slowly stilling them.

The pain turned … *fluffy* was the only word she could think of. Ganne said something else, in another language. His voice came out in a soft, flowing sing-song. She thought her horse — what was its name? — the horse — she was on a horse, wasn't she? — yes, of course, Rooster. She was moving. Was she walking? She couldn't focus. The pain had vanished under a wondrous globe of puffy peacefulness.

Ganne wasn't angry. Why would he be angry? He was her friend. He would keep her safe. Everything was fine. It would always be perfect, forever and ever.

Time blurred. Sound and motion happened somewhere else. Eventually her vision turned dark instead of white. The soft globe melted away, taking headache and dizziness with it.

Lia opened her eyes, blinking. She felt as though she'd just come off of a two day drinking binge. "Ugh," she said feebly.

The air smelled, improbably, of almond extract, bringing back memories of the one time her mother had managed to get some for baking. The house had smelled wonderful for days, although her father had complained endlessly about "that acidic stench".

Motion beside her resolved into Tank crouching down. "Awake? Good. Here." He helped her sit up and pushed a warm mug into her hands. "Drink it all at once, quick, before you notice the taste," he advised.

She obeyed, still trying to bring the world into coherent focus. Three rapid gulps later the taste registered: *skunky* was too polite. She gagged and held the cup away from her.

"Don't hork it up," Tank said, taking the mug. "Think about sommat else. Think about trees. What tree do you like best?"

"*Trees?*" someone muttered in incredulous tones.

Trees. Trees. There were trees just visible beyond the campsite wall. Dusk had set in, blurring outlines but not doing much to cool the muggy air. Any scent of almonds was comprehensively gone under the horrid taste worming through her sinuses. Lia swallowed hard, clenching her jaw, and managed to say, "Oak. Good ... color in ... fall and the wood ... good for ... fire and ... furn — furnit —" She gagged again. Tank wrapped his hand around her upper arm.

"Furniture, yeah," he said. "You ever build your own furniture?"

"No. I ... no." She despaired of explaining that was men's work. Women might carve final designs, or do a bit of sanding, or apply polish, but never *build*.

Were there oak trees in the Forest, at this campsite? There had been some on the northern side. Hadn't there? She couldn't remember. She thought she'd seen a creek tree, impressively old and wide-branched. Had she climbed it? She should have, if she hadn't. She missed climbing trees. There were trees here she could climb. She wanted to go climb a tree.

Tank's hand pressing on her shoulder surprised her. "Stay down," he told her. "Tell me how you build a fire?" His hand was a warm, solid pressure. Reassuring. Steadying. Calm.

"I ... twigs? and ... shavings. And then ... bigger twigs. And...." She drew in a deep breath through her nose, let it out through her mouth, then reversed that order. Clarity seeped into place. "All right. Thank you. I'm —"

She breathed in too fast and coughed, then gagged again as the memory of that taste ran back up into her sinuses. Tank's grip tightened, bringing her out of the moment's horror.

"What the fuck did I just *drink*?" she demanded once she could speak again.

"It's close as no difference to swamp muck, way I see it," Tank said cheerfully. "But it helps after you've been witched."

"After...." She blinked several times. "What are you talking about?"

He regarded her with interest. "You don't remember?"

Lia kept her focus on his face. It was a nice face. Strong bones, lots of pretty freckles, and his blue eyes were kind. He felt ... safe. She didn't want to look at anything that might not be safe, just then.

She said, "I remember sitting around the fire, and you telling me you'd stay awake. After that I'm not sure. I remember a headache this morning, and feeling really ill. Then something about Ganne ... talking to me." *Talking* didn't sound right, but she didn't have the right label for the vague murmuring that had wound around her bones. She could still feel a faint humming throughout her body.

"He walked beside you all day," Tank said gravely. "Kept you safe."

"Safe from *what*?"

"Falling off your horse," Dasin said with asperity, appearing near her feet.

She whimpered involuntarily as her focus jolted to a wider arc. The light came from a well-established fire. The sky was entirely dark, clouded over and ominous. Huge-leafed vines wound around scarred, rough-barked trees at the edges of the firelight. Further in, dark shadows shifted, rolling with the flickering of the fire. Beyond that was only inky darkness.

A hip-high wall surrounded the campsite. She recognized one chipped section of stone. She'd stayed here with Kennet on the way south. That memory helped to center her in the present moment. She looked around, blinking hard.

True to Tank's earlier prediction, there were no other travelers at the campsite. Toad, Cilif, and Ganne sat on rough benches around the fire, mugs in their hands and their backs to her. Dasin stood at her feet, still glaring at her. His face looked thinner and more sallow than usual, and his hair hung lank and dark with road dust, half escaped from its usual tidy braid.

Dasin said, waspishly, "Eat something and go back to sleep. You have to be able to ride on your own in the morning."

Provoked almost into temper, she struggled to her feet, leaning hard on Tank. Dasin's eyes narrowed sharply, focusing on Tank's arm around her waist; she removed herself from that support and stood straight and clear, staring right back at the merchant.

"I'll be ready, *s'e*," she said flatly.

"Best be," he said, and stalked away.

Tank's hand came up under her elbow as Lia wobbled. "Come sit by the fire," he said in her ear. "Don't mind him. He's in a pissy mood."

"What did I *do*?" she muttered back, allowing him to guide her to the roughly carved bench near the fire, at some remove from Dasin's seat. Ganne, across from her, glanced up once, then studiously avoided looking at her. His face and demeanor were gray, as though he'd run a mountain trail without stopping. Beside him, Toad and Cilif seemed uneasy and tired; their gazes flickered from her to Tank and back before they, too, pointedly ignored her.

Four enormous, stubby white candles had been placed at cardinal points around the campsite, just inside the pale stone walls. They burned with an eerie flame that was too steady, and weirdly monochrome. She could smell almond extract again, and suspected the aroma came from the candles. But who made candles that smelled like liquored almonds, of all things?

She looked up at Tank, raising a puzzled eyebrow. He glanced at the candles, then shrugged and ignored her implicit question in favor of the one she'd asked aloud.

"You weren't yourself," he said. He picked up a trail mug that showed signs of having been used already; shook a handful of dry soup mix from a tin into it, then filled it with water from the kettle resting at the edge of the fire. As he handed her the mug, he added, ruefully, "We're none of us up for cooking tonight. It was a rough day."

She lifted the mug, inhaling a surprisingly rich aroma: rosemary, garlic, and beef. Normally trail soups seemed flat and muddy to her, but this could have come from a fine tavern, at least by the smell. She said as much.

"Lot of people seem to think trail food has to taste like shit," Tank agreed. "Like you got to suffer while you're traveling. I don't see it that way. We spend the money on good supplies."

She took a cautious sip. It was still too hot to drink, and the mix hadn't fully hydrated yet, so the aroma was far better than the actual taste. She lowered the mug and wrapped her hands around it, relishing the warmth, then returned to her question, unwilling to let it rest. "What *happened?*"

Cilif looked up, then glanced sideways at Ganne, grinning. Ganne ignored everything but his soup, his mouth set in a thin, disapproving line.

"Eh ...." Tank said. "We had an incident, last night. You got caught up in it. You really *don't remember anything?*" He raised his voice slightly on the last words. Ganne looked up, frowning.

"No," Lia said, taking the cue and raising her own voice a bit. "I went from talking to you to being on the horse with a headache like all the gods were kicking me at the same time."

Ganne's severe expression melted into something like sympathy. He and Tank matched stares for a few moments. Then Ganne shrugged and went back to drinking his soup, visibly less irritable now.

Lia lowered her voice. "I did something to Ganne?"

"Kneed him in the tenders," Tank said, as quietly.

Lia put a hand over her mouth, appalled. No wonder the man looked like that. Gods be thanked he didn't have to deal with riding a horse.

"You weren't yourself," Tank repeated. "Let it be. Don't apologize to him, it'll make everything worse. Southern desert lord pride is a tricky thing. Let it be."

"Desert lord?"

He shook his head slowly. "More stuff you don't want to know about."

In a sudden burst of fury, she snapped, "I'm getting *really* tired of you telling me that!"

He sighed, rubbing a bent knuckle across two days worth of stubble. "Lia, are you going back to Stecatr, at the end of this run?"

"Of course I am!"

"Well, then. Most everyone north of the Hackwood doesn't know anything about what you've already faced, and there's good reason to keep it that way. If you'd stayed to the north, well ... but you didn't." Absently, he took out the tie on his braid and began unweaving his hair. "You've learned stuff I'm positive your priests didn't want you to know about. You just barely might get by with some clever wording, at this point. Anything more ... I'm well aware they're fond of ropes and trees, in Stecatr. I'd rather not have you entertaining the crows on my account."

His hair, free of the braid, reached his mid-back in shining, coppery-red waves. She couldn't help staring as he worked his hands through, untangling the larger knots. The back of her neck prickled in warning; she looked up to find Dasin glaring directly at her. She hastily dropped her gaze, her face hot as the fire.

Lia drank the soup, grimly fighting down mortification and barely tasting the rich broth. Dasin had clearly, entirely misunderstood the situation. She wasn't interested. She just hadn't seen Tank's hair down before, and it *was* remarkable. Anyone would look. It didn't mean what Dasin clearly thought it meant. Especially for Lia. He had nothing at all to be jealous about. Besides, he and Tank were both *ii'ne* as well; what in the world did he think Lia had to offer in that regard?

Which put her thoughts back to Tank's last words: *Fond of ropes and trees. That's true enough. Oh, Isla.*

Anger over that was pointless, exponentially so at this remove, and she had immediate things to deal with. She took a cautious glance across the fire. Dasin had returned to brooding at the fire. In peripheral vision, she saw Tank beginning to rebraid his hair, and caught Cilif smirking at her. Toad drooped, too tired to notice anything beyond his own nose, and Ganne was as inscrutable as ever.

Carefully neutral to avoid drawing Dasin's attention again, Lia said, "You may have a point." She kept her attention on her hands.

Tank tied off the braid and put his hands on his thighs. Dasin looked up again. The two men considered each other for a few breaths; then Dasin rose and headed to his sleeping mat. Tank's fingers dug into his thighs briefly, then stilled. Not looking at Lia, he said, "You know you can switch Halls any time you like. You just can't go back to Stecatr afterwards, more'n like. No great loss, by me, but I'm guessing you have other things to consider."

"I do," she said, flat and final.

Tank cut a sideways glance her way, then, mercifully, let the conversation die.

Lia tipped the cup, draining the last of the soup, and rose to her feet. Tank stood as well, taking the cup from her hand before she could protest. "I got cleanup tonight," he said. "You go get some sleep. Over there." He pointed to her bedroll, already laid out between Cilif's and Ganne's.

Lia blinked, setting a map in her head of where everyone would be that night, then looked around the campsite for external reference points. She startled herself with a huge yawn. "Thank you," she said muzzily, and took a stumbling step.

Tank's arm braced her a moment later, guiding her forward. She found herself sprawled on her sleeping mat. She rolled, groggily adjusting her position. Someone draped a blanket gently across her; it wasn't hers, and it was scented with something that smelled almost but not quite like lavender. She pushed her thin pillow into a better spot, yawned once more, then fell into darkness as complete as that of the surrounding woods.

Chapter Fifteen

Regardless of what Dasin liked or didn't like, Tank had set unbendable rules about traveling through the Hackerwood. Anyone overset, as Lia had been the previous day, got immediate, comprehensive support until they were fully on their feet. Anyone having the least bit of nightmare received the same, specifically and *only* from Tank himself, and the hells with any prudery or jealousy.

He'd only allowed Dasin to insist on traveling while Lia was recovering because of Ganne. The desert lord had walked beside Lia the entire day, one hand on her leg, talking in a low, sing-song voice that had begun to falter just before they reached the campsite.

Tank wasn't at all surprised when, shortly after Lia went to sleep, Ganne folded like an empty sack. He also wasn't particularly surprised when, just past midnight, the stocky desert lord began to twist and mutter in his sleep.

He roused Cilif with a cautious nudge to the mercenary's foot.

"Take over watch," he said as Cilif sat up, rubbing at his eyes and already reaching for his dagger. "Ganne's having a nightmare."

Cilif grunted and rolled to his feet, sheathed dagger in hand, and made his way to a fireside seat. He plopped down, facing away from the fire, scrubbing a hand through his already disordered hair.

"Got it," he said. "Go."

Dasin was up on one elbow, watching Tank with a frown. He said, voice whiny with weariness, "He of all people shouldn't need —"

"He of all people needs it *more*," Tank said flatly, and knelt beside Ganne. The desert lord had taken off his shirt to sleep: vividly colored, calligraphic stripes wound across his ribs and looked to wrap around his back. Tank had no idea what that pattern symbolized, but even in the low firelight, it was remarkably compelling. He made himself focus on

Ganne's face.

Given the risk of what he was about to do, Tank took the chance of voluntarily dropping into that *other* vision, aiming it to an internal acuity this time, rather than external. Hearing sharpened as sight dimmed, and his hands warmed, becoming almost excruciatingly sensitive. Ganne's troubled emotions moved in smoky trails around his body, echoing his restless movements.

Tank carefully avoided watching the abstract shapes. He absolutely didn't want to know what could give a desert lord nightmares.

Unfortunately, he could tell that Ganne was locked deep in dream. Tank wasn't going to be able to bring him out of it with a touch, even if he prodded at Ganne's mind instead of his body. This was going to get unpleasant.

He glanced up, checking the camp. Lia was far too close. At least Toad was well to one side, and Dasin was already awake.

"Dasin," he said, keeping his voice low. "Get Lia clear."

Dasin snorted, then rolled to his knees and shuffled the short distance to Lia. As soon as he reached arm's length, she sat up, drawing her dagger. Dasin stopped, leaning back, one hand up defensively.

"Shit, you're worse'n Cilif," he complained. "Come on, come on, move, get to the other side of the fire."

Lia rose and swept a glance around. Tank's increased sensitivity told him she was both checking where everyone stood and identifying any immediate danger. Without comment, she moved to the other side of the fire, Dasin and Cilif following.

Ganne was still asleep, still twitching and mumbling curses at an invisible opponent. Tank had hoped that the nearby movement might rouse him. No such luck.

Tank hovered a hand near the desert lord's bare shoulder. When that got no response, he moved it closer, until his hand settled onto fever-warm skin. Ganne let out a long, protesting sound and went still for a moment; then, abruptly, both of his hands came up, grasping Tank's arms. He rolled, still trapped in nightmare, gathering Tank in against him. Tank went limp, allowing Ganne to press close, more interested in keeping his mental shields firmly in place. A moment later, as expected, a hard push hit his defenses, which — *damnit* — didn't ... quite ... hold.

The world whited out, then went black.

Awareness returned slowly, painfully acute in everything but sight. Ganne lay tucked tight around Tank, still asleep but peacefully this time. Tank's body was a solid flare of bruises, as though he'd been tumbled across rocky scree; he could feel Dasin watching, worry sharper than jealousy for once. The fire had burned low, but was still live enough to block perception. Lia and Cilif were nowhere in range, so they were safely behind the firepit. The horses were nodding sleepily, which meant that at least Ganne and Tank hadn't drawn the attention of anything particularly dangerous.

They'd been lucky.

Toad, improbably, was firmly and serenely asleep himself. As Tank blinked awake, the old man let out a resonant snore that turned into a startled snort. He sat up, grunted, then burrowed back down again without waking. Tank heard Cilif laugh, and his own mouth stretched in a grin.

Ganne tightened his grip, shoving his hips up against Tank. He was hard, his breathing roughening and his body still fever-hot; Tank felt himself responding to the desert lord's urgency, found himself pushing his hips back — it had been *so* damn good with Alyea, he'd never matched that experience again, never had it on with another desert lord, and he *needed* —

"*Tank*," Dasin said, white-furious and crimson-alarmed.

Tank slammed back to expanded perspective with a sense of something non-physical cracking throughout his body. He untangled himself from Ganne's grasp and rolled clear, gasping. The desert lord let out a growl of protest that choked off short, then pushed up to one elbow, blinking hard.

"The *fuck?*" he snarled. "Did you just try —? *You?*" He lurched to his feet.

Tank stayed on the ground, on his back, intentionally vulnerable as he looked up at Ganne.

"You had a nightmare," he told the infuriated man, keeping his voice deliberately calm. "I brought you out of it."

He ignored the deep ache, the too-slowly fading, desperate want. Fucking Ganne would have been a terrible idea, even without Dasin right at hand. He started that thought on a loop in his head, setting it in place as inflexible truth that might — that *would* — stop him from dragging Ganne off into the shadows first chance they had. Hopefully Ganne was disciplined enough to do the same, because Tank didn't think he'd be able to say *no* if Ganne pushed him up against a tree.

Gods, that really was a bad, bad idea. I should have let him suffer through the nightmare. At least he wanted to fuck instead of fight. That thought was no comfort at all.

Ganne stopped moving. He turned his head, looking around at the people watching him. His fists slowly unclenched, his breathing evening out.

"Right," he said after a time. He looked down at Tank, his mouth thin. "Don't fucking touch me again," he snapped.

"Don't intend to," Tank said; still in the sharp clarity of vision, he knew they were both lying.

Ganne stalked away, headed for the latrine area. Tank shut his eyes, forbidding himself to follow, and let go of heightened perception entirely. Dropping back into the ordinary world felt like being smothered and shattered all at once. He rolled to his side and curled into a ball, letting out a single dry, coughing sob. Then he uncurled and climbed to his feet, brushing himself off and grateful that at least he'd been awake and fully clothed.

"That could have gone better," he said to Dasin's white-mouthed glare. "Could have gone a lot worse, too." He raised his voice, looking across the low fire at Lia and Cilif. "It's all over. No more trouble tonight. Cilif, it's your watch. Lia, go back to sleep."

He looked at Dasin again, raising an eyebrow. Dasin glanced towards the others, then grimaced and gave a single, short nod.

When Ganne returned, still grumpy but considerably less tense, Tank headed for the safe darkness of the latrines himself; and Dasin, without comment, followed.

Chapter Sixteen

The air hung thick and sullen. Even the omnipresent insects seemed disinclined to leave their leafy shelters. The horses plodded along, each showing their own irritability with the weather. Rooster *wiggled*, a whole body shimmy that didn't really go anywhere. Sin tended to go sideways at erratic moments. Blackie randomly wanted to stop moving.

Lia, Cilif and Tank all wore their armor, and even Dasin wore a short, loose chain vest. Ganne seemed entirely unconcerned about armor, but he did have a large knife in an ornate leather sheath at his side today.

Cilif had been cursing in and out of dialect all morning as he fought his recalcitrant horse. He'd finally dropped to rear position to avoid holding them up. Lia took his spot beside the wagon, putting Tank, as always, in the lead. Dasin cheerfully translated the bursts of invective for Lia, interrupting Toad's storytelling so often that the old man finally *grumphed* and declared he wasn't wasting his breath on such an unappreciative audience.

The draft pony plodded along stolidly. Lia wasn't sure if the pony — which, as far as she could tell, didn't even have a name — was too stupid to care about anything or smart enough to know that kicking around irritably while in harness would be a short road to the boneyards.

It annoyed her that nobody had given the poor beast a name beyond "the draft". She'd been thinking of possibilities for days, and hadn't come up with anything that quite suited. Maybe she should ask Toad to put his mind to it. She made a sour face, unhappy at even having had that thought. He was a *bad person*. She didn't want anything to do with him.

Someone clucked beside her. She startled; Rooster shimmied sideways into Ganne, who'd made the sound. He let out a yelp and scrambled clear, not in the least graceful. Cilif let out a hoot of laughter as Ganne tumbled to the ground and rolled clear of the big gelding's hooves. Ganne, leaping to his feet, directed a string of insults in southern dialect at Cilif, most of which Lia, by this point, knew: *poxed whoreson, nameless bastard,* and *shit-eater* was the gist of the invective. Cilif laughed again, not at all upset.

Lia brought Rooster under control, then looked down at Ganne as he turned his back on Cilif. She said, "You shouldn't startle me, *s'e*. I thought you'd already figured that out."

He grinned at her, his momentary temper gone just that quickly. "I didn't think a simple cluck would set you into a fuss."

"It wasn't the noise. It was not knowing you were there until you made the noise." At the slyly amused look on his face, Lia made an exasperated noise. He'd known exactly what he was doing and how she would react. Aggravating. Then again, occasional baiting seemed little enough punishment for her kicking him in the balls.

"I notice that the storyteller isn't talking," Ganne said. He edged round to walk between her and the wagon. Dasin glanced over with a tired frown, his earlier cheer gone, but said nothing. Ganne went on, "I'm in the mood to tell tales, myself. Since the old man's gone quiet for once, might be you'd like to hear one of mine."

Toad made a sleepy, protesting sound, then shrugged and said, "It's too hot to talk."

Lia couldn't argue with that. Even the foliage along the trail, from tree to grasses, drooped miserably. She couldn't imagine going much further in this heat. Her light leather armor, designed to give her more freedom of movement than for actual protection from serious blows, felt like a block of heated plate metal, and her whole body was dripping with sweat. If Ganne's chatter could distract her from her own misery, she certainly wouldn't object.

"*S'e* Dasin? Any requests?" Ganne asked. Dasin shook his head, his face set in sour lines.

"Well enough, then," Ganne declared expansively. "So, then, a southern legend for you." His voice shifted to the same rhythmic, formal style as Toad employed when spinning stories; his spine straightened, his chin lifted, and his stride changed to a near-strut. "We tell these tales on the trail," he declaimed, and was off:

Atop a high mountain in the western desert, with ocean far below and water scarce to all sides, an owl and a snake nested together. The snake, being a creature of the low sands, was never warm enough; the owl, accustomed to moving through warm woodlands, was also unhappy about the cold winds. The story of how these creatures came to live so high in the mountains is best told another day.

The owl lined its nest with many feathers to keep its snake friend warm, and brought it food so it need not risk the chill. The snake did not like the feathers, nor the food, but it held its peace in order to stay with its friend. The owl did not like fighting the cold winds, and the hunting was poor so far from its woods, but it held its peace in order to stay with its friend.

The two animals spoke often and long, in between the owl's hunting forays. They talked of flight, and burrowing, they spoke of rending and crushing one's prey, each convinced their way was the best method. They spoke of their gods, and the story of that discussion is, once more, best saved for another time.

Ganne paused long enough that Lia glanced down to see him looking at her with sardonic amusement. "Perhaps we should discuss our gods, another time, ourselves," he said.

"Perhaps we shouldn't," she retorted.

Ganne flashed her a distinctly predatory grin, then resumed his narration.

Inevitably, they began to discuss their respective capabilities.

The owl loved soaring high, then diving, arrow fast, to pierce an unsuspecting creature with its talons. It loved lurking in trees, watching prey pass, studying their habits and vulnerabilities. It loved the feel of wind in its feathers, it loved the way its talons gripped a branch, it loved being able to twist its head in a glorious stretch and see things behind it without moving. It thought itself the best of all animals, for no other could perform such a feat.

The snake loved its ability to skim across the ground like a lightning strike; it loved driving its fangs into prey and engulfing the still-living body. It liked the period of sleep after a successful hunt, when dreams of its much larger ancestors spun past, teaching it wisdom and slyness, conveying its history, inspiring it to be greater in the future. It loved its ability to double back on itself, to coil and to twine, and it thought itself the best of all animals, for no other could perform such a feat.

Ganne paused to take a sip from his waterskin. He grinned, his gaze tracking Tank, too far ahead to hear; shifted to examine Dasin, who wore an odd expression and seemed overly intent on the road ahead. Lia began to suspect this story was about much more than two animals on a mountain. Southern symbology was a mystery to her, but this story had the ring of Ganne throwing out a challenge somehow.

"Please don't start a fight on the trail, *s'e*," she said dryly, looking down at Ganne. He grinned up at her with innocent-eyed cheer, then tucked his waterskin away and went on:

As the two animals spoke of their self-admiration, each one found itself longing for its own specialty. The owl wished to soar through dark forests on warm winds, with no care for a vulnerable companion; the snake wished to feel the hot sand beneath its body, to coil and strike as it wished, with no need to huddle trapped in a nest high on a mountain.

"We should not have come so high," said the owl one night, reflectively. "Hunting is poor here, and I miss the forests below."

"We should not have come so high," agreed the snake. "I have not stretched for too long, and I am forgetting the feel of the desert sands beneath my scales."

"I am forgetting how to move through the close air of the forest," sighed the owl. "I am tired of fighting the cold winds. I crave an entire night to do as I wish."

"I am forgetting how to navigate the dry and the sandy, the rocks and the small hidden streams," the snake said. "I crave an entire night to fly across the sand, as you do across the sky."

The two animals agreed that they should return to their homes, even though that meant they must separate. It was best for both of them, they told one another. The owl could not live as the snake did, and the snake could not live as the owl did, and only their far remove from all of their respective relatives had allowed the friendship to endure in the first place. At that time, you understand, there was no deep hostility between creatures of the air and the ground, merely a dislike. All understood that each creature acted only according to its nature, and sensibly held no grudges over one side killing the other in search of a meal.

The owl carefully gathered the snake into its talons and soared down the mountain currents to the treeline. "I must rest," it said then, and descended to the forest floor. "Let us build a nest here, together, and see if we might stay together after all, in this place."

Ganne paused for another drink, his expression turning thoughtful now. He didn't look at anyone this time, just strutted on for a few paces without speaking. He shook his waterskin, checking the level, then shrugged and put it away again.

"This is your place, not mine," said the snake, "but for the sake of our friendship, I will try to learn the ways of hunting in the forest. At least it is warm enough that I can move about now."

And so they built a new nest, deep in the dark woods, and for a time they were content. The snake became quite effective at hunting forest mice, and the owl was delighted with its surroundings; it preened and danced, and now and again brought back choice tidbits of animals too large for the snake to hunt. The snake found those larger animals distasteful, and it had been eating food it disliked for too long.

"I cannot eat this food," the snake said at last. "I prefer the food I catch myself. What you think are treats are more suited to your diet than mine."

The owl found that offensive. "So all the times I brought you food on the mountain, you never truly enjoyed it?" it asked. "Have you been lying to me all along?"

"I ate what you brought me in order to survive," the snake replied. "Had our positions been reversed, you would have done the same."

"But you never told me you were unhappy with my offerings," the owl pointed out. "You gave nothing but praise for my efforts. You lied, and friends do not lie. You have never truly been my friend."

"I came to the mountain to be with you," the snake argued. "I did not lie. There was no other food you could offer me, and refusing it would have caused you distress."

"You did lie," said the owl. "You were unhappy and you did not tell me so. I came to the mountain for you, and I fought cold, sharp winds every day to bring you things you told me you enjoyed. I gave of myself with honesty, while you were false in your acceptance. Friends should be honest about such things. Did you truly like my feathers, at least? Did you cherish the warm bed I made for you?"

The snake hesitated, but at last had to admit it had not. "Your feathers caught against my scales," it said. "They caught on my tongue. Any time I moved, the entire nest became disarranged and you fussed over putting it together again. I did not want to make you unhappy, so I stayed as still as I could. I was very unhappy."

Even as they spoke, the feathers in the owl's nest, high above the treeline, were flung aloft. They drifted long and far before finding a new place to settle.

"Oh, for fuck's sake," Dasin said. Lia looked at him, startled. Dasin's mouth was set in a sour line as he glared at Ganne. "Really?"

"It's only a tale about an owl and a snake," Ganne said lightly, his eyebrows going up in a thoroughly innocent expression. "What are you hearing, s'e?"

Dasin shook his head and turned back to the road, still visibly displeased. Ganne grinned up at Lia and went on.

The owl and the snake argued, each growing increasingly angry. At last, they agreed to part ways for good. The snake asked, as one last favor, that the owl return it to the sands of its true home, as it was too far a journey for the snake to make alone. The owl agreed, only because it now secretly feared that if the snake remained in its hunting grounds, then one night it might find the snake's sharp fangs sinking through its feathers in vengeance over their disagreement. The snake, in turn, was secretly worried that if it stayed in the owl's hunting grounds, that the owl would one day stoop upon the snake and carry it off as a meal.

In one last gesture of trust, the owl gathered up the snake and set out for the desert below.

They arrived without incident. The owl placed the snake on the sands. The two friends said their final goodbye.

The owl stepped back, turning, and spread its wings to fly. It stepped on a horse scorpion, the size of a rat, whose venom is more deadly than that of a micru. The owl, believing the snake had bitten it, lashed out with one taloned claw and its beak, killing its friend immediately. Poisoned, dying, the owl fell to the sand, crying out to its gods to save it. The horse scorpion ran away, since neither snake nor owl was its proper prey.

The gods of the owl, of course, made no answer to its dying plea, for gods never answer such things except in the most fantastic of fables, which this is not.

The tale of the snake and the owl spread amongst all of their relatives, carried by the horse scorpion itself, although it omitted its own part in the incident and claimed that the snake had indeed bitten the owl. From that day to this, owls and snakes have been bitter enemies, and horse scorpions have hidden away from the light of day, for fear of the lie being discovered and their own people exterminated as a result.

The trail hears this tale and finds it good, and so it is.

Ganne stopped walking, bent into a flourishing bow, and came up laughing. "There you are, then," he said in a normal voice, then drained his waterskin. "Damn, I'd forgotten how long that one ran."

"You're going to get yourself stabbed in your sleep one of these days," Dasin observed, glaring down at Ganne. "You're far too fond of your own cleverness, *Lord* Ganne."

"I envy your ability to get a rise out of your audience with an apparently simple tale," Toad said, leaning to look past Dasin's back and stretching to peer down at Ganne. "I have a few of my own that do the same. I admit to professional curiosity: would you explain, perhaps, *why* it got such a reaction?"

"Nope," Ganne said cheerfully. At the same time Dasin snapped, "*No.*"

Toad sat back, startled.

Lia cleared her throat loudly and said, "*S'e* Ganne. How about you go walk with Cilif for a time?"

"Excellent idea, but it's properly *Lord* Ganne. Do try to remember that," Ganne said amiably, and dropped back.

"Thank you," Dasin muttered. "Now, everyone *please* shut the fuck up for a while."

They went on in a silence as brooding as the humid air around them.

Chapter Seventeen

By the time they arrived at the campsite, the sky was turning gray from clouds as much as from the close of day; the horses were exhausted from the heat; and Dasin was in a towering snit.

Tank wasn't in the best of moods himself. He'd heard enough of Ganne's story, despite riding ahead of the wagon, to know how sharp a stick the desert lord had been prodding with. Ganne had the trick of making his voice carry exactly where he wanted it to go, and Tank had invoked a narrow clarity in his hearing, hoping for an extra second's warning of any trouble.

Darden Family claimed snakes as their family symbol. The teyanain claimed owls. Aerthaim Family used feathers. Often, now that Tank thought about it, owl feathers. He wasn't certain about the horse scorpion. It might have been been intended to represent Tehay, long since exterminated in a fight with Darden.

Tank wasn't an expert on southern history, and neither was Dasin, but from Dasin's furious reaction he'd likely picked up on much more than Tank had. Tank had caught quite enough: the clear inference that Darden and the teyanain had been close allies at one point in time, that treachery and deceit had separated them. Also clear was the implication that their split had somehow spawned Aerthraim Family, which couldn't be true.

Could it?

Tank brooded over it throughout the day's ride, and came to no sure answer other than that he'd have to ask Ganne directly to know one way or the other; and *damned* if he would give the bastard the satisfaction. Or believe him, whatever answer Ganne offered.

Tank ignored Dasin's sullen glare as he went about the business of sorting camp. Sin made a half-hearted attempt to bite him as he put the hobbles on. Entirely expected, easily dodged. He made sure to put the draft pony between Sin and the other horses, and warned Lia and Cilif about Sin's mood.

They weren't the only travelers this time. A battered passenger wagon and chunky draft mule took up one of the spots, and far too small a fire had already been started in the large pit. A soft-faced man and a leaner, broader-boned man sat near their wagon on camp stools, talking in low voices. They waved amiably as Dasin's wagon rolled in, and after that ignored the newcomers.

Before tending to anything else, Tank took a walk round to check the wall. Last time through, one section of stone had seemed loose. This time, it looked like someone had bashed into that part hard enough to crumble the old mortar and scatter the bricks. Most of them had been roughly restacked.

He poked the stone into a tighter configuration, hoping it would be enough. Other areas of the wall featured visibly decaying mortar, too many for his poor mending skills to manage. He would put in a report about it to Kiu of the Forester's Guild in Isata. He glanced at the lowering sky, gauging how long they had before the storm broke. Not long enough, and this was a bad campsite for a heavy rain.

"Risers?" Cilif asked as Tank brought his gaze down to survey the site.

"Yeah. Risers. Have Lia help. I want the tents up fast. And Ganne, go build that baby fire up to adulthood. Fucking amateurs." He didn't bother lowering his voice. The larger of the two travelers glanced over with a scowl.

Ganne shot Tank an affronted look and huffed, "That's *Lord*, you bloody pig-fucker."

Tank retorted, "Stack the fire for a hard rain, *Lord* Ganne, and never you mind what I fuck, cause it sure as shit's hot ain't gonna be you."

Cilif let out a peal of surprised laughter. Ganne cracked a reluctant smile.

Tank didn't give anyone time to answer. "We've a rain log in the wagon, in the under-seat compartment. Cilif, you and Lia set up the tents. Show her how to use the rain risers. Toad, I've work for you this time: go fill the kettle and soup pot with water. There's a pump over there." He pointed to a narrow path, flanked by the everpresent aenstone, that wound out of sight. "Be *careful* with it. If you break it, everyone's fucked until they get an engineer out here, which could be months."

"I do know how to work a pump," Toad said, prickling as sharply as Ganne.

"*Tank*." Dasin stepped in front of him, forcing Tank to focus on his set expression. "Cut it back before someone starts bleeding."

Tank drew in a harsh breath and shut his eyes, running an internal check: pressure where there shouldn't be, and he hadn't been paying nearly enough attention. *Fucking moondark.* He took another breath, adjusting his shields. His temper subsided like water draining from a sieve.

"Sorry," he said, aiming it generally. Then, in a consciously neutral tone: "Toad. Bring the pot lid to the pump with you in case it starts raining before you come back. I don't want leaf drip in the soup. I'll get the horses settled. Dasin. Please go talk to our new friends, smooth over Ganne reworking the fire." He indicated the other travelers.

"Smooth over your own stupid shittery, you mean," Dasin grumbled, then put on a charming smile and headed for the strangers.

Tank pinched his nose briefly, reminding himself that there were more important things to hand, then headed for the horses. He kept an eye on the camp as he worked. Ganne rebuilt the fire with steady competence around the rain log: a long, heavy chunk of stonewood soaked in volatile oils. Once properly lit, the fire would burn even in a heavy rain — at least for a while.

Lia fumbled with the risers as though her hands were greased. She was awkward enough that Cilif finally barked at her to "leave off, go help with the horses, I'll do it faster alone." She retreated, shoulders stiff, and circled round to stand near Tank.

Abruptly, he realized she was trying to keep as much of her back as possible to the strangers.

He caught her eye and pointed her to stand on Blackie's far side, out of sight; then, deliberately casual, worked his way round to stand beside her.

"You know these people," he said, carefully flat.

Her face, still lined and red from the combination of the ata and the day's muggy heat, twisted briefly. "I do. I trained with the mercenary. He's ... not a good person. He has a grudge against me, and I...." She paused, shaking her head, and seemed at a loss for how to explain further. The set of her mouth turned bitter.

"You have a grudge against him too, sounds like," Tank observed. "Who's the second one?"

Bitterness became, briefly, fear; then her expression went blank. "Goldrobe," she said unemotionally. "Stecatr priest, Elrin. He knows me too."

Tank shut his eyes briefly, resisting the urge to start swearing. Not good. Not good at all. He bent ostentatiously over Blackie's back hoof to buy time to think, and realized he'd done it to move into Dasin's line of sight at the same time he caught the merchant's thin-lipped stare.

"Damnit," he muttered. "Tell me about the mercenary first."

Her shoulders went back, her eyes going hard and cold. "Isrin Nahonna," she said. "The cousin of the three we scrapped with in Obein. We were in training together." There was a resonance to the last words that Tank didn't like.

Tank paused, setting Blackie's foot down, and gave Lia a sober stare. "He tried to rape you?"

She blinked, as though she hadn't expected him to guess that. She shook her head. "He didn't get that close. Not to me, at least." Now her eyes held the same murderous chill he'd seen in Obein, warning him not to ask after more details.

"Well, shit," Tank muttered. He glanced at the deceptively pretty foliage and the woods beyond, which held a darkening cast to match the cloudy sky, then straightened and looked over at the newcomers.

Isrin, larger than his cousins and with darker hair, was picking at his fingernails, radiating boredom. Tank read him as a spoiled rich kid with a sadistic side, wanting to prey on the vulnerable. He'd graduated Stecatr, like Lia, so Tank couldn't dismiss him as a fighter.

Elrin the priest was more of a problem, in Tank's judgment. He was built soft, but watched everything with sharply assessing eyes and an attitude of ingrained superiority over any dirty common folk.

"What authority does the priest have over you, here and now?" Tank asked, keeping his voice low.

"I don't know," Lia said. "Goldrobes never leave Stecatr. Never. Which means he's after something important." She wound her fingers into Blackie's mane. Her hands were shaking. "If that something is *me* ... because I sent word I was going to Bright Bay ... ? If he's carrying a mandate from Lord and *n'sion*, I have to do anything he says."

After years of sorting out travel times and routes, calculations came fast and easy. "Unlikely," Tank said. "He couldn't have gotten here that fast. He was already on the road before you hit the Hackerwood going south. He's not here for you."

He paused, looking over the main camp as Toad returned with the lidded pot of water. Toad set the pot out of Ganne's way, then turned, caught sight of the priest, and froze. The priest looked up, his face blank with surprise. Toad's stiff posture melted immediately into a hunched, defensive stance. He bowed to the priest, looking every bit the craven fool. The priest beckoned him over, surprise melting to scorn.

The speculative expression that crossed Dasin's face said he was picking up on the situation just fine.

Humidity shifted, thickening. Tank threw another glance at the looming storm. He said, "We don't have time for this right now. You're faster with horses than I am. Get them handled, fast. I'm going to help Cilif. Never mind anything those two say or do while you're moving around. No hiding. You got work to do, and it's not fighting. I'll handle any problems."

"This isn't your problem —"

"*My* crew," he cut in. "*My* job. Get moving. Remember what I said about strong emotions. Oh, and watch out for Sin. If he bites you, grab his ear down and bite him back."

Lia laughed at that, a sharp, strained sound. Tank went to help Cilif.

Cilif glanced up, pushing humidity-straggled hair back from his forehead. "Trouble? She about went to pieces when she got a look at them folks."

"Stecatr high priest, and the merc's Nahonna," Tank said. He motioned for Cilif to pass him a riser.

Cilif's eyebrows went up. He whistled quietly, but passed Tank the riser without comment. Tank wedged the plank in place on the riser base, tapped the joining edge down, and began stringing net.

The rain risers were, as far as Tank would tell, entirely unique to his crew. They were a combination of Aerthraim engineering, Dasin's ingenuity, and a few pragmatic suggestions from Cilif. Four thick, specially milled stonewood blocks, the most expensive part of the entire setup, sat on the ground. Precisely joined boards slotted together as support and sidebar, and then a tightly strung net topped by a layer of padding made matters considerably more comfortable. They had two tents custom-designed to fit atop the risers, although most tents would do in a pinch.

Getting the entire setup compact enough to fit into the wagon, let alone two sets, had been the second most expensive part of the construction. Dasin had redesigned the wagon's undercarriage for the extra weight and storage, and they'd replaced their mule with a large draft pony.

They'd all practiced setting up in dry conditions repeatedly until there was no hesitation, and could now set it up and break it down in poor weather with minimal troubles.

Tank cast an assessing look at the churning sky. "Maybe an hour before it breaks, at most," he said. "Oh, damnit."

"What?"

"The numbers are off. I don't think Toad has his own tent. And if Ganne has one, there's no riser for it."

Along the Coast Road, they'd stayed at inns. The previous two nights, they'd all laid bedrolls out around the fire. Tank could blame missing this particular detail on the strain of maneuevering around Dasin, or being rattled over Ganne's presence, or a number of other excuses; but at the end of the day, it had been his damn job to be sure this situation didn't come up, and he'd failed.

Cilif ran a quick count on his fingers. "Two sets of risers, six people. Wagon?"

"No room. Dasin added a new clothes chest this run."

"Vain bastard."

Tank lifted a shoulder wearily.

"I've *said* we should have an extra set of risers to hand," Cilif observed.

"So have I. But that takes time and money we haven't had to spare. And we've never taken passengers before, nor a woman from Stecatr with *issues*." Cilif snorted laughter at that. Tank pinched his nose, considering. "Three high spots here. The priest has one, the other's too far from us and too close to him, but one's in our area." He pointed. "Set Lia's tent up there for Ganne and Toad. You share with Dasin. I'll stay with Lia."

Cilif gave Tank a level stare, amusement gone.

"I know," Tank said. "But I'll sort it. Trust me."

"Best do, and fast," Cilif said dourly. "Here comes Dasin. I'm off for a piss." He turned away and headed for the latrines.

Dasin nearly radiated acid as he approached. "This is one *fuck* of a coincidence," he said when he was close enough to speak quietly. "We don't run into this many people from Stecatr in a year, and there's four of them all together, just *now*? What the hells have you landed us in this time?"

Tank shook his head and made a dismissive gesture. "There are more important matters right now. Bad storm coming, six people, two risers. Someone camps on a high spot and someone shares with Lia, no way around that."

Dasin's gaze flicked rapidly over the two raised tents. Cilif returned from the latrines and began setting up Lia's tent where Tank had indicated. "I see it," Dasin said, his tone indicating a comprehensive understanding. "What do you have in mind?"

Gods be blessed, he wasn't arguing. This might go easier than Tank had expected. "Toad and Ganne can take the high spot. You stay in with Cilif. I'll take our tent, it's the largest."

Dasin's eyes narrowed dangerously. "Like that, is it?"

Abruptly exasperated, Tank pushed forward to stand close up against Dasin, forcing the merchant to look up at him. He tucked his fingers into the waist of Dasin's pants and allowed years of frustration to surface as he said, "Like *this*, isn't it?"

They stared at one another for a long moment, Dasin's expression wavering between amusement and irritation. At last, he returned the gesture, his knuckles cold through Tank's thin shirt. "So much for caution," Dasin muttered.

"I've got my limits," Tank said, not quite able to leach the frustration from his voice yet. "I'm tired of you being jealous over nothing, Dasin. If I've got to take a risk, I'd rather it be with you, not against you." He raised his free hand and ran it through Dasin's hair once, then stepped back, letting Dasin go. His temper faded, leaving a painful, scraped-thin feeling in its wake.

Dasin's expression cracked to something terrifyingly vulnerable, then returned to hard lines. He said, low and sharp, "If you fuck her, I'll tear your balls off with my bare hands."

"If you fuck Cilif, I'll do the same to you," Tank said equably.

Dasin let out a startled bark of laughter. "Ta-karne," he said, the word almost fond.

"Go rescue Toad before that priest eats him," Tank said. He raised his gaze, meeting Elrin the priest's owl-eyed stare; tilted his head mockingly, then turned his back and went to help Cilif with the last tent.

Chapter Eighteen

The dim light faded to a threatening murk just as everyone retreated into their various shelters. Ganne, swathed in a rain cloak, stayed out to tend the fire and keep watch, saying, "Rain doesn't bother me, and I can stay up for a while before I need a relief."

Thankfully, Elrin had stayed occupied with whatever he had to say to Toad, and Isrin remained sullenly uninterested in anything beyond his own nose. He'd never liked a full day's work, and he was probably exasperated at having nothing but water and tea to drink. Goldrobes were notoriously strict about abstaining from intoxicants of any sort.

As far as Lia could tell, neither of them had seen her clearly enough to recognize her yet. She prayed fervently that Toad kept his mouth shut. Also that he didn't damage her tent out of spite. She was severely unhappy about giving up her tent, but Tank had been unbending, and Dasin had backed him.

Tank's tent had high, banked sides of sturdy oilcloth over oiled leather. It smelled of horse and smoke and dirt, with an undertone of something almost but not quite like cloves. The combination wasn't unpleasant, and the padding made it positively luxurious.

Lia let out a heartfelt groan as she settled down, pushing her pack to one side to make room for her bedroll. Her arms and hands were trembling. It had been a *long* time since she'd handled four horses in a row, and while the other three had been docile with weariness, Sin had been a *beast*. She'd dodged two lazy attempts to nip, gotten her foot out of the way of a deliberately shifted hoof once, and failed entirely to dodge a sharp sideways swing of the horse's big bony head. That last might have been an accident; she'd moved closer just as he turned, and she'd been out of his proper vision for a moment. Accident or not, she'd have a bruise along her face in the morning.

"Yeah," Tank said in response to Lia's pleased noise. "This is the best tent, with the best mat. Dasin likes the extra padding." He grinned, unashamed.

Lia had seen the moment of shocking intimacy between the two men earlier; had caught Elrin's stare; had understood, the moment Tank announced the sleeping arrangement, that the entire display had been deliberate. Sleeping in a tent with an ostentatiously *ii'ne* man was marginally better, once Elrin realized who she was, than the alternative scenario. Tank had been protecting her again.

How did I ever think I could walk this line? It's impossible.

Caught between resentment and gratitude, Lia busied herself with setting up her bedroll to avoid talking to the big redhead sitting just out of reach. At least it was absolutely clear that Tank wasn't being kind out of personal interest. She was part of his crew, and he took care of his crew. Once they parted ways he'd have no hold over her for past courtesies. It was a relief.

At the same time, it was yet another unsettling strangeness that nobody in Stecatr would believe or understand. The goldrobe outside certainly wouldn't, nor Isrin.

She looked up at a faint noise and found Tank watching her with a bemused expression. "You look like something bit you in the betwixt," he said. The thick red scruff of his developing beard made him look more northern than usual, which provoked an unexpected pang of homesickness.

"Thinking," she said briefly, and fussed with her bedroll some more.

A pattering of rain began, quickly strengthening to a drumming, then to an outright roar as the sky opened up overhead. She sat back on her heels, staring up in astonishment. The sturdy tent walls shuddered under the onslaught.

Tank laughed and stretched out. "Now you see why we put up the risers," he said. "This camp is low ground."

"Are there going to be tornadoes?" Lia asked, anxiety rising sharply.

"No, not here." Tank shut his eyes. "Take a nap. Rain will break in an hour or two, before full dark. We'll be able to make a hot dinner. And deal with that priest."

Her stomach turned. She almost said *Do I have to?*

"Yes, you have to," he said without opening his eyes. At her hissing intake of breath, he glanced over. "I'm not reading your mind. It's an obvious thought." He propped himself up on one elbow and seemed about to say something else. Then he shrugged the shoulder he wasn't leaning on and stretched out again, shutting his eyes.

Lia unsteadily laced her hands together and took refuge in prayer. *Wae, keep your kindly face towards us as you bless this place with your bounty. Eki, be gentle with your vulnerable servants; Syrta, show your love and keep the waters moving away from us.*

She didn't offer a prayer to Payti. Drawing Payti's unpredictable attention risked bringing down lightning, and a fire in this situation was absolutely not what anyone needed.

Please, she added, troubled by what she was asking even as she asked it, *keep your sworn servant in good temper with myself and my companions. Let me get through this situation without harm to anyone at all, or at the least, let me be the only one to take the harm, if harm must come.*

A few more phrases begging for her family's safety, then some generous praises of how wondrous were the gods, in case they *were* actually listening, seemed comprehensive enough for now. Finished at last, she checked Tank's position and breathing, reassured herself that he was at least lightly asleep, then settled down herself, closed her eyes, and listened to the rain until it faded into dream.

Chapter Nineteen

The rain stopped before dark. Tank woke to the sound of Lia's thready snoring. He grinned up at the tent ceiling, pleased that she'd relaxed so deeply given the circumstances. He hadn't even had to push at her. That indicated that she trusted him enough to be vulnerable, and hopefully meant she'd stop being so damn prickly. There was no room for that on this small and tight of a crew.

The air smelled of damp earth, horse, wet canvas, and Lia. She hadn't bathed any more recently than the rest of them, making do with a damp cloth and one of the vials of diluted ravann oil that Dasin had apparently handed out at the southern edge camp. Tank hadn't gotten one, the only rebuke Dasin had offered over his abrupt departure and late return that night.

Perfumes and oils often took on different notes on different skin. Dasin's skin turned most oils sharp and somehow hot-smelling; on Lia, the ravann oil mellowed, losing the spicy undertone and turning more floral. He inhaled the calming scent, settling himself for the confrontation waiting outside the tent, then sat up.

Lia's snore broke instantly. She went up on one elbow, but at least she didn't grab her dagger. After a quick glance at him, she cocked her head at the unmoving tent walls, her face tightening.

"In your own time," Tank said, and rolled forward to squat-walk to the entrance flaps. "Not too long, mind." He grabbed up a thick rain cloth and went out without looking back.

There was enough sunlight left for a clear survey of the site. He saw no obvious problems. The horses and draft, while definitely unhappy about being outdoors in the storm, hadn't tried to escape or attack one another. No limbs had come down across the wall, although Tank saw a few freshly snapped pieces hanging on the far side, thankfully well clear. Water had pooled where he'd expected, and was draining where he'd expected.

The tents were untouched by the limited flooding. He'd have to check the wagon for leaks, as always, but it hadn't been visibly damaged. Better than he'd hoped for, overall.

He turned his attention to the group around the fire, which Ganne was working to relight. Dasin wasn't in evidence; neither was Toad. Cowardice or wisdom? It didn't really matter. Best to have them both out of the mix. Cilif sat with his back to Tank, watching Ganne, which only left the two Stecatr problems to study.

Elrin was a soft, broad-faced man with shoulder-length auburn hair, which was currently flattened into straggling tangles along his face and neck. He looked like a half-drowned rat, and only the carefully stitched bancti along the hem of his long-sleeved tunic pointed to his allegiances.

His hire, Isrin, had cropped dark hair that stood up in damp spikes, leaving the man's broad features clear. A sullen sneer spoiled what should have been a handsome face, and his clothes, while of a fine cut that had no doubt seemed dashing on departure, were splotchy from badly cleaned off muck. Either Stecatr Hall of Arms didn't teach their students how to clean their own clothes, or this sulky scion hadn't been interested in learning such a domestic skill.

They sat on a dark oilcloth, talking in low voices and watching Ganne suspiciously as the desert lord worked to build the fire back up from the carefully banked and covered coals.

Tank checked the fold of the rain cloth, then set it onto a soaking wet bench that put everyone, including his group's tents, into at least his peripheral vision.

Ganne glanced over his shoulder at him. "Got another rain log?" he asked, sounding harassed. "This damn quickwood doesn't want to catch."

"Just the one," Tank said, sitting down. "Storage and money don't allow for more'n that." He checked at hearing his old, coarse accent emerge. This wasn't the time to act like a street rat, or to talk like one.

Ganne grunted irritably, then stood. "Be right back," he said, and went into his tent.

Lia emerged and sat down beside Tank, entirely unarmed and unmasked. She'd tied her hair back into a neat tail, and wiped her face clean; her expression and her emotions alike were studiously blank. Tank allowed himself a tiny sigh of relief that she hadn't come out aggressively angry or afraid.

Isrin lifted his head, beginning to sneer. Then he looked at Lia's face, and his own froze in astonishment. "Lia!" he blurted. The priest looked up much more sharply, his eyes narrowing.

Lia's jaw set tight. "*S'e* Isrin," she said with perfect chill. "*S'iope* Elrin. Gods bless and hold you at this unexpected meeting."

Ganne came back from his tent, carrying a small pouch and a pair of leather gloves. Tank held back a wince; what Ganne was about to do would have the priest screaming *witchcraft*. No way out of it. That fire had to get built back up before full night descended.

Isrin reached back to scratch his shoulderblade as he looked Lia over. His mouth moved into a vicious smirk. "Oh, this is interesting," he remarked. "Very interesting." His gaze tracked across Tank, Cilif, and Ganne, then flicked meaningfully to the tents. "Five men, is it? That's a record, even for you."

Lia's hands formed into fists on her lap. She said nothing at all, her gaze unwaveringly on the priest, as though Isrin didn't even exist. Ganne put on the leather gloves, opening the bag with care, and took out a generous pinch of a chunky, ashy-blue powder. Extending his arm while leaning back a bit, he tossed the powder onto the reluctantly smoldering coals.

Nothing happened for a moment; then, abruptly, blue-green flames shot a foot high. Ganne pulled his hand back, keeping it well away from his body and the pouch in his other hand well away from the flames. Elrin scrambled to his feet, eyes wide in horrified fury, hands moving in fervent warding gestures.

"*Witchery*," he spat, as Tank had expected.

"Alchemy," Ganne said, not looking away from the fire.

The blue-green faded to a more ordinary orange. The rain log caught once more, just that easily, and the fire roared back to life. Ganne retreated to a bench and set the bag down, stripped off the gloves, put them down next to the bag, and let out a long breath.

"Better'n usual," he remarked to Tank. "I've lost eyebrows twice so far, doing that."

He tied the bag tightly shut, then took it and the gloves back to his tent. It seemed unlikely, at this point, that Toad was still asleep, which meant he was more interested in avoiding the priest than in a hot meal. Tank didn't entirely blame him.

Elrin stayed upright, his lips almost invisible, emanating righteous disapproval. "This is *unacceptable*," he announced. "Lia, I'm declaring your contract invalid. You are to come with me."

"No," Tank said pleasantly, before Lia could speak. "You haven't that authority, *s'e*." He stressed the generic honorific, letting the priest know the lack of title was entirely intentional. Elrin's plump face flushed.

"I most certainly do," Elrin retorted. "Her oath is to Hall *and* Church, and I represent the Church in this matter."

"I'll have to hear the word of Hall *and* Church before I release her from a legal contract," Tank said, mimicking Elrin's haughty delivery. "I've my own duty here, *s'e*." He hammered on the lesser honorific once more. "I'm trail lead, and I've sworn my own oaths. Unless Lia wants to break her contract with us, she's not going anywhere." He felt as much as saw her flinch, but there had never been any way to avoid that part.

Isrin's smirk turned even more vicious. "You're certainly attached to her," he said, tone entirely unsubtle.

"Oh, gods," Cilif muttered, putting a hand over his eyes. "Here we go again."

Ganne reappeared, moving to stand behind Tank's right shoulder. "One moment," he said, and his voice held both boredom and a dangerous underlying vibration. "Allow me to introduce myself properly. I am Lord Ganne Darden. In case you don't know what it means that I'm this far north of my beloved home, I'll spell it out. I have diplomatic immunity for *anything* I do between now and my arrival in Isata, granted from the king himself." He paused to take in their startled expressions. "I'll also tell you that when I offer my word to speak only truth, it is fatally dangerous to doubt me. This young woman has behaved with exemplary correctness every moment of every day. She is no whore, and no witch, and neither are the rest of us. Well." He smiled, his teeth on full, predatory display. "Except for me. I can't deny that charge."

Cilif let out a muffled snort of laughter. Lia sat still as a statue, barely breathing, her face bone-white. Tank eyed the desert lord thoughtfully, wondering if the priest or the Nahonna had picked up on the fact that Ganne hadn't, actually, given his word to speak honestly. He also suspected, considering Ganne's connection to Yuer, that the assertion of immunity was complete fiction.

"She's still breaking her oath," Elrin said through his teeth. Isrin scratched at his shoulder again, grimacing. "Will you stop that already!" the priest flared at him. Isrin took his hand away, grumbling.

"Maybe she is," Ganne said, supremely unconcerned. "I invite you to look at the odds here, *s'e*. Do you really want to face off with a witch over something so minor?" The vibration in his voice broadened. Elrin's eyes took on a hazy cast. Isrin sat still, expression blank; apparently he'd caught the full blast. Smart of Ganne to take the fighter out first.

"The odds ... yes, I do see, but...." Elrin blinked hard.

"She'll be returning to Stecatr, after all," Ganne said, tone still indifferent even as that non-vocal hum deepened. "I'm quite sure your fellow *s'iopes* will manage her evaluation just fine."

"True," Elrin said vaguely. "Very true. Well...."

Isrin grunted and scratched at his shoulder again, twisting to reach further back. Lia's face was a picture of horror as she looked from Elrin to Ganne. Stark fear began to rise in a prickly cloud around her.

"*Calm*," Tank told her, sliding the word more into her subconscious than her ears. She slouched immediately, taut muscles releasing, terror smoothing to placidity. Ganne caught Tank's eye and winked appreciatively.

A flicker of movement caught Tank's eye: a shifting beyond the campsite wall, a flash of red and gold where color shouldn't have been. Sin snorted loudly, one front hoof hitting the ground in a hard, scraping motion. Blackie moved uneasily. Rooster went on dozing, as did the draft pony and Elrin's chunky mule.

Isrin grunted again, sounding pained this time. He rose to his feet, twisting and stretching to dig at his shoulder.

Ganne looked abruptly alarmed. Cilif rose, watching Isrin with wary anxiety.

Isrin swayed on his feet, breathing heavily. His face turned splotchy, veins standing out. A moment later, he let out an unhinged, sobbing shriek and ripped his shirt off, wadding it up and frantically slapping his back with it. As though it would help him reach the spot better, he began to stumble a wide circle, clawing at his shoulder and whining in agony.

Dasin tumbled from his tent, hair and clothes disarrayed. His wide-eyed stare sought out Tank first, then focused on Isrin.

As Isrin turned again, Tank saw an ugly, oozing lump on his back.

Tank swore and sprinted for the wagon. "Ganne!" he hollered over his shoulder as he slapped open the latches on the side panel and shoved the shelf supports into place. "He's been bit. Take him down, hold him down! Cilif, help Ganne! Dasin, keep that fucking priest out of the way!"

He dropped the hinged panel onto the supports and began pawing through the supplies for his surgery kit. Bags had slid, as they tended to do, and he hadn't needed the damn thing in a while. He only kept himself from flinging supplies out of the way into the mud because he'd be the one to pick them up and clean them off if he did.

Isrin stumbled and went to one knee, yelling something incoherent. Elrin's voice rose, belatedly, demanding to know what was going on. Dasin said something — all Tank caught was the acidic tone — just as Tank's fingers finally closed around the long, thin box he'd been looking for. He yanked it out, made himself take the time to latch the shelf securely back into place, then turned to survey the situation.

Cilif and Ganne had Isrin pinned to the ground, face down, by the simple expedient of sitting on him. Lia had retreated to stand well clear, and Dasin was beside the priest, ready to haul him out of the way if necessary. So far, Elrin was just staring at his mercenary in astounded horror, making no effort to hover over him.

Tank squatted beside Isrin, examining the suppurating mass. "Spider bite gone bad," he said. "Isrin, how long ago were you bit?"

Isrin didn't answer. He lay still, head turned aside, breathing hard, his gaze glassy. Beads of sweat dripped down his face.

"Had to be within the last three days," Cilif said. "That's a Hackerwood bite. Better hurry, Tank, or he's gone. It'll burst soon."

"*Gone?*" Elrin exclaimed. "As in dead? From a *spider bite?*"

"From a Hackerwood spider bite," Tank corrected. "Dasin, I need —"

"Here." Dasin handed him a small metal flask and his shirt. "I'll go get the full bottle and bandages."

"*Witchery,*" Elrin muttered, backing away.

"Shut up, priest," Cilif snapped. "None of us need your whining just now. Go sit the fuck down."

Tank draped the shirt over his shoulder and pulled the stopper from the flask. A bitter vapor etched along his nostrils, chasing away the rotten aroma of pain-sweat wafting from Isrin. "Hold him good. He's going to thrash." He poured a careful dribble of liquor around the bite, washing and wiping away as much surrounding dirt as he could. Isrin stirred. "Hold him," Tank repeated, then poured liquor directly onto the bite.

Isrin bellowed, bucking. Ganne nearly went sprawling in spite of Tank's warning; Cilif threw himself forward, hauling Ganne upright before he went into the mud. Elrin retreated, his face ashen. Lia moved in, adding her weight to Isrin's legs.

Tank opened his kit, then hesitated. He didn't want to set it in the mud but had no stool or stand ready to use. Dasin's hand reached over his shoulder, taking the open box and holding it steady to one side.

"Bottle's beside you," Dasin said. "Try not to use it all."

Tank grunted thanks, his attention on his kit now. The equipment was relatively crude, compared to the Aerthraim ketarch tools he'd learned on, but the knives were still sharp and thin enough to get the job done. He picked out the knife with the shortest blade and leaned in close.

Cilif grimaced and looked away as Tank set the knife to skin at a slant. He drew it round the bite as quickly as precision allowed. Red blossomed, streaking across Isrin's back. The man thrashed again, with less success this time. Two fast, shallow slashes in an X over the bite, and the red mixed with oozing gray-brown, yellowing pus.

Isrin screamed, a high, warbling sound like a dying rabbit. Lia went rigid, her eyes huge in a face abruptly bereft of all color. *"Don't you fucking faint,"* Cilif hissed at her.

Isrin began to pant, sucking in and spitting out mud. Cilif stripped off his own shirt, then reached down and hauled Isrin's head up out of the mud, tucking the shirt beneath.

Ganne ostentatiously eyed Cilif's cleanly muscled torso. Cilif, noticing, said, "Oh hells no, there ain't *nothing* here for you." Ganne laughed, although it sounded forced.

Tank picked up the large bottle of liquor and poured it into the wound, careful to keep the muddy bottom of the bottle angled clear. The liquor washed away the erupting rot long enough for him to spot the tiny, irregularly-shaped black egg embedded into the flesh. Isrin tried to scream again, but his voice cracked and crumbled into a shredded moan.

"Dasin, give me the larger curve."

"Tricky," Dasin said, trading clean knife for bloody. "Looks close on the muscle."

"I know. Ganne, take this shirt, soak a big patch down with the roosh. Don't use it all, I'll need more in a moment."

"That's not roosh," Dasin said, aggrieved.

"Shut up." Tank drew a steadying breath, studying the spot with a critical eye, then set knife to flesh again. He flexed his wrist, sharply scooping the blade as though he were carving a grapefruit from its skin, then flipped the resulting bloody gob into the fire with perfect accuracy.

A vile smoke rose. Sin let out a heavy, furious snort of protest, his head low and ears flat; Blackie and Rooster were little better, and even the draft pony shifted uneasily. Isrin gagged, ropy drool soaking the shirt beneath his face.

"Damnit, I liked that shirt," Cilif muttered.

"Bottle," Tank said, holding out his hand. He poured again, dispersing the swelling tide of red washing across Isrin's back: managed a clear glimpse at the wound and let out a breath of relief. "Got it on the first cut. Thank the gods. Ganne, the shirt."

He worked the liquor-wet shirt into a small ball and pressed it into the wound, holding it there with one hand. Isrin writhed briefly, then went limp.

"I *didn't* like that shirt, fortunately," Dasin said. "Not as much as I like that *very expensive liquor* you just poured all over the fucking mud."

Tank ignored him. "He's fainted. Cilif, hold this in place."

"Aw, hells no," Cilif protested. "Have Lia do it. I need to get upwind before I lose my stomach."

"Go settle the horses, then. Lia." She moved to kneel beside him. "Hold this in place. Keep the pressure on. Thank you."

He sat back on his heels, rolling his shoulders, then handed the second bloodied knife up to Dasin, who handed back an already threaded needle. Tank motioned Lia to move her hands aside, then made short, if graceless, work of stitching up the wound.

He sat back on his knees and looked up at Elrin. "I got the egg out," he said, "so he'll be —"

"The what?" Elrin said, his face wrinkling. He began washing his hands together, blinking rapidly. "*Egg?*"

"Hackerwood insects are nasty," Tank said. He looked down at his gore-covered hands. "I have to wash. Lia, keep an eye on Isrin, keep him from rolling around if he wakes up. Cilif." He raised his voice to carry. "Once you get done settling those beasts, get some hot water and clean Isrin up, take over from Lia. Use the good thick bandages and padding. Ganne, stand watch and handle anything that comes up."

"*Egg?*" Elrin said again. He scratched at the side of his neck uneasily.

Tank began to reassure the nervous priest. Hackerwood spider bites weren't in any way subtle. Isrin must have been in severe pain for at least two days.

He glanced at Lia, reconsidering, and left the priest to squirm.

On a normal run, that might have been the end of it. If the wall had been entirely solid, that might have been enough. But once more, something moved beyond the aenstone. The air went thick and strange, staggering Tank into a few breaths of hazy paralysis.

A wicked smile spread across Cilif's face. He called out, "Yeah, eggs. You know, I seen a man once as didn't get it cut out in time. The egg, see, when it hatches, there's *hundreds* of babies as come swarming out, digging into anything close as what's alive, too fast to stop, you can barely even see the little fuckers — hey, weren't *you* scratching at sommat?"

Elrin's distress twisted into panic.

Tank shook himself out of the daze and said, too late: "Cilif, *stop.*"

Elrin gagged, then, abandoning all dignity, bolted for the edge of the campground.

"Ooops," Cilif said, his expression wavering between malice and real chagrin.

Elrin leaned on the low wall with both hands and vomited into the brush beyond, collapsing across the stone as he retched.

"Cilif, bring him back," Tank ordered sharply.

"Yeah, yeah," Cilif muttered, but moved to drag the priest away from the wall. He pulled Elrin clear just as branches began to move in the area.

Elrin staggered back from Cilif's hand. He began to scream and claw at his face. "Spiders! On my face! *Spiders all over —*" he babbled.

Cilif smacked the man's hands from his face. "Nothing there, priest. Stop it."

"Spiiiiiiiiiderrrrrrrs," Elrin wailed, and threw himself to the ground, rolling wildly.

"Gag him," Tank ordered, watching the shadowed underbrush bend in a steady, stalking trail around the campsite. Sin began to stomp a back hoof, over and over, his ears flat. Blackie and Rooster were moments from beginning to fight their hobbles. The draft pony shifted worriedly. Elrin's mule had its own head down, ears back.

Ganne, a few steps away, tracked the movement in the brush, his expression grim and one hand extended as though warding — or warning — off whatever was pushing at them all.

"Gag him with *what*?" Cilif demanded. "You want me to take my pants off, too?"

Dasin let out a nervous bray of laughter. Tank shot him an evil glare. Before he could answer, Elrin leapt to his feet, screamed once more, and in two extraordinary bounds was at, then over, the low wall.

Sin bugled and tried to rear. Blackie gave a frustrated hop, while Rooster tried to go backwards and nearly tripped himself. The draft pony and the mule whinnied unhappily.

Holding nothing back on the push, Tank aimed at the horses and demanded: "*Quiet.*"

Someone behind him gagged briefly. It might have been Ganne. Then everyone, beast and human, went silent, listening — to nothing. No sounds of crashing through thick forest growth. No screams, no panting. No birds, no crickets, no wind: only a dark, dense, satisfied stillness.

"He's gone," Tank said at last, grimly. He lifted a hand to rub at his eyes; caught himself in time to avoid smearing blood across his face. "Hells. That was too damn noisy." He surveyed the perimeter again. "And now it's too quiet. Ganne. Do you feel anything?"

Ganne stared at him for a moment, his face gray as it had been after escorting Lia all day. "Do I — you insane ta-karne, you fucking *whited me out!*"

Tank bent his head and pinched his nose hard. He'd overset a desert lord? Dear gods. That was very, very bad.

"Didn't mean to," he said.

Ganne huffed incredulously.

Tank rolled a shoulder in a half-shrug, half-apology. "Shut up, everyone. Let me listen."

It was becoming increasingly easy to drop into other-vision, to direct exactly which senses sharpened and by how much. Tank's fantasy of an ordinary life was fracturing further by the day, and the conversation with Dasin that he'd been avoiding for so long was probably imminent.

He shut his eyes and tilted his head, listening intently: *Satiation. Amusement.* Even as he picked that out, the presence faded into dark emptiness. He listened for another few breaths, than sighed and opened his eyes.

"Nothing," he said. "Everything's gone completely quiet. I think whatever was out there is happy with what it got."

Lia made a small, horrified noise, drawing into herself. She seemed to not know where to look. Whenever her gaze fell on Tank or Ganne, she visibly flinched. Cilif caught her eye and said, quiet but definite, "Stop that." Lia shut her eyes and put her head on her drawn-up knees.

Night crickets began to chirr contentedly. Somewhere distant, an owl hooted.

Ganne looked towards that last sound, his features drawing into a scowl.

"It's just an owl," Cilif said, tone shaky but mocking.

"It's never just a fucking owl," Ganne said, not taking his gaze from the dark woods. "Tank, go clean up. Dasin, go with him, make sure he doesn't fall over. I'll keep watch, I'm doing better now. Cilif, you take over watching this *seshii-ta-karne*. Lia, take a slug of whatever liquor is left in that bottle and go back to bed. You and Cilif can wash up in the morning." His stance and voice made it clear that any protests would end in bloodshed.

Tank rose to his feet, staggering a little as his knees protested. "I'll second all of that," he said, then headed for the pump, Dasin close behind.

Chapter Twenty

The priest who'd tormented Isla, who'd all but put her neck in the noose himself, was almost certainly dead. Under the terms of her oath, Lia should have rescued him from the Hackerwood, should have set her own safety aside to protect that of a senior priest of the Stecatr Church. She hadn't even tried.

She didn't feel at all remorseful. That was a terrible sign. Payti's wicked face was turned towards her. *Aspna, aspna pay'nianth, aspna*: the prayer felt thin and false. She let the attempt fade into silence.

Staring at the dimly visible tent ceiling, Lia found herself hoping that the spider bite might make Isrin lose his mind and hurdle the wall as well.

I'm losing my faith. Tank's right. I never should have gone past the Hackerwood.

Noise began to accumulate. Low-voiced conversations, footsteps, the crunching and shuffling of the fire being woken up once more. "Porridge," someone said in tones of resignation. Dasin's voice answered, indistinct. The scent of cinnamon and apples wafted into the tent. Someone applauded.

She had to leave the tent eventually. Might as well do it while there was hot food to be had.

Lia sat up, glancing over at Tank's sleeping mat. It held the same creases as when she'd gotten up for dinner the night before. He hadn't come back, then. She wasn't surprised, but it was odd that nobody had woken her to stand watch.

She finger-combed her hair into reasonable order and left the tent, yawning. The dawn sky was blessedly clear of clouds, and a faint breeze drifted through the camp as though apologizing for last night's fury. Tank and Dasin sat side by side on one of the plank benches, bowls in hand, showing no interest in anything but the food. Cilif stood looking out into the trees, apparently deep in thought, bowl held absently in one hand.

Toad, as usual, was nowhere in sight, and Ganne, once more intent on poking at the fire, barely glanced up as Lia sat down nearby.

Isrin, bedraggled and bandaged, still shirtless, sat down on a bench across the fire moments later. His pants were stiff with dried mud, his hair would have suited a shia-banse, and he winced with every movement. It took some time for his bleary expression to focus on anything in particular; when it did, his gaze locked onto the bowl of porridge in Cilif's hand.

The pot sat at the edge of the fire, three more bowls and wooden spoons waiting on another bench. Lia hesitated, then rose and quietly filled two bowls. Chunks of dried fruit and smaller bits of nuts dotted the thick oatmeal, and a warm draft of cinnamon filled the air above the pot.

Rounding the fire, voluntarily approaching Isrin, took every bit of willpower she had. She made herself put the bowl and spoon down on the bench beside him instead of flinging it into his face, then retreated to her own seat, not looking at him once the whole time.

She was almost done with her own porridge when Tank finally stirred and stood up.

"Isrin," he said. "That's a one way walk your priest took. What are you going to do now?"

Isrin raised his head. "I don't know," he said hoarsely, setting his empty bowl aside. His hand moved as though to scratch his shoulder; he winced and lowered it. "Nobody would believe me."

"Of course they would," Lia said, unable to help a certain amount of venom coming out. "They'll believe that you were witched into abandoning your sworn duty. That you allowed a senior priest to die because you fell prey to temptation."

Her own self-accusations, aimed outward, hit square; Isrin flinched. Lia looked at his miserable expression and felt no pity at all.

Tank said, "I strongly suggest you forget you ever saw us. Take the mule and wagon, go south. Disappear in Bright Bay, start over. Catch up with your craftsman cousins."

Isrin jerked, eyes widening. He glanced at Lia.

"We ran into them in Obein," she told him, then couldn't stop herself from asking: "Why are they so far south, anyway? Why are *you?*"

Isrin began to answer, then rubbed a hand roughly over his face as though waking himself up. He looked around, his habitual sneer making a faint but distinct reappearance, and said, "I'm Nahonna. I don't answer to any of you lot. I'll do as I please, and *say* what I please." He smirked at Lia, then stood and ostentatiously turned his back on them, heading for his tent.

Ganne said something in dialect that sounded a lot like the equivalent of *for fuck's sake,* and took a step towards Isrin. Lia stood, reflexively reaching for a dagger she hadn't belted on, then stopped, stunned, as Tank simply — *appeared* in front of Ganne. He'd easily been ten feet away a moment before.

Ganne went back a step, eyes narrow. He and Tank glared at each other until Ganne shrugged and backed up two more steps. "Your walk," he said. "Your mistake."

"Mine to make," Tank agreed. He made a sweeping gesture, gathering everyone's attention. "Get ready for the road. Get Toad moving, break everything down. Lia, with me."

He led her around the side of Dasin's wagon, out of everyone's sight. She could almost feel Isrin's smug grin following her.

Tank folded his arms, looking down at her. His freckled face was deadly serious. "I won't take this fight away from you," he said. "Not this time. What do you want to happen here, Lia? He's a vicious little shit, and you've seen him weak. He walks away, there's trouble ahead."

She stared at him, her vision wavering from blurry to dry even though she felt nothing at all: her emotions seemed to be missing entirely at the moment. At last she said, "You'd let me kill him?"

Tank's face went expressionless. "Yes."

"Because I don't like him?" Her heart thudded in her ears, useless prayer echoing in time to the beats: *Payti, payti, aspna, aspna....*

"No," Tank said. "*I* don't like him. *You* hate him. Question is, do you hate him enough to kill him, right here and now? I'll hold his arms while you slit his throat, and help you wash out the blood after."

Her vision blurred, her throat going too tight to speak. Emotions were dark shadows through a thick, warped piece of glass. She didn't want them. Didn't need them. Tank was being icy cold. She had to match that. She didn't want him to perceive her as hysterical.

Isrin deserved to be run through the worst of the hells five times over, but only the gods could order that. Cold blooded murder was too easy on Isrin, and too dangerous for Lia, given Payti's looming, laughing presence.

She had to trust the gods to deal out the proper punishment for Isrin's actions. She *had* to.

Lia managed a single word: "No."

Tank didn't say anything for a while, as if giving her time to change her mind. Eventually, he said, without any particular inflection, "Let's get ready for the road, then."

Emotions seeped back, bit by bit, as the miles went by and scenes from the previous night ran through her head alongside more self-reproaches. *Elrin is dead. Is it my fault? Those creatures that sense emotions, did they hear that I wished him ill? Did they come for him because of me? If I hadn't been present, would he have died? And how in all the hells do I face the Church now that I've let one of their goldrobes die without raising a hand?*

Guilt and shame itched along her spine, closely followed by growing anxiety over the future. She felt as though she were looking out over the edge of a infinitely high cliff with a beater of a wind hitting her back.

The drumming of hooves announced a rider ahead. Lia moved to the wall side of the wagon. Rooster had been twitchy all morning, and she knew her own reflexes weren't what they ought to be. Ahead, Tank did the same.

Ganne eyed Rooster warily, then angled round to walk opposite. Dark circles hung under his eyes, as though he hadn't slept well the night before. Toad, on the other hand, displayed a cheerful exuberance, although he did cast too-frequent glances Lia's way as she drew level.

A finely proportioned plainsbred with a coal-dark coat came into view, moving fast. Its rider wore blue and gold: News Rider colors. They swept by without so much as a wave.

"Goodness," Toad said, turning to watch the News Rider disappearing into the distance. "What could be so important, I wonder?"

Dasin shook his head, his expression grim. "If we're lucky," he said, "we'll never find out."

Lia swapped sides with Ganne again, resisting the urge to make fun of him for being so uneasy around Rooster. He shot her a dark stare as he went by, as though he'd heard the impulse going through her head; which started her worrying again about her part in Elrin's death.

Tank looked back, frowning, then waved her forward to ride beside him. Once she drew level, he said, without preamble, "Last night wasn't your fault, and you didn't draw anything that wasn't already watching. Isrin was a damn fool for not speaking up about that bite as soon as it happened, and Elrin was a worse fool for any number of reasons. Moondark fucks up everyone's judgment. Stop brooding. Cork it until you get to Isata, then go get as drunk and weepy as you like." His tone was definite but not unkind. "Wasn't. Your. Fault."

She let out a long breath, feeling her shoulders relax as anxiety eased. "Thank you," she said. Then, before good sense could stop her, she blurted, "Would you *really* have let me kill Isrin in cold blood?"

His face went grim. "No. If you'd said yes to killing him in that situation, I'd have fired you on the spot. But I'd still have gotten you to Isata before I cut you loose."

Rooster tossed his head and gave an odd stuttering skip. Lia patted his neck absently, thinking that answer over. "Good. I'd have quit on the spot if you'd answered any other way." She offered Tank a wan smile. "But I'd have stayed through Isata before leaving the crew."

Tank let out a short, unamused laugh.

Lia hesitated, measuring options, then said, "I have a lot of questions at this point, s'e. And I'm beginning to think that answers might be more important than worrying over what the Church will say." She was almost certainly going to have her Hall coin broken at this point, so it didn't really matter how deep she dropped, but she didn't say that part aloud.

Tank rubbed the knuckles of one hand against lengthening stubble, frowning at nothing in particular. Eventually, he said, "Maybe so. Not here, though. We'll talk in Isata."

A gigantic black beetle wobbled through the air on oversized, diaphanous wings, barely a handspan from Lia's nose. She leaned back and sideways. Rooster gave that odd little skip again, then abruptly surged into an uneven turn. She tucked in close against his neck, clinging tight as Rooster pranced out his displeasure.

As Rooster turned into range, Tank leaned over and slapped him on the nose, hard. "Knock it off, asshole!" he snapped.

Rooster set his feet and stopped moving altogether, head low and ears flat. Lia tugged on the reins gently to confirm that he'd taken the bit between his teeth. "Damnit," she said, and shot Tank a hard glare.

Dasin pulled the wagon to a halt, shouting at them in a dialect Lia didn't know. It sounded uncomplimentary at best. Tank made an exasperated sound and waved at Dasin to wait.

Tank said, "He did this to Gint a couple times. You'll have to get down and walk him for a while, he won't move otherwise."

Lia straightened in the saddle. Rooster stayed in the same stubbornly irritated posture. She sighed and dismounted, extra careful to make sure nothing snagged along the way. She had a feeling that Rooster would simply bolt, whether she was entirely on the ground or not.

"You shouldn't have hit him," she told Tank as she pulled her sword and belt free of their loops along Rooster's body. The horse stood unmoving as she buckled the sword into place around her waist, but his ears were beginning to come back up. She lifted the reins over Rooster's head. "He didn't deserve that."

"Only thing that gets his attention when he's being a fucking mule's ass," Tank said.

Lia slanted a disapproving look at him, then clicked her tongue. Rooster raised his head with serene majesty, ears up, and regarded her patiently. "You still overreacted," she said, looking up at Tank; then, deliberately harsh: "Moondark fucking up *your* judgment, maybe?"

He glowered at her. "Take rear," he said, and motioned at Cilif to come forward and at Dasin to start the wagon moving again.

As they settled back into motion, Ganne dropped back to walk beside her. Keeping an eye on Rooster, he said, "Pushing at Tank's temper, now, are you? Interesting choice. Aren't you afraid of him? Of his 'witchcraft'?" He grinned sardonically. "I know you saw that jump of his. You about fainted, didn't you?"

She looked at him sideways and didn't answer.

"You northerns and your gods," Ganne went on, cheerfully ignoring her silence. "Endlessly suspicious over perfectly ordinary matters, declaring that anything you don't understand is against what your gods want. Letting your priests tell you how to live." He clicked his tongue disapprovingly.

Lia bit the inside of her cheek, admonishing herself not to react.

"Southerners, now, we're pretty much agnostic," Ganne said, scratching at his chin. He'd shaved recently, and the beginning stubble looked like smudges of dirt against his skin. "We admit that gods exist, but they're mainly ceremonial."

Lia frowned darkly at him. "How do your priests allow that?"

Ganne waved a hand airily. "No priests for us. We have dedicated god servants, called

Callen. Heh. Bloody Kaenic. 'Called Callen'. Anyway. Remember that healer at the Edge camp? Kwri? He's *comosain*, Callen of Comos. They're supposed to be neutral. Can't say I believe that. Every Callen I've met has been neck deep in one plot or another." He glanced sideways at her. "Are your priests any better than that?"

Lia considered that for a few steps, turning over possible responses, and finally decided to keep silent.

Ganne grinned briefly, as though he'd read her brief struggle like a page in a book. Then his expression turned pensive. "I should really start learning more about your northern gods, instead of making fun. I know the basics, but it doesn't make any sense to me. You have eight gods?"

"Four," Lia said. "Each with a dual nature."

"Syrta, Payti, Wae, and ... what's the other one?"

She shouldn't be talking about this to a southern heretic. She ought to direct him to a priest, in part to ensure that his heresy didn't drag her from the proper path, and in part because the Church declared that laypeople simply couldn't be trusted to provide accurate answers.

There were too many miles of road left to antagonize him, though, and she was already straying far from the proper path. Answering his questions didn't matter all that much.

"Eki," Lia said. Reflexively, she lowered her voice, glancing over her left shoulder. Ganne made a stifled sound of amusement.

"That's like tossing salt over your shoulder, is it?" he inquired. "You can't even name your gods without some little protective twitch? Really?"

Lia's temper rose. She said, coldly, "I don't want to talk about this any further, *s'e*."

"*Lord*," the man said, humor instantly replaced by an ominously brittle tone. "Lord Ganne. I will have that honor from you, *s'a*; I've bloody well earned it."

Lia set her back teeth together for a count of five, then said, deliberately flat, "I don't want to talk about this any further, Lord Ganne."

"Well, I want to hear about it," Ganne said, instantly cheerful once more. "If you like, I'll pay you to talk to me. Or you can look at it as an attempt to convert a southern heretic witch lord." He flashed her a wide, insouciant grin that froze, a heartbeat later, as he turned to stare at the brush to their left.

A sharp crackling erupted, the bushes past the wall beginning to whip about as though caught in a high wind. Rats swarmed across the wall: *enormous* rats, their humped backs nearly to Lia's knee. Rooster reared, squealing. Lia dodged as the big horse kicked out, losing hold of the reins as he spun. She yanked out sword and dagger as two of the big rats came at her.

They had brown fur mottled with unlikely moss-green, although that might have been debris from their charge through the brush. Their long teeth and black eyes both seemed too large for the streamlined skulls, and their paws were tipped with short, sharp red claws. They hissed and chittered as they ran towards her. The closest one leapt into the air, aiming right at her chest.

She brought the sword round, slicing into its neck hard enough to knock it away in a spray of blood; twisted the blade back around to meet the second rat's charge, her wrists protesting the maneuver. The creature swerved, angling away before she could hit it.

Somewhere far away, Tank yelled something — a name, a command, maybe a curse. Her hearing was distorting, her vision narrowing: she spun, searching for that second rat.

Ganne had a wickedly curved dagger in each hand, slashing at three rats circling him. Rooster screamed again, kicking the rat Lia had been looking for. The rat went flying. Unfortunately, it flew right into Ganne, who went sprawling with a startled yell. The nearest rats pounced immediately.

Lia's sword took one across the hindquarters. It screeched and tumbled clear, turning to flee across the road. Another swing went wide but still took off an ear: that rat turned to leap at her, teeth bared. Before she quite knew what she was doing, she bared her own teeth and screamed at it, days of frustration and fear erupting out into the sound.

To her surprise, the rat staggered back, ears flat. It stared at her with terror-glazed eyes, then spun and fled across the wall. The third rat, its eyes just as frantic, scrambled clear before Lia could even raise her sword, disappearing over the wall and into the brush with the others. More rats poured out of the woods a moment later, but these seemed uninterested in anything but crossing the road.

What the hells did I just do? She stared after the swarming rodents, too shocked to move. Then Cilif was there, hoisting Ganne to his feet and shoving him into a stumbling run towards the wagon. Lia could hear the draft pony squealing and Dasin cursing.

"Get up against the wagon," Cilif shouted to Lia. "Get your back to something!"

"Everyone, get clear!" Tank bellowed. He was standing in the stirrups, watching the flow of rodents. Sin was nearly dancing under him, snorting hard and clearly wanting to charge forward into the fight. "Back, *back*, damnit, let 'em by, they're not attacking —"

"Hells they're not," Cilif muttered, half-supporting Ganne as the two men leaned hard against the wagon. Lia noted, distantly, that the draft pony had stopped squealing.

"They're running," Dasin said. He stood on the bench, gripping the top of the wagon for balance. Lia had never seen his face so pale. "Gods — *Tank* —"

"Dasin, shut up and hood up the draft!" Tank snapped.

"I just did!"

"Good! Shut up! Everyone be quiet! Let 'em run. Stay close to the wagon. Watch the wall!"

Lia looked round for Rooster. The rangy gelding was still wildly stomping and kicking at the fleeing rodents, sheer hatred in every movement. The ferocity astonished her: most horses would have fled, not attacked.

Cilif had, at some point, hitched Blackie to the wagon. The horse stomped the ground, flat-eared and taking occasional nips at the tether.

The last of the rodents leapt across the wall on the far side of the road, leaving churned, blood-splattered dirt in their wake. Rooster turned and turned, head snaking low, searching for more opponents. Lia didn't even bother trying to grab the reins. Rooster was so wound up he'd deliver a real bite without intending to. Blackie began to savage his tether in earnest.

With no warning at all, a long-legged creature stepped casually over the wall, stalking into the middle of the road some ten feet behind Lia. Easily eight feet tall, it looked like a stork with hard, metallic feathers, a misshapen beak, frothing white crest and demonic red eyes.

Rooster shrieked and backed up. Tank's horse bugled a clear challenge, fighting Tank for the bit. Blackie yanked hard: the tether stretched, strained, then snapped.

The monster spread elegantly crenellated wings, leathery arms emerging from the folds. Filthy black talons unfolded as skeletal fingers flexed. It opened its wide, white beak, revealing tiny ridged teeth, and screamed, eyes fixed on the horses.

Blackie staggered sideways and almost went down. He caught his balance just as Cilif grabbed his bridle and hauled him closer to the wagon. Distantly, Lia realized Ganne was on his knees, vomiting.

The bird turned its elongated, tightly feathered head in a slow arc, its flat red eyes regarding the humans with regal indifference. It paused, its attention fixing on Tank this time, and let out a low churkling sound. Spreading its wings again, it flexed three-fingered hands as it paced forward, ignoring everyone but Tank.

Unbelievably, Tank hadn't drawn his sword yet. He wasn't even looking at the bird, but at the ground in front of the wagon.

Lia tossed her sword to one side, then shifted her hold on the dagger and dropped into a fast tumble that brought her up behind the creature. Every creature had vulnerable points. She just needed to find the right spot —

There. From a crouch, she lunged upwards, thrusting her long dagger into the space where the stork-like leg met the armored body.

The scream this time was a shattering sound that knocked Lia back as though struck by a exceptionally large hammer. She managed to roll to her feet and face the creature, dagger still in hand.

The creature hissed at her, an entirely un-avian sound, as it balanced awkwardly on one leg. Lia had far too clear a look at those impossible teeth and far too intense a waft of the worst breath she'd ever faced. She staggered back a step, gagging; then, yielding to a sudden impulse, shrieked back at it as she'd done with the rats. It emerged much more thinly than before, and a stinging, acrid taste flooded her mouth.

The bird-demon-*thing* hopped backwards, eyes slitting into an evil glare. It spun, heaved itself over the wall, and vanished into the thick undergrowth. Dark blood formed an uneven, snaky trail across the road in its wake.

A thundering wave of nausea walloped Lia a moment later, a lightning headache blurring her vision. Every single one of her muscles simply stopped cooperating.

The world around her went wavy, then gray, then, finally and solidly, black.

Chapter Twenty-one

Tank relaxed his grip on Sin's reins and drew in a deep breath as he looked around. Dasin was unconscious on the ground, drool leaking from the corner of his mouth. The draft pony stood calmly, turning its hooded head back and forth in slow, blind sweeps. The thick panic hood, another invention of Dasin's, featured heavy padding around the ears and was stuffed with calming herbs. It had never been tested quite this severely.

Cilif and Ganne were down, toppled across one another in a tangle of limbs. Ganne's clothes were ragged and drenched with blood. Cilif was less torn up, but his clothes, dark with blood, were well past saving. Blackie stood over them, tail swishing and ears half-back, watching the woods intently. Rooster stood near Lia, not as ferocious a guardian but unwilling to go far from her all the same.

Sin shifted, snorting, and pawed the ground again. Tank let him pace in a full circle, bleeding off the last of their shared rage as the horse slowly calmed.

Toad crawled out from beneath the wagon, his hair and clothes rumpled and filthy from his dive for cover. He looked around, wide-eyed. "What ... what was all that?"

That, Tank didn't say, *was something that shouldn't ever have happened in broad daylight, even on a moondark run. That was me damn near overset, and a desert lord completely overset. That, right there, was Trouble, and worst of all, we're out of diomersha candles.*

Instead, he said, nonchalantly, "Welcome to the Hackerwood." He dismounted, looping the reins over the saddle hook, and patted Sin's neck. "Stay put," he told the horse. Sin flicked his ears and regarded him with regal indifference.

"On my way south there was nothing like that," Toad said, shaky but stubborn.

"You got lucky, then," Tank told him. "And this time you got unlucky. Come over here and hold Sin's bridle strap so he doesn't bolt." Sin was far too well trained for that, but it would give the man something to do besides fret.

Toad shot a decidedly unhappy glance up at Sin's big frame, then looked at the sprawled figures. After a moment of visible hesitation, he said, "I'm more use helping the wounded. I'm ... I'm an apothecary."

Tank narrowed his eyes, irritation climbing. "Got a kit in your bag?"

"A limited one, but yes." Toad avoided Tank's gaze.

"Why the fuck didn't you tell us you had that training up front?" Tank demanded.

Toad clicked his tongue a few times, one cheek puffing out, then said, reluctantly, "Because I'm not allowed to practice it any longer. *S'e* Tank, we haven't time right now."

"True enough. Look at me. Meet my eyes. Tell me how competent you actually are." Tank caught the man's gaze, dropping a push into the last words to force honesty.

"I'm very good," Toad said without embarrassment.

"All right." Tank dropped the compulsion. Toad blinked rapidly, shuddering, then put out a hand defensively and backed up a step.

"Don't," Toad whined. "I don't deserve witching!"

Tank bit the inside of his cheek to stop himself from apologizing. He said, harshly, "Start with Dasin —" Toad began to protest, pointing at Ganne. Tank overrode him. "Do this my way, damnit! Dasin first. Ganne second. Lia third, Cilif last. *Don't* touch the bloodbird's blood." He paused, struck by how ridiculous that phrase sounded, then went on. "Don't touch any cast feathers. Blood and wounds from the rats are safe enough. Tell me if you need more supplies: roosh, needles, what have you. We've got plenty. Get working. I'll sort out the horses."

Toad retrieved his bag from beneath the seat of the wagon. With a last, wary glance at Tank, he crouched beside Dasin's limp form.

Tank drew in a long breath and whistled loudly: *tweeeeee-tweee-twoooo*. Sin's ears twitched, and he snorted irritably, his ears flicking. Rooster and Blackie looked round at Tank, recognizing the signal; hesitated, then slowly picked their way over to him, angling to stand so they could see their riders. He pulled treats from Sin's saddlebag, talking to the horses in a low, soothing voice, repeating praise and reassurances until their twitchy tension eased.

Toad finished checking Dasin over, waved smelling salts under his nose, and helped him sit up. The draft made an unhappy noise. Its tail lifted, and Dasin rose as though propelled by a spring, stumbling clear of the wagon to vomit just shy of the wall.

Tank didn't laugh. He had no humor within reach at the moment. Focusing on gentle, deliberate movements, he began checking the horses for wounds. Rooster's legs were liberally splashed with rat blood. That wasn't a problem, it could be washed off tonight, but he also bore several bites and cuts. Tank patted him reassuringly, marking the spots in his mind, and moved on to examining Blackie as Toad knelt beside Ganne.

"*Tank*," a familiar voice said. That particular collection of hell condensed into human speech — the voice of the only human-inclined elder ha'ra'ha he'd ever met — was one Tank would never forget.

It also wasn't *speech*, as such, arriving somewhere south of Tank's left ear and inside his head at the same time. If it had been literal speech, Tank would likely have whipped to his feet and taken off running in whatever direction he happened to be facing at the time.

Tank splayed both hands on Blackie's warm shoulder and focused on keeping utterly still so as not to spook all three horses. "No," he said aloud. "Don't you *fucking* tell me you're involved in this debacle, Deiq."

Not the wisest greeting, but he honestly couldn't help himself. Tank had cherished fond hopes of never hearing that smoky, cynical tone again.

I'm still at Peysimun Fortress. A faint echo ghosted erratically through his words, but amusement came through clearly. *Alyea says hello. She misses you.*

Tank sucked in a sharp breath, terror and fury fighting for dominance. The horses shifted uneasily, responding to his tension. He caught control of himself with grim ferocity and said, "Return the greeting, if you would. What do you *want, ha'inn?*"

There's trouble ahead.

"You sure it's not *behind?*" Tank muttered savagely.

Ahead. A sense of strain grew in the words, echoes multiplying: *You have to ... needs to know. Alyea wanted me to warn ... someth ... changed in ... Hackerw ... wall isn't ... I can't see —*

Deiq's voice faded, sputtered, and stopped.

Tank stared blankly at Blackie's stirrup for a while, idly working bits of dirt from the metal grooves. At last he said aloud, "Well ... shit."

Chapter Twenty-two

The bird-creature loomed above Lia, an impossible, metallic construction. She stabbed, aiming for the weak spot where leg met body. The bird dodged out of the way. She sprawled forward, off balance, rolling to get to her feet. An enormous glittering head thrust against her, knocking her to her back. It opened its beak, displaying disproportionately large, serrated teeth.

Lia began to suspect this was a dream. The creature couldn't possibly close its beak if its teeth were that large. Fear froze her in place regardless, death a handspan from her throat.

Someone shouted. The bird spun, letting out a horrible, piercing scream. It charged at Tank, its wings spread wide enough to block out the sky and the sun and the trees and the universe.

Darkness eclipsed everything.

Darkness resolved into a narrow Stecatr alley and a goldrobe priest.

Lia was on her feet, shivering; angry, terrified, but not sure why. The priest's face was hazy. She didn't try to bring it into focus. Didn't want to see ... the name escaped her ... didn't want to see that face again, even in a dream.

He's dead. He's dead. This is a dream.

The priest remained in front of her. She looked at his hands instead of his face. They were surprisingly wide and callused: a farmer's hands, a worker's hands, not at all suitable for one of the soft elite of the Church.

They weren't a priest's hands. They were her mother's hands.

"Lia, I worry about you," Lia's mother said. "You should have stayed back and let that creature kill Tank. They already had their eye on him. You could have come home safely if you'd just followed the rules. Now you have their attention. What happens to your sister if you get yourself killed in someone else's fight?"

Lia's sister Kia perched on the low roadside wall, her pale hair tucked under a paler head scarf, a pad of paper in her lap, industriously sketching away. "You promised to bring me paints," she said *without looking up. "I can't paint the blood unless you bring me a proper southern red. Why aren't you home yet?"*

Kia lifted the paper and turned it around, displaying a strong, harsh sketch of the bird, its eyes bright green and slitted like a snake's, its mouth open, a long snake tongue hanging out. It looked sad, rather than deadly.

"That's not what it looks like," Lia said. "It's a monster."

"I don't have the right paint," Kia answered. "And you're not here to tell me how it looked. Why aren't you home yet?" Her lip quivered in a pre-crying pout.

"I'm on my way. I promise."

"You can't come home," their mother said. "You made your choice. You left. You went too far, you've gone beyond the rules. You're lost to us. All you can do now is try not to be lost to yourself."

The demon bird appeared behind Kia, its beak dripping with blood. It let out a high-pitched caw that sounded remarkably like "Lost! Lost!"

It drove its savagely pointed beak into Kia's neck —

Lia awoke with a stifled scream. She jerked up onto her knees, panting harshly, one hand over her mouth. Her stomach roiled as visions of splashing, gouting blood ran through her mind. It felt as though the dream were reluctant to let her go: a dragging weight pulled at her to lay back down, to slide back into the arms of that horror, to watch her sister die.

She slapped herself, hard. The ringing shock and pain chased away the thick overlay.

"Holy *fuck*," she whispered as her breathing and pulse finally began to slow. She'd never had a dream that specific, that vivid, that terrifyingly bizarre.

Real memory filled in around the dream sequence. She *had* stabbed the bird, its blood spurting thick and oily along her arms. She'd fainted, and woken to find Toad wiping her face with something that smelled like alcohol. She'd snatched the bottle and cloth away from him. Tank had stepped in, directing Toad to go check Cilif over.

"Strip," he'd said, dropping her pack at her feet. "Get anything cloth off, toss it into the woods far as you can pitch it without going near the walls. Forget modesty. Nobody's looking. Wipe every bit of that blood off you and your armor. We have spare clothes if you need any. Any cloth with the bloodbird's blood on it gets pitched. Toss the ata. If you don't have another one, too bad. Pour some of the roosh over your hands and hair when that's done, and run a comb through, too." His expression was grimly uncompromising.

There hadn't been much conversation as the group pulled itself raggedly together and trundled onward once more. Tank rode in a constant, looping circle around the wagon, alert and ferocious. Sin, reacting to his rider's mood as much as to recent events, snapped at Rooster and Blackie several times in passing, and twice there was nearly a fight.

At first Toad walked, having ceded his space on the wagon bench to Ganne. As Ganne drooped more and more miserably, Dasin pushed an increasingly rapid pace. Toad finally came up beside Lia and touched her leg lightly to get her attention, his expression pleading as he looked up at her.

Cilif was nearly as shaky as Ganne, and Tank was far too tense to take on a passenger. The old man's hand had been hot and dry in hers as he scrambled up. Thankfully, he'd had the sense to keep entirely silent, except for a small squeak when Lia wheeled Rooster sharply away to avoid a fight with Sin.

The day's ride had been an eternity of terror and tension and steadily growing aches. After setting up camp, Tank, that ferocious expression still in place, had pointed Lia and Ganne to their tents. She'd gone without argument. Someone else would take care of Rooster, and his tack, and everything else. She only had to go to sleep.

Which she'd done.

Now she knelt, shaking from the intersection of nightmare and memory, watching shadows dance against the tent wall. Someone had built the fire up high and bright. Tank and Dasin were talking in low voices. She stared at the tent flap, her hands fisted tight in her lap.

You have any dreams, you see anything odd, you tell me — me, not nobody else, right off, Tank had said.

She didn't want to share the dream with him. She didn't want to talk about watching her sister murdered. But more than that, she didn't want to go back to sleep right now. Another nightmare might break her completely.

Lia tugged her clothes straight and pushed the tent flap open, looking out cautiously. Toad was a dark lump to one side, quietly snoring. Dasin and Tank sat on a log by the fire, facing one another. Firelight caught highlights from Dasin's pale hair and skin, and lit Tank's hair and beard into a mat of glowing threads. Dasin, leaning forward with his hands on the log, was radiating a nearly tangible anger. Tank looked stubborn, his hands splayed on his knees.

They both looked sideways at her. Dasin's lips actually peeled back into a silent snarl. Tank waved her forward.

"She's already awake," Tank pointed out as Dasin glared at him. "From that scream, I'm guessing she had a nightmare." He put up a hand as Dasin's glare intensified. "*Ha'vash, ha'ne,* Dasin!"

Lia, remembering how Ganne's nightmare had gone, didn't blame Dasin one bit for his reaction. She settled on a different chunk of log, putting Tank between her and Dasin, and studied the fire as though it were the only thing of interest in the area.

All around the camp, tree frogs and black crickets cheeped and chirped, their songs sawing across one another in mild cacophony. Smoldering ash flaked along the edges of the blazing logs, puffing into tiny explosions from time to time as sap or other moisture popped.

"You just want an interruption," Dasin snapped. "So go *take care of her,* then!"

Lia bit her tongue and forced herself to let Tank answer that. Something more was going on here than surface jealousy, and Dasin was very obviously spoiling for a fight.

Tank glanced at Lia. He said, "No. She's awake, she's reasonably calm, she can wait." He rolled a shoulder, then folded his arms. "Keep going with how pissed off you are at me. I don't much care what anyone hears at this point."

The words had the sound of a long-delayed line being drawn. Dasin's knife-sharp glare confirmed that impression. His voice held a familiar, just-before-violence resonance as he said, "Fine. I will. She ought to know you're a lying sack of shit anyway."

An owl drifted by, its mournful call momentarily bringing everyone's gazes up to search the overhead shadows. When it faded away, Tank said, "I didn't lie, Dasin. It wasn't safe for you to know —"

Lia let out a snort, unable to help herself. Both men looked at her. "Why does that sound like such a familiar line?" she said. It came out more defensively than she'd intended.

Dasin smirked meanly. "Yes, he does like to play the protector, doesn't he?"

Lia dropped her gaze back to the fire, wishing she hadn't spoken.

"It's not that simple," Tank objected. "If he's right and there's trouble ahead, it'll focus on me."

Lia wondered who *he* was, in this instance. Ganne, probably. Movement to one side caught her eye: a blacksnake slid lazily along the wall, dipping and curving in its silent hunt. It rippled down to the forest side and disappeared.

Furious color surged into Dasin's face. "Of course it will. You're always the center of everything, aren't you? Well, you're not the center of anything for me, not anymore. You're fired. Pack your shit and go over the fucking wall again if you want. Go deal with whatever this is by yourself. I don't want to ever see you again. Leave the horse, you don't deserve it anyway."

Lia froze, doing her best to be not worth noticing. Tank turned his head sharply to frown at her, then let out a hard breath. He said, "Dasin, be reasonable. I need to get the crew safe out of the Hackerwood."

"I don't care what you think you need. I'm not listening to you any more."

The crickets and frogs paused, leaving a dangerous, rolling silence. Lia sat up straighter, worried for an entirely different reason now; then they began again, and she let out a quiet breath of relief. Tank and Dasin seemed too caught up in their argument to have noticed.

"Dasin, we're on a moondark," Tank tried again, tone falling into a wearily patient cadence. "You're not thinking clearly. Wait until we get to Isata before you —"

"*No.* I've been wanting to ditch you for a while now. This is as good a time as any. You're — you're just holding me back." Dasin's face set into stark, chill lines.

Tank's expression went oddly shadowed, as though that had hurt more than anything else Dasin had said.

Lia shut her eyes, tucking into herself, listening to her breathing; channeling fear into a crystalline awareness of internal ticks and clicks. Her heartbeat. Her pulse. The popping in her left ear. The clicking of her toes as she flexed them.

The owl sounded off again, farther away.

She wondered what it would be like if Dasin and her father ever faced off in a mutual rage. Probably not much would survive that encounter. Priana had warned her: *Dasin's got a temper, and a mean, dark streak. Don't cross him, or the redhead.* Apparently Priana had known exactly what she was talking about.

What had Tank done to rouse such ire in Dasin, when everyone should be too exhausted and sore to have any emotions at all? Probably best not to ask. Probably best not to know.

Keep your head down, get through it, move on. That incantation had gotten her through training at the Hall of Arms. It would work here, too.

Lia heard Tank stand. A vibrant, dark anger filled the air briefly, then dimmed. "All right," Tank said, scarcely audible. "I still think you're being overset. But if that's what you want, fine. Get me my pay, and come morning I'm out of your life."

Dasin didn't say anything. Tank moved away, going to the wagon. Lia sat very still, not at all sure whether a hasty retreat to her tent would be seen as a weakness. She was deeply shaken by the anger still washing through the air. It felt entirely too much like the brewing storm of her father's rages, on nights when things got broken and people got hurt. Back before he'd stopped drinking. Back before she'd made the mistake of going to Scarpy for help.

"Lia," Dasin said. She opened her eyes to find a petty meanness in his expression. "You're fired too. I don't need you. Tank's the one hired you; he's gone, you're gone. Come morning, clear your gear and go. Leave Rooster, he's mine."

Lia sucked in a sharp, gut-punched breath.

Dasin flicked a hand at her in dismissal, then stood up and strode to his tent, his back rigid.

Lia looked up at Tank, who'd paused in rummaging through supplies to watch Dasin storm off. The big redhead pinched the bridge of his nose, then took his hand away quickly, expression going even more sour.

"Damned habits," he muttered. "Stop me when I do that, would you?" He paused, sourness turning to ruefulness. He cleared his throat and tried again: "Sorry you got caught up in that. Come morning, he might calm down and at least realize you'll have to be walking alongside until Isata, and that Cilif can't handle two extra horses alone. There's no damn sense in his head right now. Don't leave without making him pay you, though."

"What are you going to —" She stopped short as the nighttime chorus from the forest fell silent. Tank lifted his head and squinted out into the darkness.

Dasin emerged from his tent with three small leather bags, a large flask, and a pipe. He hurled one bag at Tank, who caught it with a lunge and a snort of annoyance. Dasin tossed the second bag, underhand, to Lia.

"Your pay," he said, then went, pointedly, into Cilif's tent.

The frogs and crickets restarted.

Tank muttered something under his breath, then shook his head and closed up the wagon, leaving everything inside. "Godsdamned moondark," he said, then came and sat on a nearby log, straddling it to face her. "Tell me about your dream."

"What, *now*?"

"Dasin's going to smoke aesa and drink mountain lightning and bitch to Cilif until he passes out. Toad's out cold. So's Ganne." He motioned to another lump at the edge of the firelight that Lia hadn't noticed. Apparently Ganne had decided to sleep in the air as well. "There's no rush for either of us. And your dream might be important. So yeah. Now."

"Why would my dream be important?"

"Just tell me." His face had taken on stark angles, and a smoldering anger lurked in his blue eyes.

Not wanting him to explode at her, she told him about the dream. He listened, expressionless and intent. When she finished, he put up a hand to signal silence, then scratched his chin for a while, frowning in thought.

"'You've got their attention'," he repeated. "Are you *sure* about that wording?"

"Yes." The black snake reappeared, looping gently over the wall and descending into the camp, where it idled along, a darkness among shadow, for some distance before lifting back up and over.

Tank's voice dropped to a low mutter, scarcely audible: "And Ganne's in no shape to take over. *Damnit.*"

The smell of aesa drifted through the air, faint but distinctive, along with the murmur of men's voices. Dasin's bitter tones predominated. Tank's mouth drew thin.

The hair on the back of Lia's neck prickled as the night creatures went quiet yet again. *Perfectly normal, an ordinary predator moving around, that's all.*

She said, defensively, "It was just a dream."

Tank gave her a rueful sideways glance. "Not on a moondark run it's not." He nodded to the still-quiet night, frowning, then relaxed as the noises resumed.

They fell silent, both staring at the fire, brooding over their separate thoughts.

"Why did Dasin fire you? Us?" Lia said eventually, deciding she deserved to know that much.

"I had a warning from an old acquaintance about trouble ahead," Tank said, not looking at her. "I felt I should tell Dasin about the warning, but that meant telling him about the old acquaintance."

Lia frowned, looking around the campsite.

"The person in question is several hundred miles south of here," Tank said. His mouth quirked into a half-smile. "Which meant I had to explain some other things I haven't wanted to talk to Dasin about. He got understandably upset."

The prickling along the back of Lia's neck turned painful. "Wait. You spoke to someone hundreds of miles away? Just … just now?"

"A few hours ago," Tank said. "But yes." He rubbed the back of his neck. "You needn't look at me like that. You're not some ordinary mercenary, yourself. There's the way you fight. The way you know how to fade out of being noticed. And then there's the question of why you were completely deaf to that bloodbird's attack when it sent the horses sideways, dropped Dasin and Cilif flat on their asses, foxed me, and overset a fucking *desert lord*." His expression was granite-hard now, his hands tense on his thighs.

"I don't understand anything you're saying," Lia said helplessly.

"The *hells* you don't," Tank snapped back.

"You two," Cilif said from behind them, "are fucking ridiculous, you know that?"

Lia jumped up. Tank started to his feet.

"You're yapping fit to wake the birds, and you're being so pissy *I* can feel it," Cilif said, sitting down beside Lia. "Dasin's asleep," he added, flexing his hands meaningfully. "I got tired of his ranting."

Tank's eyebrows rose nearly to his hairline.

"He won't remember," Cilif said. "I know what I'm doing. *Tela-taba*. Did he really try to fire you?"

Tank sat down, waving Lia to follow suit. "Yes. I'm out. So's Lia. Come morning, you're on your own."

Cilif snorted dryly. "That's not how this works," he said. "Dasin ain't the boss. He's been let to think he is. I know better. Ganne knows better. Yuer made it clear. We don't move a step without *you*. Especially not in this damn place." He glanced at the surrounding trees with a grimace.

"Yuer said that?" Tank said, looking completely stunned.

Cilif shrugged, scratching at his developing beard. "Not in so many words. But Dasin ain't worth shit without you beside him. He'd be drunk twenty out of twenty-four, and trying to fuck a diseased cat during the remaining hours."

Tank let out a bark of startled laughter.

Cilif grinned briefly, then went on, "I ain't letting him override what you say, or following him without you alongside. I'm staying with you, and so's Ganne, an' that wagon won't move without us if I got to chop the wheels. Isata, well, that's to talk about then. But it's not happening now."

Tank shook his head, bemused. "I didn't know you felt that way."

"You miss a lot, believe it or not," Cilif said. "Dasin pushes your head right up your ass half the time. Never mind. Go get some sleep. We'll sort Dasin out come morning. Go on, I'm good to stand watch."

"You're sure?" Tank said, rising to his feet even as he asked the question.

"I sure as shit ain't going back in to listen to him snore and whine in his sleep, and I ain't interested in waking him up. He already made one bad pass at me, I'm out of temper for fending off another. Go. Snuggle up with Lia, get back at Dasin for being stupid." He looked at Lia and laughed quietly. "You could pass for a fire right now, you know that?"

Lia ducked her head, desperately wishing for the security of her ata.

Tank, ignoring the byplay, said, "I don't think Dasin would welcome finding me in his tent come morning."

"Likely not, but as he's in *my* tent at the moment, I'd say the hells with what he likes," Cilif observed. "Go get some damn sleep already."

Tank went into the tent without a backwards look.

Cilif made a low, amused sound, then picked up a stray branch, pulled out a knife, and ostentatiously began whittling. Lia retreated to her own tent, suddenly too tired to focus beyond a sense of shamed gratitude over not having to share. As she settled down, her chest eased, the lingering sense of danger finally fading away. She took a deep, relieved breath and stretched out on her sleeping mat, reassured by the ongoing forest songs.

Darkness chased her into silence almost immediately.

This time, she had no dreams.

Chapter Twenty-three

Tank woke alone and sweating. The walls of the tent glowed with dappled sunlight, and the air was thick and humid. He'd slept past dawn.

He rolled onto his back, listening. Horses whuffled, pans clicked, and the smell of coffee drifted through the air. No shouting. No fighting.

Hauling himself up into a crouch, he ran his hands through his hair. His fingers encountered small twigs and bits of leaf: not unusual for this point in the trip. He needed to brush it out properly and re-braid it. Usually Dasin took care of it while on this leg of the trip, providing them both a badly needed stretch of quiet, shared companionship. That seemed unlikely to happen now. Maybe Lia....

A surge of heat hit his groin at the thought of her hands on the back of his neck, and he swore under his breath, yanking at his hair to distract himself. *Not happening*, he told himself. *Stop being a fool. She's Stecatr, and you're ... you. Nobody with half a bit of sense would want you. That's why you've been with Dasin for so long.*

He grimly worked out the worst of the knots and tied off a low tail to keep the mess out of his face, then ran a hand through his scruffy beard. Grit and oil slid against his fingers.

"Damnit anyway," he muttered, and left the tent.

The entire crew sat around a low fire, drinking coffee from metal trail mugs. A pile of dishes in a bucket indicated they'd already eaten breakfast. As the last person awake, Tank was responsible for washing up. He hadn't dealt with that duty in quite a long time.

Bright and sullen bird calls bounced through the air. He'd never bothered to learn what bird made what song, but it was a pretty enough sound, if a bit of a racket. Feathered forms hopped and whistled through the brush, too hidden and quick-moving to identify, but he caught the bright crimson of a murder-bird and the distinctive white and black stripes of a woodcutter.

Nobody looked at him as he emerged. Dasin was glaring at the cup in his hand. Toad seemed engrossed with studying his hands. Cilif rose, not quite ostentatiously, and went to tend the horses. Lia nearly leapt up to follow.

So there had been an argument. Probably a loud one. And he'd slept through it! In the Hackerwood! He cut a sharp glare at Ganne. The desert lord smirked and sipped coffee, admitting nothing.

"Huh," Tank said, to Ganne as much as to anyone else, and went to the necessary. When he returned, he edged round to a seat between Ganne and Toad, at a carefully calculated angle to Dasin.

Dasin flicked a dour glare at Tank, then went back to staring at nothing, his hands tight around his mug.

"We've finished the coffee," Cilif called out cheerfully. "Price you pay for sleeping in."

Tank grunted. He glanced over his shoulder at the wagon, considering whether to make another pot, then let it go as too much trouble.

"So I'm told you're actually the one in charge," Dasin said abruptly, not looking at Tank.

Toad looked from face to face anxiously but said nothing. Lia had withdrawn into herself, nearly unnoticeable unless Tank looked straight at her. He really needed to talk to her about that tendency once everything calmed down.

A blackwing bird darted across the campsite, its dipping, flittery flight briefly drawing everyone's attention. Cilif smiled a little, an unguardedly warm expression.

Dasin's voice went even more sour and taut. "Would have been nice to be clear some time ago on how *I'm* secondary to *you*."

Tank began to wish he'd stalled by making the coffee after all. "It's as much a surprise to me as to you, Dasin," he said, keeping his tone level.

Ganne snorted. "Seriously?" he said. "I saw that before we were on the road an hour."

Dasin flicked him a bitter glare. Tank pinched the bridge of his nose, steadying his own temper. "Not helping, Lord Darden," he said, deliberately using Ganne's formal title. Ganne blinked, then inclined his head in recognition of the warning.

"So what are your orders, then, *s'e Tank*?" Dasin said, venom in the words.

Tank felt his teeth grind together. "Damnit, Dasin," he said, "could you at least not make this any worse?"

A squirrel with unusually dark fur hopped up onto the wall, looking around curiously. It sniffed the air, nibbled on something in its agile little paws, then turned and sprang away into the woods.

Dasin, back straight and face stiff, stared at Tank, ostentatiously waiting on an answer. Tank could feel the broken bits shifting beneath Dasin's outward anger. He barely stopped himself from apologizing for being the one to deal that damage.

Cilif abandoned any pretense of checking hooves and came back to stand nearby, arms folded. Lia wavered, then determinedly focused on her work, but Tank could tell she was listening.

Cilif said, tone precise and cold, "How about I save time? We always knew a moondark run was a shit idea. Turns out it's more shit than we thought. Lord Ganne there got knocked on his ass last night, he's still wobbly. I feel like I got run through a grain mill sideways. Tank and Lia are the only ones properly on their feet. Firing them was probably the stupidest decision Dasin's made to date."

Dasin's eyes went dangerously cold. Tank put a hand over his own eyes briefly, unable to think of a way to stop the imminent explosion.

"Don't even start with me, Dasin," Cilif said. "This is where you sit and take it. You're brittle, and you're mean, and you're jealous, and it fucks with your common sense on a good day. This isn't a good day, and you're not thinking straight, so I'm overriding you. Fire me if you want, but we're sticking together until we get to Isata. Whether you throw us all out and we walk different ways at that point is a question that don't need to be handled right now."

Tank stared at Cilif, completely at a loss. The dark-haired mercenary stood planted square and solid, his arms folded across his chest, seeming to take up considerably more room than usual. Dasin's face was splotched with shocked, helpless fury, his hands tightly fisted.

Ganne's voice slid under and through the moment, thinly compelling. "*Calm,*" he said. Then, breaking any chance he'd be listened to, he added: "We're not alone."

Tank jerked to his feet. Before he could so much as take a step towards a weapon, a crackle of brush came from all around the campground at once. Everyone froze.

A bloodbird slowly, deliberately stepped over the shielding wall and stood within the campground, staring at them with emotionless black eyes. A second followed, then a third. Each bird had slightly different markings. Each one wore a silver chain around its neck.

Four. Five. Six. They arranged themselves into a perfect semi-circle, the woods at their back: wings held tight against their sides, heads high and regal as any predator that knew itself to be supreme.

Balby had assured Tank that bloodbirds only ate bugs and fruit. Looking at the surrounding arc, Tank no longer believed it. He'd never seen this many in one place. He'd also never been seriously troubled by any Hackerwood creature, after he'd made Balby that stupid promise to stay his side of the walls, until this trip.

He *was* certain that while the bloodbirds had a basic intelligence, it wasn't enough for this organized presentation. Someone much more clever was in charge, and if that person wasn't Balby, her protection had just catastrophically failed.

What if she'd been killed? The thought was horrifying. *My son ... oh, gods, oh dear and holy gods, my son.* His muscles tensed with wanting to hurt something.

The horses shifted nervously but stayed quiet; not at all the right reaction, which meant someone or something was holding them still. Someone like a desert lord. Tank glanced between the horses and Ganne questioningly, and received a baffled shake of the head in response.

Someone cleared their throat from the direction of the road. Everyone twisted round to stare at the man standing in the middle of the entrance. Two bloodbirds flanked him, smaller and paler than the others. They wore no chain Tank could see.

"Good morning," the man said, strolling forward into the camp proper. He had dark, scarred skin and elaborately braided dark hair; he could almost have been a child by his height, but the glitter in his eyes was entirely and maliciously adult. "No, no, please don't get up." It was, distinctly, a warning. "I'm perfectly happy for you to sit comfortably."

Everyone sank down onto the nearest seat. Tank could barely hear anyone breathing, even himself.

"Good morning, *s'e*," he made himself say, and hated the catch in his voice.

The man's dour expression widened into a small, brief smile. He crossed his arms, tucking his hands up into the sleeves like a priest, then stood quietly, allowing them to take him in.

The top of the man's head might have reached just Tank's sternum, had Tank been standing. He wore simple clothes of black and green, a long-sleeved tunic over trousers. No belt, no ornamentation, no jewelry. White scars ran across his face and down his neck, and Tank would have put money that they continued all across his body. Not random; definitely a pattern. At a guess, a complex series of tattoos had been removed.

Tank held back a shudder at the thought of how much that extensive of an application would have hurt — and how much worse removing the marks would have been.

"I see that none of you know who I am by sight," the man said. "That might make things more difficult. I know who you are, however, and none of you particularly matter to me unless you refuse me what I want." One of the small bloodbirds at his side opened its beak, tongue darting out as though tasting the air. It looked a great deal like the creature was laughing.

Tank said, prompting, "And what do you want, *s'e*?"

The man's dark face drew into a severe expression. "My title is *hadinn*," he said. "Hadinn Evkit, formerly head of the teyanain."

Ganne let out a sick, choking sound. "Oh dear gods," he muttered.

The hadinn's gaze flicked to him, severity shifting towards amusement. "Indeed," he said. "To the question: I want, first of all, *him*."

He pointed at Toad.

Toad let out a faint bleating sound, face blanched with terror. Jolting to his feet, he turned wildly in place as though searching for somewhere to run; then he dropped to his knees and shouted at Tank: "Sanctuary! Help me! I claim Family rights! Protect me!"

Tank regarded the old man with bemusement. "What Family are you claiming?" he asked, more to satisfy his curiosity than because the answer actually mattered.

"F'Heing!" Toad squeaked. "I'm working for F'Heing Family! You, you have to honor, you have to, they'll be angry if you let him hurt me!"

Ganne let out an explosive, derisive snort. "That's not how this works, you utter fool!"

Both of the smaller bloodbirds clacked their beaks menacingly. Toad scuttled further away.

"I am not interested in harming you," the hadinn said, cocking his head to one side. "We merely need to have a private discussion, you and I. Dinas?" He raised a hand in a lazy, airy wave.

A man appeared behind Toad. Tank had time for a startled impression of bright blue, red, and yellow; time for Toad's scream to begin to register. Then both men were simply gone, the air empty of sound in their wake. A faint *thunk* of air shifting crossways, like a door closing, evened the pressure in Tank's ears.

Knives appeared in Lia's hands, thin throwing blades he hadn't known she carried.

"Hold," Tank said loudly. "Drop the knives. *Nobody move.*"

Lia let the small blades tumble to the ground without hesitation. Something warm and painful tugged at Tank's chest at that unquestioning trust.

Evkit smiled, a brief, unfriendly expression.

Tank tested words in his head, then said, very carefully, "*Hadinn*, may I ask why you wanted the northern man?" No sense giving him Toad's name, in case he'd been lying about knowing who everyone was.

"You know what teyanain are," Evkit said, his gaze fixed on Tank again.

"He bloody well better," Ganne muttered.

Tank drew in a breath to admit that he was, in fact, largely ignorant on that point beyond certain basics: that teyanain were a xenophobic tribe, that they had occupied the Horn before the *disruption*, as Yuer had called it; mostly, that nobody wanted to talk about them. People turned odd colors and changed the subject when teyanain came up.

Before he could say anything so dangerous, Alyea's presence wound through a space somewhere between memory and the present moment. His breath stuttered and cut out as a scene unfolded:

Drums boomed, east, north, west, south: torchlight and shadows, the first steps of a deadly precise ceremony. Evkit stood watching Alyea, his face sober and solemn; Deiq stood watching Evkit, his expression appalled and furious.

From there, a flurry of memories not his own washed through his head in a matter of seconds. Several things made sudden, terrifying sense.

"*Formerly?*" Tank blurted, his voice emerging far too high and shaky.

Ganne muttered, "And he joins the damn party at last."

Evkit reached out his right hand and ran bent knuckles along the bloodbird's feathers. It churkled contentedly, tipping its head back to let Evkit stroke the underside of its neck. Evkit smiled at the creature fondly, then dropped his hand and turned his attention back to his audience.

"My daughter led an uprising against me," Evkit said. "I was stripped of my power, and had to begin again. After a time of reflection and recovery, I chose to come here to rebuild my power. This is now my land, from the *Rohasoi* to the eastern marshes. As the Horn once was, the Hackerwood now is; every stick, every stone, every road and resting place is mine to command."

Ganne sucked in a harsh breath, his skin taking on an unlovely cast.

Evkit smiled at the desert lord, rocking back onto his heels slightly, then to his toes. "Indeed." He settled square again, still smiling.

"That's a bold claim, hadinn," Dasin said. "How exactly are you going to enforce ownership on the king's roads?"

"Holy gods, Dasin, *shut up*," Ganne said, not bothering to switch to a southern dialect.

Evkit laughed and put his hands out to touch his malevolent-eyed escorts. "I enforced my will throughout the Horn for many years, against powers much stronger than your king," he said, motioning to the aenstone surrounding the campsite. "These walls mean nothing to me. I have mastery of all barriers and borders on my land."

"I accept your authority, hadinn, as does my crew," Tank said hastily, before Dasin could fracture the moment with ill-timed aggression. Usually Dasin was the one pulling Tank back. The reversal of that dynamic alarmed Tank as much as anything else in front of him at the moment.

Evkit's gaze settled on Ganne. The desert lord bent his head without speaking. Apparently that was good enough; Evkit crossed his arms and said, "S'e Tank, you and your remaining crew may leave my lands, but you may not travel this road again until you negotiate terms with myself or my representative, Dinas." His gaze shifted to Dasin and took on a speculative cast that Tank didn't like one bit. "There is one negotiation I wish to offer now, however," Evkit added, inclining his head at Tank.

Tank decided that comment shifted the power balance enough to allow him to stand without causing offense. He moved slowly as he came to his feet, watching for signs that he'd misunderstood. Evkit tilted his head to look up at him unconcernedly.

Please don't mention my son, please don't mention my son ... As much as Tank ached to ask that very question, last night's fight with Dasin was far too raw yet. Throwing that revelation onto the table right now risked launching Dasin into a violently manic state. Given Alyea's memories of Evkit, they'd all be dead a few moments later.

Evkit cocked his head, his mouth twitching sideways into a dry smile. Tank bit his lip and tightened his shields, not at all sure his slip had been accidental.

"What negotiation is that, *hadinn*?" Tank said, more steadily than he'd expected.

Evkit's eyes gleamed with sly humor. *I see the broken places in your lover,* his voice said in Tank's mind. The words carried a dry, ancient feel, underlaid with a molting-snake smell.

Tank's jaw went tight with instant anger at the intrusion. He dropped his head down and forward like a bull readying to charge, glaring at Evkit.

I can heal your lover, Evkit said. A gently windy, shuffling sound accompanied the words.

Tank froze. "What —" he started, then swallowed and carefully redirected to: *Why would you do that, hadinn?* Distantly, he wondered what his own mental voice sounded like.

Evkit paused, his gaze moving to Dasin. When he spoke, the words evoked centuries-dry dust sifting through shattered glass. *What happened to you, to both of you, should not have been allowed. I lost myself in pride and in ambition, and I ignored my oaths to protect and deliver justice.*

Tank stared at the small man, a wild mix of emotions lacing through his chest. Nobody of any power had ever offered that much of an apology for Tank's childhood. They'd been repelled, or revolted, or horrified. Even Eredion of Sessin, the only desert lord Tank had ever considered close to a friend, had flinched away from facing the reality. None of them wanted to see their own kin as culpable. Nobody wanted to accept that their own careless ignorance had enabled the katha villages.

Evkit's gaze sharpened back to Tank. They stared at one another for a few moments. Then Evkit said softly, *I cannot extend the offer of healing to you. You have already been shaped. Your lover has only been shut. And what I offer is not free.* The old-snake smell returned, and the sense of a sly smirk.

"Of course not," Tank muttered aloud.

No good asking questions about that *shaped* and *shut*. He wouldn't get answers, and he was uncomfortably sure he already knew anyway. That bitch-witch Teilo must have done something to Dasin. Tank had never considered that possibility before, but it made horrible, sickening sense.

Snake molt and scale oil in his voice, Evkit said, *Work for me and I will heal your lover.*

I already have an employer.

Not any longer, Evkit said. *I have sent someone to remove him. You are familiar with her, I believe ... and with her son.*

Tank hitched in a sharp breath and found himself moving forward. Evkit's smirk vanished, and his escorts opened their beaks wide, hissing warningly. Tank managed to stop after two long steps, which put him far too close but still out of the bloodbirds' reach.

He said, *That's too close to a threat, hadinn.* Then, aloud: "You don't want to start a scrap with me, *hadinn*, no matter what power you claim."

Ganne let out a loud, shocked whoosh of breath. "We're all going to *die*," he muttered.

Evkit regarded Tank with marked wariness. After a moment, he reached out to touch the bloodbirds again, stroking their necks until they stopped hissing. *Work for me, and I will heal your lover,* he said. *I also promise to protect your son far better than his mother has yet managed, and to ask little in return for that service. We may not have tea at hand, but I swear to this as though we stood in full ceremony.*

Tank bit the inside of his cheek, slamming the door on the questions crowding his mind. He tried not to think about the inference that Balby hadn't done well by their son.

I will heal him, Evkit said a third time. Tank heard the ritual weight of that final repetition. *Your lover will be ... not immediately nor entirely whole, but able to heal. The price will not, I think, be onerous: I have work in mind that matches your abilities and temperament.*

What, you want me to beat people up for you? Tank said, scowling.

Evkit laughed. Silently, he answered, *You think far too narrowly of your capabilities.*

"No," Tank said aloud, pushing out a palm in instinctive rejection. He added, *I'm not a desert lord, or anything close to one. I rejected that path.*

Your desires on this point mean nothing. Evkit's voice was stern now. *You cannot undo what the hakraiknin did to you — and all she did was prop open a door to your heritage. Like your one time mentor, Allonin Aerthraim, you are as close to a desert lord as an unbound human can be, whether you learn to use it or not. That makes you tremendously vulnerable to those of more skill.* He paused, then added, *You just faced me down. Do you think that means nothing? You will never be ordinary. Never.*

Tank barely heard most of the speech. "My ... heritage?" The word felt thick and strange in his mouth. Nobody had ever accused him of having a *heritage* before. That was for people who ... people who mattered.

Tank wasn't at all happy with himself for that thought, but this wasn't the time for internal argument.

"Another time," Evkit said, grinning as though they were discussing nothing more important than whether to meet for breakfast. "I must keep something back for future negotiations." He added, *But I will tell you, with no attached obligation, that your father is the important part of your particular line.* He paused, and the serpentine dryness expanded, musty and stifling.

No — the sensation wasn't that of an ancient snake. It was feathers. Long feathers, shifting and scraping against each other: owl feathers, skeletal with age. He sucked in a hard breath and folded suddenly trembling hands up under his armpits.

"*Tank,*" Dasin said sharply. "What's going on?"

Let us return to discussing your lover, Evkit suggested. *Allow me to show you why you should accept my offer. Regard him a moment.*

Tank turned. A faint overlay blurred the air, and then Dasin *changed.* Now he had gaunt, sallow skin that stretched thin over knobbly bone. His hair went limp and loose, as though unwashed for months. His hands shook, and his eyes turned dull and dark.

This is his soul you see now, Evkit said. *He is dying in small pieces. You cannot save him from this decay.*

The blur clouded, cleared again to reveal an exuberant smile amidst clear skin and shining hair, Dasin's eyes bright with excitement and wonder. Muscles filled in. Sallow skin turned tanned and glowing.

Tank's breath stopped in his throat. He'd never seen Dasin so fucking *happy.*

This is what could be, Evkit said simply, and went quiet.

The overlay vanished. Dasin stared at Tank, eyes narrow and hands knotted into fists in his lap: a familiar stare, with a tic starting beside one eye and that particular tilt to his head that signaled *hurt or be hurt.*

If ... the word echoed through Tank's thoughts for several repetitions, a beginning searching for a complete sentence. Words refused to connect to that *if.* His chest hurt; his insides went hollow for a long, dizzy moment, as though they had fled to join that too-brief golden vision.

Dasin. My son. My father? *Godsdamnit.* The hook was set, and Evkit obviously knew it.

He drew a long, aching breath and said, "You have a deal."

Evkit bowed, palms flat together, thumbs against his chest. Straightening, he said, without emphasis, "Dinas?"

A flash of color appeared behind Dasin, who had time to rise to his feet, half-turning, hands coming up in a fast defensive move Tank had drilled into him — *Gods, how long did it take for that to be instinctive, years of insisting, years* — and then Dasin was gone, as swiftly as Toad had disappeared.

The crunching sound of air turning sideways hung in the deathly silent air. Tank's mouth opened for a shout, but his voice failed him entirely.

"What the *fuck!*" Cilif said at last, as loud and furious as Tank wanted to be. "What did you *do?*"

Tank stared at the empty space where Dasin had been, then turned to look at Evkit.

Who was, of course, gone, along with his escort and the arc of bloodbirds.

A moment later, Sin snorted, his head going down and forward, ears entirely flat. Rooster seemed paralyzed still, his eyes wide, shifting his weight in tiny increments. Blackie shook his head, looking utterly bewildered. The draft pony remained stupidly placid.

Another, or maybe the same, squirrel hopped up onto a different section of wall and sat up on its haunches, surveying the camp with bright-eyed interest.

Lia, with a sharp head-shake as though emerging from a daze, edged clear of Sin and went to soothe Rooster. Ganne sat deathly still, biting a knuckle, eyes wide enough to show the whites. Cilif was on his feet, hands clenched, glaring at Tank and visibly ready to attack if he didn't like the answer to his question.

"What just happened?" he demanded.

Tank curled his fingers loosely, flattening fingertips against the heels of his hands. "He'll be back. They'll both be back. He won't hurt them."

"I don't fucking care about the storyteller," Cilif snapped, "but Dasin better fucking come back. You might be balls-all in fighting monsters, but he's solid on making the money to fucking *pay me.*"

The squirrel popped back into the woods, tail twitching furiously.

Tank's hands tightened. "I know," he said. "He'll be all right." By the glare Cilif delivered, the words hadn't come out anywhere near to convincingly. "Enough. There's work to hand. Horses first."

Cilif snorted, chin going up. Ganne, dropping his hand from his mouth, looked up at Cilif and said, thinly, "Calm down, or *I'll* calm you down."

Cilif swung to face the desert lord, aggression in every line of his body. "Don't you fucking try me," he snarled.

Ganne, without changing expression, raised a hand slightly. Cilif backed up a step, then knelt and bent his head. "Lord," he said to the ground.

"Correct," Ganne said. "Go care for your horse."

Cilif rose and went to Blackie without another word. Tank pinched the bridge of his nose and turned away from Ganne, deliberately setting aside conflict in favor of productive work. He took a moment to consider Sin, who was no longer quite as furious but still far from docile, then began a slow approach, murmuring calming phrases.

"How long is ... is the hadinn keeping Dasin?" Lia said, voice low but carrying. Beside her, Rooster remained nearly frozen in place, skin twitching as though plagued by flies. "Are we waiting here for him?"

Tank pulled his attention away from the tight line of Sin's head and back. "I don't know," he said, then: "I suppose so." He cleared his throat. "Let's ... how about someone make a pot of coffee. I could about kill for a cup right now."

Coffee would help. Or, at least, it would keep things from getting any worse. He clung to that slightly irrational belief with everything he had.

Intersection: Intention

The sitting room was the warmest room in the house, which meant it was where Yuer spent the majority of his time. He'd long since learned to nap in his chair. The dining room had become his servants' domain, in part because Yuer rarely ate and in part because his gnarled hands had difficulty grasping utensils. The colder the room, the more difficulty his persistently aching joints presented; refusing the humiliation of being fed meant eating his meals in the sitting room, where the heat eased the fine tremors and the pain.

Nothing ever eased his smoldering fury.

Betrayed. Banished. Crippled. And now the one solace he'd created for himself, the tiny empire so carefully built and managed, was eroding around him. That sexless whore in Obein was stealing business that rightfully belonged to Sandsplit; and the fewer market sales, the fewer the visitors to Sandsplit, the lower went the perfectly reasonable tithe Yuer asked for in return for his benevolence.

Yuer stared at the man before him. Almost as short as a teyanin, but with nearly albino coloration and a stocky build, Gens ran the Sandsplit market. He'd never shown Yuer much deference, and today was proving no different. He stood square, his hat in his hands, displaying his bristly-short white hair: it had begun to retreat in spots, and his scalp, like the rest of his body, was spotted with brown age marks.

Gens kept his gaze to one side and down, not looking Yuer directly in the eyes, the one deference Yuer absolutely insisted on.

"*S'e* Yuer," Gens said, his fingers tight around the brim of his hat. "I know this is intrusive …."

"Intrusive, no," Yuer interrupted. "*Brazen*, yes. *Disrespectful*, yes."

Gens' thin lips pursed. "I don't mean to be any of that," he said stubbornly. "But *s'e*, with all possible respect, this isn't *working*. I'm barely managing the upkeep as it is. Tightening down is driving people away. We've got to be more generous." Yuer opened his mouth for a retort. Gens, unbelievably, interrupted *him*. "You said once, *s'e*, to tell you if I thought you were above and beyond wrong. I remember you saying that, as part of our first talk. I've never done that before. I'm doing it now."

Gens' hands were white-knuckled, the brim of his hat buckling under the pressure.

Yuer sat back in his chair, blinking slowly. "I see," he said. "So you wouldn't agree, for instance, that removing Prianna and destroying the Obein market is an option."

Gens' gaze jerked up at that, startled and appalled. He met Yuer's eyes for the briefest moment before turning his head swiftly away. "Ah ... I wouldn't agree on that, no," he said, voice strained; very clearly aware that Yuer hadn't been joking in the least.

"I'll consider what you've said." Yuer rearranged the lap blanket slightly, as an excuse to look away. "I'll send for you to discuss this further."

Gens backed up a step, bowed hastily, and retreated with commendable dignity.

Yuer took several calming breaths, then said to the empty room, "Next, please."

A rangy, scarred man stepped into the sitting room. He wore light clothing of fine materials, precisely cut to highlight his build, and his dark hair was carefully styled in waves to match current Bright Bay fashion. A fresh bruise swelled under one eye, and he moved with delicate care, as though from a recently aggravated injury.

"*S'e*," he said, clipped and resentful. "I would have come for a simple message, you know. No need to kidnap me."

"I can't steal what I already own, Gint," Yuer said, letting his voice go dangerously flat.

The man's chin lifted even as color began to leach from his tanned features. "I've done everything you've asked for years now, *s'e*."

"Until now," Yuer retorted. "I particularly wanted you on this run. They put a *woman* in your place, and one from Stecatr, at that."

"I fell ill!" Gint protested, chin dropping to a sulky posture. His gaze flicked across Yuer's face every few seconds, a nervous tic he likely wasn't even aware of. "I can't help being ill. They chose to go on without me."

"So you didn't choose to involve yourself in a bar brawl that left you unfit for the road?" Yuer inquired sardonically, then held up one hand as Gint began to answer. "I'm not only relying on Dasin's word for that, of course."

Gint blinked several times. Then: "I ... it was ... it wasn't my ... uh ...."

"It wasn't your idea? You didn't mean to get into a brawl? You thought you'd win, so it wasn't a risk?" Yuer put barbed cruelty into the words. "Whatever excuses you may attempt to present are inadequate. You failed me."

Gint backed up a step, losing his remaining color. "*S'e*, I'll go after them," he blurted. "I'll go replace the outsider —"

"It's far too late for that," Yuer said. "Do you know, I wonder...." He cocked his head to one side. "I wonder if, perhaps, you deliberately made yourself ill? Deliberately put yourself into a dangerous brawl, allowed yourself to get badly hurt? I've been sensing a certain reluctance from you lately. You seem increasingly fond of your appearance." He motioned to Gint's fashionable attire. "Are you, perhaps, hoping to gain an employer among the nobles of Bright Bay who can protect you from me?"

Gint's expression took on a frantic tinge. "No, *s'e*, no, of course not, I'd never —"

Yuer lifted a hand. Gint shut up.

"I'm disappointed," he told the mercenary. "All these years of paying you so well, and you betray me at such a moment."

Gint backed up, muscles tensing to whirl and flee. "No," he said. "No, you can't —"

A bulky form loomed behind him. At Yuer's nod, the door guard grasped Gint's arms from behind. Gint screamed, entirely undignified, and thrashed to get free; but Yuer always hired his door guards based on a capacity for brutal efficiency. Gint swiftly wound up on the floor with a knee in his back and his arms pulled just shy of popping out of the sockets. Tears streamed down his face, his breath coming in rough pants and occasional whines.

"*Can't*," Yuer said, smiling now, "is not a word one safely says to me."

Oh, if only he could pull strength from the mercenary! Unfortunately, Gint had no trace of the heritage Yuer needed for that. Not for the first time, Yuer deeply regretted his own failure in capturing Tanavin's obedience to the necessary level. Dasin had the big redhead entirely claimed, and Tanavin's own barely-banked fury made any attempt to draw from him supremely unwise.

A *presence* distorted the edges of his awareness.

Yuer pulled his head back like a turtle withdrawing into its shell, his eyes falling nearly shut, and scanned his territory. His current favorite, a broad-faced, coarse-haired young man, dozed in his room, completely content. His pet Aerthraim was in her attic room, busy working on plans for Yuer's latest notion. Her whole mind was thrown into the challenge. The cook was working on dinner, the housekeeper was out for the day. The remaining outside guard....

Ah.

The guard had spotted someone coming toward the cottage. *Child/strange/caution* and *danger/sympathy/helpless* resonated along Yuer's inner ear.

He sat up straighter, intrigued. What in the world was a child doing coming to his door? Especially one that exuded enough eeriness to unsettle a guard hired for a distinct lack of imagination?

This held far more potential interest than punishing a useless hireling.

"Be done with it," he said to the guard holding Gint.

Gint let out a screech of protest. There came a brief flurry of tussling, a thick cracking sound, and the mercenary lay still, head at a sharp angle. The guard gathered himself to his feet, glanced once at Yuer for permission, then scooped up the body and left.

The child that came into the sitting room not long afterwards was of indeterminate age. Above toddler, below puberty, was Yuer's best assessment. He'd never bothered to lean about children, knowing he'd never have any of his own.

The boy's thin build held promise of filling out in a few years. He had bright dark eyes and a head of glossy red hair. He appeared, superficially, to be uninjured, but that grave, thousand-year stare was one no child wore when wholly innocent of pain.

Yuer looked at the lines of the boy's face and sucked in a breath before he could stop himself. He'd *just* been thinking wistfully about Tanavin. The gods had to be laughing. He shivered a little, truly excited for the first time in years, in a way that had nothing do with sex.

"Have a seat," he told the boy. "What's your name, child?"

The red-haired boy moved forward, but rather than sitting, he put a hand atop the head of the chair and regarded Yuer without fear or flinching.

"My name doesn't matter," he said in the light tenor of youth. "I'm here to tell you something important."

"Are you trying to threaten me, child?" Yuer inquired, smiling tolerantly; knowing that the ruin of his face made it more like a leer.

"No." The boy dropped his hand and advanced three more steps. "I have a message. Will you hear it?"

"Allow me to order tea," Yuer said. "Messages are better conveyed in comfort, I find."

The boy shook his head and moved forward another step, his gaze steady on Yuer's face. Abruptly alarmed, Yuer stretched out his will to summon a guard, and found himself blocked. He shoved himself upright, leaning forward to glare at the child, who smiled with such virtuous innocence that Yuer's blood ran cold.

"What's your message, then?" Yuer grated, no longer feeling the least bit indulgent. "Deliver it and get out!"

"The Calcen is no longer the Calcen," the boy said. "The hadinn carries none of the promises and obligations of his former life."

Yuer stared, the words simply refusing to make sense for a moment. Then he found himself on his feet, lap blanket falling away, exposing his withered, twisted legs. "*Evkit?* You, you of all people, work for *Evkit?*"

"My mother does," the boy said. "I follow my mother's wishes."

Yuer took a staggering step forward, opening his mouth to summon aid, and found his voice stolen away.

The same blank wall met his renewed effort to use other methods to call his servants. He reached to the sides, to the top and to the bottom, and found an intangible pressure wrapped entirely around him. With a surge of effort that left him dizzy, he found the external connection point. It led not to the boy, but outside.

Yuer wasn't sure whether to be relieved that the boy didn't, after all, have the strength to do such a binding, or to be terrified that whoever stood outside could cast one through solid stone walls onto an unseen target.

It didn't matter. Whoever stood outside, they were *outside*, and this boy stood barely out of Yuer's reach. He might be blocked from using his mind and voice to summon his guards, but nothing yet stopped his body. A good lunge would have his hand on the child, allowing him to sidestep the binding and pull, drawing hard and fast, gaining the strength to fend off his unseen, unwanted guest.

At the end of it, Tanavin's child would either be dead or bound to Yuer's will, and, if his guess was right, whoever stood outside as well.

The boy looked up at Yuer, his expression faltering to confusion. *"S'e?"*

Yuer lunged. His hands wrapped around the boy's upper arms before the child could dodge, not that the foolish boy made any such attempt.

It felt as though a streak of lightning tore through Yuer's body. Muscles spasmed and failed, dropping him to the floor. He thrashed to a sitting position. Unable to kneel, he wound up in the undignified position of sitting on his ass, twisted legs stretched out before him. He stared up at the child, both shocked and furious. *That* had come entirely from the child, and indicated a level of innate strength and power beyond what such a slight body should hold.

The boy had to be bound to Evkit. There was no other answer, no other source that could disable Yuer so easily. The boy was, in essence, an athain. If Yuer hadn't been quite so alarmed, he'd have been utterly fascinated by multiple aspects of that possibility.

"Evkit swore an *oath,*" Yuer spat. "He swore never to send anyone to bind me. I've *earned* that safety!"

"The Calcen swore an oath," the child said. "The hadinn has not."

Yuer sucked in a shaking breath. This, then, was the beginning of a new negotiation. "What terms are being presented this time?" he inquired, forcing his voice steady.

The child considered him gravely, then said, "None."

Dark eyes, now laced with shifting, silvery threads, locked onto Yuer's.

Oh dear and holy gods, this isn't from Evkit, the teyanain don't have this skill or heritage, this is … this is from one of the old lines. I thought, everyone thought, it was erased … oh dear gods, does this come down from Tanavin, or from the mother?

Gold would have been deadly. Silver was much worse. Yuer could feel his thoughts beginning to shred, unraveling like ribbons on a strong breeze. He had no defense at all against this.

No, he tried to say, tried to deny the forming compulsion. He tried to jerk his gaze away, to punch out. *No, no, no….*

The slow slide of silver was a pattern. It meant something terribly important. If he looked for another moment he'd understand it. He'd see the deep secrets, the ones he'd paid so much for but never received.

"Well done, son," a woman said, close to hand. "Now the final knot."

Yuer almost broke free at that, some distant part of his mind grasping the immensity of the danger yawning before him. Then the pattern changed, acquiring hard corners where curves had been, pulling him into a desperate need to *understand….*

"There," the woman said. Her voice felt like smoky silk, rich with satisfaction. "And a slight push to finish the binding. Yes, of course I'll help you. All you had to do was ask."

A painful wrenching sensation ran through body and mind alike, shredding away his hard-won yet crippled gift. Yuer tried to scream: found himself unable to feel his body, unable to know if he'd been permitted so much as a mumble.

Light inverted to a thick darkness laced with silver fractals.

"You thought to make a slave out of my son," the woman said, silk replaced with razors. "See, now, how it is to be *my* slave."

A chill, ragged laugh cut across the final word, an entirely inhuman sound.

The woman gave a cry of surprise, and began to speak: a name, or a word, something beginning with *tee*. Her voice cut off abruptly.

The pattern broke. Darkness turned thin, lines of light beginning to striate through.

"*I* think not," a new voice said, colder than ice, more abrasive than a sandstorm. "You've done quite enough already, child of the edgelands. I will take him and teach him properly. He never should have been left with *you* at all."

Yuer reached for a thread of light with intangible hands. It slid away from his clumsy lunge. Two more attempts, each more careful, and he finally felt the line shivering in his grasp: ghost to ghost combining into just real enough. He worked ethereal fingers into the middle and began pulling it apart, expanding the gap, pulling himself into the clarity it represented.

The first woman said something in an unfamiliar dialect. No, not entirely unfamiliar. He knew that accent, knew the words without knowing how: *Oh, fuck you, bitch!*

The new stranger answered serenely, in the same dialect. The woman let out a short, shrill scream. A body collapsed to the floor. Yuer froze, unsure of the consequences of visibly regaining his wits.

In that pause, he came clear on what dialect they'd been using. *Aerthraim.* They'd both been speaking Aerthraim dialect. He'd picked up enough, from his pet's absentminded muttering, to recognize it. *Oh gods, if you exist, oh good and holy gods, help me....*

In Kaenic, the new stranger said, "I won't kill you, edgelands child. I should. I know I should. But there, I'm soft hearted still. I'll probably regret that. But I'll take your child, to replace the one stolen from me. You can always have another. Humans are so *fertile*, after all. Be sure to tell your new master to help you with that."

A harsh, cawing laugh sounded after those words, thick with the taste of a bitter joke Yuer didn't understand. Air thumped from a displaced weight, and the binding broke. His vision returned, along with awareness of his body. He was sprawled on the floor, drooling thickly. Past caring about humiliation, still caught in the narrowness of fear, he scrabbled to a sitting position and looked around frantically.

To Yuer's right, the boy stood with a very nearly blank expression, hands in tight fists at his sides. To Yuer's left was a tall woman with long silver hair and smooth dark skin. She looked young: twenties, maybe thirties at most. He didn't need the gift to know that was only a seeming. He also didn't need the gift to sense the power dripping from her, to register an intense *presence* the likes of which he hadn't felt since his failed blood trials.

She turned her head to look at him, her smile cruel.

"Where is my mother?" the boy demanded.

Not taking her gaze from Yuer, the woman said, "I sent her back to her master. She's unharmed. You will travel with me for a time, and when I've taught you what I have to teach, you may go back to her if you wish." Her disdainful tone indicated her opinion of that.

The boy, without bothering to argue, headed for the door. Smiling even more widely, the woman put out a hand. The boy froze, then slowly backed up and turned to face her.

"You will travel with me for a time," the woman repeated. Silver patterns began to slide across her dark skin. The boy's eyes widened, his expression turning distinctly greedy.

Yuer's heart nearly failed. *Another one? Impossible. Impossible!*

She said, "I have things to teach you that your mother cannot, and your new master cannot. Give me the time to explain before you decide whether to leave." The silver lines faded, and she dropped her hand. "First I must deal with this." She fixed her attention on Yuer.

"Spare me!" he rasped, completely beyond dignity. "I'll serve you!"

Her laugh sliced through him. "*You*, failed one? You who should have died during the trials you tricked your way into? No. You are useless to me." A brief, considering pause; then she added: "Hm. Perhaps not entirely useless. You hold memories of my pupils, don't you? That's why I'm here, you know. I tracked them to your door. I'll take those memories from you. Then, since I was kind enough not to kill the edgelands child, and since I am hungry...."

Silver lines swept into a dense network across her body and filled her eyes.

"Here, child," she said to the boy. "See how this is done. Watch, now."

Agony swept through his body; doubled, redoubled, quadrupled, gaining definition, becoming black-laced flames: and he abruptly knew, beyond any doubt, who this woman — what this *creature* — had to be.

His own incredulous, manic laughter followed him into a final silence.

Chapter Twenty-four

Coffee hadn't helped. Neither had polishing tack, catching up on various mending projects, going through inventory, and a dozen other small tasks Tank invented to keep everyone busy throughout the endless day following the hadinn's appearance with the bloodbirds and his disappearance with Dasin.

Cilif maintained a smoldering silence, frequently glaring at Ganne, who completely ignored him. Ganne sat gray-faced, occasionally poking at the fire but mostly staring at nothing in particular. Lia stayed as far away from everyone as she could and spent most of her time fussing over the horses.

Night fell with no sign of Dasin. Dinner was a sullen, reluctant affair. They retreated to their respective beds with nothing of substance said. Tank emerged from his tent well before dawn, murderously cranky and exhausted: he'd spent the night spent jerking awake at every small sound. Cilif and Lia joined him not long after, and Tank put on coffee and porridge without speaking. He didn't bother adding the fruits and spices Dasin preferred. It was too much work, and he didn't care enough.

Just past dawn, the bloodbirds stepped back into the campsite, forming their solemn arc. The horses snorted uneasily, shifting in place, but to Tank's immense relief made no serious objection.

A teyanin dressed in bright colors appeared among the bloodbirds, cradling Dasin's limp body in his arms. It should have looked absurd. Dasin was considerably taller, and dead weight besides. Somehow the small man retained both his dignity and Dasin's, as though he held nothing heavier than a large stick.

Tank started to his feet and took a hesitant step. At the teyanin's nod of permission, he lunged the rest of the distance to take the burden on himself, nearly kneeling to lift Dasin clear.

Dasin felt light in Tank's arms, as though his bones had turned hollow and all fat burned away. His skin was sallow and hot. He trembled unceasingly, his eyes moving rapidly behind closed lids.

"We were not properly introduced yesterday," the teyanin said. "I am Dinas, the hadinn's second." He moved back three slow paces. "You will leave the Forest now. None of you may travel this road again until you are told your way is clear. You will be contacted when the *hadinn* wishes to speak to you. I am directed to tell you to continue on your planned route, and to offer this by way of compensation for any necessary delay during the time of healing."

Dinas drew out a small pouch and set it gently on the ground, then straightened, surveying them all. As his gaze came to Lia, he smiled.

"Greetings, grayhand," he said. "Ask your master to send us a representative for negotiations. You would be acceptable. If he sends another, advise him that an understanding of the south is entirely necessary in a representative. If you are chosen, you may wish to consult with...." He paused, glanced at Tank, then said, "With this one."

Tank bit his lip, relieved that Dinas hadn't said *Tanavin*, then cut a sideways glance at Lia, thinking: *Grayhand?*

She avoided his gaze.

Dinas looked at Ganne. "Lord Darden. Tell your *reh* that the hadinn would speak with him. You may stand beside him as second, when the time comes."

Ganne's chin came up, his back stiffening. "I do not have contact with the *reh*," he said flatly.

"You will take the message to him yourself, all the same," Dinas answered, unruffled. "You may attend to your business in Isata, but come back to this campsite within ten days. I will bring you as close as I can to your home lands."

Ganne made a harsh noise of protest, but subsided under Dinas's dark stare.

"You will do this thing, if you wish your Family to be able to move through our lands as planned," Dinas said. "You will return to your home, and speak to your *reh*, and bring him to the southern border of the Hackerwood. All desert Families are being similarly contacted. Many northerns of note are being contacted. This is no small endeavor, desert lord. You will do your part, or see your Family's plans cut apart utterly."

Ganne's teeth dug into his lower lip, his face stark.

Dinas turned his attention to Cilif. His expression went thoughtful, than a bit sad. "You are clever, mercenary. You have avoided stepping into matters larger than yourself, so I have no requirement to place on you at this time. If you continue alongside these men, however, you will be drawn into their troubles. I make no remark as to whether that is good or ill. I only think you deserve the warning."

Cilif bowed his head.

Dinas returned his stare to Tank. "I am directed to say that the northern healer will be returned as well, in time. The *hadinn* wishes to speak with him, not harm him." He looked at Lia. "There are misunderstandings between you and the healer that ought to be corrected before he leaves this life."

Lia opened her mouth, her expression nearly a snarl, then dropped her chin towards her chest in sullen acknowledgment.

Dinas smiled and passed another gaze round the group. "May the gods hold you all gently," he said. "Now, kindly leave this place at best speed."

"Gladly," Tank muttered in the wake of displaced air. Once more, the horses made unhappy noises. Sin stomped a back hoof, and even the draft pony flattened its ears briefly, but that was the end of their reaction. The bloodbirds stepped backward without taking their obsidian stares from Tank, and disappeared soundlessly into the woods.

Tank let out a long breath, looking down at Dasin's slack features without really thinking about anything at all for a few moments. Then: *able to heal.*

Worth it. Had to be worth it.

It better be worth it, or I'll rip Evkit's guts out his mouth.

"Load up," he said, not raising his gaze from Dasin's face. "Let's get the fuck out of here already."

Chapter Twenty-five

The first sight of deadman's moss, late the following morning, came as an almost physical relief to Lia. Everyone else seemed to feel the same way. Spines straightened, the pace picked up; even the horses stopped their restless bickering.

Cilif had taken over driving the wagon. Tank rode beside the wagon, holding Dasin, loose-limbed and groggy, before him. Ganne had reluctantly mounted Blackie and taken point. He wasn't a bad rider, for all his professed disdain for horses. All the same, Lia was fairly sure most of the credit had to go to the horse. Both of the black geldings seemed the type to make even a poor rider look skilled.

Lia stayed to the back, nerves taut, and prayed to the kindly face of Syrta to keep her steady.

The day passed without incident or other travelers. The night's campground was empty but for them. The weather and the ground both proved dry enough not to bother with tents. Tank set up his tent, took Dasin inside, and only emerged, briefly, for food.

As on the previous night, nobody spoke. No stories were told, no laughter or jokes tossed about. They ate, agreed on guard shifts that didn't involve Tank and Dasin, and went to their beds in silence.

The night passed without incident. No nightmares, no strange creatures, no voices. The night creatures seemed muted and erratic. No owls called, no snakes went by. The very air felt flat and bland.

In the morning, as they sat round the fire with coffee in hand, Tank emerged from his tent. He poured himself a mug and sat down, wincing a bit. Everyone tried to look at him without looking at him.

Lia suspected he'd slept in his clothes, as they were not only the ones he'd worn the day before, but badly creased and rumpled. His feet were bare, and as that was safer to look at than his face, she noticed he needed to trim his nails.

Tank snorted, then said, "He's still half-dazed. Since you're all being so careful not to ask. No, I didn't get shit for sleep. No, he didn't say a word. Yes, he thrashed and kicked all night. I'm bruised from knee to tit."

Cilif chuckled and began to say something. Tank leveled a suddenly freezing stare at him. Cilif snapped his mouth shut and looked away.

"I can handle getting us into Isata," Tank said. "Ganne, once we're past the southern guard, I'm assuming you don't mind bidding us farewell?" His feet flexed, toes digging into the soft ground.

Ganne scratched his stubbled cheek, grimacing. "I'd hoped for an introduction here and there. But...." He glanced at the tent. "I think I'll manage fine on my own, all things considered."

"Good. Cilif. Are you leaving us in Isata?"

Cilif shrugged uncertainly. "Haven't decided yet."

Tank's voice turned crisp. "I'd like you to stay, but I won't hold it against you if you don't. But figure it out soon. Lia, I know you want to leave in Isata."

She looked up, startled. "I never said —"

"Oh come on, even *I* saw that," Cilif said roughly.

Tank held up a hand. "Lia, I can't hold you any more than I can hold Cilif, but I'd like you to stay as well."

"And what about what Dasin has to say about it all?" Cilif demanded.

"If he fires us all, then that's what happens," Tank said flatly. "I have to go on as though we're on routine."

He put one foot over the other; glanced down with a grimace and straightened them to side by side. Then he drew a long breath, visibly gathering his temper under control.

He said, "Get the camp broken down, get ready for the road. Same as usual once we reach Isata — eh. I'd better go through it." He glanced at Lia. "We'll be lodging at the Round; it's an inn and stables that caters to merchants. Stables are in the back, there's a barn with guards and all for the wagon. It's on the west side of town. Cilif, you're covered for two days if you decide to leave. Lia, same for you. We normally stay for three, but I don't know what's going to happen this time around. And I don't know if the full Market is running right now. Dasin's the one keeps track of that calendar." He cleared his throat. "Questions?"

Cilif began to speak, then shook his head and went back to sullen silence. He began hacking the ground lightly with one booted heel.

Ganne said, "I don't have questions as such, but I'll have my say. I don't know what you agreed to, but I can tell you it was a mistake. *Anything* involving that man is always, always a mistake. When he went walkabout, the entire southlands just about shit itself. That he's now, apparently, the northern kingdom's problem is making me want to laugh and weep in equal measure. Don't tell me what bargain you made with him. Don't tell me anything you said to each other. I already have to tell my people he's claiming the Hackerwoods, and they will *panic*. Do you understand what a bad idea it is for Darden Family to panic? To be told we can't go through the Hackerwood until our *reh* deals with him?" He flung out an arm to point into the woods. "To find out that Yuer is being removed entirely, that all of our negotiations are useless now? Not to mention what I have to tell them about *you*." He glared at Tank, who glared back with ice to match the man's fire.

"You don't tell them anything about me, is the answer to that," Tank retorted. "Or do we get into a scrap right here to sort that out?"

The desert lord tensed. Tank's muscles bunched. Cilif let out an ear-splitting whistle that shattered the rising hostility. Both men turned frosty glares on Cilif.

"My turn to say *enough*," Cilif said. "We're still in the damn Hackerwood, and it's barely the outside edge of a dark moon. Either you're overset or you're being assholes; either way, knock it off."

Lia decided to take a chance on asking questions by way of distraction. She said, pushing her own voice into the strained air, "I don't understand most of what you just said. What's a *reh*?"

Ganne and Tank exchanged another long, measuring look. Then Ganne said, "We're the only ones with a reh. It's a unique position. He's something like a loremaster, something like a priest of the Sun Lord, something like a powerful nobleman." His voice turned brittle: "The reh does not travel. He doesn't talk to anyone but the head of Darden Family. I'm going to get myself killed or disowned trying to fill that bastard's demand." He turned his glare back to Tank.

Tank drained the last of his coffee, then stood. "Cilif's right. Enough," he said, tone definite. "Time to get moving."

Ganne stomped off to pack up his kit, muttering under his breath.

"Break camp," Tank said. "I want *out* of here."

"You and me both," Lia and Cilif said simultaneously. They exchanged rueful glances and shrugs, then went about the business of getting ready for the road.

Chapter Twenty-six

Dasin stayed silent, eyes vague, through the entirety of rolling into Isata and deploying everyone to the necessary tasks. It wasn't until Tank shut and latched the door to their room and turned to look at the limp form he'd laid on the bed that he saw Dasin watching him with a clear, sharp stare.

"So how long were you faking it, then?" Tank said. He leaned a shoulder back against the doorframe and crossed his arms.

"Not long," Dasin said. He paused, working his mouth as though at a bad taste, and shut his eyes. Tank waited, caught between stoic misery and sharp anxiety.

The room smelled of lavender, vinegar, and cinnamon. Not the best combination, but Tank had put up with worse. A large window in need of cleaning let in smudgy light.

The Round was normally better than this. Tank distracted himself with contemplating whether to complain, to whom, and what wording to use.

At last Dasin said, "I don't know. Time's a little strange just now. How long has it been since you gave me to that bastard?"

"Two days." Tank considered several remarks and questions, but discarded them all as too provocative or too bland. In the end, he said nothing more, watching Dasin's lean features as he lay quietly, staring up at the ceiling.

"I won't say you made a mistake, exactly," Dasin said. He blinked, alertness fading. His eyes slid closed. "But ... you don't understand ... what you've ... dnnnn." A heavy snore rattled through the room seconds later.

Tank said, under his breath, "Well, that's nothing new."

He watched Dasin sleep, tracking the small twitches that crossed his face, trying to see signs of change. At last he admitted to himself that he wouldn't know anything at all until Dasin woke up properly. More, even with exhaustion running heavy along his muscles, he was too anxious to sleep. He'd drive himself mad sitting around staring.

He tucked his pack under the bed. Dasin's pack, along with the bags and boxes that he insisted on having close to hand at any significant stop, Tank lined up neatly along one wall. Then he checked round the room: window secure, good; no sign of rats or roaches, excellent; door hinges solid metal and strong, perfect.

Refusing a backwards glance, he let himself out, locking the door behind him, and kicked the key back under the door. If Dasin was still asleep when he returned, it was an easy enough lock to pick.

Tank wasn't at all surprised, on reaching the inn's common room, to find Lia sitting on a bench near the door, arms crossed. She might have been waiting for him, or brooding on what to do, or avoiding the vinegar smell in her own room. There was no telling, and he didn't much care. He waved her to her feet without comment and went on out the door.

She followed him, silent and patient in a way that reminded him of a stalking asojacau. He could almost see the questions she'd been holding back, like a faint haze that came and went around her head. He blinked and rubbed his eyes, chiding himself for the fancy. That was something a desert lord might be able to do. Not him. Never him.

Evkit's words coiled, smoky with amusement, in his memory: *Your desires on this point mean nothing.*

Tank grunted irritably, picked up the pace, and stopped looking back at Lia.

Isata sprawled haphazardly across an irregular landscape. In an abrupt elevation shift, the road from the Hackerwood sloped up and split into eclectically angled passages. The steepest hill in the city wasn't claimed by the Lord of Isata, nor even the Northern Church, but by the News Rider Hall, a building that looked more like a southern fortress than a scribe-center. Horses came and went from that quarter of the city at regular intervals, riders and mounts alike garbed in the bright blue and scarlet of a neutral news-carrier.

Neutral. Right. Tank snorted softly. *Well, they're trying to do better these days, I suppose.*

The best drinking establishment in Isata was the Silver Goose, located near the foot of the News Rider Hall hill; and the best place to sit and stare out over the city was about halfway up that same hill. If one didn't mind ducking past a thornbush or two.

Tank didn't mind. He swung by the Goose to get two flasks — one of honeyed *ibitt*, and one of full strength mountain lightning. The former was made from the latter, and both were rare this far north. Tank had convinced Dasin to bring two precious barrels of mountain lightning along on the last run. They'd taught the barkeep how to make *ibitt* with it, on a promise that one barrel would stay reserved for them alone. Dasin had sweetened the deal with two large bags of mulling spices.

The Goose was a decent enough place, with wide windows that let plenty of light and air through when the shutters were open on good days. They used reasonable oil in their lamps, served hefty portions of bread and smoked meats alongside their ales, wines, and liquor, and was the only place Tank had ever seen that required patrons to move outdoors to the patio to smoke.

Even so, he wasn't in the mood to watch his tone or volume, or to worry about being overheard. He put down a silver round for a loaf of fresh-baked hearth bread, a wedge of hard cheese, and a chunk of smoked sausage in addition to the liquor, then waved Lia out the door. As they returned to the road, he handed everything over to her.

At a gnarled old oak, he turned from the road, holding aside aspen branches for Lia. She paused a moment, studying the brush thoughtfully, then ducked ahead of him. Somehow, even with one arm holding a bundle of food and flasks, she managed to eel through to the clear spot he'd been aiming for. He followed her this time, bemused and intrigued.

A large, flat stone that jutted out over the drop made a perfect seat and table. They sat with their legs hanging over the edge, looking down over the steep, rocky scree below. To the south, the line of the Forest ran thick and implacable. To the east lay what looked to be a relatively affluent neighborhood; to the northeast, rows of shops with colorful awnings. Farther to the east lay the terraced open market area, and beyond that, the road towards Arason emerged from more randomly arranged buildings and snaked up a hill.

Tank methodically began to cut the cheese and meat into pieces, setting it in neat piles between them.

"Have you been here before?" he said as he worked, rotating one hand in a tight circle to indicate he was speaking to this specific spot.

"No," Lia said. "But I grew up finding spots like this to hide. I could see where people have pushed through before." She flashed a grin at him. He let himself return the smile and drew a deep breath of clean, quiet air, a weight fading from his shoulders. A hawk floated over the terraced market, tilting gently, the sun catching golden gleams along the edges of its wings.

"I've never been to Stecatr," he said. "I had in mind it was — well, Assiasan's not much on random greenery. It's mostly rock and terraced farms."

"Stecatr's a fair bit like this," Lia said, looking out over the buildings sprawled below them. "It goes *up* a lot more. I still can't believe how much ground space these buildings use. But there's a lot of forest in and around the city. It helps with the blizzards, I think. Syrta holding off Eki, is how the priests put it." She looked down at the sliced food uncertainly.

"I grew up in sand and rock," Tank said. He stacked slices of cheese and meat together and handed it to her, waiting until she took it before he went on: "I'd never even heard of snow until I came to Bright Bay. The nights can get damn cold, mind you, and there's ice at times, even hail. But there isn't ever a proper snow. At least not where I lived."

"I'd never heard of tornadoes before coming down through the hills," she admitted. "They sound *terrifying*."

"They are." He passed her some bread and cheese. "I like hard cheese. The south only makes soft cheese. Curdled, fermented stuff, what you'd call cottage cheese or curds, I think. From goats, usually."

They ate for a time in silence, watching a wake of buzzards circling over the southern woods. The cheese was a good hard Arason cheddar, the meat a well-spiced Isata dried sausage; the bread, made from locally ground flour, had a hard crust and fluffy insides. The sharp and the oily tastes meshed with the soft bread in a way that demanded respectful attention.

Eventually, Tank picked up the two flasks and held them up to check the marks. Lia let out a demurring sound, shaking her head.

"Oh, no," Tank said, letting his voice go flat and unfriendly. "This is likely the best chance I'll get to talk openly. So if you want me to answer your damn questions, you listen by my rules. And my rule is: we drink."

He unstoppered the flask of mountain lightning and took a hefty swallow. Acid, brass, and cinnamon washed through his sinuses; after swallowing, he inhaled contentedly, feeling the harsh notes softening.

When he lowered the flask and held it out to her, she took it and drank without protest. He watched to make sure she swallowed, and checked her eyes as she returned the flask: watering slightly, and she breathed out hard, but she hadn't coughed or choked. So she knew how to drink strong liquor. Good on one hand, unfortunate on the other. He probably couldn't get her drunk fast enough to avoid answering at least some of what she wanted to know.

He uncapped the ibbit, drank, inhaled fumes of honeyed gold, then passed it to her. This time she was smiling as she handed the flask back. "That's *good*," she said. "What is it?"

"Same as the first, mountain lightning, but cut with tea and honey. Mountain lightning is...." Tank looked up at the clear sky, which was worth looking at all on its own and not only as a distraction as he considered the complex geographical and cultural explanations tied into the term. Isata rarely had weather quite this clear, and from this vantage the blue seemed to go on forever, so deep that he could turn upside down and fall into it with a hop.

He blinked free of that fancy before it made him dizzy.

"Quality hard liquor," he said, recalling the question. "Worth its weight in gold, some places."

"Can I stick with the second one?"

He laughed. "No. It's traditional to switch. Eat some more. It'll sneak up on you." He capped and set aside the liquor, then leaned back on his hands, looking out over Isata and enjoying the warmth of the sun on his face.

"How was the ale cold?" she said unexpectedly. Her face tinted slightly when he stared at her. "In Bright Bay," she clarified. "The beer Sanben had me buy you. It was cold."

"Ah."

Well, that wasn't the worst place to start, even though it wasn't nearly as simple a question as it sounded. Tank went back to looking at the city as he thought through how to answer that. Lia let the silence alone, nibbling at the food absently as she waited.

Eventually, Tank said, "First up, there's no such thing as witches. I don't even know for sure that I believe in gods." He caught her flinch out of the corner of his eye and waited until he felt her relax into reluctant acceptance of that statement. "What there is ... what there are, is creatures that...." He paused, grammar tangling in his mind and mouth, then tried again. "There's these creatures called ha'reye. Powerful enough to squash us like ants, live hundreds if not thousands of years, manipulate the elements as easily as a human being's thoughts and actions." He stopped. Lia had let out a grunt like she'd been gut punched. "What?"

"Nothing," she said. "Go on."

Tank regarded her sideways, dubious, then shrugged and went on. "They've never claimed to be gods. And the southern gods don't have anything to do with them. They're not the same, I mean. Or drawn one from the other. I don't think. Eh. I'm making a hash of this."

He frowned up at the sky, watching a large bird circling close by. He'd never paid much attention to theology, and he didn't feel any regret over that now, but it did make this a difficult conversation. How to explain the Three, and their Callen? How to explain the intersection between gods, ha'reye, and ha'ra'hain? Not to mention the southern reverence towards desert lords, created as intermediaries between ha'reye and ordinary humans.

Lia sat very still. He could feel her watching him. "What are ... *hahreh?*" she said, scarcely audible. "Was that, were those bird creatures ...?"

That was an opening he could work with. "No. Those were bloodbirds, and those were bad, but nothing like what I'm talking about. I don't think anyone knows what ha'reye actually look like. They're ... they're old creatures. *Old*. One is a ha'rethe, more than one is ha'reye." He emphasized the correct pronunciation for her. "They live far underground, where the land turns to fire. You'll never see one. But they've interbred with humans, over the...." He paused, considering the actual scale, then said, simply, "Over the years. Half-breeds are ha'ra'hain, singular ha'ra'ha. They look human, if they want, or if they're down the line a bit. And ha'ra'hain can mess with the elements, or close enough. So, that cold ale in Bright Bay? There's a lot of folks with a trick or two, like chilling down a drink. We call 'em partials. They just got a bit, nothing too dangerous. Mostly find them to the south, because there aren't any ha'reye to the north."

As far as I know, he thought, then wondered where that had come from. He'd never even considered the possibility before. The notion sent a chill down his back.

"The *aichin*," Lia murmured, as though something had just come clear.

"That's a kind of ha'ra'ha, I think, yeah. You talking about those two here in Isata? Thought so. Dasin and I stayed there our first time through. Didn't suit us, so we moved to the Round." He paused, sorting through what he could say, and decided to leave out any details of that trip. Instead, he said, "They're prickly about questions, but they're not ... they're not *dangerous*, as such. They like jobs where they can stay awake for a long time at a stretch, and they're nasty fast in a fight. Just leave 'em alone. Most partials look a lot more human than that. And I never saw aichin anywhere but Isata. For all I know, those are the only two in existence. Partials are odd."

He sat up and reached for the liquor again. Lia took her turn without hesitation.

Tank eased back onto his elbow and said, "Like I was saying, they're not gods. The ha'reye. I've killed one. Well, hurt it badly, at least. It was in Bright Bay, turning the King completely insane. And the Northern Church was right up alongside, meddling, making everything worse." He paused, then risked a loaded question: "Did the Purge reach Stecatr?"

"Not really," Lia said, her voice thin and dry. "We heard stories. And some of the priests who didn't like what King Oruen was doing came to Stecatr, because we're the most pious city in the north. They swear the stories are exaggerated."

"They aren't," Tank said, acidic. "Don't trust any priests that were in Bright Bay during the Purge. The things they did ... none of them are innocent. They didn't just leave, Lia. Oruen threw them out, to avoid holding some damn ugly trials. Ninnic was a fucking *monster*, and they egged him on." His hands hurt. He glanced down to find them white-knuckled fists.

Lia's chin sank to her chest. She looked, suddenly, much older and more worn.

"Yeah, well," Tank said after a moment, relaxing his hands and regaining his composure. "You see why I didn't want to say anything about this. You're no happier for knowing, are you?"

"No," she said, low voiced. "Are you a ... a partial, then?"

That question brought him up short. A tenday ago, he would have laughed at the idea. Now, with Evkit's comment about *heritage* fresh in his mind, he couldn't dismiss it so easily. "I honestly don't know," he said.

He deliberately ate a piece of bread, slugged down two more shots, and passed the flasks off to Lia once more. As she handed them back, he registered that the weights weren't right. She was faking her swallows. The liquor in his own system sped him past caring or commenting on that. *Fuck it, her loss.*

He said, "I've never wanted to be seen as anything special. I don't want to live my life being looked at sideways. I like to fight, I like to travel, I like to stay very far away from the true south. That's all I want out of life."

"And Dasin," Lia said, then put a hand to her mouth as though she hadn't meant to say that.

Tank laughed bitterly. "Now you see why we're drinking," he said, and tossed back another round. "Nah, don't try to keep up with me at this point," he told her as she held out a hand with a resigned expression. "I'm fucking pissed and I'm about to get fucking pissed."

Now that was a sentence that only made sense in Kaenic; southern dialects had no equivalent word. *Angry, drunk,* and *urinating* all in one sibilant package. It was a glorious, glorious word, *pissed.*

Tank let his head hang back, looking up at the clear blue sky, and breathed deeply for a time.

"Who was that man? Ha ... Hadinn Evkit?" Lia said.

Tank sighed and let himself down flat on the rock, drawing his feet up to rest on the edge. "This needs a geography lesson. Remember the docks in Bright Bay?" He breathed in sharply, catching himself before he said *Where you were tracking Toad.* She still didn't know he'd seen her there. "There's two sets of docks, west and east. To the south of Bright Bay is — *was* — an area called the Horn. The Horn was the only land passage to the southlands."

She made a small sound. He paused, and she said, tentatively, "The southlands ...?"

"Eh ... right." He shut his eyes, sorting out terms and geography, then said, "Furthest south to furthest north, everyone draws the line of what's *south* and what's *north* differently.

Irritates me no end. But look —"

He sketched in the air with both hands as he spoke, drawing lines and curves, forming a clumsy, invisible map.

"You got the Jungles, way south of here. The desert southlands, the true south, where all the Families are — another time," he added as she started to say something. "That's a whole jug an' a half on it's own. Lissen. Jungles, desert — that's what *I* mean when I say *southlands*. Land narrows into a neck between that and Bright Bay, where the northern kingdom proper starts. That neck is the Horn. Was the Horn. 'S pretty torn up now."

Lia made a soft noise, as though about to ask a question. Her thin face was intent and thoughtful, her hair tousled by pushing through the alders. He let himself briefly enjoy the sun-gilding on her pale hair, then shook himself back to sense and waved a hand to stop her speaking.

"Nemmind that. Another time. So, look, Bright Bay sits with water to west and south and some east, right? The Coast Road runs along the coastal southlands, and it splits — one road goes out to the swamps, one to the docks, one road goes up through the Hackerwood, where we went, yeah? Then there's all your northlands, where we are now —" He motioned vaguely. "Right? Yeah? So you, from way up by the mountains, you call anything past Arason the *southlands*, right?"

"South of the Hackerwood," Lia said.

"Okay. So. I mean south of the Horn when I say southlands, you mean south of the Hackerwood." He breathed deeply, attempting to focus. What had he just been saying? Horn. Right. "You were asking about Evkit. He's one of the teyanain. He was in charge of them, the ones in the Horn, they've controlled the Horn since, I dunno, since the first fire was lit, probably." He shut his eyes, aware that the liquor was making him incoherent. "Gimme moment."

He made himself sit up and eat a few bites of bread and cheese. As he ate, he pulled old mindfulness rituals through his mind, steadying himself as Allonin had taught him to do so many years ago.

"Don't think about that bastard," he muttered.

"What?"

"Huh? Oh — nothing. I was talking about the teyanain, right? Right. So. They're like self-appointed judges that think they ought to be making the rules. They kept control of all the traffic between the southlands and the northern kingdom for a long damn time. Now it's different. It's messy. Real messy."

He ate another piece of bread, chewing without enthusiasm. Lia was frowning deeply now, but at least she was keeping her questions to herself. He allowed himself another bit of watching her, taking in the way her concentration brought out the sharp lines in her face and shoulders. She wasn't at all unattractive, once the ata wasn't in the way.

He blinked lazily and refocused on the conversation before she could notice him looking.

"Lord Evkit was in charge of the teyanain before the Horn went to shit. The teyanain are ... they're...." Tank shut his eyes briefly, trying to find the right words. "They're terrifying.

Like a tornado, yeah? Scary. Pop up out of nowhere. Lots of damage when they're angry. I think, a real long time ago, they used to sort of be in charge. Like judges or sommat. I think maybe *they* still think they ought to be the ones deciding right and wrong."

Tank sighed and sat up again. He weighed a flask in one hand, then shook his head. More would risk loosening his tongue a step too far, spilling things that didn't need to be said. He would start answering the questions Lia didn't know how to ask.

He went on: "Anyway, a while back, there was a thing that happened. A big — thing." He waved a hand in the air, frustrated at himself. There was simply no way to explain something he didn't entirely understand himself. "The Horn collapsed. Where the teyanain and Lord Evkit lived. And a lot of the southlands, the southeastern coast past the Horn, that collapsed too. There were these waves ... docks were destroyed, huge chunks of Bright Bay was destroyed, the southeastern coast got smashed to shit."

Tank picked up the mountain lightning flask, took a drink, passed it to Lia, then took a swig of *ibbit*. She drank both without comment and handed them back.

"Evkit dissa — disserpreed. Disappeared. The teyanain too. Sounds like Evkit's daughter took over in the Horn. I've never met a teyanin before, never really paid attention to the talk, since it didn't concern me. I wasn't ever going back through the Horn, wassnn', wasn't, ever going back south, so I'd never need to know anything about them. I thought." He snorted. "I should know better by now. So. Did I answer your question?" He squinted at Lia, feeling puzzled and bleary.

"Not really," she said, an odd expression on her face.

"Too bad. I'm done talking." He lay back down on the warm stone again, breathing deeply. "Gods, it's nice here. Quiet. Smells good. I like the, the, whatever that flowering bush over there is." He waved his right hand vaguely.

"The bush isn't what you're smelling," she said, sounding bemused. "It's a false cherry. That smell is the spiraling moth vine on the tree over there."

He managed to focus. "Huh. I never even noticed. Small flowers. You sure it's not that big fuffery — fluffy — bush?"

"Positive."

"Huh. All right." He let his head back down. "Just a nap," he said indistinctly. "I need some time away from that fucker. Every time. Every trip. Always need."

Time flickered. He was vaguely aware of snoring, vaguely aware of drifting aromas: sweet syrup from the spiraling moth vine, tangy smoke from the meat, a greasy underlay from the cheese, acidity from the liquour, and the mixture of soap and horse fustiness that infused Lia's clothes and hair.

Warmth grew, sun beating down with relentless attention. He rolled, drowsily trying to find shade, and fetched up against Lia. She laughed a little and moved aside. He scrunched into the shady spot she'd occupied and went back to sleep.

Chapter Twenty-seven

Tank snored, a whistling sound that was more amusing than annoying. He rolled, bumping into Lia's hip every so often, as though trying to push her from the rock. She pinched his earlobe each time, a trick she'd often used on her sister, and he grunted, turning to his other side.

Leaving him wasn't an option. Even if there hadn't been that steep drop right to hand, it would have been ... *rude* wasn't quite the right word, but it would have to do. So Lia sat still, looking out over Isata, making sure Tank didn't roll off the cliff, listening to the traffic clattering up and down the hill a long stone's throw to their backs, and thinking about what Tank had said before passing out.

So Idisio, that *person* she'd met in Arason, was a ha'ra'ha. Not entirely human, but *demon* didn't properly fit either. *Demon-spawn?* The Stecatr Church would use that term. Tank would, by definition, be a demon-killer. That would make the Church happy. He was also most definitely, under their definition, a witch. That would negate any goodwill.

A train of wagons lumbered in from the south, probably loaded with dried fish, sea salt, and various pickled things. More than likely, some also carried bins of shells and sand, which sold for increasing profits the further north one went.

Another thought turned over in her head, one so vast it took her some time to properly work around the edges and see it in its entirely.

Oruen threw them out, to avoid holding some damn ugly trials.

Ninnic was a fucking monster, and they egged him on.

The things they've done ... None of them are innocent.

The priests that had come from Bright Bay to Stecatr claimed they'd been fighting the Purge, but from what Tank had said they'd been actively involved in *fomenting* it.

Who do I believe? The Church I grew up with, or a mercenary I only met a matter of a tenday or so ago?

Lia felt a wave of nausea roll through her gut. She stared hard at the glossy leaves of the moth vine until the sensation passed.

The southern priests had trickled into Stecatr bit by bit over the past few years. They'd slowly taken over the Stecatr Church, claiming that serving at the Bright Bay tower gave them more status. Nobody could properly argue with that. Nobody had *known* there was no Church presence in Bright Bay any longer. That alone was explosive news to bring home, and Lia was entirely certain the priests would forbid her to speak of it.

The newly arrived priests had sharpened the rhetoric about being careful of demons and always obeying the gods. They increased penalities. Restrictions. Punishments....

Her heart ached, remembering.

As piece after piece linked together, it seemed stunningly obvious that the newly arrived priests had been doing their level best to recreate the Purge, on a smaller scale, in Stecatr.

Why?

A dry, cynical voice answered: *Because they could.*

She couldn't refuse the new belief, no matter the pain involved. *The Stecatr Church* lied. *Our own priests lied to us. The priests who daily invoke strict and loving obedience to the gods. The priests my mother bakes her special bread for. The priests my father kneels before as examples of the most righteous path.*

A faint red tinge, more of a feeling than an actual color, began to form in the back of Lia's mind.

Tank cleared his throat. She opened her eyes, startled, to find him looking up at her with a pensive expression.

"I get the feeling," he said, tone neutral, "that you're starting to understand why everyone's been so damn careful in what to tell you if your priests might object to your knowing a thing." He sat up, slowly, and rubbed a hand across his eyes, then glanced at the steep drop near to hand, his mouth twisting. "Thank you for staying."

"Why hasn't anyone *stopped* it?" she demanded, not caring if the question made sense.

Tank looked at the sky as though considering that question. In the end, he said merely, "I should get back. I didn't plan on leaving Dasin alone that long." He rose to his feet, staggered slightly, then steadied himself and held out a hand to help her up.

She glared up at him, not moving. He sighed and dropped his hand.

"Don't brood and steam about it," he advised. "We'll talk again later, yeah? It's a long road north. There's time. Go get some sleep." He turned without waiting for an answer and walked away, a bit unsteadily.

She dropped her head to her knees and stayed: far too unsteady, herself, to risk standing. She also suspected that if she had to walk back beside him, she might haul off and punch him to vent her growing frustration.

Better, much better, to sit still and merely daydream about it.

Chapter Twenty-eight

Dasin wasn't in the room, which had been left unlocked. His bags and boxes were gone. A neatly folded note sat propped against the oil lamp on the desk, the key beside it. Tank took a look round, checking for signs of intrusion in the sparsely furnished room. His own pack hadn't been moved. The vinegar smell had faded, leaving cinnamon as the dominant note. The window had been wiped clean, turning blurry light into wide, warm rays, and both inside and outside shutters stood wide open.

Half-formed thoughts swirled through Tank's mind. *Is he —? Did he —? Am I —? Are we —?*

He scrubbed a hand roughly over his eyes, locked the door behind him, then picked up the note.

Tank —

Get some sleep. I've taken another room. We set up at the market in two days. Do your rounds when you wake up.

— D

Tank read the note three times, his mind slowly going blank. At last, he dropped it to the floor, pried off his boots, and drew the inside shutters closed. He collapsed onto the bed without bothering to undress.

Dawn light squinting through the shutters woke him some time later. He lay on his back, staring up at the ceiling and blinking slowly. No hangover. Not even a headache. That was nice, if surprising.

He put out a hand, found empty space beside him, and remembered. Lay still a while longer, gaze unfocused, taking inventory of various bruises and aches that had accumulated over the past few days. At last, he sat up slowly, wary of dizziness, and reached for his boots, then paused and reached for the chamberpot instead.

That handled, he went about making himself presentable. He brushed out his hair, felt through the strands to check the curl, and left it loose. It needed a trim, and he needed a proper bath. He'd get both at the same time. In the meanwhile, the first person he had to visit on his rounds significantly appreciated long, loose hair on men. Catering to small matters like that made larger ones considerably easier, and Dasin's jealousy rarely overwhelmed his pragmatism.

Tank pulled out his small jewelry box and poked through the contents. He normally didn't wear any, but Isata was a place where his personal preferences had to come second to proper presentation.

Jewelry carried specific meanings south of the Horn. Dasin always wore multiple earrings when he was showing off, although he was careful to stick with neutral metals and stones. Tank rarely wore more than one earring. It felt like claiming status he hadn't earned and didn't want, even in the northlands where such things held much less weight.

Today, he settled on a single silver hoop in his right ear, the wire so thin as to be nearly invisible. A set of leather wrist bands, inset with bands of copper. A wide copper ring on the third finger of his right hand, matching silver band on the left. He considered his two necklaces, then left them untouched.

Dark brown trousers, a white shirt that laced down most of the front, and his good walking boots made for a sturdy enough outfit to manage walking all over this bloody town. As a final touch, he drew a small design in black ink on the left side of his neck — the southern symbol for *fire*, although no northern would likely see anything but spiky, foreign writing.

The people he needed to deal with today liked to feel superior. Tank now looked sufficiently barbaric, by Isata standards, to satisfy that. As an extra benefit, the display would warn away most thieves and opportunists.

Not for the first time, he wondered if he ought to get a tattoo. Not for the first time, he shuddered at the notion. He had enough permanent marks of the past on his body already. He didn't need more.

Reflexively, he reached back, feeling across what he could reach of the thick scars from nape to tailbone, as though to assure himself they were still there. Ghost-images, memories he didn't want to remember, tapped at the edges of his consciousness. He dismissed them impatiently.

Never mind. That was a long time ago. It's over.

Although ... He touched the scars again, thoughtful now. Alyea had similar marks. It didn't take much attention to bring up her memories of the stripping pain, her determination to endure, and her humiliation as she broke, far sooner than she'd expected. That had been before her transition to a desert lord, of course. These days, the whip would have been shoved sideways up the wielder's nether regions before the first swing.

Tank had Alyea's memories of the trials, and some time past them. *I literally have the training of a desert lord in my head. Why have I been ignoring that?*

Well, he knew that answer: he'd wanted to be ordinary. He hadn't wanted that power, that responsibility, that danger. But ... *Your desires on this point mean nothing,* Evkit had said with supreme confidence. Maybe it was time to stop hiding from what Evkit, among others, apparently saw in him, if only to be sure he could properly defend himself and his crew.

It all starts with the attitude, Alyea said, a ghost-voice laughing at him without malice.

All right, then. Tank straightened his posture to a desert lord's easy confidence, shook away lingering doubts, and swept out into the city to do his rounds.

Isata stood at a critical trade junction. Four major roads led from the city: the Forest Road, the North Road, the Midlands Road, and the West Road. Each road led to, and through, such different regions that the Lord of Isata had designated specific groups to work with and guide travelers. Each group kept up to date with the latest news and law changes relevant to their area, provided maps and specific supplies, and sometimes hired out guides for groups needing extra support. And each group deeply appreciated travelers who stopped by to offer updates on their way through town.

The head of the Foresters, a woman named Kiu, stood as tall and broad as Tank, with coarse dark hair clipped short and equally dark skin and eyes. She sat at a rough table near where the Forest Road entered the city, under the shelter of a wide-branched white oak tree. The previous day, Tank had waved at her as they went by, signaling that he'd come back to talk later. Kiu had narrowed her eyes at Dasin's limp form and glared in a way that said: *You'd damn well better.*

Now, she greeted Tank with a wide smile, taking him in from head to foot with a gaze at once appreciative and cold. She motioned to the bench seat in front of her table and raised an eyebrow pointedly.

Tank sat down, resisting the impulse to braid his hair back out of his face. He didn't waste time with pleasantries. Kiu preferred short and blunt speech. He said, "The former head of the Horn teyanain has taken over the Hackerwood. He's called hadinn Evkit now. Sounds like he's going to allow regular traffic, but for anyone of note, there's no going in or out without his permission. You'll want to send someone to start negotiations, if there hasn't already been an approach."

Kiu's eyes narrowed thoughtfully. "I take it your information comes first hand?" Tank nodded. "And does that have anything to do with why you were carrying Dasin in yesterday with him looking like a sack of cooked oats?"

"Well, yeah." Tank scratched his collarbone uncomfortably and changed the subject. "It was a moondark run. Things got complicated. We had a batch of woodrats and a high-red bloodbird come over the wall at us in broad daylight. Everyone survived," he added as her expression turned alarmed.

"You got lucky."

"I know. I suggest warning travellers not to go alone, and especially without guards. The walls are starting to crumble at more than one of the campsites."

Her lips thinned, a deep frown crossing her face. "I'll pass the word. Might be able to convince Lord Tiyh to send out patrols of Lordguards or Hall trained over the short term. And I'll send word to the King. Again. Maybe he'll finally *do* something about the walls." Her tone was ferociously bitter.

"I'm going to the Hall of Arms next," Tank told her. "I'll let them know."

"Good luck talking to anyone of note," she said, her mouth drawing aside cynically. "Front desk might as well be manned by rocks for all the help they are. But I have a feeling *you'll* get through like a greased eel, won't you?"

Tank didn't say anything to that. Nearby, a northern firebird screeched challenge at someone who'd come too close to one of the warehouses. A child screamed, then wailed in hysterical terror: so, it had been an ignorant fool who'd thought the bird was for petting, and been stupid enough to bring their child over for a look. Tank had seen that before. It never failed to astonish him how careless some people were of their children.

Kiu ignored the sound. She frowned off into the distance, clearly thinking. "Is it possible this Evkit —"

"*Hadinn* Evkit."

She paused, her attention focusing on him. He could see her working through the implications of his correction. Her neck muscles tensed, but she was smart: she didn't look around for lurking teyanain.

At last she rubbed her nose, blinking slowly. "Yes. *Hadinn* Evkit. Is it possible he weakened the walls deliberately?"

"Maybe?" Tank rocked a hand, palm-down, to show uncertainty. "I don't think so. I think he's still consolidating his power, to be honest."

Her gaze turned speculative.

He added hastily, "It's not a good idea to try interfering before he can settle in all the way."

She snorted, looking disappointed. "Well, then. Anything else?"

Tank hesitated. Kiu's eyes narrowed again. Reluctantly, Tank said, "A Stecatr priest we ran into went Forest-crazed and jumped the wall. His hire is, was, a Stecatr mercenary. Likely their church will blame him for not saving the priest. I told him to go south and stay there, but he's got a snake up his ass. I don't know which way he'll jump."

"Mm." Kiu's thick eyebrows slanted into a thoughtful frown. "I remember that priest. He'd never gone through the Forest before. He tried to tell me I was spinning folk tales." She laughed a little. "Not smart, coming to me for information and then making fun what I have to say."

"Speaking of information," Tank said, turning the topic. "Any news?"

"A bit," she admitted, and began filling him in on various matters. He listened, mentally marking what Dasin needed to know about sooner than later, what was amusing gossip to pass along at a moment that needed a light touch, and what Tank needed to follow up on himself. Assuming their routine held. If, if, if.

There were enough items on the followup list to make Tank look up at the position of the sun in the sky, grimacing. Today and tomorrow would involve a lot of walking, talking, and being *seen*. He hated Isata. It was the most complicated town they dealt with, which was likely why Dasin loved it so much.

Kiu motioned with a closed fist to indicate she'd given him everything she had to say. He stood and offered a formal bow. As always, she chuffed laughter. When he straightened, her eyes were gleaming. "You do have lovely ... shoulders," she told him. "That hair of yours is quite something, you know." She flexed her fingers.

He put on a practiced smile and withdrew before she could say anything more explicit. *Stay on her good side, let her flirt,* Dasin had said, *but don't encourage her or we'll have a hell of a mess to sort out.* He hadn't needed to specify that the mess would largely be his own fury.

Once out of Kiu's sight, Tank stopped long enough to braid his hair back. Loose and rough, but it would do.

On the way to the Isata Hall of Arms, he swung by a small food cart that sold a particularly good seared corn dish. Rich with rosemary, butter, and salt, served with a wedge of flatbread, it was an easy and filling meal. On consideration, he picked up a small, expensive jar of spiced apple preserves as a bribe, tucking it into his belt pouch. The added weight banged against his hip, and he set a hand on the pouch as he walked to keep that to a minimum.

Isata, like every major city, had multiple Halls. The News Rider Hall was the flashiest, literally as well as metaphorically: it had recently been fitted with enormous, perfect glass windows. Given its spot atop a high hill, it made an easy landmark when giving directions. The Merchants' Hall, nearly in the middle of Isata, ran parallel to Market Row, with extensive warehouse space for long term storage. There were also Green and Craft Halls. The former split into sub-Halls for forestry, farming, hunting, and the like. The latter separated into as many directions, from clothcraft to candies.

To Tank it seemed far too complicated. Even Dasin complained occasionally about the extensive negotiations needed for a traveling merchant to get inventory and supplies. Since Dasin absolutely refused to pay for any membership beyond his tithes from market sales, which he also grumbled about handing over, Tank wasn't at all surprised at his difficulties.

Thankfully, all Tank had to deal with was the Isata Hall of Arms. Located close to the Hackerwood, it wasn't a particularly impressive building. The two-story stone building, designed for function rather than aesthetics, was really an outer shell around training grounds. Hall trained could take a room along the western edge; classes ran along the eastern edge; administration along the northern side. The southern side had no doors nor windows, in tacit acknowledgment of the looming woods less than a mile away, and the rooms along that leg offered storage and mending services.

The intake officer of the day was a man Tank had dealt with, and bribed, in the past. He brightened expectantly on seeing Tank and slid the book across the counter.

"I love that I never have to write it all out for you," the officer said as Tank filled out the required information: his name, employer's name, current date, contract terms. At least he could put "same as previous" there.

"I need to see Aster," Tank said as he dotted the last period.

The man said, with entirely inappropriate joy, "Oh, now, he's a busy man...."

They argued a bit for the look of the thing. Tank quietly put the preserves on the corner of the desk, keeping his hand on it as they spoke; the man developed a pleased smirk and suddenly discovered an opening, "Just for a few minutes, mind, he really is scheduled out today, don't get me in trouble." Tank lifted his hand from the jar and smiled at how quickly it was whisked into hiding.

Aster, the sub-Head of Hall, was a short man, spare and taut and pale. He looked up with a frown as Tank came into his office. "What's this? I'm busy."

"It's important, *s'e*," Tank said, then offered a formal bow to underscore the statement.

"Very well," Aster said, waving Tank to a chair in front of his heavy oak desk. "Make it quick. I've a meeting with Hall Master Hendle and the Lord of Isata this afternoon, and I'm not nearly ready for it." He glanced down at himself ruefully, taking in the sweat-stained undershirt and ragged leggings. "My *kehair* should be here any moment to dress me."

In the south, Aster would have said *kathain*. Tank liked *kehair*. It didn't have the ugly weight the first word held for him.

Tank briefly outlined what had happened in the Hackerwood and, in broad strokes, his understanding of the shifting power balances. Aster listened with a still, set expression.

"Thank you," he said when Tank finished. "I'll let Master Hendle and Lord Tiyh know."

As Tank withdrew, the kehair bustled in, a young woman with her arms full of rich fabrics and boxes of accessories. Aster sighed noisily. Tank grinned and got out of there.

Dasin should be handling the visits to the Green and Craft halls. Tank hesitated, debating whether to try tracking Dasin down in spite of the note. He decided against it. The day was drawing on, and he was uncomfortably aware of his own stink. He wanted a private bath, to soak for a while in gloriously hot water and scented soap and *silence*.

Then ... *then* he'd go find Dasin, and find out where matters stood.

Chapter Twenty-nine

Last time through Isata, Lia's stop at the Hall of Arms had been a perfunctory visit, a matter of writing her name in the book and listing her current contract holder and rate of pay. This time, the clerk glanced at her entry and said, "A moment, *s'a*, please. Head of Hall wants a word with you."

She blinked, taken aback. Tank had signed in well before her. Had he said something to draw her to such lofty attention?

"Why?" she asked.

"You think I know? I don't ask what isn't mine to care about." He relented. "Far as I know, it's nothing bad. Come on, this way."

The smell of oil, metal, and leather trailed through the air as the clerk led Lia to a large, plain red door reinforced with thick metal banding. It bore more than a few dents and chips, as though someone had actually tried to break in at some point. The clerk rapped briskly on the door, then motioned Lia to enter.

Two large glass windows let in late morning light, shimmering across several large-leaved vining plants trailing from baskets hung near the ceiling. The room smelled of fresh-turned dirt and wood shavings. A bench before the windows held bags of both, along with small gardening tools and pots of tiny, misshapen trees.

A rack of more familiar gear took up another wall: swords and armor, and a workbench with a chain vest spread out into several pieces. Most of the equipment clearly needed repair and cleaning.

A thick red rug covered most of the stone flag floor, and a solid blackwood desk sat against the far wall. There appeared to be no chairs other than the one the large man behind it was rising from.

Lia settled her stance to endure standing for a while and bowed politely to the man before her. "Master," she said. "Lia of Stecatr. I'm told you wanted to see me."

He raked his hands through graying hair, smiling. "You can call me Hendle," he said. "In public, it's Lord Hendle, or Lord of Westhall if you must be entirely formal for some reason. But I don't bother with formality in private." His smile faded to a more pensive expression. "I meant to meet with you when you came through town before. I was caught by events and missed the opportunity." He glanced around, frowning. "They've taken my guest chair again. Gods only know what they're going to return this time." He sank down into a perfectly fluid cross-legged sit on the carpet, motioning Lia down with him.

She complied, mildly bewildered. "What they'll return?"

"I set my senior students to develop challenges for the novices," Hendle said. "My guest chair is apparently an excellent opportunity to learn how to handle being attacked while seated. None of the other chairs will do, this year." He sighed. "The previous class decided my hallway was an excellent place to stage battles in tight indoor quarters. Before that, I had students climbing all over the roofs and devising ways to attack from the air. That was an interesting year, to be sure. Taught me to be damn careful about accepting Aerthraim students, for one thing."

"So that's what happened to the door," Lia said, at a loss for any other remark.

Hendle's broad face stilled, taking on a hard cast. "No," he said. "That was from a disagreement with the Lord of Isata, during the Purge. I refused to turn over a Hall-sworn who'd offended some goldrobe or other, and he tried to force the issue."

Lia stared.

Hendle shrugged, his cheerful mood returning. "I won, in the sense that we drove the fools off our grounds and held our independence, but it's made for a few delicate moments, politically, in the years since. So." He studied Lia, his blue eyes thoughtful. "I'm told you ran into some troubles during training."

Lia sorted out her answer with care. "There were students who didn't like my being there. I had to get creative in defending myself a few times. Nobody was seriously injured, and my Hall master backed me on each incident."

"'Creative'," Hendle repeated, a small smile pulling at his mouth. "I like that word. It certainly matches the stories I've heard of you. I'm wondering where you learned that, though, because while Coy is a ferociously good teacher and Hall master, he does stick to the tried and true paths."

"I grew up scrapping on the streets," Lia said easily. "Poverty teaches you to use what you have. I'm a fast learner."

Hendle bent his head to one side, his smile unwavering, and said, "Nice evasion. Perhaps I ought to be honest, myself, and tell you that Carter and I have lunch at the Bald Goat once a tenday. I'm entirely aware of your connections, *s'a* Lia."

Lia ducked her head, feeling color bleeding up into her face again. This conversation was quickly turning into a nightmare of vulnerability.

Hendle's mouth moved in a faint smile. "I believe in protecting my people," he said matter-of-factly, "and I believe that every Hall sworn that walks into this city is one of my people while they are here, no matter where you're signed. I protect my people from the scheming of Church, Lord, and underground alike, and that means knowing a great deal about how the world works. It means I sit down to dreadful lunches in seedy taverns with criminals and dry meetings with pompous nobles and even drier conversations with the few priests who linger in this city. I do not choose sides. I do not break confidences. As my door shows, that is not always a safe path to walk."

"Aren't you — I'm sorry, Master, aren't you sworn to the city's defense?" Lia was too fascinated and bewildered to hold on to her embarrassment. "I thought all Halls ...?"

"Hendle, please. And yes. We support the Lord of Isata, when called upon. But my priorities are *my* people first, *then* the city, *then* the Lord's particular requests or requirements." He paused, then added, "And after those, the king and kingdom."

Lia sat wordless, stunned by that entirely backwards recital.

"I've been forced to understand a lot about politics in order to hold that line," Hendle said. He scratched his scalp absently, then wiped his hand on his trousers with a grimace and glanced at the windows. "I don't have much time today. Let me cut to the quick point: you can't stay with Stecatr Hall."

"What?" Lia stiffened, instantly and deeply offended. "Because of my connections?"

"Not at all. Think about how you gained that coin, and what I'm quite sure you've learned since then. I'm told you're reasonably clever. Work it out for yourself." Hendle laced his hands over his stomach and regarded her patiently.

Lia inhaled slowly and, with an effort, shut out everything but the question to hand.

Start at the beginning. The king in Bright Bay had issued a decree that women could train at every Hall of Arms throughout the kingdom, overriding the traditional independence of the cities in such matters. The Lord of Stecatr had, unexpectedly, backed the new rules and refused to bend to the furious priests.

The Stecatr priests were more internally divided than most people suspected, notably between the newly arrived southern priests and those born and bred to the high northlands. Scarpy had taken advantage of that thin wedge of discord to set the priests arguing amongst themselves, fracturing their ability to push Stecatr's Lord to their will. His help had meant more debt for Lia to pay off, of course.

Even before that, Lia had gathered information for Scarpy, both through open activities and more covert ones, as payment for keeping herself and her family safe. She knew perfectly well that Scarpy had been attempting to set up a shadow government of thieves and smugglers, ranging across multiple cities, with himself in charge. Her journey from Stecatr to Isata, as guard for mechant Kennet, had in large part been cover for her bringing messages to Scarpy's counterparts in Arason and Isata.

If Hendle knew that plan existed, he would know it had failed, and why.

In addition, Hendle almost certainly had the news on what had happened in the Hackerwood by now, and that she'd signed with Dasin and Tank. He would know more than Lia did about how the local balance of power had been shifted by the hadinn's appearance and declarations.

Would the teyanin lord taking over the Hackerwood affect *Stecatr*? She rubbed at her eyes as her mind balked at further analysis. It was all too tangled.

She said, unable to prevent a nearly rude edge to her voice, "Please, Master Hendle, just tell me why you think I should break my oaths, put my family in danger, and leave my sworn Hall. I feel like I have a hundred pieces and no frame for the puzzle."

Hendle regarded her with an odd expression. "I suppose that's fair enough," he said. "Here's your frame, then: you're a target. You were a target before you even set foot on the road south, and now you're in the middle of a mess and even more useful as an object lesson. Bluntly, you're too good for Stecatr. Your Church will burn you out with the nonsense of having to prove yourself over and over, if they even allow you to do so fairly in the first place."

Object lesson. Yes, she knew what that would look like. And the implication that Master Coy wouldn't, or couldn't, protect her from the priests, cut like a knife to the gut.

"Thank you for warning me, Master, but I can't break my oaths."

"Stop calling me that. And don't go back," Hendle said plainly. "Coy is willing to help quietly relocate your entire family."

Lia stared, breathless with shock as the knife twisted at an unexpected angle. "He *what?*" She gathered her composure. "No. They can't. Won't. My father wouldn't go. His whole life is there. His career."

It was absolutely impossible to picture her father anywhere but in Stecatr. Not to mention that it would be a hot day in midwinter before he walked away from his precarious climb through the city guard, from drunk brawler to trusted captain, for *her* sake.

Her father wouldn't ever know, if she could help it, how much she'd paid to make that ascent possible.

Lia pushed old, gray resentment aside and shook her head vehemently. She said, "I don't believe the Church would allow that, either. They'd be losing too much face."

"They don't have to know in advance," Hendle said blandly. One eye slid down in a conspiratorial wink.

Lia drew in a sharp breath. This was too much, too fast. "Master Hendle, I don't know what to say."

"Say you'll switch your Hall to Arason, at the very least," Hendle said. "Either Isata or Arason, and I'm thinking you'd do better with Arason, given the complications stirring here."

"My father won't go," Lia said again, floundering for the right words with which to explain. "And I have — I can't —"

Heat flushed up her neck and her ears rang. Dimly, she realized she was getting angry. Really, truly *angry*.

"No!" she snapped, her true objection finally coming clear. "Stecatr is *my home*. I won't skulk away for my own safety!"

Hendle's face went expressionless. "And what is it you think you can do, other than decorate a tree for some manufactured slight?" he said, tone desert-dry.

"I don't know," she said tautly. "I don't *care*. I couldn't live with myself for running away. There has to be *something* I can do to stop this!" She drew in a great breath, then allowed herself to say it: "Something I can do to take the bad priests out of power."

Silently, she sent a fervent apology to all the faces of all the gods. But surely, *surely*, they couldn't be happy about their words being twisted and used to harm their followers?

Hendle's voice could have cut stone: "That's what most of the people who died in the Purge in Bright Bay a few years back thought, too. These aren't foolish men, *s'a*. They have a good grasp on their power already. You can't march up and unseat them for the wanting of it."

Lia looked down at the carpet and didn't say anything.

Hendle sighed, a great gusty sound. "I thought as much. All right. I'm taking one part of this out of your hands. You *are* signing over to Arason. Coy will tell the Church he forced your transfer. He'll come up with plausible reasons, so no blame falls on you. Then you'll be out from under Stecatr Hall, *and* Stecatr Church, authority. It won't make Stecatr *safe* for you, but a small shield is better than none."

Lia began to protest. The iron look in his eye silenced her.

"I'm short on time," he told her. "I'll say only one more thing: there's more happening than you know about. Stay with your current contract through Assiasan, and check in with the Hall there for further directions before returning to Stecatr. You'll need to have a meeting with Head of Arason Hall, too, when you arrive there. That is all an official order, *s'a* Lia. In my role as Head of Hall, liaison to King Oruen, representative of this and that and whatever title you want to consider important, I am giving you an *order*. One which supersedes any oath you may have made to any entity in Stecatr, human or god."

Hendle hoisted himself to his feet, brushing bits of lint from his trousers, and scowled at her forbiddingly.

"Master —" *It's not that simple,* she wanted to say. *You can't wave away my oath to the gods like that!* She had a feeling he wouldn't have any respect for that stance, though.

"*Hendle*," he corrected her sharply, then waved at the door. "You may *go*."

She stood, reluctant. "M — Hendle," she said again. This time he motioned, irritably, for her to speak. Abandoning her first, useless protest, she tried: "I don't understand — why *me*? Are you helping relocate anyone else from Stecatr?"

"I already answered the first question, and I'm not answering the second question," he said. "Now, *go*, before I pitch you out a damn window to get you out my way."

She bowed hastily and beat as quick a retreat as dignity allowed.

Chapter Thirty

Tank, despite his best efforts, couldn't find Dasin that night or the following day. His first assumption, that Dasin had taken a room somewhere else in the Round, ran into a stolid denial by every member of the staff that might or might not have been purchased with a generous donation of coin. Dasin's usual spots to brood all came up empty. The Green and Crafts Halls admitted that he'd been by, but refused any details beyond business related information. Cilif professed ignorance. Lia was genuinely ignorant. The spots where Dasin routinely networked were as unhelpful as the Round and the Halls, and Tank wasn't quite desperate enough to start looking through the whorehouses and taverns.

He considered it, though.

Well, fine. Let Dasin hide. Clearly he had enough of his wits back to manage himself, and he'd be at the market tomorrow, according to that note. Tank would corner him then. In the meanwhile, he had the rare opportunity to walk through Isata without obligation.

It was a haphazard town, with steep hills breaking the wide, pleasant roads of the south into winding slopes. Buildings, mostly wood frame, remained largely one or two stories, and a great deal of landscaping wound throughout the city. There was even a public garden, and a zoo, neither of which Tank had ever visited before.

He chose the garden as the less depressing prospect. After paying a frankly outrageous price for entry, he wandered among rose bushes, topiaries, herbs, and an abundance of flowers he had no name for. The plants looked healthy, there were plenty of shady and plenty of sunny spots, the air smelled good, and the paths were clean. He didn't feel the need to know anything more than that.

The other visitors, or patrons, as they probably preferred to be called, strolled through in pairs and groups of perfumed elegance. Ladies wore thick-heeled, lace-up boots, puffy dresses of fine materials, acres of jewelry and wide-brimmed, overly decorated hats. The gentlemen tended towards puffed, slashed breeches and shirts that looked like a cross between a tunic and a pointed tabard; somewhat fewer but larger pieces of jewelry; and caps with a floppy, baglike tail into which they tucked their hair.

One and all, they regarded Tank with expressions ranging from horror to indignation. He stepped politely out of their way at every encounter, refusing to show the sourness building in his stomach.

Tank let himself rest on a sun-drenched bench for a time, watching the play of afternoon light as a combination of a breeze and swarms of insects shook leaves and flowers on nearby bushes. The air smelled sweet and humid. Tank had nothing he had to do, nowhere to be. Nobody he had to appease, please, or otherwise cater to.

He straightened his back, shifting slightly until his body caught a still, centered sensation, and waited there, patiently, as his spinning thoughts settled into a tidy line in his mind's eye.

One at a time, now.

My son. Nothing to be done about that. A scythe of pain swept through Tank's calm. He wobbled, blinked back tears, and recentered himself.

Dasin. Not much to be done there either, until tomorrow. Possible outcomes splayed out like a hand. Tank considered them, reorganized them by likelihood, then set them aside for later.

Lia. Tank blinked again, staring at the nearby, bee-bothered flowering bushes with a sense of deep bewilderment. What in the world did he need to think about regarding Lia? About to dismiss that thought from the line, he paused.

She's going to leave, because this is all too much of a mess for her. She should leave. It would be best for her. But ... I don't want her to.

Tank shut his eyes, breathing through his nose, nostrils pinched. "She's my fucking hire," he muttered under his breath. "It's your own fucking rule, you horse's ass."

The *Dasin* thought metaphorically sat up, scowling.

Tank grunted and broke the trance, annoyed and impatient. "Fuck this," he said, and stood just as a group clad in complementary arrays of silver and lilac swept by. They startled back, the two men immediately moving between Tank and the four women. Tank, bench at his knees, couldn't back up and didn't want to this time.

"*S'ieas,*" he said, using a deliberately cultured accent. He bowed to the women, pointedly ignored the men, and took his leave before his fist could accidentally push someone's face in.

Chapter Thirty-one

Isata's Market wasn't as grand as Bright Bay's, but it was much more tidily laid out, especially compared to the chaos of the city at large. Careful planning had resulted in wide terraces and streets, as well as dividing the market into permanent and temporary districts. Craftsmen of the more odiferous trades were on the lower terrace, finer trades on the top tiers. Temporary stalls ranged from the lower to the middle terraces.

Dasin, of course, had one of the best spots, right by the stair leading up to a row of fine tailoring shops. After testing the wind direction, he set up a small incense dish on a hanging tray, securing it to one of the thick wooden canopy supports. As it began to burn, a rich aroma threaded through the air, a completely unfamiliar scent that managed to evoke intangibles: *sunlight, luxury, beauty*.

"What *is* that?" Lia asked, astonished. Once more, as per market rules, she was unarmed but for her daggers, and therefore wasn't wearing her ata.

Dasin grinned, clearly pleased at her reaction. "Blend I came up with," he said. "Well, with help from an *inasia* — incense creator. It's based around oil of thopuh. Thopuh is a southern tea." His cheer faded. He breathed deeply, as though needing the scent to steady himself; then he motioned her to leave her spot at the forward corner and come around behind the table.

Up close, lines of strain marked his face. He'd missed a spot of stubble near one ear, and his nails were chewed back nearly to the quick. "S'e," Lia said, alarmed, then hesitated on what to say next.

"I know," Dasin said irritably, pushing a stray lock of blond hair from his narrow face. "I've seen you watching me on market days. You know what you're seeing, don't you? You've been trained to handle a table."

"Kennet taught me a bit on the way south," Lia admitted. "But I'm not all that good."

"Doesn't matter if you're as good as I am on my best day," Dasin said. He turned over an empty crate and sat on it, shoulders sliding into an exhausted slouch. "You'll do better than me right now, is all that matters. I can watch for thieves just fine while sitting here. Ah, here we go."

The smoke had drifted gently out along the terrace. Heads turned, people changing direction to track down the beguiling aroma. One, then three, then five customers arrived, and soon Lia was so busy answering questions and exhanging goods for money that she had no time to ask more questions.

Dasin stood, for particular customers, to offer a vibrant smile and hearty greeting, then sank back down, nearly gray with the effort, as soon as they departed. He kept up a steady stream of commentary and advice between customers, filling in things Lia hadn't known to tell people and correcting her mistakes. His usual cutting tone was entirely absent, replaced with a weary, pragmatic dryness.

"You're doing well," he said during a lull. "I didn't think you'd heard quite that much of my patter, much less memorized it."

"Thank you," she said, absurdly pleased by the praise, then rolled her neck to release accumulated tension.

He watched her with an odd, sly expression. "Do you know, I think you're actually enjoying it," he remarked. "You certainly don't look quite as rigid as you usually do. I might have you do this again."

She shot him an alarmed look. He laughed and directed her attention to an approaching customer.

By noon, the bright blue of the morning was dimming to a gray foreboding, and more than one nearby merchant was beginning to pack up or move easily soaked items further under cover.

"Won't be a full day," Dasin said, heaving himself to his feet. "Tank and Cilif should be here soon. I'll have them help pack everything up, and you can go on and do something more interesting than this. There's a zoo, I'm told." He rubbed at his eyes, blinking hard. "Might not be much fun in a rainstorm, of course."

"Are we staying another day?" Lia asked tentatively.

Dasin looked at the gathering clouds and shook his head. "If it's raining tomorrow morning, we'll take another day to rest. If it's clear, we'll travel on. We're out of routine, so the people who usually look for us are elsewhere. There's no money in staying." He wobbled a bit and put a hand on the table edge for support, then shot a sharp look her way. "You don't tell anyone," he said. "You especially don't tell Tank I had you helping today, or why. Get back to the front."

"Yes, *s'e*." She stepped around the table obediently.

Dasin took a deep breath, stood up straight, and became the shining beacon of charm she was used to seeing, moments before Tank and Cilif appeared around a corner.

"Storm coming in," Tank said briefly once he came within easy speaking range.

"Lia hasn't eaten anything yet," Dasin said, chill and precise. "Go walk her over to get a meal at a stall that won't give her dysentery. Get something for yourself, too. Cilif can start the breakdown, you come back to finish and load."

Tank's face darkened, as though about to protest. Cilif said, barely audible, "Best do. I got this."

Tank shrugged, an entirely hostile gesture, and took Lia's elbow in an uncompromising grip, steering her away before she could say anything herself. "So he's in a mood, then, is he?" Tank inquired as they walked. Hard, angry lines had settled into his face.

"You could say that."

"He say if we're staying another day?"

"If it's raining, we'll stay. If it's clear, we'll leave." She tugged her elbow out of Tank's grip; he startled a bit, glancing down as though he'd forgotten, then gave her an apologetic grimace.

"It won't rain," he said with absolute surety. "Here."

The food stall before them exuded a wealth of savory, spicy, oily aromas. Lia's mouth immediately began to water.

"Rice is good here," Tank said. "Best avoid the red rice, though, if you're not used to southern spice levels. Anything with *red* in the name is best avoided, for that matter. Get the green rice and black beans, I'd say." He dug a silver round from his belt pouch and handed it to the food vendor, who grinned amiably. "Red and black for me," he told the man, who began scooping large spoonfuls of a violently crimson batch of rice, and ebony beans dripping with greasy liquid, into a large wooden bowl lined with a thick flatbread.

"Green and black," she said when the vendor looked at her, and received a similar, emerald hued, bowl for herself.

"Come on," Tank said, pointing to the terrace edge behind the stall.

Lia followed him without protest, sensing that his temper was still on a very thin edge even though she didn't understand why. They sat down side by side, legs dangling over the drop, and ate in silence for a time. The rice was sweeter than Lia had expected, with a strong garlicky undertaste. The earthiness of the beans was overlaid with a vinegar tone that matched well with the rice. It reminded her of southern food, and she said as much.

"Yeah, that vendor's from south of the Horn," Tank said indifferently. "I don't trust most of the folks selling local style food around here."

He glanced up at the darkening sky to the west. The local clouds still lofted by in pale pillows overhead, but even they were acquiring an ominous graying edge, and the top layer was beginning to pick up speed.

"About an hour, maybe two," Tank muttered, then: "You'll have to walk through a bit of rain, but with market out for the day, you've time this afternoon to find another contract. If that's what you want to do." He looked out over the lower tiers of the market, lips thin as though to stop himself saying more.

Lia rested her bowl on her knee and looked at Tank's profile. He'd shaved his developing beard, and his face once more looked young and sharp, the freckles standing out in the sunshine. His hair was tightly, if simply, braided back into a looped queue; she found herself remembering it down and loose, glowing in the firelight, and had to look away.

She said, "I'm guessing that you've already looked to see if there are any available."

Tank blinked, swinging a startled glance at her that slid towards sullen a heartbeat later. "Seemed a good idea, since I know more on who to ask than you do."

His tone made it nearly an insult. She chose to ignore that. "That's true. Thank you for taking the time to ask around. What did you find?"

Tank looked away again, sour-faced. "I found two worth your time. One slower, one faster, but the slow one leaves tomorrow and only goes to Arason, and the fast one doesn't leave for another tenday. Three more groups going up the River Road or Plains Road, alongside unsworn or offering crap pay. I wouldn't advise those, myself."

A babble of conversation broke out behind them. Lia twisted, looking over her shoulder, and saw a pudgy, middle-aged woman arguing with a taller, thinner man, shaking her finger up in his face. Several bystanders added their voices to the matter. A bulky man with dark skin and all-white clothing pushed between the couple, separating them; a young woman who looked a great deal like the older one came forward and pulled her away. The men stood in low-voiced conversation for a few moments as the crowd dispersed, then headed in opposite directions.

Tank said, dryly, "I've seen a similar fight with different people damn near every trip through. She cheats on him, he cheats on her, he tries to poison her, she tries to destroy his reputation, he's killed her pet rabbit, whatever. It's every accusation you can imagine, and I don't think a word of it is true; because if you noticed, there are two youngsters skimming the crowd."

Lia blinked, annoyed with herself for not seeing that. She'd gotten out of the habit of watching for such things. "And nobody's caught on yet?"

Tank shrugged and went back to eating.

Lia looked out over the market for a while. Then: "What do I get for staying?"

"A fucking headache," Tank muttered. "My thanks. A crew you already know. Damn good pay. I can't renegotiate that, by the way, talk to Dasin if you think you can sweeten him into obliging." Lia drew in a sharp breath at that. Tank cut a sideways glance at her, his mouth twisting. "Sorry. That didn't come out right."

"No, it didn't," she said, letting her voice go flat. "Is there even a crew for me to belong to in the first place?"

"Far as I can tell." Tank's chin tucked towards his chest, then he straightened. "You spent all morning with him. What do you think?"

"I think he wants to forget anything ever happened," Lia said bluntly.

"Of course he does." Tank raked loose strands of hair from his face, tucking them around his ears. "Of fucking course he does." It wasn't a rebuke, but a rueful acknowledgment of an old pattern.

Before she could stop herself, Lia asked, "Is he still *sane?*"

Tank drew in a sharp breath, then laughed without humor. "He never was," he said. "Neither am I."

"That's not what I meant and you know it."

He sobered, his hands forming briefly into fists. "Sane enough, far as I can see," he said. "Only thing that matters to you is, if Dasin cuts us loose and you're stuck for a contract, I'll take on the obligation of getting you back to Stecatr. Not because you're incapable, but because that's a long and expensive road without a contract. So are you staying or leaving? Because I need the afternoon to find a replacement if you're out."

The other options he'd listed weren't attractive. She'd already completely ruined her reputation as far as the Stecatr Church was concerned. Traveling alongside Tank and Dasin was at least a known situation, and while the thought called up a mixed ball of feelings, Tank was, indefinably, *solid*. She trusted him, more than she probably ought to.

Lia met his steady stare for a handful of heartbeats. There was no warmth remaining in his tone, and his face could have been carved from speckled granite. She said, "Staying. At least through Arason." Given that she was apparently switching Halls there, it seemed smart to leave herself negotiating room.

"Same damn answer Cilif gave," Tank grumbled. "Be at the stables tomorrow before dawn, then." He pulled his heels up to rest on the edge, then levered himself to his feet with acrobatic grace. He left without another word, taking the bowl back to the vendor on his way past.

Lia ate the remainder of her meal in pensive silence, and offered a steady litany of prayers to all the kindly faces of all the gods that she hadn't just made a soul-destroying mistake.

Chapter Thirty-two

The question kept resonating through the back of Tank's mind: *Is he still sane?*

Well, that's the fucking question of the day, now, isn't it?

Dasin didn't seem all that different — and yet, there was something *off* in the way he held himself, in the overly tight focus of his gaze and the unusual speed at which he reacted to small movements. He met Tank's gaze without flinching, but there was a hardness in his eyes that warned against asking questions yet.

It would sort out. It always did, in the end. They'd had more than one flaming row, over the past years, and faced off multiple bizarre situations together. It always balanced. He had to trust that it would once more.

Trust. Hah. For once, it's not my *trust that's the problem....*

Isata not being as kind as Obein about overnight security, Tank loaded the stall contents into two handcarts and, alongside Cilif, took them to the warehouse. Dasin had reserved a wide stall for wagon and goods alike, leaving them room to unload and reload without standing in the aisle or edging through tight spaces. The warehouse design was ingenious, in Tank's opinion: wagon stalls were built at angles, not straight, which allowed a horse to be backed up to the wagon or carriage, harnessed, and then smoothly off along the wide aisle and out the doors. Even better, both front and back of the stall could be opened, allowing a simple pull-through process on arrival. This particular warehouse didn't offer adjoining stables, unfortunately, but it was still an excellent layout.

As they unlocked the stall door, Dasin said, "Is it going to rain tomorrow?"

"No," Tank said. "It'll be a shit night, I think, but it should blow out by morning."

"We'll take to the road, then. Let's pack everything up." He wasn't meeting Tank's gaze. Tank couldn't decide whether that was a bad sign or just Dasin being tired and cranky. "Actually," Dasin added, "Cilif can do that just fine. You go on. You still look exhausted. Go get some rest."

Tank turned a hard stare Dasin's way, entirely failing to catch his eye. "What's going on with you?" he demanded.

"I'm simply not in the mood for your cheerful company," Dasin said tartly. "Feeling jealous, are you?"

"Oh, hells no," Cilif butted in. "Don't you put me in the middle of that. For one, neither of you are my type, and two, I don't even *have* a type. So don't go using me as bait, Dasin."

"You don't have ... what?" Tank stared at Cilif, honestly bewildered.

"I don't fuck," Cilif said, pronouncing each word distinctly. "So I object to being used in this particular game. Right? Good. I'm off to meet a friend." He turned and walked out of the stall without another word.

After a long silence, Dasin said, "Well, shit."

Tank leaned against the wagon and let out a helpless burst of laughter. "Well, shit," he agreed cheerfully. "That sorts that, I suppose." He stepped back, turning to survey the bags and boxes, then began loading with practiced efficiency.

Dasin worked alongside him, silent but at least not sullen for the moment. As they tucked the last box into place and began closing doors and latching locks, Dasin said, "I want to be alone tonight."

Tank tested the last padlock, then stepped clear of the wagon and checked the lock on the back door to the stall; waved Dasin out ahead of him, shut the front stall door, checked that he had the key, then snapped the heavy padlock on that door shut.

"Dasin," he said then. "I need to —"

Dasin turned and walked away.

Tank stood still, watching Dasin's retreating back. A strange sort of silence grew in his mind: a lack of thought, almost a lack of being. He blinked several times, breathing with care.

What the fuck did Evkit do to him?

A warning prickle ran across the back of his neck, hard and sharp: someone stood behind him. Tank turned, sharply, gathering will and shields.

"Lord Eredion Sessin," he said a moment later.

"Just Eredion," the stocky man facing him said. He stood some distance away, well out of reach, and his hands were pointedly folded over his stomach. He'd gained weight since their last meeting, and looked softer, calmer, and considerably more sober than Tank remembered. He'd abandoned all his desert lord and Sessin Family status markers: no bracelets, earrings, rings, or necklaces at all, and his clothes, while of fine cut and fabric, held no sigils or symbols or rank either.

Tank barely stopped himself from demanding, *What are you doing here?* That wasn't the most important question to ask. "What do you want *this* time?" he said instead, with a deliberate lack of warmth.

Their previous encounters had, one and all, pitched Tank into situations ranging from unpleasant to outright dangerous. Silently, he promised himself he wouldn't let the man push him around this time.

Eredion's dark face crinkled into a surprisingly genuine smile. He said, "I had a talk with Lord Ganne of Darden. You quite impressed him."

A nearby stall clattered open. A tall young man led a feather-hocked draft mule into the aisle, then slid and padlocked the stall shut. Tank and Eredion moved aside, both offering amiable smiles. The groom ignored them entirely as he went by, murmuring to his charge in a steady monotone.

Tank found himself studying the beast for details he could relay to Lia later. She might know if that long leg hair was in any way normal for mules. Tank had never seen it before.

Once they were alone again, Tank said, "Lord Ganne didn't particularly impress me."

Eredion's smile widened. It held none of the cynical exhaustion Tank was used to seeing from the man. Apparently Isata had mellowed him considerably.

"Yes, well. Not much does, as I recall. But to answer your question, you have an audience with the Lord of Isata."

Tank blinked. "I do? When?"

Eredion's teeth flashed: not as white as they had been, but still mostly straight. "Now."

"Now", of course, never actually meant *now*, not when dealing with nobles. The Lord of Isata was famous for presenting himself in eclectic garb and behaving with a certain unfashionable coarseness, but he was still the ruler of the city and one did not appear before such a man in ordinary clothing.

Eredion took Tank to his apartments, which took up the entire top floor of a sprawling building near the Lord's complex. A stout woman met them at the door with a smile, grasped Tank's elbow firmly, and steered him to the bathing room before he could protest.

"Tank, this is Abi, my *daimaina*," Eredion called after them, voice filled with laughter. "Be nice to her. She knows her job." The bathing room door shut on the last word, and the woman pointed to the full, steaming tub with brisk insistence. The air smelled warmly floral and a bit spicy, not at all an unpleasant combination.

"Don't bother with a blush or a brush-off, my boy," she told Tank, folding her arms. "We don't have time for either, and I'm well aware you're no innocent."

Tank shrugged and stripped without protest. His long legs fit in the tub, to his relief, and when she offered absolutely no reaction to his scars, he allowed himself to relax under Abi's unhurried competence. The soap was soft, with a smoky-sweet aroma.

"Smoked vanilla," Abi said when he asked about it. "New regional specialty."

Vaguely, Tank considered asking after contact details to pass along to Dasin; decided it was too much trouble, and went back to enjoying the moment.

"There now," she said, sooner than he'd expected. "That'll do, and Rin can do your hair while I find you suitable clothing. Your boots looked good enough, they'll be clean by now, but you'll need proper jewelry."

"No," he said reflexively as he stood, taking the towel she handed him. "No jewelry."

"Yes, jewelry," Abi said flatly. "You've status enough to be called in for an audience with the Lord of Isata, and you won't shame Eredion by walking up naked of any markers."

He met her dark green eyes, measuring her determination, and sighed. "Yes, *s'a*. As you say."

Abi pointed him to a chair, then swept from the room. He finished drying himself and looked around for his clothes. Not a stitch in sight. He folded the towel neatly onto the chair and sat down resignedly.

A tall, gangly young man with nondescript brown hair edged into the room, carrying a box of grooming tools and blinking anxiously. "*S'e*," he said with obvious relief on seeing Tank. "My name is Rin. I'm Eredion's *kehair*. You'll permit me to do your hair?" His own was neatly, simply cut, and a small sapphire and silver hoop sat high in his left ear.

"Go ahead," Tank said.

Rin pulled up a small side table and began fussing about with the contents of the box, avoiding Tank's gaze.

"Is there something wrong, *s'e*?" Tank asked.

Rin gasped and stammered, knocking awkwardly against the table. Tank reached out and steadied it before it toppled. "Oh! Thank you. Ah, no? No. Nothing's wrong, no." He cut Tank a swift, hungry glance from beneath long eyelashes. "I'm sorry, *s'e*. I've seen you about, on occasion, and, well, I've always wanted to make your acquaintance." He attempted a shaky smile.

Seen me about? Oh, for the love of the gods, that's thin. Tank did his best not to roll his eyes. "So Eredion's had you following me when I'm in town, then?" he said, neutrally.

Rin startled back a pace. "Um! Well, I...." He dropped his gaze to the floor. "Yes," he admitted in a small voice. "I'm sorry, *s'e*."

"I'm not upset," Tank said. "That's the way of things. You don't need to pretend to be meek, either, it doesn't impress me." He cleared his throat. "I believe we're short on time?"

Rin straightened, drawing a deep breath, and visibly calmed. "Yes, *s'e*," he said. "If you'll hold your head so — thank you. Hold still, please."

His initial flutter over, he moved with swift precision, trimming, brushing, and weaving Tank's hair into a neat series of interconnected braids more elegant than anything Tank had ever dared attempt before. It was the hairstyle of someone *important*, and as the young man's fingers brushed the nape of his neck, Tank found himself desperately wanting to turn and catch Rin up in his arms by way of distraction from how terrifying that felt.

Not the right time, he told himself, then ground his teeth together on realizing that he was still entirely godsdamned naked, his scars — and his arousal — on full display. *I should have put the damn towel over my lap instead of under my ass.*

Tank shut his eyes and covered himself with his hands, feeling a wash of crimson climb up his neck. "*Shit*," he muttered under his breath, then more clearly: "Ah. Rin, I'm sorry. Ehh...."

"It's the way of things," the young man said, broad amusement in his voice. "You needn't apologize for reacting." He slid a finger slowly along Tank's neck; Tank inhaled sharply. Rin laughed and went back to arranging Tank's hair.

Tank set his teeth together and tried to think of something tedious. It didn't work. He was far too aware of Rin's fingers moving through his hair.

"There," Rin said at last, pulling a final cord tight, and came around to stand in front of Tank, surveying him thoughtfully. He grinned, evidently satisfied with his work. Then his gaze moved lower. No longer playing at being nervous, he moved forward a step and stared down into Tank's eyes.

"*S'e* Rin," Tank said, and found himself unable to say anything more.

"I'm not a whore," Rin said softly. "I'm not a kathain. I'm not a slave. I'm offering you this not at anyone's direction, but because I *want* to." He paused, then added, "*Gods, do I want to. You're gorgeous.*"

A shock ran down Tank's spine at the savagery in those last words. Had Dasin *ever* used that tone? If so, it had been a long damn time. *Gods, no, don't think of him right now — wait, wait, damnit, I need to say no — damnit —*

Rin dropped to his knees and pushed Tank's hands aside. Tank tried to voice a hasty, polite refusal. The words stuck in his throat for a heartbeat too long. Instead, he wound up setting his hands lightly on the back of Rin's head and letting out a long, agonized moan.

"Ah, *gods*," he said, and then again, some time afterwards.

Rin slipped from the room, smiling, while Tank was still catching his breath. "I'll see about those clothes, and some coffee," he said over his shoulder, and shut the door quietly behind himself.

Lord Tiyh was a head shorter than Tank and several pounds lighter than Rin. His skin sagged as though his frame had once supported considerably more weight, and his eyes were a sharp, dark green. He impatiently waved aside Eredion's formal bow and pointed them both to stools set before the dais. His own chair was of pale oak, and featured simple, graceful lines without ornamentation other than the large wolf's feet at the base of each leg.

"Lord Tiyh," Eredion said. "I'm grateful you've made time for this audience in your busy schedule." In, apparently, his own concession to needing status markers, emerald and silver studs ran along the curve of his left ear, and a single silver band graced his right thumb.

Tank didn't know the symbology of that particular pattern. His own earrings were thin gold hoops with a small black stone, thankfully only a single, bottom set; a wide gold and silver braided bracelet on his left arm; and a choker-style gold chain that he dearly wanted to rip off.

Eredion's daimaina had dressed Tank in unexceptionable gray and copper colors and clothes of a simple but sophisticated cut that made him look born to the nobility instead of the streets. The knee-high, charcoal-colored soft boots laced up the front and had far too thin a sole to support anything but indoor court functions.

"You should be." Lord Tiyh frowned at Tank. "Eredion, I know you insist that he's southern, but he's as fire-and wind-marked as a true son of Stecatr."

"I may have heard that once or twice," Tank said. He intended it to come out amiable; somehow it went the other way, into cutting coldness.

Lord Tiyh stared at him, eyes narrowing, then said, "That's why you've been able to move around freely in my city for so long. Quite simply, nobody could believe you were really a southerner."

Tank lifted one shoulder and said nothing.

"There's also the small matter that he hasn't done anything, before this, to bring him to your attention," Eredion said, acidic. "Lord Tiyh. *Please* don't waste your time trying to bait this young man. I assure you it won't work."

Tank heard the warning clearly, and tightened his hold on his temper.

Lord Tiyh sat back in his chair, rubbing a knuckle across his lower lip thoughtfully. "Very well. You have been peacefully ordinary, as Eredion points out. Now, however, you've walked the beginnings of a crisis into my city. I tend to take notice of people who do that." He dropped both hands to the arms of his chair and drummed his fingers.

"Could you specify what crisis you think I've brought in?" Tank said, chill and precise, and heard Eredion groan lightly beside him.

"How about *neither* of you bait one another, and we might get through this talk before nightfall and without having to call any guards?" Eredion suggested. "Tank. Be so kind as to tell Lord Tiyh about your trip through the Hackerwood with Lord Ganne of Darden. Lord Tiyh. Be so kind as to not interrupt until Tank's finished his story."

Lord Tiyh's frown lightened to a rueful expression. "I wonder sometimes how King Oruen put up with you, Eredion." The words held no real bite, and Eredion shrugged in response.

Tank said, keeping his voice emotionless, "I've been working for some years as a guard to *s'e* Dasin, a merchant who represents Yuer of Sandsplit. This particular trip, *s'e* Yuer directed us to escort Lord Ganne of Darden Family through the Hackerwood into Isata. Our responsibility for his well being and whereabouts ended when we reached this city, Lord Tiyh. If he's done something regrettable, it's no business of ours."

Lord Tiyh's thick eyebrows drew down sharply. "Neatly worded, but missing the bulk of what I want to hear about. I understand there were some unusual incidents along the road. I'd like your version. Do be mindful that I've already spoken to Lord Ganne." His mouth set in a straight, warning line.

Tank paused, sorting words into sense, then offered up a carefully edited version of events.

When he finished, Lord Tiyh leaned back in his chair. "Again, very neat. You're careful with your words. That's a good thing. Most of the people I deal with could use lessons in not wasting half my day with blather." His cold stare stayed on Tank's face, searching, as he spoke. "I'll do you the same courtesy. I've already begun negotiations with representatives of *hadinn* Evkit. They've indicated that your employer would be an acceptable liaison, should he choose to take up residence here; perhaps even a *preferred* liaison."

"*Dasin?*" Tank said before he could stop himself. His shoulders went taut. "Pardon me, Lord Tiyh," he added hastily.

"So you weren't aware of that offer. Interesting." The lean man flicked a glance at Eredion. "You were wrong for once, Eredion."

Tank cleared his throat. "Lord, *s'e* Dasin was unwell when we left the Hackerwood, and I needed to rest. Once we both recovered, we were busy with the market, and with preparing to leave tomorrow. We haven't had much time to talk."

Lord Tiyh lowered his chin, rubbing his nose with a knuckle, then straightened. "I'm told Dasin spent some time with hadinn Evkit, although Lord Darden was a bit vague about that situation." He raised an eyebrow inquiringly.

Tank felt his back go rigid. *Damn* Ganne for letting that out. He said, "Forgive me, Lord Tiyh, but that's a personal matter."

Lord Tiyh barked an incredulous laugh. "I'll give you a moment to reconsider that answer."

"*Tank,*" Eredion muttered warningly.

Tank fixed his stare on the wolf's paw foot of Lord Tiyh's chair, and said, in the same tone, "*Eredion.*"

Lord Tiyh said, "I'm not generally given to threats. But I can always make an exception."

Tank could feel Eredion's glare on the side of his face. He shrugged one shoulder, hard and hostile, and said, "Dasin and I share a.... an unpleasant childhood history. Hadinn Evkit is aware of that history." His throat closed for a moment, but nobody said anything. "He indicated that he considers himself, in part, ethically responsible. For not preventing certain ... events."

Eredion made a faintly incredulous noise. "*Evkit?*"

"Childhood history," Lord Tiyh said, more quietly. "Would that be —"

Eredion cut in sharply: "It would be inappropriate to discuss that further. I know what Tank is referring to, and that'll have to be enough for you, Lord Tiyh."

The Lord of Isata grunted sourly, but didn't argue. "So this has what to do with Dasin's visit with hadinn Evkit, then?" he said instead.

Tank said stolidly, not looking up, "He offered to help Dasin recover from ... from his own experiences."

"But not to help *you,*" Lord Tiyh observed archly.

Tank felt threads of fury staining his face. He set his teeth together, ducking his head, and shot Eredion a scathing sideways glance.

The desert lord cleared his throat. "I'd advise not pushing further, Lord Tiyh. I believe that's enough of an answer."

Lord Tiyh made a dissatisfied sound deep in his throat. "Very well. Leaving that aside, then. I'll tell you *my* understanding of the situation. *S'e* Dasin, who has only presented as a merchant of herbs and simples up to this point, has now been in private contact with an entity of considerable power who's abruptly declared sovereignty over the land on my southern border. He has been named as a preferred ambassador to this new and entirely unwanted neighbor. Of course, I began inquiring about Dasin, on hearing that, and I discovered certain matters involving *you, s'e* Tank. It's quite astounding what finally asking the right questions of one's advisors can produce."

Tank's stomach sank. Lord Tiyh's glare moved to Eredion, who managed to look both apologetic and unrepentant, then snapped back to Tank.

"Between wild rumors and verifiable incidents, the information I've been given about the two of you to date, when put beside the destabilization of the Forest and Coast Road areas, is *not making me happy*." His voice dropped nearly to a growl on the last words.

"Tank, don't you dare say what you always say," Eredion muttered as Tank opened his mouth. "He *will* fling you into the stocks."

Lord Tiyh's eyes gleamed with savage agreement.

I'm just a mercenary, hung at the back of Tank's mouth, then dissipated. It wasn't true any longer. It never really had been. Time to let that old dream go, and accept what the hadinn had said: *You are as close to a desert lord as an unbound human can be, whether you learn to use it or not.*

Tank carefully adjusted his posture to a dignified self-possesson, and saw Eredion's eyes widen in appreciation. He said, "I understand you're unhappy, Lord Tiyh. I'm not the reason things have...." He paused, carefully redirected away from *gone to shit:* "...gotten complicated. That's purely hadinn Evkit's doing. I just happened to walk into the web at the wrong time." *Story of my life,* he didn't add.

He paused again, checking Lord Tiyh's expression, and Eredion's. The former's expression was stony, the latter's cautiously approving.

Encouraged, Tank went on, "There's a fair bit about myself, and about Dasin, and about ... well, other matters ... that I can't or won't talk about, whatever threats you make. I'm guessing you already knew that, if you asked Eredion about me. Which means you didn't call me here just for information. So, then, what would you have me do?"

He allowed himself a moment of pride at managing to deliver that pre-emptive refusal and redirect without the least bit of aggression in his voice or posture.

Eredion let out a soft breath of relief.

Lord Tiyh sat quietly, considering. At last he said, in the same neutral tone as Tank had used, "I would have you *and* Dasin out of the area while I get a handle on this mess. There may well be a place for you both once the debris settles, but at the moment I would vastly prefer to work with a person who carries fewer complications than either of you."

"You won't want to be sending Eredion, then," Tank said, then bit his lip. "Pardon, Lord —"

Lord Tiyh let out a harsh caw of laughter. "Ah, but this is Lord Eredion of Sessin, whose name strikes a young and arrogant Darden lord near to wetting himself," he said, abruptly cheerful. "This is the man who held his own against a mad king and then against a very angry sane one. This is the man who killed a demon who'd taken over Bright Bay, evicted the Northern Church, then turned his back on his own Family shortly before an epic disaster that destroyed nearly his entire bloodline."

Tank cut a startled glance at Eredion. The desert lord avoided his gaze.

"Complications are relative," Lord Tiyh said, more calmly. "One trait Eredion has, above all else, is a nearly absurd sense of loyalty once he decides he's found a worthy target. I do what I can to live up to his opinion of me, but I'm not fool enough to let that stop me from using his skills and reputation for the good of my city. And he knows that. Don't you, Eredion?"

Eredion sighed heavily and bowed. "Yes, Lord. I believe you have other matters waiting your attention. May we withdraw?"

Lord Tiyh waved a hand, leaning back into his chair. Eredion bowed again, more deeply. Reluctantly, Tank followed suit, then let the desert lord hurry him from the room.

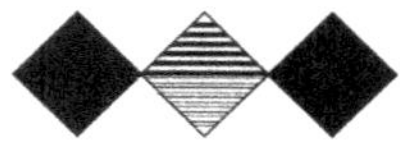

"That went about as well as could be expected," Eredion said some time later, over a platter of steamed vegetables and noodles.

Aromatic sauces ranged along each side of the dish, some dark and oily, others pale and so dry as to be almost crumbly. Tank picked through the ones he recognized, tipping them in small measures onto his own plate. He didn't quite feel up to trying something new at the moment. At least he'd been able to swap out the absurd court boots for his own, sturdier ones, which comfort thinned his temper considerably.

"So you're the one who actually killed the ... was it a ha'rethe, or a ha'ra'hain?" Tank said, not looking up from prodding his food around. "I always wondered about that."

"Ha'ra'ha, but one damn near to being a First Born like Deiq." Eredion hesitated, then added, "Its parent was the ha'rethe that Aerthraim Family evicted."

Tank's hand spasmed, nearly knocking the plate from the table. Eredion's hand shot out to catch it as Tank scooted back from the table, staring in horror. "Please tell me you're fucking with me."

Eredion gently resettled the plate on the table, then sat back and wiped his hands clean with a napkin. "No."

Tank's breath shuddered in his chest. Eredion, studiously patient, brushed the spilled food to one side and once more cleaned his hands. Finally, Tank said, "Just when I think I can't hate them more, something always comes up to prove me wrong."

Eredion looked up, his eyebrows quirking. "You do have a complicated relationship with your Family, don't you?"

"I don't have *any* fucking relationship with Aerthraim Family," Tank gritted out. "Back to my question. Are you the one who killed it, after all? I've been thinking all this time that I did that. I suppose I should have known better."

"You weakened it," Eredion said, sobering. "We wouldn't have had a chance, without you going in first."

Tank couldn't help scoffing at that. "You make it sound voluntary on my part!"

Eredion shrugged, spreading his hands. "It's done," he said. "To get back to your question, yes, I'm the one who was quietly given the credit. I'm not entirely sure who landed the actual, final blow. The moment was chaotic, to say the least. It's more accurate to say I was the one left standing, the one who dragged everyone else out to the healers."

He blew out a harsh breath through his nose. Tank measured his own breaths and stayed quiet, knowing Eredion wasn't done.

"Three of them died," Eredion said quietly. "It was very messy. I still don't like to talk about it. I will say that if not for you, it would have been completely impossible." He paused, as if sorting out words, then finished, "You'll note I've never asked you any questions about just exactly what the hells you did, and how. Please return the courtesy."

Tank made himself eat a few bites, not really tasting anything.

Eredion put his hands flat on the table and drummed his fingers, still flat, briefly. "Since we're finally abandoning your pretense of being nothing out of the ordinary, however, I do have questions. And since I'm not Lord Tiyh, and I'm no longer Sessin, and I'm only theoretically a desert lord these days, but I *am* still one of your best allies in a mess, I'll thank you to indulge me by answering plainly." He pushed aside his untouched plate and leaned back in his chair, looking tired and old. "Have you seen Allonin lately?"

"No," Tank said, giving up on his own food. He drank some water, idly admiring the expensively simple goblet. "Have you?"

"Seen, no. I've heard from him on occasion. He's managing matters below the Horn, along with his sister. Neither of them will come north at this point, or go up against Evkit. That's been made plain. Allo's sister, Azaniari, is liason between Aerthraim Family and Lord Cuna of the Horn teyanain, and she's mending that longstanding breach with admirable skill. Allonin is being less visible, but doing a similar job to keep the Families at large from each other's throats."

"He's doing a piss poor job between Darden and F'Heing, then," Tank observed. He speared a piece of steamed carrot and ate it dispiritedly.

Eredion let out a short laugh. "They're not literally assassinating one another in the streets, or invading each other's territory, so I'd say he's doing quite well."

"Was it his idea to have Darden relocate? Sounds like his sort of trick."

Eredion sobered. "I'm not sure," he said. "It does, doesn't it? And it's a good solution, Tank, to be honest. You never saw the western coast. They were always damn thin on resources. Once the Horn went, and Deiq's Farms died out — no, he's not maintaining them any more," he added as Tank looked up sharply. "They're entirely human-supported now, and some of them have failed catastrophically. Mostly on the west coast."

"No bias there, I'm sure," Tank muttered.

Eredion sighed. "Gods only know. Have *you* heard from him?"

Tank's jaw tightened. He shrugged, knowing he'd already given Eredion the answer with that involuntary moment of tension. "Yeah. In the Forest. After the bloodbird attack. He threw his voice into my head and told me there was trouble ahead. He got cut off. I'm guessing he was talking about Evkit, and that's who stopped him reaching me."

"Probably. It's astounding he got through at all." Eredion turned his attention to his food and ate, frowning thoughtfully, for a time. "So there's no help coming from him either. All right. Idisio —"

"*No*," Tank said, sitting up straight.

Eredion regarded him calmly. "I was about to say, he's most definitely not going to help. He's been quite clear on his desire to remain within his current territory and to be left alone. I assume you've spoken to him yourself."

"No. I've avoided that part of Arason, and he's avoided me. It's better that way."

Eredion's eyebrows rose. "Interesting," he said, sounding like the Lord of Isata. "I expect he'll want to talk to you this time through, given recent events."

Tank stared at his plate, refusing to meet Eredion's gaze. "We're already planning to leave in the morning," he said, hoping to distract the desert lord from that topic.

Eredion snorted, obviously spotting the attempt. "Well, and so," he said. He sat back and brushed at invisible crumbs on his trouser legs. "Get Dasin out of here, and winter over in the north. Assiasan or Stecatr, I'd say. I can give you coin —" He paused, watching Tank's face. "Allow me to help," he added, more softly. "Please. I'd rather be entirely sure you weren't at Dasin's mercy at the moment."

Tank dragged a rough breath past his teeth and nodded once, feeling as though the motion broke something deep inside his chest.

"That aside," Eredion said, his voice returning to hard pragmatism. "There's the matter of Yuer being replaced. I noted your extremely careful wording on that part. In full confidence, then, kindly fill me in on what you left out. *Completely*."

Tank looked up at the ceiling, at the floor, at his unfinished food, desperately seeking some distraction. Eventually, he met Eredion's direct stare.

"There's a girl who served at Aerthraim Fortress while I was there," he said, flat and harsh. "Balby. We were as close to friends as I could manage, at the time. She left before Allonin took me to Bright Bay. We crossed paths again at a Horn tavern. We ... well." He looked away, unable to endure Eredion's intent expression. "She apparently went on, afterward, through Bright Bay and into the Hackerwood, and took up service there —"

"She *what*? How is that even *possible*?"

Tank's already overstretched temper snapped. "Don't fucking ask *me*!" he yelled, years of frustration cracking his voice. "First I knew of it was when I was idiot enough to jump the wall to rescue someone and ran damn near face first into her *and my fucking son —*"

His voice broke entirely.

Eredion sucked in a sharp breath, face abruptly ashen.

Tank put both hands over his face and let out a deep, hitching cough. His throat felt raw.

Eredion made a low, distressed sound. "*Tank*."

"Dasin doesn't know," Tank said through his fingers, voice rough and shaking. "He *can't* know. He hates this girl so much — *so* much. And she made me swear never to go into the Hackerwood again, a promise bound in blood. I couldn't even *try*. I think I'm only able to *talk* about it now because of Evkit moving in and breaking whatever power she had when I last saw her. I think he sent her to kill Yuer. Or kidnap him. Or something. Balby is ... I don't know what she is. I thought she was human. I'm not so sure these days."

Tank drew in a deep, shaky breath, keeping his eyes nearly shut, because if Eredion was looking at him with pity it would be unendurable.

Eredion said nothing for some time, waiting while Tank regained his composure —
and, very likely, collecting his own balance as he sorted through the new information.
When Tank finally sat up, Eredion said, gravely neutral, "Thank you. We've known —
every entity whose lands border the Hackerwood has *known* — that there are creatures
of considerable power in the Hackerwood. The stories of a deal struck by Wezel in order
to make a path through to the northlands are entirely true. Our part of that compact is to
stay out of the Hackerwood and to stay silent about what we know. Their part is to stay out
of our lands."

Eredion paused, visibly searching for words. Tank used the quiet to pull himself
together, gathering panic and fury to one side, slipping into a shakily centered calm.

At last, Eredion went on, "It's slightly terrifying that Evkit apparently overcame this
power and is in charge now. That's not something anyone ever considered as a possibility.
We expected Evkit to force a war, overt or shadow, with his daughter to get the Horn back
under his hand. *This*...." He shook his head, then made a sweeping gesture with one hand,
as though shooing something large away. "I'm guessing that Evkit will put this girl in
charge of the coastal southlands in Yuer's place. If she was able to serve whatever creatures
have been running the Hackerwood all these years, she's entirely capable of cowing several
small human towns and villages."

Tank put a hand over his eyes as he visualized the resulting political and trade maps
in his head. He said, slowly, "That would effectively extend Evkit's hold well past the
southern Hackerwood border, cutting Bright Bay off from the rest of the kingdom." His
stomach sank. "Dear gods. And there's unrest to the north ... the kingdom would shatter
completely."

"It wouldn't take much." Eredion rubbed a hand over his face and swore in multiple
dialects. When he'd exhausted that, he said, "Gods, this is more of a mess than I expected,
and I knew it was going to be bad."

Tank made his voice nearly monotone, to keep it from fraying again. "Let me go, Lord
Eredion. Let me get Dasin out of here. Give me a chance to find out what Evkit did to him.
Let *me* get out of here, before I go tearing through the Hackerwood like a lunatic on a
hopeless quest. Leave me, leave *us*, alone for a while. One last time. Please."

Eredion sighed. "There's a pouch on the table by the door, with your street clothes and
money in it," he said. "Take it on your way by. No obligation. It's all yours to do with as you
wish. Keep the clothes and jewelry, too. They're a gift."

Tank rose to his feet, scooped up the bag, and left the room without looking back.

Chapter Thirty-three

The trip from Isata proved unremarkable other than the occasional downpour. Lia already know, from her previous journey in the other direction, that this road was lined by a procession of small villages with barely an inn or stable worth the name. She knew, too, the meaning of the occasional bird calls that ran through the brush alongside empty stretches of road, and smiled a bit in satisfaction that the local thieves remembered her so clearly.

Cilif cut her a thoughtful glance after the second coded warning echoed through the air. She met his gaze with a deliberately innocent expression; he snorted, amused, and let it be.

At each village, Dasin set up and sold for an hour or two after arrival, much as he'd done at Kybeach. That left enough time in the evening for Lia to work with Rooster, smoothing out the various small twitches he'd acquired after the trip through the Hackerwood. Tank and Cilif did the same with the two black horses.

For the most part, Cilif camped on the edge of town with the horses, while Dasin took a room and Lia the common-room floor, more from a lack of lodging than a need to conserve coin.

Tank didn't seem to be staying with Dasin, and he wasn't catching a corner of floor. Night after night, he saw everyone else settled, then vanished on his own errands, stony-faced and uninformative, reappearing at dawn to order the day's travel.

The second day, Tank turned them down a thin, rambling road to a village even further from the main road than usual. Dasin's narrow-eyed glare indicated it wasn't a planned destination. Tank ignored him with magnificent disinterest and bartered with a farmer for the use of an empty field for the night. Once camp was set up, he pulled three wooden practice swords from the wagon and pointed Lia and Cilif to a spot well clear of the fire.

"Time to see what you've got, northern," Tank said, his tone brisk. "Stretch."

"About time," Cilif said cheerfully. "I was getting *bored.*"

After everyone had loosened up, Tank handed out the swords, then stepped back, angling his across his shoulder to indicate the first match was for Lia and Cilif.

Cilif promptly tossed his sword aside, grinning widely and flexing his hands in not-quite suggestive motions. Lia shrugged and lobbed her sword to join his. The other mercenary moved in, reaching with his longer arms to grapple. She dodged, circled, and kicked out once, hitting him high on the inner thigh with sharp precision.

Cilif let out a startled curse and went down on one knee. He leaned back fast to avoid Lia's following high kick, then scrambled back to his feet, circling her much more warily now. "Not just your knees to watch out for, then," he said, and tried another rush.

She met it with the same manuever. This time he yelped as he went down, but bounced up much more quickly.

"Don't you fucking *dare* nail me in the tenders," he snarled, backing up. "You were damn close that time."

"I hit what I aim at," she said with deliberately maddening calm.

He growled and came at her again, keeping his hands close to his body this time, clearly ready to grab her leg should she try that kick again. She moved aside, stepping out of his reach, just ahead of his punches. When he finally leaned too far, she came in beside him, chopping down with the side of her hand above his right elbow.

Cilif yelled, outraged and hurt all at once, his right arm briefly limp below the elbow. He spun, ready to tackle her; she was out of reach before he began to move, and delivered one more precise kick that sent him sprawling.

Lia stepped back several paces and waited. Cilif rolled, moaning, and glared at her. "You're not supposed to fucking kill me, bitch! That fucking *hurts!* The hells did you *do?*"

Tank said, "It's called *micruna* in the south. Snake strike." His gaze stayed on Lia, thoughtful but not startled. "The inner thigh is a spot most people don't think about, but especially for folks who've been on a horse all day, it's damn painful spot to hit, let alone twice in a row. And it's not particularly easy to *do* when you've been on a horse all day, even after stretching."

"You did say you wanted to see what I could do," Lia said, unable to resist.

Cilif complained, "Bitch, did I *ask* to be your proving ground? You coulda *said* you had southerner training!"

Tank grinned. "You did say you were bored, Cilif," he pointed out.

Cilif offered an obscene gesture.

Tank gently lowered his own practice sword to the ground and moved clear of Cilif, beckoning Lia forward. Cilif groaned and hauled himself further out of the way, muttering to himself.

Lia watched Tank's eyes, well aware that he had considerably more skill to call on than Cilif's cheerful bar-brawling technique.

She didn't get a blink's worth of warning when he moved. He was up against her, twisting her arm behind her back, yanking her off balance, and dumping her into the dirt with his knee planted in her mid-back before she could do more than gasp.

She thumped the ground with one hand, not in the least ashamed to concede in the face of that speed. He released her and stood, moving clear, and waited for her to regain her feet. Then he said, "I'm going to move more slowly this time. Stop me."

Her attempt to block his grip failed. She managed to twist free, suspecting he was allowing it. She tried for a calf-kick. He moved aside with ease, then hooked his own foot around her extended ankle and yanked her off-balance again. A hard push to her shoulder overset her, and she barely turned the flailing drop into a safer tuck and roll.

When she stood, Tank was smiling like a wolf presented with a fresh meal. "Cilif," he said. "Go make dinner. This is going to take a while."

"Gladly," Cilif said, and retreated.

Tank worked Lia ruthlessly: testing, pushing, never saying a word, never losing that savagely pleased smile. Just as she was beginning to consider pleading exhaustion, or throwing up on him, he called a halt. She dropped to the ground, trembling and lightheaded. He looked down at her for a moment, then turned away and went to claim his share of dinner.

He hadn't even been breathing hard.

The following nights went much the same. Wherever they stopped, Tank pulled her, and sometimes Cilif, aside to some deserted field or empty barn to spar. Once they were done sparring, he bowed, gravely amused, and retreated to wherever he was spending his nights while Lia limped off to sleep on a hard common-room floor and Cilif stomped off to complain at the horses.

Lia expected Tank to tell them what they were doing wrong, or give them tips on how to meet his attacks more competently, but all he did was repeat the same basic moves at various speeds. Sometimes he let them twist free of a hold, other times he used their struggles to knock them further off balance and, inevitably, to the ground.

In fact, Tank didn't say *anything*, which Lia found incredibly annoying and even Cilif commented on grumpily. She soon began to suspect that Tank was using their sparring time to release his knotted tension over Dasin. With that in mind, she decided it was probably for the best that he wasn't making any comments.

Dasin wasn't talking much, either, and his tone, when he did, was uniformly vicious. He didn't ask for Lia's help again, and entirely refused to let Tank stand guard while he bartered and sold among the villages. Cilif stayed by his side more often than not.

Lia, unexpected swathes of free time on her hands even with Tank's brutal sparring sessions, began, idly, to refine her stitching technique when mending her clothes. After a time, it turned to tentative patterns; nothing as fine as what her mother could manage, of course, but not too clumsy, either.

She was thinking over whether to add a flowering design along the hem of an old shirt as they arrived at the outskirts of Arason. Outlying farm cottages rose high and chunky through a chill early morning mist, their already sober colors dulled further by the gray air. The resonant chime of church bells drifted through the air, deeper and earthier than the brassy clang of the Stecatr Church bells.

"Ghost morning," Cilif said from her right. He ran a hand through his mist-damp hair, slicking it back out of his eyes.

She blinked and glanced at him. "What?"

"Ghost morning," Cilif repeated. "Locals call days like this a ghost morning. They stay indoors until it burns off. Say there's soul-sucking creatures that come out in the mist. They think the mist comes off'n the Lake. That's why those innkeepers gave us goose-eyes when we left before dawn."

"Superstition," Lia said firmly. She pressed her lips together, trying not to think of the strangeness of her previous encounters here. "There's no way this mist comes all the way from the Lake. There's enough high ground between here and there to make that impossible. It's low ground here, and wet. That's all."

Cilif laughed softly. "Well, *impossible* isn't a word you use around this town. The land here doesn't follow what ought to be."

Lia glanced over her shoulder at the wagon trailing some distance behind. Dasin slouched sullenly on the bench, wrapped in a thick, hooded cloak. Tank rode beside him, sitting very straight in the saddle, regal and frosty. She turned back to watching the road.

"I think they're fighting again," she said.

"Nah. They're still not *talking*. That's a bit worse. But they'll work it out. They always do." Cilif yawned.

They plodded on in amiable quiet, listening as birds slowly awoke around them.

Abruptly, the mist thickened around them, too swift a change to be natural. Lia reined her horse to a stop, drawing her sword, and heard Cilif doing the same. The horses stood placidly. From behind them, Sin nickered as though in greeting.

The mist faded away as quickly as it had formed, leaving the road clear and gilded with early sunlight.

Lia let out a shaky breath. "What the fuck?"

Cilif grunted. "That wasn't about us, I don't think," he said, glancing over his shoulder. "Likely a message to one or both of them two back there. Let's keep moving."

Lia couldn't help yet another glance back as she sheathed her sword. Tank had pulled Sin well clear of the wagon. Dasin was sitting up straight, hood thrown back and face fairly blazing with fury as he glared at Tank, who was returning an entirely too bland expression.

"Let 'em work it out," Cilif repeated, sheathing his own sword. "Let's go. I want a real bed tonight. My bruises want it even more." He shot Lia a sour smirk and nudged his horse ahead.

Intersection: Jurisdiction

Idisio found it satisfying to see Tank startle as the mist rolled in around him. Tank was easy to anger, difficult to surprise. It felt like a petty victory, but he took it as one owed all the same. Tank bloody well should have come to visit before this point.

A hard, spiky shield built from Tank's familiar, protective anger enveloped not only the redhead, but Dasin and the wagon as well.

Idisio backed up instantly, startled. Tank hadn't been nearly that skilled at their last encounter. Clearly, despite his protests of preferring a sword in hand, he'd been training in less tangible defenses. If his range was that extensive these days, he was even more dangerous than he'd been years ago.

Dasin batted at the air, shredding the shield with that one simple, irritable gesture, and glared at Tank. The redhead startled, then snapped into an icy indifference, as though to say *I knew he could do that, of course I knew.*

Idisio backed off further, surprise moving to caution. *Dasin* had developed abilities of his own? Given what he'd seen as the pair moved through Arason over the past years, the revelation didn't make him at all happy. If it hadn't been for Tank, he'd have forbidden Dasin passage long ago. There was something treacherous and dark in Dasin that made Idisio's gut twist warning.

Tank, despite his very good attempt to cover, clearly *hadn't* known Dasin could do such things, hadn't expected it: meaning this was something new.

Which wasn't good. Not at all. Not with the tales Idisio had heard lately.

A moment's focus brought Idisio back to the safer ground by the Lake. He stared out over the mist-swirled waters for a time, considering.

He'd have to insist on a visit this time, from Tank at the very least. But not the two of them together, in case it turned into a fight. Not because Idisio might lose — hah! No.

Not even with Tank's expanded capabilities, and certainly not *here*, at the center of Idisio's power. But he might have to hurt them past recovery, and that would be awkward on a number of levels.

Idisio sensed a motion to his left, a familiar resonance. He turned, deliberately slow, and offered the young woman a mild smile. "Cera."

No point in *Good morning* or *How are you*. Human greetings had already slipped into being meaningless to him. Acknowledging her presence was all the courtesy she needed, or expected. Her official role, assigned by the Arason Council, was his human liaison. It hadn't begun well, but they'd formed a reasonable partnership eventually.

"Spice bread and fresh milk on the counter," Cera said, similarly sparse. She understood how to talk to him. "West sent four jars of apple butter; her daughter has a fever and bad cough."

"Fair trade. I'll take that."

"The Lord of Araison would like a word. He's concerned about Stecatr."

Idisio sighed, tilting his gaze to the lightening sky, and breathed in through his nose to test the moisture in the air. "Yes. After I see West. I have things to discuss as well."

He held out his hand, signaling an end to the conversation, and drew Cera in against his side. She tensed, turning to look at the cottage.

"She's sleeping," Idisio said. Ceria relaxed immediately.

Not for the first time, he reflected that the townspeople really weren't comfortable with Galliana. It wasn't surprising, after everything the community had been through, but it did make training her more difficult when humans routinely flinched in her presence. She'd already begun to show clear signs of resentment. Fortunately, she was also sleeping a lot. Not uncommon, from the records he'd found, for young ha'ra'hain coming into their power. He hadn't slept so much during his awakening, but he had spent that time deep in meditation. Perhaps that had served the same purpose.

They stood there, looking out over the Lake, for some time. Idisio inhaled Cera's scent: goat milk and white lilac soap, the blend he preferred her to use when she came to see him. Beneath that, if he focused, he could pick out a lingering tinge of sweat and mildew. Only the very rich could entirely shed that odor. He went back to enjoying the smell of the soap and the complex reaction of the fragrance with her natural skin oils.

She stayed silent, matching her breathing to his, her mind and emotions serene. After a time, he sighed and let her go, offering another neutral smile. "Thank you."

"My pleasure, *ha'inn*," she said, bowing deeply, then retreated, returning to town to go about other duties.

He'd stopped asking humans not to use his title. For one, it unsettled them far too much, especially *here*, to insist on familiarity. For another, the title was not only his due, but a useful reminder of his responsibilities. She understood him well enough to only use it once, at the end of a visit. That was enough.

The Lord of Araison would be using it *constantly*. He grimaced, rubbing a hand over his face. At least he had the audience with Tank to look forward to. Tank wouldn't be scraping in poorly concealed awe. If he used the title, it would be more a curse than a courtesy.

Idisio's irritation lifted into a pleased grin at the thought, and he decided that he actually *was* looking forward to seeing the surly bastard again.

Idisio grabbed his bag from the cottage and set out for West's farm, whistling cheerfully. A few steps later, he paused as a *presence* caught his attention. He turned to scan the area with eyes and mind, every sense alert: it vanished as quickly and completely as the fog he'd drawn across Tank's party.

Dasin, pushing back? No. Idisio couldn't credit the merchant with that level of power. Certainly not Tank: he would be instantly recognizable. It wasn't the teyanain who kept watch over Kolan, the unstable priest who'd loved Idisio's entirely mad mother. It wasn't the *chekk*. If they returned, they'd have no reason to skirt around. They'd simply walk right in.

No, that presence had been someone new, an unfamiliar power skulking about the edges of his territory.

Idisio suspected he'd only sensed the intruder because they'd slipped briefly.

Not good. But did that necessarily make it *bad*? Strange creatures routinely moved through Arason, unseen by most humans. So far, they'd all noted Idisio's presence, offered a respectful nod or other marker, and withdrawn to other hunting grounds. This might well be the same.

Idisio checked his wards: solid. Untouched, untroubled in any way. Galliana was still sleeping. She wouldn't stir for hours yet, and when she did, she'd stay within the cottage until he returned.

Was it safe to leave her, with a strange force tickling the boundaries? Intuition, when questioned, said *Yes*: the intrusion had nothing to do with Galliana, and wouldn't disturb her. Was it directed at Idisio himself? *No*, but that answer wobbled uncertainly. The Lake? Did this involve the Lake and its slumbering occupant?

Silence.

Idisio frowned up at the sky, displeased. Then, with a resigned shrug, he collected his bag and went on his way. If this new presence had anything to do with the Lake, there was nothing *he* could do about it. Best to stick with what he could reasonably affect, and let trouble, in this instance, manage itself.

A silvery, hyena-like shiver of laughter strung through the air. Idisio checked again, scowling, and physically turned in a circle as he tried to pinpoint the source of that sound. Something about this felt increasingly familiar, and he didn't like it.

Ordinary birdsong, ordinary air, ordinary aromas. Nothing at all unusual.

"Quit fucking playing games," he said aloud. "This is my territory; come out and face me if you want a chance at welcome."

He waited. Nothing at all happened, and nothing continued to happen.

Intuition stirred, bringing something entirely unrelated to his awareness: Lia was nearby. She'd returned to Arason, despite his warnings. There was no chance Galliana would miss Lia's proximity, when she awoke; she'd been restless with want for weeks.

Idisio growled under his breath and resumed walking, setting a rapid pace. It was going to rain soon, and he wanted to be home before that point — and well before Galliana roused.

Chapter Thirty-four

Arason, for all its through traffic, was primarily a self-sufficient farming town. The entire northwestern edge was entirely taken up with sprawling fields lush with everything from corn to wheat to herbs, the southwestern dedicated to livestock of dizzying variety. Being a farming town meant endless farming celebrations, which could be useful for sales but more often proved frustrating from the sheer chaos that they tended to provoke in the town's routine.

For once, as far as Tank could tell, they'd caught Arason between significant dates. No banners or bouquets were in evidence, although a few enterprising residents had begun setting out woven willow baskets filled with dried gourds. Tank was fairly sure they were meant to represent Syrta's bounty or some such. He thought about asking Lia, then considered Dasin's ongoing touchy mood and decided not to risk causing problems.

He wondered, idly, if desert lords ever ran into this sort of delicate balancing act between confidence and uncertainty, pushing and backing up. It seemed unlikely. They had servants to take the brunt of their bad temper, after all. They didn't have to worry about upsetting lesser mortals.

In the back of his mind, Alyea laughed and said, *You know better than that.*

"Yeah, well," he muttered aloud.

It wasn't really her, he knew that, just a ghost echo of an encounter where they'd shared far too much. Still, it was oddly reassuring, rather like having a friend that wouldn't ever turn on him. He wondered if she ever found *his* voice in *her* mind, and wasn't sure if he liked that idea.

The merchant quarter backed up against the northwestern farms, and was flanked on one end by Arason's Merchant Hall complex and on the other by inns and taverns. The Merchant Hall was a sprawling collection of buildings that provided stables, merchant housing, and private taverns as well as warehouses. Dasin did pay fees for membership here, in large part for the networking access, but also because membership was much more conditional on reputation and connections than on coin.

Membership also gave Dasin, as a verified merchant, access to private rooms that Tank wasn't allowed into. With the mood Dasin was in, Tank found that notion disquieting, but there was nothing he could do, especially if Dasin wouldn't even talk to him in the first place.

They settled horses and wagon at the Merchant Hall complex, and rooms at the Nine Bees Inn at the other end of the market. As soon as that was managed, Dasin disappeared without a word, presumably — *hopefully* — to visit his contacts among the farmers or to network with his fellow merchants.

Dasin hadn't taken a room at the Bees, and Tank hadn't asked where he was lodging. After that morning's display, Tank wasn't all that interested in talking to Dasin, himself. He needed time to sort out what Dasin had done.

Tank had been working for *days* on strengthening his ability to shield. He'd actually been quite proud of his progress, and nearly smug about how fast he'd thrown up a ward around not only himself, but Dasin as well.

Right up until Dasin had, with one annoyed gesture, shredded it to wisps.

Only the wide-eyed stares from Cilif and Lia had stopped Tank from launching into aggressive confrontation on the spot. Dasin had *never* displayed any such skill or strength in the past. He was definitely sensitive; he'd heard the Hackerwood creatures on occasion, and when he really focused, he had an uncanny ability to pick out far too much of what Tank was thinking.

But waving aside a strong shield even quicker than Tank had built it? No. That was entirely new, and a touch terrifying, considering that it had to come from whatever Evkit had done to him. Or worse, undone.

Cilif nudged Tank's shoulder with the knuckles of one hand. "Quit brooding," he said. "You've company."

Tank blinked, abruptly aware that he was sitting on a bench outside the Nine Bees, staring into space like a moonstruck. Cilif sat beside him, stubbled face amused. A gawky young woman stood well back from them, hands laced together over her stomach, waiting patiently.

"*S'e* Tank?" she inquired once he looked up at her.

"Yes. Sorry." Tank brushed loose hair back from his face and regarded her with polite inquiry. "Something you want from me, *s'a?*"

She bowed gravely. "Master Onda asks for a word, if you would be so kind." As Tank stood, she added, "The invitation extends to your two mercenary hires."

"'Invitation', huh," Cilif said resignedly, and heaved himself to his feet. "I'll go track Lia down. I think she's still inside."

The young woman bowed again, then turned and left. Tank sat back down and studied the early morning sky while he waited for Cilif to corral Lia. By the time they emerged from the inn, he'd decided it would rain, and hard, by early afternoon at the latest.

"What's this about?" Lia asked. Either she'd relaxed enough to start leaving her sword behind, or Cilif had rightly pointed out that an audience with Head of Hall was a bad place to bring weapons.

The tan lines on her face had evened out, and her hair had lightened; she looked considerably leaner and stronger than when she'd first sat down across from him in Bright Bay, and she regarded the world with much less fear. The sparring sessions along the road had done them all good.

He recognized the shirt she had on as one she'd worn several times before, but there was a newly embroidered line of tiny blue flowers along the sleeves and hem, which perked up the plain garment no end. He repressed a smile, not wanting her to know he'd noticed.

"Not sure what it's about," Tank said, waving them into motion.

Cilif gave him a hard glance. "Sure you aren't."

Tank shrugged, matching strides with Cilif. "If you want a guess, the news from Isata ran Hall to Hall and well ahead of us. There's enough trouble in the truth of things to make Master Onda call us in, not to mention what's likely been distorted by rumor and gossip along the way."

"But why are *we* going along?" Cilif said, scowling. "Sorry, why were we *invited* along?"

"You're witnesses to what happened," Tank pointed out. "And you need to check in anyway, yeah? Call it a combined trip and quit fussing at it."

Cilif shook his head, unamused, and went on in silence.

They cut along a side road to avoid the crowds of Merchant Row. The cobbled road narrowed and curved through high banks lined with flowering plants. Tank, pointing to a thistly plant sporting a crown of white flowers, asked, "Anyone know what that plant is? Always caught my eye."

"Hawk weed," Cilif said. "My grandmother always said it was good for keeping mice away."

"I think it's poisonous," Lia said. "I wouldn't handle it without gloves. I don't know, maybe the mice eat it and die?" She shrugged. "I never heard that about the mice. I was told farmers work it into the soil for better crops."

"Till sommat poisonous into the ground where you grow your food?" Cilif said, incredulous. "You lot aren't half mad up there."

"How about that one, with the purplish leaves?" Tank cut in, pointing.

Lia shot him a suspicious sideways look, as if checking for mockery. "Loose-duck."

Simultaneously, Cilif said, "Speedweed."

They stopped walking and stared at one another.

"*Loose duck?*" Cilif said. "You're *joking*."

"I'm not," Lia said, a flush crossing her face. "Don't look at me, I'm not the one that named it! Why do you call it speedweed? That's just as strange!"

"It gets your guts moving when you're stuck. Does the job right fast." Cilif shook his head, muttering "*loose duck*".

Tank said mildly, "I imagine it would work the same on waterfowl as on humans. Possibly even more strongly, given body mass differences."

Cilif burst out laughing. "Good gods, the picture that paints! All right, all right, I see the sense. All right. That one there, that's redfern. And snake vine."

"We have something similar called trumpet vine," Lia offered, pausing to examine the delicate plant more carefully. "This has red flowers, though. Ours has bigger leaves and white flowers."

"What do you have south of the Horn?" Cilif asked, looking at Tank.

"No idea," Tank admitted. "I never paid any attention."

"I never used to," Cilif said, then launched into a story about getting to know a woman in Isata with a wildly prolific flower garden.

They spent the rest of the walk contentedly discussing plants, even though Cilif cut a wry side-eye at Tank on occasion, as though to say: *I know what you're doing.*

The Hall of Arms in Arason had waist-high stone walls around the complex that rose into a simple, wide arch at the entrance. A generous road led to the right, clearly for cart traffic; a crushed-stone footpath wound to the left, edged by neatly trimmed bushes and the occasional oak or beech tree. The center path, wide enough to accomodate a small parade and edged with ankle-high stone blocks, consisted of neatly laid pavers.

Tank liked the Arason Hall of Arms almost as much as the one in Bright Bay. In some ways, he liked this one better. There was certainly more attention to the landscaping here, and a surprising sense of peace he would have thought more common within a church.

The buildings themselves sprawled across a hillside, three smaller buildings and a larger, all set into the hillside in such a way as to blend in to the overall line of the hill. A large, sand-filled outdoor training circle took the place of a central courtyard, and the entire complex was neatly paved, with not a blade of grass evident between the bricks.

The training circle lay empty and neatly raked out when they arrived. Three trainees moved about outside, carefully trimming hedges and depositing the clippings into a large bin. They glanced indifferently at the newcomers and continued their work.

Tank looked up at the sky, squinting a bit, tracing the thready clouds overhead and comparing that to the moisture in the air. The day was currently bright and warm, but that wouldn't last for long.

The largest building rose well above the hillside it was set into, with a level underground for the trainee barracks and equipment storage. The topmost floor held libraries, classrooms, and staff quarters, leaving the central floor for the Head of Hall and administrative chambers.

An amiable young man met them at the door. He glanced at Tank's red hair and said, "Here to see Head of Hall, then? She's expecting you. This way."

"I'm going to dye my hair one of these days and see how many people don't recognize me," Tank muttered under his breath as they followed.

"You'd have to powder your face, too," Cilif said, laughing as Tank growled at him.

They came to a stop before a plain wooden door. Recalling his insight when facing down the Lord of Isata, Tank checked his posture and drew himself into a neutral-but-confident stance. The attendant knocked in a precise pattern, then opened the door and waved them in.

Master Onda, Head of the Arason Hall of Arms, was a short woman with auburn hair and freckled skin. Beside her stood a slightly taller man, whose unruly, thick brown hair spoke to either Stone Island or Easterner heritage. They both wore the white, gold, and blue of Arason Hall of Arms: Onda by way of a simple dress that allowed for easy movement, the man beside her in loose trousers and shirt.

"There you are," Onda said, frowning at Tank's companions. "Took you long enough." Her eyes fixed on Lia, and one of her cheeks hollowed briefly.

Tank bowed to a carefully judged degree, then straightened and said, for the sake of formality, "Master Onda, this is Lia of Stecatr Hall and Cilif of Bright Bay Hall. They traveled through the Hackerwood with me this run."

Onda pointed them all to chairs and resumed her own seat behind the heavy oak desk that dominated the small room. The man moved to stand behind her, his back nearly against the wall and his gaze unwaveringly alert. She looked them over once more, then said, "As mentioned, I'm Master Onda, Head of this Hall. That's my second in command, Elm." She motioned to the man behind her, who touched his left ear with the backs of his fingers. "I'm not going to waste anyone's time. I've heard what's going on with the western Hackerwood; it's frankly nothing I want to involve myself or my Hall with. As far as I know, it doesn't affect the woods along *our* borders. Is my understanding on that point flawed, *s'ieas?*" Her hard stare fixed on Tank.

"I don't know the range of the trouble," Tank said frankly. "Not knowing the boundaries, I can't answer that, Master Onda."

She grimaced, muttering *"boundaries"* as though it were a filthy word, then said, "Let me rephrase. In *your* understanding of the ... source ... of this situation, is it likely for matters to be pushed into ... let's say, gray areas, as far as geographical boundaries are concerned?"

Tank considered, measuring map points in his head, then said, "I don't think so. I think the, eh, source, as you say, is more currently concerned with establishing matters in the western area than in expanding out this far. I can't speak to how long that might last."

"I agree," Lord Onda said, "and so, apparently, does Isata's Hall. I believe I can safely leave that aside for the moment." Her gaze moved to Lia, and she added, in a more measured voice, "We have a more immediate situation, and a more complicated one, to the north."

Tank felt his stomach twist with abrupt dread. "No," he said, not entirely sure why.

Onda and Elm both stared at him, visibly startled. Tank made an apologetic gesture, but managed to stop himself from looking away or any other submissive movement.

"Elm," Onda said briskly, "Take *s'e* Cilif, if you would, and collect his remarks about this trip for the records. Thank you for coming, *s'e* Cilif, and don't forget to log your status before you go."

Elm ushered Cilif from the room. Lia sat stiffly on the edge of her seat, frowning at the corner of Onda's desk. Her hands were balled around one another in her lap.

Onda rested her elbows on her desk and leaned her chin on her clasped hands. Her hair, beginning to feather loose from the pins that kept it out of her face, showed strands of silver among the auburn.

Her gaze flicked from Tank to Lia and back. "*S'a* Lia. I've a message about you, from Master Hendle of Isata Hall, and another from Master Coyinue of Stecatr Hall. I'd have called you in to discuss it, so it's as well you're here already. Do you wish me to send *s'e* Tank away while we speak? If you intend to keep your contract with him, he'll have to know, in any case."

Tank tensed. Onda immediately looked over at him, her head tilting warily. He made himself exhale and loosen his muscles. "She's not committed past Arason, Master Onda. I'll leave, for the sake of —"

"If it's about my Hall status," Lia said, voice thin but steady, "speak freely."

Onda flicked a glance at Tank as he settled back into his seat; then, resting her chin once more on her hands, considered Lia. "Are you making that commitment now, then, *s'a*?"

"No. Not yet. But I'd rather avoid having to explain it over again, if I do."

Tank made an impatient gesture, muttering "*Tela-taba*," before he could stop himself, but managed not to follow up with any apologetic gestures this time.

Onda smiled and sat up, spreading her hands flat on her desk. "Do you know that saying, *s'a* Lia?" she asked. "I'm fond of it, myself. 'Play the game that's on the table,' if you translate it more or less literally. In essence, he's saying 'get on with it already.'"

Tank kept his spine still and met Onda's searching stare without flinching.

Her smile slipped away to a more serious expression. She said, briskly, "Both Isata and Stecatr recommend that *s'a* Lia change her registration to Arason Hall of Arms."

Tank pursed his lips in a silent whistle. Lia stared at the corner of the desk as though it might offer up holy revelations, or perhaps rescue.

Onda went on, "From all I hear, *s'a* Lia, you're an excellent addition to any Hall roster. You're more than welcome here, *if* you're willing to sign over. I'm aware you've been ordered to do so," she added with some asperity, "but I'm not willing to have someone sign under duress. Hendle is overbearing at times, and it wouldn't be the first time I've refused to obey his ever so kindly commands."

Lia said, not looking up, "I swore to the *gods*, Master Onda. That's not so easily set aside."

"You won't be abandoning that oath. Arason Church supports the move."

Lia's head jerked up. She stared at Onda, wide-eyed and pale. "They can't!" she blurted.

"Of course they can," Onda said mildly. "Arason's long gone along a unique path all its own, but our priests are as honestly sworn as your own. *S'iope* Brehan, in fact, was set in place with the recommendation and recognition of your own Stecatr Church. If *he* says a thing can be done, then that's an end to it in my view."

Lia looked even more miserably confused than before.

"Lia," Tank said, as the silence stretched, "I'd say —" He stopped, catching himself before self-confidence could tip into arrogant assumption. "Well, do you *want* to hear what I think? It's properly none of my nevermind."

Lia shot a sideways glance at him, her mouth twisting in a sour grimace. "Go ahead."

"I'd say do it, then. Arason's a *damn* good Hall."

"Why, thank you," Onda murmured.

Tank inclined his head, mindful of the dignity he was trying to make second nature, and said, with more care, "If you have three major Halls telling you to switch, including your own, that's serious. *And* the Church? That...." He paused, checking Onda's expression to be sure he wasn't overstepping, checking his own balance, then went ahead and said it: "That means they all think staying with Stecatr will get you killed."

Lia kept staring at the desk, her mouth a thin line; visibly not surprised, which told Tank a great deal about her conversation with Master Hendle in Isata.

"Lia, your family can be relocated to Arason," Onda said. Tank's eyebrows went up. "Your father has a good reputation. I'll make a place for him here, or there's a spot open on the Arason High Guard."

"As captain?" Lia said. Her eyes blazed with a ferocity Tank hadn't seen since the tavern fight along the Coast Road. "He's *earned* that rank! He deserves to keep it."

Onda considered, one knuckle resting against her chin, her gaze turning abstracted. "Perhaps," she allowed. "He may have to accept second or third captaincy for a time, but it shouldn't be too difficult to get him close to that mark."

Lia frowned, confusion replacing the anger. "We don't have those ranks. I don't understand."

"First captain is in charge, second captain backs him and takes over if he's unwell, third captain is a reserve position. We tend to like redundancy here, *s'a*, as we've faced having large swaths of ranking leaders becoming abruptly ... unavailable." She waved a hand to dismiss the subject. "You can ask around for the relevant history, if you like. But right now, I need an answer. Will you sign over? I already have your release from Stecatr Hall on file."

Lia straightened, eyes widening in clear alarm. "Am I without a Hall?"

"No. It only goes into effect when you sign over to us."

Lia looked up at the ceiling, at the desk, at her hands. Finally, she let out a short sigh. "Yes. I'll sign over."

"Excellent." Onda smiled reassuringly. "Don't look so miserable, *s'a*. We have a constant stream of jobs coming through here, milder winters than Stecatr, and training available in everything from Stone Islands to Easterner fighting styles. Our Hall stays busy, but we always have enough rooms and food, and even a spot for drinking, so you'll never have to stay at an inn unless you want to." She tilted a sardonic glance at Tank, adding, "We're in negotiations for a proper *aqeyva* master teacher to stay for a time, as well."

"I have to go back to Stecatr for Winter Festival," Lia said, head lowering stubbornly.

Tank needed a moment to compose himself after Onda's casually lobbed remark. *How in the shadow of the Sun Lord did she manage to even* start *negotiations for that?* He barely managed to keep the question behind his teeth. This wasn't the time.

Onda considered Lia's glum expression for a few moments, then splayed her hands on the desk before her. "Yes, well. Stecatr's a bit complicated just now." She looked at Tank. "Since you're here, we might as well throw this conversation the rest of the way into the frying pan. *S'e* Tank, what does Lia know about you?"

Tank's spine stiffened, his chin rising. He looked down his nose at the woman, unable to help the chill in his stare. She returned it ice for ice.

"He's a witch, under Stecatr terminology," Lia said before anyone else could speak. "Maybe they'd call him a demonkin." She cut a glance at Tank, and her tone sharpened as she looked straight at Onda and added: "You can't send him to Stecatr. They'd kill him." As though that had exhausted her courage, she dropped her gaze back to the corner of the desk, her lips so tight they nearly vanished.

Tank audibly choked. "And *why* in the hells would I go —"

Onda snapped her fingers, cutting him off.

"I'll get to that question in a moment," Onda said to him, then looked back at Lia. "Normally I'd agree with you. However, you're both missing an important bit of information." She sighed and leaned back in her chair, folding her hands over her stomach. Her gaze settled on Tank as she went on, "There are increasing signs of ha'ra'hain or possibly even ha'rethe activity in Stecatr. And given *s'e* Tank's history —"

"Oh, *fuck no*," Tank said, standing. His chair shoved sideways with the force of his motion, nearly toppling over. He glared at Onda, who regarded him without the slightest alarm.

"Don't yell at the messenger, *s'e* Tank," Onda said.

He turned on his heel and walked out without answering.

Chapter Thirty-five

Widow-beetles and wittlers chirred and clacked, falling silent briefly as Lia passed. A thick stand of berry brambles lined one side of the path, trees rising from the briars every so often. Lia named them absently as she walked: oak, maple, butternut, scrub birch, red poplar.

She paused on seeing that last. It was a rare tree in Stecatr, more at home in the warmer, more fertile downlands. This one was showing signs of strain, the bark blotched, the veins of some leaves yellowing. Possibly a bug infestation: more likely too sharp of a weather shift, too often.

This is my home, now. Or at least where my oaths bind me. The ceremony had been brief and dry, releasing Lia from all promises and obligations to the Stecatr Hall — and Church, to her surprise, because *s'iope* Brehan, the tall, freckled Arason priest she'd met on her way south, had shown up. He had laid out, with exacting and at times embarrassing clarity, what Lia was now free of and what she was bound to.

"I swore an oath to the gods," she'd said, voicing her protest at last. "This feels like … like humans twisting the words, the will, of the divine to suit their own ends."

Brehan had looked at her for a long moment. Then he said, very calmly, "That would be what the Stecatr priests did. I'm correcting their mistake."

And that had been the end of that.

Brehan gave her an offical document with the same precise wording as his verbal recitation, to hold in case of argument. "I'm going to send a copy to the Church myself," he'd said, expressionless. "I think it best they have time to accomodate the change before you show up in town, don't you?"

Lia hadn't argued. Years wouldn't be long enough for a civil welcome, never mind a matter of a few tendays, and Brehan likely knew that as well as she did. *Stone wears to sand faster than these priests forgive interference,* her mother had grumbled once, and the phrase had stuck in Lia's head.

I'm free. At least, free of the absurd parts. No more ata. No more celibacy. No more vulnerability to malicious rumors.

Her family, unfortunately, was far from safe. She'd effectively rejected the Stecatr Church, rejected the generosity of the Lord of Stecatr that had allowed her to set foot on this road in the first place. She'd transferred her loyalty and, perhaps worse, her tithes, to another city. Her family would absolutely be targeted by the Church for retribution.

She'd penned a hasty note to her parents, advising them of her change of Hall, trusting that they would understand the implications immediately. Then she'd found a News Rider headed to Stecatr and paid extra for direct delivery. It was all she could do. That, and pray.

This rambling walk around the western outskirts of Arason was proving less than useful for prayer. She pushed aside worry and set the words to match the rhythm of her steps: *Gods, please protect my family. They don't deserve to suffer for the mess I've gotten myself into.*

A shadow passed overhead. Lia looked up, discovering the clear sky rapidly filling with dark clouds. Abrupt humidity thickened the air. She swore under her breath, searching frantically for shelter: the path split ahead, the slanted roof of a barn visible to the right behind a thick holly hedge.

On trotting briskly around the glossy-leaved bushes, she found herself on the edge of a sprawling farmyard. Pigs, chickens, and swassons took up large, wattle-fenced enclosures in which were neatly constructed shelters. Several multicolored ducks waddled about as they pleased. A sturdy northern draft horse grazed in a lightly fenced area. It lifted its head to consider Lia's approach, then went back to cropping grass.

The main house, some distance away, was a long, irregularly shaped single-story building, set into a hillside. A generous field of sunflowers flanked the house on one side, an equally large field of herbs on the other. The barn Lia had spotted mostly held farm equipment and was half open to the elements, the other half closed off for a stable and storage.

A young man came out of the barn, pausing as he noticed her. He was short and pudgy, with thick hair and eyebrows. "Oy," he said, waving her over. "What's the need, *s'a?*" He glanced up at the sky. "Ah. Got caught out walking, then? Afraid of melting?"

"Not hardly," she said acerbically. "Pardon me for troubling you." She began to turn away.

"Nah, hey, come on then," he said. "It's like to be a hard storm. Not something to walk in. I've got to put Bucket into the barn anyhow, come on in and sit out the storm with me. It'll pass fast enough, this time of year."

A hot wind laden with speckles of moisture ruffled her hair. The young man shooed the livestock into their shelters, latched the doors, then slipped a bridle over the draft horse's head and led him into the barn, beckoning Lia to follow.

Inside was tidy and clean, thick with the smell of horse and straw. Lia sneezed once, then sat down on a small stool and watched the young man settling the draft in his stall. Rain began to patter on the roof, a rising wind pushing it into erratic bursts.

The young man came out of the stall, latching the half-door with care, and hung the bridle up on the hook by the stall. The light in the barn faded as the rain increased to a relentless hammering. He shrugged and pulled another small stool over to sit near Lia.

"I'm Reun," he said, touching a knuckle to the top of his left ear, the local gesture of introductory respect.

She duplicated the motion. "Lia. Thank you for the shelter."

A harsh rattle overrode the rain for a few moments. They both looked up at the roof. Reun said, "He was right. As usual."

"Who?"

"*Ha'inn* Idisio. He had a foretelling. Said it would hail today, and that I'd meet someone new. I didn't think that would happen, seeing as I've too much work to do to go into town, and we don't get visitors all the way out here, but there we are, and here you are." Reun smiled, a bit awkwardly. "My sister's sick, see, so he came out to —" He paused, frowning at her. "You look straight odd. What did I say?"

"I've met him," she said, steadying her breathing. "He's a bit unsettling."

"Aye, yeah, he is that at times," Reun agreed. "But he's done more right by us, on the whole, than the Northern Church ever has, and that all by himself. I'll not hear a word against him."

Lia lifted a hand in what would have meant apology back in Stecatr. "No disrespect," she said. "I'm just … I'm from Stecatr." The words felt sour on her tongue, but it was the quickest way to explain.

Reun relaxed a bit, although amused contempt crossed his thick features for a moment. "Ah, well then," he said. Lia bristled. He raised an eyebrow and repeated, with an entirely different inflection: "Well, then?"

The two words, somehow, contained multiple questions: *What of it?* and *Can you blame me for laughing at you?* and *Am I wrong to think you superstitious and ignorant?*

She looked down, thin-lipped, and didn't answer.

They sat in silence for a time, listening to the heavy rain and wind battering outside.

"He said I was to tell you something," Reun said eventually. "The *ha'inn* said so, I mean."

Tension gathered back in her body. "Yes?" she said, not meaning to be quite so curt.

Reun cut her a sideways look, clearly amused even through the murky gloom. "He said you can visit, if you like. Said there's someone waiting to talk to you. There's no offense if you don't, he said, but the door's open."

Lia sucked in a sharp breath, abruptly caught in a swirl of emotions.

"Eh, well," Reun said. It seemed to be his version of a neutral sound to cover awkward moments.

The rain began to ease, the wind dying down in steady increments.

"Not much longer to it," Reun said, glancing up at the roof again. "I'd go by the high path on your way back to town. The one you came in on has low spots that'll be flooded after that mess. I'll point you to it. Wait a bit more, is all." He sighed. "Gods grant the hail didn't entirely destroy the crops," he added under his breath, clearly talking to himself.

She searched for something to say, not wanting to be rude. Before she formed anything useful, Reun stood up and walked back to the stall, running his hands over the hanging bridle and clicking his tongue.

"It's early in the year for hail," Lia said, feeling entirely stupid even as she said it.

"It is," Reun said, not turning. "But that's what happens, I suppose, when the world gets turned around." He looked over his shoulder at her. "The *ha'inn* and his like, they've been holding the weather steady," he added, as though that were a perfectly reasonable thing to say. "And now they're not. So the world's deciding what it wants to be without guidance."

Lia stared at him. He spoke so casually of something only the gods could order! Granted, *she'd* gotten somewhat used to such startling concepts being treated lightly, but how did a poor farmer on the edge of town know anything about what she'd understood to be carefully guarded secrets?

Reun turned all the way around to face her. "This is Arason, *s'a*," he said. She couldn't tell if he'd taken offense; the light was too poor and his accent too thick. "None of us here are ignorant of the old ways. Not when we've had a *chekk* on our flank for generations, and a ha'rethe napping in our largest lake."

"What's a *chekk*?"

"Community of ha'ra'hain. Ours left a while back, for whatever reason. No idea where they went. Some of us would surely like them back. Nobody pushes much at a town with that sort of ally to hand. But we've the *ha'inn* now, at least, and that's a great support." He regarded her steadily. "He's not *safe*, mind you. Not for us, and surely not for outsiders. I'd think long and careful before taking that invitation. Not my place to say, I know, but there, and so, I've said it." He shrugged.

She blinked, uncertain how to respond, and glanced to the door without meaning to. Reun motioned her up.

"Come along," he said. "Rain's stopped enough. I'll set you on the road back to town."

Chapter Thirty-six

In Bright Bay, in the grip of such profound rage, Tank would have gone looking for a fight in the slums of the city. Even Isata had places to blow off temper with a good brawl. But he couldn't let loose here. Not after that clear warning on the inbound road that Idisio was watching him this time through.

At least Lia had been wearing her face mask on the way in. Hopefully the ha'ra'ha hadn't registered *her* as anyone worth paying attention to.

A treacherous thought snaked by: *She really is, though.*

"Damn it all anyways," Tank muttered, and went to find Dasin, hoping he'd be luckier than he'd been in Isata.

Dasin wasn't at his preferred bar, secondary bar, or favorite whorehouse. At which point, naturally, the storm broke. Tank was stuck fending off offers that he *really* wanted to take advantage of; only the absolute certainty that he'd be even angrier afterwards stopped him cold. None of the whores had anywhere near the sincerity of the kehair in Isata, but one woman, a redhead with a sharp sense of humor, planted herself beside him and presented a damn near identical act.

She almost convinced Tank to take the risk. Then a newly arrived customer glanced over with eager interest and exchanged a familiar wave with the woman, jarring Tank back to reality and refusal just in time.

Tank managed to escape once the storm passed, without causing offense or having his pocket picked. That seemed likely to be the best win of the day.

Dasin wasn't, in the end, at any of his typical sulking or socializing spots. It was entirely possible he'd paid at least two of the people Tank questioned to respond with blank-faced negatives, but short of starting the brawl Tank was trying to avoid, there was no way to be sure.

Cilif might have been able to use his rough humor, and several rounds of drinks, to turn Tank's bleak mood around, but Cilif was nowhere to be found either. Lia would be worse than useless, given his own conflicted feelings about her. And Tank had just stomped out of the Hall, so going back there to spar with someone seasoned would send his temper all the way through the ceiling of the sky.

Tank actually found himself tempted to investigate his longstanding suspicions regarding whether teyanain were in residence, keeping an eye on Idisio. *I'm not far from the Lake. If they're here, they'd be easy enough to taunt out of hiding....*

The thought shocked him out of his rage into a glacial, breathless moment.

Gods and nightmares. He shivered, like a horse twitching away flies. "I'm not that fucking tired of life yet," he muttered under his breath, and forced himself not to listen for a quiet, huffing laugh.

Tank tilted his head back, breathing in damp air and looking at the cloud-studded sky with grim concentration. He couldn't tell if it would rain, or hail, again today. His intuition felt raggedy. Smoldering anger chilled to a more somber unease.

"Almost a desert lord," he said to the sky. "What the fuck is that good for, at the end of the day, if I can't even find Dasin when *I* fucking need *him* for once?" Belatedly, he glanced around, deeply relieved to see nobody within hearing range.

Idisio would probably have useful answers to at least part of Tank's frustration.

Idisio was the last damn person Tank wanted to ask for or about anything at all, much less how to be *nearly a desert lord*. But his only other option was backtracking to Isata to beg Eredion for help learning what he could and couldn't do, so....

"Fuck it," he said, and turned his steps towards the Lake.

Chapter Thirty-seven

The true Ghost Lake valley lay farther to the east of Arason than Lia had expected. Getting there involved climbing a steep hill and two smaller ridges, ducking under a number of overhanging branches, and very nearly turning an ankle on a loosely graveled slope.

She was beginning to suspect that she'd taken a wrong turn onto on an old hunting trail when the woods finally fell away behind her, leaving her with long grass to either side and wide wooden steps leading down.

Far below lay an impossible lake.

A swirling, iridescent mist filled the space where water should be. A widely spaced arc of simple cottages and small barns stood a hefty stone's throw back from that lapping fog. Most had a distinct air of abandonment. The cottage closest to the stairs, however, had a small, neatly tended garden, a recent roof patch, fresh paint, and smoke rising from the chimney. A wide patio with a table and chairs fronted the house.

A man and a woman sat on the patio, mugs before them. They looked up at Lia without apparent alarm. The man waved a hand in welcome and beckoned her to come down. Neither of them stood. The woman sipped from her mug as though indifferent to Lia's arrival.

Lia hesitated, then put her spine straight and moved forward. This was what she'd come for, after all. It would be cowardly to turn and bolt, even if her knees demanded, for a moment, that she do exactly that.

As Lia descended the long flight of stairs, setting her feet with care because the wood was still damp from the recent rain, she noticed that all of the buildings were set at an angle. The front doors never directly faced the lake, and the abandoned garden spaces were on the side furthest from that shining fog. A large pile of chopped wood formed a half-wall along one side of the brick patio of the occupied cottage, and the table stood over a large, empty firepit. The four chairs were sturdy and simply made. The clay mugs on the table were not skillful work; they were lumpy and uneven, with a white and blue glaze smeared across.

It could have been any village, any simple country couple.

Except for that lake. Except that she knew neither of them were human. The homey touches just made it all so much worse.

She drew to a stop just shy of the line of brick, gathered her courage and said, "*Ha'inn* Idisio." She bowed, hoping she'd guessed the right angle. Then, straightening: "Gally. Eh, I beg your pardon. *Ha'inn* … Galliana?"

Idisio's mouth crooked into a dry smile. His chestnut hair was drawn back into a loose braid, his skin tan as a farmer's. He wore only a long, simple tunic belted around the waist, and no shoes. It reached to his knees, and Lia found herself obscurely relieved by the fine hair along his legs. Demons didn't have leg hair, did they?

"Thank you for the courtesy, *s'a*," Idisio said before she could wander too far down that thought path. "I'm normally not fond of formality, but until I'm sure you understand the situation, it's probably safest to keep proper manners. You are correct: Galliana is, indeed, a ha'ra'ha, therefore her title is *ha'inn*. Gender doesn't affect that."

Gally sat silently studying her mug, not so much as glancing up, even at Lia's tentative greeting. She wore the same simple tunic as Idisio, although it fell longer along her legs, and a silver bangle graced her left ankle. Her dark hair had grown; like Idisio's, it was gathered to the back of her neck in a simple braid. A black earring sat high in her right ear.

"I can see that you've learned something about ha'ra'hain since our last meeting," Idisio said. "Good. Please, sit." He offered a sharp smile as she obeyed. "Galliana. You may answer. Remember the terms, please."

Gally raised her head, and her gaze raked hungrily over Lia, never quite meeting her eyes. "Hello, Lia," she said in a subdued voice, then her hands tightened around her mug and she dropped her attention to the table.

Lia blinked, not at all sure if she'd imagined the flash of gold lacing through Gally's eyes and deeply unsettled by the intensity of that brief survey.

"Good. Thank you, Galliana," Idisio said, then aimed another dry smile at Lia. "No, I'm not being condescending, *s'a* Lia."

Involuntarily, Lia pushed back in her chair. "You're reading my thoughts?"

"Only the loudest of your surface thoughts," Idisio said calmly. "You have no training at all in being quiet, do you?"

Lia inhaled through her nose, nostrils pinching, then withdrew into herself as though trying to avoid notice. Idisio's thin eyebrows rose, his smile becoming more genuine.

"Some training, then," he amended. "Not bad. Do you have any notion of how to shield?"

She swallowed hard, then shook her head. This conversation was not matching even her vaguest expectations. "I'm from Stecatr, *ha'inn*," she said, once more hating how much that explained.

He offered no reaction at all to that. "Shielding is much like being quiet," he said, "and serves much the same purpose. Being quiet helps to avoid the notice of predators; shielding protects you once they've noticed you."

Lia couldn't help darting a glance at Gally, who sat as motionless as though frozen.

"We're both predators, *s'a*," Idisio said softly.

Lia jerked her gaze up. His dark eyes immediately hazed with gold. A feathery heat trailed down Lia's spine, and she found herself leaning forward.

Idisio blinked, turning his face slightly away. "Oh, that was a bad idea, *s'a*. Never meet my gaze straight on like that. Or any ha'ra'hain's."

She sat back in the chair, bewildered and shaken.

"We're predators," Idisio repeated. "You remember Galliana as a simple village girl. You remember traveling with her, laughing with her, sleeping beside her."

Even though the last words had been as neutral as the previous ones, Lia's face went hot. Gally glanced up with a sly smile, aiming her gaze at Lia's shoulder, then went back to withdrawn stillness.

Idisio let the moment hang, his own expression sober. At last, he said, "I'm aware Galliana tried to seduce you, and you refused. *S'a* Lia, I'm going to repeat myself once more, and I do hope you truly hear me this time: *We are predators*."

All embarrassment drained away, replaced by a growing, stark fear.

"There. Now you're understanding," Idisio said. "You refused Galliana something she wanted. She hasn't forgotten that, or forgiven it, and now she has the strength and skill to *take* what she wants. So I'm not being condescending when I tell her 'well done'. I'm *teaching* her."

Lia's breath hitched in her throat, her hands squeezing into tight balls.

"Shielding," Idisio said placidly. "That will help, I think. Close your eyes. — *S'a*, if I wanted to harm you, your guts would already be spread across the patio. Close your eyes. Thank you. Take a moment to feel the stone under your feet. Put all your attention on the physical connection to the ground. It's often easier with bare feet, by the way, but we're not stopping for that."

Lia's hands, still balled into tight fists in her lap, ached with strain. She couldn't focus on anything, for a moment; then, consciously stepping sideways into that quietness once more, she dropped her awareness to her feet.

"Good. Now imagine that stone flowing up around you, forming a wall, enclosing you on all sides, including overhead. Keep that connection with the ground in the forefront of your mind."

The resulting image felt as crude as the clay mugs on the table, and somehow smothering.

"Push it out a bit," Idisio said. "You've made it too tight, and too heavy. Give yourself arm's length in all directions, at least, and thinner stones." Lia adjusted the image, frowning with concentration. "Good. That's a start. Now, keep your eyes shut, but can you hold that and talk?"

Lia cleared her throat, her eyes twitching with the need to open them. She could *feel* the danger sitting across from her now, as surely as she'd ever sensed an ambush during Hall training. "I'm not sure," she said, then bit her lip, steadying the wall in her mind.

"Keep trying," Idisio said. "Remember to trust that I won't attack you, and neither will Galliana. You're still under the grace of ignorance."

After a few more shaky attempts, Lia was able to say, "Why are you teaching me this?"

"For your own safety. Open your eyes. Don't look directly at me, or at Galliana."

Lia looked down at her white-knuckled hands.

"You don't have to use stone every time," Idisio said. "You can use the sound of birds singing, or the feel of rain, or the smell of your favorite herbs. Whatever resource you have to hand is the best. There's no use trying for stone in the middle of a lake."

Lia glanced sideways at the swirling vapors of the Ghost Lake.

"No," Idisio said sharply. "Don't *ever* use that, or anything like it. Very, very bad idea."

"I wasn't going to," Lia said, voice raspy. "Thank you for teaching me, *ha'inn*. I think I might best withdraw, with apologies, at this point."

Gally looked up. Lia barely turned her gaze aside in time. A thick impact rattled the invisible wall she'd built, and she gasped, scrambling to shore up the structure.

"Galliana," Idisio said sternly.

Gally shot him a smoldering, resentful glare. "*No*," she said, her first word since Lia's arrival.

Idisio met Gally's stare. A shimmering, razor-edged sense of power rose between the two. Lia tucked away deeper than she'd ever done before, unashamedly terrified.

"That's enough," Idisio said, and Gally flinched, bowing her head submissively. "*S'a* Lia. I need to finish explaining, and Galliana is clearly running out of patience, so please keep your very restful quiet and your shield in place, and listen."

Lia made herself shut her eyes and loosen her hands, flexing them to restore circulation. Tentatively, she wound the resulting joint aches into the wall as an intangible mortar.

"Good!" Idisio said, sounding genuinely pleased. "You're a quick study. That's good. Keep adding new sensations as old ones fade out. The more variables you have in place, the harder it is to push through a shield. Stone is actually fairly easy to defeat, for anyone who knows what they're doing." He paused. Then: "I was born here. Within the Lake itself, if my mother can be believed. But I grew up in Bright Bay, thinking myself entirely human. Finding out about my heritage, and coming to terms with it, was ... let's say, complicated and unpleasant for all concerned."

Lia inhaled through her nose, picking out something herbal wafting through the air, probably whatever the two ha'ra'hain were drinking. It was earthy, and minty, and nothing she recognized; she slathered the smell over the wall in her head like paint.

Idisio made a small, pained noise. "Perhaps not quite so strongly," he murmured. "Weave, not drench, please. — That's better. Thank you. Galliana was born in or near Orhon, very far from here. She was also raised believing herself to be human. If she'd never come to Arason, she'd think herself human still, and might well have grown old and died as such. Ha'ra'hain are complicated." There was a sense of laughter in the last words.

"So she's related to you?" Lia asked, keeping her eyes firmly closed.

"Yes and no. Again, complicated, and not a polite topic to ask about. It's enough to know that Galliana *did* come to Arason, and she now knows what she is. I'm doing my best to keep her transition less unpleasant than mine was. For everyone's sake." Idisio sighed, then went on, "Arason hosted ha'ra'hain for a long time, but the *chekk* — the ha'ra'hain community — that claimed this land left some time ago, and the town began to forget. I'm mindful enough of my human upbringing to be gentle in reminding them, and mindful that I have a responsibility for their well-being, as well. So I'm not allowing Galliana to prey upon them, which isn't always easy."

Lia went along with the graceful subject change. "Why did the *chekk* leave?"

"I don't know, and again, impolite question," Idisio said. "I don't take offense. As I said, you're still ignorant. Let's instead focus on Galliana being a predator again. Even when she thought she was human, she had enough ... extra ... in her nature that she generally got what she wanted. It's made her a bit spoiled, and that's why I'm making her sit still and silent right now. She needs more practice in accepting *no* as an answer. I think all ha'ra'hain would benefit from learning that from infancy, to be honest. You can open your eyes, if you like."

The table was round, and wooden. The crafter had brought out the grain beautifully. Lia couldn't identify the tree used, but wove the dark gold and chestnut variations into her shield.

"Very good," Idisio said, pleased. "I'm beginning to think you might survive this after all."

Once more, she jerked her gaze up, barely remembering to focus on his shoulder this time. Terror spiked through her: not stopping to think about it, she wrapped that through her shield.

Idisio sucked in a harsh breath. "*No, s'a,*" he said. "Don't use emotions. Drop it out, right now. *Quiet.*"

Abruptly, it was all too much, too complex, too alien. Her shield shattered, and Lia pushed back from the table, breathing as hard as if she'd run for miles. Gally looked up, her eyes lambent with gold overlay, and began to rise to her feet. Idisio lunged, grabbed Gally's arm, and yanked her down to the ground.

Lia found herself on her feet, backing up fast, as Idisio knelt over Gally, his face close to hers, murmuring something Lia couldn't make out.

Stay still, a voice said in Lia's mind, sharply commanding. Her knees locked; she wobbled, throwing her arms out to stay upright.

Idisio climbed to his feet, hauling Gally up with him. Their eyes were entirely black.

Lia pulled into herself like a turtle, rebuilding her shield with desperate haste from the feel of air along her goose-prickled arms, the residual damp in the air, the sensation of descending wet wooden steps.

"Sit down, *s'a,*" Idisio said, voice flat, and guided Galliana back to her chair. He waited until Lia had returned to her seat before settling down himself. "I'm going to give you a very dangerous piece of information, and I'll ask you — no. That won't be enough. I'll bind you not to pass it on to anyone else."

Lia felt a feathery tickle slide through her shield, through her skin: it coiled around her spine before she could even open her mouth to protest, flared scalding hot for a scant beat, then dissipated entirely.

"Stong human emotions are irresistably attractive to ha'reye and ha'ra'hain," Idisio said grimly. "Especially fear. We read fear as prey-weakness, and we'll almost always attack. Anger is just as bad. That reads as an attack on us, and we instinctively retaliate. Be very, very careful, *s'a*; you've used up the last of your grace from ignorance at this point."

Shaken from that searing sensation along her spine, Lia found herself sitting as still as a rabbit in front of a wolf, breathing in short gasps.

"I'm trying to stop you from getting hurt," Idisio said. "Not for your sake, mind, but in order to teach Galliana restraint. She needs to learn how to take what she wants without killing."

Lia barely tucked the sweep of fear behind her shield in time. Idisio exhaled, long and low, then let out a more ordinary, if exasperated sigh.

"*S'a* Lia," he said, more gently. "We do have the right, believe it or not. A very long time ago, ha'reye — my ancestors — formed an agreement with humans. Humans chose to serve ha'reye and to create ha'ra'hain. In return, ha'reye protected humans. That happened far to the south of where we stand, and the overall compact has been ... let's say *damaged* ... during recent events. But here, right here, this is *chekk* land. The *chekk*'s agreement with Arason was absolutely clear: within the boundaries of this settlement, I'm entirely within my rights to demand that humans do what I want. *Anything* I want. I can kill without any legal consequences at all. Human law and morals do not apply here." The last words were crisply staccato. "And Galliana, through me, holds the same right."

Lia leaned back in her chair, an icy calm settling over her. Idisio kept his thin hands splayed out on the table. Galliana sat perfectly still, looking at nothing in particular, her dark hair still disarrayed, her face smudged with dirt. One of her nails had broken nearly to the quick, another had a ragged gouge that continued up into an angry-looking scrape along the back of her hand, but she wasn't actualy bleeding. For some reason, that felt important.

"If you can accept that, *s'a*," Idisio said, "if you can accept that Galliana is your master in all ways while you stand on my land, this will be much easier. Fighting against what she wants won't end well. And I will require your specific consent for this much, and I'll offer no apology for being crude: what Galliana wants, mainly, is to fuck you senseless. Mostly because you said *no* before."

Lia inhaled harshly, looking away.

Idisio let out a rueful chuckle. "I was under the impression the interest is mutual."

"It ... was," Lia said, and sensed Gally shift slightly in her chair. "I don't much like not having a choice, *ha'inn*."

"I just said you do have a choice, on that point alone," Idisio said, tone flat. He rattled his fingers on the table impatiently. "Damnit. You're still not understanding. — *S'a*. I will be extremely generous this one time. Look me in the eye, I'll allow it this once. Now tell me, if you can, that you honestly want to leave. Tell me you don't want to take her to bed, or rather, for her to take you to bed, given what I've told you. If you leave, you can't come back to Arason. You can't ever speak to Galliana again. Not so much as one more time over the course of your entire life. So convince me that what I've said has completely broken your fondness for her. I'll let you go, and she won't follow. My word on it. Make your choice, *s'a*, and remember that I can hear lies as clearly as truth."

Idisio's eyes were a steady, cold gray, no trace of black remaining.

Lia swallowed with an effort, remembering her early encounters with Gally:

Lia couldn't help casting an appreciative glance over Gally's curves. The girl wasn't as solidly muscular as she usually liked, but there was a case to be made for abundant softness in the right spots. She raised her eyes to find Gally watching her, a mischievous gleam in her eyes.

And:

"I'm not popular around here," Gally said, "not since people figured out I'm ii'ne. And it's a small village. I can't find work, I can't even get training other than what Bemma and Anaya offer me, which I'm fortunate to have, I know, but I don't want to be here for the rest of my life. I don't want to live like this, barely tolerated." Her dark blue eyes filled with misery.

And:

Gally broke into snatches of song, bits of Church hymns and other tunes, replacing lyrics with nonsense words. Lia listened, admiring the clean tones and easy shifts, and found herself laughing more than once as Gally turned away to dance around the room briefly as though needing to bleed off excess energy.

And:

"You think I'm an innocent," Gally said, her expression turning strange and hard for a moment, completely unlike her usual open amiability. "You think I'm a bit simple, maybe, and you want to protect me. It's all right," she added over Lia's protest, with a brief, sharp smile. "It's what I want people to think...."

Apparently Lia should have listened to that part more carefully.

Aspna, gods, aspna. Eki, save me. Payti, save me. Syrta, save me. Wae, save me. Someone! A colder voice interrupted the hopeless litany: *From what? From having to make my own decisions? That's childish.*

If she'd never gone past the Hackerwood, never seen how casually the rest of the world treated what she'd been taught to regard as heresy, Lia might have been able to answer the proposition before her with strait-laced indignity.

Lia had been prepared to live a life bound on one side by pleasing the Church and on the other by pleasing Scarpy, with little room left for what *she* wanted. She'd been braced for a life of no real friendships, because being friends with men risked assumptions both from them and from onlookers, while being friends with women, innocent as that would look on the surface, held a much more intimate danger.

Sanben had refused to respect that script. So had Gally. *S'iope* Brehan, on Lia's first journey through Arason, had shattered Lia's assumptions about priests and the role of the Northern Church in the larger world. Tank, Dasin, and Cilif had entirely upended Lia's understanding of relationships, ethics, and heresy.

Lia wasn't sworn to Stecatr any longer. She could follow Arason Church rules, rather than Stecatr, and *they*, very clearly, knew about the resident ha'ra'hain, but hadn't made it part of her new oath to avoid them.

Lia knew it for thin reasoning even as uncertainty steadied towards rebellion. She found herself wanting to *make a statement*, which sounded even more absurd. Taking a woman to bed would be a statement. Letting a ha'ra'ha, a *predator*, take her to bed went far beyond *statement* and well into *suicidally stupid*.

She discovered that she didn't particularly care.

Lia looked at the neat row of entirely empty cottages; the weird lake; the long flight of stairs leading back up the hill to safety; and ruefully admitted to herself that she'd made her choice before ever descending those steps.

She met Idisio's eyes again, and watched the gray slowly bleed into a satisfied, smug darkness.

Chapter Thirty-eight

Tank was on the top step of the stairs down to the Lake when the first scream shredded the air.

The descent was far too steep to risk leaping, but he managed to *bounce*, haphazardly, two and three steps at a time; slipping on the damp wood, windmilling his arms for balance, cursing the lack of a handrail. Halfway down, a board cracked under the force of his landing. He staggered, leaned too far, and fell: whipped his body round to thud into a painful crouch, arms out wide for balance, four steps from the bottom.

He froze, staring.

Lia was entirely naked and *intimately* tangled with another unclothed young woman, one with considerably greater curves throughout and an aggressive passion in her movements.

Well, shit, Lia's definitely ii'ne, was Tank's first, rather disappointed thought. Then: *That wasn't a scream of pleasure*, followed immediately by *That's a fucking ha'ra'ha she's fucking and Idisio is right there* watching —

Bemusement became fast-rising fury as Lia twisted, her tear-streaked face briefly visible, and let out another spine-shivering scream. Idisio turned to face Tank, his eyes flooded with black from edge to edge, and held up a hand, forbidding, warning —

"*Fuck you, ha'ra'ha, she's mine*," Tank bellowed, and leapt.

Calculation caught up, belatedly pointing out that he was far too high to make this jump, his knees wouldn't take the landing, and he was about to sprawl out and make a horse's ass of himself in front of someone he didn't want laughing at him.

None of that mattered, because a moment later Tank went sideways, midair, as though slapped by a gigantic hand. He landed hard, rocky ground kicking the air from his body; gagged, wheezing, and forced rage and panic alike to *stop* until his spasming muscles could calm.

Lia whimpered, once, like an overwhelmed, overtired child.

Then there was silence.

Idisio crouched in front of Tank, his gray eyes still stained with black. "What in the *hells* possessed you to try that?" he inquired mildly. "Have you decided you're ready to die? I'm happy to grant that wish, if so." The black spread, then contracted, as though Idisio were fighting to control his own temper.

Tank managed to haul in a breath, let it out in a word more air than sound: "*Mine.*" He didn't mean it in any way as a sexual claim, but couldn't form words to draw that distinction.

Idisio's fair eyebrows rose, then sank into a pensive frown. "You're claiming her as — ah. As under your protection, not as in a relationship. Right?"

"*Mine,*" he husked again, by way of agreeing.

Idisio let out a sound somewhere between exasperation and amusement. Tank sucked in another, easier breath and began delicately levering himself upright, pausing frequently to gag for air.

"Take your time," Idisio said, and went away.

Tank sat still, vision swimming. *Concussion. Damnit.* He focused on breathing, his eyes half shut. *Probably at least one cracked rib.* He moved his feet gingerly, hissing at the shooting pain in his left leg and right knee.

The smell of ravann tea announced Idisio's return.

"Peace," the ha'ra'ha said. He handed a lopsided clay mug to Tank very carefully, avoiding direct contact, then backed up and crouched well out of reach. "No harm. *Ha'vash, ha'ne.* Truce. Yes?"

Tank nodded blankly and sipped the tea without protest.

"I added something for the pain," Idisio said after a few moments. "In case the taste is off."

"Just taste blood," Tank rasped, touching the corner of his mouth tentatively. He blinked at the red on his fingers and held his breathing carefully shallow. Definitely at least one cracked rib. *We'll be late for the road,* he thought fuzzily. *Dasin's going to be so pissed....*

Idisio grinned, a sharply derisive expression. "Never mind Dasin," he said. "Focus, Tank. Why are you claiming Lia? How do you even know her?"

Tank lifted a startled gaze to the ha'ra'ha. "She's on my crew," he said, and held back a barking cough at the stunned look on Idisio's face. "You didn't see her? She came in with us!"

Idisio scowled. "I honestly wasn't paying attention to anyone but you and Dasin. Arrogant and careless of me, I suppose."

Tank breathed past the urge to laugh, knowing he'd start coughing and that would go badly. "Didn't you *look*?" he said. "At something other than the outside show?"

Idisio made a face. "That's crude, 'eand I'll put it down to the concussion and the drug," he said. "But no. I avoid seeing human thoughts as much as possible. It's gotten even more unpleasant with time. Never mind. You're claiming her?"

"My crew, my people, my protection," Tank said. The words came easier, as long as he remained careful to keep his tone mild. His head seemed to be clearing, although a worrying grayish squiggle worked across his vision at random moments. "Mine. *Mine*, ha'ra'ha."

"Like a lord, then," Idisio said. He tugged at his lower lip thoughtfully. "Is she going to understand what you're trying to invoke here, Tank? Do *you*?"

"She's not my kathain, you *ta-karne sanahair*," Tank growled, then gagged for breath as muscles began to spasm.

Idisio waited patiently until Tank's breathing steadied. "Take it easy," he said. "The medicine will ease the pain, but it's not all that strong. I understand perfectly well you're not claiming her as lover, servant, or slave. But Tank, you're in *my* territory. You don't have any titles or rank. Your abilities are insignificant while you stand on my land. You aren't, in any way, a threat to me or to those under my protection. So why, exactly, should you claiming Lia as under your hand mean anything to me?"

Tank stared. Idisio stared back, his gray gaze mild.

"Yes," the ha'ra'ha said after the silence had stretched for a time. "I'm very different these days." He sighed and rubbed the bridge of his nose.

"She didn't deserve — that," Tank said. He set the mug down on the slope beside him, wincing.

Idisio smiled wryly. "You missed a lot of better moments."

Rage rose, hot and fast, and sent Tank's muscles into spasm again. "Not ... right ... *fucker*," he panted as breath came and went.

"Oh, calm down," Idisio said a bit irritably. "She chose with full knowledge of what might happen. Listen. I can help you, heal you, if you let me, but it's still not particularly easy for me. If you lash out at me while I'm trying to help, I'll kill you before I can stop myself. Purely by reflex. Do you understand?"

Tank dragged air past his clenched teeth and glared. Idisio glared back, a very human expression of annoyance, with nothing *other* in the air.

"You can't help *anyone*, nor protect them, if you're pissing yourself with pain on a hillside miles from town," Idisio pointed out pragmatically.

Tank shut his eyes, his jaw so tight he thought his teeth might shatter. He jerked his head once in surly agreement.

"Thank you," Idisio said. "I have to touch you. Hold still."

Tank gathered anger and fear alike into a tightly leashed bundle, keeping it walled off from the feel of Idisio's fingers tracing light and quick across Tank's body.

"Yes, cracked ribs, two of them," Idisio said absently. "Twisted kneecap, wrenched ankle ... there's an old shin strain here too. Concussion, abrasions ... all right. I've got the map. This is going to hurt like fire, so remember I'm helping you, please."

Tank blinked, drawing in breath —

— and liquid fire poured through his body, searing him from inside out and from the outside in simultaneously. He choked on a scream, found himself unable to thrash in protest, lost his hold on the fury and terror: drew back for a last, suicidal attack —

The pain stopped with a nearly physical *snap*, like a stick bent too far finally breaking cleanly in half. Tank let out a long, shivering moan, hazily aware drool was dripping down his chin, and fainted.

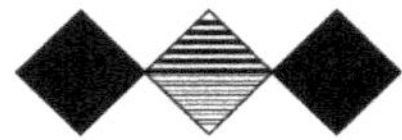

That could have gone better, Idisio observed, his tone light with laughter. *But as it also could have gone much worse, I'll take it. Wake up, Tank. Nap time's over.*

Warm, late afternoon sunbeams slanted across Tank's face. Overhead, the sky was a peaceful, empty blue. Crows and grackles argued in the underbrush. A squirrel hissed irritation at an intruder, then chirped and leapt away, its tiny body making an outsized amount of noise.

Tank drew in a deep exploratory breath. Finding only a faint, bruised ache, he pushed himself up to a sitting position, wary of dizziness. He flexed his hands, turning them over to examine the entirely unscratched flesh, front and back, breathing very consciously. An ant crawled across one wrist. He leaned over and pushed it gently onto the ground.

"Thank you," he said at last. "Stay out of my head."

Idisio's tone was blandly neutral. "You're welcome. Lia's back at her inn room with no memory of what happened today. As long as you don't prod at it, she won't remember. Tell her she got drunk and passed out, she'll be malleable to that."

Tank lowered his gaze, tracing the slope down to the viridescent Lake. He didn't want to look at the ha'ra'ha. "That's probably best. Although I don't actually *know* what the hells happened today."

Idisio made a thoughtful, humming sound, then said, "On her way south, Lia traveled with what she thought to be a slightly odd young lady from Orhon. The young lady, Galliana, turned out to be one of my lesser kin, and I took her in for everyone's safety. Lia, unfortunately, had already developed an affection and a protective streak for the girl, and Galliana had grown very ... let's call it fond ... of Lia in turn. Neither of them were willing to let it go, and I can only bend Galliana to my will so far. When I sensed Lia was back in town, I decided a tightly controlled meeting would be the safest option, so I offered up an invitation." He made an annoyed noise deep in his throat. "If I'd realized Lia was in *your* crew, I would have made sure you were occupied elsewhere today."

Tank looked up sharply, scowling, but didn't say anything aloud: he didn't need to.

Idisio lifted a shoulder wearily and said, "No, it wouldn't have stopped me from inviting her if I'd known. Galliana fixated on Lia, and I cared more about that than about any harm to a human I didn't even know. I don't regret it, Tank. It let me teach Galliana something she needed to understand, and it helped her balance considerably. In human terms, it made her more sane." He made a face. "That's not at all the right way to say it, but I can't come up with anything better." He stared down at the Lake, expression pensive.

"You're a cold bastard these days, aren't you?" Tank said bitterly.

Idisio's thin shoulders moved in another pained shrug. He said, "There was a *chekk*, a community of ha'ra'hain, here for a long time. They left before I was even born, but I found their hidden record books, and a few of the town's accounts survived the Purge. There's a recorded instability in the Ghost Lake line. My mother never got any help for her ... imbalance. I'm doing my best to keep Galliana from going that far sideways. She *has* to be able to coexist with the human community here. She can't leave, she's not nearly stable enough yet. I can't leave either. This town is my responsibility." He bent his head, scrubbing his fingers through his hair. "I'm not as cold as you think," he added, more quietly. "I understand your claim, and I'll honor it from this point forward."

"Oh, shit," Tank said, remembering. "Lia's swearing over to Arason Hall of Arms."

Idisio's head came up sharply, his eyes wide and darkening. "That's not a good idea."

"Stecatr would kill her to prove a point," Tank said bluntly. "There's politics involved, *ha'inn*. And speaking of politics, I'm told there's quite possibly another of your sort wandering around up there lately. Know anything about that?"

"Not enough," Idisio said ruefully, but made a cutting-off gesture to stop further questions.

They sat in silence for a while, watching the sun shift gently towards the horizon. Tank let himself breathe, tracked the tiny bits of healing still working through his body, and allowed himself an entirely unexpected moment of peace.

Whether Idisio couldn't attack him or wouldn't attack him made no difference. They had a truce in place, and here of all places, nothing of lesser power would attempt any sort of attack. Tank could *rest*.

Idisio snorted lightly, looking at him sideways as though hearing that thought, but offered no comment. Tank smiled at the sky and leaned back on his elbows, letting out a long sigh.

As the sun began to spread into an orange-gold evening display, Idisio said, tone muted, "Go away, Tank. Take the road north and don't come back to Arason. Don't let Lia come back. I don't care if she's sworn here, keep her *away*."

"Why?"

"Because I *can't* choose you, choose humans, over kin. Not again."

Tank's back went rigid at the anguish in Idisio's voice. "Lifty —" he said, involuntarily reverting to the old nickname.

"*No.*" Idisio rose to his feet and plunged down the slope towards the line of cottages without a backwards glance.

Tank heaved himself to his feet, considering the wisdom of following. After checking the glowing horizon, he grunted irritably and turned to labor up the stairs instead.

Chapter Thirty-nine

Lia woke with a splitting headache, vomit-sour mouth, and the threads of nightmares just barely beyond recall clouding her focus.

She sat up, hiccuped, and put both hands over her aching eyes. Why had she gotten so drunk? She never drank heavily. Something must have happened.

No. I don't drink like this. I never, ever do this. There was something else going on, something familiar about this dizzy, sick sensation. She put a hand down, testing: a bed beneath her, cotton sheet and pad over what felt like a corn husk bottom layer. So, not a cheap room, not a tent, not the commons floor.

She blinked, looking around with slitted eyes, taking in the simple room around her, the drawn curtains — another sign that this wasn't a cheap inn — her pack, and boots, sitting beside the bed, yesterday's clothes neatly folded across the nearby chair. A thick wool rug in a cheerful shade of red covered a large part of the floor.

Memory sifted back, bit by bit. Arason. Tank and Dasin and Cilif. She'd gone all the way to Bright Bay. Evkit and his bloodbirds in the Hackerwood; the huge, terrifying bloodbird looming at the edge of camp; the way she'd felt the next day — ah. That was what this felt like. And the day after she'd stabbed the one on the road through the Hackwood itself.

I was fucking witched again? *Unbelievable.* And in Arason, no less. She blinked gummy eyes, then rubbed them clear. Judging by the light coming around the edges of the heavy curtains, it was at least mid-morning. She should have been awake and at the market stall by now, which meant someone had decided to let her sleep in.

So someone had known she'd been witched. Instinct said Tank was involved, because, damnit, he was always involved with that sort of thing. Had *he* witched her? No. She wasn't sure why, but she was entirely certain of that much.

She flexed her hands, fury washing away the haze; swung her legs over the side of the bed, and launched into getting dressed, her hands starting to shake. She needed to confront *someone*. Anyone.

This was once too godsdamn *often*.

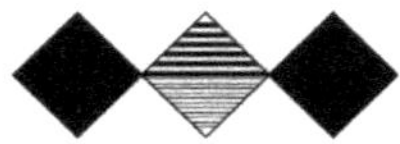

Lia had been wrong on one point: it wasn't midmorning, but late afternoon. She'd slept the entire day.

By the time she reached Dasin's stall in the market, she'd remembered enough to make her shaky with horror as much as with anger. She'd gone to Ghost Lake, for some bloody ridiculous reasons she couldn't quite recall. She'd sat down at a table with Idisio and Gally — she was too furious to give them titles, not in the privacy of her own damn mind. Idisio had said ... something. A lot of something. It wouldn't come clear.

But she'd had sex with Gally. That was absolutely clear, although the specific details were more than a little hazy. *What in the eternal love of the gods was I thinking?*

Lia stormed through the market, belatedly realizing she'd left both sword and ata behind. Not that she needed to wear the ata anymore: that thought stopped her aggressive stride for a frozen moment. She'd sworn over to Arason. Because ... because....

They all think staying with Stecatr will get you killed.

She stared at that memory for a moment of appalled horror, then shook her head, hard, and started moving again, although more slowly this time.

Her memories were remarkably scattered, much more so than in previous encounters with being witched. That argued for Idisio being behind it, and for him to have pushed very hard indeed to make her forget something.

When she finally arrived at Dasin's stall, Tank and Cilif were working to break everything down for the night. They weren't packing for the road, which meant they were staying at least one more day; boxes and bags were being sorted to easily pull out and reset in the morning.

Dasin took one look at Lia's set face and stopped moving. "Tank," he said, "handle it."

Tank turned, his eyes widening at whatever he saw in Lia's expression. "Right. Cilif?"

"Got it," the burly man said. "Go."

Tank shut his eyes and pinched the bridge of his nose. Then: "Lia, hold a moment. Dasin. Tonight —?"

Dasin wouldn't meet Tank's eyes. "Alone."

Tank dropped his voice to a low rumble: "*Dasin.*"

Dasin didn't look up. "Not tonight," he said, tone turning brittle. "Tomorrow's the last market day for us. Let's get through that first."

Tank hesitated, then leaned behind the table and snagged up a basket. He motioned Lia to follow, an imperious gesture that left no room for argument.

"Have you eaten?" he said as he began walking.

"No."

"Me neither. This way."

"I'm not hungry," she began, irritated.

Tank turned to face her, scowling forbiddingly. "My rules, remember? We eat. We drink. *Then* we talk about whatever's chewing your hair."

She duplicated his sullen shrug of moments before. This wasn't, after all, the place for a screaming fight, much as she'd have liked just that; and Tank was her best option for figuring out what the hells had happened the previous night.

Tank ignored her as he worked his way through the food section of the market, collecting a generous basketful of meats, cheese, bread, fruits and slightly wilted greens from various vendors. He wedged in two large flasks of liquor, then led her to a spot at the far corner of the market. The few tables were largely unoccupied, and the people remaining were making clear signs towards leaving.

Tank dumped out the basket contents, laid the lining cloth across the scarred table, then set out the food and drink with precise attention. Lia's irritation shifted into bemusement.

"That's a lot of food," she said. "Are you expecting company?"

Tank drew his belt knife and began slicing hard cheese into a neat row of tiny planks. "This is restful. And given how solidly you were sleeping earlier, I'm expecting that this'll be the first food you've had all day. Strip the thick center stem out of the spinach, if you would."

"Good grief, it's like being at home again." Carelessly, she dropped the wilted spinach leaves beside the cheese. Tank picked up the leaves, arranged them into a fan pattern, and laid them down gently. "Are you *serious*?"

"Restful," he said again, and passed her the carrots and his knife. "Trim the ends and leaves, they're clean enough."

She obeyed, increasingly bemused, and made an effort to stack them neatly when she finished. Tank offered a mild smile of approval.

Once all the food was arranged to Tank's satisfaction, he held up a finger. "You pray, yeah?"

The simple question incited a complicated anguish. She'd prayed every day of her life: for the gods to keep her in favor, for them to keep their dark faces turned away, for her family to remain safe, for a path out of the trap she'd landed herself in before she'd even passed puberty.

More and more, she found herself feeling as though their dark faces were, in truth, turned on her, but had no idea of what she'd done to deserve it. She'd been taught that once that happened, it could only be flipped back with extensive purification ceremonies.

Not everyone survived being purified. Especially of late.

Maybe there was another way. Maybe the Arason Church had a different belief. A wave of shame hit her at allowing herself such a selfish, nearly heretical hope.

Tank's eyes narrowed as though he'd heard her thoughts; then his expression went neutral. "Praying ain't something I do often," he said, his accent considerably less refined than usual, "but now and again, it's good to remember there's something more'n us out there. You mind if I lead? It's a short one."

"I thought you said you didn't believe in the gods."

"I said I wasn't sure if I did," he corrected. "Anyway, I don't know that prayer has as much to do with the gods sometimes as it's just ... *taking* a moment." He shrugged. "Lemme say it out already, yeah?"

She nodded, tightness strident throughout her body, and folded her hands together.

Tank set his hands flat on his thighs, his back straight, and shut his eyes. He said, with absolute sincerity, "Thank you, Comos; thank you, Ishrai; thank you, Sun-Lord. We've survived another day. We've food before us and friends around us and money in pocket. We have shelter, we have our health, and we have a reason to wake up in the morning. We haven't had to kill anyone today. Thank you, all Three, for all of those things, and may we never take any of it for granted." He relaxed his shoulders, leaning back a little, and opened his eyes to signal he was done. "You got anything to add?"

Lia stared at him, lost for words, then pulled herself together. "No. No, I think that covered it well enough. It's an unusual prayer, though."

"I don't like the traditional words, and I don't feel like singing right now. Eat." Tank picked up a spinach leaf the size of his hand and began rolling cheese and meat into it. Lia watched him, bewildered — *singing?* — then began copying the assembly as neatly as possible.

"I've never tried this before," she said, examining the small bundle of food thoughtfully. "Is this a southern thing?"

The conversation drifted through differences in cultural approaches to food for a time, and a discussion of the peaches he'd bought, which didn't grow farther south and which Tank liked beyond, he said, all reason. She knew he was lightly distracting her any time she began to think about the reason she'd come to talk to him; she allowed it, not at all sure what she'd wanted to say anymore.

Finally, though, her mood darkened past avoiding. "Tank," she said. "I need to —"

"I know. Time to talk for serious. Here." Tank held out one of the flasks. "Drink. It's a northern rotgut, sommat I can never pronounce."

She took a cautious sip. "Gin. Not hard to pronounce at all."

"Yeah? I thought it was that warbullya stuff. My mistake."

"*Warhbhuia?*"

"Yeah, that."

She took another, thoughtful drink. "No. You got cheated, if you paid for that." She set the flask down, frowning, and met his eyes.

He claimed the flask and took a hefty swallow. "All right," he said, setting it on the table between them. "Talk." His tone was brisk, his expression nearly blank, as though to avoid provoking her in any way.

"You're trying very hard to keep me calm," she said. "Which tells me you know something about ... what happened. Were you —" She breathed in sharply, sudden cold sweeping down her back. "Did *you* —" She choked, unable to finish that question.

Tank reached out and wrapped his hands around hers. She froze.

"*Lia*," he said, in his trail captain voice. "I have never, and will never, lay a hand on you against your will or when you're out of your senses. Don't you fucking *dare* put that on me. *Ever*. Now tell me what you remember."

There was a vibration to the last words that pulled all restraint and confusion aside. She related how she'd woken, what she remembered; as she talked, tears spilled down her face. He kept hold of her hands, now tightly fisted within his grasp.

The gaps were the worst part, overflowing with the terror of the unknown. Unsaid, but wavering through every word, were questions she couldn't say aloud: *What did Idisio do to me that I don't remember? How could I have let him* watch? *How could Gally have let him watch? Are they demons after all? Am I tainted, cursed, disgraced forever?*

Tank let her stammer it out, let her shiver and cry, his hands warm and solid around hers. When she fell silent, he let her pull her hands back and hunch into trembling misery.

By the time she caught her breath and sat up straight again, he was quietly slicing bread. "Eat," he said, handing her a piece.

She took it, too exhausted to protest, and ate slowly, reaching out and picking up bits of cheese and cured meat to go with it. Without really thinking about it, she picked up the flask and drank down a good half of what was left before Tank took it away.

"Enough," Tank said. "There's more to get drunk on, but wait until this talk is clear first, yeah? So, then." He sighed through his nose, very nearly an irritated snort. "First up, Idisio never touched you. Don't know if that helps any."

Lia stared at him, flushing rapidly towards fury. He held up a hand.

"I arrived at the end," he told her. "Pure chance. I tried to intervene and got slapped down hard." He dropped his hand to his ribs, wincing.

"Then how do you know?" she demanded.

"Because he wouldn't," Tank said with absolute surety. "Anything sexual that happened was all your friend."

Lia cut a fast glance around to check for eavesdroppers, her mouth tight. "Gally," she said, scarcely audible. "She's — she's one of them."

"She's a ha'ra'ha, yeah. Young and untaught, sounds like." Tank began to shred a piece of bread, frowning down at the crumbs. "From what I saw, you ... well...."

"I'm *ii'ne*," Lia said, the word sticking in her throat. She cast another hasty glance around, then swallowed and repeated it, more defiantly this time.

"Really?" he said, deadpan, then grinned at her startled glare. "You're looking at the wrong person if you want a reaction about that, Lia. No, what matters to me is whether you were *willing*. Did Gally force you? Do you remember?"

Lia stared at him, her mouth shaping soundless words, then: "No. I don't think ... no."

She shut her eyes, concentrating, and recalled Idisio saying: *You do have a choice ... Tell me you don't want to take her to bed, or rather, for her to take you to bed, given what I've told you.*

She shivered a little as the gin hit, blurring dignity and caution. "No. I made a choice. I knew ... I know what Gally is, but I didn't care." She straightened, defiance stirring. "I was ... I *am* ... sick and tired of living by what the Stecatr Church calls right."

Tank swept the crumbs into a pile, frowning at them. "All right," he said finally. "So, you weren't raped. Idisio didn't touch you, and you were willing with Gally. Meaning neither Arason Hall nor Arason Church will interfere. What else? You're still twisted up. Keep talking."

"It's all so muddy," Lia said, defiance draining away. "I don't like not remembering everything properly."

Had she really just said that about the Stecatr Church? Gods, what was the matter with her? It had taken less than six months to overthrow a lifetime of learning. She must have been born weak, for things to flip in her head so quickly.

"Gone is gone," Tank said pragmatically. "I don't like it either, but you'll remember when it's time, or maybe never. I can say Idisio has honor. A sideways honor, by our way of thinking, but it's there. He wouldn't have witched you into an oath or pressed you into anything you didn't want to do already. So not remembering words...." He flicked his fingers dismissively. "Let it be."

Lia wavered, nearly convinced. Then she said, stubbornly, "But I woke up feeling like I'd been in a brawl and not knowing how I got back to my room. Why would he make me forget *anything*, if there's nothing that happened against my will? And why do I *hurt* like this? I feel like a disjointed chicken!"

Tank stirred the pile of crumbs with one finger, his expression grim now. "Because ... well, there's a thing ha'ra'hain do. It's hard to explain."

As though that had opened a door in her head, Lia abruptly remembered more of what Idisio had said, after her decision to submit to whatever Gally asked of her. That decision alone turned Lia's stomach, now. *What was I thinking?*

Idisio had been brutally clear. *She's going to hurt you, s'a. That's unavoidable. I'm going to try to keep her from going too far when she starts to feed on you, but you have to remember to ...* words blurred, inaccessible. Then came an intense memory of wild, uncontrolled pleasure switching, without warning, into a screaming, searing agony ... *howling, unable to break free, lost in the tangle of want/not want....*

Tank glanced up, his eyes wide and shocked. "Damnit," he muttered, then: "*Quiet,* damnit, *quiet.*"

Lia pulled into a surprisingly easy silence, and rested there until she stopped shaking. Then she said, fighting nausea, "He told me. I remember. The ... the *ha'inn*. He *said.* He said she'd hurt me. He said something about ... feeding?"

Tank spread his hands flat on the table, meeting her eyes. "Yes. That." He paused, then asked: "Did you — so, then, he told you beforehand what she would do. Did you agree to *that?*"

Lia shut her eyes and pressed her face into her hands, then sat up, resolutely stiff-backed. "I'm not sure. I remember him saying there was a way it wouldn't hurt. I don't remember what that involved. I think I agreed to try."

"I'm guessing it didn't work. You were screaming when I showed up." She flinched. He set his jaw and went on, "I'm pretty sure you're scrambled because he pushed too hard, trying to remove your memory of that part." His hands formed fists on the table, an old, dark anger stirring in his eyes. Then he took a deep breath, and his expression smoothed out.

"What *is* it?" she asked, tone wavering, not at all sure she wanted this answer. "The feeding? I don't remember if he explained that."

"I don't know," Tank admitted. "Our energy? Our —" He hesitated, biting his lip as though unwilling to finish that thought.

"Our *souls?*" she demanded, appalled.

"No. Maybe. I don't know! I just … look, I was a target myself, once. I didn't know what was happening at the time, didn't even have as much explanation as you got. I panicked and hit out and ran away." He glanced up at her, then blanched at whatever he saw in her expression and looked away hastily. "I don't think it's souls they're after, no. I suppose you could *ask* one of them, but I'm surely not about to."

"No," Lia said, choking back the bubble of terrified laughter rising in her throat. "No, I wouldn't either."

Tank pinched his nose again, squinching his eyes shut. "It's not simple, Lia. Nothing ever is, with ha'ra'hain. Idisio made you forget what happened because Gally hurt you, and Idisio doesn't like to cause humans pain. He was *trying* to be kind."

She dropped her hands to her lap, her gaze settling into an unfocused bleakness. "I knew as soon as I woke up that something was wrong. I remembered enough to put together that I'd been witched again — he's done that to me before —"

Tank's eyebrows went up. "He has? When?"

She waved the question aside, abruptly wanting shut of the subject entirely. "It doesn't matter. But once I sorted out that it had happened again, all I could think of was coming to talk to you."

Tank looked startled, then pleased. "That was a good choice," he said. "Better than some you could have made, at least. So did I answer enough of your questions for now? It's almost dark, and I don't like talking on some things at night if I can help it."

She looked at the argent, gold, and scarlet-tinged clouds spreading across the western sky, considering. "I suppose so," she said. "I've a lot to think through."

"Yeah." Tank tilted his head, studying the sky himself. "It's going to rain again tonight," he said. "We've got maybe three, four hours left of clear weather. One more day of market, then we're out of this damn town."

Lia picked up the flask and drained it in three long swallows.

Tank laughed a little and uncapped the second flask. "Yeah," he said. "I think I'll join you."

Intersection: Historian

"I am going to tell you a story," Tath said. She ran the new name through her head a few more times, testing, then smiled, satisfied. *Ghost* was a good enough name to take, considering how many people likely assumed her dead. She could always adapt it for any given situation: *tathni, tathqi, tathsay.* She looked out over the valley below her, pleased, and adjusted her vision to see through the dark as clearly as if she stood in daylight.

The Ghost Lake swirled with the steady exhalations of a creature from the beginnings of time. Closer below, untidy grass and scrub rambled along the uneven, rocky slope. Even closer, the thick bark of a mature oak branch supported Tath and the boy comfortably.

The boy hadn't shown any particular joy in climbing, but he'd shown no hesitation, either. Once securely perched on the branch, he began gently touching the damp bark — it had rained earlier in the night — as though exploring the texture. His expression remained locked in a blankness she knew all too well, the neutrality of someone trained from birth to be invisible in all ways.

He still hadn't given Tath his name. Well, she hadn't given him a choice about following her, so that was fair enough. Here, though, sitting in a tree high above the nest of one of the last living ha'reye, it was time to settle things between them, to gain his trust if possible.

Tath was very, very good at gaining human trust.

The boy looked at her, after a moment, and gave a scant eyebrow twitch to show interest, the movement barely visible under his mop of unruly red hair. So, he knew how to adjust his own eyesight. She'd suspected as much. Good. Very good.

Tath returned her attention to the Lake, letting the boy's curiosity build.

Earlier in the day, when Idisio had briefly sensed them, she'd been able to shoo the ha'ra'hain on his way without incident. Idisio really *should* have recognized her touch. He'd obviously grown complacent from thinking himself entirely safe, lazy from having such enormous power a few steps away. He'd learn the downside of that soon enough.

On the other hand, perhaps having to rebuild so completely had altered her own signature presence. That was something to investigate. It could prove quite useful.

The lesser kinswoman, Galliana, was damaged: nearly blind and deaf, compared to Idisio. She was entirely useless as a guardian and so of no concern at all. The full guardian, far below, was deeply asleep, still recovering from the massive surge of effort that had started so many things and ended others.

It was safe enough to sit here for a time, safe enough to enjoy the trickle of power rippling like a warm fire against her feet. She could tell that the boy felt it too. He was holding himself back, with admirable discipline and caution, from exploring it.

Very promising. His father would have been waist deep in the muck and screaming for help by now.

"It's a story of long and long and long ago," Tath said. "A story of when I was your age, more or less." She paused, allowing herself a sigh only because the boy would expect such a sound. "I was born to a family of no particular note, in a place of no particular importance. I had dirt for a playing floor and thatch for a roof, bird eggs and gruel for my meals. I had stones and sticks to lay out into patterns for my games."

She looked sideways at the boy. He stared at the Lake.

"Have you ever played the pattern-games with sticks and stones?" she asked softly.

He hesitated, then nodded without lifting his gaze from the slow swirling below them.

"Don't focus on that area too much," she advised. "The guardian is sleeping right now, and we aren't ready to wake it yet." Not that they *could*, not without intention and a great deal of personal pain, but the boy didn't need to know that.

Still, too much focus on the Lake might draw Idisio's attention, which didn't suit Tath at all. On a second look, Idisio *would* recognize her, even in her new form, and that would interfere with her developing plans.

The boy lifted his gaze to study the valley, occasionally looking up at the cloud-littered sky.

"You know the game, then," Tath went on. "One day, I began to realize I was building patterns with purpose, not merely playing. That the patterns I created meant something. They were a language that I thought nobody else understood."

He looked at her then, ducking his head slightly to screen his eyes with bright red strands of hair.

Tath smiled. "Yes, I thought you'd have done that as well. You did well, back there, with the failed one."

He swung his gaze away, his shoulders hunching a little. He'd been oddly reticent about taking part in the feast. Apparently his mother hadn't allowed him that pleasure before.

Tath hadn't forced it. He'd come to understand the need eventually. Perhaps he simply wasn't quite old enough yet; this many generations removed from the source of his heritage, the time to full maturation might well have changed.

"One day," she said, letting him avoid her, "one of the elders of my family — everyone there was family, you understand, there were no distinctions between *mother* or *aunt* or *sister*, not in the sense of status. There were only those elder and those not elder. And the elders held the power, such as it was in our very small and unremarkable home place. One of the elders, then, came across me as I built my patterns."

The boy's shoulders went back, tension sharp in a thin-boned frame.

"The elder asked me questions about what I was creating, and I had no reason not to answer. He was family, he was elder. He seemed not at all upset, merely curious. I told him everything." She paused again, looking down at the Lake, then shut her eyes and produced another deliberate sigh. "And so I was sent away to a greater home, with remarkable people who knew a great deal about the patterns I had been creating. From there, I was sent away again, to even greater people, and then yet again."

The boy beside her sat very still, but a question hung unspoken in the air.

"I was treated well," she said, as gently as she could, and caught the tiniest shiver from him. "I suspect you weren't as fortunate."

A long silence. Then the *tiniest* sniffle.

Tath waited without speaking until the ambient misery cleared from the air, then went on, "I was pronounced elder once I reached my physical maturity. I stood as equal to those many times my age, and we worked together for the good of many families. I learned the ways of water and of air. I learned what I could of fire and of earth, but those elements never listened to me so well, nor did I hear them as strongly. I had the strongest touch with water. Stronger than any of the elders, stronger than anyone in any known family at that time. So when the voices began to call, I was the first to hear them."

The boy turned to look at her, his dark eyes wide with understanding. She kept her expression mild, and let him examine her face until he retreated once more into studying the clouds.

"Those were, of course, the ha'reye emerging," she said. "Others heard them, soon enough, but the ha'reye preferred to speak to me, as I was the one they knew first. I took guidance from the other elders, but I was at the age of wildness, and full of pride, and I made mistakes." She looked up at the sky herself, letting out a real sigh this time. "I was not nearly cautious enough in the agreements and promises I made. I trusted those I should not have trusted, and was betrayed, over and over. Most recently I was abandoned, by one I had foolishly begun to trust despite knowing better. Abandoned to die in a nest of creatures who wished to use my life to strengthen themselves. But I was the stronger. I am always, *always* the stronger."

She paused, thinking back, with great satisfaction, to the crumbling of the earth, the distracted confusion of the *attiara*, and her own excellent ability to play dead. It had been far too chaotic, in that moment, for the creatures to look closely. They had taken her appearance for fact, and so fled the collapsing Qisani without her.

The most difficult part had been winding a sufficent portion of herself to the surface of the destroyed temple complex. Then had come the tedious process of luring small creatures within reach, rebuilding her strength, moving aside more collapsed rock as she slowly, so slowly, worked towards escape.

She could have gone looking for the one who betrayed her that last time: De'sta'haiq — Deiq — currently comfortably ensconced as master of a desert Fortress with that *stupid* human woman, Alyea, by his side. She could have razed the entire structure down to the molten core of the earth, shredding Deiq into a real death in the process.

That would have been simple. Too simple.

Her desire, her goal, had come clear at last. She wanted, she *deserved* more than simple revenge. She'd suffered enough, as a follower. She'd more than earned the reward she'd been promised in return for submitting wholly to the ha'reye, so long ago: to become as a god herself. To rule this ragged world, to shape it, at last, into *her* vision. The ha'reye were gone or dying out at last. It was her time, her turn.

She'd nearly left it too late. The only remaining location that might hold the last burst of power she needed was not in the remains of the southern jungles, which the teyanain had so recently swept clear with genocidal passion, but in the harsh, untouched northern mountains.

This boy beside her might well be the key to her proper ascension. She had to gain his trust.

He shifted slightly, the tiniest sign of restlessness. She'd been quiet for too long. She went on, moderating her tone to reassuring sobriety: "So I am here now, with you, and I have suffered for many human lifetimes. And so you are here with me now, and your ancestors and mine have caused you great suffering, in your very short life, for reasons drawn from my long and long and long ago mistakes."

The boy said nothing. Tath allowed the silence, patience being one of the most enduring lessons she'd learned over the centuries. What he said or asked or did next would tell her how well she'd done on hooking him in. If he wasn't ready yet, well ... she would have to wait, and try again, that was all. This was far too delicate a matter to force as she'd done with Tanavin and Dasin.

Stars speckled the sky overhead as clouds dissipated. A brisk chill washed through the air, dropping the temperature to what humans would consider uncomfortable. The weather near a ha'reye's nest never obeyed normal laws of nature, although generally it went in the other direction: hot, not cold.

There was quite a bit strange about this particular nest. She considered staying to study it. But that would mean causing and managing quite a lot of fuss, and it would be a distraction from the all-important task of gaining the boy's trust ... and his name.

As the moon began to turn towards its own bed, the boy said, "What do you want from me?"

Young as he was, he knew how to hear human lies. Tath wasn't willing to risk breaking his fragile trust to find out if he could hear hers. Choosing her words with care, she said, "I want to teach you properly, as I was taught. I want to give you that gift."

He sat very still, and his voice came very soft as he asked: "And what then?"

Tath smiled and said, quite calmly, "Tell me the name your mother gave you, that I may teach you. Without that, I'll answer no more questions."

He met her gaze. Slowly, his expression became as feral as her own: "Jacale," he said. "My mother calls me Jacale."

Intersection: Disorientation

Chill night air startled into fog as it encountered the considerably warmer Lake vapors. Out in the hills to the south, a wofic howled: a long, rolling question with no immediate answer.

He wondered whether he could, if he tried, understand the beasts of the world. But understanding his fellow humans was difficult enough on the best of days. He didn't particularly want the burden of more comprehension.

Another wofic howled belated response, the sound more deliberate than the first call. Much closer, warm air moved behind him. He held still, knowing himself entirely safe. Only one being besides himself ever walked this path. Even the newly arrived, younger ha'ra'ha hadn't ventured to the southern side of the Lake yet.

"Kolan," Idisio said from a polite distance. "You're out late tonight."

Kolan. Yes, that's my name. He blinked at the swirling vapors a stone's throw from his bare feet and smiled at the ha'ra'ha's careful tone. "I'm not having a fit," he said without turning. He didn't say: *yet.* This close to the Lake, a fit was inevitable. "I need to talk to you, and this is the only safe spot."

"That's a relative concept," Idisio said dryly. "Please come back away from there. You know that makes me nervous."

Kolan bowed slightly to the power slumbering far beneath their feet, then backed up several deliberate steps before turning and selecting a large boulder on which to perch, one that put his back to the Lake.

"Having me that close won't wake it," he said, as he'd said before.

Usually Idisio's answer was, "I'd rather not take the chance." Tonight, the young ha'ra'ha hesitated, then came around to stand before the boulder, looking him over carefully.

"I'm more worried about you," Idisio said, no levity in his voice at all. "I'm afraid that one of these days you'll keep going."

Kolan looked over his shoulder slowly, considering the slow, iridescent swirl gleaming in weak moonlight. "No," he said. "That doesn't tempt me, Idisio."

"Then why *here*? You know perfectly well we can talk privately anywhere you like. Sometimes I think you enjoy worrying me."

Kolan smiled. "You sound like a querulous grandmother," he said. "And why here ... because *here*, I know you won't lose control and hurt me. It's too close." He motioned vaguely to the Lake behind him, and didn't say the other truth: that while he didn't, truly didn't, want to touch that shimmering not-water, staring at it was very close to an addiction. It reminded him of the dark, and the fire, but in an odd way. Free of pain, but filled with terrible beauty.

And sometimes, just sometimes, he felt Ellemoa sitting beside him, her hand in his, entirely at peace. Those brief moments were worth any amount of risk.

Idisio drew in a sharp breath. "Oh, Kolan," he said. "You still think —"

Kolan interrupted gently. "Never mind. I have to talk to you about something important. I've tried to explain this before. I think I have the words right this time."

He drew a breath, frowning to himself, and reached for the arrangement he'd patiently worked out. Idisio stood still, waiting, his concern a thin, acrid haze in the ambient.

Kolan said, slowly, "Arason ... isn't ... *stable*. You being here is keeping it from fraying completely, but you're only one ha'ra'ha. You can't do this alone. That's why an entire *chekk* settled here. That —" He hooked a thumb over his shoulder to indicate the Lake, "that is not a normal nest, and the land ... here ... doesn't ... *like* it."

He could feel cohesion fading as Idisio's growing alarm muddied his clarity. He let out a faint, strangled sound, desperately grasping after rehearsed words, and caught only a fragment.

Knowing it was out of sequence, but afraid to lose it entirely, he said, "That's why I have to leave. With Tank. And you, later."

Idisio's breath hissed through his teeth. "Kolan —"

Kolan dropped his chin to his chest, breathing strained. "I've lost it," he muttered, anguish blazing through his chest like a live coal. "I'm sorry, I'm sorry, it's gone again ... gods, gods, *please....*"

He felt as though the multicolored vapors of the Lake were drifting into his head, scattering sense and vision alike. The faintest trace of fire slid along the back of his neck.

No, no, not again, please, not again....

Idisio was saying something, but the words were green-gray suka taffies that melted away into nonsense as soon as they emerged. A wofic howl, far closer than before, came through clean and clear and sharp, a lifeline back to rationality: he gripped it, swinging his *self* back into control, shutting away the past. Words returned, arranged across the inside of his mind as though inked on a freshly prepared page, crisp and perfect. The letters began to shiver even as he stared at them.

"No," he said hastily, cutting across whatever Idisio was saying. "No, no, I've got it again, wait. You need the *chekk* back here. You can't leave. Not ... yet ... but...." He was losing the thread. Idisio having to leave, eventually, was a complicated, painfully distracting topic. He pushed his focus onto what mattered *now*. "There's no chance Tank would track down the *chekk* without. Without. Because — there's a chance they're —" he wobbled, words sliding again, then pounced on the remnants and shouted them out, anxiety swamping self control: "— *involved! Because! Chance of involved! Chekk! Stecatr!*" He managed to moderate his volume, but not the inane scattering of the words. "Fight, I can, I know — need someone who — fear isn't. Isn't afraid. They need *me!* Stecatr! Have to go! Maybe! Involved!"

He fell silent, panting like an overheated wofic and not at all sure he'd made his point clearly enough.

After what seemed a long time, Idisio said, "That's not only extremely dangerous, I suspect that Tank won't let you travel alongside."

"Church," he rasped. "Orders. Priest. High."

Idisio let out a wordless, wondering murmur, then said, "Oh, now *that* is jumping straight out into the middle of the fire."

Kolan laughed a little, breath coming easier, and sat up straight. "Only way," he said, rubbing his chest gently. He set his fingers between his upper left ribs and focused on the reassuring, steady thump of his heart. "Already asked. Already agreed. Already set."

"Kind of you to at least tell me before you wandered off," Idisio said, tone desert-dry. "Kolan, this is a *terrible* idea. You're not nearly stable enough for this, no matter what act you put on to fool the Church."

"It'll be better — away," he said, voice wobbling. He could feel the slant growing in his mind, the heavy pressure that would send him away from himself for hours or days at a time. It *was* better, further from the Lake. He'd proven that to himself, over and over. *Don't forget. Don't forget. This is a good idea. It* is.

There was something else he was supposed to say, something terribly important, but it was gone, fading, melting away like mist under strong sunlight.

"Godsdamned fool," Idisio said, and then he was there, his hand tucked around Kolan's upper arm, half-lifting him from the rock. "Come on, come on, let's get you in to lie down. Damnit, you can't even walk properly —" As Kolan stumbled, legs disobeying, the ground refusing to stay flat beneath him; as his ears filled with a wet-cotton pressure. "Kolan! Don't fight me, let me move you!"

Kolan nodded blankly, granting permission for something he couldn't grasp but knew he needed. A moment later his knees simply gave out, muscles failing; but instead of falling into rock-studded scrub, the colors of the world shifted, then shifted again, and he knelt on a tidy stone patio.

Idisio knelt beside him, a shaky arm around Kolan's shoulders. "Gods, you're hard to move, even willing," he said. "I'd intended to get you back to the church, but I barely pulled you across the Lake."

The wofics howled again, a duet this time, question and answer braiding together. The sound cleared the fear and fog from Kolan's mind, leaving him empty of all energy.

"This is ... good ... enough," he said, the words blurring on his tongue. Then he folded over sideways to curl up on the cold ground and went, comprehensively, to sleep.

Chapter Forty

As the last of the boxes landed in the rented hand-wagon and the cover latched down to secure the cargo, Tank's mood soured from foul to nearly savage. The hangover had taken until noon to clear. He was hungry, and angry without a clear target. Lia, who Dasin had excused on some errand or another that morning, hadn't come back. Cilif had the day off, meaning Tank had dealt with the entirety of a long day's market, alone with Dasin and unreasonably resentful of it.

Dasin, for his part, hadn't sniped at Tank once. He'd been studiedly neutral, focused on the customers and scarcely saying a word to Tank all day. Far from being a relief, it had only increased Tank's anxious tension. Dasin typically waited until the perfect moment for a devastating remark.

Dasin wouldn't let him go without saying *something* hurtful. At the very least, the promise of *later* would be pushed out one more time, just to see if Tank would accept it.

Tank didn't know if he would. Flatly, bleakly, didn't know.

He checked the load one last time, then wordlessly moved to take up the handles.

"Tank," the merchant said just before he began to lift.

Here it comes. For a moment, Tank considered ignoring Dasin and trundling the load off to the stables to sort it back into the wagon for departure in the morning. Arason, like Obein, provided tables, controlled the flow of traffic to cut down on distraction and mess, and secured the market after hours. The wagon was stored in a well-secured stable catering to merchants. Not cheap, but they could afford it. Today's profit alone, from what Tank had seen, easily covered their fees, the mercenaries' pay, rooms at the Nine Bees Inn, and meals for the past three days.

Arason was a reliably good market, but the slog to and from the stables at start and end was hell on Tank's back. He wanted to get it over with, then retreat to a tavern with decent food and strong liquor, far from aggravating ha'ra'hain, looming political messes, and Dasin.

"Tank," Dasin said again. Tank grunted, letting go of the cart handles, and turned. "What?"

Dasin's face held a startling chill, his eyes clear and sharp. "Tonight. It's time to talk."

"Good to know your schedule's finally clear," Tank said, unable to stop himself.

Dasin's expression didn't change. "I may deserve that," he said, then held out a small wrapped bundle. "You haven't eaten. I'm not letting you haul that cart anywhere until you do."

Tank stared at him, speechless. Slowly, he accepted the bundle and unwrapped it to reveal a *disdis*: thin flatbread spread with a lightly spiced meat and olive filling, then rolled into a tight cylinder.

It was one of Tank's favorite foods. He didn't know of a single shop or baker in Arason that made it. He looked up at Dasin, bewildered. "Where did you ...? *When* did you?"

"Now and again I'm not a complete asshole." Dasin gestured at the sandwich and turned away to lean pointedly against the side of the cart, setting his weight in such a way that Tank wouldn't be able to move the cart until Dasin stood up.

It wasn't the best *disdis*, definitely made by a northern with no real understanding of southern spices, and the bread was dry rather than spongy, but Tank's eyes still burned with conflicting emotion as he ate it. He took his time, as much to show respect as to make sure it wouldn't bounce right back up from his unsettled stomach.

As Tank wiped his hands on his trousers, Dasin shifted upright. "Meet me at the Red Ox Inn," he said. "When you're done sorting the load. Room five. Get something decent to drink, there's a place across the street." He walked off, back very straight.

"Yes, *s'e*," Tank muttered under his breath, sarcasm driven by long habit, and began trundling the cart towards the stables.

Tank took a detour past his room at the Nine Bees to grab a few small items he might want, and to smear his lower back with a layer of hot paste to keep his muscles from seizing up. It was a typical southern remedy, and smelled strongly of hot peppers, thus the name. Dasin had worked with a northern alchemist to tone down the potency of the smell considerably without losing therapeutic effectiveness. Now Tank could walk down the street after applying it without causing aromatic suffering to innocent bystanders, and ordinary soap took the oils from his hands.

Fortunately, the Red Ox wasn't all that far from the Nine Bees, and there was indeed a liquor shop across the street. The shop had no name, only a sign nailed up beside the door, featuring a roughly painted wine jug and a symbol Tank didn't recognize. He took a moment to look at the door frame, trying to keep the inspection casual. He caught at least two thief marks he was sure of and four more that he couldn't interpret.

The door opened while he hesitated. A short woman looked up at him, her dark face sardonically inquiring. Her long gray hair was roped into thick braids laced through with gold thread, a clear warning that customers needed to mind their manners. "Will you be standing here until it rains, *s'e*? I'd rather you came in if you're going to buy, or find another staring spot if you're skint."

He blinked down at her, then forced a smile. "I'm sorry, *s'a*. It's been a long day, and my thoughts ran away with me. Please, I'm looking to buy. May I come in?"

She stepped aside, pointedly holding the door open for him. He ducked under the slightly too low lintel with a murmur of gratitude.

He half-expected to be told "Oh, you're that redhead I was told about, there's a blond merchant as said to sell you this particular, high end, *expensive* liquor." The woman merely stared at him, waiting. He stumbled through asking after what he wanted, negotiating the price, and draped the raffia-wrapped bottles in their woven carrier over his shoulder without seeing a single spark of recognition in her eyes.

As the door shut behind him, he heard the definite sound of a bolt being thrown. He blinked at the dark sky, uncertain as to the time. It had been fifth bells at market close today. Taking the cart to the stables, he'd heard sixth. At the Nine Bees, had he heard the seventh? It was dark enough to be nearly ninth. It wasn't late enough in the year to be dark so soon. Wait, they were on the road late this year, his calculations were off.

Tank stood still, breathing through his nose, collecting himself against a sourceless sense of dread. After a moment, he shook himself and strode for the door of the Red Ox.

Tank was well into the room and setting his purchases down on the small writing desk before he saw the whore. She was in a chair behind the swing of the door, obviously placed in the only spot out of direct sight as one entered.

She was tall and freckled, her hair a shade darker than his own ferocious red. He recognized her from his time waiting out the rainstorm the previous day: she'd been the one to sit stubbornly beside him, plying him with sharp humor followed by a delicately pressed invitation that had damn near overcome his reluctance. Belatedly, he recognized that had more than likely been on Dasin's directions.

His temper flared. He shot Dasin a glare and turned on his heel to walk out, fury muffling thought. A step later, his anger spluttered, oddly pale. Two more steps, and it was simply gone, leaving behind a chill wash of bewilderment and disorientation, a sense of having shoved at a wall that fell away at the first touch.

Tank turned to stare at Dasin. "What?" he said, in complete disbelief. "Did you just ...?"

Dasin's expression was as coldly neutral as before. "Please sit down, Tank." He motioned to the desk chair, then settled in a cross-legged sit on the bed.

Tank obeyed, not quickly: testing for compulsion, ready to break free at the first suggestion that his will wasn't his own. He felt no resistance, even when he moved sideways as though going for the door, so he settled in the chair and nodded, with scant politeness, to the whore. "*S'a*," he said.

She smiled back at him, half-mocking, with genuine amusement in her eyes.

Tank fixed his gaze on Dasin, letting his face settle into harsh, cold lines. "Talk, then."

"Don't try to walk out on me before we've finished talking. This is important, Tank."

Tank's lips compressed into a thin line. "I hold the right to quit afterward, if you piss me off enough," he retorted.

"You've always had that," Dasin muttered. He forced a wan grin, then motioned politely to the whore. "Tank, may I present Nea. She's one of my informants in Arason."

"We've *met*," Tank said savagely, trying not to glare at the woman. Then: "*Informants?*"

Dasin's smile was more genuine this time. "So I heard. And yes. Whorehouses are wonderful places for gossip about all things mercantile."

"And political," Tank said, no less sharply than before.

"Of course." Dasin drew his knees up and wrapped his thin arms around them, ankles still crossed. He'd rarely been so casual in his posture, certainly not in front of anyone but Tank. "Don't ask why I didn't tell you that I've developed informants. You didn't want to know. You just wanted to be a mercenary, and you wanted me to be a herbs and simples merchant. I tried to let you have that. I would have ... I would have walked away from Yuer, if you'd refused, back in Sandsplit. I tried to say no, myself. I ... I couldn't." He swallowed hard, ducking his head, then visibly forced himself to raise his eyes again to meet Tank's astonished stare.

Able to heal, Evkit had said. Tank had almost never been allowed to see this much vulnerability in Dasin, and certainly not in front of ... *company*, he decided, or *Nea*, because *whore* was becoming not only tedious but emotionally troubling.

He'd been one himself. He didn't have the right to sneer.

Able to heal. Was this what it would look like? Tank wasn't sure if he liked it or not.

Dasin cleared his throat. "I'm ruined as a merchant," he said. "After the last of the commitments clear in Assiasan, I have no idea what I'm going to do."

"What about your contacts?"

"None of them will talk to me anymore. Rumors are already going wild, the entire damn supply chain is spooked, and at the end of the day we're still southerners. With Yuer out, I've got nothing left to work with. There's a raggedy edge of a chance that our contacts in Assiasan are less anxious. It's the only reason I'm willing to take the chance on the trip. We have to have *somewhere* to stay overwinter. That's why we're here to talk." His gesture included Nea. "There are things you need to know about what we're walking into." This time the *we* only meant himself and Tank.

"Maybe Lia —"

"How could she help?" Dasin said with a snort. "Whatever nonsense I spun for Yuer, Stecatr Hall or not, she's still a barely tested mercenary with no contacts herself. She's useless."

Tank shrugged, conceding the point.

Dasin waited a beat, then let out a hard breath and said, "I didn't know until today that you had a history with the Arason ha'ra'ha."

Tank glanced over at Nea worriedly. "Dasin...."

"Who do you think was my source for that tidbit?" Dasin retorted. "Also, this is Arason, Tank. They're very familiar with the Ghost Lake and its residents. I've known there was a ha'ra'ha here, but as far as I knew, it had no reason to be interested in us, and since you always damn near went invisible when we came this way, I figured you knew the risk and it was safe enough. I didn't know you *knew* one another."

They were on more familiar ground now, with that irate tone in Dasin's voice. "I didn't know how to tell you, at first," Tank said. "And then, after a while, it would have pissed you off that I didn't say anything sooner, so." He shrugged.

"I don't know much," Dasin admitted. "One day, maybe, we can sit down and you can tell me the details of how you know this ha'ra'ha."

"Maybe," Tank said, but privately: *Not a chance in all of the Northern Church hells.*

Dasin laughed a little, as though he'd heard that. Tank, startled all over again, checked and tightened his shields.

"You'll notice I'm not using names," Dasin said, amusement fading. "That's on Nea's suggestion. She claims I'm far too free with my words."

Tank blinked at Dasin, at Nea, at Dasin. "*What?*"

Nea laughed. "I see him more relaxed than I think you generally do, s'e," she said with a sly smirk.

"Damnit, Nea," Dasin said, scowling at her. "No, Tank, I'm not using her that way. We smoke aesa together, and talk."

Tank bit his tongue to avoid saying anything openly rude.

Dasin glanced at Nea, rubbing the knuckles of one hand over the back of the other, a deep frown crossing his face. He said, "I started collecting informants like Nea after our first trip through the Hackerwood. It was pretty obvious that you weren't as ordinary as you kept insisting. You always made it sound like everyone had gotten overexcited about whatever you got involved with, when Allonin took you to Bright Bay. You're persuasive. I believed you. But after that trip, after you —"

Dasin's glance flicked to Nea, and he shook his head slightly. Tank found that a relief; at least Dasin hadn't confided everything to a ... *to Nea, damnit, stop being a shit.*

Dasin went on, "After that trip. I knew you'd been lying. Lying *a lot.*" His voice was a dose of desert-winter: cold and bleak, gray and gritty.

Nea's expression went entirely blank, her gaze fixed on nothing in particular.

"I had to," Tank said, scarcely above a whisper. "Dasin, can we please not...." He threw out a hand to indicate Nea. "Please."

Dasin's mouth twisted. "I'm not saying anything she doesn't already know. She's my main informant, Tank. She's been tracking down stories about you for years now, finding out the things you wouldn't tell me."

"I didn't know you were doing that," Tank said. He already felt emotionally bruised. *Lying a lot.* The accusation felt brutally unfair, but Tank couldn't escape the basic truth of it. Or the truth that he had no particular regret over that choice.

He was actually more irritated that Dasin had gone around behind him, spying and sneaking after information Tank didn't want him to have. He'd made that boundary perfectly clear. Why couldn't Dasin have left it alone?

Tank had tried so hard to avoid unnecessary lies, worked so hard to make the few necessary lies as solid as stone. Finding out that Dasin had been grinding quietly away, wearing stone to sand, felt like a tremendous betrayal.

"You wanted me to be ignorant," Dasin said without any particular venom, chill fading to a more neutral tone. "I never have been certain why that is." The end of the sentence ended in a lift that was more invitation than question.

"Do we *have* to talk about this in front of —" Tank looked sideways again at Nea, who grinned at him sardonically.

"I live in a town with an active ha'ra'ha and a sleeping ha'rethe, and I've been researching *you* for a while now," Nea pointed out. "I'm not likely to be shocked by anything you say. Spill it, sweetling." She tilted an eyebrow and worked her fingers with deliberate innuendo, smirking.

Tank lifted a shoulder briefly, surrendering, and said, "Because my encounters with ha'ra'hain have been *bad*, Dasin. I don't like remembering, let alone talking about it. Desert lords are just as bad if not worse." He paused, searching for the right words, then added, "It's like falling into a crevasse of trash. A rotten, jagged mess."

Dasin nodded slowly. "I thought it might be something like that. But I can't play at being ignorant to soothe your ego any longer. Do you know the history of Arason, Tank? Why you first met an Arason-born ha'ra'ha in Bright Bay, if Nea's information is correct?"

Tank flinched, then shot a hard glare at Nea. She shrugged, smiling at him with innocent cheer, and said, "Just doing what I was paid for. Couple folks in Bright Bay remember him, and remember you, and remember you crossing paths at least briefly. Took some digging, mind you, and I'd like the confirmation directly: was he *really* a street thief?"

"I strongly suggest never mentioning that again," Tank said dryly. "In fact, I'd suggest you never look into anything involving his history ever again, not even to get more on me."

"I'm well aware of the dangers," Nea said, her perky smile fading to a stern expression worthy of a loremaster. "I learned very little about him. He went from Bright Bay all the way south to Scratha Fortress, not long before half the Horn went into the sea. I know he came back afterward, and broke the southern gates to Bright Bay, and killed over a dozen people before disappearing again, only to turn up *here*. We're all being very cautious around him, *s'e* Tank. Very, very cautious. So far, he's been reasonable to work with, but we're surely not willing to test that." She paused. "But that wasn't the question, was it? Dasin asked if you know why he wound up in Bright Bay, of all places."

"I don't know, and I don't want to know," Tank said through his teeth. "It's never been important for me to know."

Dasin said, "Too bad. It's a necessary run up to what you have to know now. Nea, go ahead and tell him. Start back a ways, give him the background."

Nea's relaxed demeanor evaporated. Scholarly and dry, she recited, "In the days of the

Purge, Isata and Arason suffered extensively from the Church's excesses. In Arason, much of the local church leadership was removed as heretics and traitors, replaced with more zealous *s'iopes*. They managed to turn Arason's government inside out, forcing a number of critical members of the Lord's cabinet and staff into hiding, flight, or execution." She paused, a sharp crease appearing on her forehead. "They liked burning," she added, teeth showing in a savagely unhappy wince.

Tank looked down at the floorboards, his own jaw tight as Alyea's memories rose in the back of his mind. *They liked burning* ... yes, Alyea had seen that in Bright Bay as well. He blinked hard, pushing that aside, and lifted his gaze to focus on Nea once more.

"Arason wasn't accustomed to defending itself, at the time," Nea went on. "We'd always had the *chekk*, and the ha'rethe. But the *chekk* had left, all but one, and there was a ... a situation...."

Her words slowed as she picked her way through with more care.

"I don't really understand the details, and the people who lived through it won't even discuss it. But best as I can gather, zealots and soldiers from Bright Bay got into a scrap with the Arason Church. When it was over, most of the local church leadership was dead or fled, Ellemoa — the last remaining member of the *chekk* — was gone, and the ha'rethe was asleep. *Deeply* asleep. Even the liason-line couldn't feel its presence."

Nea looked at the single window, left open to the evening chill, and shivered a little.

"Ellemoa," Tank said, sitting up straight. "That's Id — that's the ha'ra'ha's mother. Was." Ellemoa was, most definitely and thankfully, dead.

Liason-line he left unquestioned, fairly sure he could guess. No desert lords here, no kathain, but there was a ha'rethe, and there had been a group of ha'ra'hain. Some analogue of the former two would be necessary.

Nea scratched her freckled cheek absently. "Yes. She wasn't quite right in the head."

Tank snorted. "You can *definitely* say that again," he muttered.

Nea's gaze turned sharp with interest, but after a glance at Dasin, as though for permission, she let it go. She went on, "While she was here, Ellemoa stayed to herself in her cottage. We never really knew her, but she was still one of the *chekk*. We thought she was bound to help us in need. As it turned out, she might have been behind our priests being killed. In any case, it took a while and a deathbed confession or two to realize that when she disappeared, she'd had a child in her arms."

Tank's breath felt cold in his throat. "She fled to Bright Bay?"

"Apparently so," Nea said. "No idea why, and no idea why she apparently then abandoned her child to grow up on the streets." She shrugged. "That's the end of what I risked learning on that point. I sorted out more about local history from there, and I believe this next bit is what Dasin particularly wants you to hear."

Dasin drew his legs up once, looping his arms around them. He looked gaunt and gray, as if listening to Nea narrate old history was somehow painful for him. "You needed all that lead up to understand this part," he said.

No longer reciting, Nea's tone now reflected a deep personal investment. "Bright Bay and the priests kept sending troops, because they believed the ha'ra'ha and his mother were still here. Arason was being torn apart. Our defenders were gone. Nobody would help us. So, we helped ourselves."

Her eyes were bright with malice, but she didn't stop to explain what helping themselves had involved. Tank found that he really didn't want to know.

"Isata went through something similar, but by that point we were strong enough that we could reach out to help them. We've been close allies ever since, not that the King ever knew." She paused. "Still not a good idea for him to know," she added warningly.

"I can see that," Tank agreed.

"So, then. Ninnic was removed...." Nea tilted her head, shooting Tank a sardonic glance. He shrugged wearily, not in the least willing to discuss his part in that. She laughed at him as though she'd expected that reaction, and went on: "King Oruen stepped up and dismantled the Church, sending all the priests scurrying out to any shelter they could find. Some wound up in Salt City, those marshes out to the east of Bright Bay. Most got pushed up through the Hackerwood. Isata gave them little welcome, the villages between here and Isata had nothing to offer, and when they came to Arason they found that the Church now bows to the Lord, not the other way around. The Lord of Arason put some harsh restrictions on the Church, once we cleared up the mess from the Purge. A few priests accepted that, and stayed; those that wouldn't bow to our conditions kept going, and wound up —"

"In Stecatr," Tank said, his mouth thinning.

"And Assiasan, but that didn't last long. The people and the Lord of Assiasan aren't tolerant of outsider arrogance. The Church there never really took hold. So those priests eventually retreated to Stecatr, too."

Tank covered his face with one hand.

"Some of them would have known about ha'reye and ha'ra'hain," Dasin added, entirely unnecessarily.

There are increasing signs of ha'ra'hain or possibly even ha'rethe activity in Stecatr.

Fuck, fuck, fuck. Tank made a faint motion with one hand for Nea to go on.

Her voice filled the room without being loud. "If Ninnic hadn't died when he did, I expect Isata would have led a revolution to separate the lands north of the Hackerwood from the southern coastal area. It was a near thing, waiting to see how King Oruen proved out. It's still chancy. There's a lot of bad feeling yet. Arason, in particular, would be delighted to never again host royal troops. So would Assiasan. Their argument is that during the years of the Purge, they received no kingdom support but still had to pay outrageous taxes and host soldiers without warning. After Ninnic's death, supposedly in a show of support for King Oruen, Assiasan immediately kicked out every single remaining Northern Church priest. Who, of course —"

"— went straight to Stecatr," Tank muttered. "Yeah."

"Yes. Assiasan, for whatever reason, is *still* getting shorted on support. They're strongly considering whether they're better off declaring themselves independent, like Kismo. They've the ability to hold off a siege, once prepared. Believe me, they've been preparing." Nea paused again. "There's talk they're quietly minting their own coins," she added.

Dasin sucked in a sharp breath, eyes narrowing.

Nea tilted her head, apologetic. "I only just heard that before I came here."

Dasin flicked a hand to dismiss his moment of annoyance, then turned his attention to Tank. "So now you see the problem," he said.

"Yes. Gods." Tank rubbed his eyes with the backs of his hands to stop himself from pinching his nose. Assiasan had just gone firmly off the table for overwintering. If the city was that volatile, just going there to drop off their commissions was dangerous. Staying for months, trapped by blizzards, was out of the question. Arason was out, because of Tank's history with Idisio. Small villages or towns were too high a risk to stay at for long, given attitudes about *ii'ne*, incontinent gossiping, and the overall lack of privacy that came with everyone knowing one another. Which left....

... Stecatr.

Tank fought the urge to get up, walk out, and keep walking until he found a place where none of this existed.

Nea's mouth twitched into a faint, understanding smile. She said, "Another piece I just learned, although I've had time to tell this one to Dasin, is a rumor that the Stecatr Chuch has managed to find a ha'ra'ha or similar creature to bind to their will, or one that's working with them willingly."

Tank lowered his head, breathing deeply. He should have known that information had no chance of staying confined to Lord Onda's office. Walking out there hadn't made any difference; walking out here wouldn't do any more good. He was doomed to get tangled up in the middle of the mess in Stecatr.

You're going to change things, Rania had said, back in Orhon. *And they're going to change you.*

Tank hadn't expected that change to be something he hated quite this much.

After a brief silence, Dasin said, very quietly: "Thank you, Nea."

She murmured something neutral and rose. Her skirts brushed lightly against Tank's arm as she edged past him to the door. He stood, guilt washing over him, and said, "*S'a*, thank you. I'm sorry for my rudeness."

Nea smiled at him, sardonic, and said, "Come and see me to apologize properly, before you leave town." She tipped him a salacious wink and was out the door before he could respond.

Tank locked the door, then busied himself opening one of the bottles he'd brought. Dasin watched without speaking; took one of the small cups Tank held out to him and sniffed the contents with care.

"Good choice," he said. "Don't open them both. Save one for the road."

Tank raised an eyebrow, surprised.

Dasin smiled and inhaled the vapors arising from the liquor once more. "I'm not planning on getting skunk drunk, or letting you get that way tonight."

Tank tossed back his own cup and poured himself another. "You'll be answering some godsdamned questions now," he said flatly.

Dasin's smile widened to a sour smirk. "I plan to," he said. "Oh, I do plan to. I suspect you truly won't like the answers."

Chapter Forty-one

The Plains Road ran long and erratic, curving round for no visible reason and sometimes in ways that took it up, rather than around, a steep hill. A day's travel north of Arason, the trees and brush were noticeably thicker to the west than to the east, and the temperature was already dropping.

Lia found herself relaxing into the chill damp, even as Tank and Dasin began to grumble. This was familiar weather, coming up into her favorite time of year. She'd been born a midwinter child during a wild storm, and had always been happiest once the leaves began to fall. Too, it allowed her to add a bit more padding under her hauberk, which always made her more confident in its protection, irrational as that might be in practical terms.

Rooster also seemed to be in a better mood. It had taken hundreds of miles and a lot of work, but Lia felt that they were, finally, a team.

A few russet and gold leaves presented a splotchy announcement that at least one good cold snap had already come through this area, and flocks of black-winged geese heading south darkened the sky on occasion. Tank looked up at them, every time, with a sourly wistful expression, as though wanting to grab a ride back to his own preferred territory.

The strange priest who'd joined the crew at the last moment usually looked at the geese with a nearly blank expression, as though he weren't quite sure what they were but was afraid to ask anyone. He looked at a lot of things that way, including his own hands.

"This is Kolan of Arason. He's coming along on Church orders, backed by the Hall," Tank had said the morning of their departure, his face like granite, displeasure nearly steaming from him. "He'll come with us until the split to Stecatr."

Kolan stood behind him, hands folded, smiling blandly, looking at nothing in particular. He was of average height and thin, with a distinctly ragged appearance in spite of perfectly adequate trousers and tunic. One of his ears was cut: not thief-cut, as the missing piece was high along the arc. He wore no jewelry at all, his thin brown hair was trimmed short, and he was going bald in front.

Cilif had surveyed the priest and shrugged acceptance. Dasin, to Lia's surprise, had smiled as serenely as the priest and said, "Far be it from me to argue the Church's dictates."

Tank had aimed a frozen glare at Dasin, then drew in hissing breath through his teeth and began hassling everyone into final preparations for the road.

Kolan rode on the wagon alongside Dasin. On occasion he walked, at varying speeds: discarded his sensible walking boots to sprint ahead, laughing like a child; ambled so slowly that Dasin called a halt to allow him to catch up. He rarely matched pace with the wagon, said little even when spoken to, and used the fewest possible words when he had to speak. He seemed more interested in the plants and animals they passed than in the people around him.

Lia grew accustomed to scooping up the priest's discarded shoes. More and more often, he went barefoot.

"Touched," Cilif muttered. "Church sent us a gods-touched. He'll wander off a cliff along the way, and you won't catch *me* going after him when he does."

At one point, Kolan walked alongside Lia for a time, far enough away to be well clear of the horse but close enough to speak. "Good weather," he said, looking up at the sky for a few steps. He stumbled, caught himself, and laughed ruefully. "I'm sorry. I'm not used to normal courtesies. One does still talk about the weather as an introduction, right?"

Lia couldn't help grinning. At the lack of cloth shifting with the movement, she touched her face, still surprised by finding it bare. "Yes," she said. "That's one topic, certainly."

"Oh, good." A flock of geese went overhead, honking noisily. Kolan paused to watch them, falling behind a few steps, then caught up with a stride somewhere between a skip and a lope. Rooster looked sideways at him, snorting distrustfully. Kolan smiled at the horse and made a deep clucking sound. Rooster whuffled and went back to ignoring the strange priest.

"Do you like geese?" Lia asked, more for something to say then out of real interest. Most of her attention remained on the trail. Something was itching at her spine, a sense of trouble ahead.

"Not particularly," Kolan said. "They shit everywhere, and it stinks. Oh, I'm not supposed to say words like that in front of women, am I? I'm sorry. But they fly in great big families, and work together, and that's not something I've ever experienced. So I admire that, a bit."

"Don't worry about cursing in front of a mercenary, no matter our gender," Lia said dryly. "You won't shock or offend any of us that simply."

"That's good to know," Kolan said with apparent sincerity. "About half a mile ahead, by the way. On the left, behind a stand of holly and thornbrake."

Lia stared at him, bewildered. "What?"

"The ambush you're sensing." He blinked up at her, then turned away to examine a vining plant at the side of the trail.

Lia stared another moment, then nudged Rooster into a trot to catch up with Tank.

Tank listened, frowning. When she finished, he cast a sharp glare over his shoulder at the meandering priest, then sighed. "All right," he said. "Might as well believe him." He raised his left fist, thumb sticking out, and twisted it round so his thumb pointed to the left, jerked his elbow twice, then dropped his hand back to the reins. "Go on as though you don't know," he added, motioning her to return to her place. "And tell that damn priest to stay out of the middle of it."

As Lia turned Rooster to circle back behind the wagon, she caught an alert nod from Dasin and a less enthusiastic acknowledgment from Cilif. The priest smiled sunnily up at her as she came back into position beside him. He said, "I'll stay out of the way, don't worry. Is this jasmine?" He held up a piece of three-leafed vine.

She bit her lip, then said, carefully, "No, *s'iope*, it's poison ivy."

"Oh!" Kolan studied the vine for a moment, seeming disappointed. "I did think we were a bit north for jasmine. Oh well." He tossed the piece to the side of the road, then held out his hands, examining them. "Steady your horse," he said absently.

Lia tightened up on the reins and nudged Rooster sideways without hesitation. A moment later, the priest's hands burst into flame, a thin layer of flickering blue and orange rippling from wrist to fingertips.

Dear gods ... Payti ... no, that's far too aspna, not safe at all. She's far too unpredictable when actual fire is involved. Maybe Eki? No.

Lia simply didn't know who to ask for protection from this unprecedented display. *Gods hold me safe*, was the best she could manage.

Rooster stepped sideways again, more because of Lia's involuntary pressure than from fear. The horse seemed not to notice the flames at all, which was very nearly as unsettling as the feat itself.

The flames disappeared. Kolan rubbed his hands together and said, "That should take care of any oils." He paused, then sank slowly to his knees. Lia reined Rooster in, ready to dismount, but he waved a hand at her and said, "I'm well enough. Go on without me. I'll catch up. I'm having a ... a moment." He flapped his hand again, closing his eyes, and leaned forward to put his forehead on the ground.

Lia hesitated, but a glance back showed no traffic close enough behind them to be any bother, and the bandits, if the strange priest was right, were well ahead. He'd be fine. She nudged Rooster back into motion, trying to ignore the guilt stinging at her.

It occurred to her, a short time later, that she'd been more confounded than frightened. But by that point, the ambush had launched, and the momentary thought slipped past and was gone between one clash of blades and the next.

Chapter Forty-two

The ambush came right where Tank had expected: a narrow spot in the road, where the trees and brush hadn't been cut back in too long. A high bank to one side, screened with holly and thornbrake, gave bandits a grand perch, and an ancient oak tree with a massive limb overhanging the other side of the road served as a second vantage point.

Tank had looked for an attack there every trip, and had been mildly disappointed at getting through with no troubles. Apparently someone with a grasp of basic strategy had finally come into command in this area.

He caught the flicker of movement and began to rein in a scant moment before an arrow buried itself in the road a stone's throw ahead of Sin's nose.

The big warhorse's ears went flat. Tank ordered, "Stand, Sin!" in his sharpest tone. Sin stomped a back hoof once, unhappy, ears still flat, but stayed still. Tank raised a hand, signaling a halt more for the look of the thing than because he thought anyone needed the order, and tilted his gaze to look up at the man perched on the oak branch, bow ready with another arrow. He had short dark hair, a broad face, a limber build, and a chill smugness to his expression.

"Greetings, travelers," the bandit said. "There's a bit of a local tax just come into effect. A gold round a head." He smirked.

"Come down and get it," Tank said, smiling easily, and put a hand to his belt pouch as though ready to hand over the money. "You alone, mind you, I'll not hand good coin to one of your lackeys."

The man laughed. Something about the sound went straight into Tank's hindbrain and *twisted*. He found himself looking at the line of the man's leg and hip. The way he sat on the branch, entirely sure of his balance, so confident, was immediately fascinating.

What would he be like in bed ...?

Holy gods, what am I thinking? This is not the time!

"Ah, you're negotiating," the bandit said. "And you're trying to be clever. No, *s'e,* you take that money bag of yours and toss it over that way, to land under that birch tree, see? And someone'll take a look to see if you've got enough to cover the tax."

Gods, that voice. What would it sound like in my ear? ... maybe if I give him enough money we can ... talk ... I think I'd give him anything he wanted, if he let me touch his....

What in the Sun Lord's name is wrong with me? The man's robbing us, for fuck's sake, focus!

Sin moved under him, uneasy, ears still back-tilted but holding discipline.

"Do I get change?" Tank inquired, relieved that his voice, at least, remained calm. The man laughed again.

"Clever, clever," he said. "Such a sense of humor. Toss the bag to the tree *now, s'e.*"

Tank suspected that if he'd been standing, his knees might have buckled. *The strength of that command! He's a partial, has to be, but how in the hells is he coming this close to oversetting me?*

The man startled, his eyes narrowing as he looked past Tank. The arrow tracked to a new target.

"Oh no, my dear," he said, his lip curling into a sneer. "No, your master's got no favor with me."

"Too bad," Lia said. Even as she spoke, something small and sharp whipped past Tank's head. The man in the tree loosed the arrow with a shout that cut off into a harsh gurgle as his throat blossomed with red. Rooster's outraged shriek overlapped it all, as did the trampling of brush and shouts from Cilif and Dasin.

Arousal *finally* died as the man fell from the tree and thudded to the ground, bow cracking beneath him.

Tank took a moment to check for adversaries ahead, then spun Sin neatly about to see what was happening behind.

Lia was nowhere to be seen, but a trail of trampled brush indicated that Rooster had bolted. The arrow had gone into the ground close to where Lia had been. Two bandits were attacking Cilif at one side of the wagon. A third was in the process of vaulting up onto the wagon bench after Dasin.

Dasin's hands glittered with knuckle-knives. He swept one hand sharply into his attacker's face. The man screamed and fell back, clutching at his eyes. Blackie reared and kicked out, sending one man sprawling. The remaining attacker faltered and fell back, but Cilif kicked Blackie forward and rode straight over him without pause.

Someone screamed out in the brush, a high, female voice. Tank caught Dasin's eye. The merchant swept a hand out to indicate Tank should follow that scream. Cilif took Blackie to a position in front of the wagon, alert for more attackers, and made the same "go" motion.

Tank rode well around the downed bandits, wary of attacks on Sin's legs, and followed the trail Rooster had left. The horse shouldn't have bolted. Rooster was better trained than that, Lia a better rider than that, and certainly they shouldn't have gone straight into the woods instead of along the road.

Had the bandit's voice somehow spooked both rider and horse? Had the man falling from the tree shaken Rooster's training? Had Lia, for some odd reason, chosen to flee? Not having seen the moment of flight, Tank had no idea.

The trail didn't go very far before breaking into a clearing occupied by a rough campground and the remaining bandits.

Two women, one heavily pregnant; a toddler; a young man with terrible acne brandishing a sword too big for him. One man sitting on a stump, stained bandages wrapped raggedly around his left leg.

Lia and Rooster were nowhere to be seen, but another broken trail led out the far side of the campground. Tank glared down at the terrified faces watching him.

"The *fuck* are you people thinking?" Tank shouted at them savagely. They shrank under his glare. The young man dropped the sword, then, crimson-faced, snatched it back up and pointed it at Tank.

"Don't you come any closer!" he yelled, sword wobbling in his grip. "You stand right there, you're surrounded, there's twenty men right behind you!"

Tank snorted contemptuously. "I don't give a shit about you lot," he said. "I'm collecting my hire. You might want to go collect *your* men from the road, in case any of them have life left to save."

He nudged Sin forward as he finished speaking, pointedly angling around the boy. The heavily pregnant woman wailed, took an unsteady step, then sank to the ground, her face a pasty color. The other woman, ignoring her, gathered her skirts and headed for the road, dragging the boy with her.

Tank kept going. He couldn't save the world, and he certainly had no interest in helping a pack of fools who'd made one poor choice too many. At least he knew, now, that it hadn't been Lia who'd screamed. That loosened the knot of worry in his chest.

The shattered brush ended in another, smaller clearing, one as much tumbled rock as clear space. It looked like a building had been torn down nearby and the debris heaped here. Lia sat atop Rooster, both completely still, their attention fixed on something in front of the big gelding. Rooster was breathing hard. Lia's hair and clothes were a wonder of brambles and twigs, while long stripes of tickweed decorated Rooster's body.

Tank reined Sin in as he entered the clearing, uneasy at the transfixed attention of horse and rider alike. He angled Sin to come around from the side, the horse picking his way delicately through unstable rock mounds, then reined in again as he saw what had caught Lia's attention.

A small man, the top of his head barely level with Rooster's shoulder, stood smiling up at Lia. He had dark skin and neatly braided hair laced with small blue stones. One thin hand held Rooster's bridle. He seemed to be speaking softly to the horse.

The man — the teyanin, he couldn't be anything else — looked up as Tank came into view. "*S'e,*" he said gravely. "*Ha'vash, ha'ne.* Peace."

Sin shifted, ears flicking rapidly. One hoof caught against a rock with a harsh click. The teyanin looked the horse in the eye and said something in a dialect Tank didn't recognize. Sin settled down, standing as placidly as if in a stable stall.

Tank drew in a difficult breath and dropped his chin slightly. "Peace," he said. "Can I have my hire back, *s'e?*"

"He stopped Rooster," Lia said, a bit dazedly. "He — I couldn't think, I couldn't get a grip on anything, with the branches, and I wasn't expecting — and he just stepped out in front of us and said something, and Rooster stopped on the spot — I almost went over —" Her hands began to shake. "That priest," she added, seeming surprised at herself even as she said the words. "He's — he's — there's something not right about him."

The teyanin laughed. "That is very much true," he agreed. "That is why we watch, and are here to catch willful horses on occasion." But he said it all in the southern tongue, with an eye on Tank.

Tank shut his eyes for a moment. *They're watching Kolan. Of course they are.* "And here I was thinking that something, just once, might be simple," he grumbled.

The teyanin laughed again, a clear sound without malice. "We stay out of your way, *s'e,*" he said, still in southern dialect. "You will not see us unless the priest becomes dangerously unbalanced. He will not harm you or yours. Our word on it." He looked back at Lia, still smiling, and patted the side of Rooster's jaw gently. "You take her back now, yes? I show you path without angry people. Ah. Wait, please." He reached into his belt pouch and withdrew a small, twine-wrapped bottle stoppered with cork. Removing the stopper and holding the bottle up to her, he said, in Kaenic, "You drink, *s'a.* You trust, you drink. You have shock. This help."

Lia turned a hazy-eyed stare on Tank, clearly unwilling to make any risky decisions for herself. "Go ahead," Tank said. "He's called truce, it's safe."

Lia accepted the bottle with a shaking hand and tossed the contents back like a shot of liquor. She coughed once, eyes watering, and blinked several times, then sat up straighter and cleared her throat.

"All right," she said, voice hoarse but clear. "Good enough. Let's go while that lasts."

"Until tonight," the teyanin said, smiling, and turned Rooster gently towards a barely visible path out of the clearing. He reverted to southern dialect as he added, "Maybe longer. She is not teyanin. Who knows? Might stay up all night." He slanted a mischievous wink back at Tank.

"Wrong tree, wrong season," Tank said flatly in the same dialect.

The teyanin shrugged, cheerfulness not dimmed in the least, and merely said, in Kaenic, "This way, please. Duck head, maybe. Low places. Teyanain path."

Chapter Forty-three

It took Lia half an hour to pick all the debris from her hair, and easily twice that to clean Rooster's hide, even with Cilif's help. Her shirt had enough tears in it that she set it aside to mend later, grateful that she'd bought an extra one in Arason. Her trousers weren't as bad, once the tickweed and bramble fragments had been brushed off. She'd need to sit and mend them next time they stopped early enough, but they'd do for the road. She had another, carefully clean pair on hand for market days. Her boots were scratched, but it was nothing a thick coat of polish and a night near the fire wouldn't cure.

It was her own fault. She'd thrown the *ishi*, seen the man fall, and something inside her had twisted. She must have jerked or kicked or moved enough to upset Rooster, and the big horse had promptly taken off. She'd been startled, her arms unaccountably jelly for the one critical moment when she might have grabbed control back. After that she'd been too busy ducking branches to focus, then Rooster had just *stopped*. She'd nearly gone over his head. On recovering her wits, she'd found a small, dark-skinned man holding Rooster's bridle, smiling up at her as pleasantly as though they'd met at a social for a dance.

Lia shuddered, pushing away the memory of that smile. It still terrified her, and she still didn't want to think about it.

Dasin steered them to camp in a fallow field, near enough to a farmhouse that the wife came out with a large pot of beef stew and four loaves of freshly baked bread, followed soon after by her husband. They clearly knew Dasin, Tank, and Cilif from previous trips, and accepted Lia and Kolan without hesitation. Dasin, after gravely handing over a small basket of neatly packaged herbs, invited them to sit by the fire and catch up on various news.

Lia listened with half an ear, occupied with eating. The thick, hearty stew was loaded with fragrances and textures so familiar it made her want to weep. She still felt ridiculously shaky.

I killed a man.

The potion swirling through her body made it possible to act normal, but tremors came and went in her hands at odd moments, and she found herself remembering moments of intimacy with Gally that brought a fiery blush to her face.

I killed a man. I need to talk to a priest. And, gods, did I actually do that with Gally? I definitely need to talk to a priest.

She looked at Kolan, as she had throughout the afternoon, and shook her head dubiously.

Lia could feel Tank's attention every so often as he unobtrusively checked on her. Cilif did the same, less often and much less subtly.

Nobody had spoken after the ambush. Dasin had set a brisk pace, and everyone had been stern and unhappy. Even the priest sat quietly on the wagon bench, hands folded together, apparently praying. He'd knelt, on rejoining them, to touch the blood on the ground; looked at his hand for a long moment, then wiped it clean on a tuft of moss and gotten up onto the wagon bench without a word.

"You're a neat hand with a throwing knife," Cilif had said as they started moving again, his voice scarcely audible.

"I'm useless with a bow," she said, as quietly. "I'm not awful with a slingshot, but better with throwing things by hand. I'm mean with a skipping-stone."

Cilif didn't laugh, but he didn't say anything else, either.

Over dinner, he brought it up again: "Those knives," he said. "I been thinking on them."

She glanced meaningfully at the nearby farmers. "Later."

Cilif went back to eating his stew in silence.

The farmers withdrew not long after that, and Dasin excused himself to bed with an ostentatious yawn. Tank and Cilif stayed put, both shifting on their seats to stare at her directly.

"Well?" Cilif said. "Those weren't no normal throwing knives."

Tank put out a hand to signal *wait*, studying Lia's face. "Was that the first time you killed?"

"Yes." She blinked hard, eyes suddenly damp, then shut them against a wave of nausea. "There wasn't any choice," she said into the reddish darkness.

"You're right," Tank said. "There wasn't. Thank you for not hesitating. It could have gone ugly."

Lia drew a breath, feeling steadier from his dry lack of reaction, then looked at Cilif. "The knife I threw is called an *ishi*," she told him. "It's a throwing knife, but it's rounder than most. Better for throwing at opponents above you."

She opened her long sleeves to show the shortblades strapped to each forearm, then lifted the outer flap she'd sewn into her belt pouches to conceal the *ishi*, two on each side. One was missing, now. She hadn't been able to find it in the scrum after the attack.

After tucking everything back into proper concealment, she folded her hands across her stomach and met their gazes, trying not to look angry or defiant.

"That's a thief's weapon," Tank said, voice as flat as his expression. "And you gave him a thief-sign."

"I'm not a thief," she said, dodging the question as best she could. "I'm working with my strengths, which are being quicker and lighter on my feet than my opponents, surprising them with weapons and tactics they don't expect me to have, and making fast decisions under pressure."

That hung in the air, as Tank's expression went from flat to thoughtful and Cilif's face broadened into a reluctant half-smile.

"And you learned that in the Stecatr Hall, did you?" Tank said at last. "And that code sign?"

"I learned to work with my strengths, yes." She rubbed her right forearm, barely keeping herself from digging her nails in for a satisfying scratch.

"Did you learn to use those *particular* strengths through Stecatr Hall?"

"No," she said, then decided not to drag it out. "I'm a Stecatr grayhand."

Cilif's smile disappeared. He cut Tank a slightly anxious sideways glance.

"You already *know* that," Lia went on. She shot Tank a pointed stare. "I don't know why you haven't pressed the point. You knew in the Hackerwood! I've been waiting for you to say something."

"So've I," Cilif admitted. "Thought you'd cut her out in Isata, for sure."

Tank scowled. "I've had other things on my mind," he said, then grunted as though remembering something. "Wait."

He twisted to reach for his pack, pulling out a small bag. Sorting out the knots took a few moments and some irritable muttering, then he had the bag open and was stirring the contents with one hand. His scowl deepened as he pulled out three small metal objects: a cylinder, a blank coin, and a pyramid.

"Chabi pieces?" Cilif said, obviously bewildered.

"This is the pouch the hadinn gave me, back in the Hackerwood," Tank said, staring at the pieces. "There's a lot of large-value coin in there as well. I'd actually forgotten him giving it to me." He rolled the game pieces around in his hand thoughtfully. "No inscriptions on any of them."

"Fair warning that he's playing a game?" Cilif suggested. Tank shrugged and put the game pieces back in the pouch, tying it off and returning it to his pack without further comment.

"It'll all show out eventually, I expect," Tank said, back to being sour, and motioned for Lia to continue.

Lia plowed on, wanting to get this extremely uncomfortable conversation in the ground. "I'm not a pickpocket, house burglar, or con artist. My involvement with the Stecatr underground is a very personal story, and it doesn't affect the job you hired me for."

Tank's mouth set in a thin line. "I'll judge that for myself."

She set her own jaw and gave him stubborn for stubborn. "No. That part of my life has nothing to do with my work for you. The details beyond that aren't your business, *s'e* Tank." As he drew breath to speak, she added, "I'm sworn as your employee through Assiasan.

After that, *if* you're coming to Stecatr with me, we can talk about this. Not until then."

It was the first time she'd mentioned the idea of his coming with her. Perhaps not the most graceful way to introduce the subject, but it was out and done now.

Cilif blinked hard, glancing back and forth between them with a slightly stunned expression. Tank let out his drawn breath in a slow hiss, frowning as he studied Lia's face intently.

"Someone put steel up your spine," he said at last.

"I suppose so."

Tank considered another moment, then smiled grimly. "Good. You'll need it. We'll talk about the future another time." He rose. "Cilif, you're on first watch. Wake me, then I'll wake Lia. Get some sleep, tomorrow's that shit hill everyone hates." He turned and went into the tent he shared with Dasin without a backwards glance.

Lia let out a long, quiet breath of her own. Cilif snorted. "Steel up your spine is about right," he noted. "Didn't ever think the soppy newling I met in Bright Bay would stand up to himself in a temper."

"Didn't have a choice," Lia said.

Angering Tank had become an insignificant risk compared to what lay ahead for her in Stecatr. She was only Tank's hire through Assiasan, and that wasn't so very far away. She could feel the power dynamic between them shifting already, as her thoughts turned towards a much larger problem than guarding a small spice caravan: *Saving my family. Interfering with the dominant political entity in Stecatr. Surviving, myself. Oh, and there might be a ha'ra'ha wandering about in Stecatr.*

"No," Cilif said, voice muted. "I don't suppose there was."

Lia rose and went into her own tent. In the privacy of the darkness, she curled into a tight ball and shivered, eyes damp, until she fell asleep.

Lia woke surrounded by warmth, both from breath in her ear and a presence at her back. Reaching back for the curve of Isla's hip, she found a considerably leaner haunch under her hand, and froze. "What?" she said, still half asleep. "Gally? Isla?"

A thick arm lifted slightly from where it had been tucked around her, but otherwise the other person stayed still. "Tank," a low voice said. "Breathe, Lia, no harm, *ha'vash*." His voice sounded muzzy with sleep.

She blinked, obeying without conscious intention, and thought about her breathing for a time as her mind cleared towards wakefulness.

"You were having a bad time in your sleep. Yelling out," Tank said as soon as she tensed again. He kept his arm loose, ready to let her push clear. "You didn't want to wake up, but you wouldn't settle unless I had a hand on you. Remember, I'm the best at sorting nightmares, I've done this for Cilif and Dasin often enough."

She didn't move. The warmth and solid pressure against her back felt wonderful, and it was hard to remember it wasn't Gally nor Isla, hard to resist burrowing back against him, to keep her hands from reaching back to feel —

No. Damnit, no. I'm not interested in him. He's certainly not interested in me.

"It's not even close to dawn yet," he said. "You want me to leave you be, I'll go. I think your nightmares are over for the night."

She realized she still had her hand on his hip, and pulled it back hastily. "Eh — that — probably best," she muttered, scooting forward a bit. The shock of chill air against her back woke her up further. *Oh gods yes it's for the best he goes, and fast. What was he* thinking?

He's so damn warm *... and, mmmmm, I wonder what it* would *be like....*

"Goodnight," he said, then shifted round and out of the tent without another word.

Lia tucked the blanket more closely around her, shivering with sudden cold. A pang of regret tightened her chest. Tank wasn't unattractive. He was kind at the most unpredictable moments, and in the strangest ways. She found herself trusting him more than she'd wanted to.

He would have gotten along well with Isla. She cut that thought off fast, pushing the pain away into its well-worn prison.

She would have been warm, had he stayed. Warm and safe. There were worse things in the world. And maybe....

Stop it, you idiot, Lia told herself, and toppled back into sleep.

Chapter Forty-four

Dasin didn't complain when Tank returned. While they weren't in the Hackerwood any longer, things had been strange enough on an ongoing basis that the rule about nightmares stayed in place without a word needing to be said.

All Dasin said was: "She settled?"

"Yeah." Tank drew Dasin up against him, simultaneously relishing the warmth and wary of rejection. At least here he didn't have to worry about keeping his hips back, as he had with Lia. She'd probably have reacted very badly to waking with an erection pressing against her.

Dasin chuckled a bit, pushing *his* hips back into Tank's groin, and said, "Shame we had to kill that thief." He twisted, reaching down. "If Lia hadn't intervened, I was about to offer to give the tax out in trade."

Tank sucked in a sharp breath. "You felt it too? I was —"

"Gods yes." Fingers moved, pressure applied. Tank let out a strangled moan. Dasin had been *insatiable* since Arason, as though determined to test Tank's limits. "I'm guessing he had what the locals call *witch blood*."

"Yeah, a partial — *uhhh*."

"Quiet, now," Dasin said, sardonic and delighted all at once. Tank laced his fingers into long blond hair and yanked gently by way of retort.

Some time later, Tank stared into the darkness of the tent, listening to Dasin snore, and tried to think of how to phrase *What the hells has gotten into you lately* tactfully enough to avoid disrupting matters back to older patterns. Gods knew, he didn't want to lose this generous mood Dasin was in, but it was so unlike him that Tank was beginning to feel a cold thread of fear.

A thought nagged at the back of his mind: something he'd forgotten, something relevant, something deadly important.

"Tank, may I present Nea. She's one of my informants in Arason ... I can't play at being ignorant to soothe your ego any longer."

Memory of the conversation filled in: patchy, unpleasant, but not nearly enough to match his heavy unease.

"You'll be answering some godsdamned questions now."

"I suspect you truly won't like the answers."

Then ... nothing. Nothing at all. Tank's next memory was of getting the crew ready to roll the following morning.

Dasin turned over, his arm draping across Tank's shoulder, and the warmth of his breath in Tank's ear brought back thoughts of that breath lower down — and of that damned bandit. Even hours later, even with the man *dead*, remembering his voice and the line of his hip lit up every nerve in Tank's body.

Everything else vanished as Tank wrestled with the urge to wake Dasin. Test *his* limits.

He let out an exasperated snort, annoyed with himself. Dasin stirred and rolled tight up against Tank. His hand wandered over Tank's hip and across. A moment later, he laughed, murmuring something Tank didn't quite catch, and began again.

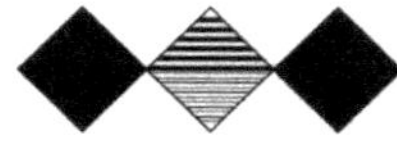

Hells Hill, as more than one traveler called it, was the work of an entire day to climb and descend. In bad weather, it was a nightmare. In good weather, it was merely unpleasant. To make it worse, the hill seemed to have its own weather, which changed without warning. A fair morning was apt to to end in a drenching downpour. Tank had even seen hail once.

There was absolutely *no* camping at the top, or anywhere along the way. Some bright-eyed fool had planted a graveyard atop Hells Hill. Even if Tank had been iron-souled enough to chance sleeping a stone's throw from a grave, the villages to either side of the hill would have been outraged.

Local legend warned of restless spirits roaming well beyond the hill during moondark nights. Some tales promised that staying on the hill overnight would net you a meeting with someone you had loved and lost. Others spoke of bargains to be made with the spirits of the hill, but that sort of meeting was as tricky and dangerous as dealing with an actual devil.

It sounded like superstition, but Tank also saw threads in the tales that made him think of ha'reye, ha'ra'hain, and their pets. So they broke camp, well before dawn and with a stolid expectation of not stopping until well past nightfall. As Lia and Cilif dismantled tents and bundled everything into its proper place, Tank checked tack, traces, hooves, wheels, load distribution, and everything else he could think of.

Dasin sat lordly and aloof in an uncertain circle of flickering torchlight, sipping his last cup of coffee and ignoring everyone. The priest sat quietly to one side: praying, meditating, half asleep, Tank couldn't tell and didn't much care.

As Tank ran his fingers through Sin's mane one last time, more from ritual than worry, he heard Dasin's voice:

You want to know what Evkit did to me. I'm going to tell you. And you're going to hate it.

Tank blinked, taking his hand from Sin's mane, and turned to look at Dasin. The merchant wasn't looking his way and showed no signs of having spoken. And the words *hadn't* been spoken, or at least, hadn't been spoken in the *now*. They felt like memory, not mindspeech. Dasin *had* said those words, some time ago. When? *When?* And *why* —

Tank turned back to Sin, running his fingers through the stallion's coarse black mane, fighting the impulse to stride over to Dasin and shake him until sense rattled out into his grasp. How in the hells could he have forgotten that conversation — well, that was an easy answer. He wouldn't have. Which meant *someone* had altered his memories.

Not Dasin. It couldn't have been Dasin. But there were teyanain lurking about.

A black stain surged into the edges of his vision. His mind filled with the calming litany his teachers, long ago, had drilled into him for moments like this. *Stop, stop, stop, breathe, breathe, breathe, think, think, think ... stop, breathe, think ... stop, breathe, think, stop, breathe, think ... stop, stop, stop....* and around again, carefully counted and cadenced, designed to force him to look away from rage.

It took a wretchedly long time to pull back from the edge of mania. But there were innocents here, and teyanain watching. Losing control wouldn't get him answers.

Stop, breathe, think. Stop, stop, stop. Breathe, breathe, breathe. Stop, breathe, think ... no, he'd skipped a step. *Stop, breathe, think. Stop, stop, stop. Breathe, breathe, breathe. Think, think, think. Stop, breathe, think.* There. That was right. He could feel his spine relaxing in tiny increments.

Tank inhaled slowly, stroking Sin's mane, focusing on the feel of coarse hair against his fingertips. He let the breath out as slowly, locking his temper down. *Then* he turned, casting a deliberate gaze across the group. Dasin had finished his coffee, cleaned up after himself, doused the torch, and climbed onto the wagon. The thin light of the partially hooded lantern showed that Lia and Cilif were already mounted, talking in low voices and almost ostentatiously not looking at him.

The priest stood out of reach, his hands folded across his stomach. What Tank could make out of his expression seemed entirely placid.

"When you are ready to let the anger rage," Kolan said when Tank met his gaze, "come speak to me. I can help you manage it safely."

Tank began to smile, halfway between sour amusement and contempt.

Kolan lifted his chin and said, "I was imprisoned with Ellemoa. Idisio's mother." His eyes slowly filled with shifting threads of black.

All amusement fled. Tank felt his muscles shift into combat readiness. Sin dipped and swung his head briefly but made no sound. The priest stayed perfectly still, his eyes now a neutral color in the dim light.

"So that's why they sent you along," Tank said, tone nearly a growl.

"I asked to travel alongside you," Kolan said. He shut his eyes, dipped his chin;

breathed deeply, then straightened his neck and looked at Tank, his eyes paler than before. "I believe it is my correct path. I will not harm you or yours, nor will I allow you to harm others, without due cause."

"What's due cause?" Tank said bitterly. "And this from a northern priest, no less!"

The priest's mouth quirked in a strangely mournful expression. "Do not judge me by my peers," he said. "I am merely myself, *s'e*. I will help you when you are ready. Remember that." He nodded deeply, almost a bow, then turned away without a word and circled round to climb up onto the wagon seat beside Dasin.

The merchant looked over his shoulder at Tank. Tank shrugged roughly and swung into the saddle, ignoring the unexpected and very unwelcome stinging at the back of his eyes.

Chapter Forty-five

Her second trip over Hells Hill very nearly convinced Lia to never take the North Road again. Kennet, with a lighter load and an energetic mule, had easily managed the tedious haul between dawn and dusk. Dasin's heavier wagon and slower draft pony trudged along the steep incline at a pace that an ox could have managed in its sleep.

News Riders and other travellers thudded past, calling out cheerful greetings. Dasin, walking alongside the draft, seemed entirely unbothered by their slow pace. They were all walking. In part because of the steep incline, in part because going any faster than the draft was a pointless endeavor.

"Merchant Dasin," Lia said at one point, after careful consideration of how to ask the question. "May I ask why we didn't take the Plains Road straight up to Assiasan?"

"Easterners," Dasin said briefly. "I don't like dealing with 'em. Plains Road is more easterners than northerns."

Lia hesitated, but seeing no hint of a frown, took a chance on pressing. "I've been told that easterners and southerners were very alike," she said.

Dasin laughed, once, short and sharp. "No. Nothing like. Careful saying that around anyone from a desert Family. You'll get yourself strung up by the toes."

Lia dropped back a few paces as a less than graceful end to the conversation. That brought her up alongside Cilif, who grinned at her wearily and said, "You're lucky he's in a good mood. That was the hells own loaded remark."

"I didn't mean —"

"I know." He waved her half-formed apology silent. "Nah, it's a point of pride with most from south of the Horn. They're prickly about being called barbaric. You ever seen an easterner?"

Rooster chose that moment to crowd Lia sideways. He and Blackie snapped at one another, lips peeled back. She twisted out of the way, cursing, and hauled him around as Cilif pulled Blackie clear. They spent several minutes walking the irritable beasts on opposite sides of the road. Finally, Cilif mounted Blackie and set him at a trot up the hill to bleed off his agitation. Lia did the same, downslope. By the time she'd turned and caught up to the wagon again, Rooster was nearly cheerful, Blackie placid.

They walked the horses side by side without incident for a time.

Cilif repeated his question: "Ever seen an easterner?"

"Yes."

"In Stecatr, or on the road south, or what?"

"One in Stecatr, years ago," she said. "Two on the road south. I didn't speak to any of them, only saw them in passing."

"Heh. Well, you ever get close enough to talk, keep that mask you used to wear handy. They *stink*. Don't bathe but once a year at a guess. They put grease all through their hair and on their skin. Fucking disgusting. I mean, we ain't no prize right now, but we're dainties compared to the best of the easterns I've ever come within range of. Their idea of fancy food is to bury unseasoned meat in jars underground for months, pull it out, then eat the maggots."

Lia made a face.

"Yeah. Don't compare that to southerners." Cilif slapped Blackie's neck companionably. "*They* at least roast the maggots."

Lia let out a sharp, barking laugh. Tank, catching the sound, turned and circled back to them, Sin moving restlessly beneath him. "Horses are shitty today," he observed.

Cilif said, entirely bland, "Yeah, well, it's this damned hill. They always do hate it. We're talking about easterners. Lia don't know much about them."

"Rough people," Tank said, scratching his cheek. "They like fighting. Men, women, and children. They'll take any chance to cry offense, and they're dirty fighters. Winning a fight is serious stuff for them. You don't like tangling with unsworn, you definitely don't want to go up against an easterner. *I* wouldn't want to. They're not at all slow about killing."

Sin pranced irritably. Tank turned him aside and took him on a short trot, then returned.

He said, "We went up the Plains Road our first trip to Assiasan. Came out of it with cracked ribs and a couple of new scars, lost half the cargo and our draft mule. Never did that again. Not worth it. Rather take the North Road and walk this hill."

"That's so different from what I've been told," Lia said. "I was taught that easterners are Syrta's children. That they have a connection to the earth, and a wisdom about healing."

"Maybe so," Tank allowed. "They do work as healers, as I hear it. Whether they're any good at it I don't know. I suppose they must be, for the villages and towns to allow them in. But they're territorial, and they consider the Plains Road *theirs*. We're outsiders, and it's not worth our time and risk to make them our friends."

"Who'd want to?" Cilif said, pulling a face. "Eurgh."

Rooster darted his head at Sin abruptly, teeth bared. Tank hauled on the reins and Sin went sideways with a disgruntled snort.

"*Fucking* horses," Tank growled. "I fucking *hate* horses sometimes." Lia laughed. Tank glowered at her. "It's all right for *you*," he said waspishly. "You love 'em, don't you?"

"I grew up —" She stopped, catching herself. "Yes. I do."

Tank regarded her sideways for a moment, then shook his head and moved up to ride beside the wagon. Rooster lifted his head, as proud as if he'd won a war all by himself, and walked with a distinct prance for some time.

"You don't like talking on yourself," Cilif observed.

"No," Lia said, then laughed at his exasperated squint. "There isn't much worth telling. I grew up poor, fell in with the grayhands, signed up for training at the Hall of Arms when it opened to women. Spent some time with horses because it's hard not to, in Stecatr. There are three major horse breeding and training farms there." She pointed to the draft pony. "That's probably a Stecatr-bred horse, or at least one from a Stecatr line. Most of the horses you see News Riders using are from Stecatr. It's one of our major exports."

Cilif perked up, interested. "I didn't know that," he said. "Or, well, I think I heard sommat, but I didn' t know it was that extensive. Tell me more?"

Lia found herself relaxing, and felt Rooster settling under her, as though infected by her mood. It had been a *long* time since she'd had a friendly audience for that topic. "I'll chew your ear off," she warned, grinning.

"I've got two. I can lose one." He returned the smile, a bit awkwardly.

"All right, then. Remember you asked for it...."

Toad was waiting for them at the top of Hells Hill, with not a teyanin in sight.

He wore gray and blue clothes of a style that would fit in any northern city, pristine and new in appearance. His straw hat was gone, replaced by a much smaller cap of an odd style that sagged to one side like a tiny sack, and he wore knee-high, laced boots of fine leather. He looked entirely rested and entirely calm, but his eyes were bleak and dark with a new, deep pain.

He and Kolan stared at one another, ignoring everything else. Finally, the strange priest smiled, sunnily cheerful, and wandered away to braid Rooster's mane as though nothing more important existed in the world.

Toad looked at Dasin then, his face wrinkled in worry. "There's something very wrong with that man," he said.

"Welcome back," Dasin said dryly. "We're well aware, trust me. Get up on the damn seat, we've little enough daylight to be going on with as it is. You can fill me in as we go."

As the old man scrambled up onto the wagon, Dasin shot Tank a look that didn't just speak loudly, it shouted entire volumes. Tank spread his hands, grimacing, then motioned everyone forward once more.

Lia dropped to the back of the group, trying to decide whether to be relieved or offended that Toad hadn't spared her more than the briefest glance.

Halfway down the hill, the clear sky turned muddy with clouds. Tank swore as he looked west, then: "I didn't see that coming. Double pace, *now*."

Travelers headed up the hill, likewise, took one startled glance at the sharply building weather and turned tail for shelter lower down. Dasin knocked the downhill brake loose and shook the reins hard: the draft lunged into a lumbering trot. The wagon slewed wildly at the abrupt shift of pace, and Lia heard glass and thin wood breaking inside. Tank swore again.

"Damnit, don't destroy *all* the profit from this run!" he hollered. Dasin lifted a hand in a rude gesture.

By the time the steep hill ran down to a gentle slope, the sky was nearly black. Heavy, cold rain pattered down around them. As they reached the outskirts of the small village nearest the hill, patter turned to percussion, the road morphing to a field of muddy gravel, and the draft subsided to a stubborn, exhausted plod. Rooster's stride was off. Lia had a strong suspicion he'd picked up a stone.

To make matters worse, the stables were already full of equally annoyed travelers, as was the inn, and nearly every farm in the area had already given shelter to the overflow from the inn. Dasin finally found a farmer willing to let them set up tents for the night in the flat spot between his hay barn and tool sheds. Thankfully, most of the area was neatly paved with thick red block, angled to run water into a nearby ditch. Still, enough dirt washed across for the rising water to be dark with mud.

Lia did her best with the still-unfamiliar risers, but in the torrential rain and poor light, she could barely see what she was doing, and seemed cursed to drop everything she picked up. Tank, exasperated, finally shooed her out of the way.

"Go check on the horses," he snapped. "Their hooves, in particular. Get their feed bags and blankets on. And try to find something *resembling* high ground to picket them at, they oughtn't to sit on this paving overnight. Once this damned storm clears and the stables open up, we'll have to spend a day over putting everything back to rights. Maybe two. Pray to whatever gods you like that they don't take a cold from this shit weather."

"This *is* the high ground," Lia said, blinking and squinting against the water streaming down her face. "I can see about buying hay from the farmer, to put down on the pavers for them." There was nothing to say by way of reassurance about the horses' health. Lia knew perfectly well that the sturdiest draft could go down sick from a chill breeze if hit just right. The matter was entirely with the gods at this point.

Tank nodded once, sharply. "Do it."

While the rest of the crew, even Toad, worked to put up tents and settle the horses, Kolan stood to one side, face tilted to the sky, apparently entirely content. Tank went over to talk to him at one point. Lia didn't hear the conversation, but Tank's body language went from impatient to incredulous, then into irritation. At last he stomped away again with a dismissive wave. Kolan, unbothered, went back to staring up at nothing.

When camp was as handled as it could get, Tank motioned everyone into a tight circle. "We've too many people and not enough risers again," he said. "We picked up extra tents in Arason, but there's only one spot that won't be in muddy water. The others have to go on the risers, so we're at three tents again."

"What about Kolan?" Cilif asked, scowling at the priest.

"He's said he's fine out in the open," Tank said, irritation strong in his tone. "I'm not about to argue. Lia, you take the bare spot, and Toad comes in with you. I'm with Dasin. Cilif, you're on one of the risers, and if Kolan changes his mind, he'll kip in with you. This storm feels likely to last all night, but I think it'll turn more to wind than rain by midnight. Might be some hail. You'll have to manage on trail bars for the night, but we'll do a proper breakfast. Dasin's paying for meals once we get into the local inn. We're staying a day, maybe two, get some rest and sort out damages to the horses and stock." He stepped back, waving everyone off.

Lia stood frozen in place, staring at the big redhead. She'd expected him to share with her again; at least she knew she could trust him. She would even have accepted Cilif, especially after today's long talk and his open interest in what she had to say. But Toad? No!

"Tank," she said, her voice cracking, then said it again, more steadily and with more volume. She tried to find a way to say *I'll kip in with Cilif instead*, but that sounded far too brash, too laden with implications. Cilif wasn't *ii'ne*, and although she was fairly sure he'd be respectful, there was no way to keep that statement from sounding like an invitation she didn't intend.

Before she could sort out words, Tank stepped in close to her, his scowl forbidding under the hood of his heavy rain cloak. His hair was plastered in wet strands across his face, as though he'd given up trying to push it aside some time ago, and his beard streamed water down his neck and into his shirt.

"Get the fuck over it, Stecatr," he said harshly. "We don't have time for this shit."

He turned away without waiting for an answer. Lia glared after him, panic bubbling in her chest. He'd *never* spoken to her that way, never called her that mocking name. Apparently, what she'd thought of as a budding friendship had been nothing more than a distraction while he fought with Dasin. Now that the two men were, very clearly, back on good terms, Tank had no compassion left over.

Fucking southerners. Fucking men. *The hells with the lot of them. My mother was right.*

Lia turned sharply at a tug on her sleeve, her glare settling on the priest.

Kolan said, "Be at calm. It will be a grace." He paused, his eyes pale and distant for a moment. "I'm sorry. The words aren't right. There's no harm. There will be no harm."

He dipped his chin to his chest, abruptly taut with clear frustration. Something seemed wrong about him, something more than his usual strangeness. It put a sharp chill up Lia's back, colder than the rainwater already slicking her spine.

"Close enough," Lia said. "I get your point."

Kolan raised his head, and even in the dim light his eyes seemed to glow. Lia took a reflexive step back.

"You're safer with your countryman, tonight," the priest said, quiet but distinct. Then he turned and walked away.

She stared after him, completely numb to anything but a fragmented sense of being far out of her depth. Even after everything she'd seen, everything she'd learned, the dread of witchery still wrapped round her bones, nearly impossible to push aside.

If Toad was *safer* company than Tank, tonight....

Lia wondered if she ought to warn Dasin to be careful. The thought brought bitter laughter to her throat.

Toad touched her arm, cautiously, bringing her attention back around. The old man's features were pinched. "Lia," he said. Somehow the one word carried volumes, as did his miserable expression. She let out a long, harsh breath, then headed for her tent, waving him along in her wake.

Somewhere in the subsequent fumbling through packs for dry clothes, turning their backs for what privacy could be had, and then wrapping themselves in blankets and bedrolls, she realized what had been so off about the priest.

He'd been completely dry in the midst of a torrential downpour.

Chapter Forty-six

Warm for the first time in hours, reasonably dry, and entirely exhausted, Tank lay on his back listening to Dasin's even breathing and wondered, vaguely, what the hell was wrong with him.

He'd snarled at Lia more out of guilt than actual irritation. She might be Arason sworn now, but the fear of a lifetime would take more than a tenday to ease. Her hesitation hadn't been at all unreasonable. Putting her in with Toad, given their mutual antagonism, was a bad idea, arguably a selfish decision.

He *should* have set her with Cilif. They'd been getting along well of late, and given that Cilif wasn't at all interested in anyone, he wouldn't force her into anything. But there was no way to put them together without *someone* misunderstanding, and as the most likely misunderstanding would come from Toad, it had seemed like solid logic to put Lia and Toad together and make them finally sort out their damn issues.

Tank couldn't offer himself as an option this time. The way Dasin had been tackling him lately, there was *no* chance Tank wouldn't grab in his sleep. That would end badly, to say the least.

And *damn*, he'd been hungry to get laid. For all his sourness in daylight, Dasin was a fiend when he let go, and the torrential rain meant safety. Nobody would hear or see a thing. *Quiet* and *limited movement* weren't essential in a storm like this. Opportunities like that were rare along the northern road. Tank was more than happy to grab them with both hands, as it were.

He was actually grateful that it was unlikely they'd have the privacy for anything particularly vigorous over the next few days. He needed time for a few sore spots and overworked muscles to heal. He might have to ask Dasin to lay off entirely for a day or two.

From desert to flood, he thought wryly. *Enjoy it while it lasts, I suppose.*

He gently shifted Dasin's head to a better angle on his shoulder and let out a long, contented breath. Things could be worse. Things could, most definitely, be worse.

The rain was easing, the wind kicking up in rasping bursts that rattled loose boards and rolled small objects across the courtyard around them. Tank lay quietly, listening to the random sounds, thinking of nothing in particular.

You're not going to like the answers ... You're going to hate it. You're going to hate me.

Tank's breath caught in his chest as memory danced around the corners of his contentment. He didn't want to remember. Didn't want this one, peaceful moment disrupted.

You won't remember this. Won't want to. You'll keep forgetting, because I want you to, but you'll remember eventually. I can't hold this forever, more's the pity.

Tank shut his eyes, setting his teeth together until his jaw ached, and breathed hard through his nose. *Not now,* he told the pressing memory. *Not now, for fuck's sake. Please. I need this moment. I need this peace. Please.*

Something metal crashed against the side of the barn nearby, clattering along for some distance. The wind rose to a shriek, then died back to a hoarse moan.

Dasin's voice returned. *You don't need me, Tank. You're going to realize that soon. You'll be much better off without me. I've always known that. And ... I'll be better off without you.*

Tank tilted his head back, until he felt the strain in the front of his throat. *Godsdamnit. Gods*damnit....

Those few sentences put Dasin's recent generosity in a new light. He was getting ready to walk away. Probably to go walk alongside Evkit. Or maybe not.

Dasin didn't know — or did he? — that Tank had already agreed to act on Evkit's behalf when called on at some murky future time. *Did* Dasin know that? Was that the reason he was walking away? Was *he* unwilling to share that particular master with Tank?

It didn't make sense, and it made absolute sense, and Tank was no longer the least bit relaxed. Resentful anger with multiple roots tightened his muscles and rolled Dasin from his shoulder. Dasin snorted, complaining, and half sat up.

"What —" he said, blurry, then drew in a sharp breath. "Tank...."

"*What did you do to me?*" Tank grated.

Dasin said nothing for a long moment. Shutters rattled in the distance, barely audible under the rough wind. At last, Dasin sighed. "Not yet," he said. "Let it go, Tank. Wait until we're in a proper room. We'll talk again then. Let it go. Forget. Go back to sleep."

Anger wobbled, slowly losing its edge. "Dasin," Tank said, more plaintively this time, "what did you do? What are you *doing?*" He tried to gather his anger, tried to fight the buzz already invading his mind.

"*Sleep and forget,*" Dasin said, his voice blending with the raw murmur of the wind, and Tank did.

Chapter Forty-seven

The rain stopped some hours before dawn, but the wind remained fitful. Uneasy and resentful, Lia slept poorly, jerking awake often and half-sitting up to check that Toad was still tucked up against the other side of the tent. He slept without moving, damn near rolled into the wall of the tent and snoring softly. Apparently he wasn't the least bit concerned by *her* proximity, which irritated Lia in a tired, childish way.

At one point, Lia woke and heard voices. She put them off as wind-thrown distortions, or farmers moving about to secure things knocked loose by earlier gusts. Closer to dawn, she woke again and heard the murmuring more clearly: the hair stood up on the back of her neck and her bladder suddenly felt overfull.

It wasn't human. She didn't know how she knew that. She tried to scold herself against night terrors and wild imaginings, but her heartbeat refused to slow and her hands wouldn't stop shaking.

She shut her eyes and listened, putting aside disbelief, focusing with grim patience.

Wind howled. As it died, words emerged, sounding something like *shia ne kallena fee sshin* ... then the wind built again, in a way that should have obscured the next words but merely underscored them instead.

Come talk to us, northern of Stecatr. Come out and talk. Come, come out ... shia, shia, kalle, kalle, ssheee ... Then the wind buried all sound as it rushed and roared, sending branches creaking on the tall oak trees nearby, tumbling small things to bang along the barn walls.

Lia fought to hold her bladder control. She heard herself whimpering like a child, and bit her lip savagely to stop the noise.

Toad coughed and sat up. "Lia? Child, are you all right?" He made a brief, annoyed clicking sound, then added, "My apologies. I ought not have called you child. But what's the matter?"

"I have to piss," Lia said through her teeth, then surprised herself with raw honesty: "There's something out there. I don't think it's human." She'd intended to point to the weather as a reason not to go to the latrine, and wasn't at all sure why she'd blurted out the truth.

Toad went completely still, barely breathing, as though he were listening intently. "I don't hear anything," he said. "But that doesn't mean there's nothing there. This is a bad spot." Fabric shifted and scraped. "Wait a moment, only a moment. Here."

She sensed his outstretched hand and met it with her own. He deposited a fistful of what felt like pebbles into her palm.

"Put that on," he said. "I'd meant to give it to you earlier, but, well." He let out a huffing sigh. "It's to protect you. Put it on, and I'll go with you."

"What can *you* do against a ghost or a monster?" Lia demanded acerbically, running her fingers gingerly over the pebbles. Moving them around revealed that she held a necklace of roughly polished, irregularly sized beads, generous enough in length to slip over her head easily. "What is *this*?"

Toad clicked his tongue again. She could almost see his irritated frown despite the blank darkness. "Likely nothing but run for help," he said, "but that's not such a poor thing to have, now is it? I have to use the latrine as well, anyway. And the necklace is a … a talisman, if you will. It makes it harder for those — *things* — to see you, to affect you." He hesitated, then put a hand on her arm, gripping with sudden urgency. "Tuck it under your shirt, so it touches your skin, and don't tell anyone you have it. Please."

Lia bit the tip of her tongue, holding herself silent against conflicting impulses. She really *did* have to piss, with a painful ferocity, and improbable as it seemed, she was certain that Toad was telling absolute truth this time. She draped the necklace over her head and tucked it under her shirt. The beads felt warm against her skin. Whether that meant anything, she'd have to ask later. For the moment, she began working her boots onto her feet, and heard Toad doing the same.

"Why do you say this is a bad spot?" she said as she rolled into a crouch, beginning to reach for the tent flap.

"It's too close to the graveyard, too close to the hill itself," Toad said without hesitation. "Shia-banse are the least of the worries when the local spirits are stirred up."

"I don't think it's ghosts," Lia said tightly as she ducked from the tent.

Scarcely audible, she heard the old man mutter: "Neither do I."

The latrine wasn't far from the barn, and she'd memorized the route for exactly this eventuality. Still, with so little light in the cloud-scudded sky, she moved with care, splashing through endless puddles and intensely grateful neither boot had yet sprung a leak. She kept a hand outstretched, sweeping her feet occasionally to check for wind-rattled obstacles. Toad labored in her wake, breathing heavily and grumbling to himself.

The wind died down as they walked, leaving an eerie stillness. They heard no whispers, no voices, not even snores from human or animal. They made it to the latrine without incident, and took turns standing watch.

Toad emerged yawning loudly and muttering about the ill effects of trail cooking. "I'll be glad for a good Stecatr diet again," he said as they trudged back toward the tents. "Rice and beans, feh! Doesn't agree with me at all, not with those damn spices they insist on adding. A bit of salt is enough for any meal, you ask me. Rather have oatmeal and apples. Nice, steady —"

He paused, grabbing Lia's arm. She froze, of two minds about allowing him to touch her, but listened intently, squinting into the moonlit shadows around them for any sign of trouble.

The wind was moving again, tiny whispers rilling around corners and under low-set gaps. Lia listened for words in the whispers, every muscle in her body going tight. Behind her, someone said, "Lia."

She yelped aloud and spun, reaching for a dagger she'd left back in the tent, then fell back a pace, shoving Toad away as she readied for a blind fight.

"It's only me," the voice said. Fire flared, a low blue light along outspread fingers, to show the Arason priest standing several paces away. "Ha'vash, ha'ne. No harm. I heard them too. I asked them to leave, but they want to speak to you. I'll be with you, there's no danger."

"*Witch*," Toad snapped. He began to back up, then hesitated as though about to push forward instead.

"No," Kolan said. "Lia? Will you come?"

"What are *they*?" she demanded, still taut.

"You'll see," Kolan said equably. "*S'e* Toad, go on back to the tent. You'll only get in the way. Go on, go back to sleep."

To Lia's surprise, the old man turned and shuffled away without protest. "Did you witch him?" she asked, scowling after him and wondering if she should wake Tank.

"Yes. He was about to make matters difficult. Will you come? Alone," he added, as though hearing her thoughts.

"You admit to witching him but say you're not a witch?" It occurred to her that if Toad had been wearing the same necklace of beads that he'd pressed upon her, it had just proven useless against at least one sort of witchery. That didn't bode well for its overall usefulness.

Kolan said, patiently, "*S'a*, there isn't time for discussing distinctions. Dawn is near. Will you come?"

Lia shrugged, tight-lipped, and followed the priest and his handful of blue fire to the edge of the small farming village.

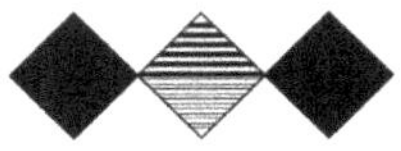

Hells Hill was not where the locals buried their kin. A scattering of small headstones within a hip-high, stacked-stone wall enclosure at the edge of the village stood mute testimony to dozens of lives lost early and late. The wind pipped and squeaked past the stones, shifting loose twigs and sodden bouquets into a slithering tumble. A faint, steady blue glow hung over the entire graveyard, just enough to see it clearly.

Lia stood arm's length outside the wall, staring in with horrified fascination, then checked, squinting hard at the wall itself. The light was too dim to be sure, but a cold certainty that the wall was at least partially built of the rare, opalescent stone Stecatr called godstone settled in her chest. Godstone was, as a matter of faith and folklore alike, an effective ward against demons.

Reflexively, she pulled one palm over her stomach at a slant towards her heart, then traced the signs of all four gods across her chest.

Kolan said, mildly, "You really ought to be past that, *s'a*. Ah. They're here. I suggest courtesy." The fire on his hands flared briefly, then disappeared.

Between one blink and the next, the blue within the graveyard coalesced into four uneven, man-height blocks, leaving the bulk of the graveyard darkly shadowed once more.

Northern child of kin, a voice said. *We see you.*

Northern child of kin, a slightly different voice said. *We hear you.*

A third voice: *Northern child of kin, we feel you.*

A fourth: *Northern child of kin, we welcome you.*

Lia stood frozen. A meaningful cough from Kolan recalled her to her senses. She bowed deeply, muttering something about the blessings of the gods, not knowing quite what the words were even as they came out of her mouth.

Kolan sighed deeply, which she supposed meant she'd scrambled it completely. The blue — creatures? — seemed unbothered. Their shapes moved vaguely from rectangular to rounded and back at irregular intervals, never quite the same. It hurt her eyes and her head to watch the pulsing movement.

The voices overlapped, each saying a slightly different thing: *We ask you to visit our kin/ your kin/all kin, in the mountains/in the place of rest/in the final home. We wish you to witness for us/bring word of us/beg for our release from our kin/your kin/all kin. We have guarded this bridge/ gathering place/resting place for long enough.*

The voices combined briefly: *We are weary.* Then, once more unevenly braided: *We ask for peace/reward/ rest. We would have reached for the other/nearer kin/stronger kin but that one cannot hear us/is empty/is gone within itself.*

The voices faded to silence. Lia stood gaping at the glowing forms, her mouth actually hanging open. She frantically sorted out the various requests to find the sense, then gave up and said, "Sorry, *what*? Northern kin? All kin? *Nearer kin?*"

The forms seemed to shrink and condense slightly, their color deepening. *You have not been told of us.*

Lia found herself remembering Cousin Anaya's gimlet stare as she accused: *I don't suppose your mother's even spoken of us poor farmers to you, has she?*

"Um," she said, floundering as badly now as she had then.

Kolan stepped forward to stand beside her. He said, placidly, "She is not to blame for the lack of her elders. And your northern kin, not she, is — are? — responsible for holding her elders to account. Ask only if she *will* bear your message, and have faith that she will understand it in the proper time." He withdrew a measured step, hands folded across his stomach.

Lia stared at him, her eyes wide with beginning panic.

"Courtesy," he admonished mildly, motioning past her. "Tell them if you will do as they ask."

She brought her attention back to the glowing forms and said, "I'll carry your message, but who do I take it *to*?"

Before she even finished the question, the glow flexed once, as though in a sigh of relief, then disappeared entirely. Dark closed back in, terrifyingly silent. A moment later, the wind returned, building from swirls to driving spears laden with chill rain.

"What the *f*—" Lia caught herself, unwilling to swear this close to a graveyard, and clutched after Kolan's shoulder with a shaking hand. "What was *that*? What did I agree to?"

Kolan stood still for a time. At last, his muscles shifted under her hand, as though he were looking around. He said, plaintively, "I ... *s'a*, I don't understand. I'm very sorry. But where are we? How did we get here?"

Lia let out a shaky bray of laughter, unable to help herself. "Of course," she said. "Of course. It's all right, priest. Come on. It's nearly dawn. Let's go see if anyone around here is awake enough to make coffee yet."

Chapter Forty-eight

Tank dreamed.

It was, at first, a familar dream: *Bird-figures stalking through underbrush, circling, watching, coming steadily nearer. But the colors were blue and green, not red and gold, and the trees were wrong. Even more strangely, Dasin stood watching the birds, arms folded and not at all concerned, while Tank shook and shivered in panic.*

"This isn't the Hackerwood," Tank said. "Dasin, where are we?"

"No, it's not," Dasin said, not turning his head. "Go back to sleep. It's fine. They're only going to eat you. It won't hurt if you're asleep."

Tank backed up a step, then whirled to find a gigantic cobalt and emerald bloodbird before him. Its beak gaped wide, rows of serrated teeth clearly visible as it let out a very human, if manic, laugh.

He grabbed for his sword and came up empty. Dasin, still not looking at him, said impatiently, "Stop being a fool. It'll be over quickly if you don't fight."

"Fuck that," Tank said, and ran.

Trees flew past him, the ground rolling by more quickly than he'd ever run before. He leapt over a log and found himself running across the tops of the trees. A fierce wind shoved him this way and that. He heard the grackling of the strange bloodbirds as they hunted him from below, unable, for all their gigantic wingspan, to loft into the sky after him. In the distance, tall mountains gleamed a cold, beckoning ivory.

He would be safe in the mountains. The bloodbirds couldn't go there. He had to reach the mountains. The stone there would protect him.

Dasin appeared and shoved him, hard and contemptuously. Tank found himself back on the forest floor, surrounded by the gaping, hungry mouths of several bloodbirds.

"Time to eat," Dasin said cheerfully.

As the first beak began to close over his face, Tank screamed and woke, still screaming, thrashing against Dasin's embrace.

"Tank! Tank," Dasin said. "*Tank.* Stop, it's me, it was a dream, you're safe, you —"

Still dazed with panic and betrayal, Tank lashed out with a vicious blow that sent Dasin sprawling. The imperative to run wrenched his muscles, and he scrambled out of the tent and several steps across the cobbled courtyard before chill air shocked him into clarity.

Lia, Toad, and Cilif, all holding steaming mugs of coffee, stared at him in open astonishment. Kolan was nowhere to be seen.

And Tank himself was quite thoroughly naked.

Lia's face bloomed with dull color as she jerked her gaze away. Cilif began to roar with laughter. Tank, holding what dignity he could manage, ducked back into the tent, ferociously ignored Dasin — who huddled in a corner of the tent, face washed out, shaking with reaction — and yanked on last night's trousers and shirt. Then he retreated back into open air, barefoot and tousled, his own shivering panic still far too close to the surface.

Dasin emerged some moments later, rumpled but dressed, glaring fit to kill. Anger, as usual, had trampled over fear in short order. Tank circled to the far side of the courtyard, away from him, grabbing the mug of coffee from Lia's hand as he went. She made no protest, her face still the color of a ripe tomato. Cilif burst into renewed laughter. Tank swatted at him, growling, which only made the big mercenary laugh harder.

"Didn't think his morning, ah, *face* would scare you into streaking after alla these years," Cilif gasped, still grinning.

"I had a nightmare," Tank said flatly, then drank down most of Lia's coffee in one gulp.

Dasin's glare lightened. "Oh," he said. "It's been a while since you had one so bad as to *deck* me."

Tank shrugged, surly and unwilling to apologize in the wake of Cilif's continued chuckling and Lia's mortification.

Toad cleared his throat. "Ah," he said, "The inn has two rooms open now. I took the liberty of reserving them for you. I believe the stables are open again, as well. And, ah, I've found a farmer who'll let me take a corner of his kitchen for a night or two." He looked around, frowning a little. "I don't know where the priest went, after he and Lia found us all coffee."

"He'll be back," Cilif said comfortably. "Wandered off to take a piss or sommat."

Lia's expression shifted to a different emotion, one more starkly fear-based than her earlier mortification. Before Tank could ask after that, Dasin came up beside him and shoved at his shoulder.

"Come help me examine the wagon for leaks," he said. "And tell me about this damn nightmare so it lets go of you." He pulled the cup from Tank's hand and gave it back to Lia, scowling.

"Look over the horses," Tank said, ignoring Dasin. "Lia, Cilif, get them moved into the stables and take the morning to sort them out properly. I'm not moving on until everything's been cleaned, dried, mended, and oiled, from hoof to hoofpicks. Lia, you take care of Sin and Rooster. Cilif, you get the draft and Blackie." Cilif *hmphed* but made no argument.

"*Alli-furdath*. We'll stay two days," Dasin declared. "We all need the rest. Now come *on*, Tank."

Once around the far side of the wagon and out of sight from the group, Tank said, in a rough undertone: "Sorry. But don't — I can't talk about it. Not yet."

Dasin pushed Tank's shoulder, more gently this time. "Asshole," he said without venom.

"Yeah, well." Tank set his fingertips lightly against the side of Dasin's face. "Gonna bruise?"

"No. I rolled with it well enough."

Tank withdrew before Dasin could push his hand away. "Good to know you listened when I taught you that."

Dasin began to bristle, then paused, regarding Tank with an odd expression. "I do listen to you," he said, very quietly. "More than you realize."

Tank set his lips together and tapped at a jagged, hairline crack where the roof joined the side. "We'll need to patch that."

"Yes. That's four spots now. Need to find a proper cartwright."

"Yes. Might be one here. I'll ask around."

They went on checking for leaks in blessedly neutral silence.

Chapter Forty-Nine

Toad, without asking, began unsnarling Rooster's tangled mane as Lia checked Sin's hooves. The big black gelding, visibly dispirited, gave no protest at Lia's handling. Rooster fussed. The old man soothed Rooster, inexpertly but well enough to sort out the majority of the mess by the time Lia set the last hoof down. Sin swung his head round and bumped Lia gently as she stretched to ease the knots in her back. Since she didn't have a carrot, she settled for scratching Sin's narrow, fine nose.

They'd decided to sort the grooming outdoors, in full daylight. The work would be easier, and Lia's nerves were still frayed enough that daylight felt substantially safer. Besides, the stable was still clearing out stalls from the previous night's tenants.

"That black horse is getting old," Toad said, picking fluff from the comb and dropping it on the ground with a displeased grimace. "Look at this silver creeping in. He ought to be retired." If *he* remembered anything about the priest sending him off to bed, he wasn't showing it, and Lia was disinclined to ask.

"No," Lia said, looking Sin and Blackie over and thinking back to her conversation with Cilif the day before. "They're neither of them all that old. I'm not sure why there's gray showing up, that's odd."

Straight from the king's stables, and a prime bloodline, Cilif had said during their conversation the day before. *Ask Tank about it one of these days. It's a wild story, if you can get it out of him. Maybe tell him what you told me, that might get him to open up.*

She wasn't at all sure she *should* have told Cilif about her family, but done was done, and now he knew more about her than anyone outside of Stecatr, and most people *in* Stecatr.

Her father, Korin Eller, should have inherited the job of caretaker to the Feninta stables, second only to the Lord of Stecatr's own horses in quality. Korin had been the eldest, and *his* father had been a traditionalist about such things. But the head of Feninta had liked Lia's uncle better: he was fair-haired and easy to talk to, a sharp contrast to Korin's dour intensity. There had been an incident or two, young men jealous of one another battling for pride and prominence. When their father died, the matter had settled in favor of Korin's younger brother.

Korin, furious, had rejected an offer of a lesser spot at the stables and gone into the city proper, to join up with the prestigious Outriders — mounted guards who routinely rode patrols from Stecatr to the nearby villages and towns, making sure the roads were clear of any trouble and that communications stayed open.

Lia hadn't been so careless as to tell Cilif the rest of it: starting with her own birth coming markedly too soon after the marriage, it wasn't a story to share. She'd talked horses, and just that small bit of family history. That had been more than personal enough for both of them.

A sound nearby recalled her from brooding: Toad, clearing his throat. "Lia," he said, frowning at her worriedly, "Are you quite all right? You look — well, you're just standing there."

She blinked at the brush in her hand. "Thinking," she said. She looked at the big splotchy horse for a moment, then began brushing him down. "Thinking about when I learned to take care of horses."

"Ah." Toad began rubbing Rooster's nose, digging his nails in. The horse leaned into it, eyes drooping half-shut. "How old were you?"

"Not much more than a toddler, if you believe my mother."

Lia's uncle had apparently said that even if Korin was determined to reject family, there was no reason for Elsa and Lia to suffer from his pride. It had been a stormy point of contention for most of Lia's early life, until she'd grown old enough to pretend a complete disinterest in horses while sneaking off to the stables every chance she had.

Her uncle faded out of her life over the years, taking to the road to sell the best of the yearlings and search out new bloodlines, but she'd become friends with the new stable manager, who not only allowed her visits but let her ride out among the morning string on occasion. And, of course, had her endlessly grooming horses by way of training and payment alike.

Remembering her lessons now, she focused on brushing Rooster down with brisk efficiency.

Toad said, "I was honestly surprised when you signed with the Hall of Arms. I thought you'd go to the Feninta stables and work towards becoming manager there."

"I thought about it," Lia said. "But it was less of a confrontation for me to take up the sword." It would most certainly have been safer, in hindsight, to take the — hah — stable route.

What in all the hells am I going to say to the priests when they ask me about demonic encounters? Just because I've changed Halls doesn't mean they won't pull me in for an accounting. She barely suppressed a frustrated sigh. It had seemed so simple in Arason, but the much more complicated reality pressed harder by the day as they traveled further north.

She wished she dared ask Toad if he remembered Kolan's hands flaring blue in the windy darkness. *Too dangerous. Let it be.*

Toad laughed a little, wryly. "I suppose it would have been, yes. What a thing."

Lia finished cleaning Rooster, checked over Sin one last time, then stowed the grooming supplies away. Cilif had already led Blackie and the draft into the nearby stables.

She turned to look at Toad. "So tell me the truth, then," she said. "I suppose I should apologize first."

Toad's amusement faded to a dry weariness. "You only believed what you were told. I'll take the apology, but I was never really angry at you, Lia. Come." He motioned to the remaining horses. "We should bring them into the stables, yes? I think they have the stalls ready now. Cilif just waved at us."

Horses settled, fed, and checked over one last time, Lia and Toad joined Cilif outside on a wide bench to examine and oil tack. It was a peaceful task, broken only by occasional murmurs to look at a spot for a second opinion or a request to pass the oil bottle or rag. Lia watched for signs that Toad was looking for a chance to break away for a private conversation, but he seemed entirely content to work quietly.

Finally, Toad said, "I was born in Bright Bay." He lifted his gaze, looking south. "I left because I was a fool, and proud. Beyond that, you don't need to know. I wound up in Stecatr because I fell in love and followed the girl home. I managed to impress her enough that she disregarded her family's wishes and married me." His throat worked in a hard swallow. "Linera. Her name was Linera. She was ... she was *everything* for me."

Cilif's hands stilled. He cut the old man a sharp sideways look. "That's a rare love," he said.

Lia frowned, intensely uncomfortable. She hadn't intended to have this talk with an audience, and Toad was jumping straight into very personal matters, but she couldn't think of a way to protest without sounding childishly petulant.

Toad's mouth went tight, then relaxed. "I would have died for Linera," he said simply. "But I was still proud, and in my work as an apothecary I offended the wrong person, and so, instead, she died for me. Someone had intended to poison me. She drank it instead. And then I was blamed for killing her, and I —" He shut his eyes, bowing his head, and breathed hard for a few moments. At last he went on, "I was so angry, wild with anger. I made things much worse, and put the seeming of guilt around my own neck. And so." He motioned vaguely at himself, a sweeping, head to foot sort of motion. "I managed to escape actual hanging, but I was forbidden to have anything to do with medicine ever again. The Church took half of my belongings as penance, Linera's family took most of the rest, and I fell into whatever work I could find to keep a meal in my stomach and a roof over my head come winter. Storytelling always had been a side interest of mine, so I took that up. It worked out well enough."

"Did you ever find out who'd tried to poison you?" Cilif asked interestedly.

Toad cut a glance at Lia. "I believe so," he said. He hesitated, then, slowly, went on: "I'd found out something dangerous involving the head of the grayhands. I believe he ordered —"

Lia stood up, dropping the bridle in her hands onto the bench.

"*No*," she said. Not loudly, but definitely. "Don't even try that, old man. Don't you dare. That's a *lie*."

Toad looked up at her, expression sad but set. "This is why I never told you before."

"You're a fucking *liar*," she said, then turned on her heel and walked away.

Lia walked, seething with fury. The town was far too small to contain the number of strides she needed to take. She found herself headed out into the tangled forest, following what might have been human paths. She'd never taken much interest in learning about tracking, and had no idea of local wildlife in any case.

Her skills were more city-based. She could scale the side of a building in Stecatr and dance across the rooftops, swing through an open window or shimmy up a lattice to a safe observational post. At least, she'd *been* able to, when smaller, skinner, and lighter. She still tried to stretch, still tried to stay limber, but resuming that sort of work, at the level she'd once done, really wasn't wise.

Liar. Scarpy had been right. Toad was manipulative, amoral, and entirely dedicated to himself above all else. He'd poisoned his wife, talked his way out of it, then hastily squirmed under the protection of sufficiently powerful people to avoid pursuit by anyone who disagreed with the official ruling. She'd been foolish to even consider trusting him.

Scarpy had saved Lia's family. He'd saved *her*, more than once. She'd have been put under lock and key by enraged parents or priests, if not hanged long since, if he hadn't intervened; but he'd arranged matters so that her family never heard the first whisper about the incidents.

A new, cynical voice in the back of her mind whispered that she wouldn't have *been* in danger if she hadn't been on errands for Scarpy in the first place, so it really was the least he could do to pull her out.

She shook her head, angry at herself for such a disloyal thought, then paused, looking at a gnarled old oak tree.

A leap brought her to the lowest branch, momentum swinging her up and around in a nearly perfect transition to sitting on the branch itself. She sat still for a few moments, balancing, catching her breath and testing the strain in shoulders and rib. No damage, just unaccustomed movement. Once the muscles relaxed again, she climbed to her feet, flexed her hands, then went up several more branches like an oversized squirrel.

Lia settled on a broad branch high above the ground, breathing hard and feeling ridiculously proud of herself. Her shirt and pants were smeared with bark and lichen, she'd ripped a fingernail nearly to the quick, and one ear stung hotly from just barely not missing a knobbly spot on the trunk. But she was *up*, up high and alone, isolated and safe in a way she hadn't enjoyed in years.

Lia leaned back against the trunk of the tree and looked up at the sky, letting herself rest in the clean blue for a time. Inexorably, her thoughts turned back to what she'd just heard.

You only believed what you were told….

The pain in the old man's voice when he spoke of his dead wife had been absolutely genuine. His tone had caught her like a hook under the ribcage and nearly pulled her heart out.

If Toad loved his wife that much, that deeply, all these years later, how could he have killed her in a fit of jealous rage, or to get her out of the way, or any of the dozen other reasons gossip had ascribed to the deed? Human emotions might be tangled, complicated things, but within that plummeting depth of conviction — no. Toad wouldn't have killed his wife for anything less than a direct command from the gods, and even that he'd have fought bitterly.

If *he* hadn't killed his wife….

Lia scrubbed a hand across her eyes. Bits of bark and dirt cascaded across her face from the debris embedded in her hand, and she spent some time frantically clearing out her eyes while balancing on a suddenly far too narrow branch. Finally settled again, blinking hard through watery, sore eyes, she found herself reluctantly poking at the question.

Maybe, just *maybe*, someone had accidentally killed his wife in an attempt to get at Toad. That didn't mean the someone had to be Scarpy. He'd never approved of poison.

That cynical voice prodded at her: *Are you sure about that?*

She stopped, frowning at her hands, and began to carefully brush debris from her skin as she considered. What had Scarpy actually *said* about poison?

Never trust someone who's used poison to kill. He'd also said, more than once, *Poison is a woman's weapon.*

A woman's weapon….

Had the intent been to blame Toad's *wife* for the poisoning?

Lia stopped picking at the debris, shocked nearly breathless at the thought. That would have worked. Gossip already said she'd had a lover, that Toad had killed her in retaliation. Gossip said that the priests had understood that sort of anger enough to forgive him the crime.

They wouldn't have forgiven a woman wanting her husband out of the way so that she could have her lover by her side. She would have hung, alongside whatever man seemed the likeliest candidate, regardless of any protests of innocence. Even if she'd been released, she'd be ruined forever. Nobody would ever believe anything she said … just as nobody believed anything Toad said these days. In that regard, who'd actually died was irrelevant. If the goal had been to silence Toad and prevent his wife from speaking whatever she might have known, it had been successful.

And … Scarpy hadn't *said* he'd never use poison. He'd told Lia not to use it. He'd said not to trust anyone who used it. But he'd never *clearly* and *definitively* spoken to whether *he* would use poison himself. Or whether he might direct that it be used. One thing Lia knew very well indeed was that Scarpy delighted in splitting words into fine threads.

What had Toad found out? What could possibly have been that dangerous?

Oh gods. I actually believe him.

Lia leaned back against the trunk of the tree, eyes once more swimming with tears of an entirely different agony.

What do I do now?

Chapter Fifty

"That nightmare," Tank said, and stopped.

Dasin looked up, his hands stilling. He'd been sorting through his packs, frowning and grumbling to himself. He didn't say anything in response, just straightened his back and gave Tank his full attention.

Tank looked out the inn window, studying the trees. The glass was thick, and flawed enough to distort the view into a near abstraction. "It was about you."

Dasin drew in a deep breath, let it out, but remained otherwise silent.

"I was being hunted by bloodbirds. And you threw me to them. You wanted them to eat me." Tank cleared his throat, feeling foolish. In the light of day, the dream sounded absurd, and not at all worthy of his panicked waking response.

The room smelled faintly of apple vinegar and lingering pipe smoke; the wooden walls held several scars, as though from a fight, and the bedspread showed two old, irregular stains. For all that, it was still one of the better rooms at this particular inn.

Dasin sat down on the bed, a deliberate move to put himself lower than Tank. They'd been together long enough for Tank to understand small motions like that clearly. He still didn't say anything.

Tank looked down at Dasin, expecting mockery. To his surprise, Dasin was regarding him with clear sympathy.

"It's been a hell of a road," Dasin said quietly. "I haven't been the kindest partner, maybe." He looked down at the thin blanket he sat on, one hand twisting it gently, then let it go and returned both hands to his lap. "We've both told each other a lot of lies over the years, haven't we? Lies of sand and lies of stone, as the saying goes."

Tank stared, unsure how to respond to that. Once more, *What the hells did Evkit do to him?* ran through his mind. This was supremely unlike Dasin.

Dasin watched Tank's face, his own expression briefly miserable. "I'll give this another try, I suppose. He told me the truth," he said. "Evkit did, I mean. About Aerthraim family and the katha villages." He looked at the bedspread again, tracing one of the old stains with a finger, then straightened his back and neck and met Tank's gaze again. "You knew. And you didn't tell me."

Another try? But that question could wait. Tank's neck muscles strained with the need to look somewhere, anywhere else.

"*What* did he tell you," Tank said. Not a question, but a flat, hard statement that admitted, in itself, how bad this was.

Dasin's voice was as level as he said, "Aerthraim Family created the katha villages. To see if they could —" He stopped, breath rough, then went on: "If they could create desert lords without ha'reye involved. Because since emotional and physical pain is *apparently* an integral part of the *fucking* blood trials, it might be the key to unlocking —" He stopped again, as though unable to continue; crumpled the blanket in both hands, then forced out a bitter ending: "— *abilities.*"

Tank didn't say anything. Couldn't, against that acid rage.

"And *godsdamn* them, apparently they were *right*, or at least right *enough*," Dasin said. He made as though to rise, pulling the blanket along; glanced down at his hands, let go, then sank down again. He tilted his chin defiantly high and glared at Tank, a hot gleam in his eyes.

"Yes," Tank said. It didn't seem a good time to add: *And too godsdamn many were broken beyond repair along the way.* He'd known several such. Their blankly witless stares frequently featured in his nightmares.

Dasin glared, white-faced, as though he'd heard that thought. All he said aloud was: "And you didn't tell me any of that."

"No." Without apology. There was no point. No words to salve this.

"Why?"

It was a simple, flatly spoken word, with no anger, no grief, no emotion at all. Tank found himself floundering in the face of it. He'd expected this moment, always inevitable, to involve a good deal more shouting *at* him, but while Dasin was showing plenty of emotion, it seemed oddly muted, with a sense that repetition had dulled the edge. Which was ridiculous, because this conversation had never happened before.

Something stirred, protesting that thought, then faded to silence.

At last, Tank said, "It would have hurt you too much."

Dasin showed his teeth in something less than a smile. "Your idea of pain doesn't match mine, Tank," he said. "I'd rather have had the truth, years ago, than find out I've been working for people who could do *that.*"

Tank lifted a shoulder resignedly. "You had the pieces, same as I did. I figured you didn't want to see it."

Dasin's anger faded. "No," he said. "I didn't have the same pieces you did." He bent his head and said nothing for a while.

Tank stood still, waiting. The conversation wasn't finished.

At last, Dasin said, not looking up, "Teilo worked me over. She didn't like some aspects of my ... temper." He paused again, his head moving in a slow, unsteady sweep, then sat up and met Tank's eyes. "She cut my memories off. A *lot* of my memories. I remembered enough to be angry. I remembered enough for their purposes. But what she blocked out wound up crippling me. They only kept me alive because *you* liked me, and they needed *you*. I was a reserve ... a reserve weapon ... against you. Just in case." His voice failed. He bent his head again.

Tank's blood nearly congealed. "Evkit couldn't possibly know any of that. He was winding you up."

Dasin sat up, his expression so cold and hard that Tank went back a reflexive step. "No. He didn't *tell* me anything. He just gave me my memories back. I *remember*."

An abrupt awareness of danger backed Tank up another step, a dagger in his hand before he quite knew he was drawing it. Dasin's upper lip quirked in a not-quite smile. He raised a hand, and Tank froze, unable to move.

"I was maybe ten, I think, when I — changed, triggered, whatever you call it," Dasin said, voice flattening out, losing all accent and inflection. The small hairs along Tank's arms and the back of his neck prickled in painful reaction. "Felt like my brain was breaking in half. I nearly didn't survive it — the caretakers thought I'd had a stroke. They almost put me out on the street to die in a gutter." He laughed a little. "That was probably the first time I *made* someone do what I wanted, and I wasn't even conscious at the time. Anyway. After that, anyone who tried to hurt me ... I gave them the damage they'd have put onto me, then made them forget how it happened. Because that way, they'd come *back*."

Dasin dropped his hand. Tank's muscles released. He stumbled back another step, staring in outright horror.

"That's not possible," Tank said, scarcely audible. "That wouldn't have — not more than once or twice, it would've been noticed. And with that kind of — you could have *left* —"

Dasin let out a rough, coughing sort of laugh. "I didn't want to be noticed," he said. "Tank, I *liked* being there, once I realized what I could do. I *enjoyed* turning those fuckers inside out. I wouldn't have left with Allonin if they hadn't drugged me senseless, and I wouldn't have stayed with the Aerthraim but for Teilo wringing my brain sideways before I could wake up."

"No," Tank said, utterly appalled. "No. Evkit fucked with your head, he put all this on you, it's not — it's not real, it's not *possible*." He felt as though his chest were fracturing around his increasingly ragged breathing.

Dasin, expression mild now, watched him struggling for a few moments, then said, "This is too much for you, isn't it."

"You're *not* — you're not like that," Tank insisted. His legs gave out from under him, the dagger dropping from his hand. He sat on the floor hard, staring up at Dasin in a dull haze. Thought simply stopped, held by a fierce band of gray silence. He wasn't even sure, from moment to moment, what had upset him so badly, and the slashes of clarity felt like knives carving through his flesh.

"It's too much for you," Dasin said, and sighed. "All right. At least this time went better than in Arason; I was able to say more before you broke. Maybe my third attempt will be the key. Forget what I've said, Tanavin. Forget. Stand up, pick up your dagger, put it away. There you go, everything's all right. Breathe, breathe easy and forget. I'd never hurt you, you know that. Dasin can be trusted, of course he can be trusted. Foolish, brittle, *weak* Dasin, you know he couldn't possibly ever be a threat. Relax into that, you're safe. There. Good. So. Let's start again." He cleared his throat ostentatiously. "I didn't have the same pieces you did, Tank, but I should have figured it out. You're right."

Tank blinked once, twice, not sure why his eyes were wet. He swiped away the dampness, cursing himself for showing weakness, and said, "I should have told you. I'm sorry."

Dasin, looking drawn and tired, said, "Forgiven. I don't want to talk about this any more. I need to look over the books and do a good bit of planning. Would you go check around for news and gossip?"

Tank stared, unsettled. Dasin had been so angry, a few moments ago, and now seemed nearly drained of emotion. The conversation couldn't be over yet, could it? There had to be more.

"I'm fine, Tanavin," Dasin said irritably, the old name a clear warning not to push. "Don't hover. Go. I need news. That's more important than old matters."

Tank hesitated a moment, unsure and anxious, then shrugged and said, "Anything in particular you want me to dig into?"

Dasin's mouth twisted in a moment of mocking humor. "Rebellion, religion, and routes."

Tank left without a backward look; wondering, dimly, why his back began to twitch the moment he turned away from Dasin.

Chapter Fifty-one

Toad sat in a patch of sunlight, eyes closed and chin tilted to expose more of his thin face to the warmth. He didn't open his eyes as Lia approached, nor when she sat down just out of arm's reach on the long bench.

"So," he said. "You've climbed a tree and cursed me to the hells and back, and then realized I was telling the truth."

"...Yes," she said, more than a bit startled.

"Climbing something is your usual way of handling upset," Toad said serenely. "You'll remember, please, I've known you all your life." His chin dropped. He opened his eyes to shoot Lia a sideways glance. "Besides, you're all over bark bits."

"Oh," she said, feeling stupid.

"'Oh'. Indeed."

"You've changed," she said impulsively. "You're different, in Stecatr."

Toad's eyes slid closed. He said, in a perfectly bland voice, "In a town where my reputation is lower than that of a whore's, where I'm constantly vulnerable to the Church's whims, where small children feel free to pelt me with stones and debris on the basis of adult gossip? In the place where I lost my wife, my profession, my home? A place where I'm barely a step from living in the gutter at any given time? How strange, that I should act different there."

Lia looked down at the ground, her lips tight. "All right," she said. "I've been unfair. I'm sorry."

Toad was silent for a time. At last, he sighed and said, "It's only what you were taught, Lia, and you've always been regrettably credulous in certain respects. I see that changing, and I'm glad of it. Are you going back?"

"Yes. I have to."

"You don't," Toad said, "but I understand why you think you do." He bent his head, rubbing the back of his neck without opening his eyes.

"Why are *you* going back?" Lia said impulsively. "Why not stay south, somewhere without all that — mess?"

"Because Jener lied to me, after I warned him not to," Toad said. He straightened, glancing around. "Because … it's complicated. Let's walk, please. I don't like to sit still too long, my joints get stiff."

Lia rose and followed the old man, at a casual pace, from the stables to a winding footpath that ran round the village. Holly trees and burning-bush dotted the area, with stretches of sunflowers — surprisingly few of which had been bent or broken by the storm — tall, tufty grasses, and brambly roses. The holly trees formed a definite line between the beginning of Hells Hill and the village proper. The roses tended towards a stunning shade of orange-gold, and were very large. Lia idly considered trying to bring her mother a cutting. Maybe Dasin would have some ideas on how to keep it alive.

"My wife was very ill," Toad said. "A wasting disease. Nothing I did helped. The Church healers said there was nothing to be done. I was desperate enough to look for unusual solutions, and found an old book of notes from a ketarch, which is what southerners call their enclaves of healers. Most of the ingredients were easy enough to find, but some were … strange. Distasteful." He paused, gaze briefly distant, then went on. "I made the mistake of asking around about them anyway. I soon had a visit from a Church goldrobe to warn me off my inquiries. I didn't respond to that well." His expression hardened. "Next I knew, my wife had died and I was up on charges for poison."

"How does Scarpy come into this?" Lia asked, frowning.

"He was the one to give me the book," Toad said. "He warned me not to talk to anyone about it, but I was so frantic … I broke my word on that, without hesitation, and only realized the severity of my error when the goldrobe showed up. He pressed me for my source and laid down threats, and I'd no sooner thrown him out than a grayhand showed up to tell me how angry Scarpy was at me for getting the Church involved. I threw *him* out, too, which was the larger mistake." He sighed, wrapping his thin arms over his chest, and looked up at the sky.

"How do you know it wasn't the Church that poisoned your wife, then?" Lia said, faint hope flaring in the back of her mind.

Toad smiled without humor. "Because the book disappeared the same day she was poisoned," he said. "I had it well hidden. In its place was a grayhand marker. A gray diamond with a bold 'x' in the center. You know perfectly well what that mark means."

It wasn't a death note, but it was damn close. Lia drew in a hissing breath. So the poison hadn't been intended to kill. Linera taking it, and reacting badly, had been entirely and horribly an accident.

Toad stopped to examine a double bloom on a rosebush, his fingers gentle around the huge flower. "Linera loved roses," he murmured, stroking a petal lightly, then sighed and released the plant. Waving Lia back into motion, he said, "Indeed. Not entirely conclusive, but enough for me then and now. After my trial, Jener approached me, and I've been working with him ever since. He's kept me from the streets in exchange for a bit of … creative story acquisition, let's say."

"Spying, let's say," Lia said dryly. Toad shrugged.

"It's no more than Scarpy's had you doing, my girl," he said. "Although I've probably done a bit more thieving along the way than you, from what I've seen, and I'm the better at spreading rumors." He smirked.

Lia let that go. "So what were you doing in Bright Bay? What errand did Jener have you run?"

Toad paused to look at a nodding sunflower, smiling; reached up, going to his tiptoes, to touch the lowest edge. Coming back down to stand square, he said, "I went to see my family. I have two nephews who became orphans not that long ago, and I felt myself bound to offer them whatever assistance I could. They turned out to be more capable than I expected, and already had matters well in hand by my arrival. I was ready to bring them back to Stecatr with me."

Lia studied his face carefully and decided that he was telling the truth. "But that's not all you were there for," she said, unwilling to tell him that she'd actually seen his meeting with the southerners.

Toad pointed towards the ground. Lia looked, and found a scrawny, splotchy cat curled up under a bush, watching them curiously.

"Pay more attention to the moment, Lia," Toad said. "You might be less anxious if you do."

"I'm not anxious!" she protested. Then, hearing the defensive whine in her own voice, she grimaced and muttered, "Whatever."

Toad laughed a little, then sobered. "No, I wasn't there just for family. Jener financed my travel in exchange for meeting some of his contacts along the way. He's been building a very efficient information network over the past few years. Yes, I know Scarpy's been doing that as well, and yes, I've been spiking his efforts as often as I could." Catching her expression, he made a dismissive gesture with one hand. "*You've* no standing to scowl at *me*."

She shrugged, reluctantly ceding the point. They came to the end of the meandering path; ahead lay a small, dilapidated shed and cow pasture. Without a word said, they turned and went back the way they'd come.

Toad said, "I've gone as far as Arason in his name before, but he never trusted me to go further. When I said I was headed to Bright Bay, though, he said he'd finance bringing my nephews back if I would do a task or two for him. And hinted that he could restore my good name. At the least, restore my ability to work as an apothecary."

The cat was gone from its spot. Lia made herself stop and look up at the sunflowers, inhaling the powdery aroma of dirt and pollen in the air.

Toad pinched a leaf from a bush and began tearing it into pieces as they resumed walking. He said, "I've very much missed being able to help people."

"And the medicine?"

"Yes. It's one of the ingredients I'd asked about, before." Toad's hand moved in vague indication. He dropped the leaf, deliberately pausing to step on it as though venting temper with the motion, then spoke rapidly, as though wanting to get the words out before she could interrupt: "Jener knew I wouldn't be able to resist a chance at acquiring some. He said he'd been inspired by my interest, and had found a source, *coincidentally* from the same people he wanted me to carry a message to. In combination with the other ingredients, in the recipe from that book, it would create a powerful anti-toxin. Not against external poisons, but against internal ones. It could have cured the foul humors that were killing my wife before she was poisoned. And I've met so many in dire health over the past years."

He started walking again, avoiding Lia's gaze.

"What's the name of that bush?" Lia asked, carefully neutral, pointing to a small shrub with mottled red and green leaves.

Toad gave it an indifferent look. "Variant of burning bush," he said. "Looks like someone's experimenting with combining varieties. I don't know why anyone would bother. No medicinal uses. Hardly even attractive. Now that —" he pointed to a holly with blotches of white on its leaves, "*that* is an unusual pattern."

He bent to examine it, muttering to himself, and finally plucked a leaf before coming back to Lia's side. He began tearing it apart, with precise care, as they started walking again.

Toad went on, "Jener said he had a copy of the ketarch book. He said we'd create the cure, that he saw the value of saving lives, that I deserved to be reinstated as an apothecary and together, we could change Stecatr for the better. Gods help me — damnit —" He shook out one hand, grimacing, and examined it. "Ouch. I know better. — I believed him. He can be very charming, Lia, and I wanted to believe him *so* badly. I'm a fool."

Lia couldn't tell how much of that last comment was aimed at pricking himself with a holly leaf. She found it hard to believe the dour old man she'd known her whole life was secretly an idealist. But she'd also never expected Toad to be so tenderly interested in plants.

Toad dropped the shredded holly leaf, but didn't step on it this time. He wiped his fingers on his tunic, briefly checking his hand again. "No blood. Good. I was suspicious, of course, after meeting those southern witches, so I took the medicine to the healer at the edge of the Forest, who told me it was legitimate. He did warn me that, like any strong medicine, the ingredients can be dangerous. He told me to keep it close, and to be sure of the ethics of anyone I gave it to. The hadinn ... apparently knew I carried it, and objected to its presence in his territory."

He glanced over his shoulder, gave a nervous twitch, then jerked his gaze back around and knotted his hands together before him.

"What's the medicine called?" Lia prompted, but Toad shook his head.

"That's not your never mind. It's not something anyone but a properly trained apothecary should ever handle." He paused, considering a stand of bright pink flowers with a small smile. "Coneflower," he said. "Blooming late. Very good for several medicines...." He started walking again. "I knew the package wasn't safe to give to Jener, by that point. I was planning out a lie, to tell Jener that I hadn't gotten anything from the southerners.

I thought to develop the medicine myself. I told myself I could source the remaining ingredients, create it in secret. Wishful thinking. Never would have worked. The hadinn came up with a better idea."

Lia once more made herself stop in a patch of sunlight to look at the bushes and flowers, breathing in a swirling cinnamon smell she couldn't quite source. Toad smiled serene approval. The cat appeared, stalking across the path before them without glancing their way, and disappeared into the undergrowth once more.

The pauses were, actually, restful. Lia felt her frayed nerves soothing. "What was the hadinn's idea?" she asked, beginning to walk again, more slowly than before.

Toad matched her new pace. "He replaced it with something visually identical but entirely neutral. It might as well be table salt. But it's in the wrappings and under seal exactly as before, even better than after the comosain put it back together. Jener won't be able to tell it's been swapped out. Hopefully." He snorted. "I'm not certain that Jener won't blame me regardless, but at least the worst harm to come would be my own death, and that's years overdue already."

"I'm not sure I'd trust … the hadinn," Lia said with care.

Toad shook his head minutely, cutting his eyes to one side. "The hadinn is an honorable man," he said, not raising his voice, "and he gave his sworn word. Explicitly. And as I said, if I die … well, so I do. There are none left to mourn me, after all."

Lia kept her expression mild against the itch to glance around. The old man was being paranoid. Surely there wouldn't be teyanain — teyanin? — spies lingering about *here*? Why under the fair and dark faces of the Four would any of the teyanain be lurking to watch Toad?

Her shoulders went back at a new thought. Not Toad, perhaps, nor herself, but *Tank* was certainly odd enough to be a source of interest. Perhaps the teyanain were keeping an eye on Dasin as well, because of whatever had happened in the Hackerwood. Then there was that very strange priest, who could bring flames to his hands without burning his fingers.

Yes, quite probably they *were* being watched.

"Wonderful," she muttered, not realizing she'd spoken aloud until Toad gave an abrupt bark of laughter.

"Yes, well," he said, grinning now. "You're seeing the shape of things, I expect. Took you long enough, but you got there in the end. You were quicker to catch up threads in Stecatr, but that's a fairly small world, and closed in on itself. The wider world is more complicated. You'll learn."

They reached the end of the trail, once more back where they'd started. Toad knelt, touching the ground, and murmured something Lia couldn't make out, then stood, brushing off his pants.

He looked at her, expression entirely placid. "Do you have any messages?"

She stared at him blankly.

"For your family," he clarified. "I'm headed up the road with that mad priest to Stecatr. You're bound to Assiasan, yes? So, I'll arrive well before you. Messages?"

She opened her mouth, shut it again, then said, "That wouldn't be wise, I don't think."

"Perhaps not," he said, unruffled, "but I'm as secure a messenger as any News Rider, now that we've sorted out the misunderstandings between us. Perhaps more so."

"Scarpy would have you *gutted*," she said without meaning to say it quite so brutally. "Don't go near my family, Toad. They're under Scarpy's protection, and there's no way he'd believe you benign."

"I never said I was benign," the old man retorted with a surprising flash of temper. "And my *name* is Ebeza Nahonna. I'm thinking it's about time I reclaimed myself, all things considered."

"*Nahonna?*"

"It's a name," he said, cutting her off with another warning squint. She hesitated, dearly wanting to push for answers; in that momentary pause, Toad bowed stiffly, then spun on his heel and stalked away.

"Nahonna," she said under her breath. "Fucking *hells*."

She thought back to Toad's casual remark about *relatives in the south* and *none left to mourn me*. But he hadn't said a word, in the Hackerwood, about Isrin; nor had he been anywhere in sight during the confrontation with the Nahonna craftsmen in Obein. It didn't make sense.

There would be time to think it all through later. Lia stretched briefly, cracked her knuckles, then went to check their supplies for the next stretch of road.

Chapter Fifty-two

Some two days' travel from the small village at the foot of Hells Hill, the road split once again: the sharply northeastern Hills Road to Assiasan, and the North Road, which ran northwest to Stecatr.

Toad — *Ebeza*, he'd announced with startling determination — and Kolan said their farewells at that fork, the former visibly uneasy about his traveling companion, the latter as vague-eyed and absent-minded as Tank had ever seen him. More surprisingly, Lia seemed unhappy to see Ebeza go. Apparently they'd finally had that talk they'd needed to plow through, and relevant wounds had healed. Shoving them together had worked after all. Tank felt a little smug over that.

Wasn't properly any of his business, but *damn*, Tank was curious. One day, maybe, he'd ask. Not now. He had to pay attention. The Hills Road was the longest and second most dangerous leg of the run, nearly as treacherous as the Hackerwood, although for far more ordinary reasons.

Where the North Road ran in a fairly straight line to Stecatr, the Hills Road looped and twisted around immovable obstacles on the way to Assiasan. It was a road with many small villages, each one as likely to be holding its own local celebration, on any given day, as to be holding a funeral.

As they rolled into the first village, Thentree, it became clear both were happening: incense laden smoke billowed from a funeral pyre set at the edge of a steep cliff, merry chants following in its wake.

"Oh!" Lia said, perking up. "I've heard of this! I always wanted to see —" She sobered at the frown Cilif aimed her way. He'd begun growing his beard out, as he always did on this stretch of trail, and it gave him a more menacing look than usual. "Er. Didn't mean to be disrespectful."

Dasin angled the wagon aside once the road broadened out, then stopped, waving everyone to come up to him. His face was oddly grim and strained, and he glanced frequently at the plume of smoke as he said, "This is bad timing."

"No sales, for one," Tank agreed, in part to catch Lia up and in part to see Dasin glower at him. To his surprise, Dasin just shrugged one shoulder in a distracted motion.

Dasin said, "Cilif, go check the stables and inn to make sure of our welcome. Tank, take Lia and go find out who's being sung down. I'll start going through the gift piles." He locked the wagon brake, looped the reins around the bench hook, and swung down to the ground.

Cilif trotted off without comment. Tank dismounted, motioning Lia to do the same. The roads by the funeral cliff weren't suitable for any horse larger or less agile than a mountain mule. They looped the reins over the wagon hooks, one to each side, keeping the wagon between the two horses to avoid fights.

"If it's Jein, we're in trouble," Tank observed in parting. Dasin only shrugged again and turned away.

"Who's Jein?" Lia asked as they began to walk.

The southern edge of Thentree, where Dasin had stopped, was a wide plateau heavily dotted with scrub and boulders. Three other merchant wagons were arrayed to the other side of the road, their occupants clearly also taking stock of the funeral ahead. To Tank's right, the wide road narrowed and dropped down a set of steep rock stairs, then climbed considerably higher without widening in the least. Cilif's path would lead him along the much easier public route to the large commons area, bracketed by inn, stable, News Rider post, and shops. Outsiders didn't go into the village past the commons. There was no reason to, and little welcome from the locals if they tried.

"Jein's the local ... I suppose liaison is the best word ... between the locals and outsiders," Tank said. He began descending the steps with care, one hand on the chill stone wall to their left and as always doing his best not to look at the right side drop. Here, it was little enough of a tumble over rocky scree; further up, once they began to ascend again, it would be increasingly dangerous. He'd found it best to start by not looking and keep to that the whole way.

From behind him, Lia said, "Will we be welcome to go poking our noses in, then?"

Tank smiled, pleased at how quickly she'd jumped past the obvious questions to the important one. "I will, yes. And you're with me."

They came to the bottom of the descent, walked a few steps on reasonably flat ground, them began the knee-straining ascent. Tank had seen local children scampering up this and other sharp climbs like goats, shoving and wrestling for the lead in a way that put Tank's heart in his throat but won only a tolerant smile from their parents.

Thankfully, no children swarmed past this time; probably they were all at the funeral. Thentree, a typically pragmatic Hill Road village, set a play area aside at funerals for easily bored children.

"You don't like heights, do you?" Lia observed a bit tartly.

"Not particularly. I mostly don't like the *down* part." Tank motioned with his right hand to the ever-steeper drop to that side, careful not to look.

Lia laughed a little, not unkindly, and said, "There are climbs like this in Stecatr without any wall to either side."

"Those come up along the Hills Road too," Tank said. "And in Assiasan. Some I have to go up sideways, my feet don't fit properly on the damn stairs otherwise. Not at all fond of those."

"I could see that," Lia agreed. "What —"

Tank made a quelling motion with his right hand. "I need to focus, Lia," he said. "Talk once we're on level ground again."

"All right."

They labored upwards in silence, Tank stopping on occasion to catch his breath. His thighs and calves burned by the time they reached the top, and he could feel a stitch trying to start in his side.

Lia stepped around him, entirely unwinded, and surveyed the area with bright interest. "This is gorgeous," she remarked.

Tank moved a few careful paces away from the cliff edge and turned to follow her gaze. Rocks, arranged in carefully balanced stacks, traced out a rough, labyrinthine path that swirled around a large pile of flowers and herbs. The source of the greenery was immediately apparent: a lush garden ran wide and deep not far past the labyrinth, riotous with dozens of flower varieties and even more herbs.

"That's the Ash Garden," he said, motioning, and was pleased once more to note Lia's quick glance towards the still-rising smoke and her nod of immediate understanding. "Everything up here is dedicated to use for funeral rites," he added, and waited, patiently, while she turned in place, examining the *everything* scattered across this plateau: the keeper's cottage, sheds, piles of wood, piles of flat, slate-like stone; sleds of various sizes and harnesses, a garbage pit, a latrine, and a much wider path than the one they'd just climbed, bordered with knee-high stone walls, leading at a gentle slope up towards the smoke.

"Extensive," she said at last, then looked at him inquiringly.

"They take it serious. Not grim, but serious, and they're slow to forgive outsider mistakes, so let me talk and keep your face quiet."

He turned towards the walled path into the plateau. The locals called it a bridge, in spite of it being on completely solid ground. The steep downward and upward stairs had been the first part of leaving the ordinary world behind. This area was a reflection and resting point, then one crossed the bridge to bid the departed on towards their chosen god.

Tank briefly considered warning Lia about that particular custom, as it was likely to shock or even offend her. A surge of irritation stopped the words in his mouth. She wasn't sworn to Stecatr any longer, and she'd leapt far beyond the right to get upset over theological differences. So he left it at the one comment and crossed the metaphorical bridge without looking back.

Chapter Fifty-three

Stecatr sat higher in the mountains than this small Hills Road village, but Lia could see definite similarities. The tight, steep climbs, for one; the sense of *old*, for another, as though human habitations were nothing but anthills, soon to be swept away. Stecatr, too, laid out their funeral grounds on a high plateau, with a dedicated garden, a bridge path, and pyres at the four god-corners of the funeral square.

There were also most definitely differences. In Stecatr, smaller pyres, sometimes only braziers, sat in the corners, with the actual funeral pyre in the center. Here, there were four equally sized squares, with a sunken pool in the center. The pyre to the northwest blazed high, nothing more than wood at this point, the body long since subsumed.

Braziers smoldered in the remaining three corners; the deceased had apparently been commended to Eki, the god of cold, wind, and malice. It didn't speak highly of the departed.

Lia wasn't sure how long funerals lasted here. In Stecatr, it depended on how important the deceased had been in life. Poor commoners might get a day, enough to reduce the earthly shell to bones for the *kophas*. The pyre for someone as important as the Lord of Stecatr would burn for ten days, with accompanying chants and hymns.

A scattering of mourners stood in the square, most of them grouped around the pool and singing in clear, loud voices. Now and again one or another knelt, falling silent, and washed their hands in the pool; drank from a waterskin, washed their hands again, then stood, resuming their song.

Tank drew Lia to a halt a respectful distance away. "Not Jein," he said quietly. "That's him to your left, sideways to us, big man with white hair. At a guess, his nephew's the one on the pile."

"I take it he wasn't a particularly nice man?" Lia said in as low a tone.

Tank shot her a sideways half-smile. "A bit on the selfish side, yeah."

She didn't smile back.

Jein glanced their way. His shaggy white eyebrows went up. Without a break in his singing, he raised a hand, beckoning to the mourners at the edge of the square. A thin young woman came forward, then moved past him; knelt to dip her hands in the pool, then stepped into Jein's spot as he moved back, her voice rising to take over his lines without a missed moment.

Jein knelt and wet his hands, then dabbed water on his face, collarbone, chest and stomach before standing and working his way over to Tank and Lia.

He was, indeed, a big man, taller and broader than Tank, with a ferociously bushy white beard and thick, curly white hair. His skin held a charcoal hue, and his dark eyes were thoughtful as he cast an assessing glance at Lia.

"*S'e* Tank," he said, offering a shallow bow which Tank returned. "Day's blessings."

Lia could easily see him holding forth, with that deep, resonant voice, on sermon or fireside tale with equal magnetism.

"Day's grace to you and yours," Tank answered, then motioned to Lia. "*S'e* Jein, may I present *s'a* Lia of Stecatr Hall. She's replaced Gint, this trip. I take it that's your nephew, there?" He nodded to the flaming pyre.

"It is." Jein unhooked a waterskin from his belt, took a deep draft, and tucked it back away with a contented sigh. "Were you able to find a source for that fireweed oil I asked about?"

He was going to talk business at *graveside*? Lia did her best not to react, but a lifetime of strict training as to the respect due the dead betrayed her into a small sound of dismay. Jein looked at her again, a steady, unamused expression settling across his features.

Tank said mildly, "She's Stecatr, *s'e* Jein."

"Ah." Jein's mouth creased in a familiar contempt.

Lia's face felt washed in flame. She clamped her mouth shut against her first protest. Then she said, more loudly than she'd intended: "*No.*"

Both men looked at her, visibly startled.

"I'm not a child, and I'm not a fool, to be dismissed like that," she said.

An odd, growling reverberation rolled through the back of her mind. It felt like her father, glowering over her shoulder, angry on her behalf for once.

"The beliefs I grew up with may not be yours, but it's as rude to turn your nose up at mine as it is for me to yours." She paused, not at all sure that had come out clearly; the words felt tangled at the end. By Jein's narrowing eyes, she'd been clear enough, so she went on: "I *don't* know or understand your beliefs, but I'm open to learning so as to avoid giving offense in future."

A long silence, in which Tank, tight-lipped, glanced at Jein for a reaction and Jein looked only at Lia.

At last, Jein said, "I'd have liked seeing you face off with my nephew. He could have used a good cutting to size, and nobody here had the proper edge for it to hold more than a tenday. Not even me."

He bowed to her, as he had to Tank. She returned it, her teeth set in her tongue as a reminder to use caution on further words.

"I'm on the singing down until tomorrow night, but I'll break for dinner in another two hours," Jein said. "*S'e* Tank, bring the lot of you to the cottage. We'll talk more then." He lifted a hand and turned away.

Tank let out a long, quiet hiss of air, then touched Lia's elbow lightly. "Back to the wagon."

She put out a hand, stopping him. "I'll have that apology from you, here and now."

His expression went chill, blue eyes glittering like ice; he turned his back and walked across the bridge without answering.

Lia bit the side of her tongue, irritated, then followed, disinclined to make a scene at a funeral.

Tank moved more slowly on the downward slope than he had going up, and by the time they reached level ground again, his face was set in a near-permanent wince.

"It'll get better," he muttered, apparently to himself. "Always does, always does."

Dasin was sitting on a low stool beside the wagon, a line of small bags on a shallow tray at his feet. He seemed half-asleep, but looked up in sharp inquiry as they approached. Cilif was nowhere in sight.

Tank said, "Not Jein. His nephew. Northwestern pile."

Dasin let out a weary chuckle. "No surprise there. All right, then...." He looked at the arrayed bags, leaned over to pick up two, hesitated, then lifted a third. "How'd she do?"

"Add one," Tank said, not looking at Lia. "But she's invited to dinner, so not too badly."

Dasin made a disgruntled sound and scooped up another bag. "How much longer is it going to be?"

"The singing down ends tomorrow night," Tank said.

"Two days, then." Dasin rubbed at his chest, frowning.

Cilif sauntered into view, saddlebags slung over one shoulder and a satisfied expression on his face. "Got us all in," he announced as he drew within speaking range.

Dasin looked up, his thin eyebrows rising. "At the inn?"

"Well, no," Cilif admitted. He lowered his bags to the ground and squatted, elbows on knees. "Inn's full and two merchant parties are taking up the spare rooms in the old barn. But widow Afen has a room for me, Berran agreed to take you two if you'll do some odd jobs for him, and ... Guin has a spot for Lia." His mouth drew aside a bit on this last, and he didn't look at Lia. He added, hurriedly, "But the horses are all at the stable, and Degal is taking on the wagon like always."

Lia, catching the weight of that brief hesitation, said, "What's wrong with Guin?"

"Nothing," Dasin said, "but that he's the pyre-keeper. You'll be up on the funeral plateau."

"It's comfortable enough," Tank said. "I've taken his spare cot before. He doesn't even snore."

"Not during a funeral, you haven't," Dasin said, acerbic, then shook his head and handed the bags he'd chosen up to Tank. "Deliver these. Berran, two to Jein, and Guin.

Might as well settle Lia in while you're at it."

Tank glanced at the narrow stairs down, let out a thin, whining sound, then said, "I'll take her around through town." Lia was the only one to smile at that.

Cilif hauled himself to his feet. Almost absently, he moved forward and pulled Dasin up. Tank's chin rose, a sharp frown on his face. Dasin shook Cilif off, grumbling, but avoided Tank's gaze.

Lia bit her tongue and forced herself to turn away. She went to Rooster, who stood sleepily at the back of the wagon, and began unhitching him. After a moment, Tank, still scowling, did the same with Sin. The wagon dipped and shifted as Dasin clambered up to the bench, then again as Cilif swung up beside him.

"Walk them in," Tank said, more ice in his tone than she'd heard for some time, and thumped the back of the wagon three times. It creaked into motion.

Lia put herself between the two horses as they started walking. Tank did the same. Sin tossed his head once in annoyance at having someone walking on his off-side, then plodded on without further fuss.

The air was clear and warm, black and red birds wheeling and dipping in random patterns overhead. Her hair felt sticky from the heavy incense smoke on the funeral plateau, her nose nearly clogged with the aroma. She rubbed her nose roughly, as if that might shake the coating from her inner nostrils.

"Is there a bathhouse here?" she asked hopefully.

"No."

She looked sideways at that terse answer. "Are you always this pissy when you don't want to admit you fucked up?" she inquired.

Tank stopped walking and glared at her. Sin snorted, shaking his head as though annoyed by the pause. "Don't fucking push at me right now," he snapped.

"Whatever's up your ass, it isn't me," she snapped right back.

He let out a rough, growling sound; then, abruptly, moved around to the other side of Sin and swung up into the saddle. The big horse carried him around the wagon and out of sight in moments. Nobody called after him.

"I maybe could have phrased that better," Lia muttered to herself, and plodded on, irritation fizzing along her nerves.

Rooster let out a grumpy whuffling sound, breaking her mood into a startled laugh.

"Yeah, about like that," she told the rangy gelding, and went on with a lightened step.

Chapter Fifty-four

Between the pain in his legs and back, Cilif's increasingly familiar behavior with Dasin, and Lia's aggression, Tank was well and truly inclined to walk off on his own by the time they gathered at Jein's farmhouse for dinner. Only the triple surety that he'd enrage Dasin, badly insult Jein, and miss out on some excellent cooking forced him through the slightly crooked door.

Jein had built the farmhouse some fifty years past, with the help of neighbors long since gone to their own pyres. It was a tall building, set close against a steep hill to its west, with a high-lofted barn to the east; the small farm plot and grazing for his three milk goats were sheltered by a natural dell beyond the barn. Along the back of the house, a dense band of oak, holly, and ash offered protection from swirling storm winds and plenty of deadwood for smaller fires throughout the year.

Charcoal burners came twice a year to drag off larger fallen trees throughout Thentree to their own village, set well back from the road. The results sold at a pittance to locals and a much higher price to outsiders.

The aroma of roasted meat and rosemary drifted out through shutters and doors put wide open in welcome to any wandering spirits, living or dead, who might desire solace. The lower floor served as kitchen and gathering area, with Jein's work table currently pushed to one side, cleared of his carving tools and covered with tablecloth and dishes. Neatly fitted, straight oak planks made up the floors, topped by thick braided wool rugs of red and bronze. A long trestle table, which Dasin had helped design in a such a way as to fold away when not needed, dominated the center of the room.

Upstairs were the bedrooms for Jein and his three girls, whose mother had died shortly after the youngest was weaned. The girls were bright-eyed, energetic, and deceptively pretty; each and every one equally as capable of basting a chicken or mending a fence as of beating sense into a fool.

The eldest, Ilna, met Tank and his companions at the door, beaming. She had a sturdy, curvy build, with thick dark hair and bright green eyes. Tank couldn't remember ever having seen her cross, even when swinging a heavy skillet into an overenthusiastic drunk's face. Which she'd done twice in his sight, and narrowly avoided a third when Tank yanked Gint out of the taproom before matters could get that far.

"Tank!" Ilna crowed delightedly. She flung herself into his arms like a child, although they were very nearly the same age, best as he could tell without being so rude as to ask.

He laughed, hugging her without any awkwardness, then handed her off to Cilif for the same affectionate greeting. Dasin, as always, fended the girl off with a grimace. Unbothered, she offered him a swift, cheerful bow, then cocked her head inquiringly at Lia.

"*S'e* Ilna," Tank said, "May I present *s'a* Lia of—" He caught himself barely in time. "Of Arason. Our latest hire." Unexpectedly, his stomach went sour, but the queasiness passed in moments, and he dismissed it from his mind.

"Much prettier than Gint," Ilna declared. Tucking her hand around Lia's elbow, she drew them all inside, where she lowered her volume considerably. "You can eat as you like," she informed Lia, not releasing her light grip. "Talk as you like, or go sit and be left alone as you like." She pointed out several chairs around the room, each one an example of her recital. "I don't know how it's done in Arason, but here, a funeral is a time of, well, reflection, I suppose. You've no requirement to be sociable, here in this space."

"That's a relief," Lia remarked dryly, glancing sideways at Tank.

Ilna, misunderstanding, said, "Oh, he's gotten much better." She grinned at Tank. "First time we met, he was so busy looking at *s'a* Ninie's bosom, he spilled a bowl of soup down it."

Tank cleared his throat loudly. Ilna's grin widened.

"No," she told him, "I'm never, ever going to stop teasing you about that. *S'a* Lia, are you hungry? This way, then." She tugged Lia away.

"Silver round that *they'll* be spending the night together," Cilif muttered, clearly amused. Tank shot him a dour glare, collapsing Cilif's smile into a scowl. "You and your moralizing," the mercenary grumbled.

"It's not something to *bet* on, you degenerate!" Tank retorted with unexpected heat. Another surge of uneasy acid ran through his stomach, fading as quickly as before.

Cilif smirked and walked off to collect a plate for himself.

Dasin had already eeled away, striking up a conversation with a stout woman with dark brown skin and hair set into long braids: Mena, a local herb woman, who'd put more than one medicinal blend together for Dasin's shelves. The two of them bartered and bantered for hours, every visit. A funeral wouldn't stop that.

Lia and Ilna, plates full, settled at the trestle table, already deep in conversation. Looking at the slightly stunned expression on Lia's face as she bore the full weight of Ilna's attention, Tank privately conceded that Cilif was likely right. His mood darkened even further, and he found himself turning towards the door with a half-formed notion of escaping and manners be damned.

Jein clapped him on the shoulder before Tank could take more than a step, his dark eyes shrewd. "Come on, then," he said. "Gather up a plate and a drink. There's wind wine over by the stove there. Let's go into the kitchen for a talk. You've news for me and I've some for you."

Tank's stomach lurched at the thought of food, but he forced an amiable smile and followed Jein into the kitchen, a carefully chosen plate of light foods in one hand and a mug of wind wine in the other.

Chapter Fifty-five

Lia rolled to her back, gasping. Ilna tugged a warm blanket up over both of them, breathing hard and chuckling. "Well, that was worth the time," she observed cheerfully.

Ilna's room was small, and very dark with the shutters closed. The house below was silent, everyone having gone back to the funeral plateau or away to their various families. Dasin and Cilif had left together. Tank had departed rather later, looking thunderously annoyed about something: probably Dasin.

Ilna had said, brightly, that she'd walk Lia up to the plateau, really it was no trouble.

Tank had glowered and walked out with only the briefest farewell. Lia faced a moment of reflexive, anxious embarrassment; then Ilna smiled and pressed another mug of wind wine into her hand, and Tank's mood didn't matter any more.

The door had barely closed behind the last person to leave before Ilna tugged Lia upstairs, both of them warm from wine and arousal alike.

Ilna wriggled against her now, tracing a hand along Lia's ribs. Lia captured the seeking fingers before they could hit a ticklish spot, or set off a stronger reaction, and said, "That was lovely —"

"If you thank me, I'll bite you," Ilna said, and caught Lia's earlobe gently between her teeth, unerring even in the dark.

Lia laughed, pulling away. She turned on her side. "No. But I can't stay here, can I, and it's already late."

"More's the pity," Ilna said regretfully. "All right." As Lia began to sit up, she added, "One moment — there!"

A lantern flared to life on the bedside table.

Lia froze, staring at the distance between Ilna, sprawled on her back, and the comfortably dancing flame. "You ... did you just do that?"

"Of course." Ilna rolled to prop herself up on one elbow, smiling. "I wouldn't have shown that to most outsiders, but you're from Arason, right?" Her smile faded as she searched Lia's face with increasing bewilderment. "It's a small trick. I didn't think it would be anything unusual for you...."

Lia made herself swallow back *I'm not Arason, I'm Stecatr, and that's witchery!* It was absurd for her to have that reaction, given all she'd seen and walked through on the way to this point. "I wasn't expecting it, that's all," she said, and made herself smile.

Ilna didn't return it, her expression grave.

"We should go," Ilna said, reaching for her clothes, and didn't say anything more the entire walk through town, nor along the long, broad road to the funeral plateau. Still mute, she steered Lia onto a side path, bordered by thick hedges, that discreetly circled the pyre grounds, cutting over to the ash gardens and the keeper's cottage.

The hymn currently being sung was one that Lia particularly liked, with multiple braided melodies that required skilled voices as leads, and the smoke drifting through the leaves had a warm, spicy aroma. If she'd been by herself, she'd have lingered behind the hedge for a time to enjoy both, but Ilna's brisk pace didn't allow for delays.

A tall, thin man in much-mended clothing sat on a wide bench outside the cottage, a lantern on a hook by the door catching glints from his auburn-gray hair. Cilif sat beside him, nodding as though half-asleep.

As Lia and Ilna emerged from the side path, the lanky man — presumably Guin — turned his head and stood, offering a bow. Cilif blinked awake, rubbing his face.

The hymn wound down, sliding without pause into a simpler, repetitive chant calling on the beneficent faces of all four gods. Long-handled torches burned to either side of the bridge path now. Lia thought they might be the source of the intriguing incense smell.

"There you are," Guin said. "You'll be *s'a* Lia, I take it? I'm Guin. Cot's all set up for you, fire's banked, there's lavender tea in the pot by the fire." Scrubbing a hand through his hair, he yawned enormously, cut a meaningful sideways glance at Cilif, then went inside himself, closing the door gently behind him.

"Good night, *s'a* Lia," Ilna said with precise courtesy, then turned away before Lia could do more than mumble a similar phrase.

Cilif chuckled and observed, "She likes blue basil. There's some flowering now in the Ash Garden, nobody'll mind if you cut a bit. You'll want to get back on her good side, if'n you're wanting to travel this road again."

He patted the bench beside him, more command than invitation. Lia sat down, too tired and annoyed to be polite. "What do you want, Cilif?"

"Dasin wanted to come up and sing," Cilif said. "We knew Jein's nephew well enough to stand a short turn. I'll do my bit come morning. Probably so will Tank." He yawned, himself, and scrubbed a hand over his face. "I hate those stairs. Bloody ceremonial nonsense. Feh."

Lia waited, silent.

"Yeah, well," Cilif said after a moment. "Yeah. So ... Dasin's sick, Lia. Real damn sick. And he don't want Tank knowing anything about it, which I've told him is being an ass, but he's not having it. He didn't say not to talk to *you*, though. So." He sighed and scratched his scruffy beard.

"He wasn't well in Isata," Lia said. "Something from the Hackerwood?"

"That far back?" Cilif set his hands on his thighs, frowning thoughtfully. "He came to me in Arason, asking for help keeping him out from under Tank's nose as much as could be done. He's wanted more distance, lately." Cilif paused, then added, "He's getting worse. I caught him coughing up blood on the way up to the singing."

Lia sat up straight, deeply alarmed. "You have to tell Tank!"

"Hells, no," Cilif said. "Nope, nope, and no. I am not taking on that particular beating. Don't you do it, either. I made him talk to the local herb-witch, earlier tonight. If there's anything to be done, she'll know it. Smart woman." He yawned again, covering his mouth this time. "Agh. I have to go pull Dasin out of the line and get him down to some sleep, or I'll be walking off the cliff."

Cilif stood, wobbling a bit, and absently put a hand down for Lia. She let him pull her to her feet. To her surprise, the motion brought her up against him, his arm wrapping lightly around to hold her in place. He rested his forehead against the top of her head, his scruffy beard barely noticeable at that angle.

Lia stood still, uncertain of how to respond. He smelled of dirt, and horse, and harsh soap; not particularly unpleasant, and she had no sense of any pressure or expectation. It felt, simply, like a moment of weariness and connection.

"You been a good influence, you bloody Stecatr bitch," Cilif muttered at last, then straightened. He looked down at her for a moment, expression grave. "You got up under his skin. Didn't think anyone but Dasin could ever do that. Maybe he'll finally get his head the rest of the way out of his ass." He let her go and stepped back.

She stared at him, completely confused. "I what?"

He flapped a hand at her. "Get some sleep. Two days, Dasin said, so sleep in if you can." He cast a grumpy look towards the orange-gold limned sky nearby, then headed for the bridge.

Lia sat still, trying to work through that very odd speech. Her jaw creaked under an unexpected yawn, and she admitted that clear thought was a lost cause right now. She'd think about it in the morning.

As she came to her feet, Guin swung the door open and stepped outside, frowning. Not at her; his head was tilted as though listening to something distant. "That's not good," he muttered. "Not good at all."

"What's not good?" she asked warily.

Guin barely spared her a glance. "Stay here," he said. "Go inside, latch the door. I'll be a while." He turned, leaning inside the cottage long enough to retrieve a battered hat, a lantern, and a stout walking stick, then walked off towards the bridge path without another word. He didn't bother to light the lantern first.

Lia hesitated, inclined to chase after him for no other reason than that he'd said not to; and how childish was that? Shaking her head at herself, she retreated into the cottage and dropped the bar across the door. It was all nothing to do with her, anyway. Just something going on at the funeral.

About to sit down on the cot, she froze.

Dasin wanted to come up and sing ... Dasin's sick. Real damn sick....

"Fuck," Lia said, and stood, caught between exhaustion and concern. At last, she swore again, using a handful of dialect words she'd learned from Tank and Cilif; set the bar aside, and went back out.

Realizing, after two steps, that the singing had *stopped*, she broke into a run.

Chapter Fifty-six

The air was cool, after hours in a room full of people. Tank drew in breaths of increasing relief as he strode along paths familiar enough to need no lantern. The Hills Road, while it might look, on a map, like the shortest leg of the road from Bright Bay to Assiasan, was very nearly the longest. Mainly because of the geography, which ran erratically from drop to rise, deeply vulnerable to bad weather; but also because the people here genuinely liked Tank and his crew, making it hard to ride through in any sort of haste. Two days a village was the minimum for courtesy, and with villages often less than a half day apart, that could make for a wearying long stretch of sociability.

Tank had delivered more than one child along this road, learning from harried midwives and alongside terrified fathers. He'd sat night watch over illness and injury, for animals as often as for humans. He knew every path in most of the Hills Road villages, and could walk many blindfold in a windstorm.

Another wave of ill-feeling hit. He veered to lean again a large mountain oak, his breath coming in ragged gasps, his stomach quivering like jelly. Feeling his forehead, he found no sign of fever. Either it hadn't struck yet or this was a matter of bad food.

The shakiness passed in a few more moments. He resumed walking, more cautiously than before and with an eye to good stopping points should another attack hit.

Well, if he *had* to fall ill, this was one of the best places to do so. There would be little to worry over as far as crew antics. Lia was never rowdy, and Cilif never started a brawl along this road. Without Gint's influence, Cilif had actually been considerably more sedate than usual this trip. Tank had been right in his choice to swap Lia in. He tucked that aside to throw in Dasin's face during their next petty fight.

Dasin, too, wasn't a concern on this leg of the trip. He'd never yet gone seeking trouble among the Hills villages, in part because the audience for his rougher preferences simply wasn't safely available in such small, tightly woven communities. One bit of gossip could destroy years of carefully built goodwill, forcing them to choose between abandoning Assiasan as a destination or risking the Plains Road.

Well, Dasin was surely losing Tank's goodwill in great dollops and blobs this time through. Even knowing that Cilif was entirely uninterested in sex barely blunted the edge of Tank's simmering irritation.

What would that lack of interest be called, anyway? *Ii? Io? Io'ka?* Tank hadn't even known it possible. He couldn't decide whether to pity or envy the man.

An odd weakness shivered through his legs. He stumbled to a nearby boulder and sat down heavily, panting a bit. Not a flu. Not bad food. Something else. Overtired, maybe.

Resolving the situation with Dasin felt far more important than worrying over a bit of exhausted twitchiness. There was something going on, something Dasin was keeping from him, and he'd drawn Cilif into the confidence he'd denied Tank.

I deserve better than that, damnit. After all I've done ... But he hadn't done it with expectation of *debt*, so it wasn't ... fair? No, not quite the right word. Right, that was the word: it wasn't right to complain in that vein.

Tank's legs steadied, the shaky flush fading from his body. He stayed seated for a time, looking at the stars, listening to the funeral chants, and trying not to acknowledge the brooding thought at the edge of his mind. It was like trying to ignore a horse stepping on one's foot.

He stood up, half-consciously hoping that walking would distract him, either through movement or a renewed nausea. A dozen steps later, the words very nearly printed across his vision, refusing to be denied any longer:

Dasin's getting ready to leave me behind.

Tank found himself crouched, hands splayed on the ground. He breathed in great gasps, shivering all over, unable to move. It wasn't a surprise, of course it wasn't in any way a surprise. He'd always known Dasin would walk away as soon as he was strong enough. Tank had been working *towards* that goal for years. Why would it hurt to see it near at hand?

Why *did* it hurt?

Tank forced himself to his feet, his breathing steadying. "Godsblessed fool, is what I am," he muttered, impatiently swatting his hands clean against his hips. "Need some sleep, is what."

He'd pull Dasin aside for a talk in the morning. No sense waiting on Assiasan for the conversation, no matter what Dasin might prefer; Tank didn't much care for the dance they'd been doing lately. At least he knew for sure that Cilif wouldn't let Dasin walk off without him, whatever fight might erupt. He'd be able to finish his obligation, get everyone safe to Assiasan, then step clear, if that was what Dasin wanted. Then....

... then what?

Dasin would go south to take up with Evkit, and Tank would go tamely on to Stecatr, to be the solution to someone else's self inflicted problems yet *again*....

Wait.

Dasin would go south to work for the man who controlled the *entire fucking Hackerwood*. What that would do to his Aerthraim Family standing —

Wait.

In order to work for Evkit, Dasin would have to abandon his allegiance to Aerthraim Family. No other road led from that decision.

Why am I so sure that's what he'll do? It felt like a solution to a missing equation, an absolutely correct answer without the right pieces in place to support it. *What have I forgotten? Why am I so sure I've forgotten something?*

Tank staggered sideways, fetching up against a stone wall hard enough to scrape furrows into the arm of his shirt; turned to rest his back against the wonderfully solid surface, and closed his eyes.

I didn't drink enough wine to be out of my senses like this. What the hells is wrong with me? I'm as mind-muddled as Kolan. No, not Kolan; Lia. She said something, back in ... Arason, it was Arason ... something important....

He ground his teeth together, fighting for recall. *Ah.*

I knew as soon as I woke up something was wrong ... I started picking at memories.

Tank drew in a sharp breath. "No," he said aloud. "No, he wouldn't have. He couldn't have."

He was abruptly and absolutely certain that this erratic oddness in his own head wasn't a recent development, wasn't from bad food or exhaustion. It had started ... Tank bore down on memory hard, forcing it clear.

In Arason. It had started in Arason.

Idisio. Had to be. *But how?*

The slightest use of ha'ra'hain abilities invariably triggered Tank into a violent rage. Idisio couldn't have altered Tank's memories so much. And he wouldn't. He *wouldn't*. Not to Tank.

He's a fucking ha'ra'ha. Of course he could, and would.

How was simple enough. Tank had walked right up to the shores of the Lake, where Idisio had damn near infinite power at his fingertips. It would have been the perfect time for Idisio to do anything at all, and take away the memory of it. Which could very well have damaged Tank's mind enough, even with the gentlest of intentions — as if ha'ra'hain even *understood* that concept as more than an abstraction — to explain the oddness he'd been feeling for days. The gaps in his memory.

"I'll fucking kill him," he muttered, and pushed upright, hands clenched. The journey lay clear in his mind: take Sin, never mind any explanations to anyone. Give the big horse his head, let them both run entirely loose, unchained, thundering towards vengeance —

Tank stopped, breathing through his nose hard, his entire body shivering with the need for violence.

Once, he wouldn't have stopped. Once, he would have ridden Sin into a heart attack, then leapt to the ground and continued, stealing the next horse to hand, and the next, and the next, until he could vent his rage on the one ha'ra'ha he'd ever halfway trusted, the one he'd half-to-halfway considered a friend.

But if he left, he wouldn't come back. He'd die in the attempt to kill Idisio; there was no putting a gloss on that bare fact. He wouldn't go to Stecatr to do whatever the hells he was supposed to do. He would be breaking his word and disappointing people in several directions: Dasin. Merchants in Assiasan. The Arason Guild Hall. Eredion. Lia.

Maybe the heaviest weight: Sin didn't deserve to be ridden to death in a fit of rage, on a pointless journey. No horse did.

If Tank died, he'd never find out the answers to so many questions. Heritage, father, *son —*

Deliberately, Tank drew in long, even breaths until his heartbeat stopped hammering in his ears and he could hear the drifting cadence of the funeral singers again.

"Afterwards," he said to the night sky. "I'll come back for him afterwards. I'll find a way. *Afterwards.* Not yet."

After *what*, precisely, Tank left as a hazy future shadow, unwilling to look too closely at that side of the brambles. The words served well enough as a promise to whatever gods might be listening, and allowed him to release the shivering rage straining his muscles.

For the moment.

Good enough.

Tank shook himself and set off up the path once more, no longer the least bit nauseous.

A dozen steps later, the stairs to widow Afin's house within reach, his legs abruptly went out from under him. He hit the ground hard and badly. Something snapped in his shoulder; he howled in startled pain, bladder loosing at the shock. Before he had time to feel embarrassed over that, his head cracked against the ground and everything went, comprehensively, dark.

Chapter Fifty-seven

Lia walked into chaos only barely subdued by the gravity of location. Four people, including one child, were down. A short, stocky man sprawled out, limply unconscious; a gaunt woman rocked in a glassy-eyed crouch. The child curled up on the ground, arms over its head as though fending off a blow; the last, an older man, stood frozen, staring blankly at the sky.

Easily a dozen people still stood, not singing but hardly silent as they babbled to one another, made frantic attempts to rouse the stricken people, or argued with Guin, who stood frowning at everything without any apparent attempt to resolve the chaos.

Lia searched anxiously for Dasin and Cilif, but neither man was in evidence. Had they left before or after whatever had happened here? No way to tell without asking, and it seemed a petty concern against the mess before her.

She hesitated to offer help, unsure what she could even do. She had no training in anything relevant. As she hovered, Guin turned, catching sight of her. His frown deepened; then he motioned the people around him silent and waved her forward.

"Told you to stay put," he said as she came within speaking range. "You're one of those that don't listen well, eh?"

"Yes," she said without flinching.

"Well, then. Nobody here's willing to leave to go down through town, they're howling about angry ghosts and afraid of the dark. You have more sense, or at least —" He chuckled a bit, glancing at the outraged villagers around him, who were one and all visibly displeased by that comment — "At the least *you* don't have any ghosts here to haunt you off a cliff. Go carry the word, get Mena the herb-woman up here, and tell Jein of this wreck. Go find your two that were here, see if they made it back to town. Sounds like they were still here when it happened, but damn near bolted after."

He handed her the still-dark lantern, then turned back to listen to renewed complaints about his disrespect for their absolutely understandable fear, he didn't understand, he was half in the ghost world himself, living up here, and why are we even talking to you anyway, you're not *doing* anything! *Why aren't you doing something! Anything!*

Lia escaped gratefully, pausing only to light the lantern. Unwilling to take the unfamiliar route that led out of the far side of the plateau, much less the stairs, she hurried back over the bridge and along the side path.

The air seemed very thick and still without the singing, and the once-pleasant incense took on a cloying edge. She glanced up at the dense speckling of stars in their midnight beds. Oddly reassured by their steady presence, she muttered a quick prayer to the kindly faces of all four gods. There was nothing to say that the frightened villagers were *wrong* about their ghosts stirring, after all. The unsettling encounter with the spirits at the foot of Hells' Hill had disintegrated her slightest skepticism on such things.

She found Dasin and Cilif halfway to the village. Dasin was kneeling on the ground, shivering violently. Cilif had an arm around his shoulder, hugging him tightly sideways.

Cilif looked up at Lia's approach and let out a coughing breath of clear relief. His face was pale, his eyes wild, and his hair disarrayed as though he'd been raking his hands through it.

"Thank the *gods*," he said. "This is beyond me. I can't even get him on his feet. I've been wanting to pick him up, but if he starts thrashing I'll go over, and I do *not* want to be alone in the dark with a lunatic and a fucking broken leg." He scooped Dasin up as he spoke, or tried to: the other man remained tautly compacted, impossible to manage. "Damnit, Dasin, fucking *loosen up.*"

Lia leaned in and dug her thumb in just above Dasin's bent elbow. Dasin yelped and twisted away; Cilif lunged, almost rolling Dasin up into his arms, then stood with a grunt.

"Don't you fucking thrash," he growled almost in Dasin's face. Lia was shocked to see blood smeared over Dasin's face, sleeves, and hands. Cilif saw her alarm and said, "Nosebleed. Bad one."

Dasin curled up like a child being carried by its father and laid his head on Cilif's shoulder, eyes blank. Cilif exchanged a baffled glance with Lia.

"Gods damn," Cilif muttered. "Hope to all fuck that Tank has some notion of what to do. This is so far beyond me it might as well be up the top of those mountains of yours."

They were almost to the point where the path opened up into the village proper when someone carrying a lantern hurried towards them.

"Thank the gods," Jein said. "I was just coming to find you. What's this?" He stared at Dasin with deep dismay. "Him too?"

"What?" Lia and Cilif said together.

"Well, Tank's down," Jein said. He lifted the lantern to examine Dasin more closely. "Nosebleed, hm? At least it looks like *he* didn't break any bones when he fell. There's that, at least."

"*What?*" Once more, they spoke in duet. Jein's eyes crinkled in a pained smile as he stepped back and lowered the lantern.

"Come on, then," he said. "Best take you to Mena's, have you all in one place."

"There's trouble on the funeral plateau," Lia blurted, recalled to her original errand. "Guin wants Mena up there quick. And you."

"More like this up there?" The corners of Jein's eyes creased in dismay. "Well, shit. I'll collar Ilna and her sisters, then, that's the best we have until Mena cuts loose of your two. Cilif—"

"I know the way. Go."

Jein nodded and hurried away.

Lia and Cilif stood still for a few moments, both blinking and bewildered. "What in all the good and holy," Cilif said at last, "is going *on* here?"

"She hurt him," Dasin said suddenly.

Cilif jerked, nearly dropping Dasin. "I'm getting tired of saying *what*," he observed tartly. "You getting your wits back, then?" He peered down at Dasin's blank face. "Apparently not. Who hurt who, Dasin?"

"Her own son. She — her own *son*." Dasin's body went tense, back arching. Cilif, swearing volubly, fumbled to keep his hold. Just as suddenly, Dasin went limp once more, nearly boneless, and Cilif had to switch to an entirely different tactic to avoid losing his grip.

Finally, Dasin more or less secured, Cilif blew out a harsh breath and said, "I'm beginning to really, really not want to see what Tank's like, at this point."

Lia made a rough sound of agreement. "I'm getting past worried into scared."

"Let's get to Mena's before Dasin starts thrashing again," Cilif said, and they set off again.

Chapter Fifty-eight

Tank woke to the smell of harsh soap and old sweat, his eyes gummed shut, his mouth parched, and a brutal, all-over ache that seemed wound into his bones. Trying to raise a hand to wipe his eyes clear, he found himself tied down; his instinctive response was to freeze, shoving at his muddled mind to get his wits active again.

"He just twitched," someone said from nearby. "I think he might finally be waking up."

"You've said that three times so far."

"Look at his face, the way his eyes are moving. He's listening to us." That was Lia, so the other voice, male, had to be Cilif. No, the tenor was wrong. Jein?

"Tank? You have a broken collarbone. You're tied down to stop you thrashing." Yes, it was Jein.

Tank drew in a deep breath through his nose, licked his lips uselessly, and rasped, "Water. Eyes."

"Right." A moment later, a damp cloth patted across his face, followed by a reed straw at the corner of his mouth. He squinched his eyes a few times, breaking free the last of the crust, then took several careful sips of tepid water. As he did, he heard Lia mutter, "See, I told you."

Jein snorted irritably. "Don't move, Tank," he said. "I'm releasing the straps." The straw withdrew, followed by a faint clunk indicating the mug had been set on a hard, elevated surface nearby.

Tank opened his eyes warily as the bindings fell away. He was in a small room; the one, small window was shuttered. Enough daylight seeped through the edges for him to see Lia and Jein, leaning over him with expressions matching his own uncertainty. Lia's hair was in loose, lank straggles around her face. Neither one looked as though they'd slept lately.

The bone-aches faded briefly, then coalesced around his left shoulder. "Oh, *fuck*," he grunted through his teeth, the words so mangled as to be unrecognizable. Jein offered a sour, weary grin all the same.

"Welcome to the world," he said, then put a light hand on Tank's right shoulder, as if to warn him to stay still. "You've been out for three days."

Tank's muscles bunched despite himself, sending a spasm of pain into his left shoulder. He forced himself limp, breathing hard. "Dasin," he said as soon as he caught his breath.

Lia drew back, her facing creasing into a starkly unhappy expression; half-crossed her arms, her nails digging in just below the elbows.

"Told *you*," Jein said to her, not quite smiling. "First question, hah."

"*Dasin*," Tank repeated, glaring at them both.

Lia bit her lip, her expression doubtful. Jein, his expression far more grim, said, "Left."

Tank blinked, blinked again; drew in a long breath, then let it out in a *whoosh*. His chest seemed to have been scooped out by an invisible hand, and his throat was desert-dry.

"Water," he rasped. Sipped enough to loosen his throat, then shut his eyes and lay still for a while, not speaking. "Left," he said at last. "Huh." He looked up at the ceiling, studying the lie of shadow along the rough plaster.

"I'll get Mena," Lia said, and withdrew.

Jein raised his head, watching her go, then said, "Dasin took Cilif and the wagon the morning after you fell. He left you a note and left me enough to cover your lodging and whatnot until you heal enough to follow. He told me to remind you of Gint." Jein cocked his head to the side inquiringly.

Tank moved his head in a slight, sideways nod, a wave of deep weariness flooding through him. "Figures."

Mena came in, looking completely exhausted herself. "Well, there's the last of them awake," she said with an obvious attempt at cheer. Her long braids were ruthlessly tied back and greasy, her brown face bruised dark under the eyes. She shooed Jein from the room, telling him to go get some rest already, and to make sure Lia went to bed as well, then firmly shut the door and turned to regard Tank with a thoughtful frown.

"What happened?" he asked. The words were an effort, dredged up from what little strength he had left.

"You won't be awake long enough to hear the answer," Mena said, coming to the side of the bed. "Hold still and let me look at you."

She flipped the sheet back in sections, replacing each fold before moving on to the next, examining with gentle touch not only his shoulder, but nearly his entire body. Cool air prickled skin, advising him that he was entirely naked; he couldn't summon up the energy to particularly care. Mena had seen worse than his scarred body, and in any case he was at her mercy.

At last she came to his face. "Blink. Look left. Look right. Look up. Down. Focus here." She held a hand away, then closer. "Good. The concussion's sorted. I wasn't at all sure you'd wake with any wits at all, you know. Make a fist with your right hand. Left. Yes, I know, sorry." She sighed and straightened, looking down at him pensively. "You'll heal. Hungry?"

He considered. "Yes."

"I'll have Lia bring you in some soup, and Jein help you sit up. In a bit. Right now, your eyelids are about to drop like bricks. Go back to sleep. You'll be wobbling around by the end of the day, if I know you. Sleep."

It might as well have been a pushed command. Tank faded out into hazy, unfocused dreams in which Dasin stood some distance away, half-turned to hide his face and refusing to answer any of the dream-incoherent questions Tank pressed on him. After a time, that shifted to sitting on the cliff in Isata, looking over the city and eating disdis, entirely alone, entirely naked, and quietly weeping.

He woke with damp trails streaking his face and inhaled the warm aroma of chicken soup. "Agh," he grunted, then tried to sit up and yelped at the shattering-glass feeling that raced through his left side.

"Damn fool," Jein said, looming over him a moment later. "Hold still, I'll sit you up."

He lifted Tank with a gentle sort of ruthlessness, propping pillows behind him and ignoring his panted curses. That sorted, Jein drew a chair up beside the bed, bowl and spoon in one hand.

The room was almost dark, a partially hooded lantern the only light, the hissing pop of the flame and Jein's movements the only sound. "Nighttime," Tank said, not quite a question.

"Just past midnight," Jein said. "I'm feeding you, like it or not. Until Mena gets a sling on you, she said, you're not to move either arm."

"Trade. Tell me what happened."

Jein nodded equably. "Fair. Here."

The broth was rich and savory, laden with garlic and rosemary; not hot, but pleasantly warm, as though it had been sitting covered for a time.

"Good. So. After they left my house, that night you went down, Cilif and Dasin went up to the funeral plateau to sing. Well, Dasin sang. Cilif was going to, the following morning. He was keeping Dasin company, that night."

Tank squeezed his eyes shut.

"Ah. More soup. Here." Jein fed him several more spoonfuls, then went on. "Something happened while Dasin was up there. Stories I got are a bit muddled, but sounds like Dasin stopped singing, grabbed his head, and went down on his knees. Right after that, a few other folks went sideways. Unconscious, or rocking like a bewildered child, like that. Anba and her son Deon were two of the ones affected."

Tank's stomach began to curdle. "No more soup right now. Tell me the rest of it."

Jein considered him, then leaned to set the bowl on a nearby stand. His expression went grave. "Dasin apparently stood up and took himself off pretty quick after that, leaning on Cilif hard. Guin sent Lia to fetch me and Mena. She found them two halfway back to the village, Dasin near catatonic and Cilif panicking. They managed to get Dasin down here about the time I was headed out to find them myself, because Mena and I had just picked *you* up off the ground with a snapped collarbone."

He paused, taking on an inward, abstracted expression for a few moments, then sighed and ran his hands through his bushy beard. "Mena and my three girls have been tending you and the others who went down for three days now. Dasin got up the morning after, came and looked at you for a bit, then told Cilif to pack up the wagon and took to the road with scarcely a farewell to anyone." He hesitated, then added, more slowly, "I think it's maybe a good thing he did."

"No," Tank said involuntarily, shutting his eyes again. "I don't — godsdamnit. I don't want to know why you're saying that, but I have to, don't I?" Vague words formed in the back of his mind, bits of memory he knew he didn't want to see, a conversation too painful to recall.

"Probably," Jein said with a sigh. "Deon woke up first. He wasn't ever really asleep, just curled in a panic too deep to shake him out of. We loaded him under blankets and kept ravann under his pillow, and he sat up evening of the day after and told us what Anba had been doing to him."

Tank drew in a sharp breath. "Oh, no," he said. "Oh, fuck no. No."

"Mm." Jein sat still for a while, not speaking. When Tank dared to look, he found Jein's face peculiarly blank. "It wasn't pleasant hearing. Anba woke up not long after that. She ... eh, isn't quite in her right mind. We've got her aside in as secure a room as we could find, with someone watching her all round the day and night." He tilted a bleak glance down at Tank. "You don't look surprised. Did you know?"

Tank moved his head in a slight negation, the motion setting another warning spike through his left shoulder. "No. I'm guessing something similar from the others?"

Jein nodded slowly. "Each one was hurting or had hurt ... someone vulnerable. Badly. And often." He let a breath hiss out through his teeth. "They're none of them right in the head anymore, but Anba's the only one needs constant supervision. The others are quiet, mostly. Sitting on chairs staring. Sometimes crying."

Tank shut his eyes again. *Fuck* didn't quite cover this, and he was supremely disinclined to say *Good and holy gods* in the face of their obvious indifference.

"Something Anba's son Deon said." Jein spoke very slowly and carefully now. "He says he was looking at Dasin, just before ... said Dasin stopped singing, looked like he'd been slapped, face white as a ghost. Said Dasin looked at Anba, and she went down. Said he looked at the others that went down. Deon said Dasin had on an expression of such fury that it terrified Deon into falling down in a fit, himself."

The silence seemed very long and heavy.

"Didn't know Dasin for a witch," Jein said at last, very softly. "Would have liked to've known that a while ago, Tank."

Tank licked his lip, tried to speak twice before words emerged. "He isn't. Wasn't." There was no value in clarifying that witches didn't exist, that what Dasin had done was far closer to a desert lord's capabilities than anything supernatural. "Something happened to him, this trip. On the way through the Hackerwood."

Evkit's voice snaked through his head: *Not immediately nor entirely whole, but able to heal.*

Was this what healed would look like, for Dasin? Was the vision of glowing joy that

Evkit had shown him drawn from … *this*, causing such pain, retribution against.…

The memory he didn't want to acknowledge pressed closer. "No," he said aloud, and began to raise a hand as if to physically push it back. A searing bolt of pain helpfully scrambled his thoughts and left him panting, nauseous, and exhausted.

Jein, grumbling under his breath, eased Tank back down flat. "Damn fool. Mena will have my hide if you keep on like that. Here." He set a straw to the corner of Tank's mouth. This time, the water held the floral, bitter taste of ravann liqueur. "Go back to sleep."

Tank's body felt chill and heavy. He blinked several times, trying to form words, to say something reassuring, or maybe defensive; perhaps even a plea of some sort. The powerful liqueur stole sight and words nearly at once, dropping him back into empty silence.

When he woke again, he asked for Dasin's note. Mena arrived, checked him over once more, then insisted on setting his arm in a sling before letting him have the carefully folded and sealed note. She also insisted on opening the shutters to let in fresh air and afternoon sunlight, and on Lia staying with him, both of which he one-shoulder shrugged at.

Lia took the chair by the bed as Mera departed, keeping herself politely angled so as to not see the writing.

The seal was a crude smear of candle wax. It broke easily. The words inside were in Dasin's familiar, spikily precise handwriting:

Tank—

I'm going on to Assiasan. I'll arrange for your lodging and meals along the road, and I'll be selling the wagon and stock.

I won't be there when you arrive. I'll leave your share and your personal items with the Assiasan Bank. Whether Cilif comes with me from there is up to him. I doubt he will. He's fairly aggravated with me. He doesn't want to leave you.

I'm leaving you behind, in part, because I can't hold you bound any longer. If you haven't already, you can remember now, and rage as you like.

I know you won't accept it, but I am sorry.

—Dasin

Tank read the note three times, each time more slowly; then, with great precision, ignoring the spikes of pain in his shoulder, tore it into tiny, fluttering pieces on his lap. He looked up at Lia, who was regarding him worriedly, and said, "Get me. A fucking. Drink. Hardest they have. *Now.*"

She rose without hesitation. He fixed his attention on the opposite wall and breathed steadily through his nose, his eyes wide and strained, until she returned with — bless her — two flasks of local apple lightning.

"Thank you," he said, accepting them with a shaking hand. "Now go the fuck away and don't let anyone come in, no matter what. *Nobody.*" He glared until her rebellious expression faded to a reluctant nod.

Once the door closed behind her, he opened the first flask and took a long drink, coughing a bit at the acrid fumes. He could *sense* Lia, on the other side of the door, taking up guard post with a stiff-shouldered mixture of worry and resentment.

He picked up a handful of shredded paper, sifting it through his fingers, watching the play of dust and light and air currents as it settled back into his lap. Took another long drink. Carefully, carefully wedged the cork back into the neck of the flask and set it into his lap beside the other.

Then he shut his eyes, leaned his head back against the pillows, and let himself remember.

Chapter Fifty-nine

It wasn't a scream. It was a guttural howl, mixing agony and fury in equal measure, a sound that Lia's hindbrain advocated immediate flight from. She actually jolted two steps away from Tank's door before she could stop. She forced herself to step back and press her shoulders against the wall.

The inhuman sound went on far past when he should have run out of breath; finally staggered, stopped, then rose again at equal intensity.

Something smashed inside the room just as Mena bolted around the corner, eyes huge in a gray face.

"What the *hells* is going on?" she shouted, skidding to a stop just shy of Lia, who'd put herself in front of the door as soon as the woman appeared. "You let me through, right now!"

Lia shook her head obdurately. "He said not. No matter what."

"He's ripping his shoulder apart, is what!" Mena yelled. "Let me *through*."

"All respect, *s'a* Mera," Lia said, setting her stance with care, "he's my trail lead. I do as he says. *And*," she went on as Mena drew in breath to yell again, "he just read that letter from Dasin. If you'd seen his face as I did, you wouldn't want to go in right now either."

Mena stared at her for a few moments, then slowly deflated. "Oh," she said. "I see. Well."

Something exploded inside the room; *crashed* was much too mild a description.

Mena went back a step, eyes narrowing. "There isn't but so much furniture in that room, and he oughtn't have the strength to throw a chamberpot, no matter how fussed he is," she observed.

The scorching howl arose, more wobbly this time.

"You handle it, then, *s'a* Lia," Mena said with abrupt decisiveness. "I'm quite sure he'll pay for what he's wrecking." She began to turn away.

"*S'a* Mena?"

The woman looked back, her expression unpromising. "What?"

"Thank you."

The howl frayed into a dark silence. The two women stared at one another, caught in reflexive listening. When no more sound emerged from the room, Mena let out a hard breath and said, "I won't say you're welcome. I'll say go make sure he's still alive." She turned and strode away.

Lia drew in an unsteady breath, stooped to collect the two flasks of apple brandy at her feet — much smoother and lighter than the rotgut she'd given Tank — and let herself into the room.

Tank was sitting on the bed, knees pulled up and staring at the wall with bleak intensity. Every other piece of furniture in the room — the stand by the bed, the chair, the heavy armoire — was in flinders, sprayed about as though each piece had ruptured from the inside out.

Lia put her back to the door, looking around in stunned silence. Tank turned his head fractionally, eyeing her sideways. He said, "Told you t'stay out."

"And I did. And now I'm here." She went on surveying the destruction, increasingly intrigued as well as bemused by her own lack of terror. "How did you manage all this?"

He blinked, looking around in dawning shock himself. "I ... I'm not sure," he admitted. "I don't remember." He pushed back on the bed, wincing and cursing, to fetch up against the pile of pillows, then added, "Probably not real smart to be in here right now, Lia. I'm not nearly done being pissed yet."

She crossed to sit on the edge of the bed, holding up the two flasks. His strained expression gentled into a wide, savage smile.

"*Now* you can stay," he said, and took the one she handed over.

Some time later, Lia dimly registered someone urging her up and onto a pallet on the floor. Some time after *that*, she woke up with an achingly full bladder and searched around for the chamberpot. It had wound up in a corner. She used it, lidded it, shoved it under the bed where it belonged, then collapsed back to sleep.

Eventually, evil sunlight wormed its way through her eyelids. She moaned and turned over away from it, curling up in protest.

"That's enough indulgence," Mena said sternly, prodding her with a booted toe. "Up, *s'a*. Up."

Lia, grumbling protest, staggered to her feet.

"Mercenaries," Mena muttered with a snort. "Come on, then, this way."

Blinking, Lia turned to look at the bed. Tank lay on his side, long hair tangled over his face in a crimson-brass screen. Someone, probably Mena, had drawn the blanket neatly over him, and a large mug of, presumably, water sat on a new bedside table.

"He'll be fine," Mena said. "When I peeled you off the foot of his bed and onto the pallet, I loaded him down with water and another dose of painkiller. He'll be out for a while, with no more fussing about. This way."

She shepherded Lia to the inn and up to the room Lia had taken at the inn. Both Tank and Lia's packs and gear were piled on and around the bed and chair. Lia had been stepping around the stack for three days and barely even saw it any longer. Mena insisted on Lia taking time for a rough cleanup with a wet cloth and fresh clothes, then hustled her down to the commons room for a bowl of oatmeal. Lia regarded the unappetizing globs dubiously, but Mena proved unyielding, pushing the bowl into her hand and leading her outside to sit on a bench to one side of the door.

As they settled down, Lia more slowly and wincingly, Mena let out a huff that could have been satisfied or annoyed. "So, he's alive," she said. "That's something, I suppose. Are you a witch, too, then?"

Lia, about to swallow, choked. It took some moments of coughing, and Mena patting her back, to be able to say, "*What?*"

"Dasin's a witch," Mena said, "and after what Tank did to that room last night, he's one too. You managed to spend the night without him doing any more damage, to you or to himself, so I'm thinking you're able to match or better him in his witchery."

"No," Lia said. She rubbed a hand over her eyes, then looked down at the unappetizing mush in the bowl. "I'm not. He was hurting over something that had nothing to do with me, and he's not the type to lay it off on whoever's to hand."

Mena didn't say anything for a time. She looked up at the sky, watching feathery clouds flitting by, her expression pensive. "It's a bad time," she said. "We needed those folks who went down. I'd like to put you to work, if you would."

"Doing what?"

What turned out to be mucking out stalls, clearing garden beds, hauling loads of mulch, and tidying up the funeral plateau; cutting up vegetables for dinner at the inn, feeding and milking several goats. If it hadn't been shadowy near-evening by the time Lia finished the array of tasks, she was fairly certain Mena would have given her more. She washed up briefly and went next door to get something to eat.

Tank was already in the tavern when she staggered in, exhausted. He sat in a corner, back to the wall, his gaze on the mug before him. As Lia sat down, the tavern girl set a basket of biscuits down on their table, stretching her arm out rather than coming up close to the table, then whisked away with an unfriendly look. Tank watched her go, his expression bleak.

"Our welcome's gone," he said. He grimaced, running a thumb around the rim of his mug. "We worked so damn hard, too. What a waste. Gods grant Dasin hasn't ruined every village along the way."

"So we're still going to Assiasan?" Lia began munching on a biscuit. It was fresh and hot and buttery, and made her want a great deal more food very quickly.

"Have to. Several things got left in the wagon I want to collect. Plus my pay, and yours. And Cilif's probably waiting on us." He picked up a biscuit, set it on the table before him, and prodded at it listlessly. "Thank you. For staying last night. I didn't expect —" He paused, shaking his head a little, and scratched at his left wrist through the sling. "It helped," he finished, very quietly. "Not being alone."

"Tell me what happened," Lia said, reaching for a second biscuit. The serving girl came back and plopped a large, dented metal bowl of stew and two spoons on the table, then flounced off again.

Tank spared it a brief, disinterested glance. "On the road," he said. "Not here." He prodded at his left wrist again. "Tomorrow, I'm thinking. We'll have trouble if we stay."

Lia regarded the sling dubiously. "I don't know that you're ready to handle Sin if he gets fractious."

"I'm not. But there isn't much by way of option. Any tolerance I might have held out for got smashed with the furniture last night." He glowered down at the sling. "You know some trick for riding like this? I already want to rip it off."

"We can tie your arm to your side," Lia said, "and adjust the sling into more of a waist wrap that you can tuck your forearm into. You'll need a mounting block, though."

"Figured as much." He dug a spoon into the soup without enthusiasm and managed a few bites, grimacing frequently, before setting the spoon aside and sitting back. "Jein said I've a room here tonight. I'm assuming you do as well?"

"I think they expect us both to stay in the one," Lia said, remembering the tangled pile of belongings on the floor.

"Of course they would," Tank said, sounding exasperated and resigned all at once. He flicked her a wary glance. "That a problem?"

"I passed out over the foot of your bed last night, and neither of us burst into flames," she said dryly, and was rewarded with a genuine grin.

"Kept my feet warm, anyway. All right. We can do this." He leaned forward and began eating stew with true appetite. "Get food when you can, at this point," he added, nudging the other spoon towards her. "Going to be an interesting trip, without the wagon as backup."

Chapter Sixty

Tank woke in the middle of the night, sitting up before he remembered not to move quite so quickly. His yelp started Lia to her feet, a lithe shape in the near-darkness: she'd left the lantern burning, turned low.

"What? Where?" Lia demanded, turning in place. He was fairly sure she had a dagger in hand, and almost chuckled.

"Nothing," he told her. "I just woke up too fast." He swung himself to sit on the edge of the bed, rubbing at his eyes. She'd insisted on taking the floor pallet because of his injury. He hadn't argued.

She huffed out exasperation. He heard the slight rasp of a dagger sliding back into its sheath, and smiled thinly at the confirmation.

"Need the chamberpot?" she asked as she reached to turn up the wick, brightening the room.

"Nah. You?"

"No."

She stood still for a moment, then, slowly, crossed to the window and pushed the shutters open. The flickering lamplight caught soft gleams in her hair. In another heartening mark of trust, she'd worn a smock to bed.

Tank had been very, very careful with his gaze at that point.

Lia breathed, "There's something...."

Tank lurched to his feet, immediately alarmed. "What?"

He moved to stand beside her, dropping his right hand on her shoulder without really thinking about it. Her muscles were tight under his fingers, but not from his proximity: her attention was entirely fixed outside. He peered out, frowning, and saw only the thin pool of light cast by the night-lantern hanging outside the inn. Cautiously, he extended *other* sight and found only the ordinary energies of bats, mice, snakes, owls, cats, and other small to medium night-prowlers.

"I don't know," she said. "I think … I think I need to go up onto the funeral plateau."

"*Now?*"

"Yes." She turned and began catching up bits of outer clothing and boots. Tank, bemused, painfully whipped round to put his back to her as she stripped out of the smock and began dressing in day clothes.

"Wait. Lia. *Lia!*" He put enough trail-captain command into the word that he heard her stop moving for a moment. "I'll go with you, but I need help with my boots. Please."

She began dressing again. "Sit down, then."

After a cautious glance to be sure she was properly covered — mainly because he didn't want *her* getting upset at memory, come morning — he sank onto the bed. He'd slept in day clothes, both too tired and too wary, with Lia in the same room, to undress entirely. At the moment, he considered that to have been a very good decision.

She worked his boots onto his feet as gently as possible, then wrapped the sling tight. He set his teeth in his tongue to stop the hisses of pain as his shoulder jolted. He wanted more of the pain medicine, gods he wanted more. Which thought lit up warnings in his brain.

I didn't ask closely enough about what's in that medicine, he realized. That could be a whole different set of trouble, given his history, but that would have to wait for morning. Right now he was nearly chasing Lia out the door and down the stairs, growling to himself at the pace.

The village lay still and quiet under moondark, swathes of bright stars and the lantern in Lia's hand the only light. Tall firs loomed as black cones; shorter, wider hill juniper and oakbush spread out in patches of deep shadow. The air smelled of old smoke, pine sap, and a sweet night-blooming flower of some sort. Lia would probably know the name.

He didn't ask.

They walked from packed dirt through softer stripes, over gravel paths and wooden-planked temporary bridges laid over eroded spots. Tank let himself be aware of the different textures underfoot as a way of not worrying over what madness had infected Lia this time, and let the silence be. The slope to the plateau was hard-packed dirt and old gravel needing a refresher, less unkempt the further up they went.

The empty funeral plateau had an eerie, still beauty. Any signs of the recent gathering had been swept away, the paths raked clean and straight, braziers heaped with clean charcoal, fresh torches set at each corner. Lia paused to turn the lantern up further.

Her head tilted like an asp-jacau listening to some high-pitched sound, then she set the lantern down and strode decisively to the pool in the center. She stopped well out of arm's reach of the edge, and said, simply, "I'm here."

"*Gods,* Lia, *what* are you doing?" Tank demanded sharply. Then *something* shimmered the air over the pool, a not-emptiness, almost but not quite blueing the air. He sucked in a breath, startled, and opened other-vision: blue, yes, a wavering blue spiral.

With opened vision came awareness that the — whatever it was — had turned its attention from Lia to himself. Tank backed up a step, then forward two, starting to raise a hand to drag Lia back.

Northern kin-children, a voice said. *I see you. I hear you. I feel you. I welcome you.*

It wasn't precisely mind-speech, but it definitely wasn't verbal. The words sent an unpleasant vibration through Tank's clenched jaw.

"Lia," he said, "Get *back* from there."

She shook her head, patting the air beside her in a *wait* gesture. "I give you gods-greeting," she said to the distortion over the water. "May all kindly things look upon you with favor, and all ill things turn away from your path."

The distortion squinched down, as though in a clumsy bow. *The blessing is a gratitude. Is grateful. Is appreciated. You have seen our more southern kin, at the place of great pain. You bear their message, you witness for their weariness, you witness for their pain. I am not weary, I am not seeking rest, release, I ask for no message to be carried. I ask only for a witness to my pain.*

Tank wasn't at all sure who the creature was talking to. The words seemed equally aimed, and equally alarming. "What southern kin?" he said. "What message?"

"That's me," Lia said, tone muted. "At Hells Hill. I'll explain later."

Two northern near kin are enough to listen, to lift, to witness this pain from me, the creature said. *Will you do this gratitude, this gracefulness, this kindness?*

"Lia, *don't,*" Tank said, real fear flaring through him. "Don't *ever* say yes to something like that —"

"I will," Lia said, ignoring him. "Speak as you like, I will listen."

It is less burden with two to share, the voice said. *I do not wish you harm, and the larger kin has the greater strength for this.*

Lia looked over her shoulder at Tank, eyebrows raised. In the light cast by the spirit-thing, with other-sight open, he could see that her eyes were fully dilated. *Overset, damnit, entirely overset.* At the same time, not quite. She had her wits clear; she was simply — hah, nothing simple here — in an altered state, a nearly manic high of refined perception. He'd hit that point once or twice in his life. When she came down from this, it would *hurt.*

Lia said, "I'm pretty sure this has something to do with whatever happened up here the other night. This is some sort of guardian for the funerals, and it's hurt. Can't you feel it?"

The better question, in Tank's opinion, was *How can* you *feel it?* No time for that right now.

Tank shut his eyes, grimacing, and shifted other-vision to a different slant. The shifting form had four long spots where nothing moved — slashes, either frozen or cut out, Tank couldn't quite focus to see.

"Godsdamnit," he muttered. "Fine. Yes. I'll listen." With the bleak thought, *If this goes sideways I will fucking skin you.*

Tentatively, he approached to stand beside Lia, once more putting his right hand on her shoulder. Surprisingly, the touch grounded him, sending fear to one side and allowing him to focus clear-eyed, rather than knocking him sideways into shared mania as he'd expected.

"We have *got* to have a talk once we get on the road," he muttered. Her shoulder moved in a faint shrug.

The creature began to speak.

Not so much *speak* as *show*. Images, emotions, and sensations unrolled through what seemed like Tank's entire body: *Gathering up those present into its protection, holding the space for their mourning, filtering the grief into something pure and healing.* Flames, smoke, blessed song with which it swayed and played, delighted by the shifting air and emotions. Not predatory in any way, merely an innate, simple, joyous acceptance of the moment, and a gentle trickle of that serenity back into the mourners.

Tank had never experienced anything even remotely like this. Tears built, spilled down his face, drawn out not by grief, precisely, but by an overload of *center/clarity*. He could feel Lia weeping as well. Neither of them moved to wipe their faces, both lost in that spiraling *rightness*.

Then a dark blotch entered the singing, a tangled density of pain, guilt, and anger that far outstripped the more diffuse grieving around it. The joy hesitated, stuttered, then refocused to flow around this new presence, obeying its mandate to heal and protect. The blotch — it had to be Dasin — reacted with unexpected speed, lashing out to grasp intangible with intangible, slicing darkened energy through lighter energy, drawing it into itself — himself —

Gods, Dasin, what have you done?

The stolen pieces spun out, even as the creature recoiled, forming a thread-thin connection to every other person on the plateau. Four of the threads flared deep, bloody red. Every other connection dropped on the instant, the red lines thickening to ropes, to hawsers, to massive logs of braided energy. One by one, the connections sprouted a furious array of thorny spikes which swirled forward, piling into the people at the end. Then the lines simply dissolved.

Ghostly screams wailed, both human and not-human. Silver-gray flickers rose from the ground throughout the funeral plateau, twining around the shocked, slow-moving humans. Those, too, dissipated quickly.

The last bloodstained connection dropped. The creature coiled, sinking into the pool and down deep, deep, as deep as it could go; fleeing the unaccustomed pain, purpose shattered, fear biting into its being for the first time ever. It had never before caused pain, much less been *used* to cause pain.

Forbidden, forbidden, horror, agony, shame, so much shame, bewilderment....

Silence.

A glimmering awareness of something, something *solid*, something *right*, something that would understand and heal the splintering pain. The creature began trying, cautiously, to reach out, to coax the rightness closer, to send out a plea.

And here you are now, it said, moving from images to words, and went silent. Tank had the impression of several deep breaths being taken and exhaled in increasing relief. *Ahh. I thank you.*

The empty spots filled in, the creature once more a spiralling, dancing whole.

Tank realized his fingers were digging into Lia's shoulder, his breath coming in ragged pants. She stood entirely still, breathing evenly, and said, "Thank you for your trust. Gods hold you gently."

It is enough that you did, northern near-kin, and that you forgive me, the guardian said, and dissolved back into the water.

Tank staggered back, releasing Lia's shoulder. She turned and caught his wrist, pulling him forward in time to stop him from going over on his ass.

When he recovered his breath, he gently freed his hand from Lia's hot grip. "That was ... certainly something," he said. He looked up at the stars, blinking hard, and wiped residual moisture from his face. "Don't ever do something like that again when I tell you not. You could have gotten us both killed or overset into being killers."

"But we weren't," she said reasonably, and turned away from the pool. "Let's go back to bed."

Sight still open, he heard echoes of a deep shock in her calm, and suspected that once she settled down, she'd either break apart or have a screaming nightmare. The night wasn't nearly over.

He let out a long, shaky sigh and followed her back to the inn.

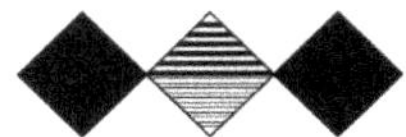

Lia began to thrash, an hour later, letting out the cry he'd been waiting for.

Tank hadn't gone to sleep, stubbornly propping himself up against the pillows to wait for the inevitable. She'd nearly collapsed on the cot after getting both their boots off, still fully dressed herself, which he considered a gods-granted mercy given what lay ahead. He also hadn't doused the lamp, which was getting close to guttering at this point. He'd have to remember to thank the innkeep for the unusual gift: most rooms only got candles or a standing oil lamp, not a carrying lantern. He wasn't sure why they'd been given it, but was intensely grateful all the same.

He swung to put his feet on the floor and leaned to turn the wick up, bringing more visual clarity, at least, to the situation; rubbed his good hand over his face, considering his plan one last time. Then, keeping the push below the threshold of waking her but unstoppable all the same, said, "Lia. *Get up on the bed.*"

She didn't so much stand as lurch and flop. Swearing as quietly as he could, teeth clenched, he managed to get himself back against the pillows and Lia tucked up against his right side. The effort left him panting and hazy for a while, genuinely wishing for the pain medicine now and not caring what was in it.

Should have taken it as soon as we got back, damnit. Too late now. Being in pain might come in useful, after all. He'd wound himself far too open, up on the plateau, and knew he wasn't entirely back in his right mind yet.

Lia had stopped thrashing, at least. She curled up against him, her head on his good shoulder, breathing more easily but shivering now and again. She wore a beaded necklace of some sort under her shirt; the small hard pebbles pressed into his skin as she leaned into him. Odd that he'd never seen it, which implied she kept it carefully hidden. Eh, probably something religious.

Her shivering turned more pronounced. He couldn't pull a blanket over them, since the scuffle of getting to this point had knocked the sheet all over. Tentatively, he focused on *being warm*; she let out a hungry moan and pressed closer, her hand splaying out on his chest.

Shit — no, no, no!

A more basic part of him argued in the other direction. He overruled it harshly and tried to reverse what he'd done. Either he failed or it was too late, because her hand trailed up to his face, encountered the thick beard stubble, and froze.

Abruptly, Lia let out a squeaky sound of horror and recoiled. Ready for that, he had his arm braced to hold her from going over the edge of the narrow bed. The pull on his collarbone put him crosseyed and whining.

"Tank? What —" The pressure, thankfully, eased as Lia realized what was going on and pushed forward against him, taking her weight off his arm.

"Stay still a bit," he said through his teeth. "Please. *Please* fucking hold still."

Her breath, at the current angle, was nearly into his ear. He hadn't known he could be in this much pain and this painfully aroused at the same moment. He needed to tell her to move her damn head to one side. He couldn't make himself do it.

"I had a nightmare?" Lia said, soft-voiced, and turned her head a bit, as though checking where she was. It didn't set off any more pain, and *thank gods* it took the edge off to have her breath going to his beard instead of his ear. Her voice went bewildered: "How did you get me up on the bed?"

"Compelled you," he said, then let out a gasping whine as she brought her attention — and her breath — back around. "Holy *gods*, Lia, breathe through. Your fucking. *Nose.*"

She recoiled again, not as strongly as when waking up. "What? Why — *what?*" Her voice went acid with understanding: "Let me go."

He unwound his arm. She skittered off the bed, fetching up against the wall with a slight thud, and stared at him, one hand covering her mouth. Her pale hair was tousled, sticking up in spikes and curls. He found it oddly adorable.

"You're crossroads," she said. "Not *ii'ne.*"

He adjusted his position, bringing his right arm back to a balanced spot, and held his teeth shut, more interested in breathing through the waves of agony than in answering her.

"You *lied.*"

He rested his head against the pillows and said, not looking at her, "Tell me the nightmare while it's still fresh. Say it out."

A silence hung, in which Lia made more than one choked-off sound of angry disbelief. He began to think her trust entirely broken, that she'd sweep up her gear and take another room. Leave him behind, as Dasin had done.

He waited, patiently enduring the overlapping aches from body and mind, to see what she'd do.

At last she said, "Dasin was beating you. And you were letting him. And the — the blood that came out was — was clear. Turned blue. Turned into that —whatever that spirit thing was. And it, it ate Dasin."

His eyes popped wide open on the first sentence. By the last, he was frozen in place, his breath difficult and thin. The silence, this time, was far more prickly with charged tension.

"Your nightmare," he said, very slowly. "Your nightmare was about *me?*"

She shrugged away from the wall and sat warily on the edge of the bed, her hand coming up to her own collarbone — no, to check the hidden necklace. Belatedly, she ran both hands through her hair, smoothing it out somewhat.

"Dasin never touched you again, after the Hackerwood, did he? I mean, not to hit you," she amended at his huff of laughter. "Whatever Evkit did to him, he stopped hitting you. Or you stopped letting him."

"Little of both, I think," Tank said. His breath began coming more easily, and the words pulled up surprisingly little pain. Not none, not by a long ways, but not the red tinge he would have expected. "Mostly, I think, he stopped needing it, and I started thinking...." He paused, frowning at nothing as he put words together in his head. "I started thinking I'm not so small as that," he finished dubiously. The words weren't quite right, but they were all he had just then.

Her smile was rueful. "You're not small at all, Tank."

He let out an amused snort. "That's not what I mean."

"I'm not talking about your size," she said. "I'm talking about *you.*" She put a hand to her chest, then dropped it at his slow, narrow-eyed inhale. "I'm glad he stopped. I think Cilif might have chucked him upside down into the latrines by this point if he hadn't. *I might have.*"

Tank shut his eyes again. "It's not simple. We'll talk on the road, yeah? I need, you need, some sleep. And I need to stop thinking —" He bit his tongue, hard, before the rest of the sentence emerged: *I need to stop thinking about hauling you into my lap and getting my hands all over you.*

Lia jerked as though to bounce upright, then paused and managed to stand without making it a retreat. "Yeah," she said. "We'll talk on the road."

He winced at the edge in her voice. *I deserve that, maybe.*

With a sigh, he settled into a fragmented, aching, and entirely unrestful doze.

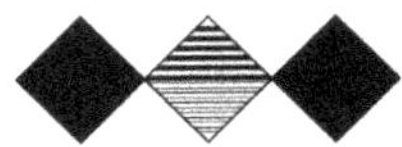

Mena was kind enough, despite her obvious irritation with Tank, to be sure he had a good supply of painkillers, an extra sling, and a few other frequently needed, small medical supplies that had left along with Dasin's wagon. Jein, or maybe his daughters, made sure they were well supplied with trail fare, a half wheel of hard cheese, and two loaves of fresh-baked bread. Rooster being more tolerant of extra loading, and Tank being in no shape to navigate the bundles in any case, most of the largesse wound up draped in bags along the splotchy gelding's sides.

Ilna pulled Lia to one side and had a low-voiced conversation with her that left Lia looking, if not happy, at least less cow-eyed every time she glanced the girl's way. Tank figured he'd ask about that on the road. It would be something to pass the time, anyway.

None of the other villagers spared Tank more than a dark stare in passing. Lia came under a less harsh but still unfriendly regard. She seemed utterly indifferent, not only to that, but to anything not requiring her attention. Her face was tinged with gray and deeply bruised under the eyes, and she moved with the stiffness of someone badly beaten the night before.

Tank wasn't feeling all too limber himself, but he had years of practice in ignoring accumulated agonies both physical and emotional. He let Lia handle most of the loading and all of the tacking up, found a large rock to serve as a mounting block, and steered them out onto the road without a backwards glance.

Sin, as though understanding the delicacy of the situation, seemed to be moving more gently than usual, and put up no fuss at all. Tank said to the serenely flicking dark ears, "You'll have the *best* damn mash I can get you, soon's I can, asshole."

"Tell me what's ahead," Lia said. "Village tonight, or camping? What's the trail like? How far to Assiasan? And —"

Tank held up his good hand, managing a wry smile. "Yeah, all right, hold on. I'll tell you all of that, but don't load up so many questions that I forget what the first one was, yeah?"

She fell silent, but aimed a sullen glance sideways at him.

He sobered, considering, then said, "There's a village less'n a day's ride ahead, another within reasonable ride most places. I don't know what our welcome will be anymore, anywhere up along the way."

A News Rider hurtled towards them from the north, beast lathered and rider filthy. Tank and Lia moved aside. Sin whuffled irritably as the dappled horse sped past, but thankfully didn't make the restless shimmy such things often provoked. Maybe he did, somehow, understand Tank's current fragility. Wouldn't be the first time Sin had surprised Tank with what seemed uncanny awareness.

"King's Rider," Tank said, turning Sin to watch the departing courier. "I'm starting to get real uneasy about what's going on up north."

He reined Sin around and nudged back into a gentle amble. His shoulder hurt enough that he wanted to take his time and get used to the strain before trying a faster pace.

"You think Dasin's going to poison the entire road ahead against you?" Lia asked, frowning at Rooster's ears. "Is he that mad at you? And why?"

"Maybe. He's not mad at me, so much as ... damnit. Let me figure out where to start."

They rode for a time in silence, moving aside for faster travelers coming up from behind them, watching southbound wagons and riders going past on the other side of the road. Lia stayed sullen and indifferent, wincing from time to time like someone with a bad hangover pushed into full sun. Bit by bit, though, she started to look around with more interest, her body loosening up with Rooster's amiable pace.

The Hills Road ran through ever-changing terrain. They passed from narrow cliff cuts to wide, grass-laden plateaus, through dense stands of alder and across streams too small to need a bridge. A number of heavy wooden bridges, both flat and arched, spanned larger streams and gullies. Dozens, if not hundreds, of birds hopped and peeped and darted by; squirrels were busy collecting fallen berries, nuts, and tearing at the enormous white mushrooms that sprouted throughout the underbrush.

Tank briefly reined in, waving Lia to do the same, as a particularly large blacksnake lazed sinuously across the road, completely unconcerned about the horses a stone's throw away. The horses, more surprisingly, didn't react at all.

"Definitely getting you some prime mash," Tank muttered, wishing he could lean forward to pat Sin's neck. He considered asking Lia to identify various plants and birds as they rode, then dismissed that as too obvious of a stalling maneuver.

Finally deciding there was no other way than to start at the utter beginning, Tank cleared his throat and said, as unemotionally as possible, "I grew up in what's called katha villages, down south. Dasin did too, in a different one."

"Servants …?" She gave him a sideways, questioning frown. Her face still looked bruised and out of proper color, but her eyes were clear and sharply interested.

Argh.

"Not quite." He cleared his throat again, his back tightening. "So, see, in the south there's—there are—honorable servants, called kathain, and that's … that sounds the same, but it … it ain't. Isn't. Up north here, kathain are called *kehair*, I think. The katha villages ain … aren't … weren't that." He made himself say it: "They are, they *were*, whorehouses. Trading mostly in children."

Lia let out a choking, horrified noise. Tank set his jaw and let her absorb it. The tension in his back was ripping his shoulder up, in any case, and he was having trouble breathing, let alone speaking coherently. Not that he'd been doing that well, slipping back and forth from street rat grammar to the clarity his mentor-then-betrayer Allonin had so relentlessly drummed into him.

Absolutely not *going to think about Allo right now.* That would involve thinking about whether he was ready to forgive the man, whether to allow Allo razing every damn katha village to the ground to be sufficient apology for tossing Tank out as bait to the crazed Bright Bay ha'ra'ha. Who'd apparently been the spawn of the ha'rethe Aerthraim Family had evicted—

Stop it. Not thinking about this, remember?

It took about a half mile before Lia said, in a muted tone, "I don't know what to say to that, Tank. *Sorry* seems beyond stupid, and useless."

"It would be. There's nothing to say. It's just a thing you have to know, to understand what's happening right now." He kept his gaze fixed ahead, unwilling to see her expression. "Dasin and I were both pulled out of our villages by … by a desert Family. We were healed as best possible, and trained up, and sent out again as their representatives." Which summary omitted a mountain and a half of detail, but was all she needed for now. "Turned out, during that training, I have some abilities, like you've seen. Dasin has them too, but they've always been real small, a bit of extra awareness, nothing to remark on."

He paused, waiting to see if she had anything to say and to let another set of riders pass from behind: three men, all on tall horses with clean lines, moving swiftly but not in a particular rush. Lia frowned after them and muttered, "Flatbrushes. Huh."

"Why 'huh'?" he asked, immensely relieved for even a small diversion from the acid he was pouring over himself.

"Flatbrushes aren't good mountain horses," she said. "They don't have the wind for sharp slopes or long rides." She shrugged and raised an eyebrow at him, tilting her head.

He was back on the hook. "Dasin's always been torn up about what he went through … well, so am I, sure, but he took it … *different*. Darker. Meaner."

Her sharp intake of breath told him she'd just put together a lot of pieces into a straight line. A very unpleasant straight line, in his opinion. His back went tight again, his breathing harsh. To his markedly faint relief, she left him alone until he could speak again.

"Evkit told me he could heal that darkness," Tank said, and then his throat just closed and wouldn't let more words come out. His sight blurred. He blinked hard, then again, and breathed through his nose.

Lia said, acidic, "I'm guessing that turned out double-edged and serrated."

"Mm." The constriction eased. He drew in a long breath, another. "Yeah, well. Dasin apparently got hold of his full potential, at that point. Took him until Arason to sort his wits out. He tried to tell me … in Arason, what had happened, what he'd found out he could do. Apparently I took it poorly, and he, ahhhh.…"

Tank bent his head, unable to overcome his still-shattering fury and horror to say the words aloud.

"He made you forget, like Idisio did me," Lia said. He glanced sideways. She was white-lipped and furious. "Fucking *hells*, Tank!"

"Yeah." The word came out barely audible. "Yeah," he repeated, more clearly. "Turns out he's a good bit stronger than anyone ever thought. At least, a lot stronger than *I* ever thought. He had me pretty much doing what he wanted, since Arason. Not real sure if that was, yanno, conscious, deliberate, or if it was a side effect of him keeping me from remembering."

"If you don't toss him off a cliff, I damn well will," Lia said, her face stark with anger. She moved her right hand to grip just below her left elbow, digging her fingertips in hard; glanced down with a grimace and released the hold.

Tank laughed a little, without real humor. "Yeah, well. Apparently when he went up to sing, the other night, everything kind of … broke. Those folks as went down, they'd been hurting … children, or equally vulnerable, I guess. Dasin must have felt it, because of connecting with that guardian spirit, probably. And he got mad. Pretty sure I passed out and fell when *he* snapped, from backlash of being let go from the hold. I think it was about to go anyway."

She whistled thoughtfully. "So you think he'll be attacking anyone along the way who he thinks is hurting children?"

Oh thank the gods, I didn't have to say that part myself. "Maybe. I don't know where his head's at. I don't know how he got Cilif to agree to go along, to leave us behind, for one thing."

She sucked in a hurt-sounding breath. "Oh gods."

"Yeah. So. Long answer to a short question, but there you go."

"Oh, Tank," she said, and the depth of pain in her voice nearly overset him. It wasn't pity, wasn't disgust, wasn't rejection: just a shearing acknowledgment of agony undeserved.

He reined Sin to a halt and sat still, fighting to stay upright and not go over onto the road like a sack of cooked oatmeal. Every muscle in his body felt on the verge of failing, including his bladder, and wouldn't Sin get irritated about *that*.

Lia waited beside him, her face set into grim lines he'd never seen on her before. Not speaking, not trying to *do* anything, just waiting for him to pull himself together.

Don't you fucking dare fall in love with her, Tank told himself brutally, and wrenched back control of body and mind. The part of him that had taken on Alyea's imprint said, laughing, *Oh, you're far too late on that, and you know it perfectly well, don't you?*

He growled and thumped Sin into a thoroughly painful, sufficiently distracting canter.

Chapter Sixty-one

By the time they reached the next village, which went by the relatively grand name of Stone Oak, Tank had gone a sickly white under his tan, his freckles standing out sharply. Sin seemed to be stepping with unusual delicacy, his ears frequently swiveling back. Horses could show astonishing understanding, in Lia's experience, and Sin had already proven himself possessed of a higher intelligence than most.

Lia made a mental note to ask Tank about how they'd come by Sin and Blackie next time she needed to distract him from his pain.

The stable here, much larger than at the last village, was a rough-built log building with a high, slant-roofed loft and a sizeable paddock and fenced pasture. Four horses grazed free in the pasture section, one with hoof-collars on. Two more, a glossy-coated Blackrock and a cheerful chestnut Halfpeack, were being put through their paces in the paddock. It was a wrench to turn away, but Tank was more important than watching the gorgeous flow of mane and tail and muscle.

The stable had a mounting block, thank the gods. She managed to maneuver Tank down to the ground with the help of a tall, frowsy-haired stableboy, whose eyes widened at some of the swears Tank let out in the process.

"Galno," Tank wheezed, leaning against Sin, "give 'em both good damn mash tonight, n' bess rubdown you can do. Fucking wonnerful horses."

More pragmatically, and coherently, Lia asked, "Can you fetch us help to get Tank to the inn and into a room?"

Galno nodded assent to both, and soon enough Lia was setting their bags on the floor and steering Tank onto the bed. She'd opted for a single room and to pay extra for an oil lantern rather than a simple candle, given that Tank would need regular assistance with the simplest tasks. She'd had to help him dismount once, along the way, to piss into the bushes. That had been quite the adventure, all things considered, but at least he'd been able to stand without help, so she'd gratefully kept her back turned. And she'd managed to get Tank to the outhouse before taking him to the inn, so hopefully anything more ... *substantial* was done with. If not, ah, *handled*.

When she'd left Stecatr, she'd have blazed red with embarrassment at anyone else saying such a coarse thing. For her to be thinking it, cool and clear-eyed, was ... something to ponder another time.

She still didn't want to think about the previous night's revelation. *Crossroads, not ii'ne*. By the look in his eyes, he'd also been interested in her for some time. A tenday ago, the realization would have brought horror, shame, and terror for what it meant to her reputation and Hall standing. Now....

Well, she wasn't thinking about it now, that was all. Neither of them were in any shape to have a sane discussion on the topic.

She dug out the painkillers from his pack, measured it into a mug of water by his weak-voiced instruction, and saw him across the threshold to sleep. Then she sat back on the chair, blowing out a heavy breath of air, and scrubbed her hands through her hair, letting out a few choice swear words of her own.

I'm the one in charge now. How the hells did that happen?

Lia took a moment to look around the room. It was small, and plain, with whitewashed plaster walls that more or less covered the rough logs that made up the frame of the inn. The bed was a log frame as well, with a thick straw tick under a heavy cover and thin sheets. If the night turned chill, she'd have to throw Tank's bedroll over him. She didn't look forward to sleeping on the uneven plank floor, given that there were no pallets available here, but it wouldn't be worse than cold, rocky ground.

At least the room was on the first floor. Getting Tank up and down stairs would have been nearly impossible.

I'd really love to throw Dasin off a cliff. Maybe after poking a few holes through his thick skull with a very sharp object.

Feh. Not useful.

She checked on his breathing and skin tone once more, then let herself out to find a meal — and to find out how poor a reception Dasin had left them.

Early fall air ran crisply chill under the late afternoon sunlight. A stand of oakbush served as separator between inn and stable; taller holly and mountain oak traced a rise towards the tavern. Like almost everything else in this village, the Stone Oak Tavern was mostly log frame, but its windows were larger than those of the similarly named inn, and the ones set high up were thick, wavy glass. At ground level, the shutters sat open to show empty space in the frame. The aroma of pipe and log smoke drifted out, along with the savory greasiness of roasting meats and the sharp tang of beer.

A larger, stone building stood across the commons — which was, here, a wide swath of close-cut grass amid random gravel patches that might once have been a design. From the comparative elegance of style, Lia guessed the building to be the home of a local magistrate or small lord. None of the villages she'd passed through to date had boasted anyone of specific significance. A blacksmith might be the local authority, or an innkeep, but there hadn't been anyone *dedicated* to leadership. That was for the towns, which held implicit authority over any villages within a certain distance; in turn, cities had a say in how nearby towns managed themselves.

Theoretically, anyway.

Another leg of the roughly square commons held another well-designed stone building, whose wide wooden doors were embossed with large bancti symbols. Lia eyed the church warily, then ducked into the tavern, putting off the question of obligations for after she'd settled her growling stomach.

There were few people in the tavern at the moment. She chose a seat near the door, handed over a silver round to the pock-marked server, and asked for a second serving to be brought over to the inn later. That required another silver round, an outrageous price, but there was no value in trying to shepherd Tank over for a meal. Lia wasn't inclined to walk far after this, herself. She'd been steadfastly ignoring an array of aches all day, and it was starting to wear her down.

The fare was a trencher of spit-roasted chicken, garden peas, and slab-cut potatoes. She drew a mug of water from the common barrel and tucked in. The trencher was nearly empty when a big man thumped down on the bench across the table from her, smiling awkwardly.

"Evening, *s'a*," he said. "Traveling alone, like?"

"No," she said. He was unshaven, his hair lank, and there was a gleam in his dark eyes she didn't care for. "Not alone, and not available, *s'e*."

"Now, that's unfriendly," he remarked, but his gaze drifted across her thoughtfully. "You don't even know me."

Silently, she dug her Hall coin — replaced, in Arason, with one bearing the sigil of that Hall — from her belt pouch and held it up. He blinked at it, then scowled in clear disappointment.

"Figures," he grunted, pushing himself upright, and turned away, muttering, "They're all *ii'ne*, apron-tied, or mercenary these days. Can't find nothing fun round these parts."

Lia grinned sourly at his back and finished her meal in peace, reflecting, with a mixture of amusement and *bemusement*, that he hadn't frightened her at all.

Fortified by the meal, she knocked on the priest's door on the side of the stone — well, the Stone Oak Church, she supposed — building. As in all churches, the side door was smaller and considerably plainer than the front entry doors, but a simple carving of ivy that wound along the frame added a touch of unexpected charm.

Late as it was, torches still flared to either side of the door, so someone was awake; and the front doors were shut, so there was no service going on at the moment.

A thin man with long pale hair caught back into an untidy tail opened the door and greeted her with a politely neutral, "Evening, *s'a*," and an inquiring look.

"Lia of Arason Hall, previously of Stecatr Hall," she said, holding out her new Hall coin. "Evening, *s'iope*."

He looked at the coin without moving to take it, then back to her face. His light-colored eyes held no particular expression. "Yes?"

She caught a breath in, realizing her mistake. This priest didn't know anything about her status, her history. No flags had been sent up this road, apparently. Hard on the back of that thought came another: she had good reason to talk to this priest beyond seeking official approval.

"I've need of confession and counsel, *s'iope*," she said. "If you've the time. I know it's late, but I'll be on the road again come morning."

He moved back, holding the door aside for her, and she entered a small foyer, barely wide enough for one person to pass through and no more than four steps long.

"Through and to the right, *s'a*," the priest said. "There's a padded bench. Do you require a screen?"

Stepping through into the larger room beyond, she considered that question as well as the nave she'd just entered. Wide enough for a service of fifty people, she guessed, with simple, sturdy benches aimed to the far side of the room, where a similarly styled priest's podium took up center position on a raised dais. Two more raised sections ran along the sides of the room: for the chorus, she guessed.

The most ornate item in the room was the wide chandelier, its white candles lit and dangling crystal pendants gleaming. "This is a lovely nave, *s'iope*," Lia said with sincerity.

"I'm sure it's nothing as grand as you're used to," the priest said, moving to stand beside her. "Hardly even any art to speak of."

Not paintings, no, but the carefully paneled walls had the designs of all four gods neatly carved at exactly measured distances; linens with intricate cutwork draped the priest stand and blessing table; and the floor was built from wide, smooth wooden planks varnished a glossy charcoal color.

"I don't know," she said, turning to meet his curious gaze. "I think there's more beauty in simple things, lovingly presented, than in glitter put out for a show."

His thin mouth quirked into a real smile at that. "Thank you, *s'a*." He cleared his throat. "I'm sorry, my manners are poor tonight. I'm *s'iope* Birch. Welcome to my church." He motioned to their right again. "As I asked already: would you like a screen?"

Two wide-bottomed benches, each with thick red padding, sat well over arm's length apart. Set against the wall near them was a finely woven wood and withy screen, with thicker pieces of wood that obviously served as feet stacked beside it.

"Some petitioners find themselves easier able to speak of their troubles if they can't see my face," *s'iope* Birch said. "It's no mark of anything in particular, only a grace for your ease."

"No," Lia said, looking at the screen thoughtfully. "No, I don't think I need that, thank you."

They settled on the benches, facing one another. Birch folded his hands in his lap and bent his head to murmur an opening prayer. To her surprise, Lia was able to join in word for word, finding no differences. Well, it was a simple enough bit of gratitude, there wasn't much to vary.

"The gods are thanked, and my hands are open to hold your troubles," the priest said then. He turned his hands cupped palm up, raising his head to regard her with what seemed sincerely interested inquiry.

Lia drew in a long breath, another, then began: "Give me guidance, s'iope; I've killed a man and been touched by witchcraft...."

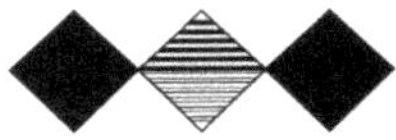

Mindful of the advancing hour, she kept the tale short and specific: first the bandit kill, which the priest agreed was unavoidable and had prevented a greater harm, then the more difficult encounters at the foot of Hells' Hill and in Thentree. She picked her way through those explanations cautiously, mentioning Kolan, Dasin, or Tank as little as possible and without using names when she had to allow for their presence.

She *didn't* talk about what had happened in the Hackerwood, or the hadinn, or Tank's explosive rage of the previous night. Those matters weren't ... *relevant* was the wrong word. Perhaps *solvable in this venue* came closer.

Birch's expression told her he'd seen the omissions clearly enough. Thankfully, he didn't press after revealing details. He leaned in and listened with intent neutrality, his eyebrows rising on occasion, and said nothing until she signaled that she'd finished talking. Then he sat back, rubbing one ear, his expression abstracted.

"The matter of killing," he said eventually, "is easy enough to set aside with a bit of prayer by way of penance, and I suspect you've been doing that already anyway. No?" He cocked his head, a faint smile ghosting across his thin mouth. "All right, then, recite the creed against harm four times a night, and the obedience creed twice a night, for the next tenday. Also, look for ways, going forward, to raise up the life of someone laboring under poor choices, that they might not meet such an end."

That was surprisingly fair, in Lia's opinion. She nodded gratefully.

"The matter of the spirits ... Eh." Birch cupped his hands palm up on his thighs again and studied them as though searching for an answer. "You weren't witched. You were allowed into the presence of a great and sacred secret." He bent his head, murmuring something under his breath, then stood. "Come this way, please, s'a Lia. I think in this case, it's easier to show first, explain later."

He led her along a narrow, dark hallway, and down a flight of stone steps. Lia kept a hand to the right side wall and listened carefully to Birch's occasional warning murmur. A heavy door creaked open, releasing a gust of chill, damp air.

"Watch for the sill, it's a handspan high, then four steps forward and stop."

She moved as directed and stood still, no solid surface other than the ground within reach. Darkness never particularly bothered her, but it *did* surprise her that she had no anxiety over her current vulnerability. The priest could dart behind her, shut and bar the door, and be gone before she even saw him moving; and nobody knew where she was.

He wouldn't, though. That certainty lay bone-deep. She was safe, standing here in the cold darkness with a priest of the Northern Church.

Now *there* was a sentence she wouldn't have believed six months ago.

A pale shimmer laced the air, building into a moon-bright glow and revealing a wide-mouthed well in the center of a small, stone-walled room. An instantly familiar blue light hovered a good four feet above the well.

Lia went down on her knees without really thinking about it. "Gods hold you gently," she said, then turned her head and frowned up at Birch, who stood with his hands folded over his stomach, regarding the light with a pensive expression.

"You can get up," he said. "It's not quite awake. Another two days, I think, before it's time for this one to speak. They're all a bit different."

She rose, brushing off her pants legs. "*S'iope?*"

"If you'd seen nothing, I'd have been both disappointed and relieved," he said distantly. "It's a burden, *s'a*. A responsibility I wouldn't wish on anyone. But there you go, and here we are. It's far too cold down here. Let's return to the nave."

He bowed to the light, touching his knuckles to his lips and murmuring something Lia couldn't quite make out, then led her back aboveground.

Settled on the benches again, he said without preamble, "The gods cannot touch the world directly without destroying it. They must work through their faithful and their servants, but nothing requires those to be human. Or properly alive."

Birch considered Lia's expression, his own thin lips drawing to one side.

"This is not normally knowledge given to those not sworn to the Church, as you might imagine."

"No," Lia said, the word sticking in a dry mouth. "I can see that. I ... *s'iope*, please don't ask me to swear into the priesthood."

"No, indeed!" Birch said, his face lighting with abrupt laughter that made him look ten years younger. "No, *s'a*, I had no thought of that. I think you'd be entirely unsuited to the robes. I will ask you to keep what I'm saying to yourself."

"That I can swear," she said fervently.

"Good, then. So. There are creatures, human and not, who, knowingly or not, serve the gods to a surpassing degree during the course of their lives. Some choose to continue in that role after their passing, and become...." He motioned down, indicating the hidden well below them. "I will admit that's an extremely simple version of a much more complicated tale. Where are you bound to, from here?"

"Assiasan."

"Ah. Good. Two more villages up, in Torion, there's a woman named Saspen. Tell her I sent you, and she'll finish explaining properly. Best give her at least two hours." Birch's pale eyes gleamed with amusement. "For now, I'll reassure you that you're not demon-touched nor witch-rattled, and that the spirits you've encountered are not only safe but sacred. Treat them with respect and honor, fill their requests as best you can, and the gods will be entirely pleased with you." He paused, a frown flitting over his thin face, and added, "You said you're originally from Stecatr, if I recall?"

"Yes." Lia braced herself for the all too familiar look of pitying contempt, but the priest looked pained, instead.

"Ah. I'm ... not quite sure how to put this, *s'a*, but...."

"Don't tell the Stecatr Church priests anything about this conversation, or what prompted it?" Lia supplied dryly. "Already figured on that."

Birch's good humor flashed once more, bright and merry. "Indeed. They're a bit difficult, aren't they."

"I've had several people pressing me to never go back," Lia admitted. "I have to, though. In fact, *s'iope*, that's another matter to ask you about, if it's not too much."

Birch cocked his head inquiringly.

Lia gathered and sorted words, then said, "I've learned a great deal since leaving Stecatr this past spring, mostly that the ways I grew up with, the, the beliefs I grew up under, aren't held the same everywhere else. I'll be going back on the wings of winter, and boxed in by weather when I arrive. The Stecatr Church is likely to be unhappy with me on several points, and I have family to think of."

Birch sat quietly, entirely sober now, his hands once more cupped up on his thighs.

Lia hesitated, trying to find any better way to ask; then gave up and said, in an unintentional wail: "What do I *do*, *s'iope*? How can I refuse my priests in favor of another path without offending the gods? How can the beliefs be so *different*, a handful of miles apart? It doesn't make *sense*. What's the *truth* of it all?"

Birch bent his head and allowed the pained vibrations from her voice to die back to stillness before straightening to meet her gaze. "S'a Lia, any man or woman who claims they know the truth of the gods is lying," he said bluntly. "Any priest doing so ought to be kicked off a cliff, in my eye. That's not what we're here for. That's not our job, nor it is proper for us to declare that only one path to grace exists. The world is very large and very strange, and I must believe, since the gods created it so, that they wish us to come to them as through a colander, not through a tight funnel."

Her heart seemed to bounce in her chest. "*Yes*," she said without meaning to, then sat back, astonished at her own ferocity.

Birch's smile returned, his eyes gleaming with answering passion. "There, *s'a*," he said. "Now you know your path, and that will lead you to the rest of your answers."

He rose, motioning Lia to her feet as well. She stood, dazed, feeling as though Sin had clipped her head with one of his big hooves.

"It's ... it's just that?" she said, bewildered. "Nothing more than ... that simple?"

"Simple is best seen by looking over one's own shoulder at the path behind." Birch put his hands on her shoulders, his skin radiating dry warmth. "Gods hold you on the road forward, tomorrow and all of your days, and may your discoveries along the way help to heal the world."

While it wasn't quite the blessing she'd grown up with, it was *better*. That, and the genuine warmth in the delivery, brought a blurriness to her vision.

"Thank you," she said in a small voice. "You as well, *s'iope*. Thank you."

"Mind the sill," he advised, voice coolly pragmatic as she turned towards the short passageway leading to the priest's door. "There's a bit of a lip from this side."

Just shy of the door, she glanced back into the visible slice of the nave, collecting one last, wondering moment of peace; then stepped up and out into the quiet, chill evening air, lighter of stride than she could remember being for some years.

Chapter Sixty-two

As much as Tank hated to admit it, having his food brought to him came as a stark relief. He wasn't sure if Lia had said something or word had spread from the inn to the tavern, but the roasted chicken and potatoes had been cut into manageable chunks and the trencher sat in a wide-bottomed clay bowl. Setting aside pride in favor of hunger, he thanked the serving girl — Ussi, if he recalled the name right — who'd brought it. She dipped her knees and twinkled at him.

"That's a real nice lady you have along this time," Ussi observed. "When t'other ones ran through without you, figured I'd be facing off with that Gint again. An' as Dasin said as you had a broken sommat or other, I didn't know as if I'd have to ask my brother to stand by me while I worked."

Tank couldn't keep himself from a pained wince that had nothing to do with his collarbone. "That's not the first remark like that I've heard along the way," he allowed. "Seems like I ought to have let him go a while ago." At least that answered the question of how she'd known to cut up his food.

"Seems like," she returned with another pretty smile, and took her leave.

Tank, with a sigh, bent his head and ate. At least, from the sound of it, Dasin hadn't done anything to offend these people.

A lot of at leasts *starting to pile up,* Tank reflected moodily, setting his empty plate aside and considering the chamberpot. *At least* Dasin seemed to be thinking with a bit of sense and kindness. *At least* he didn't have to wrangle Gint in the face of this disaster. *At least* it was his collarbone, not his leg. *At least* Lia hadn't abandoned him in the face of his longstanding deception. Although the deception, *at least,* could be argued as being to her benefit, during those early days when she'd been jumpy as a half-skinned rabbit.

He stood, smoothing his increasingly rumpled and stained clothes, then gingerly worked his way to the nearby outhouse. Stone Oak had nothing so grand as an indoor anything, in that regard. Well, maybe the priest house did, and the village lord. Those two loftily grand stone buildings ill suited the rest of the ramshackle village, in Tank's opinion, but the people within seemed nice enough, and were strictly, honestly mindful of the residents' wellbeing.

Tank and his crew had actually gone to services on occasion: once for a birth celebration, twice for funerals. Stone Oak had a much smaller funeral space than Thentree's, meaning the crowd of singers had to take up a different spot than around the actual pyre. It wasn't at all a bad space, and Birch was mild enough, although something in his pale stare always made Tank a bit itchy under the collar.

Tank devoutly hoped he wouldn't have to attend any more funerals on the way north.

He left aside brooding and focused on the sharp discomfort of managing clothing and sling without dropping anything into the privy. Once he'd managed the necessary, he settled on a bench outside the inn, breathing in the mild air, listening, watching, and trying not to think too much.

The leaves of a nearby poplar had already begun to splotch with yellow. Tank grimaced. That was generally something seen on the way back south, not a good ten days shy of Assiasan. They were running out of time to get somewhere before the fierce winter winds he'd only ever, so far, heard about set in.

I wonder ... wandered through his mind without any particular tag attached to the end. Tank looked at the feathery clouds drifting lazily overhead and let the thought drift alongside them. It was the sort of beginning that needed a quiet, patient wait to coax out the ending.

A faint pain ghosted along his shins, an old ache long since healed.

Healed....

Huh.

I wonder....

"Desert lord," Tank said aloud, thoughtfully, and squinted at the sky. "Huh."

After a few more moments of considering the notion, he rose and made his way back to the room.

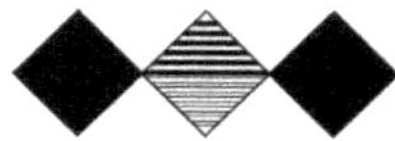

Mindful of the many things that could go wrong in the attempt to do something wholly untaught, and the agony when Idisio healed him, Tank made sure the shutters stood open to the night air and the door firmly shut. He shifted the small table and oil lantern well out of arm's reach, in case he thrashed off the bed, and set the water pitcher, mug, and pain medicine against the base of the wall near the head of the bed.

He sat on the bed, letting the red ache behind his eyes subside and his breathing steady. How long had it been since Lia left, and when would she be back? He wasn't at all sure, and it seemed a terrible idea for her to walk in on him screaming, if this went wrong, or to interrupt him midway through, if it went right.

Tentatively, he moved to stand in front of the door, sorting through Alyea's memories of this sort of thing. He laid a hand on the frame, hesitated, then *decided* nobody would come through until he was ready to allow it. Nothing seemed to happen. He shifted his hand to more of a grip than a palm-touch, dropped into *other*-vision, and tried again.

This time, a silvery netting flickered across the doorway, then faded away. He could still feel it there, an intangible barrier as good as anything, he thought, a desert lord could manage.

"Well, then," he said, pleased with himself, and went back to the bed.

As he sorted himself out against the pillows, vision flickered from ordinary to *other* and back. He'd never tried holding it while moving, much less while in pain. He let it drop until he was comfortable, rather than risk using up his limited strength.

Finally settled, left arm riding easy in the sling, he began to breathe in a quiet, even pattern. *Let it go. Let it all go. Be still.*

Slowly, silence eased in around him, body and mind. Nothing existed except his breath, his heartbeat, the thrumming pain of his collarbone.

Slowly, slowly, he turned vision inward, opened himself to himself. Ragged red lines laced throughout his torso, neck, and head. The center point of the tangle, of course, lay along his left collarbone, obscuring the actual break under an unquiet swirl of crimson.

Slowly, slowly, *slowly* he eased down amongst the mess, leaving himself no space for doubt, letting intuition run him in a way he'd rarely risked. The bone stood out white and solid, surrounded by gray-blue-silver lines and splotches that he guessed were nerves and muscle. And there was the break: a thin spot occupied by that dense red knot. Trailing red threads looped and wove through muscle and nerve, pulling close things meant to be set apart and pulling apart things meant to stay together.

Tank slipped amongst the tangle, the lines almost tangible against his hands as he teased them apart, guiding and unwinding and —

A *presence* flared, pale blue and silver and definitively female: *Lia*. He nearly lost his place, nearly stepped sideways out of the trance; caught himself in time enough to reset his grip and resume the steady, ticklish task.

One thread worked loose. Another. A third. And —

— as he'd expected, a flare of shredding pain hit, as it had in Arason during Idisio's healing. He could feel the muscles in his throat going raw from a high scream, but, lost in the overheated razor-dance throughout his body, he couldn't hear anything.

Then the knot dissolved all at once, the pain stopped with an intangible *snap*, and, also as had happened in Arason, Tank felt himself going woozy. He had barely enough clarity left to release the binding on the door before he fainted.

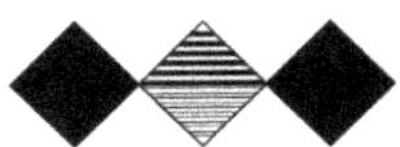

"If we get to Assiasan without a pitchfork-waving mob at our heels, it'll only be from me talking fast and lying a lot," Lia said waspishly some time later, when Tank roused and blinked around wearily. "What the fuck was *that?*"

Tank swallowed in a dry throat and reached down to scoop up the mug of water. He drained half of it and sat up to find Lia staring at him white-faced and incredulous. The lamp — a thick-bottomed, sturdy one not at all suited for carrying — was brighter than he'd left it. She must have turned it up.

Belatedly, it occurred to him that she must have paid extra for the lamp in order to make caring for him easier. He ought to reimburse her for the expense.

"What did you *do?*" she breathed, much more quietly, her hand on her chest as though to stop her heart from leaping right out.

Bemused, he looked around, then at the mug in his hand. In his left hand.

"Ah," he said, blinking rapidly. He switched the mug to his right hand and flexed the fingers of his left several times. "Damn me, it worked." His shoulder still ached ferociously, but it was a bruised sort of hurt, now, not the stabbing agony of a broken bone.

"You were screaming like a dying rabbit," Lia said. "I couldn't get the door open. The innkeep was about to go get a sledgehammer when you finally stopped screaming and the door popped open. Took me a lot of lies before he was willing to go away, at that point." Her face set in grimly unfriendly lines. "Bit of a disadvantage there, you being well liked and me being unknown."

Tank shoved back against the pillows and tried to keep his tone neutral in the face of her ire. "Gar? Big man with no chin? Hah. Yeah. He mostly likes Dasin. What did you tell him?"

"I said you'd been having nightmares and that you tended to piss yourself and he was welcome to help me clean it up if he liked. He lost interest about then."

Tank dropped his head back and let out a croaking laugh. "Fucking hells. Of all the — *Lia!*"

"It worked," she said. Her severe expression unbent towards a smirk. "And you owe me for that bit of fast talking."

"I'd say you owe *me* for the embarrassment, but as that's on the mild side for me, and as I'm not likely to be back, I'll let it pass," he said, then let out a looser laugh. "Gods damn. I wouldn't have thought of that particular lie. Thank you."

"Back to the question of *What did you do,*" Lia said, crossing her arms. The hard glint resurfaced in her eyes.

"Eh." Tank rolled his shoulders gently, right then left, and found his mouth stretching in a flatly goofy smile. "I apparently healed myself. Wasn't at all sure it would work."

She stared at him, shaking her head slowly. "One of these days I'll understand you," she said, "but that's surely not going to be today."

"Well, it worked," he said a shade defensively.

"And if it hadn't? If it had gone to the worse? Or left you mind-broken? You could have at least waited for me, rather than let me walk up and hear you shrieking like that. I thought you'd had another breakdown, that you were about to do something ... stupid."

Tank drew in a sharp breath, swinging his legs around to sit on the edge of the bed.

"With all I've been through, I've never yet wanted to kill myself," he said, holding her gaze. "I'm not about to go there for *Dasin*, of all people."

It hurt surprisingly little to say, and the sting was more of a long-hidden truth finally breaking free.

Lia looked away, shoulders hunching. The shadow of an old pain floated around her like a dark aura for a moment, then vanished. "You should have waited," she said, her voice thin and harsh.

About to say: *You couldn't have done anything to help*, he paused and looked at what the second half of that statement would have been. Best left silent, or not? Not, he decided finally, and said it: "I was afraid I'd hurt *you*."

She inhaled through her nose, then roughly pulled the chair around to sit on it backwards, her arms resting on the uneven top rail. Given the small size of the room, it put her close enough for him to reach out and touch her hand. He scooted back instead, folding his legs up into a cross-legged sit and putting his hands palm up on his thighs. For some reason, that brought a lopsided smile to Lia's face.

"Thank you for sending food over," Tank said before Lia could speak. "And for all the help, the last day or so. I'm still —" He rubbed his left collarbone gently, wincing. "Still hurts like I've been stomped on. I'll need to take it real easy for another tenday at least, I think. But the break seems to be closed up. More'n I expected. I thought I might be able to, I dunno, stiffen it up to keep it from being so damn tender while it healed."

Lia said, tone muted, "You're welcome. I have a question."

"What's that?"

"Are you still my trail lead, or are we traveling as equals at this point?"

He started to answer that, stopped mid-word; started again, then shut his mouth and dropped his head into his hands. "Fuck," he said through his fingers.

"Mm." He heard her scratch-drum her short nails against the rough wooden chair back in a slow, thoughtful rhythm. "You never said what you're expecting to find, in Assiasan."

"Not Dasin," he said, sitting up again. "Cilif, maybe. A bundle of my gear and a bag of coin. Maybe another note saying *I'm sorry but it's better this way*. That's about it."

She let out an unamused snort. "It *is* better," she said bluntly. "I'd swing a brick to his tenders while he was asleep, given the chance."

He leaned back on his hands, then hissed at the sharp twinge and sat up straight, rubbing his left shoulder again. "Given what he can do now, probably not the safest notion," he observed. Then, dropping his voice a notch, "Lia, about last night."

"Don't," she said, level and flat. "Don't apologize. I do understand why you left me thinking you were *ii'ne*. And really, for all intents, you *were*, at the time. So it wasn't wholly a lie."

"Ehhh." He made a face, not liking that phrasing, but decided to let it go. "All right. But thing is, you *are*, so it's ... eh. Rude? Inappropriate? Insulting? Something, anyway, for me to ... I don't even know."

He rubbed his hands across his face, fingers rasping through beard well past stubble.

Need to shave. And now he *could.* That was a vast relief.

Lia didn't say anything. He looked up sharply and surprised an odd expression on her face. "Lia ...?" he said, eyebrows rising.

"Right now," she said, as though testing each word, "you're a mess through and through. And I'm ... I'm sorting out some new thoughts, myself. So can we put this conversation aside for another day? Without anything implied or inferred, either side," she added hastily.

He stared at her, blinking as he ran *that* through his own head a few times. "Yeah. Yeah, we can do that."

"Good." Her stern reserve lightened into a rueful smile. "You staying trail lead, for now, feels smartest. I don't know anything at all about the road ahead, or about Assiasan, for one thing. Once we get to Stecatr ... If?" She tilted her head inquiringly. "*Are* you coming to Stecatr, Tank?"

He held up his hands, fingers spread, and examined them, turning them slowly front to back a few times. "I think maybe I'd better," he said at last, dropping his hands back to his thighs. "I think maybe I don't have much choice at this point, not if I want to live with myself."

"I can understand that." She stood to drag the chair back around against the wall, then caught up her bedroll and pack, looking down as he let out a surprised, questioning sound. "I'm going down to the commons," she told him. "You don't need the help anymore, and there's room to spare."

"Don't," he said before sense could stop him, and grimaced at the way her eyes narrowed. "I'm not at all sure that this mending will hold, for one, and for two, that I won't have a pissing nightmare after all."

"Thin," she observed.

"I don't like being alone at night," he said bluntly. "Never have. Damnit —" Keeping his gaze matched to hers felt like driving needles through his eyes. "I am, as you noted, a fucking mess. And I fucking trust you. So. Please." He gritted the last word out between his teeth.

Slowly, she lowered her pack and bedroll, let out a long sigh, then turned to sort herself out for bed.

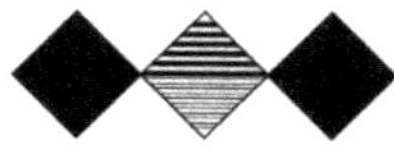

Neither of them, by the grace of whatever gods existed, had nightmares. At Lia's suggestion, Tank put the sling back on in the morning and did his best to play-act as though his collarbone was still broken. He made sure to hand over an extra silver round to the innkeep and another for Ussi, since he and Lia were leaving too early for him to bring the dishes back himself. Gar was honest enough that he'd bring the money directly to Ussi, and was clearly still uneasy about the previous night, since he didn't protest about his own tip.

Or perhaps Gar thought it was meant to cover replacing the straw tick. Tank muffled a snort of laughter at the thought and barely remembered to need help scrambling atop Sin.

Damn, Lia had quick wits and a savage humor on her, now that she'd finally loosened up.

Are you still my trail lead? After Assiasan, the answer to that would most definitely be *no*. What then? *That's to find out when we get there*, he told himself firmly. Lia was right. There was plenty to mange without throwing that on the pile.

Still, he found himself grinning at the pale dawn as it brought the trees from shadow to shape to drying leaves clicking in a light breeze. Not the chill wind of the Bright Bay dockside where he'd first encountered Lia, still further from the overheated, stagnant air of southern summer they'd ridden through together from there. Ahead lay deeper cold, and stronger winds, and higher, more dangerous paths in more than just the geographical sense.

For the first time in he couldn't remember how long, he was, from head to toes, *happy*.

Took damn well long enough, Alyea's ghostly imprint commented dryly. He laughed, and nudged Sin into a cheerful canter, moving towards the day ahead without the least impulse to look back.

Chapter Sixty-three

Torion turned out to be an expansively terraced village, very close to town-sized. There was little truly level ground; most paths ran at a distinct slope, and numerous flights of stairs had been cut into the rock to access various levels.

The main road through town boasted two inns, two taverns, a large stable, a bakery, and a hot spring bathhouse. At an angle to the main road, and significantly downslope, were a tanner, blacksmith, carpentry shop, dyer, and a repair-of-all-sorts craftsman's shop. Another branch, leading upslope, led one to a weaver, tailor, cobbler, cheese shop, apothecary, community hall, and a building that Lia could only describe as *not quite not a church*.

Squat and round, with a wide patio wrapped round one half and a tidy garden the other, the building was painted a cheerful blue, with a yellow door and shutters. The door itself wasn't square, but rounded as though to match the building, and the bancti symbol in the center of it was a thinly traced outline rather than a proudly elaborate display. Tank had confirmed that it was, in fact, the local church, then laughed at Lia's bewilderment.

The building was far too small to hold services. Apparently those were held at the community hall. As were birth celebrations, funerals, legal disputes, coming of age celebrations, contests for everything from baking to wrestling, various holidays — and weddings, one of which was in progress when Lia and Tank arrived.

Tank's face lit up at the news. "Unida and Vier? Wonderful!" he said with unusual emphasis. The stout innkeep laughed at him, in a way that implied an inside joke.

The innkeeper looked at Lia sideways, his grin spreading to include her in the humor, and confided, "Unida's had a *passion* for this one." He nodded at Tank, who shrugged stolidly. "It's gotten damned awkward at times. We're all relieved to see her finally settled."

"I believe I'll pass along my well wishes and stay clear," Tank agreed, prompting a laugh from the innkeep.

"Best choice," the man said amiably. "Anything more than the room today, *s'e?*"

"I'd like dinner and breakfast sent over from the Black Daisy," Tank said, neatly stacking three silver rounds on the desk. The innkeep looked at it with raised eyebrows, then sideways at Lia once more, his gaze much more thoughtful this time. "I'd rather not be obvious that I'm in town, given the wedding."

The innkeep nodded once, entirely serious. "I'll make sure the staff knows. *S'a*, will you be staying secluded as well?" He managed to say it without any salacious implication, although his mouth tugged to one side afterwards.

"No," Lia said, determinedly neutral. "If you could direct me to Saspen, I'd appreciate it."

"Ah, no, I'm afraid not. She's the one officiating the wedding, see."

Lia bit her lip, irritated with herself. Of course Saspen would be a priest. Birch hadn't said so explicitly, but the inference should have been clear enough. "When will she be available, do you think?"

"Ehhh." The innkeep considered, frowning. "Late afternoon, maybe towards evening. But ... I don't know that it'd be the best time, tonight, to talk to her."

"Why not?"

"It's a *wedding*," the man said, as if the answer should be obvious. "Once her duties are done, she'll be as drunk as the rest."

A priest, drunk? Lia thought but managed not to say aloud.

Her expression must have shown her incredulty, though, because the innkeep laughed again and said, "If it's important, *s'a*, I'll send a boy over to see if the *s'iope* can be pulled clear for a time. Given everything." He nodded at Tank. "You're leaving in the morning, I take it," he added. "Catching up to Dasin, are you? Funny thing, he said you were behind because you'd been injured."

"I was," Tank said calmly. "It wasn't as bad as it looked at first."

"Ah, well, these things happen," the innkeep said. "Seems odd he'd have left you behind, is all, you two always been insep'rable." He glanced at Lia again, pointedly, then inclined his torso in a not-quite bow. "I'll send that messenger and have *s'iope* Saspen come up to your room, if that's agreeable."

Lia hesitated, then said, "That's fine. Thank you."

Tank, after murmuring neutral parting phrases, steered Lia up to their third-floor room, his weight raising creaks and dull protests from the wood floors.

"Must have been *very* awkward," Lia said as they went.

"Oh yes. That girl don't understand *no* real well."

"By chance, does Vier have red hair?" she asked innocently.

Tank growled at her.

"I'll take that as a *yes*."

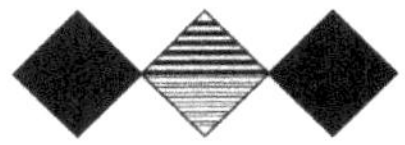

Insofar as Lia still held any expectations for how a priest of the Northern Church should look or behave, Saspen met none of them. Female, first of all; short and dark-skinned, for another. Dressed in garish reds and yellows, for a third, in a very southern style. The sleeves were slit and puffed to show most of her thin arms, and she wore indecently tight leggings under a silky skirt which had been slit up the sides far enough to leave nothing to the imagination.

"*S'e* Tank," she greeted them gravely, her dark eyes assessing them in a fast sweep that left Lia feeling more exposed than if she'd worn clothing similar to Saspen's. "*S'a* Lia, I believe?"

"*S'iope,*" Lia returned with a nod,

Saspen took the only chair — which Lia had been sitting in before Saspen's arrival — turned it round and sat, her arms across the back. Tank's mouth quirked, and he cut a glance at Lia, apparently remembering their discussion of two nights ago where she'd done the same. "What can I answer for you, *s'ieas?*"

Tank bowed, more respectful than usual, and motioned to Lia as he said, "Lia's the one with the questions, *sio* Sansa."

Lia blinked at the deeply informal address, then again as Tank moved deliberately back to perch on the bed, out of her line of sight. The priest's gaze fixed on Lia, attentive and questioning.

Lia had *intended* to explain to Tank before the priest arrived. Somehow there just hadn't been a good opening. He'd probably be irritated with her for not telling him sooner.

Well, consider it payback, she thought with a flare of sardonic amusement. She said, "I, uh. I spoke to Birch. *S'iope* Birch. In Stone Oak. And ... he told me to come speak to you. About...."

No, that approach wouldn't work. Lia paused, then sighed, rubbing a hand over her face, and moved to sit on the bed beside Tank.

"It's a long story. Let me start where it begins." With care, she repeated the tale she'd given Birch in Thentree.

Saspen listened with the same quiet intensity Birch had displayed, her eyes narrowing thoughtfully on occasion. Tank shifted his weight now and again, as though stopping himself from getting up to pace, and made a faint grumbling sound twice, but stayed silent overall.

Lia stopped at the end of her visit with Birch, then directed an inquiring look of her own at Saspen.

Saspen said nothing for a while, her gaze abstracted. Tank stirred again, then sighed deeply and went still.

"So you're Sighted," Saspen said, her gaze coming back into focus. She looked Lia over with considerably more attention. "And from Stecatr. Well."

Her gaze flicked to Tank. She seemed to hesitate, then shook her head slightly and looked back to Lia.

"Birch gave you a good basic understanding of what the spirits you've been seeing are: people sworn to serve the gods, who chose to continue that role after their mortal passing. They're not all human, and the gods they served in life are not always the ones we recognize today."

Tank drew in a hissing breath through his teeth. Saspen's mouth quirked.

"Oh yes," she told him. "There have been many more gods than the Three and the Four, over the millennia."

This time Lia was the one to suck in a harsh breath. "*S'iope*," she said, not quite protesting but feeling entirely out of her depth.

Saspen spread her hands, and Lia noted that her fingers were longer than they should have been, the nails an oddly blue color that didn't come from paint. "Humans have not been here for very long, *s'a* Lia, all things considered. You already know about the ha'reye and ha'ra'hain; they were old before humanity began. And even they were not the first, although they'd like you to think so."

This time both Tank and Lia made protesting sounds. Saspen's thin mouth stretched in a dry grin.

"There's a reason this isn't discussed with laypeople," she said, folding her hands together atop the chair back. "Stecatr, in particular, has utterly rejected this part of our world's history. To be fair, there are so few of us with the Sight that it's easily dismissed as hallucinatory nonsense. Tank, I'm assuming, since you're part of this discussion, that you've decided to face your heritage?"

Barely moving her head, Lia looked sideways at Tank. His expression remained amiable as he said, "Beginning to think I don't have much choice, *sio*."

"You never did," she agreed, "but I surely wasn't going to be the one to tell you so." She paused, frowning. "Dasin went through in a troubled state of spirit I hadn't seen in him before. Is that related?"

"It's a story of its own, *sio*, and I'm not ready to tell it just yet," Tank said with, from what Lia could see, surprisingly little tension. "But we're no longer traveling together."

Saspen nodded, accepting that with equal calm. "I thought as much." She made a dismissing gesture with one long-fingered hand, then grinned, catching Lia staring at the motion. "Yes, I'm what most people call a partial. I know my heritage for ten generations back, and the Sight passes along matrilineal lines, in my case. Some families run patrilineal." She aimed a pointed glance at Tank.

He stiffened at last, his voice turning flat. "*Sio*, these are the most words we've ever exchanged, so how do you know anything at all about me?"

"That I haven't spoken to you doesn't mean I haven't been watching and listening, and asking questions in the background," she returned, her voice dropping in kind. "You've always stood out, Tank, to anyone with the Sight. So does Lia, although I'm guessing—" She squinted at Lia, tilting her head slightly. "I'm guessing you're new to this?"

"Brand new," Lia admitted. "I only started seeing uncanny things ... recently."

"Have you recently had close contact with a ha'ra'ha or ha'rethe, by chance?"

Lia opened her mouth, shut it, then let out a soft grunt of dismay. "Is *that* why ...?"

"It's often a trigger," the priest said. "The Sight, and other abilities, are latent in more people than you'd think." She rested her chin on one wrist, her gaze abstracted again. "Tank, can you see the spirits, as Lia does?"

"I did, in Thentree," he said with audible care. "I don't know if I would've thought to look, on my own. I think maybe she sees them more easily and clearly than I do."

"Very likely," Saspen agreed. "Where is your mother's family from, Lia?"

"Orhon."

"I thought so. That community has a very strong connection to their guiding spirit. Does she have older siblings?"

"No, she's an only child." Lia bit a knuckle, frowning as she sorted through memory. "She never told me anything about this. But on my way south, I stopped into Orhon, and her name ... made people react in a way I didn't understand."

"Horrified or happy?"

"A little of both, I think. Mostly happy to see me. A lot of people asked if she was coming for a visit soon, and my cousin tried to set me up with a job that would keep me in town. I needed to continue south for reasons of my own, so I said no."

"That's a shame, in a way," Saspen said. "But I doubt you'd have triggered without your encounters along the road, whatever they were, so perhaps it's to the good. Still, your mother shouldn't have been allowed to leave. If you're Sighted, so is she."

Lia looked away and didn't say anything. She'd long since done the math, and knew exactly why her mother had married and relocated to Stecatr. But there had never been the slightest indication of anything unnatural — supernatural, she corrected herself. Then again, Stecatr being Stecatr, and Lia's father being how *he* was ... it really wasn't surprising at all.

The priest had been watching her closely. She said, "Now that you know, you have a duty. A responsibility, if you'd prefer that word. You're not just Sighted, s'a: from what you've said, you're a full Seer. You'll see the spirits again, and again, and again. They'll expect you to do as you've already done: listen, bear witness, carry messages. Occasionally, perhaps, something more. I don't know," she added, holding up a hand to stop Lia from speaking. "I'm not a Seer. I see them, but imperfectly, and I've never heard them. You do, so you have the burden of care from now on. It's not enviable...." Her mouth twisted. "But neither is it avoidable."

"How ... rare ... is this ability?" Tank asked with audible care.

"Extremely," Saspen said. "I've said all I'll say on that." She stood, returning the chair to its former spot. "Tank. One more thing. Dasin came to me with a message for you. He said to wait until after Unida was safely wed, then to find you and say: You're welcome."

"For what?" Tank said in clear bewilderment.

"No idea," Saspen said. "He did take the time to sit and speak with the girl before he left, though. Whatever he said calmed her down, thankfully. I'd been starting to wonder if she'd bolt at the altar." She shrugged, then offered a polite half-bow to Lia and Tank in turn, and let herself out.

The silence hung for some time before Lia said, acidic, "Four guesses on what he *said* to her."

"First three don't count," Tank agreed, rubbing his face roughly. "Damnit, Dasin."

"Is this his way of trying to apologize?"

He grunted, then said, "Probably."

"Is it working?"

"No." Tank paused, grimacing, then admitted, "Well ... maybe a little."

Chapter Sixty-four

Given the dubious but broad hint left by Dasin's message, they risked going to the nearest tavern for a proper meal that evening. Tank steered them to a corner table and settled with his back into the safety of the wall join, trusting Lia to run interference if it became necessary. Catching her sardonic grin, he returned a rueful one of his own; she understood what he was doing, and saw the sense of it. Thank the gods. He had no shame at all in doing everything he could to avoid Unida. The girl had been fucking *unstoppable*. If Dasin had actually influenced her out of her obsession with Tank, it might just slant Tank's mind toward a bit of forgiveness after all.

Maybe.

The serving girl took Tank's coin and returned with tankards of beer and a trencher of roast lamb, potato dumplings, and steamed carrots. Lia waited until they were alone to sniff at her drink, make a face, and set it carefully aside.

"Not fond of beer?" Tank said, draining half of his. Hoppy, as most of the mountain ales tended to be, and a bit smoky. He'd had better, but also far worse.

"I prefer wine," Lia said, spearing a carrot with her eating knife. "Sanben made me try every possible skunk brew on the way south. Only one I ever liked was that ginger-gold in Bright Bay."

"Yeah, that's the best out there," Tank agreed, and bent his attention to demolishing his portion of the trencher.

They ate in companionable quiet for a time. Then, abruptly, Lia stood, turning fast, her hand going to the hilt of her dagger. "Stop," she said, in a level tone that managed to cut through the nearby conversations.

Silence fell, spreading throughout the tavern. The tall young man who'd been approaching their table went back a step, smiling easily, hands out with palms up. "No harm," he said. "A question only, *s'ieas*, if you'd allow it."

Lia moved aside a step, flicking a questioning glance at Tank. He nodded shortly, pushing the almost empty trencher aside and wiping his hands on the coarse tablecloth. "Sit, then," he told the young man, pointing to the chair Lia had been using. Lia moved to stand behind the newcomer's shoulder, her arms folded.

"I understand you're both mercenaries — oh, forgive me. My name is Kerry."

The young man smiled engagingly. His coarse, dark brown hair was tied back in a simple braid, and he had southern features but for a snub nose. His clothes were clean and well-fitted, although careful mending showed in a few spots. Tank couldn't place his accent, but it didn't sound local.

"I believe you're Tank and Lia, yes? I was told to seek you out." He waved a hand towards the bar, vaguely, as though to indicate who'd sent him over. "I'm traveling, you see, and I'd like an escort to Assiasan. I'm advised you're traveling in that direction."

Tank considered, frowning. "What have you been doing for escort so far?"

"I've walked alongside various groups," Kerry said, waving his hand again, this time in a lazy spiraling motion. "I found myself left behind by my latest companions. Something of a disagreement, and then a hangover interfered with my plans to mend fences before they left me behind." He grinned cheerfully.

Tank didn't trust that grin one bit. "What takes you to Assiasan on the wings of winter, *s'e*?" he said brusquely, hoping that rudeness might get rid of the man.

"I like that phrase!" Kerry said, brightening further. "I hadn't heard that before." He seemed to mutter it to himself a few times, as though fixing it in his head, then looked up again. "I study words, you see." He paused, taking in Tank's expression, and sobered considerably. "Or perhaps not. I'm a scholar. I study words. The origin of words, what they mean in different cultures, the way spelling has diverged ... Don't worry, I won't rattle on about it. But that's why I'm going to Assiasan. I have a contract, I suppose you could say." He picked at his lower lip, eyes squinching almost shut. "I can't speak on details, I'm afraid. But I do need to get there in good time. And I can pay!" His infectious grin reappeared. "I forgot to mention that, didn't I? Sorry. I can offer you a generous price. A silver round a day? Each?" His face wrinkled into a worried expression. "That *is* generous, isn't it?" he added anxiously. "I was told that would be generous. But perhaps I was misinformed?"

Tank blinked, sorting through the barrage of words and questions. "Ehh," he said, and looked up at Lia. She tilted her head to one side thoughtfully, then shrugged; back to him, then. Wonderful. "Do you have a horse? Tent? Road supplies of any sort?"

"Yes, no, and not much," Kerry said promptly. "I'm afraid a good deal of my supplies went ahead with my former companions. I'd planned on buying more. But I do have a horse. Maybe you saw him in the stables? Big, rangy, dark and splotchy beast. Tends to bite."

Tank remembered seeing a horse like that. It had looked to be taller than Sin, which might not go over well on the trail if both horses were aggressive.

"Oh, he only bites people," Kerry added, as though guessing Tank's thoughts. "He's entirely indifferent to other horses. No trouble at all, just don't get too close to him."

Tank began to pinch his nose, caught himself in time and changed it to scratching his jaw. "There are at least six more days to Assiasan. Likely more, if weather turns or other delays come up. Are you sure you can afford twenty silver, if things go poorly, *s'e* Kerry?"

Kerry's eyes narrowed, his friendliness evaporating. "I am."

Lia snorted. "You need a keeper just for being damn fool enough to offer that answer in a crowded tavern," she observed.

Kerry's smile returned, an amiable, lazy expression. He didn't look up at Lia. "Do we have an agreement, then?" he asked, watching Tank.

"We're leaving at dawn," Tank said, not putting any welcome in his tone. "If you're there when we ride out, you have an agreement. I'm not waiting on you any more than your former crew did."

"I'll be there." Kerry glanced up and back at Lia, his smile undimmed. "Excuse me, *s'a*," he said to her. "I'd like to get up and go away now."

She moved aside, blank faced but her hand once more on her dagger. Kerry wound through the tavern crowd and out of sight.

"He'll be mugged before he gets two streets over," Lia predicted, sitting down again.

"Not here." Tank considered his nearly empty mug. "Not saying thieving's unknown along this road, but something as ... as obvious as a mugging isn't really done, here. Too tight of a community, and too strong an awareness of how badly they need this route to be safe in order for travelers to pick this over the Plains Road." He drained the last of his mug, prodded disinterestedly at the remaining food, then stood with a grunt. "I'm off to sleep."

"Good idea."

They walked back to the inn without conversation, Tank too tired and frustrated to risk a wrong word starting a fight, as it so often had with Dasin; and Lia, apparently, too lost in her thoughts to notice his own silence.

Tank woke some time before dawn and lay still, on his back, staring up into the dark without any particular focus. He could hear Lia breathing steadily on the bed. The inn had been kind enough to provide a thick mat to keep the chill off, and he'd slept on far worse surfaces.

They'd fallen into an easy routine, each careful of the other's privacy and modesty, switching off who took the floor without argument. Tank stayed dressed, as much because he wasn't quite ready to reveal his scars as for Lia's own comfort. Lia, rather surprisingly, continued to change into a smock. At least he hadn't lost that much of her trust.

They both needed distance when being woken, and both of them slept lightly. Dasin had been a heavy sleeper; Tank had been able to get up and move around without waking him. With Lia, he had to stay very still until he was ready to get moving.

It wasn't an unpleasant change, as it forced Tank to fully wake up inside his own head before his body began moving. Clarity came slowly but steadily, dream haze forming into more cogent thought: the day ahead, the stranger who'd be traveling with them, the likely weather in the coming days; running over questions of feed, horseshoes and tack in his head, then moving to human food and gear.

Abruptly, it was all entirely too fucking tedious to think about while laying motionless in the dark. He sat up, hearing Lia jerk to alertness immediately, and said, "Get up. I want to show you something."

She grunted muzzily. He turned his back until the sound of her fumbling into clothes had stopped, then reached for his boots.

There was enough gray light in the air to make their way without help. Lia was groggy and uncoordinated, for all her quick waking. He stopped her from walking into a doorframe on the way out, and pulled her upright twice when she staggered on uneven ground.

Early rising villagers raised their hands in greeting or called a quiet "Morning," as they went by. Tank responded in kind but kept going, as did the villagers.

"Where are we going?" Lia asked.

"You'll see."

She grumbled at him. He grinned and turned her up a steeply sloping, narrow dirt path edged with brush in need of trimming back. She grumbled more loudly as they pushed past overhanging branches, tripping against rock stubble and thickly twining ground vines.

Tank caught her upright twice more, nearly going over himself the second time as a rock shifted unexpectedly under his foot.

The path opened up to a wide, deep ledge just as Lia's grumbling took on a sharpness that indicated she was losing patience. Tank kept a hold of her arm as they emerged, just in case, but she stopped well clear of the edge, her stance instantly more alert as she looked out over the drop.

They were high enough in the hills that the forest below looked like a fragmented, dark carpet in the pre-dawn gray. A ragged band of clouds ran along the horizon, just beginning to turn colors at the bottom edge.

Tank urged Lia to sit, and settled beside her. "I like coming up here, when I've the chance," he said. "Best spot I've found for watching the sunrise along this part of the road." It had been a better way of starting the morning than facing Dasin's erratic temper, but he didn't say that.

Lia pulled her knees up to her chest, wrapping her arms around them, and said nothing, her attention entirely on the valley below them. As the light grew, the dark mat of forest became an array of points and tufts emerging from a thick silvery fog. A hawk lofted into the air and swung through a series of lazy curves overhead, as though claiming the pale sky for its own.

The thin gold-orange at the bottom of the clouds grew into a crimson-gold blaze that seemed intent on taking over the entire horizon. Silvery blue streaked through the clouds, highlighting their ragged edges. A massive flock of small, dark birds rose, swirling well clear of the hawk, then descended back into the fog.

The silence felt as though it hung a bare moment from becoming joyous clamor, the world caught motionless just before tipping over into the ferocity of being fully alive. Tank drew in a deep breath, then another, savoring the contradictions.

As the gilded display faded towards a steadier, neutral blue, Lia stirred and said, in a subdued tone, "Thank you. That was gorgeous."

Tank hoisted himself to his feet. Lia did the same before he could offer her a hand up. Not, he thought, out of pride, but as though the existence of such a courtesy hadn't even occurred to her. She watched the slow feathering of fog through the trees below for another moment, as though mesmerized, then let out a long sigh and turned away.

"I'll show you a spot in Stecatr like this," she said, "only for sunsets." An odd expression crossed her face, as though she'd said something unintentionally personal.

Tank didn't say anything. He kept his demeanor carefully neutral as he led her back down the trail, and kept his mouth shut to conversation as they sorted out their gear and a quick breakfast: strong tea, toasted bread and a chunk of ham, here, rather than the oatmeal common to lower elevations.

As they left the inn, laden with packs and saddlebags as though they were horses themselves, Tank came to a sharp halt.

A buxom young woman with pale hair and a determined expression stood outside the inn, her arms folded. A gangly young man with auburn hair stood beside her, radiating patient resignation.

Unida had her long hair braided back in a married woman's style, a newlywed's white cap on her head and a gleaming silver ring on her right hand. Tank eyed her warily all the same.

"Good morning, *s'a* Unida," he said. "I understand congratulations are in order."

Lia moved to stand beside him, expressionless. Unida glanced at her with a dismissive eyebrow flick, but her new husband considered the sword at Lia's side with distinct caution.

"I'm married now," Unida informed them, her chin rising.

"Congratulations," Tank and Lia both said simultaneously, but Unida didn't even pause to hear it before going on:

"I've come to tell you I've a good man now, who can protect me and take care of me. So you can just stop chasing after me." She tossed her head.

Tank blinked witlessly. Lia let out a faint, smothered sound that might have been hastily cut off laughter. Unida's new husband looked even more resigned than before, his shoulders hunching slightly.

"If you don't leave me alone, he'll stand up for me," Unida went on. "I won't have you bothering me any more."

Tank raised an eyebrow at the other man, who shrugged minutely, as though to say: *I know, I'm lost as well*. "I'll do that, *s'a*," Tank said, finding his voice at last. "I surely wish you both all the best." He directed that more to her husband than to Unida.

"Mind you remember," Unida said, then turned and flounced off, nearly dragging her husband along.

If Tank's arms hadn't been entirely encumbered, he'd have put his hands over his face. He said, gruffly, "It's too fucking early for this shit," and started for the stables, ignoring Lia as she began to laugh.

Chapter Sixty-five

Lia thought she would remember the final stretch of their trip to Assiasan for the rest of her life. Stecatr had no match for the wildly tumbled, exuberant hill landscape. Rivulets and streamlets wandered underfoot, slicking and soaking stone and earth; the horses had sticky clay mud halfway up their legs most evenings that took an hour to clear out.

Wide streams, too shallow for bridges, often had patches of built up gravel to serve as a ford. Hefty piles of gravel on each side offered mute testimony as to how often they needed to be repaired. The larger streams, and on one memorable occasion a fast-churning river, had sturdy bridges that arched above the water, with old, dark moisture stains marking how high the water could get during snowmelt season. Lia found the height of the waterline entirely unsurprising. Stecatr had a thick wall to its west that shielded the city from the nearby river for that exact reason.

The villages and towns, focused on self-sufficiency, displayed far more interest in keeping their homes and local streets in good repair than the main travel roads and outsider-catering areas. Residents regarded transient merchants and haulers with tolerant indifference, took coin for the generally poor lodging and resupply, and wished all outsiders on their way with goodwill and overall disinterest. Tank admitted that Dasin was probably one of the only merchants to find this route successful, as his more southern herbs and teas were considered fascinatingly exotic.

Dasin hadn't, apparently, left any further bad feeling behind him. At Tank's advice, they kept to themselves, left generous tips, and moved on the next morning whenever possible. Bad weather swept through twice, forcing a delay, and Lia's monthlies hit with unexpected savagery, putting her in bed for two days. Tank sat with her, sometimes quiet, sometimes telling her about previous trips up the Hills Road: mostly just, patiently, *there*.

Most of his stories involved merchanting negotiations and manipulations, times

Dasin had triumphed on a deal and times he'd lost badly. Bits and pieces Tank had picked up along the way about local economies: sheep, wool, produce, wood, stone, and a quality hard liquor called *hillschalk* were abundant and frequently exported. Windy Plains wheat flour, dried southern fruits, and any soft, non-animal sourced cloth sold well along the route, but not honey, tools, or trinkets.

There were few full sized horses to be found among the locals, but quite a few ponies and draft mules; once back on the road, Lia pointed out different breeds and their features, and asked, finally, about how Tank and Dasin had come by their fine black horses. But she chose her time poorly, and he shrugged the question aside with a scowl.

Kerry remained sunny and talkative, closely questioning a number of warily baffled residents as to their local sayings, specific dialects, and word choices. More than once, Tank or Lia had to intervene to untangle the ire caused by an inadvertently offensive question on Kerry's part. Eventually, Tank ordered the young man to stop asking entirely, which put Kerry into a mild sulk for a day, the only sign of temper he ever showed along the road.

More than anything, the land was frankly gorgeous. Huge granite boulders increasingly dominated the landscape the further north and up they traveled. Many had been hammered apart or exploded to make way for the road, and the weathering striations gleamed bright with streaks of mica and quartz. Lia scooped up water-tumbled quartz pieces as gifts for her mother and sister; they were prettier than anything she'd found on her wanderings through Stecatr, often tinged with pink or purple and with an odd frostiness that made her think of snow caught within the rock.

Isla would have loved them. The thought brought surprisingly little pain, only a fading ache: and one night, when they'd camped out in the open and Kerry had wandered off to stare at the stars on his own for a while, she rolled the small stones about in her hands and told Tank the story.

Isla had been her first lover. Lia didn't remember, now, who'd started the relationship. She thought it had probably been Isla, with her bright, passionate spirit and fearlessness. They'd spent every possible moment together for close on two years, careful to present only as best friends to any public eye. Isla had been older, her family passed on or moved elsewhere. She'd lived in a small apartment near the markets, working for a local baker. It had been long hours and hard work, but she'd honestly enjoyed it and had been steadily setting money aside.

Lia had only held one thing secret from Isla: her work for Scarpy. His assignments often sent her scrambling across rooftops and crouching in shadows as she gathered information throughout the city, finding the weaknesses of merchants and middlemen, crafters and catchpoles. The information she gathered maintained Scarpy's leverage over a wide swath of the city.

He'd kept her clear of the Church, for the most part, but as the priests became more severe, their clashes with tradespeople and nobles alike increased sharply.

As she told the story, she privately shook her head over how she hadn't put the pieces together sooner. Tank's wry look more than once indicated he shared that sentiment. But

Lia simply hadn't been willing to think about the implications, hadn't been willing to put in more than the barest effort by that point, and she'd always, as her mother often remarked, been very good at not seeing what she didn't want to see. And her mind had been so full of Isla's smile as to leave no room for any sort of critical thinking.

Even so, without putting a precise reason on *why*, she'd started looking for ways out — of Stecatr, as much as of working for Scarpy. She pressed Isla to leave with her. Isla refused, commenting that it would gut Lia to leave her family. Which, while true, hadn't mattered to Lia at the time. She'd had some vague notion of living a happy, safe life *somewhere else*. There had to be a place where they weren't always worried about being caught out as *ii'ne*, where such a discovery wouldn't carry increasingly harsh penalties. Somewhere close enough that she could still come visit her family....

Lia didn't include, as she unrolled the tale, her much more foolishly optimistic thoughts that surely she'd paid enough for Scarpy's help. She'd believed that Scarpy couldn't possibly be so cruel as to force her to stay in Stecatr. She'd thought, for some unfathomable reason, that Scarpy was *benevolent*, that she was *special* in his eyes and her well being mattered to him more than his personal power and profit.

She'd held to that, if in fading increments, right up until she'd finally heard Toad — Ebeza's — tale and done some concerted thinking about actual events, shorn of romanticism.

Tank didn't need to hear any of that, though, so she focused on telling him about Isla.

Lia was never sure, later, if Isla had known what was coming. Certainly they'd been drifting apart, Isla unaccountably withdrawn and claiming exhaustion from her work. Quite likely Isla had been trying to push Lia away to keep her safe; quite likely she'd seen what was coming.

Lia had been perched high above Isla's apartment in gray pre-dawn, brooding over the odd distance between them, waiting to see if Isla came out of her building with another lover on her arm, when the priests arrived.

She'd watched in dawning horror as Isla was led through the streets; followed the procession to the Church doors; wormed her way as far into the building as she could safely go without being caught. The priests took Isla into a room below the Church, the one where they took sinners for confession and *redemptive cleansing*.

For most of Lia's life, social shame had been the largest danger of being hauled in by the Church. The priests always posted a list of names on the front of the church, indicating who'd been accused of what sin, and whether they'd been found guilty or not, and whether they'd repented sufficiently to be forgiven. The accused either came back out, shamefaced, to face the scorn and ire of their former friends and neighbors, or they were turned over to the city guards for the Lord of Stecatr to judge.

Recently, the list had stopped including the repentence status of the accused. Even more recently, just before Lia signed up with Stecatr Freewarrior Hall, the Stecatr Church began to imply that merely being brought in meant the accused was, in fact, guilty.

The accused started coming out with wild eyes and shaken nerves. They never spoke of what the priests had said or done, and they all became wary and withdrawn, as though expecting to be taken up again at any time.

Increasingly, they'd stopped coming out at all.

Those who never returned were said to have failed the purification rituals, or it was announced that they'd chosen to go to the gods for their redemption. Lia, looking back now, saw a growing pattern of fear among the people she watched, a reluctance to trust one another.

The relationship between the Lord of Stecatr and the Church became strained to the point of being nearly combative. More than once, someone was arrested and taken away by the Palace or City Guard just before the priests arrived on their doorstep.

Isla hadn't come out.

Scarpy had refused to save her.

The royal decree that women throughout the kingdom could be mercenaries came in, was instantly opposed by the Church and as immediately championed by the Lord of Stecatr. Lia had signed up on the spot, forcing Scarpy to support her on that point — at a price.

Lia's fight with her father over her choice had scared her younger sister Kia into literally hiding under their bed, at which point Lia's mother had grabbed Kia and left the apartment entirely. Lia had stomped out not too long afterwards, and it had taken until the end of her training for her father to regain any sort of civil behavior towards for her.

Lia had never seen Isla again. The list only gave Isla's name and the accusation of *obscene behavior*. Neighbors and supposed friends refused to answer questions or even speak of Isla at all, and by then Lia knew better than to go asking the priests anything.

Tank said nothing during Lia's halting recitation, asking nothing, his face expressionless and eyes mostly shut. When she finished, he set a large, warm hand on her shoulder, fingers digging in, and let out a long sigh through his nose.

She shut her own eyes and bent her head, letting the quiet soothe the raw spots of awoken memory. "Thank you for listening."

His hand tightened a bit more, then lifted away. "You're welcome."

She found herself relieved that he made no other response, no empty threats, no outrage, no reassurances. As he'd said about his own past, there was nothing *to* say. It was a thing that had happened, that was all. He'd borne witness to her pain much as they'd done for the spirit in Thentree, and Lia found, to her mild surprise, that it was enough in her case as well.

Kerry wandered into camp, amiably content with his starwatching, and the matter was entirely dropped.

The next day, Tank called a halt by a broad, meandering stream deep enough to merit a bridge. He dismounted and disappeared upstream for a time. When he returned, he handed three small, river-tumbled rocks to Lia: speckled red granite, cut through with bands of pale quartz.

"Only one spot I know of along here has a band of the red alongside the right sort of stream to wash them smooth," he said with an odd, quirked smile. "I've always liked 'em."

She closed her hand around them and stared down at him. He shrugged at her and remounted.

"You're giving the others away, right?" he said without looking at her. "Figured those you might keep for yourself." He turned a sudden glare on Kerry, who snapped his mouth shut on whatever comment he was about to make and looked away with an ostentatiously innocent expression. "Last village ahead," Tank added, nudging Sin into motion again. "After that it's Assiasan."

"Ah!" Kerry said with immediate interest. "I've actually never been there. Please, do tell me about it!"

"Us," Lia seconded. "It'll be my first time there as well."

Tank visibly relaxed, settled deeper in the saddle. "Assiasan is all about stone," he began, and rolled on, as the miles went by, into detailing out the industries and the infighting, the architecture and the artists, the farming and the food.

Lia found herself startled by the breadth and depth of Tank's knowledge. She'd expected more of a "this is where we sell shit and head back home in a hurry" approach.

He cast her a dry glance once or twice, apparently sensing her surprise, and finally commented, "I'm the one does the scouting around and a good bit of the lower to middle class networking. Dasin manages — managed —" His mouth twisted briefly. "He's better with the richer, more mannered folks. Assiasan's complicated, so I had to dig in a bit."

"Not just a mercenary," Kerry murmured, drawing a sharp stare from Tank for some reason.

"No," Tank said after a moment, still frowning. "It's always been easier to let folks think so."

Kerry bent his head and smiled, apparently to himself, then asked a question about local slang that distracted Tank from his odd mood.

Chapter Sixty-six

By the time the road widened and flattened towards Assiasan's gates, Tank was entirely sure that Kerry was more than an eager, innocent linguist. Or etymologist, or lexicographer, all of which terms Kerry used to describe himself but which Tank was *fairly* sure were all entirely different disciplines. He certainly played the part well. His passion was unfeigned, his knowledge solid: but there was something more underlying the man's exuberant fascination with everything around him. Little comments like that *not just a mercenary*, echoing Tank's long standing, so recently abandoned defensiveness, fell out a bit too often for coincidence.

He risked looking the man over with *other* vision once, only to find a gray blankness. Kerry turned to stare at him instantly, his eyes ice cold and face set in dangerous lines. Tank withdrew: Kerry relaxed into his usual amiability and looked away. Tank never tried again.

Tank decided he'd be not only relieved, but deeply reassured if the man went his own way in Assiasan as promised. The last thing they needed was yet *another* godsdamned complication.

Lia seemed to feel the same, judging by her caution in answering Kerry's endless questions and the way she unobtrusively kept an eye on him. If Kerry noticed her attentive wariness, he made no indication. Which, after that momentary not-quite-confrontation, meant absolutely nothing, in Tank's opinion.

Kerry was *devious*, under the prattle, and at the very least a partial. If he hadn't been so tall and gregarious, Tank might have suspected the man of being a teyanin. As it was, he wondered after desert Family connections, and watched in vain for signs supporting that theory.

As it happened, the weather turned foul shortly before they reached that widening of the road, high blue sky losing its color rapidly as dark clouds piled in and the wind picked up. Tank swore, motioned Lia and Kerry to the far right side of the road to let a heavily laden wagon rumble hurriedly past; checked incoming and outgoing traffic patterns, then hustled them into the city at a pace that allowed for no sightseeing. The gate guards had already ducked into their station houses, abandoning any pretense of checking for incoming trouble. Tank didn't blame them. The temperature was dropping fast, and Sin twitched restlessly beneath him.

Assiasan was a city of terraces and tiers, the entrance road falling roughly halfway up the overall arrangement. Tank pointed his companions onto a leftward, upward circling road that led to the next tier, not because it was the correct destination but because it had the most overhung, sheltered areas for this sort of weather. Sin jerked sideways twice, nearly unseating Tank, as the wind blew large, light bits of debris past. Rooster did the same four times, but Lia seemed to have no trouble keeping her seat; she moved with the horse as though she'd known the jolt was coming each time, and had Rooster back under hand with impressive speed. Kerry's long-legged beast, hilariously — to Tank's mind — named Hope, seemed entirely unaffected beyond a bit of increased ear flicking.

Tank led them to a large courtyard with tall buildings on all sides and wide stone bridges overhead at varying elevations. It was one of the rich areas Dasin frequented, and Tank had spent enough time waiting on Dasin in the area to have taken refuge here from late-summer storms on occasion. The bridges were sturdy enough for light cart traffic, and wide enough for two teams side by side and foot traffic to manage comfortably. More than one was at least partially covered, itself, against foul weather.

Assiasan's winter, from the stories Tank had heard, were brutally cold and prone to blizzards, ice storms, and incredible heights of snow. Everything was designed around making movement during bad weather possible, if not always easy, and stone masons here were deeply admired and honored.

Tank angled them up against a blank wall under the lowest bridge just as the rain broke: a silvery sheet of cold a half step from becoming ice. Tank's long-sleeved shirt, thicker than the one he'd worn further south, proved entirely inadequate to the ferocious cold. Lia dug a hooded cloak from her saddlebags and tucked it around herself, holding the still unhappy Rooster steady with her knees and a constant murmur of reassurances.

Kerry seemed unaffected, his expression almost beatific as he stared out at the thundering downpour.

Tank dug out his own rain cloak and wrapped it around himself as best he could. Sin being in no temper to be patient with more flapping things in his peripheral vision, he nearly found himself flung off or danced out into the rain while he struggled. Lia watched with no trace of mockery, looking rather as though she wanted to offer advice or help but was wise enough to know it wouldn't be well received just then.

Finally sorting out the cloak and Sin's aggravation, Tank rubbed a hand over his face and glared out at the sour weather. Rain splattered and misted over them as the overhang proved less useful than he'd expected.

"I have no idea how long this'll last," he said. "I've never been good with northern weather."

Lia squinted, considering. "I think not long. It'll come and go in waves for hours, but we should have a break soon. Where are we *going*, anyway?"

Tank started to answer, stopped, rubbed his face again, and sighed. He'd been both trying to think about, and avoid thinking about, that very question for days.

"There's a stable two tiers down," he said finally. "Caters to merchants. We've a standing account there." He glanced sideways at Kerry. "Don't think they'll take you, though."

The man didn't turn his gaze from the rain. "I'll make my own way from here. Thank you for the escort." He shook his head as though returning to himself at last, and dug a small, well-tied pouch from one saddebag. "Your pay, *s'ieas*." He tossed the pouch to Tank, who caught it at the expense of another round of protest from Sin; then, without a backwards glance, Kerry rode out into the rain and was lost to sight.

Tank let out an explosive, irritated breath, as much at Sin as at his own continued unease over Kerry. Having the man out of sight felt even *more* dangerous than his direct presence. "That's done with, at least," he said.

Lia's sideways glance spoke to her own uncertainty on that point, but she didn't say anything other than, "And after the stables?"

"Nearby merchant hostel, called the Gray Rose. If Cilif's waiting on us, he'll have taken a room there."

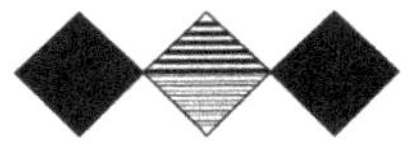

Cilif had. And had, apparently, left firm instructions to be notified the moment Tank walked into town, because he was downstairs waiting when they arrived.

The Gray Rose was a tall, blocky structure with small windows on the lower floor and larger, heavily shuttered ones on the upper stories. During summer, the shutters were left open with a removable horn or oiled paper screen set in the frame; at this point in the season, the opening would be filled with layers of thick cloth padding and sealed tightly against the cold winds.

Tank deliberately set down his various bags — Lia had insisted on carrying the heavier ones, as his still-healing shoulder had started to spasm from the chill — took off his wet raincloak, lifted Lia's from her hand, and hung both dripping cloaks on the rack by the door, before fully focusing on the grim mercenary waiting for them.

Cilif had cut his hair brutally short, shaved, and looked to have lost weight, giving his broad face a starker, meaner cast. He nodded to Lia, looked Tank over without apparent surprise at the lack of injury, and said without preliminary greeting, "I booked rooms for you across town. You'll be wanting them, I think."

Lia bent her knees and slid her load of saddlebags and pack to the floor, wincing and rubbing her shoulder. "I'm not carrying all this across town, Cilif!"

Tank raised an eyebrow and pointedly glanced out the small, thick glass windows at the rain once more pissing down outside. They'd made it through the stables and almost to the inn during a break in the storm. "I'd have to agree with her on that," he said.

Cilif's grim expression remained unchanged. "I'll have a carriage waiting by the time you leave."

Tank raised both eyebrows, then lowered them into a deliberate scowl.

"Lia, you might want to wait here," Cilif said. "With the gear. Load it into the carriage, when it gets here. I'll bring the rest to you once it stops being so shitty outside. Room's held for a tenday, we've time to sort out the next direction. Tank. This way." He turned and headed for the stairs.

Tank let him get halfway up before following, a horrible suspicion festering in his gut. Lia stayed behind, as suggested. Tank couldn't decide if he appreciated that or not, but it wasn't his decision and he had a feeling that her thoughts were running along a similar vein to his.

Cilif stopped and waited for him at the landing, then went up another flight and turned to the left, fetching up at the end of the hallway, in front of the last door. "I figured out some of the story and kicked the rest of it out of him along the way," he said then, meeting Tank's eyes. His own held a deadly sort of patience, a snake-stare without any conscience at all. "You do whatever the fuck you want. He's all yours. I'll mop up as needed."

Tank barely had time to draw a breath before Cilif swung the door open and stepped aside.

"Cilif, no...." he said, the words nearly strangling in his throat.

Cilif's only response was to poke him in the back hard enough to send him stumbling into the room, then to swing the door quietly, firmly shut between them.

Dasin sat tied to a sturdy chair in the middle of the room, hands firmly bound behind him and a thick gag that covered his entire mouth holding him silent. One side of his face was marked with fading bruises, and Tank had a feeling he had at least a split lip if not a missing tooth or two under the gag and beneath his clothes. The merchant stared at the floor sullenly, refusing to acknowledge Tank's entrance, but one knee tensed and twitched as though he were fighting not to bounce it anxiously.

Fucking hells, Cilif.

Tank shut his eyes for a slow count of ten, inhaling, then exhaled for as long, studying Dasin with a blank sort of thoughtfulness.

Whatever I want. Huh. Cilif wouldn't have made that offer unless he'd already made arrangements to cover any eventuality. Which ... was interesting, and amusing, and terrifying, all at once. *When did he decide I mattered this much? What did I even do to deserve this sort of...* Tank wasn't at all sure if the right word was *loyalty* or *friendship* or *batshit insanity*.

Whatever I want. What he *wanted* was for Dasin not to have lied. Not to have made the choices he'd made. Failing that, he wanted to stop the far too familiar, raggedy pain of betrayal. He'd spent years holding his hand and his temper, years building his patience, *years* letting himself be the one hurt because, knowing how Dasin's history, and his own, would twist so much as a shove, he couldn't stand to deal it out himelf.

All of that, and he'd still been played for a fool. Taken advantage of. *Lied to.*

Dasin twitched, then straightened, squinting at Tank through watering eyes. Not tears, but physical discomfort: Cilif had most definitely done the hells own job working Dasin over. Tank wondered, absently, how long Dasin had been tied up like this, waiting on their arrival.

Dasin jerked his chin, cutting his eyes down to the gag, then back up to glare at Tank.

"Do you know," Tank said, still caught in a strangely emotionless haze, "I don't know that I want to hear anything you have to say." He located another chair, pulled it around and sat on it backwards, and propped his chin on his folded arms.

Hitting Dasin would have been intensely satisfying, but Tank, remembering the exploded armoire, didn't trust himself to start any sort of fight just now.

Dasin's glare intensified, then faded. He looked down and away, eyes sliding nearly shut.

"Turns out Lia's a Seer," Tank said, not really planning the words. Dasin's gaze jerked back up, wide and startled now. "Mm. Yeah. She took care of healing the spirit you fucked up in Thentree, so you owe her for that. Not to mention leaving her, of all people, to take care of me, of all people." He paused as Dasin looked away again, hectic color flushing across his pale features. "Yeah, no, nothing happened there, so fuck you for leaving me in that mess, too."

Dasin's head bent. This time, Tank thought it might actually be honest shame.

Again, words emerged without conscious forethought: "You said you needed me. I only fucking stayed because I believed you."

Dasin's head came up again, his eyes protesting.

"Yeah, that wasn't always a lie, I know." Tank moved his forehead to rest on his arms, breathing hard, then straightened again. "Gods *damn* you."

Dasin managed a shrug and an eye-squinch that managed to convey complete agreement.

Tank stared at him for a long moment, a mixture of emotions battling in his chest. Finally, he stood, drawing his belt knife. Dasin blanched, eyes going tight shut and every muscle winching taut.

Tank cut the ropes and gag, then stepped back several paces and sheathed the knife.

Dasin stayed still, trembling, for a few breaths. Then he slowly shook free of his restraints and stood, wobbly and nearly panting with released anxiety. Tank stood, arms folded, and let Dasin get his bearings and balance.

When Dasin finally met his gaze, Tank said, "Say what you have to say."

Dasin licked his lips gingerly; puffed and split, as Tank had expected, but no teeth appeared to be missing. "I already said I'm sorry," he rasped. "I'm not who you wanted me to be. I'm probably not even who *I* wanted me to be."

Tank didn't say anything.

"I was so ... so fucking angry, when I remembered." Dasin's lips thinned. He winced, putting a hand to his mouth. It came away bloody. "Godsdamn Cilif."

"He left you alive for me to handle, instead of kicking you off a cliff direct," Tank said flatly. "Best be thanking him, not damning him."

Dasin lowered his gaze by way of answer, his shoulders hunching. "He took me by surprise," he said to the floor, then shook his head and straightened, some of his old arrogance returning. "Alive, dead, it doesn't matter. We're done, you and I. I'm sure you're glad of that. I won't say I am, but we're both better off going our own ways at this point."

"You're going back to the Hackerwood?"

"Only place I'll be welcomed, isn't it?" Dasin retorted, chin rising. "Cilif's going with you, he's already made that plain, and I'm surely not staying *here*, nor in Arason. Without Yuer's influence, without *you*, what else is there? Aerthraim? *Right*." He made a bitter face and spat to one side. "You know, Evkit told me I'd be left without options, and to come back when that happened. I told him he was wrong. That you'd never...." He stopped, looking away again, his eyes nearly shut. "Never mind. I was wrong."

"You fucking *ii shhha* empty-sacked *ta-karne micru*-faced *sanahair*," Tank said levelly. "Don't you fucking put this shit onto *me*."

Dasin met Tank's stare. "I'm right about one thing, always have been. You'll be better off without me."

"On that, we're agreed. Is that everything?"

Dasin swallowed, then shrugged, hard and defensive. "I'm assuming you're not going to kill me at this point," he said, a familiar arrogant edge in his voice, "so yeah, you can go fuck off to something better already. Or *someone*."

Tank drew in a sharp breath, turned for the door, and felt Dasin relax behind him.

Don't hit him, don't hit him, don't —

How much of that resolve, over the years, hadn't actually been his own?

"*Fuck it*," Tank muttered, then spun back, took two long strides, and swung with purely and unchecked physical force. Dasin crashed into the wall several paces away and slid to a limp heap on the floor.

Tank spat once on the floor between them, then left the room without bothering to see if Dasin was still breathing.

Chapter Sixty-seven

What Lia had seen of the city before the thundering rain closed in had been very different than Stecatr's architecture. Assiasan had considerably more terracing, for one, and more bridges that connected upper building stories. Even given Lia's limited understanding of masonry, the stonework was magnificent: not only sturdy, but *elegant*, often inscribed with elaborate designs and flourishes.

The roads were wide, and not set nearly as far above the walkways as in Stecatr. Multiple drains carried away the rushing rain water to points unknown that probably emptied into a nearby lake or river. A number of the walkways were at least partially covered as well, allowing the business of the city to continue even in bad weather.

This was a city of *anyway*, Lia decided. Whoever had selected this high, inaccessible spot to build a sprawling city had looked at all the very good reasons against and decided to do it anyway. The people here moved with an innate defiance: *This land wants to kill us with snow and ice and rockfalls, fuck that, we'll survive it all any way we can.* And certainly any merchants opting to travel to Assiasan, either along the Hills or Plains Road, exemplified the stubborn attitude of: *This is a pain in the ass sort of road but we're going to do it anyway.*

The trip across town to the new inn took some time, trundling up and down and across a convoluted path. "Not a straight line to be had in this city," Cilif said as they rattled on. "Especially not in bad weather. Hire-on carriages love and hate this sort of rain. They get more custom, and charge more, but then they have to get through it, and have to go different ways for best speed and to avoid flooding."

"I saw a lot of drains, earlier," Lia said. "Don't they keep the flooding down?"

"Yeah, where they exist. Or aren't blocked or broken. They've been asking the king to send engineers for years now. The drains were built by southerners back at the city's founding, as I hear it, and nobody here has the right understanding of their system to do more than fuck it up if they try to fix it themselves. Which they have. And did."

Lia looked Cilif over, in the cold dim light, then said, "You look like shit."

"Not surprising." He frowned at the thick glass window on his side of the carriage, currently fogged over. "Hasn't been a real fun time."

"What happened?"

Cilif turned his head and studied Lia with unexpectedly flat, blank eyes. "I beat the shit out of my employer, is what happened. And then sat on him so Tank could come finish the job." He looked at the fogged window again, making no effort to wipe it clear.

Lia, shaken by that frozen stare, let the conversation die at that point, and Cilif made no effort to restart it.

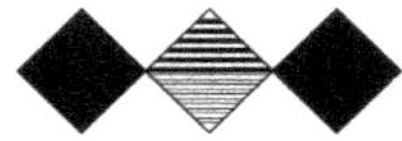

When they arrived at the new inn, which bore the odd name of The Mountain Pocket and an even odder attempt to illustrate that name on the sign, Cilif helped carry everything up to the third-floor room. Then, with a short nod and a recommendation for Lia to stay put, he departed, presumably to return to the first inn and find out how things had gone.

Cilif had only arranged one room, but at least this one had two frame beds with thick mattresses, each with its own nightstand, and the air held comfortable warmth. The savory smells drifting up suggested that the kitchen lay almost directly below and the staff was busily preparing dinner.

Lia stared around, taking in details with widening eyes: a solidly built desk to one side offered writing supplies, from inkwell to paper to wax, with a chair to match the desk; metal sconces holding thick white candles, set on the nightstands and mounted on the wall to either side of the door, offered light; and a well-stuffed, wide-seated lounging chair offered lazy luxury.

"How much is this room *costing?*" Lia muttered, fingering the thick featherbed in wonder. And for ten *days?* She suspected that even with her generous pay, just one night would knock a hole in her savings. Surely this wasn't all coming out of Cilif's pay?

A rap on the door caught her out of bemusement. She opened it to find a tidily dressed, clean-faced maid with steel-gray hair and a cheerful demeanor.

"There's a bathing room downstairs, *s'a,*" the maid said. "Your guardsman said to get two of the tubs ready, one now an' one in a bit while. You're the first, I'm supposing, and it's ready if you are."

Lia blinked, held back a protest that didn't make sense even to her, and nodded. "Thank you, *s'a.* I'll be down directly."

"Turn left at the bottom of the stairs," the maid said before offering a short curtsey and departing with a sure, rapid stride.

Lia shut the door and stared at it for a few moments. "Ten *days,*" she muttered, then shrugged and began pulling clean clothes from her pack.

By the time she got back to the room, nearly limp from an extended soak in a tub large and deep enough to allow for hot water up to her collarbones, Tank had come and gone, judging by the disturbed saddlebags and splotches of rain drip on the floor. Lia couldn't find it in herself to care where he'd gone and when he'd return. She crawled into the bed she wanted, tucked up under the coverlet, and passed out.

She woke some time later to a room lit by the candle on the night stand by Tank's bed. He was in the lounging chair, dressed in clean if wrinkled clothes, eyes shut and breathing evenly, too straight-backed to be asleep. The air smelled of the herb-infused inn soap, and his hair was loose and damp.

Lia watched him for a little while, then tucked back down and went to sleep again.

Next time she woke, the candle still burned, but Tank was in his bed and asleep, judging by the faint snores. Now the room smelled of their wet clothes, the wet leather and horse fustiness of the saddlebags, and an underlying, chill raininess. Wind rattled and moaned outside, splatters of rain blowing erratically against the shutters.

She rested amidst the interlaced sounds, her eyes sliding shut. Half-mazed by the contrast of the freezing chill outside and her warm, dry, and *incredibly comfortable* bed, she drifted off once more.

Next time she woke, the candle was coming near to the guttering point, and Tank was twisting with a nightmare.

Lia left her warm nest without hesitation, pausing at the foot of his bed to poke Tank's leg. He kicked, as she'd expected, and thrashed upright, one arm coming up at an angle to fend off an attack. She stayed clear, waiting and shivering, until he dropped his arm and blinked around blearily. His hair, tangled and matted, gave him a wildly drunken appearance, but she smelled no spirits on his breath, and his eyes, while dazed, were clear of intoxication.

"The fuck?" he rasped, then managed to focus on Lia. "The *fuck?*" he repeated, with an entirely different inflection.

Lia glanced down at herself and hastily tugged her smock back into place. "You were having a nightmare," she said, doing her best to ignore her flaming mortification.

Tank, propped up on one elbow now, stared at her for a few breaths. Eventually he shoved upright and to lean against the headboard, rubbing both hands over his face. His fingers caught in his knotted hair; he freed his hands, dropped them to his lap, and grunted irritably.

"Going to cut it all the fuck off one of these days," he muttered.

Lia grinned and went to find a comb; when she brandished it at him, an odd expression crossed Tank's face. He obediently turned and bent his head, though, as she settled on the side of his bed, and silently endured her patient picking at knots. Neither of them spoke until the coppery mass of hair was once more straight and sleek. Lia began to braid it back.

Tank put up a hand to stop her.

"It'll just get tangled up again," Lia said pragmatically.

"I know." He twisted to lean back against the headboard again, regarding her with that same unidentifiable expression. "I'll braid it up myself. It's a ... I have a ... I react. Back of the neck, for me."

She sat still, mildly surprised at her lack of embarrassment or fear. "Tell the nightmare out, then, since you're settled."

He grinned lopsidedly. "Settled, no. Wouldn't say that. Nightmare ... no. I don't need to talk this one out." He shut his eyes, amusement fading. "Lia. That talk we need to have, you and me. Probably best you move off a bit, unless you want to have that discussion right here and now."

Reflex pushed her back and to her feet; then she stopped, stuck between conflicting impulses. Tank stayed motionless, his eyes closed and hands relaxed, but the tilt of his head held more tension than his voice had done, and she could see his jaw working in tiny spasms.

"Why *me?*" she blurted. "Given — everything — why me?"

The guttering candle popped once and went out. The darkness immediately felt very thick and very cold. Lia crossed her arms and shivered. Tank gave a short, harsh grunt of distress. She heard him thrash, then a clanging sort of thunk as the metal candle holder went over onto the floor. Tank swore, breathing hard.

She reached out and found his shoulder, gripping it reassuringly. "Give me a moment, and I'll —" *Get the other candle lit* never made it out.

Tank's hands came up, one then the other as he twisted and pulled. After a flurry of coverlet and sheets, she found herself tucked up tight, her back against his chest, under the covers, his face buried in her hair and both of them shivering.

"Hold still," he said thickly. "Gods, I'm sorry, I didn't mean to do that, I'll — give me a moment, I'll let go, I just need a moment of — gods, *gods* you're warm, and that fucking *sanahair* — this fucking weather — *gods*." He tucked his head a bit further, pressing his forehead against the back of her head, and muttered, "I am so fucking *tired* inside my head."

Lia stayed quietly limp, trying not to think about the fact that for once, he hadn't gone to bed with clothes on — *any* clothes, from the feel of it. She certainly didn't feel warm. Her feet were particularly icy, and she angled them clear of Tank's legs.

Tank's shivering eased, his own body heat rising enough to dispel Lia's chill. She found she had no interest in pulling away to her own bed, where she'd have to rewarm herself and the sheets. Besides, Tank was still tense. Best to let him talk it out. She made a mildly inquiring noise by way of a prompt.

He set his cheek against her head, his breath stirring her hair, and said, "I decked him. Dasin. Cilif left him tied up and gagged. Said I could do ... whatever I wanted. So I let Dasin go, let him have his say, then knocked him across the room and walked out."

Lia listened to that pause, measured the edges in Tank's voice. "Cilif would have let you kill him."

"Yes. And cleaned up after for me, and never mentioned it again. Gods only know why."

They lay in silence for a while. Tank's breathing evened out, his heartbeat thumping steady against Lia's back.

Eventually, Lia said, "Because you're worth it, and Dasin isn't."

"Funny," he said absently, lifting his head as though to look down at her. "Same answer I was going to give you, just now."

His breath heated the space by her ear as he spoke, and she inhaled sharply at her entirely unexpected reaction. *Oh, damn....*

Tank grunted as though struck. His arms tightened around her to a nearly painful grip, then loosened. He leaned his head away, then swore in an unfamiliar dialect and shoved himself back, opening a cold gap between their bodies. He pulled his hands entirely clear.

"There's that question answered at least," he rasped. "Damnit, Lia, this is *not the fucking time.*"

"Why not?" she said before good sense could shut her up.

He laughed a little, breathlessly. "Because I'm out of bridle." At her puzzled sound, he clarified: "No restraints. It's too easy for me to ignore a *no* with how badly I want...." He made another thick sound, then: "*Please.* For both our sakes. Go."

She began to shift her weight, reflexively obeying the near-order, then stopped. "No."

Tank went dangerously still, then let out a hoarse, fluttering laugh. "Caught me there, didn't you? Ehhhh. All right, then. Give me a moment. I fucking *refuse* to be out of my head for this."

Lia set her teeth together against a mixture of terror and desire at the intensity of his last words. *Am I making the worst mistake of my life? Maybe.*

... Let's find out.

He inhaled, long and slow; exhaled the same way, and repeated that several times.

"All right," he said finally. "You're sure? You gotta feel you can say no, if'n you need to. Damnit — sorry —" He cleared his throat, then, more clearly: "You can say —"

She flipped round to face him by way of interrupting. He was a vague outline of dark against less-dark. "I know. If I need to say no, I'll make it stick."

"I believe you," he said, voice smoky with amusement. He found her hand, laced his fingers through hers briefly, then rolled onto his back. He pulled her hand to his chest, necessarily tugging her up against him in the process, untangled his fingers from hers, and put both of his own hands behind his head. "Your choices, now," he breathed, and fell silent.

His chest was very warm against her hand, and lightly fluffy with curls. She propped herself up on her other elbow and slid her fingers in cautious patterns. His breath caught twice, his body twisting slightly, and she felt her own heat in response.

Her hand slowed, then stopped, at a sudden wash of doubt, shame, and fear: *This isn't really me, he's influencing me somehow, or maybe Dasin planted the suggestion in my mind along the way. I don't like men, I never have, this can't be happening. I need to get out, get away,* run ....

"Say it out," Tank said softly, not moving. "You can bolt, after, but say it out first."

She opened her mouth and surprised herself with a bitter sob. One of Tank's hands came out from behind his head; he gripped her shoulder, the same carefully neutral touch he'd used after she'd told him about Isla.

"How do I know you haven't," she began. Her throat choked up into another, deeper sob. "Why didn't *I* know?"

Apparently understanding both garbled questions just fine, Tank said, "I swore to you I never would, and I can tell if anyone else influenced you. You're acting on your own, Lia. As for the other — did anyone even tell you crossroads was possible, before you came south?"

"No. I had no idea, until I saw Kennet...." She lifted her hand from his chest and made a vague gesture neither of them could properly see in the darkness.

A rough laugh bumped through him. "Run into Madage on the way south, did you? Heh. Them two never pass up a chance to have fun together. We camped with them once. That was one wild damn night." He sobered, as though at a darkening memory, then sighed. "Anyway —"

"Did you —?" Lia blurted, then put her hand over her mouth in renewed mortification. *Good gods, we're in bed and he's naked and that was absolutely the rudest thing I could have asked — almost asked, please gods he didn't understand that one.*

Tank let out an odd little hum, like a laugh that didn't quite make it all the way out. "Nah. Dasin doesn't — didn't — share like that. But they were noisy, and Dasin took that as incentive." He paused. "I don't get embarrassed about this stuff," he added. "Don't you get that way, not on my account. Ask what you want." He put his hand behind his head again, and his voice dropped back to smoky: "*Do* what you want."

She sucked in a sharp breath as another wave of reaction ran through her at that tone, and ran her fingers tentatively through his long, loose hair. More questions came to mind, but none that wouldn't either kill the mood entirely or end up with answers she didn't actually want to hear. Well, one.

"Tell me," she said, leaning in to speak into his ear, "no ... *show* me ... what you like."

He reached for her hand, and did.

Chapter Sixty-eight

The Mountain Pocket was a much higher-end inn than Tank had ever stayed at. Even Dasin's tendency to flaunt his wealth had been overridden by sheer financial practicality; a tenday's stay here would have wiped out every bit of profit from even an excellent run. For Cilif to have chosen *this* place both intrigued and alarmed Tank.

Besides the well-appointed rooms and luxurious baths, the Pocket had an extensive kitchen and dining hall, open to the public, and as Tank discovered, crowded even just past dawn. He was able to secure a table through pure luck, as a group of well-dressed patrons rose to leave just as Tank stepped into the hall. A server snagged Tank with a bright smile and a beckoning motion and steered him to the still-cluttered table. Another server slipped in just ahead of them with a basket, rapidly cleared the dishes and wiped down the table, then waved and departed.

Slightly bemused, Tank sank down with his back to the wall. A basket of bread sticks landed on the table in front of him; yet a third server, an attractive, heavyset young man, beamed at Tank as though seeing his best friend for the first time in years.

"Welcome, *s'e!*" the new server said. "We've rock eggs today, and stuffed hearth bread. For drinks we have Black Mountain coffee, First Day cider, berry tea, mint tea, or sweet milk, and if you're looking for something harder to wake up with, we've just got in a fine batch of Silver Mountain mead and one of golden lightning, and of course we always have black ale and crystal wine on hand." He tilted his head inquiringly.

Before Tank could answer, Cilif wove around the young man and took a chair. "Rock eggs and mint tea," he told the young man. "For both of us. Leave it to him, he'd try ordering oatmeal."

The server grinned and whisked away.

"What the fuck are rock eggs?" Tank asked, deeply suspicious.

"You'll see." The dark blotches under Cilif's eyes were less pronounced, and he'd taken more care with his clothing than usual. In fact … Tank squinted at him.

"Are you in *bespoke?*" he demanded, incredulous.

Cilif held out a long arm, looking down at the sleeve with clear satisfaction. "Ordered this last time we came through," he said. "You like it?"

Tank leaned back, looking Cilif over thoughtfully. The longsleeved shirt, a deep blue, had ornamental stitching in a slightly lighter shade, and the cuffs gathered at the wrist before flouncing out almost to the tips of his fingers. The material looked to be the sort that seemed thin but held warmth, and the cut was definitely tailored to Cilif's broad build.

He didn't bother leaning over to see the pants. If Cilif had sprung for this good of a shirt, the rest would match. "Impressive," he said. "Suits you. Also, what the hells?"

Cilif folded his arms, smirking. "Your reaction's everything I hoped for."

"Where in all the hells are you getting all this money?" Tank demanded, motioning to their surroundings.

"I don't *spend* it, for one thing," Cilif retorted. "Dasin pays — paid — damn well, and I hang on to it. I also made an investment or two here and there along the way, and they've paid off."

Tank's stomach sank. He covered it with a ferocious scowl. "What sort of investment?"

"Please." Cilif's chin went up in clear offense. "The way you're looking at me! Feh. Drysalter supplies, mainly. There's a consortium started up in Arason, just expanded into Assiasan. I ain't a merchant, but I've picked up a thought or two, traveling alongside Dasin for so long."

Tank relaxed, shrugging at Cilif's sardonic stare. "So you don't need to hire on anywhere, is what I'm seeing."

"Feh. Well, I suppose not, but that never had nothing to do with nothing. I like to be moving." Cilif looked up as their server returned. Two absurdly large plates laden with softboiled eggs in cheerful ceramic cups, shredded potatoes, and a pile of some darkly speckled meat shaped into balls were set down between them, accompanied by two large ceramic mugs of steaming-hot tea. Cilif held up a gold round; the server grinned even more brightly as he took it and darted away again.

Tank stared at his plate suspiciously. The soft boiled eggshell was a worrying tan-orange color, the potatoes had a green and red powder sprinkled across, and he couldn't tell what animal the meat had come from. At least the tea was recognizably mint.

"Cilif …." he said, not trying to hide his skepticism.

"Try it," Cilif said, delicately cracking open his egg to reveal bright orange where there should have been white and a bright red where there should have been yellow.

Tank grumbled but obediently applied himself, on the basis that as far as he knew Cilif had no reason to want him puking up his guts or trapped in the outhouse. The egg had an oddly smoky taste, strong but not unpleasant, with a familiar spicy kick that brought an unwilling smile to Tank's face.

"Cook here studied to the south," Cilif said between mouthfuls of his own food.

"Figured you'd recognize the spices."

The potatoes had the same flavor, if muted by salt and an oddly sour tang that, again, wasn't unpleasant; and the meat, whatever animal it came from, was rich and savory.

"All right," Tank said. "It's good. Thank you."

Cilif grunted satisfaction as he cleared the last of his plate. He drained off half of his tea before sitting back to look Tank over. "You look less like shit than I thought you might, after yesterday," he observed. "Finally take her to bed, then?"

Tank grimaced and shrugged.

Cilif cocked his head to one side, seemingly caught between laughter and surprise. "So ... yes, but?"

"Wasn't ideal," Tank said. "She wouldn't stop *thinking*."

He'd come damn close to losing his temper by the time he'd given up and sent her — *gently* — back to her own bed for the night. And once she'd finally started snoring, *he'd* gone to visit the Pocket's indoor latrine, after which his temper had been considerably better.

Cilif let out a short bark of understanding laughter. "I'm not real surprised by that —"

Tank lifted a warning hand as Lia appeared in the doorway. Cilif fell silent, twisting to see, then waved Lia over. Their server appeared while she was hesitating over where to sit.

Cilif nudged her unsubtly to Tank's side of the table and said, "She'll want the hearthbread, I'm thinking, and I dunno, Lia, you like sweet milk or mint tea? Or sommat else? Berry tea?"

"Mint tea sounds good." She smoothed back her short hair, awkwardly not looking at Tank. "Thank you."

Cilif's eyes gleamed with amusement, but he said nothing aloud. The server nodded and went away.

"This place is ... it's *nice*," Lia said, looking around with a slightly lost expression. "Why *here*, Cilif?"

"It's been a shit road. I figured Tank deserved a bit of nice, an' we can't very well let him be all alone, now, can we?" The smirk Cilif had been holding back crept out at last.

Somewhat to Tank's surprise, Lia just leveled a flat look at Cilif and showed no sign of embarrassment. "Just the one room?" she said. "Going to be crowded."

Cilif sobered. "Nah, I've got t'other room for me," he began, then paused as the server deposited a plate and mug in front of Lia, who grinned in apparent delight. To Tank, it looked like a thick piece of bread wrapped around the same sort of items that had been on his plate, only all mushed together instead of separated.

"My mother makes this on special occasions," Lia said. She took an experimental bite, then coughed, eyes watering, and added thickly: "Not this spicy though!" She took a gulp of tea, made an agonized face and set the mug down hard enough to splosh. Waving her hands in agitation, she swallowed, then whined in pain. "Fucking hot!" she wheezed.

Tank burst out laughing, rocking back against the wall, echoed by Cilif's rumble of amusement. Lia glared at them both, rubbing her throat.

Once they wound down, Cilif said, "I held the one room ten days out acause I didn't know what we'd be doing next. I wanted options. This ain't a city where you want to be without a reservation for somewhere to sleep. Better pricey and crowded than out on the street or at one of the grubber inns."

Tank nodded rueful agreement. Lia asked, "Grubber inns?"

"Place for the poor. Folks grubbing for a living, bits and pieces of anything they can put their hands to. Picking up trash. The like. Not real safe places to stay. So, Lia, you aiming to leave out to Stecatr, then?"

Lia lowered her head and took a few bites of her breakfast before answering. "No," she said at last. "I've been thinking on the timing, and I won't get there before full winter sets in. If I'd left at the crossroads with Toad — Ebeza — I'd have made it in plenty of time. But going back south from here and then up the North Road to Stecatr, it's too far. I didn't realize ... the maps didn't show how hard the Hills Road is. I thought we'd be a tenday faster at the least, even without the delays we ran into. The roads will be too risky by the time we get close to Stecatr. And I don't particularly want to go back *downslope* on the Hills Road right now."

Cilif nodded, visibly unsurprised. "I figured that out a while ago," he said. "You didn't seem in a mood to hear it, though."

"I'm not inclined to rush back down the way we came either," Tank agreed. "We normally take a good two tendays here, to recover as much as for selling. The Hills Road can get brutal."

"Two tendays would put us straight into the first of the snow winds," Lia said to her plate, her shoulders hunching. "I don't even want to think about what the Hills Road would be like at that point."

"So we're overwintering here, then," Cilif said. He leaned back in his chair and folded his arms. "All right. I've found three contracts we can take, room and board included on all of 'em. I've a preference, but I'll keep it to myself until you hear the choices yourselves. They all run more or less the same length, through spring melt. Pay's different, but so are the situations."

"Hold on," Tank said. "First of all, what happened to the wagon and horses and all that? Did Dasin sell them?"

"He didn't get the chance," Cilif said. "They're still being held. I wouldn't of let him sell Blackie, in any case, an' I'm moderately fond of that damn mule by now."

Tank didn't want to ask. He had to know. "So what, Dasin's ... walking? Or is he still in town?" He managed, just, not to ask: *Is he still alive?*

Cilif nodded a bit, as though guessing at the unvoiced question. "That's another reason not to rush on. I set him on the Hills Road before I came to breakfast. He ain't moving too fast or too happy, but there's a weaver's caravan headed south as took him on last minute for a bit of extra consideration." He rubbed his fingertips together. "I told him don't look back or I'd finish him as you didn't do."

Tank bit his lip and met Cilif's hard gaze directly. "Are you sorry I didn't?"

"Nope. But I'm not as forgiving as you are. I gave you a chance. Next one's mine."

They stared at one another, Cilif unwaveringly icy. Tank tried to make himself want to argue, but only a bleak silence met his internal search for guilt.

Lia cleared her throat. "Cilif, how did you avoid Dasin influencing *you*? I can't imagine he stood still for any of this."

"That's a damn good question," Tank said, startled that he hadn't thought of it himself.

Cilif put a hand to his chest with a grimace, then glanced around the crowded room and said, "Let's take this elsewhere."

Tank rose without protest and led the way upstairs to their room.

Cilif took the desk chair, Tank the lounging chair, and Lia perched on the closest bed, which happened to be Tank's. Cilif rubbed his nose, the corners of his eyes wrinkling, but kept his observations to himself. Tank, interpreting the amused gesture just fine, briefly wished he'd been able to open a window to air out the room.

Lia seemed oblivious to the exchange. She watched Cilif with unsettling intensity. "You were about to say," she prompted.

"Dasin tried influencing me, but it didn't take. I think he couldn't get a hold on me because of these." Cilif drew out a necklace of dark cord threaded through several lumpy blue stones. They weren't gemstones; apart from the lack of luster, they looked distinctly like a composite of some sort. Tank narrowed his eyes, not quite frowning as he mentally compared them to aenstone and came up with an unsettling answer.

Lia nodded as though unsurprised and drew out a matching one. "Toad? Ebeza," she corrected herself.

"Yeah. He said not to—"

"—show it to anyone." Lia nodded again, then glanced at Tank apologetically.

"Where did *he* get them?" Tank demanded, increasingly sure that he didn't like where this was going.

"I don't know," Cilif said. "I have a guess, but I don't know for sure."

"Had to be Evkit," Tank said, and put a hand over his eyes. "That fucker. That *fucker*. He knew what was going to happen."

Silence fell as everyone, very carefully, didn't ask aloud why *Tank* hadn't been given one.

Tank swallowed, then again and again, refusing both rage and tears. Finally he dropped his hand from his face and said, with chill precision, "So, then. Dasin's done and gone. Evkit's to deal with later, if at all. We're wintering over here — *we* being all three of us, yeah?"

He waited for Lia and Cilif to nod. Cilif's expression had returned to the deadly chill of earlier. Tank caught his eye and held it; Cilif grimaced and eased down into a more moderate temper. Lia, thankfully, had finally learned how to shield her emotions, and while he could see the tiny signs in her face and posture, she wasn't letting her own anger spill out.

Tank went on, not giving anyone time to interrupt: "We've the wagon and contents to sort out, and stabling and keep for the horses and draft mule. At least two deliveries to make first," he added belatedly. "I'm assuming Dasin didn't get to that?"

Cilif shook his head, his gaze briefly going distant as though once more reining in his ire.

"So. Two deliveries. Maybe three. Sell off the merchandise. Lia. You can run the table. I know you did it for Dasin once before." He grinned without humor at her startled expression. "People talk, and I'm generally the one they talk to. So, I'll check the market schedule, we take a table, sell off the herbs and anything that ain't nailed down or walking. I make our apologies to anyone as might be annoyed at losing their supplier for southern herbs and simples, and we take on a job as gives us bed and board overwinter."

He shifted to full, crisp trail captain voice, mindful of his accent and deliberately quashing the remnants of his own temper:

"Time to talk about those contracts. You said you had three in mind. Tell them out, if you please. What do we have that's *indoors?*"

Cilif's back went straight, his chin coming up in reflexive response to that tone. Tank could feel the man locking back into a detached calm, and the simmering energy in the room dropped several notches.

Shifting to a more comfortable position on the hard chair, Cilif said, "Three. Right, then. On we go with that. First up, there's Bluenesk House ...."

Tank reflected, ruefully, that he wasn't actually trail lead any longer and oughtn't be so firm about issuing orders. But it moved things along, and he wasn't in any sort of temper for fussing about on side matters.

Side matters. Once upon a time, side matters had involved whether Gint had gotten into a brawl again or if an angry serving maid was about to descend on them; whether the innkeep wanted damages from their last trip through or if Dasin was going to start a fight today. Not questions of *Why did a dangerous man box me into his service and then put me in a position where I got damn near destroyed and wound up parting ways with —*

He stopped the thought and the once-more rising anger, setting it aside for later. Something important lay in that question, and he didn't have time for it right now.

"— that one pays the best," Cilif finished. "Next contract is from someone with a better reputation, though ...."

Tank blinked irritably, realizing he'd missed the bulk of the detail, and made himself focus.

"Senn Rosweir," Cilif said, which name focused Tank's attention admirably.

"Stop," he said, more harshly than he'd intended. "You approached *Rosweir?*"

"No. I went through listings at the Hall." Cilif frowned at him, visibly puzzled. "You have a history there I don't know about?"

A package for Esna Rosweir was one of the *very discreet* special deliveries Tank had to handle. "You could say that," Tank admitted. "It's not something I can talk about. Confidential. Private."

Cilif considered for a moment, then said, "Rosweir's contract offer is for six guards, four months. Room, board, stable space, a clothing and gear stipend, one day off every five, basic overwear in house colors supplied — tabard, I think they wear here, or some sort of sleeveless tunic — and the pay runs six to eight full silver a day. Higher end for experience and for a team as already knows how to work together. Mostly indoor work, sounds like, with a wander out through town on occasion. Two already signed up, leaving room for us 'n one more."

Lia's eyes went wide and bright. "*Eight?*" she breathed. Tank could almost see her running calculations in her head. "That's —" She shut up, glancing at Tank with a guilty grimace.

"That's well above what we paid you," he agreed, not taking offense. "Assiasan is an expensive town. Adjust your expectation of local prices: eight here would be about the same as what four likely would have meant to you when I hired you on."

She sobered, frowning as she worked through that. "Still damn good," she said after a few moments.

"It is," Cilif said. "Especially with all the extras. Four, with the extras, would've gotten my attention. Six to eight?" He shrugged. "I'm surprised it ain't already entirely snapped up."

"You shouldn't be," Tank said. "Rosweir's ... a difficult household. I'd rather avoid them."

"All right. So, Bluenesk, Rosweir, and then there's Howdlein as the final option. That one's offering five, no extras beyond room and board, one day off in eight, regular escorts around the city to high level events and meetings. Only two spots, though, and no women." He turned a hand palm up at Lia, grimacing.

"Run over Bluenesk again," Tank said.

"Four full and six bits, room and board, three spots, guarding the ten year old family heir. No stable space, no stipend, one day off in ten." Cilif paused and glanced over at Lia. "I've picked up rumors about Bluenesk over the years. The brat's likely being guarded from his own damn family. They're an ambitous bunch."

"That's a shit deal," Tank observed grumpily.

"Been open for over ten days, looks like, with no takers," Cilif agreed. "Might be able to negotiate higher based on that."

"Doubtful. I've paid attention to the gossip too." Tank scowled at the floor. "Let it be for now," he said at last. "We have to go through the wagons and sort out final deliveries and all that first, anyway." He rose to his feet, abruptly restless to be *doing* rather than *talking*. "Is it still pissing down outside?"

"Dry and warm." Cilif stood as well. "Are we moving back to the Rose?"

"Probably best," Tank said reluctantly, not missing Lia's briefly unhappy expression. "But maybe not for a day or two. You're right. We've all earned a bit of luxury."

Cilif grinned. "Right along what I was thinking." He tilted a dry glance at Lia. "Shall I set you up with a separate room, then, and kip in here myself?"

Tank didn't give her a chance to answer. "No."

Lia's chin came up, her face flushing. Cilif let out a sharp laugh and backed up, putting his hands up by his shoulders, palms out. "You two get on with that talk," he said. "I'll go sort myself out. Meet you at the stables." He swept from the room.

"You do *not* get to —" Lia began, standing up as though ready to grab her gear and walk out after Cilif.

Tank, in a very flat voice that had nothing at all of a push in it, said, "Lia. Stop."

She hesitated, then took the chair Cilif had abandoned, once more sitting on it backwards and resting her arms on the back. Her hands curled, fingers digging into forearms in a nervously defensive posture. Tank sat down, deliberately measuring his movements to be as non-aggressive as possible.

"None of those contracts put any one of us in charge of another," he said, and watched her expression shift from anger into bemused wariness. "I'm not in charge of you right now, either. Not trying to be. But we aren't done, Lia, you and me. Last night didn't go well. That's all right. Doesn't mean it never will. It was too soon for me, to be honest. Give me a few days to sort out how fucking pissed off I am, give us all a few days to figure out where we're hiring on." He paused, then added, "It's comfortable, sharing a space with you. I'd rather not disrupt that, myself. My temper's too damn thin. So there's my say on it. Now, you tell me yours."

She was looking down at the floor by the time he finished, her hair falling over her face in a fine, pale screen. He set his hands flat on his thighs against the urge to move forward, lift her chin, move that hair aside and look at her ridiculously pale northern eyes. Put his hands on her shoulders. Move his hands down ....

Oh, you're completely overset, aren't you? Alyea said, laughing at him. He batted her memory-ghost presence away irritably; it faded, trailing mirth.

Lia drummed her fingers against the back of the chair, head still bent. "I thought you'd expect," she began, then stopped, her head lowering further.

Tank let the silence hang for a few beats, then said, "No. Never. We could fuck a hundred times and I still wouldn't *expect*."

She twitched at that, not quite a flinch; caught by the deliberate crudeness, most likely. As he'd intended. It brought her back straight and her head up, and she pushed her hair aside to meet his gaze.

"This isn't what I expected," she said. "This ... none of this. You want honest, I don't know how to figure any of this. The spirits. Dasin. You." She paused, then, as if the thought had just clicked, blurted out: "Was Cilif wearing *bespoke?*"

Tank let out a sharp bark of laughter. "I said the same. Looks good on him."

"It does." She ran her hands through her hair, scrubbing her short nails against her scalp in a *Focus, damnit,* sort of movement. It left her hair in just-woken-up disorder.

Tank held back a smile and waited gravely for her to finish sorting out words.

"I don't want to stay here," she said at last, all in a rush. "I'm worried about my family, about ... It feels like if I wait here over winter, it'll be too late, but I don't know too late for *what.* And it's already too late. So. I've that to work out, myself, and that's ... where my mind kept going, last night. Trying to think if I could, after all, if I left right now and went through my savings to hire on fresh horses along the way. I know," she added as he began to point out the impossibility of that idea. The Hills Road only kept remounts for News

Riders and King's Riders, and few enough of those at best. "I *know*. But I'm worried. And this …." She made a sweeping, comprehensive gesture. "Cilif had a good phrase. This is all so far outside my experience it might as well be up top of the highest peak of the Scarpane Mountains."

Tank considered, then stood, watching her reaction carefully, and moved forward until he was just within her reach. She looked up at him, wary but unalarmed; he held out a hand. She took it and let him draw her to her feet, but resisted a gentle tug, so he let go and stepped back.

"We've a wagon to unload," he said, tone as neutral as he could make it. "Horses to check on. Contracts to sort out. That's within your experience. Start there. The rest will either take time or someone else's actions to settle. Put your sword belt on, make sure you've got those throwing knives on you, and let's go."

She stood still for a moment, blinking up at him, then grinned, abrupt and sharp. "I can work with that. Thank you. And … Tank. Thank you."

He paused, hands tangled in the straps of his own sword harness, and set his teeth in his tongue until the abrupt snarl of emotions settled down. "You're welcome," he said then. "Let's move before the weather shifts again, yeah?"

"Yeah."

Not long after that, they stepped out into the warm sunny day, moving in companionable quiet. It took two blocks and a number of startled glances from passersby for Tank to realize that despite the difference in their heights, they were walking in near-perfect step. He grinned wolfishly, far more content than he'd *expected* — hah — to be, and echoed Alyea's amusement at himself.

Damn fool. Entirely a damn fool.

But he was walking lighter than he had for years, with far more — call it *balance*. Balance was a safe sort of word. He was balanced, almost as though he was getting ready for a fight, ready to move in any direction, but *inside*. He couldn't recall if he'd ever felt that way before without a generous dose of aesa being involved.

Lia, too, seemed much more relaxed than when they'd first met, much more certain of herself, despite the doubts she'd just confessed. She'd surprised him several times along the road. He had a feeling she'd keep on doing that as she adjusted her own balance.

Cilif had presented the most unexpected surprise. There was something deeper going on there, between the moments of casually gleeful behavior and the moments of worryingly cold, murderous rage. He seemed happier to be free of Dasin than Tank would have expected, while being oddly unmoved by the freedom offered by his wealth. There were most definitely changes going on there, as well, and plenty of surprises lining up.

For the first time in his life, Tank found himself looking forward to not knowing quite what was going to happen next. "No more lies," he said aloud, startled by his own words.

"What?" Lia said, breaking pace and looking up at him inquiringly.

"Nothing." Privately, he considered the words. *No more lies*. No more worrying what Dasin, or Cilif, or Lia, did or didn't know. No more trying to be *just a mercenary*. No more maneuvering to keep his childhood a secret. No more lies to shield anyone else, either.

Surprises didn't need to be inherently dangerous anymore.

It sounded like it was going to be a *fantastic* experience.

Letting another broad grin unfold, Tank matched his step more closely to Lia's and strode without hesitation towards the day ahead.

Intersection: Interpopulation

Far in the north of the largest single remaining landmass on the entire planet are a range of mountains that have collected legends since before humanity's birth. These mountains, once called the Cold Teeth, later named the Spine of Ice and Stone, currently named the Scarpane Mountains, reach across the entirety of that section of continent, firmly dividing the thin line of frozen tundra and much wider stretch of arctic wasteland from the succession of more temperate zones to its south.

For the humans, there is nothing beyond the Scarpane Mountains. They have never found a way around, over, through, or under the massive barrier. They have built precarious cities against the very toes of the rough stone hills, defying sense and legend alike. They keep secret shrines to old gods and wonders, prophets and lords, and tell themselves that will keep them safe.

They would not be so sanguine, did they ever realize the reason they are unable to bypass the mountains to their north.

It would be natural to assume them perfectly capable of conquering a simple mass of stone, bending it to their will, pushing through in their eternal curiosity, their never-ending explorations. After all, humans found a way into and through the dense, long-forbidden jungles that lie to the extreme south of this continent. They drove a wedge through the tangled forests that belt the continent's midriff, and found a way to negotiate with the creatures that lived within each of those areas.

That will never happen with the Scarpane Mountains, for a very simple reason.

It is not a geographical area that features inhabitants.

It is an inhabitant with areas of geographical features.

Intersection: Intensification

Balby hung upside down, her blood trickling like a slow benediction to the ground below, and thought about water.

Water had always defined her world: the presence of it, the absence of it. At Aerthraim Fortress, she had climbed the southeastern towers and stood, face tilted to the sun, gathering what vestiges of ocean wind found its way to that height. As moisture gathered for the rainy season, she had happily volunteered to work outside, relishing the unpredictable, drizzly days and the rolling, clinging fog draped across the uneven landscape.

During the heat of the dry seasons, virtually imprisoned within the thick stone walls, she had gone a bit mad on occasion. The mahadrae being famously severe, the consequences for Balby's misbehavior weren't pleasant at all.

She'd finally left, unable to stand being punished for her nature one more time. In the Hackerwood, so like and yet unlike the Jungles, she'd worked her way into a position of power, her nature not only accepted but honored. She'd begun teaching her child the way to grasp that power, with hopes that *he* would rise higher than she'd managed. She had aimed for him to rule the Hackerwood, in due time.

The humans had a saying about pride. She couldn't recall it, but felt that it would be appropriate, whatever it was.

Blood sheened her skin like sweat as her breathing roared in her ears.

The hakraiknain had called her an edgelands child. That was true enough, but at the same time far too shallow. She'd lived near the edge of the Jungles, behaved at the edge of proper behavior, followed an edge of puzzlement into dangerous territory both physical and mental.

Balby should have listened to the elders. Should have stayed in the humid air near the Jungles, properly connected to the vast web of community that served the greatest of the surviving ha'reye. But that road was forever closed, the Jungles seared to ash, her community destroyed past rebuilding.

"Excuse me," a mild voice said. "Are we boring you?"

Balby opened her eyes, blinking, and noted thoughtfully that none of the blood had tracked across her eyes.

"I see that we are," the man before her said, as gently as before.

He was short, even at an upside down, pain-fogged angle. He wore a thin, plain tunic and leggings that left the bulk of his arms bare. They were covered with vivid white scars where ceremonial tattoos had been removed. His eyes and skin were dark, his expression unreadable.

He said, "Well, that's enough of that, then. I suspected pain wouldn't be the proper expression of my displeasure, not without the binding of your true name, but it had to be tried. Dinas."

Slowly, solid ground came up beneath her, the bindings cut away. She lay sprawled on cool dirt for a time, her hands splayed across the loam: feeling the energy within, listening to the small movements of tiny lives nearby.

Eventually, she drew in a steadying breath and rose carefully to her feet, not bothering to brush herself off. She offered a deep bow and held it, entirely placid. "I do understand that you are displeased with me, hadinn Evkit."

"You may rise," the hadinn said, his voice cold.

She straightened, setting her gaze up into the tree branches latticed overhead. She watched squirrels twisting through impossibly small openings, darting round trunks after one another. Bits of leaf and bark scattered through the air in their wake.

"Lord," Dinas said, a voice of light and joy currently drawn thin and gray. "Lord, you cannot hold it against her that she failed against such an opponent."

There came a long silence. "No," hadinn Evkit said at last. "I suppose you are, as always, correct." He paused. Perhaps he sighed. She couldn't tell. "Given that truth, I will allow you to carry on with our agreement: you will return to the Coast Road, replace Yuer, and rule the area in my name."

"No, my lord," she said, still watching the antics of the squirrels.

"*Excuse* me?" He sounded more surprised than angry. People streaked with their own blood generally did not say *no* to Evkit.

"There is a more fitting punishment for my failure, lord," she said, carefully calm.

"*Is* there? Do tell."

In spite of her best intentions, her calm shattered as she said: "I will go after my son, and kill the *bitch* that took him from me." She drew in a long breath, fighting to regain a critical, icy detachment. Emotions were a weakness, with this man more than most.

The hadinn laughed quietly. "You can't kill her, child," he said. "She was the First of those who were called to serve, and she served well enough and long enough to become true ha'reye-kin. If you ever see your son again, he'll be hers entirely, and turned firmly against you."

Another breath, and calm returned. "Yes, my lord." A squirrel paused, clinging to the underside of a branch, and seemed to look directly at her for a few moments before scurrying away again. "I know, my lord. That's why it's a better punishment."

Evkit laughed, more harshly this time, like the caw of an amused crow. "Interesting. Allow me to think on that."

"Yes, my lord." One of her legs began to shake, threatening collapse. She lowered herself to the ground and eased into a reasonably comfortable position to wait.

A conversation happened then, in a language she didn't understand, between the hadinn and Dinas. She listened as the words rose and fell, idly tracking the tight and the loose moments, not even trying to understand the meaning.

After a time, hadinn Evkit said, "I will allow the Coast Road to manage itself. That will be more interesting, in the end. Go, then. Chase a story that has already left you behind. I release you from your debt of failure, that you may pursue the impossible, because it amuses me in this moment and because Dinas is asking it of me. But should you ever set foot within my territory again, it had best be with your son at your side and the hakraiknain's head in your hand. Or you *will* find out what I'm capable of when I am not being boring. I can find your true name, if I truly wish to. Dinas."

Balby shut her eyes and bowed her head in submission. When she opened them, she sat at the edge of the Hackerwood, the buildings of Arason within sight. Her body was clean of blood, her injuries mended, and a neat stack of clothing sat beside her.

She exhaled and inhaled carefully for a time, allowing herself to let go of all pride. Allowing herself to be *human* for a short time: and found it surprisingly restful to let herself, finally, panic.

Glossary

Pronunciation in this glossary is marked out as different from northern to southern dialect (*n:* / *s:*). When there is no distinction noted, either both areas use the same pronunciation, or the word is not shared across cultures.

Many words in the southern language include the glottal stop, which is rendered here as ʌ. A glottal stop involves closing, to some degree, the back of the throat. The glottal stop generally indicates that the original, full word involved a "k": for example, "ha'ra'ha" was once "hakrakha"; "ha'reye" was "hakreye", etc. Many humans have abandoned even the glottal stop and slur across the gap.

Aenstone (*n:* **ann**-stone / *s:* **ayn**-stone)**:** An Aerthraim Family-created stone composite. In sufficient quantity, aenstone blocks psychic communications, inhibits the use of psychic abilities, and weakens ha'ra'hain and ha'reye.

Aerth (*n:* **ar**rth / *s:* **aer**-th)**:** Rough translation: *feathers, freedom, flight*. The exact meaning is dependent on dialect and context.

Aesa (*n:* **ash**-ah / *s:* **ay**-sah)**:** A common plant whose leaves, when dried and used in a pipe, produce a mild euphoria. Illegal north of the Hackerwood, questionable along the Coast Road, entirely legal south of Bright Bay.

Alli (**ahl**-lee): **1.** The number *two* (southern). **2.** A simple two-pipe instrument, usually wooden, occasionally metal.

Aqeyva (*n:* **ark**-vah / *s:* ack-**ee**-vah, *alt.* ahh-**keh**-vah): A combination of martial-arts training and meditation disciplines.

Asp-jacau (asp-jack-**how**): A slender canine with long, thin snout and legs. Its short-haired coat tends toward fawn or brindle coloring. Its excellent sense of smell is primarily used to detect dangerous snakes and drugs.

Athain (ath-**ain**): Lit. translation: *spirit-walker*. Teyanain specially trained to manipulate energy and psychic forces. Considered holy by their people.

Bene (**beh**-ne): **1.** The number *three* (southern). **2.** A relatively simple three-pipe instrument. Like the *alli*, it is most commonly made of wood.

Calcen (**khal**-czen; *fem.* Calcana: khal-**zay**-nah): The title the Horn teyanain use for their leader. It is considered a gross offense for outsiders to use the term.

Callen (**call**-en): One sworn to the service of a southern god.

Chabi (**chah**-bee): A game whose underlying principles, moves and strategies reflect the principles of survival in a dry, hostile environment. In chabi, different types of pieces represent wind, water, goods, and money. Different areas of the board represent compass directions, fortresses, fire, air, and water.

Chekk (check): A community of ha'ra'hain openly living above ground. Genetic deterioration generally turns any such group into a human community within three generations. Also, the combative nature of ha'ra'hain makes creating a balanced community a tricky process.

Chichi (**chee**-chee): A small, hand-held clapper style of drum, generally a lightly hinged or tied striker and a metallic or wooden "head."

Comos (**Cohm**-ohs): One of three gods honored in the southlands. Represents neutrality, balance, and questioning energies. Linked to the season of winter, the colors white and brown, and curiosity. Followers are called *comosain*.

Daimaina (day-**may**-nah): Housekeeper for a desert Family. Generally but not always shares the Head of Family's bed. Holds considerable power in her own right, but in a sharply limited sphere. Male version is *daiman*.
Dashaic (Dah-**shay**-ick): Alt: Dasta tea. Dasta powder turned into a thick, potent syrup.

Travels better than the powder, but is more difficult to produce and thus more expensive.

Dasta (**Dahs**-tah): A drug originally developed by the ketarches, whose use has altered significantly over the years. Once a powerful healing tool, now often used as an addictive aphrodisiac and hallucinogen.

Datda (**Dat**-dah): One of three gods honored in the southlands, Datda represents negative energies, change, and death. Linked to the season of high summer, the colors red and black, and the emotion of anger. Commonly called "the Sun Lord." Followers are called *dathedain* and are almost always trained as assassins and spies.

Eki (**eh**-key): One of the Four Gods of the Northern Church pantheon. Represents Wind.

Four Gods: The pantheon of the Northern Church: Eki (Wind), Payti (Fire), Syrta (Earth), and Wae (Water). Each has a dual nature (good/evil).

Hadinn (hah-**dinn**): Approx. translation: *Ancient justice*. The title Lord Evkit of the teyanain took when he lost his claim to *Calcen*.

Ha'inn (*n*: **haynn** / *s*: properly: hah-∧**inn**; more commonly: **high**-inn): Lit. translation: *Honored One*. Reserved for ha'ra'hain.

Ha'ra'ha (*n*: **hrah**-hah / *s*: hah-∧rah-∧hah); plural ha'ra'hain (hah-∧rah-∧**hayn**): Person of first or second generation mixed heritage (human and ha'rethe). The next two generations are called *lesser ha'ra'hain*. Any descendants below that point are called *partials*.

Ha'rai'nin (*n*: **hrah**-hahhn-een / *s*: hah-∧**ray**-nin); plural ha'rai'nain (as prev., but with *nayn* as last syllable): One who has dedicated his or her life to serving the ha'reye, on the promise of eventually gaining the power of a first generation ha'ra'ha.

Ha'rethe (*n*: **hrah**-rett-ee / *s*: hah-∧**reth**-ay); plural ha'reye (as prev., but replacing last two syllables with one: *reyy*): Lit. translation: *golden eyes*. An ancient race, predating humanity.

Hat'naa-iti (hatch-**nahh**-eeet): Lit. translation: *deep, empty fragility*. Indicates intense spiritual vulnerability.

Ish (isshh): Prefix indicating feminine/female aspects.

Ketarch: (**Kee**-tarsch): Organized groups of healers who focus on preserving old healing lore and researching new ways of healing. Generally found within desert Family fortresses, as their work takes a lot of financial support.

Jungles: Also called *Forbidden Jungles*. An area of tropical rainforest far to the south where the majority of the ha'reye and their human devotees lived before the recent catastrophe.

Kaenic (kay-nick**):** The most common Northern Kingdom dialect.

Kaenoz (kay-nohz**):** Approx. translation: *kingdom*.

Kath (kath**):** Approx. translation: *servant*. Used with a variety of modifiers to indicate occupation and status.

Kathain (kath-**ayn**): Personal servants to a desert lord.

Ke (keh): Prefix or suffix indicating masculine/male aspects.

Kehair (**kee**-hair): Northern term for a manservant of the chamber.

Ketarch (kee-tarsch): Organized groups of healers in the south who focus on preserving old healing lore and researching new ways of healing.

Kophas (**khop**-pahs): A box to hold the bones and ashes from a cremation ceremony. A similar box, in the south, is called a *kop*, but holds purely bones.

Libaurni (lib-**arn**-ee): A southern fighting ship, found primarily along the western coasts. Can hold up to a hundred men and is the fastest ship currently known. F'Heing owns most of these, with Kismo in second place, Darden a thin third and Toscin a very distant fourth.

Mahadrae (mah-**hahd**-ray): Rough translation: *chosen mother of the free people*. Proper title for the female leader of Aerthraim Family. A male leader would be *mahadran*.

Micru (mick-**rue**): Rough translation: *small death*. A small, black and tan striped viper found in rocky desert areas. Its poison is instantly fatal even to large animals.

Payti (**pay**-tee): One of the Four Gods of the Northern Church pantheon. Represents Fire.

Purge, The: A recent time of trouble in the Northern Kingdom, marked by lunatic kings, sociopathic advisors, and numerous very bad decisions all around.

Ravann (rah-**van**; alt., rah-**vahn**): Similar to lavender in appearance and scent, but tends towards a darker leaf color, white flowers, and a slightly more acrid odor. Only found south of Water's End. Adapted for desert living, very hardy.

Reeven (**ree**-vehn): A ghost that seeks to possess living humans whenever possible.

S'a/ S'e/ S'ieas /S'ii: Respectful, gender-specific address designators.

Sanahair (sahn-ah-**hair**): Lit. translation: *shit boy.* The word ties into an obscure southern joke about kicking the person ranked just below you until there's only the chamber-pot contents left to kick.

Sessii ta-karne, I shha (Sessy tah-**carney**, ee shh-**ha**): rough translation: *You noxious, useless (castrated) little prick!*

Sheth-hinn (shethh-**hnn**): Assassin.

Shia-banse (she-ha-**bannss**): See *Tath-shinn.*

Shiaq'ree (shick-*ray*): Lit. translation: *concealed unlife.* Indicates the presence of creatures which present dangers far beyond the physical realm.

Sio, Sionno (see-**oh**-noh): Polite address between priests of the Northern Church. Laypeople must use *s'iope.*

S'iope (*n*: sigh-**ope**-ay/*s*: s-ʌ**igh**-o-pay): Lit. translation: *beloved of the gods.* Polite address by laypeople to priest of the Northern Church. Disrespectful nickname: *soapy.*

Suka: A sweet syrup used in various candies and desserts.

Swasson (**swahh**-sohn): A flightless meat bird, frequently bred for size.

Syrta (**seer**-tah): One of the Four Gods of the Northern Church pantheon. Represents Earth.

Ta (tah): Prefix implying masculine aspects. Usually involved in insults (see *Ta-karne*).

Ta feth kii (tah fethh key): Approx. translation: *stop shitting around.*

Ta-karne (tah-**carn**-ay): Insult. Approx. translation: *asshole (male).* Female version is *ta-neka.*

Tas-shadata (tahz-shah-**dah**-ta): Approx. translation: *fool, coward, idiot.*

Tath-shinn: Approx. translation: *ghost of a female madwoman* or *assassin* or *murderer.* Implies that a woman who would kill is insane, overly male, and impossible to handle even after death. In the upper northlands, a similar creature is called a *shia-banse*: the ghost of a woman who died while under the influence of evil.

Te (teh): Prefix indicating formality and honor. Genderless.

Telabat-nia-tabalet (tehl-lah-**baht nee**-yah tahb-ah-**leht**): Approx. translation: *play the game that is on the table*. Like many southern sayings, it involves a play on words. In this case, *telabat*, the game one is playing at the moment, and *tabalet*, the table one at which is currently sitting. *Nia* is a linking verb that has no real definition in and of itself.

Teyanin (tay-ah-**nin**); plural: teyanain (tay-ah-**nayn**): A small, xenophobic tribe of humans which retreated to the mountains of the Horn after the Split. Originally the judges and lawmakers of the entire southlands, they're now considered the guardians of the Horn.

Wae (way): One of the Four Gods of the Northern Church pantheon. Represents Water.

Warhbhuia (wharr-**bee**-ha): An expensive northern liquor.

About the Author

Leona R Wisoker writes a variety of speculative fiction, from experimental to horror, from fantasy to science fiction. Her writing ranges from bizarre and quirky to serious and horrific. She makes a point of aiming for moments of humor throughout her writing, in past because she grew up believing herself completely bereft of a sense of humor.

When not writing, she is pursuing a horticulture degree, experimenting with new recipes, and slowly updating a house in the woods.

Leona's web site: leonawisoker.com

About the Publisher

The Scribbling Lion, LLC, is a bookstore that aims to support small press and self-published authors of quality via online and convention based sales. It is only a publisher in the narrowest sense, that of producing owner Leona R Wisoker's books, and has no plans to expand beyond that scope.

Take a look at the fantastic assortment of other authors on sale, and at Leona R Wisoker's other books, here:

https://www.thescribblinglion.com

About the Artists

Christina Yoder, cover artist, is a fine artist and graphics designer who has worked in the commercial industry for over 12 years. She is also a fantasy/SF/and Horror artist.

For more information, please visit: https://www.artdragon.net

Monica Marier, the artist behind the maps, is a caffeinated writer, artist, mother and eccentric. On weekdays, she's a co-founder of Tangent Artists, a webcomic company where she writes and does art for 3 comics series. She is also a co-author of the popular "Handbook for Saucy Bard" series. She fervently hopes for an eighth day of the week to be instated so she can sleep. Monica currently resides in Northern Virginia with her husband and two kids. She is often seen walking down the sidewalks of Historic Warrenton, muttering character dialogue to herself.

For more information, please visit https://monicamarier.com

Other Titles By Leona R Wisoker

Children of the Desert series

Secrets of the Sands

Guardians of the Desert

Bells of the Kingdom

Fires of the Desert

Servants of the Sands (I & II)

Kingdom of Salt series

Lies of Stone

Novellas:

Fallen City (The Scribbling Lion)

Salt City (The Scribbling Lion)

Short Stories:

"Dragon Child" (*Galactic Creatures*, Sparkito Press, 2013)

"Silver and Iron" (*Sha'Daa: PAWNS*, MoonDream Press, 2014)

"Leftovers" (*Cats in Space*, Paper Golem Press, 2015)

"Scorpion's Choice" (*Sha'Daa: INKED*, MoonDream Press, 2016)

"Shadow of the Infinite" (*Society for the Preservation of CJ Henderson*, eSpec Books)

"Duck, Duck … Goose!" (*Andromeda Spaceways Inflight Magazine*)

"Alternations" (*Futures: Fire to Fly Magazine*)

"The Silver Tree" (*Abyss & Apex Magazine, October 2023*)